GROTESQUE

NATSUO KIRINO

GROTESQUE

TRANSLATED BY REBECCA COPELAND

ALFRED A. KNOPF NEW YORK 2007

THIS IS A BORZOI BOOK
PUBLISHED BY
ALFRED A. KNOPF

Translation copyright © 2006
by Natsuo Kirino

www.aaknopf.com

Originally published in somewhat
different form in Japan as *Gurotesku*
by Bungei Shunju in 2003.

Library of Congress
Cataloging-in-Publication Data
Kirino, Natsuo, [date]
[Gurotesuku. English]
Grotesque / Natsuo Kirino ; translated
by Rebecca Copeland.—1st ed.
p.   cm.
"A Borzoi book"
"Originally published in Japan as Gurotesuku
by Bungei Shunju in 2003"—T.p. verso.
ISBN: 978-1-4000-4494-8
I. Copeland, Rebecca L., [date]   II. Title.
PL855.I566G8713 2007
895.6'35—dc22   2006048594

Manufactured in the United States of America

FIRST AMERICAN EDITION

CONTENTS

Calculated at a rate of 120 yen to the U.S. dollar, the monetary figures in this book would convert approximately as follows:

¥1,000 = $8
¥5,000 = $40
¥10,000 = $80
¥50,000 = $400
¥100,000 = $800
¥1,000,000 = $8,000
¥10,000,000 = $80,000

In Japan the school year begins in April and ends in March of the following year. It consists of three terms, separated by short vacations in the spring and winter, as well as a monthlong summer break. Students attend elementary school for six years, middle school for three years, and high school for three years.

GROTESQUE

ONE · A CHART OF PHANTOM CHILDREN

Whenever I meet a man, I catch myself wondering what our child would look like if we were to make a baby. It's practically second nature to me now. Whether he's handsome or ugly, old or young, a picture of our child flashes across my mind. My hair is light brown and feathery fine, and if his is jet black and coarse, then I predict our child's hair will be the perfect texture and color. Wouldn't it? I always start out imagining the best possible scenarios for these children, but before long I've conjured up horrific visions from the very opposite end of the spectrum.

What if his scraggly eyebrows were plastered just above my eyes with their distinctive double lids? Or what if his huge nostrils were notched into the end of my delicate nose? His bony kneecaps on my robustly curved legs, his square toenails on my highly arched foot? And while this is going through my mind, I'm staring holes in the man, so of course he's convinced that I have a thing for him. I can't tell you how many times these encounters have ended in embarrassing misunderstandings. But still, in the end my curiosity always gets the best of me.

When a sperm and an egg unite, they create an entirely new cell—and

3

so a new life begins. These new beings enter the world in all kinds of shapes and sizes. But what if, when the sperm and the egg unite, they are full of animosity for each other? Wouldn't the creature they produce be contrary to expectation and abnormal as a result? On the other hand, if they have a great affinity for each other, their offspring will be even more splendid than they are. Of that there can be no doubt. And yet, who can ever know what kind of intentions a sperm and an egg harbor when they meet?

It's at times like these that the chart of my hypothetical children flashes across my mind. You know the kind of chart: the sort you would find in biology or earth science textbooks. You remember them, don't you, the kind that reconstructs the hypothetical shape and characteristics of an extinct creature based on fossils discovered deep in the earth? Almost always these charts include full-color illustrations of plants and beasts, either in the sea or against the sky. Actually, ever since I was a child I was terrified of those illustrations because they made the imaginary appear real. I hated opening those textbooks so much, it became my habit to search out the page with those charts first and scrutinize them. Perhaps this proves that we are attracted to what frightens us.

I can still remember the artist's re-creation of the Burgess Shale fauna. Derived from the Cambrian fossils discovered in the Canadian Rockies, the chart is full of preposterous creatures swimming around in the sea. The *Hallucigenia* crawls along the sediment on the ocean floor, so many spines sticking out of its back you might mistake the creature for a hairbrush; and then there's the five-eyed *Opabinia* curling and contorting its way around rocks and crags. The *Anomalocaris*, with its giant hook-shaped forelimbs, prowls through the dark seas in search of prey. My own fantasy chart is close to this one. It shows children swimming through the water—the bizarre children I have produced from my phantom unions with men.

For some reason I never think about the act that men and women perform to produce these children. When I was young my classmates would make fun of boys they didn't like by saying things such as, "Just the very idea of touching him makes my skin crawl!" But I never thought about it. I would skip the part about the sex act and go right to the children and the way they would turn out. Perhaps you can say I'm a little peculiar in that regard!

If you look closely you'll notice that I'm "half." My father is a Swiss national of Polish descent. They say his grandfather was a minister who moved to Switzerland to escape the Nazis and then died there. My father was in the trade business, an importer of Western-style confections. His line of work might sound impressive, but in fact the products he imported were poor-quality chocolates and cookies, nothing more than cheap snacks. He might have been known for these Western-style sweets, but when I was growing up he never once let me eat one of his products.

We lived very frugally. Our food, clothes, and even my school goods were all made in Japan. I didn't go to an international school but attended Japanese public elementary schools. My allowance was strictly supervised, and even the money allotted for household expenses fell short of what my mother felt was adequate.

It wasn't so much that my father decided to spend the rest of his life in Japan with my mother and me. He was just too miserly to do otherwise. He refused to spend a single cent unnecessarily. And he, of course, was the one who determined what was and wasn't necessary.

To prove my point, my father kept a mountain cabin in Gunma Prefecture where we spent the weekends. He liked to fish and just put his feet up while he was there. For the evening meal it was our custom to have *bigos*, prepared just the way he liked it. *Bigos* is a Polish country-style stew made of sauerkraut, vegetables, and meat. My Japanese mother hated fixing it, of that there can be little doubt. When my father's business failed and he took the family back to Switzerland, I hear my mother cooked Japanese white rice every night and my father scowled each time she set it on the table. I stayed behind in Japan by myself, so I can't be sure, but I suspect that was my mother's revenge on my father for his *bigos*—or, on second thought, for his stingy selfishness.

My mother told me that she once worked for my father's company. I used to indulge in romantic visions of a tender love blooming between the young foreign owner of a small company and the local girl who worked for him. But in fact, as the story goes, my mother had been married before, and when that didn't work out she returned home to Ibaraki Prefecture. She worked as a maid in my father's house, and that is how they met.

I had wanted to ask my mother's father to give me more details, but now it's too late. He's senile and has forgotten everything. In my grandfather's mind, my mother is still alive and remains a cute little girl in middle school; my father, my younger sister, and I do not even exist.

My father's Caucasian, and I suppose you could describe him as small-framed. He isn't particularly attractive, but he isn't ugly either. A Japanese person who met my father would have a difficult time trying to pick him out on a European street, that much is certain. Just as all "Orientals" look the same to whites, to an Oriental, my father was just your typical white man.

Shall I describe his features? His skin is white with a ruddy touch. His eyes are memorable for being a faded, mournful blue. In a flash they can gleam with cruel intensity. From a physical standpoint his most attractive feature is his shiny brown hair with its brilliant golden luster. It's now gone white, I suppose, and balding at the crown. He wears somber-hued business suits. If you ever see a middle-aged white man wearing a beige button-up raincoat even in the dead of winter, that would be my father.

My father's Japanese is good enough for an average conversation, and there was a time when he loved my Japanese mother. When I was little he would always say, "When your dad came to Japan he planned on going home as soon as he could. But he was struck by a bolt of lightning that left him paralyzed and unable to return. That lightning was your mother, you know."

I think it's the truth. Well, I think it *was* the truth. My father and mother fed my sister and me on a diet of romantic dreams just as though they were giving us candy. Gradually the dreams wore thin, until in the end they wasted away to nothing. I'll tell that story in due course.

The way I saw my mother when I was little and the way I see her now are completely different. When I was little I was convinced that there wasn't a woman more beautiful than she in all the world. Now that I've grown up, I realize that she was just average-looking, and not particularly attractive even for a Japanese. Her head was large and her legs short; her face was flat and her physique poor. Her eyes and nose crowded her face for space, her teeth stuck out, and she had a weak character. She yielded to my father in everything.

My father controlled my mother. If my mother ever talked back he would lash out at her with a volley of words. Mother was not smart; in fact, she was a born loser. Oh? Do you think I'm being too critical? It never even occurred to me. Why am I so unforgiving when it comes to my mother? Let's just keep that question in mind as we go along, shall we?

The one I really want to talk about is my sister. I had a sister who was a year younger than me. Her name was Yuriko. I have no idea how best to describe her, but if I were to come up with one word, it would be *mon-*

ster. She was terrifyingly beautiful. You may doubt that a person can be so beautiful that she is monstrous. Being beautiful is far preferable to being ugly, after all—at least that's the general consensus. I wish I could give people who hold that opinion just one glimpse of Yuriko.

People who saw Yuriko were first overwhelmed by how gorgeous she was. But gradually her absolute beauty would grow tiresome, and before long they would find her very presence—with her perfect features— unnerving. If you think I'm exaggerating, the next time I'll bring you a photo. I've felt the same way about her all my life, even though I was her older sister. I have no doubt you'll agree too.

Occasionally I have this thought: Didn't my mother die because she gave birth to the monster Yuriko? What could be scarier than two ordinary-looking people giving birth to a beauty beyond all imagination? There's a Japanese folk tale about a kite that gives birth to a hawk. But Yuriko was no hawk. She didn't possess the wisdom and courage that the hawk symbolizes. She wasn't particularly cunning, and she wasn't evil either. She simply had a face that was diabolically beautiful. And that fact alone surely worried my mother no end, what with her own ordinary Asian features. Yes, that's right, it annoyed me too.

For better or for worse, my looks are such that you can tell at a glance I have some Asian blood. Maybe that's why people like my face. It's just foreign enough for the Japanese to find interesting, and just "Oriental" enough to charm Westerners. Or so I tell myself. People are funny. Faces that are imperfect are said to have character and human charm. But Yuriko's face inspired fear. The reaction to her face was the same whether she was in Japan or overseas. Yuriko was the child who perpetually stood out from the crowd, even though we were sisters and even though we were born within a year of each other. It's strange, isn't it, how genes are transmitted so haphazardly? Was she just a mutation? Maybe this is why I imagine my own hypothetical children whenever I look at a man.

You probably know this already, but Yuriko died about two years ago. She was murdered. Her body was found half naked in some cheap apartment in the Shinjuku area of Tokyo. They didn't know who the murderer was at first. My father did not get upset when he heard the news, and he didn't return from Switzerland either—not even once. I'm ashamed to say that as his dear beautiful Yuriko grew older, she degraded herself with prostitution. She became a cheap whore.

You imagine Yuriko's death shocked me, but it didn't. Did I hate her murderer? No. Like my father, I really didn't care about learning the truth. Yuriko had been a monster all her life; it was only natural that her death would be unusual. I, on the other hand, am perfectly ordinary. The path she followed was clearly different from mine.

I suppose you find my attitude chilling. But didn't I just explain? She was a child who was fated from the beginning to be different. Fortune may shine brightly on a woman like that, but the shadow cast is long and dark. It was inevitable that misfortune would come eventually.

My former classmate Kazue Satō was murdered less than a year after Yuriko died. The way she died was exactly the same. She'd been left in a first-floor apartment in the Maruyama-chō neighborhood in Shibuya, her clothes in disarray. They said that in both cases more than ten days had elapsed before the bodies were discovered. I don't even want to imagine the condition they were in by then.

I'd heard that Kazue worked for a legitimate company by day, but by night she was a prostitute. Gossip and innuendo swirled for weeks after the incident. Was I horrified when the police announced that the culprit was the same in both murders? Well, to be honest, Kazue's death was far more shocking to me than Yuriko's. She and I had been classmates. Also, Kazue was not pretty. She wasn't beautiful, and yet she died exactly the same way Yuriko did. It was unforgivable.

I suppose you could say that I was the conduit who led Kazue to Yuriko and to their lengthy acquaintance, so in the long run I contributed to her death. Maybe Yuriko's bad luck somehow crept over into Kazue's life. Why do I believe that? I don't know. I just do.

I knew a bit about Kazue. We were classmates at the same prestigious private high school for girls. Back in those days Kazue was so skinny it seemed her bones would grate together, and she was known for the ungainly way she carried herself. She wasn't at all attractive. But she was smart and she made good grades. She was the kind of person who would spout off in front of everyone and make a show of how intelligent she was because she wanted to attract attention. She was proud and had to be the best at everything she did. She was perfectly aware that she wasn't attractive, so I suppose that is why she wanted to be fussed over for other things. I got a dark feeling from her—a negative energy so palpable I felt I could take it in my hand. It was this sensitivity of mine that attracted Kazue to me. She trusted me and began going out of her way to talk to me. She even invited me over to her house.

After we both advanced to the university affiliated with our high school, Kazue's father died unexpectedly and Kazue changed. She devoted herself to her studies and began to pull away from me. Now when I think about it, I realize that it was probably because she was more interested in Yuriko. My beautiful sister, one year younger than I, had been the talk of the school.

At any rate, it seems that something happened with those two. Two people who were such complete opposites in looks, intelligence, and circumstances end up as prostitutes and then get killed and abandoned by the same man? The more you think about it, the less likely it seems that you could find an account more bizarre. The incidents with Yuriko and Kazue irrevocably changed my life. People I'd never seen before would catch wind of the gossip and poke their noses into my business, bombarding me with all kinds of intrusive questions about those two. Disgusted, I clammed up and refused to speak to anyone at all. But now my personal life has finally settled down. I've started a new job, and all of a sudden I want to talk about Yuriko and Kazue so badly I can hardly stand it. I'll probably keep on talking even if you try to interrupt me; with my father in Switzerland and Yuriko dead I'm completely on my own. I feel I need someone to talk to—or maybe I just need to think about this weird incident myself.

I have Kazue's old letters and things that I can refer to, and even though it'll probably take some time to tell the whole story, I plan to keep going until I've unloaded it all—every detail.

· 2 ·

Let me fast-forward for a minute. For the last year I've been working part-time for the P Ward Office in Tokyo. P Ward is located in the eastern part of the city. Chiba Prefecture lies just across the wide river.

There are forty-eight licensed day-care facilities in P Ward, and since most are operating at full capacity they maintain waiting lists for admission. My job with the Day Care Section of the Welfare Division is to help investigate wait-listed applicants. "Does this family really need to send its child to nursery school?" That's the kind of question I have to answer with my investigations.

There are any number of unbelievable mothers in this world of ours. If there are those who feel no qualms about putting their children in day care just because they want to go out and have fun, there are also those who are so used to relying on others they have no confidence in their own ability to be good mothers. This kind of mother would prefer asking a day-care center to raise her child. There are also stingy families who won't pay for nursery schools—even though they'll pay the regular school fees—because they insist it's the responsibility of the public welfare system. How is it that mothers today have grown so depraved? The question has caused me considerable distress.

"Why is someone as striking as you involved in such mundane work?" I'm asked this time and again. But I'm not really that beautiful. As I've pointed out more than once, I'm half European and half Asian, but even so, my face is far more Asian than European and so less intimidating as a result. I don't have the model-like features that Yuriko had, nor am I as statuesque. And now I'm just a pudgy middle-aged woman. At work I even have to wear one of those less-than-flattering navy-blue uniforms! But even so, I've got someone interested in me, it seems, which has become a nuisance.

It was about a week ago that a man named Nonaka said something to me. Mr. Nonaka is around fifty, and he works in the Sanitation Division. Normally he's in Government Building Number One. But from time to time he'll make up an excuse to come by the day-care section in the Annex—which everyone refers to as the Outpost Office—and he and the section chief in my department will share a laugh or two. Whenever he stops by, he uses the opportunity to cast furtive glances in my direction.

I believe that he and the chief are on the same baseball team. The chief plays shortstop and Mr. Nonaka plays second base, or something like that. I don't much care what they do, it just makes me angry to see someone from a completely unrelated office coming over here during office hours for no better reason than to chat. "Mr. Nonaka's got his eye on you!" says my colleague, Ms. Mizusawa, who's eight years younger than I am. She's started teasing me, and this has made me even more disgusted.

Mr. Nonaka always wears a gray windbreaker, and his complexion is brown and his skin dry, probably from all the cigarettes he smokes. He has a greasy glint in his eye, and whenever he stares at me, I can feel his black eyes scorching holes in me, just as if someone had pressed a hot brand against my skin. It makes me feel queasy. And then Mr. Nonaka said, "When you talk, your voice is high-pitched, but when you laugh it's low. *Eee-hee-hee-hee.* That's how you laugh." And then he went on to say things like, "You may be polished and proper on the outside, but inside you're downright dirty, aren't you?" I was completely caught off guard. What would give this complete stranger the right to come and say something like that to me? I'm sure my dismay showed on my face. Mr. Nonaka looked over at the chief with some confusion, and then they went out somewhere together.

"What Mr. Nonaka said sounded like sexual harassment to me," I complained later to my section chief, and a look of embarrassment washed over his face. Oh, I see what's going on here! I thought. Just because I've got foreign blood in my veins, you think I'm more argumentative than a normal Japanese! Leave it to the Westerner to file a lawsuit, right?

"I agree that it wasn't appropriate to say what he did to a coworker," the section chief said, after some deliberation, making it sound as if it wasn't cause for concern. And then he started shuffling the papers on his desk, trying to look like he was putting them in order. I didn't want to start an argument, so I didn't say anything more. If I had, it would have just made him angry with me.

I hadn't brought a lunch with me, so I decided to go to the cafeteria in Building Number One, which was only a short walk away. I don't like being where people gather, so I seldom go there. But the building is new and has a very nice food hall for employees. A bowl of ramen is only ¥240, and you can get the lunch special for ¥480. The food was supposed to be good too.

I was shaking pepper over the bowl of ramen on my tray when my section chief came up behind me.

"You'll make it too spicy with all that pepper!" He had the lunch special on his tray: fried fish and cooked cabbage. The dried bonito flakes sprinkled atop the cabbage looked like metal shavings, and the cabbage reminded me of *bigos*. Scenes from my childhood played across my memory: the dinner table in our mountain cabin—silent as death, my mother looking miserable and my father eating with wordless gusto. Caught up in my memories, I must have spaced out for a minute, but the section chief didn't seem to notice. "Shall we sit over there?" he asked, smiling.

The section chief is forty-two, and because he plays catch during his lunch break he comes to work every day in his sports gear and pads up and down the hall the rest of the day in sneakers that squish when he walks. He's the kind of guy who is constantly concerned with his physique, is perpetually tanned, and is so full of vigor it's depressing. I usually don't get on well with men like that, but I found myself slipping into my usual habit. What would our child look like, if we were to have one?

If the child were a girl, she would have my fair skin. Her face, a melding of the section chief's square-cut chin with my oval face, would be attractively round. She would have the chief's slightly upturned nose and my brown eyes, and she would inherit his sloping shoulders. Her arms and legs would be sturdy for a girl, but given her vitality they'd be fairly charming. I was pleased.

I followed the chief to the table. The enormous cafeteria was filled with the chatter of employees and the clatter of cafeteria workers bustling in and out with trays and other utensils, but I felt they were all watching me. Ever since the incidents with Yuriko and Kazue, everyone knows everything. I couldn't stand thinking that they were staring at me.

The chief peered into my face. "About what happened earlier," he began. "Mr. Nonaka didn't mean anything by it. He was just trying to be friendly, I suppose. If that's sex-harass"—he used an abbreviation—"then half of what any man says would qualify, right? Don't you think so?"

He was grinning at me. His teeth were short, like those of plant-eating dinosaurs, or so I thought as I gazed at his mouth. I was reminded of the illustration of the Cretaceous Period. Our child would probably have a row of teeth like that. If she did, the shape of her mouth would be inelegant. Her fingers and her knuckles would be conspicuously stubby and, on her large hands, would be too angular for a girl. The child that the section chief and I would have had been cute earlier, but now she had transformed into something else completely. And I was growing angrier by the minute.

"Sexual harassment, I'll have you know, also includes assassinating another person's character in that way."

My protest was delivered rapid-fire, but the section chief countered in measured tones. "Mr. Nonaka was not assassinating your character. He simply stated his observation that your spoken voice and your laughing voice are different, that's all. Now clearly it's not appropriate to tease someone that way, so let me apologize for him. Will you let it go? Please?"

"All right."

I acquiesced. I didn't think there was any point in continuing the discussion. There are perceptive people and there are dimwits. The section chief fell into the latter category.

He chewed his fried fish with his short little teeth, the thick coating of batter scattering over his plate with a dull rustling sound. He asked some harmless noninvasive questions about my workload as a part-timer. I answered perfunctorily. And then suddenly he lowered his voice.

"I heard about your younger sister. That must have been awful."

This is what he said, but what he meant was that, on account of Yuriko, I must be particularly sensitive to what others say and do. I've met his type any number of times—the kind of man who thinks he can get away with pretending to know how I feel. I pushed the white onions that were floating on top of my ramen aside with my chopsticks and said nothing. Onions smell, so I hate them.

"I didn't know a thing about it; boy, was I shocked! Wasn't her killer the same man who was arrested in that Office Lady Murder last year?"

I glared at the section chief's face. The corners of his eyes were turned down and virtually dripped with curiosity. The child that I would have with the section chief had now become crude and hideously ugly.

"It's still under investigation. They can't say anything conclusive."

"I heard she was your friend. Is that right?"

"She was a classmate." Had Kazue and I ever been friends? I would have to give that idea further consideration.

"I'm really interested in the O.L. Murder, as they call it. I suspect you hear that from a lot of people. It just boggles the mind. What would drive her to do something so shocking? How could she have had such dark impulses? I mean, wasn't she a career woman employed by some construction-firm think tank in Otemachi? And a graduate of Q University on top of it. Why would such an elite professional become caught up in prostitution? You must know something about it."

So there it was! Yuriko had already been forgotten. If a woman who is beautiful but has no other redeeming value turns tricks until she's ancient, no one gives it a second thought. But Kazue's turn to prostitution left everyone racking their brains to figure out why. A career woman by day, a prostitute by night. Men everywhere were beside themselves trying to work that one out. That the section chief would lay bare his curiosity in this way struck me as particularly offensive. He must have noticed my expression because he began to stammer out an apology.

"Oh, I'm sorry. I'm being callous." And then he added, as a joke, "It's not sex-harass, so please don't be angry!"

Our conversation shifted to his Sunday baseball games. When he invited me to come watch one sometime I nodded appropriately and finished my ramen, making every effort to appear nonchalant. Finally, I understood. Mr. Nonaka wasn't interested in me. He was interested in the Yuriko-Kazue scandal. Wherever I go those scandals pursue me.

And just when I thought I had finally found a worthwhile job! I was tired of this worrisome chain of events at my workplace, but I didn't feel like resigning. It wasn't just the job. It was that a whole year had passed since I'd started working there, and I found comfort in the regularity of the hours.

After I graduated from the university and before I took the job at the P Ward Office, I did all kinds of things. I worked for a while in a convenience store, and I went door-to-door trying to sell subscriptions to a monthly study guide. Marriage? No. I never gave it a moment's thought. I'm really proud to be a middle-aged, part-time, unattached freelancer.

That night, before I went to bed, I fantasized about the child I would have with Mr. Nonaka. I even drew a picture of it on the back of an advertisement leaflet. The child was a boy with very dry skin. He had Mr. Nonaka's fat gabby lips and short stocky legs that made him swagger when he walked. From my side he took big, bright white teeth and tapered ears. I was pleased to see that the boy's features gave him a demonic look. And then I thought about what Mr. Nonaka had said to me. "When you talk, your voice is high-pitched, but when you laugh it's low. *Eee-hee-hee-hee.* That's how you laugh."

His observation had shocked me; I'd never paid attention to my own laughing voice. And so I tried laughing there by myself. It'll probably come as no surprise that the laugh I produced was hardly natural. I wondered which parent my laughter resembled. But I don't have any recollection of either my father or my mother ever laughing, so there was no way to judge. This was because the two of them never really laughed much. Yuriko, too, never raised her voice in laughter. She simply smiled mysteriously, maybe because she knew smiling showed her beauty to greatest effect. What a strange family! Suddenly the events of one winter day came flooding back.

• 3 •

Let's see. I'm thirty-nine years old now, so it must have been twenty-seven years ago. We spent our New Year's family vacation in our mountain cabin in Gunma; I suppose I should call it our "vacation cottage." It was just an ordinary house, no different from the surrounding farmhouses, but my father and mother always referred to it as our mountain cabin, so that was what I called it too.

When I was little, I could hardly wait for our weekends at the cabin. But once I entered junior high it became a real hassle. I hated the way the people there made such a fuss over my sister and me and our family—silently comparing us to each other. It was mostly the local farmers. Still, I couldn't very well stay behind by myself in Tokyo over the New Year's vacation, so off I went to Gunma—reluctantly—in the car my father drove. I was in my first year of junior high; Yuriko was in sixth grade.

Our cabin was in a small enclave of about twenty or so vacation homes of varying sizes and styles clustered at the foot of Mount Asama. With the exception of one third-generation Japanese family, almost all the houses were owned by foreign businessmen who had Japanese wives. Although an unwritten rule, it was as if Japanese people were not allowed in. In sum, it was a village where Western men married to Japanese women could escape their stifling Japanese companies and come to catch their breath. There must have been some other interracial children like my sister and me, but either they were already grown up or they weren't living in Japan, because we rarely saw any young people. That New Year's we were the only children, as usual.

On New Year's Eve my family and I went to a nearby mountain to ski. On our way back we stopped by a hot spring with an outdoor bath. As always this was my father's idea. He seemed to enjoy startling people with his foreign presence.

The outdoor bath was built alongside a river. The pool in the middle was for mixed bathing, but there were pools on either side partitioned off for single-sex use. The women's side of the bath was surrounded by a bamboo hedge, so you couldn't see in from the outside. As soon as we started taking off our clothes in the changing area, I began to hear the murmurs.

"Look at that girl."

"Why, she looks just like a doll!"

In the changing room, in the passage to the bath, and even from within the steam of the bath waters, the women whispered among themselves. Old women stared openly at Yuriko without the least bit of reservation, and young women made no attempt to hide the shock on their faces as they nudged one another with their elbows. Children, too, went out of their way to draw closer and stare with their mouths agape at the naked Yuriko. That's always the way it was.

Ever since she was a baby, Yuriko had been used to being ogled by perfect strangers. She'd strip naked without the slightest hesitation. Her body was still undeveloped and childlike, showing not the slightest suggestion of breasts. But even so, with her tiny little face and her fair complexion, she looked just like a Barbie doll. To me she looked like she was wearing a mask.

I had planned to take off my clothes, fold them carefully, and then walk down the narrow passage to the open-air bath while everyone was fixated on Yuriko.

"Is she your daughter?" a middle-aged woman sitting in a chair suddenly called out to my mother. She must have steeped herself too long in the hot waters of the bath because she looked hot sitting there, fanning her pink flesh with her damp towel.

Mother's hands stopped midair as she was pulling off her clothing.

"Is your husband a foreigner?" The woman glanced in my direction. I lowered my eyes and said nothing. The idea of pulling my underwear off was now disconcerting. I wasn't like Yuriko. I was sick and tired of being the object of curious stares. If I'd been by myself, I wouldn't have been so obvious. But thanks to the fact that I was there with the monster Yuriko, I couldn't slip by unnoticed. The woman kept pushing the point.

"So, I take it your husband's not Japanese?"

"That is correct."

"Well, that explains it! I've never seen such a pretty girl!"

"Thank you." A wave of pride flashed across my mother's face.

"But it must be odd to have a kid who doesn't look a thing like you."

The woman muttered this casually as if she were speaking to herself. My mother's face fell. "Hurry," she said to me and gave my back a soft poke. When I saw how her face had hardened, I knew the woman's words had hit home.

Outside, night had fallen and the stars were out. The air had turned cold. A cloud of white steam hovered over the bath. I was unable to see the bottom of the pool; it looked eerie, like a black pond. There was something glittery and white out in the middle.

Yuriko was floating on her back in the steamy water, looking up at the sky. Women and children, submerged in water up to their shoulders, surrounded her and stared at her wordlessly. I looked at Yuriko's face and was horrified. I had never seen her look more beautiful. She was almost godlike. It was the first time I had ever had that experience. She seemed to be more an effigy than a human being, too beautiful to be a creature of this world.

Mother called out, "Yuriko, dear?"

"Mother?"

Yuriko's clear voice rang out over the water, and the eyes that had been trained on her suddenly shifted to me and my mother. They returned to Yuriko once again and then pivoted back to me: eyes that were busy comparing, their curiosity overflowing. I knew it would not take long for them to determine which of us was the superior and which the inferior. Yuriko wanted those around her to see that she was nothing like her mother and older sister, and that is why she had answered when Mother called. That's the way my younger sister was. Yes, you're right. I never once felt any love for Yuriko. And my mother without a doubt had to do regular battle with the *odd feeling* that the pink woman had just mentioned.

I stared at Yuriko's face. Her brown hair clung to her exceptionally white forehead. Her brows arched in a bow. And her large eyes slanted downward slightly. Child though she was, the bridge of her nose was straight and perfectly formed. Her lips were plump, just like a doll's. Even among interracial children, a face as perfectly proportioned as Yuriko's was hard to find.

As for me, my eyes turned upward and my nose was as aquiline as my father's. To top it off, my body was squat and pudgy like my mother's. Why were we so different? I couldn't figure out how Yuriko had managed to inherit a face that was so superior to that of both her parents. I searched madly for some trace of them in her features, but no matter how hard I looked, I could only conclude that she was some kind of mutation.

Yuriko turned back to look at me. Strangely, the beauty that earlier had been so incredible that it seemed divine had now suddenly vanished. Without thinking, I let out a scream.

Startled, my mother turned toward me. "What's wrong?"

"Mother, Yuriko's face is creepy!"

I had suddenly noticed what it was: Yuriko's eyes gave off no light. Even a doll's eyes will have a white dot painted in the center to suggest light, won't they? As a result, a doll's face is sweet and charming, yet Yuriko's eyes were dark ponds. The reason she had looked so beautiful floating in the bath was because the light from the stars had been reflected in her eyes.

"That's no way to talk about your little sister!"

Mother pinched my arm hard under the water. The pain caused me to scream again, even louder.

"If that's what you think, you're the one who's creepy!" she said, with palpable loathing. Mother was angry. She had already become Yuriko's slave. By that I mean she worshiped her beautiful daughter. She was utterly intimidated by the fact that fate had given her such a lovely child. If Mother had admitted Yuriko's creepiness to me, I wonder if I would have been able to trust her. But Mother's outlook was different. I didn't have a single ally in the family. That's the way it looked to me when I was in junior high.

That night there was a big New Year's Eve party at the Johnsons' cottage. Usually we girls were not permitted to attend the adult parties, but since we were the only children in the entire mountain resort that night, we were included. Yuriko, my parents, and I headed along the dark path to our neighbors' house. Snow was falling lightly. The trip took several minutes, and Yuriko, who loved festive displays, skipped the whole way, kicking happily at the snow.

Johnson was an American businessman who had not owned the cabin long. His face was handsomely chiseled, his hair a golden brown. He was the kind of man who looked good in a pair of jeans, like the actor Jude Law. But I'd heard that he had a few screws loose.

For example, he took an ax and chopped down the saplings that had been planted in front of the bedroom window because, he said, they blocked his view of Mount Asama. He whacked a few miniature bamboo stalks off at the root and stuck them in the ground where the saplings had been, not even bothering to plant them properly. The community landscaper was furious. Johnson, of course, was delighted with the way the bamboo looked. I remember hearing my father scoff. "Well, leave it to an American to be satisfied with short-term remedies!"

Johnson's wife was a Japanese woman who went by the name of Masami. It seems she had met Johnson while working as a flight attendant. She was a beautiful and vibrant person, but she still found time to be friendly to Yuriko and me. She was never without her perfectly applied makeup or her humongous diamond ring, even when she was out in the middle of the mountains. She wore these like armor—behavior that struck me as downright odd.

When we got to the party, I found that the Japanese wives had left the main room where the party was and were squeezed into the tiny kitchen, a habit I found peculiar. One by one they were bragging about their own cooking. It almost sounded like they were quarreling with one another.

Occasionally foreign women would visit one of the families in the resort. When they did, they would sit on the sofa in the living room, conversing elegantly, while the white men stood around the fireplace drinking whiskey and speaking in English. It was weird to see each group forming such perfectly separate spheres. Only one Japanese wife would ever enter the circle of laughing men: Masami. She'd stand at Johnson's side, and occasionally I'd hear the cloying trill of her high-pitched voice cut across the monotonous murmurs of the men.

When we got inside, Mother immediately headed toward the kitchen, as if eager to claim a spot. The men called my father to the fireplace and handed him a glass of liquor. I didn't know what I was supposed to do, so, at a loss, I trailed after Mother to the kitchen, squeezing my way into the circle of housewives clustered there.

Yuriko latched on to Johnson, leaning against his knees as he perched in front of the fireplace. She was doing her best to play up to him. Masami's diamond ring sparkled as it caught the glow of the fire and shot flecks of light across Yuriko's cheeks. Just then I was struck by a wild fantasy. What if Yuriko wasn't really my sister? What if she was really Johnson and Masami's daughter? They were both so handsome. I can't explain it clearly, but if it were true, I could accept Yuriko. Even her monstrous beauty would take on a more human dimension. What do I mean by *human*? Well, that's a good question. I guess what I'm trying to say is that it would have made her ordinary, as if she were just a sneaky little pest, like a mole or something.

But—unfortunately—Yuriko was the offspring of my own mediocre parents. Wasn't that the very reason she had become a monster who possessed a too-perfect beauty? Yuriko glanced over at me with an air of self-satisfaction. Don't look over here, you freak! I thought to myself. I had a sick feeling. When I lowered my head and let out a sigh, Mother shot me a sharp look. I imagined her saying from deep in her heart, *You don't look a thing like Yuriko, do you!*

Without warning I began to laugh hysterically. When I didn't stop, the women gathered in the kitchen all turned to stare at me in shock. *It's not that I don't look like her! It's that she doesn't look like me, isn't it?* This response, I felt certain, was the perfect counter to my mother's statement. Yuriko's existence had forced my mother and me to take up enemy positions. I laughed when I realized this. (I have no idea if my junior high school laugh was the same low laughter that Mr. Nonaka of the Sanitation Bureau referred to or not.)

After the clock struck midnight and everyone toasted in the New Year, my father told Yuriko and me to head home by ourselves. My mother was still in the kitchen and showed no signs of budging. She looked so imbecilic I was suddenly convinced that, if she was clamped to the spot, she would be able to live forever right where she was. I was reminded of a turtle we'd kept in our classroom when I was in elementary school. It would always stretch its crooked legs out in the muddy water of its tank, raise its head, and sniff the dust-laden air of our classroom with a stupid look on its face, the nostrils in its big nose quivering.

The mind-numbing *Year Out/Year In* TV show had started as I searched for my muddy boots from among the piles of shoes that had been cast off and scattered across the floor of the wide entry hall. When the snow melts, the roads up in the mountains turn to mud, so even foreigners followed the Japanese practice of removing their shoes when they came inside. My old red rubber boots were as cold as ice when I slipped into them. Yuriko started to pout.

"You can't call our cabin a cabin. It's just a stupid old ordinary house. I wish we had a fireplace like the Johnsons'. That'd be great."

"Why?"

"Masami asked if, next year, we could have the party at our house."

"Well, too bad. Daddy's too stingy."

"Johnson was really surprised about that. He couldn't believe we were going to a Japanese school. Why do we have to live like the Japanese when we look so different from everyone else? It's just like he says. I'm always being teased and called gaijin and asked if I can speak Japanese and stuff."

"Yeah, well, no use crying to me."

I yanked the door open and stepped out ahead of Yuriko into the darkness. I don't know why I was so angry. The cold air stung my cheeks. The snow had stopped falling, and it was pitch-black. The mountains were there looming over us, pressing in around us, and yet they had dissolved into the darkness of the night and were completely invisible. With no light but a flashlight, Yuriko's eyes must have turned into those black pools again, I thought. I couldn't bring myself to look at her. I became frightened just by the knowledge that I was walking alone through the darkness with a monster. I gripped the flashlight and started running.

"Wait!" Yuriko shrieked. "Don't leave me!"

Eventually Yuriko stopped screaming, but I was too scared to turn around. I felt as if I were walking with my back to an eerie pond, and something was crawling up out of it and chasing me. Angry to have been left behind, Yuriko was running after me. When I finally turned around, her face was directly in front of me. I gazed slowly over the white sculpted features of her face, now illuminated in the light reflected off the snow. Her eyes were the only features I could not see. I was scared.

"Who are you?" I blurted out. "Who the hell are you?"

"What do you mean?"

"You're a monster!"

That made Yuriko angry. "Well, you're a dog!"

"I hope you die!"

And with that I took off. Yuriko snatched at the hood of my jacket from behind and pulled on it so tightly she made me bend backward. But I still managed to give her a hard push. She was smaller than I was, and I caught her off guard. She let go and tumbled backward, arms flailing, into a snowbank along the roadside.

I ran home without looking back again and, once inside, I locked the door. After a few minutes there came the sound of pathetic knocking, just like in a cartoon version of a fairy tale. I pretended not to hear.

"Please! Open the door. It's cold out here." Yuriko was crying. "Open the door! Please. I'm scared."

"You're the one who's scary! It serves you right!" I ran to my room and crawled into bed. I could hear Yuriko banging on the front door hard enough to break it down, but I pulled the blanket over my head. Just let her freeze to death! I thought. It's true. I longed for this from the very bottom of my heart.

I fell asleep before long, only to be awakened by the unpleasant smell of sour liquor. What time was it? I wondered. My parents were standing at the door to my bedroom arguing. My father was drunk. Because of the light pouring in from behind them, I couldn't make out the expressions on their faces. My father wanted to get me out of bed for a scolding, but Mother stopped him.

"She wanted to let her little sister freeze to death," he complained.

"No, she didn't. Besides, nothing happened."

"Well, I want to know why she'd do such a thing."

"She feels inferior to her sister, that's all," my mother argued, her voice low. Listening to what she said, I wondered why I'd been born to such a family, and I couldn't stop myself from crying.

You wonder why I didn't refute my mother's claim, don't you? But maybe I couldn't deny feeling inferior. I didn't understand my feelings at the time. And maybe I didn't want to admit that I truly hated Yuriko. I mean, she was my little sister; wasn't I supposed to love her? For so long I had been in the viselike grip of this sense of duty—a sense telling me that I was indeed morally obliged to love her.

And then the spectacle I beheld in the bath that night and again at the party liberated me from the pressure I had been feeling. I couldn't put up with it any longer. I just had to say what I felt.

The next morning there was no sign of Yuriko. Mother was downstairs pouring kerosene in the stove, a sour look on her face. My father was sitting at the breakfast table, but when he saw me approach he stood up to meet me, his breath reeking of coffee.

"Did you tell your sister, 'I hope you die'?"

When I didn't answer immediately he slapped me hard across the face with his thick palm. The smacking sound the slap made was so sharp it made my ears burn. My cheek stung with pain. I covered my face with both hands to ward off future blows, but I'd fully expected this kind of reaction. He'd been hitting me ever since I was little. First he would beat me and then he'd unleash a torrent of verbal abuse. It was often severe enough to require medical treatment.

"Reflect on your sins!" he ordered.

Whenever my father chastised Mother, Yuriko, or me, he always ordered us to reflect on our sins. He didn't really believe in apologies.

At kindergarten I'd learned that when you did something wrong, you said, "I'm sorry." And then the aggrieved party would answer, "That's all right." But this was never the way it worked at my house. Those words didn't even exist for us, so punishment always escalated into a major production. Yuriko looked creepy—so why the hell should I be the one "reflecting on my sins"? I suppose my indignation showed on my face, because my father slapped me again with all his might. From the corner of my eye I glimpsed my mother's pinched profile as I toppled to the floor. She didn't try to come to my defense. Instead, she pretended to concentrate on pouring the kerosene into the stove so as not to spill a drop. I scrambled to my feet, fled upstairs, and locked myself in my room.

Later that afternoon a deathly silence stole over the house. It seemed that my father had gone out somewhere, so I tiptoed out of my room. I didn't see Mother. Taking advantage of the moment, I slipped into the kitchen and ate the leftover rice right out of the container, scooping it into my mouth with my fingers. I took the orange juice out of the refrigerator and drained the carton. Then I found the pot with the *bigos* that had been left over from yesterday's lunch. The fat from the meat had solidified on the surface in white gobs. I spit into the pot. My orange-juice-laced spit clung to the shreds of overcooked cabbage. I was pleased. My father especially liked his *bigos* with overcooked cabbage.

I looked up when I heard the sound of the front door opening. Yuriko had come back. She was wearing the same jacket she'd worn last night and a white mohair cap I'd never seen, which had to be one of Masami's. It was a little large for her and came down low on her forehead, almost covering her eyes. Masami's stinky perfume filled the room. I glanced again at Yuriko's eyes, to confirm my earlier discovery. This beautiful girl with her creepy eyes. Yuriko made not the slightest attempt to speak to me before she bounded up the stairs. I clicked on the TV and settled down on the sofa. I was watching a New Year's comedy quiz show when Yuriko came into the room, toting a backpack and her beloved Snoopy dog.

"I'm going to the Johnsons'. I told them what you did, and they said it was too dangerous for me to stay here and I should stay with them."

"How nice. Now you don't ever have to come home again."

I was relieved. In the end, Yuriko spent the entire New Year's vacation with the Johnsons. Once I came across Johnson and Masami on the road. They both waved and said "Hi," their faces wreathed in smiles. I said "Hi" right back with a big smile of my own. But in my heart I was thinking, Johnson, you idiot! And what a stupid cow you are, Masami!

I couldn't care less if Yuriko never came home. She could become the idiot child of the idiot Johnsons for all I cared.

· 4 ·

The following year, my father's shop went under. Well, no, it wasn't just his shop, it was his entire business. As the Japanese grew more affluent, so too grew demands for imported confections of higher and higher quality, and consumers began to ignore the cheap candies that were my father's specialty. Father closed his shop. He had to sell off everything in order to meet his outstanding debts. Obviously, he had to let the mountain cabin go. He even had to sell off our little house in North Shinagawa, our car, everything.

Once he closed his business, Father decided to return to Switzerland to try to make a new start. His younger brother, Karl, had a hosiery manu-facturing business in Bern and needed help in managing the accounts, so it was decided that we would all move to Switzerland. This decision came just as I was preparing for the high school entrance exams. I had set my sights on entering a top-level school, the kind of school that would never enroll a dimwit like Yuriko. I'm talking about the school that Kazue and I attended. Let's just call it Q High School for Young Women, shall we? It was the elite preparatory school affiliated with Q University.

I asked my father to let me move in with my mother's father, who lived in P Ward, so that I could at least try to pass the high school exam. And if I did pass, I could commute to school from my grandfather's place. At any rate, I was determined to foil any attempt to ship me off to Switzer-land with Yuriko.

Father frowned at my request at first, complaining that Q High School for Young Women was expensive and would cost way more than we could afford. But since Yuriko and I hardly spoke to each other—ever since the incident at the cabin—he decided my plan was the best course to follow. I had him sign an agreement stating that if I made it into the school of my choice, he would promise to provide the funds I would need to cover the cost of my schooling up through graduation. Even though he was my father, he couldn't be relied on without a written agreement.

It was decided that I would continue living in P Ward with my mater-nal grandfather, who lived alone in a government-funded apartment complex. He was sixty-six years old. A short man, his arms and legs were delicate and his physique small. There was no mistaking him as my mother's father. He was the kind of person who struggled to appear fash-ionable, even though he had no money, so no matter where he went he always wore a suit, and he slicked back his salt-and-pepper hair with pomade. The smell of pomade so permeated his tiny apartment, it almost made me choke.

I'd never really seen much of my grandfather until then, and I was nervous about the prospect of living with him. I had no idea what to say to him. But once I actually moved in, my fears became moot. My grand-father talked nonstop in a high-pitched voice all day long. It wasn't as if he needed me around for conversation, he mostly just talked to himself.

That is, he repeated the same thing over and again, chattering on and on. I suspect he was delighted to share his home with someone as taciturn as myself. I was nothing more than a receptacle for his endless prattle.

Surely my grandfather found it inconvenient to have a granddaughter suddenly deposited on his doorstep. But there can be little doubt that he was grateful for the allowance my father provided. At the time, my grandfather was living off his pension. From time to time he'd make a little extra cash by doing odd jobs around the neighborhood; he was a sort of resident handyman. But I suspect he hardly had enough to live on.

What was my grandfather's occupation? Well, that's hard to say. When we were children, my mother told us that when Grandfather was young he'd been good at catching watermelon thieves, so he decided to join the police force and be a detective. That's why I was certain he'd be strict, and I was afraid of him at first. But in fact, the opposite was true. My grandfather had not been a detective. What had he been? Well, that's what I'll explain next. It might take some time, so please bear with me.

"It's not easy for us to go visit your grandfather, because he's a police detective," my mother would say. "He's very busy. Besides, he's always got a lot of people around him who have done bad things. But that doesn't mean your grandfather is bad. No indeed. It often happens that bad people are drawn to good people. Well, for example, people who've broken the law will come by your grandfather's place to apologize and to talk about how they plan to mend their ways. But there's always someone who's just bad to the bone. That person might hold a grudge against your grandfather for arresting him, so when he comes to visit he comes for revenge. It would be dangerous for children to be around if that happened."

Listening to these stories as if Mother were describing something in a distant land, I'd get excited, imagining a scene from a television crime drama. My grandfather's a police detective! I'd brag about it whenever one of my friends stopped by. But Yuriko never looked very impressed and would always ask Mother why grandfather was a detective. I guess she didn't think having a detective for a grandfather was particularly thrilling; I have no idea what went on in her head. But my mother's answer was always the same. "Your grandfather was very good at catching watermelon thieves. His father owned giant fields in Ibaraki Prefecture—that's where the thieves lurked."

I passed the entrance exam to Q High School for Young Women just before my parents and Yuriko set off for Switzerland, so I loaded up a little truck with my futon, desk, school supplies, and clothes and moved from North Shinagawa to my grandfather's apartment in the government housing project. P Ward is in the scruffier part of downtown Tokyo, in the so-called Low City. It's mostly flat there, with hardly any tall buildings. A number of large rivers run through the ward, slicing it into smaller sections. The large levees along the rivers obstruct one's line of vision. The surrounding buildings are not very high but, because of the levees, they look oppressive. It is in fact a very peculiar area. Just beyond the levees, an immense volume of water flows by at a normally languid pace. Whenever I'd climb the banks of the levees to gaze down into the brownish water of the river below, I'd imagine all the different life-forms swirling around beneath the surface.

On the day I moved in, my grandfather bought two cream puffs from the local shop. They weren't the kind you'd get at a bakery, but the kind with the hard puff pastry shell and the custard filling that I hate. I didn't want to hurt Grandfather's feelings, so I finished it, pretending to savor each bite. As I ate I studied Grandfather's face, trying to figure out what about him resembled my mother. Although they shared the same slight build, their faces looked nothing alike.

"Mother doesn't look like you, Grandfather. Who does she take after?"

"Oh, she takes after no one, that mother of yours. Some relative long dead must have been the one to pass his looks along to her."

Grandfather pulled the cardboard cake box apart, as he answered, and folded it flat according to the directions on the outside of the carton. He tucked it, along with the paper wrapping and string, atop the shelf in the kitchen.

"I don't look like anyone either," I said.

"Well, we've got that kind of characteristic in our family."

Grandfather was a man of habit. He rose punctually at five every morning and began tending to the bonsai trees that cluttered the veranda and the narrow space of the entry hall. Cultivating bonsai trees was his hobby. He'd spend over two hours each morning tending to them. Next he'd clean the room, and after that he'd have his breakfast.

As soon as he woke he'd start prattling in the Ibaraki dialect of his hometown. Even while I was washing my face or brushing my teeth, he'd be chattering away.

"Oh, now this is a nice trunk. Look here! The strength! The age! Any number of pines like this line the Tokaidō Highway, no doubting that. How fortunate I am to have such lovely bonsai. Or maybe I've my own talent to thank. I'm sure that's it. Must be my talent. A genius has to be fanatic with a little bit of humor. Yes, that's me."

I'd glance in his direction, thinking he was talking to me, but he'd be staring at his bonsai and conversing with himself. And every morning he'd say just about the same thing.

"People who aren't really fanatics can try all they want, but they'll never have the talent and their bonsai won't look anything like those that have been raised by an old fool like me! What'll be different? Well, let me see . . ."

I finally stopped turning around when I heard him begin to talk. I had realized he wasn't talking to me. He'd pose a question and then answer it himself. I was thrilled to have passed the entrance exam and to be on my way to a new life. I couldn't care less about bonsai trees! I'd flip through the pages of the high school guide and give myself over to intoxicating images of how my life would be in my beloved Q High School for Young Women.

I left Grandfather where he was and went to the kitchen to fix a slice of toast—which I then slathered generously with butter, jam, and honey. My father wasn't here to scold me for using too much jam. I felt completely liberated! My father was such a miser he was always warning us about what and how much we ate. We could have up to two lumps of sugar in our tea, but that was all. And we could only have a thin smear of jam on our bread. If we wanted honey, all we could have was honey. And his ideas about table manners were equally rigid. No talking at the table. Elbows in and back straight. No laughing with food in your mouth. No matter what I did he'd find grounds for complaint. But even if I sat slouched and bleary-eyed over the table eating my breakfast, Grandfather took no notice. He stood on the veranda talking to his plants.

"It takes inspiration, you know. That's essential. Inspiration. 'To be infused with spirit.' Go ahead, look it up in the dictionary, why don't you. You'll see it's not just a question of possessing elegance. Elegance will animate your work, no doubt about that. But you can't just pick it up. You have to have talent too. Those who succeed have talent. And so I say, I've got the talent. I've been inspired."

My grandfather scribbled the Chinese ideographs for *inspiration* in the air in front of his face. And then he drew the characters for *fanatic*. I drank my tea and watched wordlessly. After a long time my grandfather noticed me sitting at the kitchen table.

"Is there any left for your grandpa?"

"There is, but it's cold now." I pointed to the toast. Grandfather set on the cold dry toast with great delight and gnawed at it with his false teeth, sending crumbs flying. As soon as I saw this, I knew the stories my mother told about his being a detective were lies. I don't know quite how to explain it, but even to my sixteen-year-old eyes it was clear what kind of person Grandfather was. He was the kind who thought only of himself. There's no way he ever could have chased down another man and charged him with a crime.

Grandfather's dentures were ill-fitting, and it seemed difficult for him to chew, so he dunked his toast into his tea until it was soft and soggy. Some of the bread melted away into the tea, but my grandfather gulped it down anyway.

I summoned up my courage and asked, "Grandfather, do you think Yuriko is inspired?"

Grandfather looked out over the veranda at the large black pine and answered in no uncertain terms.

"Not whatsoever. Yuriko-chan is just too pretty a girl for that. She might be a garden plant. A pretty flower. But she's no bonsai."

"So, a flower, no matter how pretty, is not inspired?"

"That's right. Inspiration is the bonsai's trump card. But it's a person who makes it that way, you know. Look over there, at the black pine. Now that's inspiration. See there? An old tree gives us a lesson in life. Strange, isn't it? The tree may look withered, but it's living just the same. A tree can withstand the passage of time. Humans are the only ones who are at their most beautiful when they're young. But a tree, no matter how many years go by, you train it and train it, and though the tree itself would naturally resist, gradually it bends to your will. And when it does? Why then it's as if life has sprung forth anew, isn't it? Inspiration resides at that point when you begin to feel the miraculous. That's the word for it in English, right? Miracle?"

"I suppose so."

"What about in German?"

"I don't know."

Here we go again, I thought to myself, and I only pretended to look back at the veranda where he was standing. I could hardly understand a thing my grandfather talked about, and listening to him grew tiresome. All my grandfather really cared about was the dried-up old pine tree that he'd plopped down smack in the middle of the veranda. The roots were gnarled and hideous and the branches were crisscrossed with wires. With the needles bunching up like helmets, the tree was in the way of everything. It had the shape of one of those old twisted pines that you see in any run-of-the-mill samurai movie. Yet it was inspired, and the gorgeous Yuriko wasn't! What could have been more perfect? I adored my grandfather for saying what he'd said. And I prayed I'd be able to go on living with him like this forever.

My grandfather, being who he was, also gained by having me around. I was soon to discover why. There were days when he'd run around in a panic putting all the bonsai in the closet. On the third Sunday of every month at eleven o'clock in the morning, a neighborhood man came to call on my grandfather. It was like clockwork. Grandfather had marked the third Sunday of the month on his calendar with a bright red circle so he would not forget. On those Sundays, as soon as he'd finished conversing with his bonsai, he would start rearranging things in his closet and moving his junk here and there. Regardless of whether it was cloudy or threatening rain at any minute, he'd have me drag my futon out and hang it on the drying pole on the veranda—so as to make more room in the closet. And then he'd start scrambling to carry the bonsai into the space he'd made. There were hordes of the things crowded onto the tiny veranda. What he couldn't squeeze into the closet, he'd carry over to the apartments of the friends who also lived in our government-funded apartment complex. For a time I was mystified by Grandfather's behavior. Why would he want to hide the things that clearly brought him so much pride?

The visitor Grandfather received on the third Sunday of every month was an old man with a gentle face. His thinning white hair was combed neatly back, and his gray shirt and brown jacket blended tastefully. Only his eyeglass frames—heavy and black—were overly conspicuous. Even though he always apologized perfunctorily for calling on Grandfather empty-handed, he never once brought over the customary visitor's gift. When the old man arrived, my grandfather would sit up straight and receive him with the most dignified posture. For some reason, he never wanted me to be around. When anyone else came to call, he would always insist on having me by his side and would go on at great length about me, clearly proud to have a granddaughter who was half European and a student at the elite Q High School for Young Women to boot. My grandfather had lots of acquaintances. There was the insurance sales-woman, the security guard, the apartment superintendent, and all the other old men who liked bonsai. They were always stopping by to visit. But it was just this old gentleman that he didn't want me to be around. I couldn't help but find this peculiar.

On the days this visitor was expected, Grandfather was nervous. He'd ask me if I had homework to do. I'd set the tea out and then pretend to return to my room, but I'd eavesdrop from the other side of the sliding door partition. Cutting short the pleasantries, the old man would start prying.

"How're things these days?"

"I'm managing. Please don't worry on my account. I'm terribly sorry you had to come all the way out to this dirty old apartment. Really, my granddaughter's come to stay with me, and we're having a good time watching our pennies and keeping things simple. Sure, we have our disagreements—she's a high school student and I'm a tottering old fool; what would you expect? But we're getting along fine."

"Your grandchild, you say? Well, you don't look much alike, do you? I wanted to ask you about her but then I thought—well, what if she's your young mistress? I'd be pretty embarrassed if that were the case, and I didn't want to be caught prying. . . ."

The old man's tone was brisk and insinuating. He and my grandfather laughed together. *"Eee-hee-hee-hee!"*

So that's it, then? I get my laughter from my grandfather? Grand-father's speaking voice was high-pitched, but his laugh was surprisingly low, even a bit lewd. My grandfather quickly lowered his voice.

"No, no, she's my daughter's child. Her father's a foreigner, you see."

"Ah, an American?"

"No. European. My granddaughter's fluent in German and French and all sorts of other languages, but she decided she wanted her educa-tion to be in Japanese. She said she was Japanese, and she intended to study in Japanese and reach her adulthood in Japan. So she insisted on staying behind when her family left. My son-in-law is with the Swiss For-eign Ministry. That's right, he's second only to the ambassador. Such a fine son-in-law he is, what a pity he can't speak a word of Japanese. Still, he says he can communicate through signs and telepathy. It's real, you know, telepathy. My son-in-law knows exactly what I'm thinking. Why, just the other day he sent me two watches from Switzerland. They're the product of inspiration, you see. Do you know the derivation for this word *inspiration*? The ideographs for it are written this way."

I bit back my laughter as I listened to my grandfather's lies.

The visitor sighed. "No, I don't believe I'm familiar with the derivation."

"I suppose you could say it's derived from a reference to that which is animated by divine or supernatural influence—a combination of elegance and strength."

"Well, then, it's a very good word, isn't it? But tell me about your granddaughter's family. Where are they now?"

"The fact is, the Swiss government sent for my son-in-law and his family and brought them back to Switzerland."

"Very impressive."

"No, not really. A job with the United Nations or with a bank would be even more prestigious, you know."

"Well, this news sets my mind at ease—at least for the time being. I'd heard that you'd started doing odd jobs, but I trust you'll behave yourself. You're not going to start swindling people again, are you? You have your granddaughter to think of now."

"No, no, no chance of that. I've mended my ways. Just look around you. Not a bonsai in sight. No, I'll never touch another bonsai again."

Grandfather spoke with great contrition. When I heard this I realized that in the past Grandfather must have used bonsai in some kind of scam and the older gentleman must be some kind of probation officer. He visited Grandfather once a month to ensure he wasn't resorting to his old tricks, whatever they had been.

Now that I look back on it, I realize that Grandfather was out on parole and the presence of a studious high-school-age granddaughter in his household must have helped make him seem more trustworthy in the eyes of this monitor. My grandfather wanted to hoodwink his probation officer, and I wanted to stay in Japan. We needed each other to accomplish our goals, so in a way we were partners in crime. To top it off, I was able to talk to my grandfather about all of Yuriko's shortcomings. These were truly the happiest days of my life.

I unexpectedly crossed paths with the probation officer shortly after that Sunday. It was during the spring Golden Week holidays, and I was on my way back from the grocery store on my bicycle. A sightseeing bus was stopped alongside an old landed estate, and the gentleman I'd seen at Grandfather's house was waving good-bye to the passengers as they boarded. Each one was elderly, and each clutched a bonsai with a look of great satisfaction. My eye was drawn to the sign hanging nearby: GARDEN OF LONGEVITY. So this is where they cultivated bonsai? I gazed at the sign, my interest captivated by the sight of the little trees. When the bus pulled away, the old man noticed me.

"Oh, what a stroke of luck to run into you here," he said. "Actually, I'd like to have a word with you, if you don't mind."

I got down from my bike and bowed politely. Glancing at the estate through the roofed gateway—which was as imposing as one you might see at the entrance to a temple—I glimpsed a magnificent house constructed in the understated elegance of the rustic *sukiya* style. Next to the house was a lovely teahouse. There was also a vinyl-paned greenhouse on the grounds, where a number of young men inside watered plants with hoses and turned up the soil. It was hardly a nursery; the Garden of Longevity had more the look of a well-kept park. The buildings, the grounds: all were sumptuous. Even I could tell that they were the result of a lavish outlay of money. The probation officer, with his crisp navy-blue apron strapped over his shirt and necktie, looked somewhat out of place, like the town mayor dressed for a day of pottery. He had traded his earlier dark-rimmed glasses for a pair of dark-green sunglasses in light tortoiseshell frames.

The officer began to grill me about my family. I assumed he was trying to verify my grandfather's story. Had my parents really moved to Switzerland? he inquired, a tinge of worry in his voice. I assured him that they had.

"What does your grandfather do all day?"

"He seems quite busy with his handyman jobs."

That was the truth. For whatever reason, after I arrived my grandfather was inundated with requests from the neighbors.

"Well, that's good to hear. What kind of jobs is he doing?"

"Oh, he gets rid of the dead stray cats people find, looks after places while the residents are away, waters plants: that kind of thing."

"Well, so long as your grandfather doesn't fool with bonsai I have no complaint. He doesn't know a thing about bonsai and has no business pretending he does. He stole pots from others, you know, and then sold them as his own. Some he bought cheap at the night market and then turned around and sold them for exorbitant prices. He stirred up a lot of trouble and bilked a lot of people out of well over fifty million yen."

I rather suspected that those bilked out of their money were somehow connected to the probation officer. He was most likely a bonsai cultivator himself, or at least an employee at this estate. And it was probably from here that my grandfather had stolen the bonsai. Maybe he started out negotiating with the estate to broker their bonsai and then ended up bilking them of their money. This old man had probably been assigned to keep an eye on my grandfather, to be sure he didn't get involved with bonsai again. It was likely that he was going to keep watching him for a long time to come. I felt sorry for Grandfather.

Hundreds of bonsai were lined up with careful precision along thick wooden planks throughout the estate grounds. Among them was a large pine that resembled the tree my grandfather prized so dearly. In my estimation, it was much too impressive and expensive even to begin to compare to the one my grandfather had.

"I'm sorry to ask, but does my grandfather really know nothing of bonsai?"

"He's a rogue amateur." The probation officer snorted with contempt, his genial expression suddenly darkening.

"But if my grandfather tricked people, they must have been extremely wealthy."

I was thinking that if there were people who were so rich they were susceptible to my grandfather's scheme, their lack of appreciation for the bonsai he adored must have made him blind with anger. I could hardly imagine that people would actually be willing to spend so much on a single bonsai; it seemed to me that the swindled were worse than the swindler. Of course, the probation officer didn't see it that way. He was furiously poking his hand though the air around him.

"Plenty of people in this area got rich off the compensation money paid when they lost their fishing grounds. This whole area used to be under the ocean, you know."

"Under the ocean?" I gasped in spite of myself, completely forgetting the bonsai. I suddenly realized that the love that had been ignited between my mother and father, and the energy it had generated, dissipated the moment conception took place. The new life-form that was to become me ought to have been released then and there into the sea that opened up between them. I'd thought that for a long time. And now at last I had found my release in this new life that I shared with my grandfather, a life that was the sea itself. My decision to live with my grandfather in his tiny pomade-permeated apartment, the fact that I had to listen to his ceaseless chatter and live in a room surrounded by bonsai, was for me the sea, the very sea itself. This coincidental congruence made me happy, and that's what led me to decide to stay in the area.

When I got home, I told Grandfather about meeting the probation officer at the Garden of Longevity. Surprised, my grandfather began to question me.

"What did he say about me?"

"That you were a bonsai amateur."

"Shit!" my grandfather growled. "That bastard doesn't know shit! That 'true oak' of his that won the Ward Prize was a joke. Ha! Just thinking of it makes me want to bust a gut! Anybody can throw money around and buy a good tree. Let him boast about his five million yen. You just look, he doesn't know about inspiration."

From that day on my grandfather spent the entire day on the veranda talking to his bonsai.

I didn't learn this until later, but the probation officer used to work for the ward office. He took a position as a guide at the Garden of Longevity, when he retired, and volunteered to monitor my grandfather's probation. He's dead now. As soon as he died, my grandfather and I felt as if a huge boulder had been lifted off our heads.

My grandfather? He's still alive, but he's a senile old man who sleeps most of the day. He has no idea who I am. I change his diapers and work like crazy to look after him, but he just points at me and asks me who I am. Occasionally he'll call my mother's name, and say things like, "Better do your homework or you'll end up a thief!" Each time I'm tempted to respond, "Yeah, well, look who's talking! You're the one who turned out to be the thief." As long as grandfather is alive, I can continue to live in his government-sponsored apartment, so I can't come down on him too hard.

Oh, yes, I want my grandfather to live a long and frugal life. It seems the word *inspiration* has completely evaporated from his brain. I wore myself out two years ago trying to take care of him, so I had to put him in the ward-managed Misosazai Nursing Home.

My grandfather really did work as a handyman, and I did more than just answer the phone for him. When I could I was happy to help him with his jobs. I really enjoyed it, especially since I hadn't had a lot of contact with people until then. Hardly anyone came to visit us when I was little. My father preferred to associate with people from his own country, but even then he rarely included his family. My mother didn't associate with others in the neighborhood. She didn't have a single friend. She never came to meet our teachers or sit in on our classes. Needless to say, she didn't belong to the Parent-Student Association. That's the kind of family I had.

I never thought Yuriko would return to Japan and ruin everything. But four months after moving to Switzerland, my mother committed suicide. Before she died I'd gotten a number of letters from her, but I hadn't sent her a single note in return. That's right. Not one.

I have a few of her letters still with me and will be happy to show them to you. As much as I read them, I never imagined she'd commit suicide. That's because I never dreamed Mother had such a hidden store of pain. Until she actually chose suicide, I never even noticed that she wanted to bid this world farewell. But what really surprised me was that Mother had the courage to take her own life.

How are you? The three of us are well. How are you getting along with your grandfather? He's much more decisive than me, so I suspect the two of you are hitting it off. I wanted to let you know, though, that you don't have to give Grandfather a single yen more than the ¥40,000 that we've promised to pay each month. You have to take care of things at your end and can't rely on us. But I'm transferring a small sum to your bank account. This is to be your own spending money, so keep it secret from your grandfather. And if he manages to wheedle a loan out of you, be sure to get him to write out a promissory note. These are your father's instructions that I'm passing along.

By the way, how's your schoolwork? I can't believe you made it into such an elite high school! I brag about you whenever I run into another Japanese person here. And although Yuriko has yet to say anything, I'm sure she is furious with jealousy. Please keep up your studies; it's great incentive for Yuriko! You can always better her with your brains.

I suppose the cherry blossoms have all but fallen in Japan. I miss the Yoshino cherries. They must have been so beautiful when the blossoms were at their peak. I've not seen any cherry trees in Bern. I'm sure they must be blooming somewhere, so the next chance I get, I'm going to ask a member of the Japanese Citizens Association. Though your father isn't really keen on my joining the Japanese Citizens Association—or the Japanese Women's Group, for that matter.

It's still cold here: you can't go out without a coat. The wind off the Aare River is chilly, and the cold so bitter it makes me lonely. I'm wearing the beige coat that we bought on sale at the Odakyū Department Store. I'm sure you remember. It's really too light for this weather, but I'm constantly getting compliments on it. Some people even ask me where I bought it. The people here really dress well. They carry themselves properly and always seem dignified.

Bern is as pretty as a fairy tale but it's much smaller than I had imagined, and this really surprised me at first. I was also surprised to find people from so many different countries living here. When we first arrived I walked through the streets amazed at everything I saw, but lately I've grown a little tired of it. Most of our money is going toward your allowance and school fees, so we can't really buy anything and have to live as frugally as possible. Yuriko is angry and claims it's all because you got to stay behind in Japan. But don't worry about it. You've got to rely on your brains to get ahead.

Our house is in a new area of the city. Karl's hosiery factory is one building over. Across from us is a building with tiny apartments, and alongside that is an empty lot. Your father's pleased because we are within the city limits, but it feels like we're on the outskirts to me. If I bring it up, however, it makes your father furious. Wherever you go in Bern the streets are orderly, and all you find are tall people speaking an incomprehensible language. Moreover, everyone is really aggressive. This has been quite a lesson for me.

Just the other day I had this experience. I'm always careful to obey the traffic signals when I cross the street, but still you have to watch for turning vehicles. As I was crossing, a car came so close to hitting me that the hem of my coat was caught on the bumper and the lining tore slightly. The woman who was driving stopped and got out of the car. I thought she was coming to apologize but she started yelling at me instead. I didn't understand what she was saying, but she kept pointing at my coat and railing on and on. Maybe she was saying it was my fault for trying to cross the street with my coat flapping open! I told her I was sorry for the trouble I had caused and went home. When I told your father about it that night he was furious with me. "You should never admit to being in the wrong!" he said. "The minute you do, you've lost the battle. You should have at least gotten money to mend your coat!" That's when it dawned on me that your father's refusal to accept blame comes from living in this country, and so this too has been a lesson.

Three months have passed since we got here. All the furniture we shipped has finally arrived, and this has offered me a bit of relief. But the furnishings don't really suit the modern apartment we have. Your father is out of sorts about it. "We ought to have just bought furniture here!" he complains. "This Japanese furniture is worthless." I tell him there's no way he can get money for new furniture, so he should just stop going on about it. But then he gets even angrier and says we ought to have discussed it beforehand. I think your father's gradually reverting to his old self. He's always angry. Now that he's back in his own country, he's even more concerned about doing things the right way, and he gets aggravated by all the mistakes I make.

Recently he and Yuriko have been going out together a lot without me. This seems to make Yuriko very happy. She gets along well with Karl's oldest son (he also works in your uncle's factory) and they spend a lot of time together.

I was really surprised to find how expensive everything is here. Much higher than I expected. If we eat out it costs more than ¥2,000 a person, and the food isn't even that good. Something as basic as nattō, the fermented soybeans that I like, costs as much as ¥650! Can you believe it? Your father says it's due to tariffs. But it seems the people here all have very good salaries.

On another note, your father's new job does not seem to have taken off quite as he hoped. I don't know if it's because he's not getting along with the other employees or if your uncle Karl's business isn't very sound at the moment, or what. But he sulks around the house as soon as he gets home, and when I ask him about his work he won't answer. If you were here with us I suspect the two of you would be fighting all the time. So it's good that you are where you are. Yuriko pretends that she doesn't notice anything.

The other day we went to your uncle Karl's for a visit. I made a plate of chirashi-zushi, *a chilled rice dish, to take along. Karl's wife, Yvonne, is French. They have two children. There's the son who works in the factory. He's twenty, and his name is Henri. Then they have a daughter in high school. They told me her name, but I've forgotten it. She looks just like Yvonne. She has light blond hair and a beakish nose. She's fat and not pretty at all. When Yvonne and Karl saw Yuriko, they were shocked. Karl said something like, "So, if you marry an Oriental you can have pretty daughters like this?" Yvonne just looked sulky.*

That reminds me. Whenever your father and I go out for walks with Yuriko, we get strange reactions. The people we meet in the park stare at us with curiosity, every one of them. Finally someone asked us what country we adopted Yuriko from. There are people here from all kinds of other countries, and apparently adoption is quite popular. When I tell them that Yuriko is my own child, they don't seem to believe me. I guess they can't accept that a shabby-looking Oriental like me could ever produce a beauty like Yuriko, and the thought makes them very angry. "You're overreacting!" your father will tell me. But I can't help it. That's what I believe. I think they just can't accept that a member of the yellow race could give birth to something so perfect. It gives me some satisfaction to be able to say, No, Yuriko is not adopted. I gave birth to her myself.

Please write and tell me how you are. Your father needs to send you an update as well. Please give my best to Grandfather.

TWO · A CLUSTER OF NAKED SEED PLANTS

· 1 ·

Tokyo, April 20, 2000—On April 19 shortly after 6 p.m., the body of a woman was discovered in unit 103 of the Green Villa Apartments, Maruyama-chō, Shibuya Ward. The apartment superintendent who found the body called 911.

The Investigations Bureau of the Metropolitan Police Headquarters, in cooperation with the Shibuya Ward Police Precinct, launched an inquiry and determined that the deceased was Kazue Satō, 39, a resident of the Kita-Toriyama area of Setagaya Ward and an employee with G Architecture and Engineering Corporation.

Judging from the marks on her neck, the Investigations Bureau has cited strangulation as the cause of death and ruled it a homicide. An investigation is now under way.

According to initial reports, the victim was last seen leaving her house on April 8 around 4 p.m., destination unknown.

Her body was discovered in a six-mat room that had been

vacant since August of the previous year. The door to the vacant apartment was unlocked and Satō's body was found faceup on the floor in the center of the room. Her handbag was recovered at the site, and though she was believed to have been carrying approximately ¥40,000, her wallet was empty. She was dressed in the same clothes that she had been seen wearing earlier that day.

Ms. Satō entered G Architecture and Engineering Firm after graduating from Q University in 1984. She was assigned to the General Research Department, where she was assistant manager of the research office. Single, she lived with her mother and a younger sister.

When I read this article in the *Tokyo Daily,* I knew immediately that it was the same Kazue Satō I had known in school. Of course, a name like Kazue Satō is not uncommon, and conceivably I was mistaken. But I was convinced. There could be no mistake. How could I be so certain? Because almost two years earlier, shortly after Yuriko died, Kazue had called me. It was the last phone call I ever received from her.

"It's me," she had said. "Kazue Satō. Hey, I heard Yuriko-chan's been murdered."

I'd not heard one word from Kazue since university, yet this was the first thing out of her mouth.

"It's such a shock!"

I was shocked too, not by Yuriko's death and not even by the fact that Kazue had called me out of the blue. Rather, I was unsettled by the fact that Kazue was laughing on the other end of the line. Her low, whispery laugh lingered like the buzzing of a bee. Maybe she intended the laugh to seem consoling, but I felt it seep into my hand as I clung to the telephone receiver. I've said, haven't I, that Yuriko's death didn't particularly surprise me? But at that moment, and that moment only, I felt a chill shoot down my spine.

"What's so funny?" I asked.

"Nothing." Kazue's response was overly casual. "Well, I suppose you're sad, aren't you?"

"Not really."

"Oh, that's right." Kazue's tone indicated that she had always been perfectly aware of how I felt. "You and Yuriko-chan weren't particularly close, as I recall. It was as if you two weren't even related. Others might not have realized you were sisters, but I picked up on it right away."

"So what are you up to?"

"Guess."

"I heard you'd gotten a job with an engineering firm after university."

"Would you be surprised if I told you Yuriko-chan and I were in the same line of work?"

Detecting the note of triumph in her voice, I was at a loss for words. I had a hard time associating Kazue's present life with words like *men*, *prostitution*, and *sex*. From what I had heard, she worked for a very reputable firm and was making her way as an elite career woman. When I didn't respond immediately, Kazue offered the following parting shot and then hung up: "Well, *I* intend to be careful!"

I stood there for some time looking down at the telephone, wondering whether the person I'd just spoken to was really Kazue. Could it have been someone else claiming to be her? The Kazue I knew had not been so cryptic. She always spoke with arrogant conclusiveness—all the while staring nervously into the face of her audience, terrified of being caught in a mistake. She was incredibly haughty when she spoke about an academic subject. But if the conversation shifted to the latest trends in fashions, restaurants, or boyfriends, she clammed up, relinquished her superiority, and sank into the background. That was the Kazue I knew. The discrepancy between her confidence and her insecurity was so great, I had almost felt sorry for her. If Kazue had changed, it meant she'd found a new means of doing battle with the world.

This is what you want me to talk about, isn't it? Of course, I fully intend to return to Kazue and Yuriko in due course, but I seem to continue getting sidetracked. I'm sorry. All these digressions about myself really have nothing to do with the topic at hand. I imagine I've bored you to tears by now, as I am sure you would much rather hear about Yuriko and Kazue.

But what is it about those two that interests you, if I may ask? I know I've asked this earlier. It's just that I can't quite understand the fascination. Is it because the man accused of the crime—Zhang's his name, a Chinese national—was in the country illegally? Is it because of the rumors that Zhang was falsely accused?

Are you suggesting that Kazue, Yuriko, and that man as well each had their own different dark infatuations? I myself do not think so. But I am convinced that both Kazue and Yuriko enjoyed what they were doing, and that Zhang did too. No, no, I'm not saying he enjoyed killing. In fact, I don't even know if he was the murderer—and I don't particularly want to know, either.

It's probably true that the man had relations with both Yuriko and Kazue. Didn't he say he bought their services for an incredibly cheap sum? Just two or three thousand yen, I think he said, less than twenty-five dollars. If that's the case, he must have had something they wanted. I mean, there had to have been some reason for Yuriko and Kazue to do what they did. That's why I imagine they enjoyed their relationship with him. Why else would they have agreed to sell themselves for such a low price? Wasn't this the means they had for waging war on the world? This is what I meant earlier in reference to Kazue. But theirs was a method beyond my abilities.

During the three years I spent with Kazue Satō in high school and the four we had in university, my family was undergoing tremendous changes. A big factor was my mother's suicide in Switzerland just before the summer vacation of my first year in high school. (I believe I showed you my mother's last letter, didn't I? I'll speak to you more about her in due course as well.)

Kazue encountered a similar experience. Her father died suddenly while she was in university. By that time she and I weren't seeing a lot of each other, so I'm not certain of the exact circumstances, but it seems he had a cerebral hemorrhage and collapsed in the bathroom. For this reason, Kazue's family circumstances and standing at school were not unlike my own.

I referred to our standing at school just now, and I think it safe to say that she and I were the only ones at our school who had undergone experiences significantly unlike those of anyone else. So it would seem perfectly natural for the two of us to be drawn to each other.

Kazue and I both passed the entrance exam and entered the Q school system in high school. As I am sure you are aware, Q High School for Young Women is extremely competitive and accepts only those with the highest scores on the board exams. Kazue undoubtedly studied hard for the exams while she was in a municipal junior high school and got in. I don't know whether it was by fortune or fate, but I made it too. Of course, my motivation for giving everything I had to pass the entrance exam was driven by my desire to get away from Yuriko. It wasn't that I was particularly fixated on Q High School for Young Women itself. But Kazue was different. Ever since she was in elementary school she had set her sights on Q High School, and as she would tell me later she devoted herself to her studies precisely so she might achieve her goal. Here lies the difference between Kazue and me, and it is a big difference.

The Q school organization extends from elementary school through university, meaning that those who succeed in entering at the ground level as elementary students can, for all intents and purposes, glide all the way up to university level without the hellish pressure of additional entrance exams. This particular kind of school structure is therefore referred to as an "escalator" institution. The elementary school enrolled both boys and girls and only admitted around 80 children. In middle school, the number of students doubled. In high school, students were divided by sex, and once again the class size doubled. Therefore, among the 160 students attending the young women's division in any given year, half would be those who had only just entered the program at the high school level, while the other half would have been there longer, either from elementary school or junior high.

The university, on the other hand, admits students from across Japan, and the number of famous people who claim Q University as their alma mater is impossible to count. Q University is so famous that my grandfather's elderly friends would all gasp in admiration at the mere mention of the name. That's because the university doesn't admit just anybody. And that is why students enrolled in the Q system—who would be able eventually to glide into the prestigious Q University—felt entitled. The sooner students had entered the system, the more profound their sense of elitism.

It is precisely because of this escalator system that parents with money try so hard to get their children into the school at the elementary level. I've heard from others that the intensity with which they approach these initial exams is near hysteria. Of course, I have no child of my own and have no connection to any of this, so I cannot profess to be an authority.

When I create my imaginary children, do I sometimes have them entering Q Elementary School? Is that your question? Absolutely not. Never. My children merely swim in an imaginary sea. The water is a perfect blue, just as those hypothetical illustrations based on Cambrian fossils. There on the sand of the ocean floor, amid rocky crags, everything engages in a survival of the fittest and all living creatures exist just to procreate. It's a very simple world.

When I first started living with my grandfather, I would dream about what my life would be like as a student at the coveted Q High School for Young Women. My imagination ran rampant, one scene unfolding after another. It gave me a great deal of pleasure, as I have already said, to indulge in these fantasies. I would join clubs, make friends, and live an ordinary life like any other ordinary person. But reality tore these dreams to shreds. Basically, cliques were my undoing. You couldn't make friends with just anyone, you see. Even the club activities were ranked and ordered into hierarchies of their own, very clearly delineated between the coveted and the peripheral. The basis for all the ranking was of course this sense of elitism.

Reflecting back on those days from my present age and perspective, it's obvious to me now. Sometimes at night while I'm lying awake in bed, I'll be reminded of Kazue for some reason and I'll suddenly be struck with a eureka-like insight, while remembering the things she once did. It may seem a bit of a distraction, but I feel I should tell you more about my experiences in high school.

Let's start with the matriculation ceremonies. I can still remember the mute amazement I felt at seeing all the new students standing petrified in the lecture hall where the ceremony was to be held. The high school freshmen were divided into two distinct groups: those who were continuing on from within the Q school system and those who had entered that year. At a glance it was easy to discern which group was which. The length of our school uniform skirts set us apart.

Those of us who were entering for the first time—each and every one of us—having successfully passed the entrance exams, had skirts that fell just to the center of our knees, in exact accordance with official school regulations. However, the half who had been in the system since elementary or middle school had skirts that rode up high on their thighs. Now, I'm not talking about the kind of skirts that the girls wear today, skirts that are so skimpy they're hardly there at all. No, these skirts were just the right length to provide a perfect balance with the girls' high-quality navy-blue knee socks. Their legs were long and slender, their hair the color of chestnuts. Delicate gold pierced earrings glistened in their ears. Their hair accessories, and their bags and scarves, were very taste-ful, and they all had expensive brand-name items that I'd never before actually seen up close. Their elegant sophistication overwhelmed the newly arrived students.

The difference was not something that would softly fade away with the passage of time. There is no other way to explain it but to say that we new girls lacked what the others girls possessed seemingly by birth: beauty and affluence. We new girls were betrayed by our long skirts and our cropped, lusterless, jet-black hair. Many of us wore thick, unflatter-ing glasses. In a word, the incoming students were uncool.

No matter how a girl might excel in her studies or sports, there was nothing she could do to redeem herself once she was labeled *uncool.* For a student like myself, the question of being cool or uncool was irrelevant from the beginning. But there were others for whom the term provoked considerable anxiety. I'd say over half the students who entered the pro-gram as high school students found themselves teetering dangerously close to the border of being *uncool.* And so each and every one of them worked as hard as she could to avoid the label and tried to blend in with the continuing students.

The matriculation ceremony began. We outsiders paid serious atten-tion to all that was said. But in comparison, the students who had come up from the elementary levels only pretended to listen. They chewed gum, whispered among themselves, and acted as though they weren't even remotely concerned with what was going on. Far from being seri-ous, they behaved like frisky kittens, impossibly precious. And they never once so much as glanced in our direction.

In contrast, the newcomers, watching the way the insiders behaved, felt all the more anxious. They began to think of the difficult life that stretched ahead of them. Faces froze and expressions grew darker and darker. Confused, they began to suspect that the rules they had followed up to the present were no longer valid. They would have to learn a whole new set.

Perhaps you believe I am exaggerating. If so, then you are mistaken. For a girl, appearance can be a powerful form of oppression. No matter how intelligent a girl may be, no matter her many talents, these attri-butes are not easily discerned. Brains and talent will never stand up against a girl who is clearly physically attractive.

I knew I was by far more intelligent than Yuriko, and it irked me no end that I could never impress anyone with my brains. Yuriko, who had nothing going for her but her hauntingly beautiful face, nevertheless made a terrific impression on everyone who came in contact with her. Thanks to Yuriko, I too had been blessed with a certain talent. My talent was the uncompromising ability to feel spite. And whereas my talent far exceeded those of others, it was a talent that impressed no one but myself. I fawned over my talent. I polished it diligently every day. And because I lived with my grandfather and had the opportunity to help him on occasion with his handyman jobs, I was decidedly unlike all the other students who commuted to high school from perfectly normal families. Precisely for this reason, I was able to enjoy myself as a spectator on the sidelines, even amid the cruelty of my high school classmates.

• 2 •

In the days following the matriculation ceremony, more and more girls began to show up at school in short skirts.

Kazue was one of the first. But her shoes and her book bag were completely out of keeping with her skirt length and marked her as an outsider. The insider students, you see, did not carry the standard-issue student satchels. They came to school with light nylon sacks slung over their shoulders, or else they carried those chic overnight bags that were still unusual at the time. Some carted along American-made day packs, while others toted heavy-looking Boston bags. Were they Louis Vuitton? Regardless, the girls who carried them looked every bit like college students en route to classes. To complete the look, they wore brown loafers and navy-blue Ralph Lauren knee socks. Some students wore a different wristwatch every day. Others let silver bracelets—undoubtedly received from boyfriends—slip out from under the sleeves of their school uniforms. Then there were those who stuck little ornamented pins as sharp as needles in their perm-curled hair or wore diamond rings as big and clear as glass beads. Even though students weren't supposed to accessorize as freely as they do today, these girls managed to compete with one another over who could be the most fashionable.

But Kazue always carried a black satchel and wore black slip-ons. Her navy-blue knee socks were most definitely standard student issue. Her red train-pass case was extremely childish, and with her black hair clips she was—in a word—uncool. She shuffled through the halls trying to hide the ungainly thin legs jutting out from under her short skirt, along with her standard-issue satchel.

Her looks were average at best. Her thick black hair hung oppressively over her head like a heavy black helmet. It was cropped so short her ears were exposed, and the coarse hair at the nape of her neck stuck out in a way that made me think of the immature feathers on a newly hatched chick. She didn't appear to be particularly dull. Her forehead was broad, her face intelligent, and her eyes brimmed with the kind of confidence you would expect from an honor-roll student raised in an affluent home. So when was it, I wondered, that she had developed the habit of glancing timidly at those around her?

I saw a photograph of Kazue in one of those weekly magazines shortly after she was murdered. It was a picture of her at a love hotel with a man, clearly a photograph with a story behind it. Kazue's skinny naked body was exposed to the viewer's scrutiny, her large mouth opened in a laugh. I stared intently at the photograph, trying to find traces of the Kazue I had once known, but all I could find was an image of her lewdness—not the kind of lewdness that erupts from excessive luxury or even from sex. It was the licentiousness of a monster.

When we first began attending Q High School for Young Women, I did not know Kazue's name and I had no interest in finding it out. At the time, all the outsiders huddled together and looked so withered and dull it was impossible to tell one from another. For a student who had worked hard to get into Q High School for Young Women, hoping all the while to be recognized for her intelligence, this must have been particularly deflating. I feel I can now understand how Kazue must have felt. She had come of age amid humiliation. She must have been in turmoil.

You want to know about my interaction with Kazue? Well, all right then. I learned about Kazue thanks to a certain incident. It was a rainy day in May. We were in gym class at the time. We were supposed to play tennis that day, but because of the rain we had to stay in the gymnasium and practice dance. We were changing clothes in the locker room when one student held up a single sock and called out, "Whose is this? Who lost a sock?"

It was the kind of navy-blue knee sock most everyone wore. Only this one had a red Ralph Lauren logo on the top.

Everyone was completely nonchalant. No one seemed to care if they'd lost something because, unlike me, they could always go out and buy another one. That's why I found it odd that this girl was making such a fuss over a lousy sock. She held it out to show her friends.

"Well, just look at it! Look!"

Laughter filled the room. Other girls drew near to see, forming a circle around the sock holder.

"Why it's practically been embroidered!"

"What a masterpiece!"

The owner of the sock had taken an ordinary navy-blue knee sock and embroidered the upper edge with red thread to make it look like the Ralph Lauren logo.

The girl who found the sock was not seeking the owner out of some charitable effort to reunite her with her lost property. She simply wanted to know who it belonged to. That's why she'd called out like that. No one came forward to claim it. All the outsiders changed their clothes in silence, and the insiders didn't speak either. But even so their faces revealed the joy they felt as they anticipated the scene that was sure to unfold when the next class period started.

English class was to follow gym. Most of the students changed back into their uniforms hurriedly and rushed to the classroom in a buoyant mood. At that moment there was no division between insider and outsider. When it came to bullying, everyone was in it together.

Only three students remained behind in the locker room, a petite insider, Kazue, and myself. Kazue was dawdling—even more so than usual. That is when I realized that she was the one who had embroidered the logo on the sock. At that moment, the insider handed Kazue a pair of socks. "Here, you'll need these," she said. The socks were brand new navy-blue knee socks. Kazue chewed her lip and looked worried. I suppose she realized she had no choice.

"Thanks." Her reply was barely audible.

When the three of us entered the classroom, our classmates acted as if nothing were amiss. The true identity of the sock embroiderer might never be known. But it had been fun. And there would be more fun to come. Even a minor moment of maliciousness swelled and spread throughout the school, growing into subsequent incidents until it became utter and uncontrollable nastiness.

Having escaped her predicament, Kazue wore an indifferent expression. On that day, as usual, her hand shot up and she was called on to stand and read aloud from the textbook. There were those who'd lived abroad and numerous students in the class who were good in English. But that didn't stop Kazue. Confident, she'd raise her hand without a second thought. I looked over at the girl who'd lent her the socks. She was looking drowsily at her textbook, her chin in her hand. I didn't know her name but she was a cute girl with front teeth that protruded slightly. Why had she helped Kazue? It disconcerted me. It's not that I particularly approve of cruelty or bullying. And it's not that I hated Kazue. It's just that I found Kazue annoying. She'd gone and done something shamelessly stupid, and yet there she sat as if nothing had happened. She was acting so audacious. Was she being shrewd? Conniving? Even I couldn't tell.

After class, as I was pulling my classical literature textbook out, Kazue came up to me.

"About what happened earlier."

"What do you mean?"

When I acted like I didn't know what she was referring to, Kazue's face flashed red with anger. *You know exactly what I mean*, she must have been thinking.

"You probably think my family's hard up."

"I don't really care."

"I doubt that. But it's just that I hate having to listen to all that crap about whether or not you've got a stupid little logo on your sock."

I understood Kazue had embroidered her knee socks not because her family was too poor to afford to buy the real thing but out of a sense of rationalism. But I thought Kazue's brand of rationalism, which tried to accommodate itself to the wealth of the school, was ridiculous. Kazue had smallness of character ingrained within her. That was why nobody liked her.

"That's all."

Kazue went back to her seat. All I could see were the brand-new socks encasing her skinny calves. This was the mark of wealth, the symbol of

Q High School for Young Women: a red logo. I wondered what Kazue planned to do next. The girl who had lent her the socks was laughing with her friends, but when her eyes met mine she turned and cast her glance down as if she'd been caught doing something shameful.

I began talking to her now and then. I learned that her name was Mitsuru and that she had entered the Q system from middle school.

And so it was that both the insiders and the outsiders began the school year without striking any compromise in their polarity. The insiders were always together in the classroom, painting their nails and shrieking with laughter. When the lunch break rolled around, they headed off together to restaurants off campus and enjoyed fabulous freedom. When school let out for the day, the boys from Q High School for Young Men would be waiting for them at the gate. Girls with college-age boyfriends would be swept away in BMWs, Porsches, and other expensive foreign automobiles. The boys who met them had an air about them that resembled that of the girls. They were stylish, exuding a confidence backed by wealth. And they were a licentious group.

One month after I entered the school, we had our first examination. The outsider students were determined not to be outdone in their studies. They'd suffered enough as a result of constant pressure from the insiders. The studious set—who applied themselves nonstop to their schoolwork and aimed to surpass the insiders—was particularly determined, but they were not alone. All the outsiders had applied themselves with special zeal to their exam preparations. Moreover, the determination to succeed was all the more intense because we'd heard that the names of the ten top scorers would be posted. The outsiders saw this as an opportunity to redeem their honor. They would be able to claim for themselves a spot among the smartest of the smart.

I had decided from the very start that the test would not be worth the effort. Because I was still relishing my newfound freedom from Yuriko, I wasn't much concerned with what happened at school. As long as I didn't come in dead last, I didn't really care about the test and consequently did not study at all. I really didn't even care if I ended up at the very bottom of the heap, if I was able to stay in school—that was all that mattered. And so I went on with my life as before—just as the insiders did their own—without really noticing the exam.

On the Sunday before the exam, all the insiders went to a friend's vacation cottage to compare their class notes, or so the rumors went. Once again, the class was divided into two entirely different groups.

A week later the results of the exam were printed out and posted for all to see. Most of the students in the top ten were—as the outsiders had imagined—members of their own group. But what was mystifying was that among the top three was a student who had entered the school from junior high. Fifth place went to a girl who'd been with the Q system since elementary school. The highest score belonged to Mitsuru. This pattern made a profound impression on all the outsiders. Even though they generally performed better than the students who had been in the system since elementary school, how was it that they could not surpass those who had entered from junior high? The most urbane, charming, and wealthy bunch were the students who had entered from elementary school. The students who were most adept at melting into the background and were best at their studies were those who entered the system while in junior high. And the ones who were ill prepared for anything were those who had started in high school. But the pattern defied the earlier expectation of this last set of students, and they glanced about with pained expressions.

"Don't you play tennis?"

Mitsuru asked me this during our next gym class. In the month following my matriculation into Q High School for Young Women, a few of the insiders had spoken to me on occasion. When it came to our tennis lessons, those students who were on the tennis team would park themselves out on the center court as if it were their personal property. Students who didn't enjoy tennis, or those who didn't want to get sunburned, would lounge about on the benches lost in chatter. And those students who, like me, didn't want to get lumped in with the benches group would loaf around outside the chain-link fence, making it seem as if we were simply awaiting our turn to play. What about Kazue, you ask? She'd hit the balls back and forth on one of the side courts with other outsiders. She hated losing and would chase after the balls with dogged determination, letting go with strange grunts and groans in the process. The students lolling about on the benches entertained themselves with derisive comments about her.

"Well, I'm not very good at it," I answered.

"Neither am I," Mitsuru answered. She was slender, but her cheeks were round and because her two front teeth were big it made her face look a bit rodentlike. Her brown hair flowed down in wispy ringlets. Her face, dotted with freckles, was adorable. Mitsuru had lots of friends.

"What are you good at?"

"Nothing at all," I said.

"Just like me, then." Mitsuru brushed slender fingers over the strings of her racket.

"But you're good at studying. You earned the top score on the exam, didn't you?"

"That was nothing," Mitsuru said indifferently. "It's just a pastime for me. I plan to become a doctor." She turned to look at Kazue. She was wearing shorts and navy-blue knee socks.

"Why'd you lend her the socks?" I asked.

"I wonder." Mitsuru cocked her head to the side. "I don't like bullying."

"Was that bullying?" I remembered how calm Kazue looked when she stepped into the classroom the next period. I doubt she had the foggiest idea that Mitsuru had saved her from bullying simply by loaning her a pair of socks. Far from it. Even if everyone had found out those were her socks, she would have looked at them all with deadly seriousness, her face set in challenge. They're just socks, after all!

Mitsuru's soft hair blew gently in the breeze, the sweet scent of shampoo wafting about her. "Of course it was bullying. Everyone has fun at the expense of those students who don't have much money," she said.

"But you have to admit, it was pretty stupid to embroider your own socks," I said peevishly. I wanted to see how Mitsuru would react.

"True. But can't you understand how she felt? No one wants to be made a laughingstock in that way."

Not quite sure how to counter my statement, Mitsuru began to dig in the dry ground with the toe of her tennis shoe. The smartest student in the freshman class of Q High School for Young Women revealed a face shaken by my words. I experienced a tiny sliver of happiness. At the same time, I found myself feeling deep affection for Mitsuru.

"Of course, what you say is correct," I said, "but I don't know that she was particularly concerned herself. Besides, what everybody in the changing room was laughing at was the silliness of going so far as to embroider a sock! I don't think there was any secret evil intention.

"When a group of people become united by a tacit understanding and decide to act, that's bullying."

"Then why is it that those who have come up through the ranks plot against those who have just entered? Why does everyone ignore it? And aren't you one of them, after all?"

Mitsuru let out a deep sigh. "Well, you're right about that," she said. "I wonder why everyone just ignores it." She tapped her big front teeth with the end of her fingers, contemplating the question. I came to realize later that whenever Mitsuru did this, it meant she was secretly pondering whether or not to say something. She raised her head with a look of determination.

"But that's not it, you see. It's because their circumstances are so different. Because they come from such different backgrounds, their attitudes toward the value of things are completely different."

"Sure. That's obvious," I said, as I watched the tennis-club girls enthusiastically sending the bright yellow tennis ball back and forth across the net. Their rackets, their outfits, their shoes—all had been purchased with their own money and were not the usual school issue. They were more expensive than any item I was likely ever to see.

"Here we have the class-based society in all its repugnant glory," Mitsuru continued. "It must be worse here than anywhere else in all Japan. Appearance controls everything. That's why the people in the inner circle and those orbiting around them never mingle."

"The inner circle? What's that?"

"Those who began attending this school from the elementary level are the true-blue princesses, the daughters of fathers who own giant cartels. They'll never have to work a day in their lives. In fact, to have a job would be a source of great embarrassment."

"Isn't that a bit old-fashioned?" I snorted in contempt, but Mitsuru continued with great earnestness.

"Well, I agree, of course. But that's the inner circle's attitude toward assessing value. It may be a bit out of touch, but they are firm in their position and so everyone else gets led astray."

"Well, what about the others around them?"

"They're the children of salary men," Mitsuru answered with a note of sadness. "The daughter of a person who works for a paycheck can never be part of the inner circle. She may be smart or have considerable talent, but that won't make any difference. She won't even be noticed. If she tries to insinuate herself into their midst, she'll be taunted. Moreover, even if she's fairly intelligent, if she's both uncool and ugly she's little more than garbage at this place."

Garbage? What kind of word was that? I was not a member of the upper classes Mitsuru described. I wasn't even the daughter of a salary man, whose status at least was assured. I clearly wasn't in the inner circle, nor was I a member of the orbiters. I wasn't sure if I even fit into the category of outsider. Then was I even lower than garbage? Was it my lot in life to stand forever on heaven's shores watching the glittering swirl of celestial bodies on the other side? I felt as if I had discovered a new and private pleasure. When you think of it, that was probably my destiny.

"There is one way you can enter the inner circle, and one way only." Mitsuru tapped her front teeth with her fingernail.

"And what's that?"

"If you're beautiful beyond compare, exceptions can be made."

Can you imagine what I thought at that moment? Of course. I thought of Yuriko. What would happen if Yuriko were to attend this school? With her monstrous beauty, who could possibly be a match for her?

As I thought about Yuriko, Mitsuru whispered in my ear, "I hear you live in P Ward. Is it true?"

"I do. I take the train in from K Station."

"There's not another student at this school who lives in P Ward. A couple of years ago I heard there was a student who commuted in from one of the neighboring wards, though."

The place where I live had once been the sea. It's a wonderful area with streets nicely arranged, home to any number of odd and ancient people. But it's hardly a convenient place to live, especially for a student who has to commute to such a status-conscious school as this.

"I live with my grandfather in a government-funded apartment building," I told Mitsuru, mostly to provoke her. "My grandpa is a pensioner, you see, so he makes ends meet as the neighborhood handyman." I didn't add the part about him being out on parole, but the impact was sufficient.

Mitsuru leaned over to pull up her drooping socks and mumbled, with little conviction, "I didn't think there could ever be such a student here."

"Even among the outsiders?"

"Outsiders? Damn, you're like an alien, you know? No one laughs at you or tries to bother you. You just go about your business without a care in the world!"

"Well, it makes me feel relieved to hear you say that."

Mitsuru shot me a big smile, revealing her large front teeth. "Okay. I'll tell you the truth—but I'm only telling you. The truth is, my house is in P Ward too. My mother told me not to let anyone know, and she rents an apartment in Minato Ward—just for me. Of course, we pretend we own it. My mother comes over every day and cleans, cooks my meals, and does the wash."

"Why do you do that?"

"Because I'd be bullied otherwise."

"Well then, you're just like them, wrapped up in your lie."

Mitsuru looked ashamed. "You're right. I hate it. I hate myself for going along with it. And I hate my mother for it too. But if you don't cooperate, you draw attention to yourself at a school like this, so you have no choice."

I was convinced Mitsuru was mistaken. She wasn't mistaken in cooperating; if she wanted to go that far who's to say she shouldn't? No, what I meant was that Mitsuru was mistaken in her earlier comments about Kazue. I can't explain it, really, but it was a case of oil and water. Kazue was never going to mix with the inner circle, but Kazue did not realize this. If students picked on Kazue, they were picking on her for her inability to recognize her place. They weren't picking on her because of where she was born or how she lived or her sense of values. That is why you couldn't call what they did bullying. Am I wrong?

Mitsuru had once been the target of bullying, so her fear of it was considerable. Because she rented an apartment in the upscale Minato Ward and hid the fact that her family was from P Ward, Mitsuru was complicit with the insiders. And among the insiders, Mitsuru was the one closest to the inner-circle students.

"So how is it you're such a good student?"

"Well"—Mitsuru furrowed her brows as if she were shouldering a heavy burden—"at first it's true that I was determined not to be outdone. But eventually I came to enjoy studying. And I didn't really have anything else I wanted to do. I never cared about fashion and style the way the others do. And I wasn't interested in boys. I didn't join a club. I didn't especially think I wanted to become a doctor either. But I'd heard that the premed club was the one the smartest students joined. So I figured, if that was the case, I might find something there that could satisfy this longing in me."

Mitsuru was honest. I'd never met anyone before who was as honest as this.

"That longing—what exactly is it?" I asked.

Mitsuru flinched and peered into my face. Her eyes were jet black and shone like the beady eyes of a small defenseless creature.

"Perhaps it's something inside me, something of a demon."

A demon? We all have our own demons, I suppose. All things being equal, I might have easily lived a life of quiet contentment without ever even being aware of my own demon. But being raised alongside Yuriko had caused my inner demon to grow to tremendous proportions. I understood why it was that a demon had lodged within me. But how did a demon come to be in Mitsuru as well?

"Are you saying that you have sinister motives, or is it that you just don't like losing?"

Mitsuru looked startled by my question. "Well, I wonder. . . ." Confused, she looked up into the sky.

"You're the strongest-minded person I know," I told her.

"Really?" Mitsuru's face flushed red. She was embarrassed. I tried to lighten things up by changing the subject.

"Is your father a salary man? That is, are you one of the orbiters?"

"Yes." Mitsuru nodded. "He's in the real estate business."

"Must be lucrative."

"He received a large compensatory sum when they bought out his fishing business, so he embarked on a new venture. Back in the day he was the head fisherman, I heard. But he died when I was young."

Even though her people had come from the sea, Mitsuru had learned to crawl on land like a lungfish, a fish that can breathe air. Without even thinking, I started to picture Mitsuru—her thin white body—crawling through the sticky siltlike mud. Suddenly I wanted to become good friends with this girl. I decided to invite her over to my house.

"Won't you come visit me sometime?"

"Sure!" Mitsuru accepted my invitation readily. "Would Sunday be okay? I have to go to a premed study session after school every day—to tell you the truth, I'm trying to get into Tokyo University Medical School."

Tokyo University! Having just learned to crawl on land, she was already aiming to climb a mountain! And thus, deep inside me a desire was born to make Mitsuru the focus of my own study. Mitsuru was a strange creature to have been born of this school, a creature who possessed a goodness and kindness that set her apart from the rest of us. And yet, within her heart lurked a demon larger than that of the others.

"I'm sure you'll get in!"

"I wonder. But even if I get in, what then? There'll just be more battles to fight."

Mitsuru was starting to say something when one of the tennis-club girls turned and called to her from the court. "Mitsuru? Do you want to take my place? I'm tired."

I gazed after Mitsuru as she set out for the tennis court. Her frame was small and her hips high, giving her body a nice symmetry. She gripped her tennis racket as though it were heavy and exchanged some words with her friend. Her limbs were so white and slender they looked as though they'd never seen the light of day. But her serve struck the boundary line of her opponents' court perfectly. The ball made a pleasant dry ringing sound as it was returned. Although I had no basis for my evaluation, I decided that Mitsuru was an incomparably good player. She was quick on her feet and used the court wisely. Surely, when the match was over, she'd be embarrassed by the fact that she'd lost herself in her play, inadvertently revealing her considerable talents. Mitsuru was no bonsai. Her beauty was not like that of a bonsai, which achieves its charm by asserting its own will in defiance of the careful bindings that lash and restrict it. How, I wondered, would my grandfather describe Mitsuru's beauty?

A squirrel. It suddenly came to me: a clever squirrel who forages for nuts in the trees and buries them in the ground to stave off winter hunger. The squirrel was exactly what I was not. I was the tree. And no doubt a woody tree at that, a tree bearing naked seeds, ovary-free seeds, a gymnosperm. I would be a pine, perhaps, or a cedar. At any rate, I would not be the kind of flowery tree that welcomes birds and insects to gather in its branches like blossoms. I was a tree that simply existed for itself, alone. I was an old tree, thick and hard, and when the wind blew through my branches the pollen stored up there scattered of its own accord. What an appropriate analogy, I thought. The realization brought a smile to my lips.

"What's so funny?"

I heard an angry voice behind me. Kazue was standing beside the water fountain staring at me. She'd been watching me for some time, I realized, and the realization left me feeling mildly irritated. I couldn't help but picture a scraggly tree when I thought of Kazue.

"It's got nothing to do with you. I was just remembering something funny, that's all."

Kazue wiped the sweat from her brow and said with a glum look, "You were sitting there talking to that girl Mitsuru, and the whole time you were staring at me and laughing."

"That doesn't mean we were laughing at you!"

"Well, I don't care if you were. It's just that it makes me angry to think that someone like you would make fun of me!"

Kazue spit the last words out with particular venom. Realizing that she was ridiculing me, I replied with earnestness, disguising my true feelings with great skill. "I have no idea what you're talking about. We were not ridiculing you or anything of the sort!"

"Oh, it just makes me furious. They're so malicious. So childish!"

"Did someone do something to you?"

"It would be so much better if they actually *did* do something to me."

Kazue slammed her racket against the ground with surprising force, sending up a cloud of dust that coated her tennis shoes, covering the white laces with dirt. The students sitting along the bench turned to stare at her but then just as suddenly returned their gaze to the ground. Most likely they had no interest in the conversation between two such nondescript gymnosperms (Kazue was also of the somber pine or cedar species, unable to produce flowers). After Kazue had glared at the other students on the bench with pent-up hostility, she asked me, "Do you plan to join a club? Have you decided?"

I shook my head silently. I'd dreamed earlier of being involved in club activities, but once I saw the way things really were at the school, I reconsidered. It wasn't so much that I minded the petty demands senior members of the clubs placed on their juniors; that was a given in any club. But here the clubs weren't strictly hierarchical. They had a complicated inner structure that ran along vertical lines as well. There were clubs for the inner-circle students, clubs for the orbiters, and clubs for everyone else.

"No, I live with my grandfather so I don't need to participate." Without thinking, these were the words that popped out of my mouth! My grandfather and his friends took the role of upperclassmen, and helping him with his handyman job was my extracurricular activity.

"What do you mean by that? Explain yourself," Kazue said.

"It doesn't matter. It's nothing to do with you."

An angry look swept over Kazue's face. "Are you saying I'm just fighting for the sake of fighting? Getting worked up over nothing?"

I drew my shoulders in and shrugged. I'd had enough of Kazue and her persecution complex. On the other hand, if she'd already figured out that much, what point was there in asking the question?

"What I'm trying to say is why does the school have to be so unfair? It's so sneaky! They've already picked the winner before the game's even been played!"

"What are you talking about?" Now it was my turn to ask.

"See, I wanted to join the cheerleading squad. I turned in my application and before they'd even looked at it they turned me down, just like that. Don't you think that's wrong?"

All I could do was stare at Kazue stupefied. She was so clearly clueless when it came to both herself and the school. She folded her arms across her chest in a sulky pout and glared at the water fountain. A steady stream of water was bubbling sluggishly out of the faucet.

"The spigot's loose!" she shouted angrily.

But she was the one who'd forgotten to twist the tap shut.

I fought back the urge to laugh at her. Not yet adults ourselves, we sought to protect ourselves from potential wounds by turning the tables on our perceived aggressors and being the ones to launch the attack. But it grew tiresome being a constant target, and those who clung to their injuries were surely not destined to live long. So I worked on refining my maliciousness and Mitsuru worked on her intelligence. Yuriko, for better or worse, was imbued from the start with a monstrous beauty. But Kazue . . . Kazue had nothing to cultivate. I felt absolutely no sympathy for her. How can I put this? To get right to the point, Kazue was supremely ignorant, insensitive, ill prepared, and utterly outmatched by the harsh realities that confronted her. Why on earth didn't she notice?

I'm sure you will once again feel compelled to note that my assessment is particularly brutal, but it's true. Even if you allow for the fact that she was still immature, there was in Kazue a violent insensitivity. She lacked Mitsuru's attentiveness, and she did not have my kind of heartlessness. In the final analysis, there was something about her that was fundamentally weak. Kazue did not harbor any demons; in that sense she was similar to Yuriko. They were both at the mercy of whatever came their way, which I found terribly predictable. I wanted more than anything to plant a demon in their hearts.

"Why don't you lodge a complaint?" I said to Kazue. "Why don't you talk about it during homeroom?" The instructor in charge of homeroom didn't do anything but take attendance and go over the day's schedule. There was hardly any point to having a homeroom. And it would be very uncool for a student to instigate a debate on some topic and try to get some kind of consensus. But Kazue leaped on my suggestion with alacrity.

"That's it! What a good idea. I owe you one." Just then we could hear the chimes signaling the end of the class period. Kazue walked off. She didn't even say good-bye to me.

I was relieved when Kazue left, and I felt lucky to have gotten through the tennis lesson without having to do anything but chat. The gym and home economics classes at Q High School for Young Women were pretty lax. The instructors only paid attention to those who were eager to be involved.

That was the pedagogical doctrine of the teachers at Q High School for Young Women: *independence, self-reliance, and self-respect.* Students were encouraged to do whatever they wanted because only they had responsibility for their own growth. Rules were lax and much was entrusted to a student's own sense of self-determination. For the most part, almost all the instructors were themselves Q graduates. Having been nurtured in the pristine purity here, the pedagogical doctrine they preached was anything but abstract. They carefully instilled in us the belief that all things were possible. A wonderful lesson, don't you think? Both Mitsuru and I secretly clung to this teaching. I had my maliciousness and Mitsuru her intelligence. Together our good points stretched and grew, and we nurtured them and struggled to stand on our own in this corrupt world.

· 3 ·

It was early one rainy morning in July when the phone call came announcing my mother's death. I'd finished making the lunch I was going to take to school and was just starting to prepare breakfast. Toast and jam with tea. I had the same breakfast every morning.

My grandfather was on the veranda talking to his bonsai, as was his habit. In the midst of the rainy season the bonsai tended to attract both bugs and mold, so they required particular attention. Grandfather was so busy dealing with them—heedless of the rain—that he didn't hear the phone.

Once the butter melted on the hot toast I had to begin spreading the strawberry jam. It was important for me to spread the jam so that the black seeds were evenly distributed, but I had to be careful not to let the jam drip over the edges of the toast. Timing was everything because it was also essential that I dunk the Lipton's tea bag into the cup twice and then remove it. I was very busy with my preparations, so I called out angrily to my grandfather when I heard the phone.

"Aren't you going to answer?"

My grandfather turned back to look at me from over his shoulder. I pointed to the telephone.

"Get the phone. If it's Mother, tell her I've already left for school."

The sky outside was gray and the rain poured down so heavily you couldn't even see the top floor of the apartment building on the other side of the complex; it was hidden in mist. Because it was so dark, we'd had the lights on since morning. Neither night nor day, it seemed spooky. It never occurred to me to ask why my mother might be calling me at this hour. The time difference with Switzerland was seven hours; it would have been midnight there. Since they never called this early in the morning, it suddenly dawned on me that maybe Yuriko had died, and my heart leaped with anticipation.

Grandfather finally picked up the phone.

"Yes, this is he. . . . Oh, hello, it's been a long time. Thank you for all you've done recently." Grandfather seemed to be at a loss for words. Seeing him so tongue-tied I figured the call was from school. I hurriedly pulled the tea bag out of my cup and placed it on the saucer. The tea was still too weak. I'd misjudged. Grandfather called me to the phone with a puzzled look.

"It's your father. He says he has something to tell you. I can't under-stand a word he's saying, It's all gibberish. But he's saying something about an important matter that he can't talk about with me."

I had never once received a telephone call directly from my father. I wondered if he was going to tell me that he wouldn't be sending any more money for tuition. I braced myself for a fight.

"What you're going to hear will probably be a shock but that can't be helped. It's hard for us, but we'll get through this—this tragedy for our family."

Father's preamble ran on and on. He was usually diligent about get-ting the order of things right, so his words would have the greatest effect on his listener. But whether it was because he'd been away from Japan and was now used to speaking his native language, his Japanese had deteriorated. Finally, in exasperation, I said, "What do you want to say?"

"Your mother's dead."

My father's voice, melancholy as it was, rose up, unveiling the confu-sion in his heart. And then things grew deathly quiet at the other end of the line, I couldn't hear Yuriko's voice in the background or anything.

"How did she die?" I asked calmly.

"Suicide. I came home just a little while ago and your mother was sleeping. She'd already gone to bed. I thought it strange that she didn't wake up when I came in, but that's happened on other occasions. She hasn't been very talkative of late. When I came closer I saw that she wasn't breathing. She was already dead. The doctor believes she swal-lowed a handful of sleeping pills this afternoon and died around seven in the evening, while no one was home. It's just so sad I can hardly stand to think of it."

Father stammered this out in faltering Japanese before choking up. "I can't believe she committed suicide. I suppose it was my fault. She must have done it out of spike."

By *spike,* my father meant *spite.*

"It's all your fault," I answered coolly. "You dragged her to Switzerland."

My words angered Father.

"Are you blaming me because you and I don't get along? Are you saying I'm in the wrong?"

"Well, you're not completely innocent."

After a moment of silence my father's anger gradually abated and his sorrow seemed to deepen. "We lived together for eighteen years. I can't believe she was the first to die."

"I'm sure it's a great shock."

"Aren't you sad that your mother's dead?" my father asked suddenly, surprisingly.

I was not sad. It's strange, but I felt I'd lost my mother long ago. I'd done all my mourning while I was little, so I hadn't even felt particularly lonely or sad when my mother left me for Switzerland back in March. When I heard she'd died, I felt she'd already left for some place far, far away, so feelings of sorrow were quite a different thing for me. But how strange that my father would ask such a thing.

"Of course I'm sad."

This seemed to satisfy him. Suddenly his voice lost its force.

"I am shocked. Yuriko too; she just got home a little while ago. She's really upset. I suppose she's in her room crying now."

"What's Yuriko doing coming home so late?" I asked without thinking. If Yuriko'd been home, she might have discovered Mother earlier.

"She had a date—with a friend of Karl's son. I had a meeting at work, and it lasted a lot longer than expected so I couldn't get away."

My father made his excuses. His words spilled out in tangled disarray. I couldn't imagine my father ever really talking to my mother. Probably she'd been lonely, but I didn't think anything of it. If people can't stand being alone, they have no choice but to die.

"We plan to have the funeral service in Bern, so we'll send you a ticket. But I'm not going to pay for your grandfather's airfare. I want you to explain this to him."

"Sorry, but I have my end-of-term exams coming up, and I can't just leave like that. Why don't you let Grandfather come in my place?"

"You don't want to say good-bye to your own mother?"

I had already said my good-bye: a long time ago, when I was a child. "No, not particularly. Wait. I'll put Grandfather on the line."

Grandfather, who had gradually figured out what we were talking about, came to the phone with a stricken look. He and my father began to talk about all the business that needed tending to. He declined to go to the funeral. I bit into my toast—now cold—and drank down the weak tea. As I was packing the lunch I'd made from last night's leftovers into my satchel, Grandfather came into the kitchen. His face was pale and streaked with anger and sorrow.

"He killed her, the bastard!"

"Who?"

"Your father, that's who! I want to go to her funeral but I can't. It's breaking my heart. I can't even go to my only child's funeral."

"Go if you want to go."

"I can't. I'm on parole. Now I'm all alone in the world."

Grandfather sat down on the kitchen floor and wept. "First my wife dies and now my daughter. What a life."

I put my hands on Grandfather's thin shoulders and rocked him gently. I knew my hands would smell like pomade afterward, but I didn't care. That's right. I felt something akin to love for Grandfather. He always let me do as I pleased.

"Poor Grandpa. But you still have your bonsai."

Grandfather turned to look at me.

"You're right. You're always so calm. You really are strong. I'm hopeless. But you, I can rely on you."

I had understood this for quite some time. In the four months since I'd begun living with Grandfather, he had begun to rely on me for the housework, the handyman work, and even his interactions with others in the apartment complex. He relied on me for everything. Forgetting himself entirely, he wanted only to care for his bonsai. He wanted this so badly he could hardly stand it.

Meanwhile, my mind was caught in a tailspin. I was trying to figure out how to keep our accounts afloat. What if Father demanded that I move back to Switzerland? How was I going to manage? Or what if Father decided to return to Japan with Yuriko and resume residence here? What then?

But neither scenario was likely. I figured my father and Yuriko would stay on in Bern even without my mother. Surely he wouldn't want to send for me, knowing I didn't get along with Yuriko. I could tell from the last letter my mother had sent that she had probably been lonely in Bern, feeling like the only Asian in the family. How glad I was that I hadn't gone with them. I sighed with relief.

Within minutes, however, I had another phone call, this one from Yuriko.

"Hello, Sis? Is that you?"

I heard Yuriko's voice for the first time in months. It sounded husky, more grown up, perhaps because she was speaking in a whisper as if worried someone else would overhear. I didn't have time for this.

"I've got to leave for school and I don't have time to talk. What do you want?"

"Our mother has just died and you're going to school? A bit cold, don't you think? I hear you aren't coming to the funeral either. Are you serious?"

"Why? Do you think it strange?"

"Yes, it's strange! We've got to go into mourning; Father said so. I'm taking off from school for a while, and of course I've got to go to the funeral."

"Do what you want. I'm going to school."

"But how sad for Mother."

Yuriko's voice was full of censure. But my eagerness to get to school had little to do with her or Mother. To the contrary, I was in a hurry because today was the day Kazue was planning to discuss the discrimination she'd encountered when she tried to join the cheerleading squad. I doubt there'd ever been anyone at Q High School for Young Women who had raised an issue like this one. It was a one-of-a-kind happening, and I would be really disappointed if I had to miss it.

It wasn't that I thought a school event was more important than my mother's death. That wasn't the point. But I was the one who had planted the seed, and I wanted to see with my own eyes how Kazue would handle the situation. My mother's death was over and done with. Even if I absented myself from school, she wasn't going to come back to life. However, I asked Yuriko about Mother's behavior of late.

"Was she acting strange lately?" I wondered.

"Yeah, she seemed to be suffering from some kind of neurosis," Yuriko answered, through her tears. "Even though she complained about how expensive rice was, she cooked up a full pot every day, way more than we could eat. She knew it irritated Father, so she did it just to make him mad. And she stopped fixing his *bigos*. 'It's food for pigs,' she grumbled. Then she stopped going out. She'd just stay at home sitting alone in the dark without turning on the lights. When I'd get home I'd think no one else was in the house and would flip on the lights and there she'd be, sitting at the table with her eyes wide open. It was creepy. She'd stare at me and say stuff like, 'Whose child are you?' To tell you the truth, Father and I began to feel she was more than we could handle."

"I got letters from her and she sounded strange, that's why I asked."

"You got letters? What did they say?" Yuriko simmered with curiosity.

"Nothing important. Why'd you call?"

"There's something I wanted to discuss with you."

This was odd, I thought, and I felt my guard go up. I couldn't help but predict the worst. The sky outside had darkened and the rain had grown heavier. I'd be soaked before I could even make it to the station. I was already too late to get to homeroom in time, so, resigning myself, I sat down on the tatami matting. Grandfather had spread newspapers out in the small room and was moving his bonsai in from the veranda. He'd left the door wide open, and the roar of the rain filled the room. I raised my voice. "Do you hear the rain? It's really pouring here."

"I don't hear it. Do you hear Father crying? He's really making a din too."

"I don't hear him."

"I can't stay here now that Mother's dead," Yuriko said.

"Why?" I screamed.

"Well, Father's definitely going to remarry. I know all about it. He's seeing a younger woman at the factory, a Turkish girl. He's convinced no one knows about it. But Karl and Henri and everyone—they all know. Henri told me, see. He says he's positive the Turkish girl is pregnant, so I'm sure Father will marry her as soon as he can. That's why I can't stay here. I'm coming back to Japan."

I jumped to my feet in horror. Yuriko was coming back? I'd just finally gotten away from her! It had only been four months.

"Where do you plan to live?"

"What about there?"

Yuriko's voice was wheedling. I stared after Grandfather, who was busily dragging the bonsai into the room, his shoulders wet from the rain, and I answered very clearly. "Absolutely not."

• 4 •

I trudged resolutely through the downpour to the bus stop. The rainwater streamed in torrents along the asphalt road, swift enough to create a channel. One false step and I'd be soaked up to my calves. The bus I always caught rumbled up the road behind me and passed by, its windows fogged white with the breath of the passengers. I could imagine the unpleasantness of the humidity inside.

What time was the next bus? Would it get me to school in time for homeroom? I really didn't care now, one way or the other. I could hear Yuriko's voice playing over and over in my head. *What am I going to do? What can I do?* That is all I could think about.

If Yuriko came back to Japan with nowhere else to go, we'd have to live together again like sisters. Without any other relatives to rely on, she'd have nowhere else to go but Grandfather's tiny apartment. The very thought of having Yuriko there gave me goose bumps. As soon as I opened my eyes in the morning, there'd she'd be on the futon right next to mine, her dark eyes looking right at me, and then I'd be having tea and toast and jam with her and Grandfather. Shit!

Yuriko would hate the smell of grandfather's cheap pomade. She'd be angered by the way his bonsai cluttered up the place, and she'd find the way we help out around the apartment complex a hassle. And as soon as Yuriko made her presence known around here, you can be sure everyone in the apartment complex and even the shopping arcades would be seething with curiosity about her. The comfortable balance that my grandfather and I shared would be shattered. Grandfather might even go back to being a criminal!

But what I hated most was the idea of being fascinated by that monster Yuriko again, of being enveloped by her presence. At no point did I feel secure. Suddenly I thought of my mother and her suicide.

I guess they can't accept that a shabby-looking Oriental like me could ever produce a beauty like Yuriko. The reason my mother chose to end her life was not because she couldn't deal with her loneliness, and it wasn't because my father was cheating on her. Wasn't it because of Yuriko? Because of her very existence? When I heard Yuriko was coming back to Japan, an unexplainable anger began to build in my head. I resented my mother for killing herself and I hated my father for his infidelity; then, just as suddenly, I began to feel sorry for my mother, and I knew a kind of affinity with her. Tears began to well up in my eyes. Out there in the rain I was able to cry over my mother's death for the first time. Perhaps you will find it hard to believe, but I was only sixteen. Even I had my sentimental moments.

I heard the swish of a car approaching from behind, cutting through the water. To avoid getting drenched I took cover under the awning of a bedding store and waited for the car to pass. It was a huge black car—the kind a government official might use, the kind you hardly ever saw in this neighborhood. The car pulled to a stop right next to me and the window came down.

"Want a ride?" Mitsuru grimaced as the falling rain struck her face. I stared at her in disbelief and she waved me in. "Come on, hurry!"

I folded up my umbrella and climbed in. It was freezing inside and the smell of cheap air freshener wafted through the car. I guessed it belonged to the driver, a middle-aged woman with disheveled hair. She turned back to look at me.

"Are you the kid who lives in the P Ward government housing?" Her voice was so low and husky it sounded as if her throat had been raked with sandpaper.

"Yes."

"Mother, isn't that a bit rude?" As she scolded her mother, Mitsuru dabbed at my wet uniform with her handkerchief. Her mother focused on the traffic signal ahead of her and neither apologized nor laughed. So this was Mitsuru's mother? Being naturally fascinated by human relationships and the way heredity functions, I stared at the woman intently, wondering what about her resembled my friend.

Her hair was unkempt and seemed to be growing out of a perm. Her skin was dusky and showed no signs of makeup. She was wearing some gray jersey outfit that you could hardly call a dress; it looked more like a nightgown. I couldn't see her feet, but I was sure she'd be wearing sandals with socks or a pair of grimy sneakers.

Could this really be Mitsuru's mother? She was even worse than my own! Discouraged, I compared her face to her daughter's. Mitsuru felt my gaze and turned to look at me. Our eyes met. She nodded, as if in resignation. Mitsuru's mother smiled, showing a row of tiny teeth that not only looked nothing like Mitsuru's but were also ill suited to her face.

"It's unusual, isn't it, for someone from around here to attend that school?"

Mitsuru's mother was a person who'd abandoned something. I suppose you could say it was reputation and social dignity. At the matriculation ceremony I'd sneaked glances at the parents of the other students. They were on the whole wealthy, a wealth they took pains to reveal discreetly. Or perhaps I should say that they were adept at displaying their wealth by keeping it hidden. Whichever way you looked at it, the operative word here was *wealth*.

But Mitsuru's mother was completely indifferent to that attitude toward wealth. Perhaps she'd espoused it earlier and then abandoned it, walked away from it entirely. The parents of the wealthy children manifested pride in their offsprings' intelligence. Even the salary workers refrained from being ostentatious. Mitsuru had told me that her mother had ordered her not to let anyone know she lived in P Ward, so seeing her mother looking so shabby was completely unexpected. I had assumed she would be the kind to make a fuss over her appearance.

"Have you been crying?" Mitsuru asked.

I looked at her without answering. Her eyes were brimming with an ill-temperedness that I'd never seen before. I had seen her demon. Just then, for a fleeting moment, I had caught hold of her demon tail. Was she embarrassed? She averted her eyes.

"I got a phone call just a bit ago. My mother's dead."

Mitsuru's face darkened. She twisted her lip between her fingers as if trying to wrench her mouth from her face. I wondered when she'd start tapping her big front teeth with her fingernail in her usual manner. I felt I was in a battle with her. But then she caved in completely.

"I'm sorry," she said.

"So, your mother died?" Mitsuru's mother looked back at me from the driver's seat and spoke in a voice that was little more than a rasp. Her manner of speech was coarse. She sounded exactly like the people who hung around with my grandfather. Frank, open, and more concerned with substance than façade.

"Yes."

"How old was she?"

"About fifty, I think. No, maybe still just in her forties." I didn't know my mother's exact age.

"Then she'd be about my age. How'd she die?"

"She killed herself."

"Why? Was it the change of life?"

"I don't know."

"A mother who commits suicide certainly leaves her children in a tough spot! You should excuse yourself from school. What are you doing out?" she said.

"True. But my mother died overseas, so there's not much I can do sitting at home."

"But there's no reason for you to be making such a fuss to get to school, especially in a downpour like this." Mitsuru's mother studied my face in the rearview mirror, her sharp deep-set eyes looked me up and down, inch by inch.

"I need to be at school today."

I didn't want to mention Kazue and her discrimination protest, so I stopped there. Mitsuru's mother seemed to lose interest in my needing to mourn.

"Wait a minute, are you half?"

"Mom! What difference does that make?" Mitsuru interrupted and I began to hear her nervously tap her teeth with her nail. "Her mother has just died. Stop asking so many questions!"

But Mitsuru's mother was not to be silenced.

"You live with your grandfather, right?"

"That's right."

"And is your grandfather Japanese?"

"Yes."

"And your mother's Japanese. So what's the other half?"

Why was she so curious? But I was enjoying her questions. They were questions everyone always wanted to ask but never did.

"Swiss."

"My, my, what a pretty pair!"

Her mother said this with a smile, but I could tell she didn't mean it. Mitsuru whispered in my ear, "I'm really sorry my mother's so rude. It's her way of trying to be nice."

"I'm not being nice." Mitsuru's mother turned back to look at us again. "You seem like a tough kid. Mitsuru's such a bookworm. It's ridiculous. I want to go to Tokyo University Medical School, she says; she's so stubborn. She doesn't want to lose to anyone. And she certainly doesn't want to be anyone's fool. That's all she ever worries about. And so she said she wouldn't live out here anymore and she went and rented her own place. In middle school she had to put up with some hateful bullying, so she's learned to arm herself. But I really wish I'd let her drop out of this god-awful school way back when."

"Why'd they bully you?" I asked Mitsuru nonchalantly.

Mitsuru's mother answered before Mitsuru had a chance. "Because her mother runs a bar, that's why!"

She pulled up right in front of the school gate, going out of her way to attract the curious stares of the other students on their way in. She was hell-bent on nettling Mitsuru. When I thanked her for the ride, she said to me, "Be sure to tell your grandpa to come by the bar next time he's out. I'll give him a good deal. It's the Blue River, right in front of the station."

I didn't know for sure, but I suspected the bar was some kind of cabaret chain.

"Are there any bonsai there?"

"Why?"

"Grandpa prefers bonsai to women, that's why."

Mitsuru's mother didn't know quite what to make of my joke and craned her neck around to say something to me, but whatever it was I didn't hear, because by then Mitsuru had already slammed the door shut. She held her umbrella over me while I unfolded my own.

"My mother's a real piece of work, huh? But she just plays at being bad. I can't stand it. Someone who goes out of their way to say hateful things like that is really a coward, don't you think?"

Mitsuru spoke in cool, measured tones. I nodded, letting her know I understood completely. She did not measure up to Mitsuru's ideal. It was the same for me. Children do not get to choose their mothers.

"Are you okay?" Mitsuru asked, with a worried look.

"I'm okay. I feel like my mother and I already parted long ago."

"I know what you mean. I feel I said good-bye to my mother long ago too. Now I'm just using her, you know, for rides and such."

"I know."

"You're a strange girl." Mitsuru glanced up at me when she said this, but then she caught sight of one of her friends waving at her. "I've gotta go."

"Wait a minute." I clutched at her blouse. She turned to look back at me. "When you were bullied, your mother said you armed yourself. How?"

"Well"—Mitsuru signaled to her friend to go on ahead so she could talk to me—"I let them use my notes."

"But then you're just letting them use you, aren't you? How can you be so nice to the kids who picked on you?"

Mitsuru tapped her big front teeth with her finger. "I'm only telling this to you, okay? The notes I lend them are not my real notes."

"What do you mean?"

"I have two sets. My real notes are much more thorough and detailed than the set I let them see. That set has a few of the important points, so they won't notice. But the notes are faked."

Mitsuru was whispering, as if she were discussing something embarrassing. And yet the tone of her voice was so buoyant she could hardly conceal her glee.

"Their audacity really disgusts me. Since it's their habit to intimidate others, they think nothing of borrowing someone's notes. The only way to defend yourself against their brazenness is to be self-assertive and strike a deal. Because I let them copy my notes, they stopped bullying me; that's the trade we worked out. Those girls are quick to catch on. They figured out right away that I was more than just some weak kid they could push around. I could be useful to them, so they transferred their aggression to another student." Mitsuru smiled faintly and shrugged her shoulders. "You don't know what the bullying was like in junior high. It was awful. For a full year not a single soul said one word to me. The only ones who talked to me were the teachers and the women who worked in the school store. That's all. Even the other kids who had entered that year bullied me. They thought bullying an outsider might make them an insider."

The first bell sounded. Homeroom was going to start any minute. We hurried off to the classroom. For the life of me I couldn't figure out how someone as cute as Mitsuru could be bullied.

"I just don't understand why they targeted you."

"Because my mother came to observe classes during the orientation period. This is the way she introduced herself in front of the entire Parent-Student Association: 'I'm just so thrilled that my daughter is finally a Q School student. She's had her sights set on this school for a long long time. I had hoped she'd get in from elementary school, but when that didn't work out I dreamed of her getting into the junior high school. I saw that she studied hard, and it paid off. Now I hope you'll all get along well with my little girl and become really good friends!'

"It was just her typical kind of greeting. But from the very next day I was the target. That morning there was a drawing of my mother on the blackboard. She was dressed in a bright red suit with a big diamond ring and alongside the drawing were the words *Finally, a Q student!* But what it meant was, whether I had entered at elementary school or junior high, I would *never* be one of them."

"I understand perfectly."

"What do you think you understand?"

"About your mother."

I wanted to add that I knew she was ashamed of her own mother. But Mitsuru frowned. "I'm sorry. . . . I mean, about your mother. With her dying today and all."

"No, it's okay. You know, we were going to have to be parted sooner or later."

"Cool. You are just so cool."

Mitsuru laughed happily. We both understood that something had passed between us at that moment which only the two of us could appreciate. From that day on I cherished a delicate love for Mitsuru.

I entered the classroom and immediately searched for Kazue. She was glaring at the blackboard, her face pale and strained with tension. When she saw me, she stood up and walked over to my desk with that jerky gait of hers.

"Hey, I'm planning to bring up that topic this morning."

"Yeah? Good luck."

"And you'll say something too, right?"

Kazue peered into my face. Her tiny eyes hemmed by black lashes pored over me. As I returned her gaze, I felt my hatred for her multiply. What a complete idiot she was. The more she screwed things up for herself here, the more I could imagine a different life for me and Mitsuru. You say my attitude is offensive? That was the way things worked in my world.

"Sure. I'll back you up." I said it, but I didn't mean it.

Kazue looked relieved. Her eyes sparkled. "That's great! What'll you say?"

"How about if I just confirm that whatever you say is true?"

"Okay. If I start, then you'll raise your hand, right?" Kazue gazed forlornly around the room as she spoke. The outsiders were all sitting smartly in their seats waiting for the instructor to arrive; the insiders were clustered in the back of the room whispering away. "Well, here goes."

Kazue turned toward her seat, looking confident. Then the classroom door opened and our homeroom teacher breezed in. She was the instructor in charge of teaching the classics, and we all called her "Hana-chan." She was a single woman, close to forty, I'd say. She always wore a nicely tailored suit of either navy or gray and a blouse with a white collar. Invariably, a slender string of pearls hung around her neck. She carried a dark-green leather notebook, and her cheeks were pale white without the slightest hint of makeup. She had entered the Q School system from the elementary level and had continued on through university, and she was proud of her heritage.

Kazue, looking flustered, rushed to her seat. I didn't take my eyes off her.

"Good morning, girls!" Hana-chan greeted the class with her rapid-fire, slightly nasal voice. She gazed languidly out the window. The rain was still pouring down.

"They say it'll clear up by evening. But I wonder if it really will. . . ."

Kazue drew in a deep breath and stood up. I watched her out of the corner of my eye. Hana-chan looked over at her in surprise. I stared at Kazue's back, spurring her on with telepathic force. *Do it! Say it!* Finally, in a voice thick with phlegm, she started. "Um, there's something I wanted to bring up for discussion. It's about clubs."

Kazue glanced at me nervously, but I acted like I didn't know what she wanted from me and rested my chin in my hand. Just then, the girls in the cheerleading squad rushed up to the front of the room. Kazue stared at them in disbelief. The girls lined up and, standing straight and tall, began to sing "Happy Birthday." In no time at all everyone else chimed in. The girls leading the singing were almost all insiders, most of them having started together in elementary school. Hana-chan crumbled into gales of laughter.

"How'd you know it was my birthday?"

The cheerleaders began waving their pompoms and pulling party crackers, followed by clapping and cheers. At the sound of the crackers, Kazue sank back into her seat. A cute student with her hair curled up in a flip pulled a bouquet of roses out from behind her back and thrust them into Hana-chan's hands.

"Oh, I'm so thrilled!"

"We all wanted to drink a toast to you, since you're celebrating your fortieth birthday!"

When had they made the preparations? I wondered. There they were, pulling soda cans out of a paper bag and handing one to each student. "Everybody, open your cans and let's drink to Sensei! Happy birthday!"

Some students were confused and wondered if it was really okay to drink in the classroom. But no one wanted to be a party pooper, so they all acted like they were having fun. I started sipping the soda, which fizzed on my tongue and made my teeth thick with sugar. Kazue grimaced with humiliation.

"Sensei, say something!" Carried away with themselves, the students urged and cajoled.

"Well, I'm just stunned!" Hana-chan hugged the bouquet of roses to her chest. "But all of you, thank you so much! Today I am forty! I'm sure I must look like an incredibly old lady to you. I also studied at this school, you know. My homeroom teacher—when I was in my first year of high school—was exactly the same age that I am today. I thought she was ancient, so I assume it's the same for you. How distressing."

"You don't look old!" one of the students shouted, and the class erupted in laughter.

"Well, thank you! It's really a privilege to have you as a class! *Independence, self-reliance, and self-respect* is a motto that will serve you well in the future. You are all blessed. But precisely because you are so blessed we can bring you up to be self-reliant and proud. So please, study hard and keep growing!"

What an unbelievably pathetic speech. But it was greeted by applause and whistles, so loud that the teacher from the classroom next door poked her head in to see what was going on. But I knew that no one was really moved. Hana-chan was just being played.

When I looked over at Mitsuru, she had her hands clasped in front of her breast and was looking at Hana-chan, her face wreathed in smiles.

Sensing my gaze, she turned back to look in my direction and wrinkled her nose at me. I felt happy, as if Mitsuru and I were partners in crime. All Kazue could do was look on, her hopes for vindication cruelly dashed by the cheerleaders.

When school ended that day I collected my things and headed outside. The sky was blue as far as the eye could see, as if the morning storm had never happened. I suddenly remembered that Yuriko would be returning to Japan, and I headed toward the station in a gloomy mood.

"Wait up!"

I turned around and saw Kazue thumping noisily after me. She was wearing bulky rubber navy-blue boots, and the students behind were poking one another with their elbows and laughing at her.

"Hey, what happened today really ticked me off. You too, huh?"

It would be more accurate to say I was disappointed, but I nodded without saying anything. Kazue thumped me on the shoulder. "So do you have to hurry home?"

"Not really."

"Well, to tell you the truth, it's my birthday today too."

Kazue had brought her mouth close to my ear. I could smell the dank sweetness of her perspiration.

"Happy birthday."

"Won't you come to my house?"

"Why?"

"My mother told me I could bring some of my school friends home with me today."

I was curious to meet her mother. On the day I learned of my own mother's death I met Mitsuru's mother, and now I had a chance to meet Kazue's.

"Please come! Just for a bit. I can't tell her no one's coming." A look of pain spread over Kazue's face, as if she was recalling what had happened in homeroom. Based on the little bit Kazue had managed to say before being interrupted, it was now common knowledge around school that she had tried to bring up the issue of the club discrimination. Here she was on the brink of becoming the next Mitsuru, the next target of torture, and she had no idea about Mitsuru's bullying experiences. No sooner had this thought crossed my mind than I heard Kazue mention Mitsuru by name.

"You're good friends with that girl named Mitsuru, aren't you? Do you think you could ask her to come too?"

I was pretty sure Mitsuru planned to spend the afternoon studying. She'd left as soon as she could.

"No, she's already gone," I replied curtly.

"The really smart students are always busy, aren't they," Kazue said, her voice full of disappointment.

"Well, get over it. She doesn't like you anyway."

My lie silenced Kazue. "You don't have to come either," she said, looking at the ground.

"No, that's okay. I'll come."

· 5 ·

We took one of the private railroad lines and got out on the outskirts of Setagaya Ward, at a station so small there was only one platform. Kazue turned down a residential street that looked exactly as I expected it would—quiet, peaceful, and lined with moderately sized houses. Although there were no expensive mansions to be seen, neither were there any clumps of cheap apartment buildings.

Tasteful plaques graced the gatepost to each residence, and just beyond were small lawns. On Sundays the fathers in these houses would no doubt stand on those lawns practicing their golf swings while the sound of pianos wafted from the living room windows. I'd heard that Kazue's father was a salary man, and I imagined he'd probably taken out a thirty-year loan to finance his house. Kazue stomped sulkily ahead as if she were annoyed to have me tagging along with her. But before long she started pointing out all the important landmarks along the way. "This is the junior high I attended; it's a municipal school," she said proudly. "Look at that old house over there, that's where I took piano lessons." Her tour through memory lane really got on my nerves.

Having come to the end of the road, Kazue waved me over to the front of another house. "This is my house," she announced triumphantly.

It was a large two-story structure surrounded by a dingy gray wall of

Ōtani stone. The house was painted brown and the roof was covered with heavy tiles. The garden was planted thickly with shrubs and trees, the lot larger and more established than those of the neighboring houses.

"What an impressive house! Is it a rental?"

Kazue looked startled by my question. Then she thrust her chest out and replied, "We rent the property, but we own the house. I've lived here since I was six."

Diamond-shaped cutouts lined the stone wall, perhaps for ventilation. I peered through the holes into the garden, which was dotted with azaleas, hydrangeas, and other common shrubs. Potted plants were jammed in nearly every nook and cranny.

"Hey, you have bonsai too!" I blurted out without thinking. But upon closer inspection I saw that what I had taken for bonsai were nothing more than "poor man's planters," as my grandfather called them, just small potted marigolds, forget-me-nots, daisies, and other flowers you see lining the front of any old flower shop.

A woman wearing glasses was squatting down tending to the flowers, waving away mosquitoes as she pinched off the withered blooms.

"Mom."

The woman turned around when Kazue called out to her. I stared into her face with curiosity. Her glasses were silver-framed, and she had the same coarse black hair as Kazue, cut in a bob that came to a point alongside each cheek. Her face was narrow and her features were more symmetrical than Kazue's.

"Did you bring a friend?" She smiled perfunctorily, and the rim of her glasses leaped up over her eyebrows. She had a conspicuous overbite; wasn't there a fish somewhere with that same kind of face? What, I wondered, would the father look like? Curiosity got the better of me, and I decided to stick around until he arrived home.

"Make yourself at home."

"Thank you."

The mother turned back to her pots. Her greeting wasn't particularly warm. Maybe she frowned on the idea of my turning up just at dinnertime. Maybe Kazue hadn't told her she was bringing a friend home. Maybe it wasn't even her birthday. Had Kazue lied to me? I wanted to ask, but before I could, she put her hand on my back and practically pushed me through the front door.

"Go on in."

Kazue's childish way of conducting herself was really getting on my nerves. Besides, I hated being touched.

"Want to go to my room?"

"I don't care."

There were hardly any lights on in the house. I smelled nothing to suggest dinner was ready. It was as quiet as a grave, not even the sound of a TV or radio. Once my eyes adjusted to the gloom, I could see that though the house was impressive on the outside, on the inside it was constructed with cheap veneers. Even so, it was extremely tidy. I didn't see a speck of dust anywhere—not in the hall, not even on the stairs. And throughout the house wafted the smell of frugality. In living with Grandfather, I had already learned to scrimp and save, so I knew frugality when I smelled it. In this house, every corner reeked of it, and yet from somewhere also seeped a sense of lewdness. It was the devotion to frugality itself that was permeated with lewdness, as if the very effort applied to economizing was wanton.

Kazue started up the stairs ahead of me. They creaked. There were two rooms on the second floor. The large room above the hall was Kazue's. Her bed was pressed up against the wall, her desk in the middle of the room. She didn't have a TV or stereo set. Her room was spartan, like a dorm room. Here and there were scattered items of clothing. Her bed was also a mess, covered with a wrinkled futon quilt.

Textbooks and reference books were stacked roughly into her bookshelf, and she'd stuffed her gym wear onto one gapingly empty shelf. Kazue's room was as cluttered and chaotic as her house and garden were trim and tidy. It suited Kazue to a T.

Completely ignoring me as I stood there staring around in disbelief, Kazue threw her school bag on the floor and sat down at her desk. There were memo cards stuck to the wall with slogans. I read them off in a loud voice:

"Only by your own power is victory possible! Trust yourself. Set your sights! Be a Q student!"

"I put them there after I did well on the entrance exam. I got in, so they're a testament to my success," Kazue said.

"Well, looks like you're quite the victor!" I said, letting a hint of cynicism seep into my voice.

But Kazue just sneered. "I really worked hard, you know."

"I didn't write any peppy slogans."

"Well, you're weird." Kazue focused her eyes on me and stared hard into my face.

"Why am I weird?"

"You do everything your own way." She spoke each word with precision and left it at that. I wanted to get out of there and get home as soon as I could. I was worried about my grandfather and the shock my mother's death had had on him. Why on earth had I come here? Regret swept over me.

I heard the sound of footsteps stealthily drawing near, like a cat climbing the stairs. Kazue's mother called her from just outside the door.

"Kazue, dear. May I have a word?"

Kazue left the room and the two of them spoke in whispers in the hallway. I pressed my ear to the door to eavesdrop.

"What do you want to do about dinner?" her mother asked. "I wasn't expecting company and I don't have enough."

"But Daddy said he'd come home early this evening, so I should bring a friend."

"Oh, I see. Is she the one who's ranked first in your class?"

"No."

"Then what rank is she?"

Their voices slipped so low I couldn't hear. Was that story about her birthday just a ruse? Had Kazue just wanted to show Mitsuru to her father? Had she tried to use me as the bait to lure Mitsuru over? I was of absolutely no value to this family, not being much of a student myself. Kazue's mother tiptoed back down the stairs. It was as if she didn't want to wake someone.

"Sorry," Kazue said, as she came back in. Leaning against the door to close it, she added, "You'll stay for dinner, won't you?" I nodded without an ounce of shame. After their little powwow I was curious to see what kind of meal they'd produce for such an unwelcome guest as myself. Kazue started flipping through a reference book, looking ill at ease. The pages were marked up and nearly black with ink stains.

"Are you an only child?"

Kazue waved her hand at my question. "No, I have a younger sister. She's studying for the high school entrance exams now."

"Will she go to Q High School, too?"

Kazue shrugged her shoulders. "She's not smart enough. But she tries so hard it would break your heart! Too bad she's not as bright as I am. My mother always says it's because she takes after her. But my mother graduated from a women's college herself, so she only says stuff like that on account of my dad. She went to a really good women's college. Still, I'm lucky to take after my dad, because he went to Tokyo University, the best school in Japan. What about *your* dad? What university did he go to?"

"I don't think he went to a university."

Kazue stared at me in stupefaction, just as I knew she would. "Well, what about high school?"

"Don't know." I had no idea what kind of education my father had had in Switzerland.

"Well, what about your grandfather then, the one you live with?"

"He didn't even go to high school."

"And your mother?"

"I think she only got as far as high school."

"Then you're their star of hope!"

"Their what?"

What could we possibly hope for? I cocked my head to the side. Kazue stared at me as if I'd suddenly transformed into an alien. Up to that point, I'm sure she thought we both shared the same desires. But Kazue was not the kind of person to care that other people might have different ideas.

"Well, you have to try your best, right? If you really, really try, you'll make it."

"Make it? Make what?"

"Why, success!" Kazue looked in confusion at the mottoes plastered over her wall. "Ever since I was in elementary school, I was determined to get into Q High School for Young Women. It's just such a perfect school. If you apply yourself, and if you're from a good family, you can get into Q High School and then you can go to Q University. It's practically automatic. And if I can finish in the top ten in the class, I can get into the Economics Department at Q University. I'll pile up a string of A-pluses, and then I'll be able to get a job in a really good company after I graduate."

"And once you enter a good company, what then?"

"What then? Well, I'll work there, of course! Perfect, isn't it? We're living in an era when even women can work at whatever they desire. My mom came of age at a time when that wasn't possible, so she wants me to do what she couldn't."

I heard Kazue's mother call up from the foot of the stairs. Kazue left the room, and as she did I detected the sharp scent of chilled soba sauce. A few minutes later Kazue came back in carrying a tray with chipped paint, the kind a delivery service would use to carry prepared food. The tray was loaded with two bamboo-slatted plates piled high with soba noodles and two little cups of dipping sauce.

"Since you went out of your way to visit, we wanted to treat you to a feast. Mother just ordered soba for the two of us, so let's eat here."

Not exactly my idea of food for guests, but I didn't say anything. I guess every household has a different concept of hospitality. I was reminded again of the miserliness that I sensed when I first entered the house.

Kazue went out and came back into the room clutching a chair with a pink cushion tied to the seat, the kind of chair that accompanies a student's desk. It was probably her younger sister's. Kazue had me sit in that chair. We lined up next to each other in front of her desk and began slurping down the noodles.

Suddenly the door burst open. "What are you doing with my chair?" Her sister, noticing me, hung her head timidly. Her eyes landed on the plates of soba and her face flashed with resentment when she realized there wasn't any for her. Her face and body were a shrunken version of Kazue's, but her hair was long and hung down her back.

"I've got a friend over. I need to borrow it for a bit. Don't worry, I'll return it when we're done eating."

"How am I supposed to do my homework?"

"I said I'd bring it back when we're done."

"You ought to eat standing up!"

The two of them squabbled without a glance in my direction. After her sister left, I asked, "Do you like your younger sister?"

"Hardly." Kazue plucked awkwardly with her chopsticks at the gummy noodles, picking them up and plopping them down. "She knows she's not as smart as me, so she's jealous. When I took the entrance exam I know she was hoping I'd fail. And if she flunks her test you can bet she'll blame it on me for taking her chair! That's the kind of brat she is."

Kazue finished her soba before I did and then proceeded to gulp down what was left of the pitch-black sauce. I'd completely lost my appetite by then and distracted myself by slipping the cheap disposable wooden chopsticks back in the paper wrapper they'd come in, pulling them out, and then sticking them back in again. Eating soba noodles in Kazue's disheveled room suddenly struck me as incredibly pathetic. The room teemed with dust, not having been cleaned for who knows how long, and it smelled like an animal's lair. I thought again of Yuriko's phone call that morning and the way she'd described my mother's recent behavior.

My mother: sitting with her eyes wide open in the dark, shut up in a room without lights. Her fragile nerves—I wonder if I'd inherited them. It would have been a blessing if they'd gone to Yuriko, but compared to me Yuriko was uncomplicated and overly forthright in her own desires. I was the one who took after Mother.

Kazue turned to me and asked, "Do you have any brothers and sisters?"

"I've got a younger sister." I answered bitterly. Just thinking of Yuriko made me bitter. Kazue swallowed. She looked like she was going to continue to ask questions, but I cut her off with one of my own. "You weren't really going to have soba for dinner tonight. What would you have had if I hadn't come?"

"Huh?" Kazue jerked her head back as if to say, Why do you have to ask such bizarre questions?

"I'm just curious."

I was interested in what kind of meal Kazue and her mother would fix. Would they make bean cakes of mud and mashed hydrangea leaves and salad of dandelion greens? Kazue's mother looked like the kind of woman who only enjoyed "playing house." She seemed so detached from the real world, performing her household tasks but more like a robot than a real person.

"Father and you and I are the only ones eating soba tonight. My mother said that she and my sister would eat leftovers. We hardly ever order out; just that little bit of soba cost three hundred yen. It's so stupid! But we got it specially because you came to visit."

I stared up at the light fixture, beginning to notice that the evening's darkness was creeping into the room. In the center of the yellowish veneered ceiling was the kind of stark fluorescent light you'd see in an office building. When Kazue had switched it on, it made a slight hissing noise, like the sound of a flying creature flapping its wings. The light ringed Kazue's profile in a black outline. Unable to resist, I asked, "Well, why did only you, your father, and I get the soba?"

Kazue's tiny little eyes sparked. "Because in our house there is an order to things. There's that test you do with a pet dog, right? You line up all the members of the family and release the dog to see who he goes to first. And the first one is the boss. It's like that. Everyone automatically knows the order of things—who has the most prestige and authority, I mean. And you accede to that order accordingly. No one needs to explain it, but everyone obeys it. Everything is decided according to this order—like who has the right to take a bath first and who gets to eat the best food. My father's always first; that's only natural, right? And then I'm second. My mother used to come second, but once I made it into the top tier on the national scholastic rankings for my age group, I got to be second. So now my father goes first, I'm second, then my mother, and my sister's last. If she's not careful, though, my sister's going to pass my mom."

"You determine the pecking order in your family based on your scholastic scores?"

"Well, let's just say we go in the order of effort expended."

"But since your mother's not ever going to take any entrance exams, isn't that unfair to her?"

Mother and daughters lined up in competition with one another. Wasn't that absurd? But Kazue was deadly serious.

"It can't be helped. Mother lost out to my father from the very start, and there's no one in the family who can best him. I've studied as hard as I could ever since I can remember. My greatest joy in life is trying to improve my scores. For the longest time I set my sights on trying to outdo my mother. You know, my mother always says she never had career aspirations, but I think she wanted to become a doctor when she was young. Her father wouldn't permit it; besides, she wasn't smart enough to get into med school. But she always regretted it. Being raised to be a woman is pathetic, isn't it? That's what she always says. She uses being a woman as her excuse for not getting ahead in life. But if you really try your best, you can succeed even if you're female."

"Are you saying that—no matter what—all you have to do is try your best and you'll succeed?"

"Well, of course. If you try hard enough you'll be rewarded."

Yeah? Well, you're in the world of Q High School for Young Women now, my dear, and no matter how hard you try you're not going to get your reward! We live in a world where almost anything you try to accomplish will be met with failure. Am I wrong?

I wanted to say this to Kazue. Moreover, I wanted to teach her a lesson. If she should ever set eyes on a girl like Yuriko and her monstrously perfect beauty, Kazue's efforts—no matter how prodigious—would just be laughable, wouldn't they? But Kazue stared at the mottoes on her wall with a look of utter determination.

"Do you think it's true because it's what your father tells you?"

"It's like our family code. My mother believes it, too. And the teachers at school, they'll tell you the same thing. It's the truth, that's all." Kazue looked at me in surprise, her little eyes mocking me, flashing with color.

"Speaking of mothers, do you know what happened to me today?"

It seemed like the right time to spring this on her. I glanced at my watch, wanting to go home. It was already past seven.

"All I know is that it was Hana-chan's birthday," Kazue replied with a laugh, and then, as if remembering homeroom, her face crumbled into a frown.

"My mother died," I said.

Kazue leaped up from her chair in surprise. "Your mother died? Today?"

"Yeah. Well, technically it was yesterday."

"Shouldn't you go home?"

"Pretty soon. May I borrow your phone?"

Kazue pointed wordlessly to the stairs. I inched my way quietly down the dark stairs toward a thin stream of light that leaked out from under a closed door. I could hear the sound of a TV. I knocked.

A man's voice called out irritably. "What?" Her father. I opened the door. The only noticeable feature in the cramped sitting room was the wood-paneled walls. Kazue's younger sister, her mother, and a middle-aged man sitting on the couch in front of the TV turned simultaneously to stare at me. The dishes on the shelf directly across the room were all the kind you would buy at a supermarket. And the dining set, sofa, and chairs were the cheap preassembled kind. If the Q gang were to see this they'd have a field day, I thought. Kazue would be toast!

"May I borrow the phone?"

"Certainly."

Kazue's mother pointed toward the darkened kitchen. There, just outside the entrance, was an old-fashioned black rotary phone. There was a small handmade box next to the phone with the words TEN YEN. Kazue's parents just sat there looking at me expectantly. Neither bothered to tell me I needn't worry about the cost. So, I fished around in the pocket of my school uniform skirt and finally came up with a ten-yen coin to drop in the box. The coin made a dry sound as it fell. Apparently, few visitors stop by this house. To charge a fee for the phone was like a sick joke, I thought, as I dialed the numbers on the stiff rotary while carefully scrutinizing Kazue's family.

Kazue's younger sister—who had been deprived of her precious chair on my account—was now sitting at the dining room table busily scribbling in a notebook she had spread out in front of her. Peering over her shoulder, her mother was pointing something out to her in a low voice. They both glanced up to check on me and then once again began to stare fixedly at the notebook. Kazue's father was watching some kind of quiz show on TV—and looking quite relaxed in his undershirt and pajama-type pants. I could tell at a glance that he just happened to have the channel turned to that particular program and although he was looking at the TV, he wasn't really paying attention to the show. He jiggled his legs up and down nervously. He seemed to be in his late forties. He was short, his complexion was ruddy, and his close-cropped hair was thinning. At a glance he looked like a pudgy little country bumpkin. I felt cheated. Since the only Japanese man I knew was my grandfather, I was curious about Japanese fathers. Besides, I'd been dying to see just what kind of person this father of Kazue's was—especially since he ruled over wife and daughters from his exalted position as Number One in the family ranking. And yet here he was, just a gloomy middle-aged man. What a letdown.

The phone rang and rang and finally someone picked up.

"Grandpa?"

"Where'd you go traipsing off to?"

The person on the other end wasn't my grandfather. It was a neighbor, the insurance saleslady.

"We've got a problem. Your grandpa's blood pressure has skyrocketed and he's taken to bed. It seems your father and your sister in Switzerland had an argument, and that's what brought it on. They've called any number of times and have got him all stirred up. Your grandpa's always been a real sucker, you know. They both managed to calm down but then he started to feel sick, and then, when you didn't bother to come home, he started worrying about you!"

"I'm sorry. Is Grandpa okay?"

"He's okay. He had the super call me, and I ran over right away. That helped calm him down. He's sleeping like a baby now. It's too bad about your mother. It's for times like this that you need insurance, you know."

It sounded like the conversation was going to go on indefinitely, so I hurriedly blurted out, "I'm coming right home." But to get home from Setagaya would require that I cross Tokyo proper. It was going to take forever.

"How long will it take you?" she asked.

"At least an hour and a half."

"In that case, you'd better call your sister before you leave."

"Call Yuriko? Is it that urgent?"

"It is. She said they have to go to the funeral parlor and she's very impatient. Anyway, she has something she has to discuss with you, she said."

"But I'm at someone's house right now."

"So? Tell them you'll pay for the cost of the call. There's no time to wait until you've gotten home."

"Okay."

What on earth would my father and sister be arguing about? All I could think was that something horrible had happened. "I'm sorry, but I need to make an international call to Switzerland," I told Kazue's mother. "An emergency has come up."

"An emergency?"

Kazue's mother looked at me warily, her eyes narrowing behind her silver-rim glasses.

"My mother died last night and my younger sister needs me to call her."

Kazue's mother looked shocked, and she turned to look at her husband. Kazue's father looked back at me abruptly. His eyes turned up at the corners and seemed steeped in irritability. The light that flashed from them was strong and suggested an intent to take on anyone who met their gaze. "That's awful," he said, in a dark, insinuating voice. "I wonder if you would dial the operator first when placing your call. That way you can ask for the charges when the call is complete. It will be best for both of us."

The first to pick up the phone when the operator placed the call was my father, who was still in a state of shock.

"We're in turmoil here; it's just *terrible!*" The last word he spluttered out in English. "The police came and asked all kinds of questions. They think it's odd that your mother died while I was out, but it's only natural under the circumstances, don't you think? Your mother had lost her mind, you know. It's got nothing to do with me. I got mad and had to argue for my own security. It was an awful conversation. Just *terrible.*" Again with the English word. "It's so sad but also very, very bitter. It's so painful to be under suspicion like this."

"Father, you mean *innocence*, don't you? You had to argue for your own *innocence.*"

"Illness? What?"

"Forget it. Why do they suspect you?"

"I don't want to discuss it. It's not something to discuss with a daughter. But they're sending a detective over at four. I'm angry as hell."

"Well, what about the funeral?"

"It'll be the day after tomorrow, at three."

My father barely managed to finish his sentence before Yuriko got on the phone. I wondered if she'd yanked the receiver out of his hand. I could hear him scolding her in German.

"It's me, Yuriko. As soon as the funeral's over I'm coming back to Japan. Father's being impossible. He said the shock might cause his Turkish girlfriend to suffer a miscarriage, so he's brought her here—to this house! With Mother's body still here! So I told the police about her. I told them Father's girlfriend was the one who was most responsible for Mother's death. That's why the detective came. It serves him right!"

"That was really stupid, Yuriko. You're turning this whole thing into a soap opera!"

"Maybe so, but this time he went too far!"

Yuriko started to cry. It seemed like they'd been in an uproar since I talked to them this morning.

"Mother's death was so sudden, no wonder Father's in shock. I don't care how many women he brings home with him, you need to lighten up. At least he has someone to help him through this."

"What are you talking about? Have you lost your mind?" Yuriko was furious. "How can you be so cold? Mother's dead! And you're not here, so you can't possibly understand what's going on. Mother commits suicide and yet he brings that woman here. In a few months you and I are going to have ourselves a little brother or sister. Of course I'm furious! Mother's death might have been caused by Father's affair, you know. It's as if he killed her himself. Or you could say it's as if that woman did it. It's the last straw. I'm cutting my ties with that man once and for all!"

Yuriko's shrill voice raced over the six thousand miles separating Switzerland from Japan and seeped out of the black telephone receiver, entering the gloomy living room in Kazue's house.

"Mother died on account of her circumstances." I laughed through my nose. "You say you're going to cut all ties with Father, but you don't have any money. If you come back to Japan, you won't have any place to live and you won't be enrolled in school."

I was trying my best to block Yuriko's return. But what the hell was my father thinking, bringing his pregnant girlfriend into the house the very day Mother died? Even I was shocked. I noticed Kazue's family sitting there in the living room holding their breaths, their eyes riveted on me. I met Kazue's father's stare head on and refused to look away. Shame on you for bringing such a conversation into my house! his eyes accused. I tried to end the call as quickly as I could.

"Okay, well, let's talk later."

"No, we have to decide this now. The police are coming any minute, and I have to go with them when they take Mother's body to the funeral parlor."

"Get your mind off Japan," I screamed at her. "It's out of the question!"

"You can't tell me what to do, you know. I'm coming back."

"Where to?"

"I don't care. If I can't stay with you, I'll ask the Johnsons."

"Fine by me. Ask away."

"You think only of yourself, don't you," Yuriko said.

That ridiculous Johnson couple: they'd be perfect for Yuriko! I felt like a huge burden had been lifted from my shoulders. As long as I didn't have to see my sister, I didn't care if she came back to Japan or stayed in Switzerland. All I wanted was to preserve the quiet life I had with my grandfather.

"Call me when you get back."

"You don't give a damn. You never did."

Upset, I hung up the phone. It seemed like we'd talked for over ten minutes. Kazue's family averted their eyes. I waited for the operator to call back and inform me of the charges. And I waited and waited and waited. I had assumed the call would come any minute. When the phone finally rang, Kazue's father got to it before I could, leaping across the room with amazing agility.

"It's ten thousand eight hundred yen. If you'd called after eight it would have been cheaper."

"I'm sorry. I don't carry that kind of money with me. May I give it to Kazue tomorrow?"

"Please be sure to do so."

Kazue's father spoke in a very businesslike tone. I thanked him and left the living room. I heard the door open behind me as I stood in the gloomy hallway looking up the dark flight of stairs. Kazue's father had come out after me. The light from the living room filtered out into the hallway in a long narrow stream through the crack he'd left in the door. But no one said a word. It was as quiet as a crypt in the living room, as if the two sitting there were holding their breath trying to hear what Kazue's father would say to me. Shorter than I am, her father pressed a scrap of paper into the palm of my hand. When I looked, it was a reminder of the amount I owed for the phone call: ¥10,800, written in crisp clear marks.

"There's something I want to talk to you about."

"Yes?"

The light from Kazue's father's eyes was intense, as if challenging me to bend to his will. It made me feel slightly dizzy. At first he spoke in insipid tones as if trying to butter me up.

"You've been admitted to Q High School for Young Women, so I imagine you're a very fine young lady."

"I suppose."

"How hard did you study for the exam?"

"I don't remember."

"Kazue has been a diligent student ever since elementary school. Fortunately she's a smart girl, and she enjoys studying. So it's only right that she's made it this far. But I don't think just studying is enough. She's a girl, after all, and I want her to pay attention to how she dresses. And since she's now at Q High School for Young Women, I want her to become more ladylike. To try, you know. And for her part she's still doing all she can to meet my expectations. So she's very dear to me. I'm praising her blindly because I'm her father. Both my daughters are so submissive that I worry about them. But you. You're different. When compared to my daughter, you seem much more sure of yourself. I work for a major corporation, and I'm a good judge of character. I can spot a person's true character a mile away. What does your father do?"

Kazue's father leered at me. He did not try to conceal the fact that he was sizing me up. I was sure he'd find my father's work of no value whatsoever. So I lied.

"He works for a Swiss bank."

"Which bank, I wonder, the Swiss Union Bank? Or perhaps the Swiss Credit?"

"I've been told not to divulge that information."

I was completely clueless and confused, but I did my best to answer with care. Kazue's father let out a short snort and nodded. A slight wave of respect washed over his face. Did he feel somewhat humbled? It surprised me to realize that I found the encounter quite enjoyable. Yes, laugh at me if you will, but I found myself saying exactly the sort of thing my grandfather, the con man, always said about my father's work. I had managed to adapt myself to this man's sense of values. I knew of no one else who was as clear-cut as he on what was worthy and what was not. But it terrified me that he would force his biased logic on me. I was only sixteen at the time, after all.

"Kazue told me you were the one who put her up to the discussion about the clubs. My daughter's the type to take everything seriously and do her best as a result. She'll apply herself naïvely to anything anyone tells her to do. And you knew this, didn't you? But I'm the one who controls my daughter, see? It's best if you stay out of it."

I tried to meet him head on. "Sir, you don't know what it's like at our school, and you don't know about my friendship with your daughter, so why would you say such a thing?"

"There's friendship, is there, between you and Kazue?"

"There is."

"But you're not an appropriate friend for one of my daughters. It's a pity about your mother. But from what I can tell, the circumstances of her death are not what one would call normal. I selected Q High School for Kazue because I knew I couldn't go wrong there. I knew Kazue would be able to make friends with good girls. Kazue's a wholesome girl from a normal family."

What he meant was that my family was not normal. Yuriko and I were not wholesome. I wonder what he would have said if Mitsuru had come.

"I don't think that's fair. I—"

"That's enough. I'm not interested in what you have to say."

I could feel the anger burning in his tiny upturned eyes. His anger was not directed at me as a child but as a separate force that threatened his daughter.

"Of course, a friendship with a girl like you might prove to be a good lesson for Kazue. She could learn more about society that way. But it's still too early for her, and you have nothing to do with our family. Besides, I have my younger daughter to think of, so I'm sorry to have to say this but I don't ever want to see you here again."

"I see."

"Please don't hold a grudge over what I've just said, either."

"I won't."

This was the first time I'd ever been so clearly rebuffed by an adult. He might as well have said, You're worthless. It shocked me.

My own father had of course wielded paternal authority within the home. But because he was a minority in Japan, he had never really been able to communicate that authority to the outside world. My grandfather was a timid convict who did whatever I told him to do. If anything, it was my mother who represented our family to the rest of society. But my mother had no influence in the home and gave in to my father on everything. Therefore, when I saw a person who used the rigidity and absurdity of social conventions as steadfastly as Kazue's father did, I was impressed. Why? Because Kazue's father did not really believe in the social values he represented, but he clearly knew that he had armed himself with them more or less as a weapon of survival.

Kazue's father obviously paid no attention to the internal affairs at Q High School for Young Women. He was utterly unconcerned with the impact this would have on Kazue or the way it would make her suffer. He was one self-centered son-of-a-bitch. That much I understood with crystal clarity, even as a high school student. But Kazue, her mother, and her younger sister lived in complete ignorance of this man's intentions or his character; yet he was able to apprehend the evil intentions that Mitsuru and I nurtured, take them for his own, and use them to protect his family. Protecting the family was nothing short of protecting himself. In that sense, I couldn't help but envy Kazue and her strong father. Dominated by her father's strong will, Kazue trusted his values implicitly. When I think about it now, I realize that the power he had over her was tantamount to mind control.

"Well, then, take care on your way home."

I started to climb the stairs, feeling as though Kazue's father were pushing me from behind. After he had watched me for a bit, he went back into the living room, slamming the door closed behind him. The darkness in the hallway felt all the deeper.

"You took long enough!"

Kazue was annoyed to have been kept waiting. It looked as though she'd been trying to stave off her boredom by doodling in the notebook she had spread out in front of her on the desk. She'd sketched a picture of a cheerleader in a miniskirt hoisting a baton. When she saw me looking down at the drawing, she quickly covered the page with her hands, just like a child.

"He let me make an international call." I showed Kazue the bill her father had written out. "I'll give you the money tomorrow."

Kazue glanced at the amount. "Wow! That was expensive. I was wondering, How'd your mother die anyway?"

"She committed suicide—in Switzerland."

Kazue dropped her gaze and looked like she was searching for the right words, then looked up again. "I know this sounds awful, but I kinda envy you."

"Why? Do you wish your mother were dead too?"

Kazue's answer was barely more than a whisper. "I detest my mother. Recently I've begun to notice that she acts more like she was my father's daughter than his wife. What a way for a mother to behave! My father only has hopes for his daughters, you know, for us—so having her around is really annoying."

Kazue brimmed with joy at the thought that she was the only one able to measure up to her father's expectations. Kazue was a "good girl," a filial daughter whose only reason for living was to please her father.

"Yes, I suppose he doesn't need another daughter," I said.

"You've got that right! And I could do without my little sister too!"

Without thinking I let out a sympathetic laugh. My own family was far from normal, a fact I well understood without having Kazue's father point it out. I realized this was something a die-hard disciple like Kazue would never understand.

As I was stepping out of the house into the dark street, I felt someone clutch at my shoulder. Kazue's father had followed me out.

"Just a minute there," he said. "You lied. Your father doesn't work for the Bank of Switzerland or anything of the sort, does he?"

The streetlight bounced dimly off his little eyes. He must have learned that from Kazue. I stood there petrified. He continued. "It's wrong to lie. I've never once lied in all my life. Lies are the enemy of society. Do you see? If you don't want me to report you to the school, you'll not come near Kazue ever again."

"I understand."

I could tell that Kazue's father was staring after me until I turned the corner at the end of the street. Four years later he would suffer a cerebral hemorrhage and die on the spot, so my chance encounter with this man would be my first and last. After her father died, Kazue's family fortunes plummeted. I suppose I was a witness to the fragility of Kazue's family, having observed it only years before its drastic demise. And yet I can still feel the way Kazue father's glare bored into my back like a bullet that night.

After a week had passed, my father called to tell me the funeral had gone smoothly. I didn't hear so much as a peep from Yuriko. Convincing myself that her plans to return to Japan had been dealt a setback, I spent the next few days walking on air. And then one evening not long thereafter, an evening so warm it felt like summer vacation had already arrived, I got a phone call from the last person in the world I was expecting to hear from: Johnson's wife, Masami. Three years had passed since that time at the mountain cabin.

"Hii-aaai! Is this Yuriko's seesta? It's meee! Masammy Johnson!"

She stretched her vowels inordinately long and pronounced the *s*'s in her name just as a foreigner would. Just hearing it made the flesh on my arms crawl.

"It's been a while."

"Well, I didn't know you'd stayed behind by yourself in Japan! You should have told me! I would have been happy to help you any way I could. How silly for you to be so reserved. Look, I was really sorry to hear about your mother. What a shame."

"Thank you for your concern," I managed to mumble.

"Actually, I'm calling you about Yuriko-chan. Did you hear?"

"Hear what?"

"Yuriko's going to stay with us! At least while she's in junior high school. We have a spare room and we've been fond of Yuriko ever since she was a little girl. She has to change schools, of course. She said she wanted to go to Q School, where you are. So I checked into it, and found out what was required to get her enrolled as a student returning from abroad, and they've agreed to admit her. I just got the news a little while ago. Isn't that great? You and Yuriko will be going to the same school! My husband's really happy about the way it's all worked out. He says Q is a really good school, and it's not far from where we live!"

What the hell was happening? I'd studied my butt off in the hopes of finally getting away from Yuriko, and now here she was seeping back into my life like some kind of poison gas! I sighed in despair. Yuriko was as dumb as a doornail, but her beauty would forever entitle her to special treatment. On that score, the Q School system was no different.

"Where's Yuriko now?" I asked.

"She's right here. Just a minute. I'll put her on."

"Hello, Sis? Is that you?"

I had told Yuriko not to come back to Japan, but here she was. Her carefree voice on the other end of the line was quite a contrast to the distraught girl I'd heard just hours after our mother had died. Clearly she was now eating up all the attention the Johnsons were dishing out and rolling in the luxury of their swank house in upscale Minato Ward.

"So are you transferring into Q Junior High?"

"Yes, from September. Isn't that great? We'll be in the same school."

"When'd you get back?"

"Hmmm, about a week ago, I guess. Daddy's remarrying, you know."

She said it casually, without the slightest bitterness, as if whatever was okay with her was okay in general.

"How's Grandpa?"

Gripping the phone tightly in my hand, I glanced back at my grandfather. He was engrossed in his bonsai, completely unaware of the conversation taking place right next to him. He'd calmed down over the previous few days.

"He's fine."

"Mm." Yuriko's response, if you could call it that, betrayed her complete indifference. "I'm really glad I didn't go stay to with you in P Ward. I'm going to try really hard to get along on my own over here."

Yeah, right. She was really going to be on her own. What a farce. With no interest in pursuing the conversation further, I hung up, utterly dejected.

· 6 ·

The events I've narrated up to this point were those I experienced personally. Yuriko and Kazue—and Kazue's father—still live in my memory. It's something of a one-sided story, but what can you expect? The only one left to relate the events is me, and here I am as healthy as can be, working in the ward office. My grandfather, as I've mentioned, has Alzheimer's and is off enjoying himself in never-never land, where neither time nor place holds any relevance. He doesn't even remember how he once devoted himself to bonsai. He sold off his beloved oak and his black pine; either that or the trees withered long ago and were dumped in the garbage.

Mention of bonsai makes me remember that there was one more thing about my encounter with Kazue's father that I've forgotten to mention: the need to pay back the cost of that international telephone call, ¥10,800.

Since I wasn't carrying much money on me at the time, I had promised to pay it back later. But that became a problem. At the time, my allowance was a mere ¥3,000 a month. After I got through buying all my necessary school supplies—notebooks and pens and such—there wasn't a whole lot left over. My father sent ¥40,000 a month in addition to tuition fees. But I handed all that over to Grandfather. I mean, after all, I was living in his apartment. Of course he squandered it on his bonsai, either buying new plants or new paraphernalia for the plants he already had. At any rate, I'd never imagined an international phone call would be so costly, and as I made my way home from Kazue's house that night, I racked my brain over how I was going to pay for it.

From time to time we'd get phone calls from Switzerland, but of course my father always covered the charge, and besides, we never talked very long. We just weren't the kind of family to have long chats. Even if I asked my father to send me the money for the charge, it would take time for it to reach Japan. I figured I had no choice but to ask Grandfather to lend me the money.

But when I got home that evening from Kazue's, my grandfather was already snoring away in bed, trying to sleep off the sudden surge in his blood pressure. The neighbor, an insurance lady, was there looking after him. "You have to pay how much? Why on earth didn't you call collect?" she snapped, when she heard about the phone call.

"You're the one who told me to call from there, remember? You should have told me then to call collect. How'm I supposed to know about international calls?"

"You're right." The insurance lady sucked on her cigarette and blew the smoke out the corner of her mouth so it wouldn't go in my face. "But still, it's awfully expensive. Who spoke to the operator and confirmed the actual charges?"

"Her father."

"What if he lied? He probably figured he could pull a fast one on you, since you're just a girl. Even if he didn't try to cheat you, most people would have felt sorry enough for you—losing your mother and all—to have covered the cost, kind of like offering a condolence gift. I know I would have. It's really the only decent thing to do. But I suppose it's a question of character."

The insurance lady was particularly stingy. I had a hard time believing that she'd actually extend charity to anyone. But still her words caused a shadow of doubt to spread across my heart. Did Kazue's father lie to me? But even if he did, I had no proof. I looked at the scrap of paper I'd stuffed in my pocket: the statement of the telephone charge. The insurance lady snatched at it with her thick fingers. The longer she stared at the figure, the angrier she got.

"I just can't believe someone would write out a sum like this and hand it to a child: a child whose poor mother has suddenly been taken from her and whose old grandfather has taken to bed ill. What a monster.

What line of work is he in? If he can send his kid to that school he must be rich. I'll bet their house is nice."

"I couldn't really say. He told me he worked for some major corporation. They did have a nice house."

"Figures . . . the greed of the wealthy!"

"It didn't seem like that."

The atmosphere of stingy frugality permeating Kazue's house floated before my eyes, and I shook my head from side to side.

"Well, then, I get the impression that he is just a run-of-the-mill salary man with a low income trying to pretend to be wealthy. If not, he's a real cheapskate!" Once she reached this conclusion, the insurance lady hastily collected her things and left, obviously wanting to clear out before I could get around to asking her for a loan. I felt an uncontrollable anger and hurled the scrap of paper with the phone charges at the wall.

The next morning when I saw Kazue in class, she immediately started to press me for the money. "My father told me to tell you to be sure not to forget about the money you owe us for the telephone call."

"Sorry. Can I pay you tomorrow?"

I can still remember the way Kazue's eyes panned over my face. She clearly did not trust me. But were they being honest with me? Still, a loan's a loan. I knew I had to pay it back. So as soon as classes ended, I rushed home and picked a plant from among my grandfather's bonsai collection—a nandina tree, one that was small enough to carry. My grandfather was particularly proud of it; he used to describe with pleasure the beautiful color of the red berries that it bore in winter months. Luxuriant green moss, as thick as a carpet, covered the soil at the base of the little tree. It was planted in an enamel-glazed pot of somber blue.

My grandfather was engrossed in a sumo bout on TV. I couldn't hope for a better chance than now, so I quietly walked out of the apartment with the bonsai. I put it in the basket of my bicycle and pedaled as fast and furiously as I could to the Garden of Longevity.

Night was falling and the garden was closing. The probation officer stood at the front gate seeing off customers. He looked surprised to see me ride up with the bonsai.

"Good evening," I said, as politely as I could. "I was wondering if you would buy this bonsai from me."

The man looked annoyed. "Did your grandfather put you up to this?"

I shook my head from side to side.

He smirked. I realized he wanted to get revenge on my grandfather. "I see. Well, I'll give you a fine price for it then. How does five thousand yen sound?"

Disappointed, I held up two fingers. "Can't you give me two bills for it? Twenty thousand yen? My grandfather says it's a fine nandina."

"Young lady, this bonsai is not worth that much."

"Okay, fine. I'll take it to someone else."

The probation officer immediately doubled his price, offering ¥10,000. I countered that the pot itself was worth that much. After he thought that over, he offered in a wheedling voice, "It must be heavy," and put his hands over mine, encircling the pot. The hard skin of his hands had the luster of finely polished leather and was strangely warm. Repulsed, I drew my hands away instinctively, letting go of the pot. When I did, the bonsai slipped between us and struck one of the garden stones, smashing to pieces. The roots of the nandina, released from bondage, sprang out in all directions. The young people who'd been cleaning up around the garden stopped what they were doing and looked up in alarm. The probation officer bent over and began picking up the pieces in great agitation, glancing at me with nervous apprehension as he did so.

In the end I got thirty thousand yen for the deal, broken pot and all. I decided to deposit the money I had left after paying the phone bill in my savings account. I never knew when I'd need to come up with quick cash for a class field trip or something. At Q High School for Young Women we were always being pressured to contribute to events, from the annual school festival to some birthday celebration. None of the other students thought anything of it. The extra cushion in my savings account would be for my own protection.

My grandfather didn't notice a thing that night, but the next morning, when he stepped out onto the veranda, he let out a heartrending cry.

"Mr. Nandina! Where have you gone?"

I went about fixing my lunch as if I hadn't noticed. Grandfather rushed into the cramped sitting room and raced around in search of the nandina. He opened the closet and then peered up on the shelving along the ceiling in the smaller room. He even went out in the entryway and rummaged through the shoe cupboard.

"It's nowhere to be found! And such a nice bonsai it was. Where could it be? Come out, come out, wherever you are! Please, Mr. Nandina. I'm sorry if I neglected you. I didn't mean to. But my daughter just died, you see, and it's been hard on me. I'm heartbroken. I'm sorry, really I am. Please come out. Please don't pout."

Grandfather searched the house like a madman, until I guess he just wore himself out. Crestfallen—his shoulders curling inward—he stared off into space. "He went off to guide her to the next world." My grandfather was much practiced in the ways of swindling others. But it never once occurred to him to doubt me or the insurance lady or the security guard or any of the other people who were around him all the time. He hadn't even the slightest suspicion. It looked like this was the end of the absurd event, so I went off to school feeling relieved. Visiting Kazue's house had been the cause of one misfortune after another.

•

When you think of it, though, my mother's sudden suicide resulted in the scattering of the entire family. I stayed with my grandfather, Yuriko ended up with the Johnsons, and my father remained in Switzerland, where he started a new family with that Turkish woman. For my father, Japan would always be associated with my mother's death. Later I learned, to my great surprise, that the Turkish woman was no more than two years older than me. She gave birth to three children, I learned, all boys. The oldest child is now twenty-four, and I've been told he plays for a Spanish soccer team. But since I've never met him and have no interest in soccer, it's as if we're from completely different worlds.

But in the world of my hypothetical chart, Yuriko and I and our stepbrothers are all swimming vigorously in the bright blue of the brackish sea. If I draw another analogy to the Burgess diagram of the Cambrian Period I love so much, Yuriko, with her beautiful face, is queen of the watery realm. So she has to be one of those animals that devours all others. That would make her the *Anomalocaris*, I suppose, the ancestor to the crustacean, a kind of creature with massive forelegs, like a lobster's. And then my younger brothers, who must certainly have dark heavy eyebrows on account of their Middle Eastern blood, would be those insects that live all clumped up in a pile—either that or jellyfish-type creatures that cruise through the sea. Me? Without a doubt I'd be the *Hallucigenia*, the thing that crawls through the mud of the ocean floor covered in seven sets of quills, looking for all the world like a hairbrush. The *Hallucigenia* feeds on carrion? I didn't know that! So it survives by eating dead creatures? Well, then, it fits me to a T, since I live by soiling the memories of the corpses of the past.

Oh, about Mitsuru and me? Well, Mitsuru went on to pass her boards at Tokyo University Medical School, just as she'd hoped. But after that her life headed in a completely different and entirely unpredicted direction. She seems to be well—but she's in the penitentiary. Once a year I get a New Year's card from her, heavily excised by the censors, but I've never once replied. Do you want me to explain? I'll be sure to do so as soon as I've wrapped up this part of the story.

To continue, then, just the other day something completely unexpected happened. I haven't wanted to talk to anyone about it, but if I'm going to continue with my account I have no choice but to reveal everything. It was about a week before the opening day of the trial. The two murders had been linked—for convenience I suppose—and were being dubbed "The Case of the Serial Apartment Murders." At first the mass media had a field day over Kazue's murder, which they referred to as the "Elite Office Lady Murder Case." But once they connected Zhang to Yuriko's murder as well, they changed their headlines. Yuriko had been murdered first, and when the case initially involved just a middle-aged prostitute, there'd been no reason even to create a headline.

We'd heard reports that an off-season typhoon was threatening to move in on Tokyo. It was a disquieting day. An unseasonably warm wind rattled through the city, growing increasingly loud and strong. From the window of the ward office I watched the gale tear through the leaves of the sycamore trees outside as if to rip them from their branches. It toppled the bicycles in the parking lot like dominoes. It was a nerve-racking day, let me tell you, and made me feel somehow on edge.

I took my seat at the Day Care consultation counter as usual. But no one came to apply for day care, and I lost myself to my thoughts. With the typhoon approaching, all I could think of was how I wanted to head home. Then an elderly woman appeared at my counter. She was wearing a smartly tailored gray suit, very subdued and classy. A pair of silver-rimmed reading glasses were perched on her nose. She seemed to be in her mid-fifties. Her graying hair was pulled back in a tight bun, and she had a severe manner, like a German woman. I was used to seeing no one but young mothers with children in tow at this particular window. I figured this woman must have come to inquire about putting a grandchild in day care, so with obvious reluctance I said, "May I help you?"

At this, the woman let out a short snort and pulled her lips back. There was something about her teeth that struck me as familiar.

"My dear, don't you know who I am?"

Even when I stared long and fast at her face, I couldn't recall her name. The skin on her face—which bore not so much as a trace of makeup—was brown. She wore no lipstick. Here was an elderly woman wearing no makeup with a face like a fish. How was I supposed to distinguish her from any other woman her age?

"It's me, Masami. Masami Johnson!"

I was so startled I let out a little gasp. I would never have expected Masami to turn into such a subdued modest-looking woman. The Masami of my memory would forever be a garish woman out of sync with her surroundings. She was the woman who strolled along the mountain paths of Gunma Prefecture sporting a humongous diamond ring, the one who wore bright red lipstick out on the ski slopes. She was the one who put her fuzzy mohair cap on Yuriko's head. A woman who wore a designer T-shirt printed with the snarling face of a leopard so realistic it terrified young children. And she was the one who spoke English with such a trill she might as well have shouted "Hey! Look at me!" But even so, I was readily convinced by her transformation that she'd come to inquire about a nursery school. So I pulled out the registration book and said, while trying my best to conceal my bewilderment, "I didn't realize you were living in this ward."

"Oh, no, I'm not," Masami responded, in all seriousness. "I live in Yokohama now. I've remarried, you see."

I didn't even know she and Johnson were divorced. In my mind, both Masami and Johnson were people I had never expected or wanted to see again.

"I didn't know. When did you get a divorce?"

"It's been more than twenty years."

Masami pulled a very elegant name card out of what appeared to be a solid-silver case and handed it to me.

"This is what I do now."

COORDINATOR AND CONSULTANT: PRIVATE ENGLISH LESSONS, the card read. And her name had changed from Masami Johnson to Masami Bhasami.

"I'm married to an Iranian who's in the export-import business. And I have my own little business enlisting English tutors and dispatching them to various assignments for private conversation classes. It's really a lot of fun."

I pretended to study her name card while I mulled it over. Why had she shown up here to see me after twenty-seven years? More to the point, why on a day like today? It was just too strange for words. To top it off, Masami was standing there beaming at me, her eyes dancing with nostalgia.

"Oh, it's so good to see you, dear! Let's see. The last time we spoke was when Yuriko called to tell you she'd gotten into Q Junior High. That must have been more than twenty years ago!"

"Yes, I suppose so."

"Well, how have you been?"

"Very well. Thank you for asking."

Thank you for asking indeed, I thought to myself bitterly, as I replied with the expected formality. It was so odd that she'd turned up here. She hadn't come all the way to tell me about her private English classes, surely! When I could hide my dubious expression no longer, Masami finally blurted out the truth.

"After Johnson and I broke up, he really hit rock bottom. He'd once been a rising star as a securities trader, you know, but once his career took a nosedive he sank to becoming one of those dime-a-dozen English teachers. And then, of course, Yuriko was murdered."

There was an edge in Masami's voice—an effort to contain an inappropriate emotion: hatred. And then, looking straight at me and my bewildered expression, she said, "You didn't know, did you, dear? Johnson and I broke up because of Yuriko."

I suddenly remembered the expression on Johnson's face as he sat in front of the fireplace in his mountain cabin on that night so long ago with Yuriko leaning against his lap, playing sweet with him. She was just a primary school student then. Johnson had always looked so handsome and self-possessed, with his tousled brown hair and faded blue jeans. I found myself imagining what the face of a child born of those two would look like. The image I concocted was so endearing, so charming, it was enough to paralyze my mind. Yuriko might have died, but she still managed to exert control over me. I couldn't stand it.

Sensing my own hidden loathing, Masami said, "Then you really didn't know. And I was so good to her, looking after her. To have her stab me in the back like that! Really, it made me so crazy I had to seek psychiatric counseling at the hospital for a while. I mean, I went to so much trouble to get her into the Q school system, and then every day I fixed her lunch, making sure it was so wonderful that none of her little friends would ever make fun of her. And the allowance I gave her was no pittance either, plus I was always certain she had money whenever she went out. Then there was the money it took to get her into the cheerleader squad, which was quite a sum, let me tell you. If I could get it back now, I would certainly try!"

So that was it. She'd come to get the money! I lowered my head in confusion, trying to avoid her eyes.

"I'm terribly sorry."

"Forget it! There's nothing you could have done about it. You and Yuriko were never close anyway. I guess you were the clever one. You saw through her all along."

I might as well have been a fortune-teller the way Masami praised me. And then she reached in her bag, pulled out a notebook, and plopped it on the counter in front of me. The cover of the notebook was plastered with a sticker of a white lily and looked very girlish. Where the seal had peeled up, the edges were dirty and stained.

"What's this?"

"It's your sister's. I guess you could call it her diary. It looks like she kept it up until the very end. I'm sorry to spring it on you like this, but it gives me the creeps. I came here today to hand it over to you. I think it would be best for you to keep it. Johnson kept it for some reason, and then one day he sent it to me out of the blue, saying he had no use for it since he couldn't read Japanese. When Yuriko was murdered I guess he suffered from a bout of guilty conscience. But he must not have realized she'd written about him in it."

Masami's lips curled down when she said this.

"Did you read it?" I asked her.

"Certainly not." Masami shook her head vigorously. "I have no interest in other people's journals—and especially not in something as riddled with filth as this one."

Masami didn't seem to notice the contradiction in what she said.

"Very well. I'll take it."

"Oh, what a relief! I thought it would be strange to turn it over to the police. And I hear the trial will begin soon, so it did cause me some concern. All right, then. I'll leave it with you. Thanks. Take care of yourself."

Masami waved a suntanned hand at me. She glanced out the window at the sky and turned briskly on her heels. I'm sure she wanted to get home and out of this unfamiliar place before the typhoon set in. Or perhaps she didn't want to spend a minute more talking with someone related to Yuriko. At any rate, she fled down the hall.

The section chief came up behind me and peered down at the notebook. "Was it a claim? Or was something wrong?"

"Neither one. It was nothing, really."

"Really? Well, she didn't look like she had any connection with day-care centers."

I quickly placed my hands over Yuriko's notebook. Once the Serial Apartment Murder Case got under way, I'd again become the target of curious stares. The section chief was already certain I was withholding information.

"Boss, would it be okay if I wrap up early? I'm sorry, but I'm worried about my grandfather."

The section chief nodded wordlessly and he returned to his desk by the window. On account of the strange dampness in the air today, even the sound of his sneakers along the floor was dull and leaden. With the section chief's permission, I rushed home, battling the wind with all my might. The gusts were so strong they practically lifted both wheels of my bike off the ground. It wouldn't be long before fall set in and we could anticipate the cold north winds. But the dampness today made my skin feel warm and sticky. And the queasy feeling in my stomach had nothing to do with the weather and everything to do with the fact that someone like Yuriko had left behind a journal.

When she was in grade school, Yuriko was so bad at composition she had to ask for help. And she never paid attention to anything around her because she completely lacked any spirit of inquiry. A journal written by such a self-absorbed dim-witted girl had to be brimming with puerile self-portraits. Yuriko could hardly compose a coherent sentence; how could she possibly have kept a journal? Surely someone masquerading as Yuriko had written it. But who? And more than who, what? What could she possibly have written about? I was beside myself with curiosity and wanted to delve into Yuriko's journal as quickly as possible.

Well, here it is. This is Yuriko's journal. To be perfectly honest, I would rather not show it to you. It is teeming with rubbish about her own messy life, but it is also replete with lies about me and our mother.

Yuriko, of all people! It just amazes me that she could write such garbage. Certainly the handwriting resembles Yuriko's. Someone must have forged it.

If you promise not to believe a word of it, I'll let you see what she wrote. But you really must not believe it. It really is a complete fabrication. A number of the Chinese characters she used in the journal were written incorrectly. And then there were places where she left out characters, and others where the characters she wrote were just plain ugly or else really hard to decipher. I've rewritten those parts.

THREE · A NATURAL-BORN WHORE: YURIKO'S DIARY

· 1 ·

I t was one in the afternoon when the phone rang. Still in bed, I answered with as much charm as I could muster, thinking it might be a customer. It was my sister. I never called her. But she called me at least two or three times a week. She clearly had too much time on her hands. "I'm busy, call later," I told her curtly as I started to slam the phone down. "I'll call again tonight," she shot back. It's not as though she had anything important to discuss. I think she just wanted to see if I had a man with me. That's the only reason she called. And I know this because the next minute she asked, "Are you alone now? I feel like you've got someone with you."

Once when Johnson had come over, my sister called while we were doing it. She left a long rambling message on my answering machine.

"Yuriko, it's me. I just had a great idea. Why don't we move in together? Think about it. Given our different schedules, it ought to work out really well. I work during the day and I'm finished by nightfall. Since you work at night, you'll be asleep at home while I'm working. And then while I'm asleep, you'll be out. If you could get home before I wake up, we could go through the whole day without ever once seeing each other. We'd really save on rent. And we could take turns cooking meals and eating the leftovers for days on end. What do you say? Don't you think it's a great idea? Which apartment do you think we should keep? I'd like to know what you think, okay?"

"Hey, isn't that your sister?" Johnson asked.

"Yep. Doesn't it just overwhelm you with nostalgia?" I answered, biting back my laughter.

"Well, she's the one who brought us together—our own little Cupid," Johnson fired back, in flawless Japanese, letting go with a laugh. We sprawled across the bed in gales of laughter, putting a quick end to our sex.

"Cupid, huh? I doubt she'd think of it that way." My ugly older sister with her warped personality! In order to put me back in the mood, Johnson reached over and nuzzled my neck. I tilted my head to the side, accepting his kisses, and gazed at the brown freckles sprinkled across his broad shoulders. His body has grown thick and heavy, and his beautiful hair is now mostly gone. Johnson is already fifty-one.

When we first met, I was still just a little girl, but even so I knew immediately that this man wanted me. Johnson couldn't speak much Japanese at the time, and I didn't know any English. But we still managed to understand implicitly what it was the other wanted to say.

Hurry and grow up! That's what he was thinking.

I will; wait for me.

Each time my older sister tormented me I fled to the Johnsons' cabin. Regardless of whether or not Johnson was in the middle of an important business call or entertaining guests, the minute he saw me his face would light up with pleasure. Despite herself, therefore, my sister deserves a good deal of thanks for sending me into Johnson's arms with her bullying. The biggest obstacle I had to confront was Masami's kindnesses. She was Johnson's wife and a former Air France flight attendant. Johnson was five years younger than Masami and was her absolute obsession. She was captivated by his financial stability and his social standing and scared to death of being dumped by him. So if Johnson was sweet on me, Masami had to do her best to act the same. She was constantly plying me with candy and stuffed animals. What I really wanted was the Revlon nail polish she had lining her dressing table. But at least while she was around I had to act like a little girl. I understood that this was for the best.

I was ecstatic, therefore, when my father said I could stay at the Johnsons' the day after my sister and I had our big fight. Johnson and I got a bit carried away and did something extremely risky. We slipped sleeping medicine into Masami's drink. Once she started snoring, we spent the rest of the night cuddling in the bed right there beside her. At other times, when Masami was in the kitchen grilling meat or something with her back turned to us, I would sit in the living room watching TV while Johnson fondled me. I'd have my jeans on the whole time, but he'd rub his hands over me down there. And he'd put my hands around his thing, once it was hard. That was the first time I'd ever touched a man there. I was convinced that Johnson would be my first lover.

From the very start I believed that I would never have a Japanese boy for a lover. In the first place, they never came anywhere near me, acting like they were terrified of me because I was half and somehow beyond their reach. But as a result, groups of them would gang up on me and play all kinds of nasty pranks. Encountering a bunch of high school boys on the train was always the worst. They'd paw at me so violently that they'd come close to yanking my hair, and I had no choice but to put up with it. One time a group of boys surrounded me and tore off my skirt. My lessons came at a very early age. I learned that in order to survive there was only one way I could fight a man.

"Well, I'd better be on my way, or I'm going to be late for class."

Johnson made a bitter face and pulled himself up, folding his enormous body into two. He was so large that whenever he lay on my narrow bed half his body jutted over the side as if it were about to slide off. Johnson was an English teacher. He taught in a classroom in front of a station on the Ōdakyū Line. It took just over an hour from here on the express train. He said about twelve women squeezed into the classroom, all local housewives.

"A fifty-one-year-old English conversation teacher is not very popular, you know. They all want some cute young fella. Why is it that the only ones in Japan who want to study English are young women? If I want to teach I've gotta go all the way to a little country town like that. Otherwise I won't have any students."

When Masami filed for divorce, Johnson lost his dignity, his good name, his money, and everything else. He was dismissed from his job as a foreign securities trader. The divorce settlement he had to pay was so exorbitant he might as well have had his skin ripped right off. His relatives, members of some illustrious family from the northeastern part of the United States, turned their back on him and absolutely forbade him ever to see me again. Masami, of course, had aired all our dirty laundry in court, telling the world about Johnson's relationship with me. "Even worse than a traitor, my husband's a criminal. He took advantage of the fifteen-year-old girl who had been placed in his care. Those two sneaked around behind my back and did their business in my very own house. You ask how it is I didn't realize what was happening, since it took place over such a long period of time? I cared for that child! I was so fond of her. I would never in a million years have imagined she could do something like that. I was betrayed not only by my husband but by that girl as well. Can you possibly understand how I feel now?"

Afterward Masami went to great lengths describing exactly how she had discovered what we were up to. She spared no detail in divulging all our little secrets. Masami was so thorough that before long even the judge and the lawyers were blushing in embarrassment.

I was still thinking about the past when Johnson, who had finished dressing, gave me a kiss on the cheek. "See you later, my darling," he said, as he always did. "Bye, honey." Our parting words—ever the same—were half in jest.

I was still going in to work at the time. While I stood in the shower, washing away Johnson's sweat and other bodily fluids, I thought back on the strange fate that had befallen the two of us. No matter how I had wished otherwise, Johnson had not been my first man. The blood that courses through my veins is far more given to lasciviousness than what someone might consider normal. My first man was my father's younger brother, Karl.

· 2 ·

It is quite clear to me now. When I was a girl I was abundantly endowed with that certain something that attracts older men. I had the power to arouse a man's so-called Lolita complex. As fate would have it, though, the older I've become the harder it is to retain this charm. It didn't abandon me all at once. I was still able to turn it on to a certain degree while in my twenties. And because I was born with a beauty far surpassing that of the ordinary woman, I'm still attractive now that I'm thirty-six. But now I work as a hostess at cheap clubs and occasionally I'll work as a prostitute. I suppose, in the true sense of the word, I've grown ugly.

My lascivious blood leaves me no choice but to lust for men. No matter how common I become, how ugly, how old, as long as there is life in my body I will go on wanting men. That's just my fate. Even if men are no longer amazed when they see me, even if they no longer desire me, even if they belittle me, I have to sleep with them. No, I want to sleep with them. It's the retribution for a divinity that no one can sustain forever. I suppose you could say my "power" was little more than sin.

My uncle Karl came to meet us at the Bern airport with his son, Henri. It was early March, and the air was still crisp with frost. Karl wore a black coat and Henri a yellow down jacket. Wispy-soft whiskers had begun to grow around his lips. Karl looked nothing like my skinny golden-haired father. He was dark and solid. If anything, with his upturned almond-shaped eyes and his black hair, he had an Asian look about him. Karl wrapped Father in a hug, happy to see him again, and then he shook my mother's hand.

"Welcome! Welcome home. My wife wants you to come over to our house right away."

Mother nodded slightly, withdrawing her hand from Karl's grasp as soon as she could. Unable to disguise his embarrassment, Karl turned his gaze on me and then backed away. In that instant I knew. Karl was just like Johnson.

When Johnson and I met, I was twelve and he was twenty-seven, so even though I could hear him murmur in his heart, *Hurry and grow up*, there was no answer I could give immediately. But when I met Karl I was already fifteen. I recognized at once the lust that lingered in his gaze, and I decided it was time to answer.

I soon became friends with Henri, who was closer to me in age; he was twenty. He took me to movie theaters, cafés, to the slopes where he skied with his friends. Whenever one of his friends asked, "Who's she?" he answered, "She's my little cousin, hands off!" But going out with Henri grew tiresome. All he wanted to do was show me off.

I noticed something strange. With boys like Henri and classmates who were close to my own age, I was not able to exert the same kind of magical power that I held over grown men. It was practically as though they did not feel my charm. To the boys I was just an ordinary girl, hardly a goddess. Even though they fussed over me, I was not able to arouse in their eyes the same kind of excitement I found in older men. Bored with Henri, I began to devise ways to be alone with Karl.

One afternoon I stopped by Henri's house on the way home from school, pretending to have misunderstood when it was we had agreed to meet. I knew at that hour Henri would still be at the factory. I also knew that my aunt Yvonne would be at the bakery where she worked part-time and that Henri's younger sister would be at school. No one else would be home. My father had told me Karl had to go home shortly after noon to meet with the accountant. Karl was surprised to see me.

"Henri won't be home until after three."

"Really? I must have misunderstood the time he said. What should I do?"

"Want to come in and wait? I could make you a cup of coffee." I couldn't help but notice the way his voice trembled.

"Well, if I'm not interrupting anything . . ."

"Not a problem. We're just finishing up anyway."

Karl ushered me into the living room. The accountant was in the midst of collecting his papers. I sat on the sofa, which was covered in plain cloth upholstery, and Karl brought me a cup of coffee and a plate of cookies my aunt had baked. The only thing my aunt's cookies had going for them was their sweetness. Otherwise, they were awful.

"Have you gotten used to your school?"

"Yes. Thank you for your concern."

"And you seem to have no problem with language."

"Henri's taught me."

Karl always wore jeans at the factory, but today he wore a crisp white shirt with gray trousers and a black leather belt. Businessmen's attire did not suit Karl; he looked stiff and uncomfortable. He sat down across from me, fidgeting, his eyes darting from my legs, stretching out from under my short school uniform skirt, to my face. The tension was growing tedious. I began to believe I was stupid to think that I could get Karl to act. But just when I glanced at my watch, he said, in a voice hoarse with desire, "Oh, if only I were Henri's age!"

"Why?"

"Because you are so charming. I've never met anyone as beautiful as you."

"Because I'm part Japanese?"

"Well, let's just say I was smitten the moment I laid eyes on you."

"I like you, Uncle Karl."

"Too bad it's taboo."

"Why is it taboo?"

Karl blushed just like a schoolboy. I got up and went over and sat on his lap, wrapping my hands around his shoulders, just as I had done so many times with Johnson. His hard thing pressed against my backside. It was just like it was with Johnson. Could something that hard and big really fit inside me? How it would hurt!

"Ahhh." I let slip a small sigh, just imagining what it would be like. That was the signal Karl needed. He plastered his lips over mine in a hungry kiss. With trembling hands he tore impatiently at the buttons on my school blouse, the hooks of my skirt. They fell to the floor around us, along with my shoes and socks.

Once he'd stripped me down to my underwear, Karl lifted me in his arms and carried me into the bedroom. I lost my virginity there on the hard oak bed that Karl shared with his wife. It hurt a lot more than I had expected, but at the same time it brought such complete pleasure that I was convinced I liked it more than I could stand.

"Oh, my God. How could I have raped a child—and my own niece at that?"

Karl pulled away from me so quickly he practically threw me off the bed and covered his head with his hands, muttering as if in pain. What was so horrible, I wondered, in what we'd just done? It had been wonderful. I was disappointed with the way Karl, who was overcome with regret, returned so quickly to reality. But for his part Karl too felt disenchanted. The awe and admiration that I had found in Karl's gaze disappeared after he had finished with me. That was the first time I noticed that the men who embrace me, every single one of them, end up with an expression of emptiness when they are done, as if they have lost something. Maybe that is why I am always in search of a new man. Maybe that is why I am now a prostitute.

After that, I met Karl on the sly any number of times. One time, I can't remember when, he picked me up in his Renault on my way home from school and drove, with me in the backseat, without looking at me once. We went to a cabin owned by a friend of his at the foot of a mountain. It was off season and no one was around. The cabin was dark and the water had been turned off. Careful not to get the carpet dirty, we spread out newspapers and had ourselves a little picnic of wine and salami slices between pieces of bread. Karl undressed me and arranged me in various poses on the white bedspread of the double bed. He took pictures with a single-lens reflex camera. By the time he finally came to join me on the bed, my passion was as chilled as my body.

"Uncle Karl, I'm cold."

"Just put up with it."

Before we started having sex, I knew it was inappropriate behavior for blood relatives. And we were blood relatives. The one person we could absolutely not let find out about our relationship was Karl's older brother, my father. We feared his reaction. Inevitably, after Karl had finished, he would mumble nervously, "If my brother knew about this he'd kill me."

Men live by rules they've made for themselves. And among those rules is the one specifying that women are merely commodities for men to possess. A daughter belongs to her father, a wife to her husband. A woman's own desires present obstacles for men and are best ignored. Besides, desire is always for the man. It's his role to make advances on women and to protect his women from the advances of others. I was a woman who was seduced by a member of her own family. Among the rules in a man's world, this was a big taboo. And for that reason, Karl was terrified.

I didn't want to be anyone's possession. In the first place, my desire was not some paltry affair that could easily be protected by some man. But that day Karl was different. He bad-mouthed my father.

"My brother isn't what he says he is. He's lousy at keeping the accounts. When I pointed this out he got angry. To make it worse, the way he treats his wife is unforgivable. He acts like she's just his housekeeper."

Karl wouldn't understand if I explained that it was Mother who wanted to be a maid. After Mother came to Switzerland, she became self-conscious about being Japanese. Every day she made Japanese dishes out of really expensive foods, and when no one could eat all she'd made she'd stash it away in the freezer. It wasn't long before the freezer was crammed with Tupperware containers filled with boiled *hijiki* or *nikujaga* stew or sliced burdock root. Those containers spoke to me of my mother's gloom and left me with an ominous feeling.

"Uncle Karl, do you hate my father?"

"I despise him. You mustn't tell anyone else, but he has a Turkish mistress. I know all about it, you see. He has a soft spot for black hair and dark eyes."

The woman was an immigrant laborer who'd come over from Germany. Unable to keep their passion for each other a secret, my father and his mistress spent their days exchanging warm glances.

"What do you suppose Mother would do if she found out?"

Karl looked pained by my question. Undoubtedly he was equally concerned with what she'd do if she found out about us. Karl and me; my father and his Turkish mistress. . . . It seemed we had a lot of secrets to hide from Mother. But there was no one here who would tell her. She'd lost all her friends when she came to Switzerland, and she was unable to learn the new language. So she retreated deeper and deeper into her shell, refusing to come out.

"I certainly don't want her to know," Karl said.

"But it's okay for me to know?"

Karl looked at me in surprise. I averted my eyes and gazed up at the dark ceiling of the mountain cabin.

My mother hated me. Giving birth to a child who looked so unlike herself threw my mother into a tailspin from which she never recovered. She was still living in shock. After I reached maturity it became worse, and when it was decided that we would move to Switzerland, my mother became the only Asian person in the family. As a consequence, my mother began to feel closer to my older sister, who was still in Japan and who was more Asian than I was, or so my mother thought. My sister's well-being weighed on my mother. She was constantly saying over and again, "I worry about that child. Do you suppose she thinks I abandoned her?"

My sister did not think anything of the sort. If my mother had abandoned anyone, it was me. I didn't look like anyone in the family. I'd been left to my own devices. The only people who paid me any attention were the men who desired me. As a child I first became aware that my existence had a purpose when I realized men lusted after me. And that's why I will lust forever after men. Before I even began to worry about homework or any of those school things, I began having secret liaisons with men. And it is men who give me the proof I need now to feel I'm alive.

One night I was late coming home. Karl had dropped me off in the back streets, afraid he'd be spotted if he stopped the car in front of our apartment building. I trudged home alone in the darkness. When I got to our apartment, I opened the door and went straight to my room. It was already after ten but the apartment was pitch-black, which I found very strange. When I peered in the kitchen, I saw no evidence of any meal. Not a day had gone by that Mother didn't make some kind of Japanese food. Thinking it odd, I went to her room and peeked in through the door. I could see Mother in the dim light. She looked like she was sleeping, so I quietly pulled the door closed without calling out to her.

Thirty minutes later when my father returned, I was in the bath, scrubbing myself clean from my evening with Karl. There was a fierce knocking on the bathroom door. Karl and I had been found out! That was the first thought that shot through my head. But that wasn't it. Father had come to tell me that Mother looked strange. He was terribly upset. As I ran to the bedroom, I already knew in my heart that Mother was dead.

When we lived in Japan, Mother had never once allied herself with my sister against our father's bad moods. But once we got to Switzerland, she thought only of my sister. I despised my mother's spinelessness. I hated her negligence.

This is what happened once. I invited a number of my classmates over to our apartment to hang out. My mother refused to leave the kitchen.

"I'd like to introduce you," I pleaded, as I pulled her out by the hand. But she shook me off and turned her back on me.

"Just tell them I'm the maid. I don't look like you, and trying to explain will be a hassle."

A hassle. That was Mother's favorite word. Trying to learn German was a hassle. Doing something new was a hassle. My mother remained so unaccustomed to Bern that she easily got turned around whenever she ventured out into the city. It was not long, therefore, until her personality began to undergo some kind of collapse. But I still do not understand what drove her to want to die. By then she was in such a desperate state that even a tiny event would have been enough to push her over the edge. Was it the steamed rice that she didn't prepare well the other day? The high cost of *nattō,* fermented soybeans? Or was it my father's Turkish mistress? Perhaps my affair with Karl? I really didn't care. By then my curiosity about my own mother had already dwindled.

But this much is certain. Both Father and Karl experienced a brief moment of relief with Mother's death. And then they each began to worry that perhaps it was knowledge of their crime that led her to her suicide. They had to live out the rest of their lives in a battle with their own feelings of guilt.

That wasn't the case for me. What her death brought me was a clear understanding of the consequences of adult selfishness. It wasn't my fault that my mother and father had produced such a beautiful child, such a miracle as myself. And yet I was the one who was forced to shoulder the burden. I'd had just about enough of it. I certainly did not want to get saddled with the responsibility for my mother's death. So when my father brought his Turkish mistress into the apartment, I was relieved because it gave me an excuse to demand that I be allowed to return to Japan. I didn't care if I didn't see my elder sister. She hated me anyway. Besides, Johnson had finished his business in Hong Kong and he was waiting for me. Why couldn't I stay with him? I was no longer a virgin, and I wanted to see what sex would be like with Johnson. I wanted it so badly I could hardly stand it.

For a nymphomaniac like myself, I suppose there could be no job more suitable than prostitution; it is my God-given destiny. No matter how violent a man might be, or how ugly, at the moment we're in the act I cannot help but love him. And what's more I'll grant his every wish, no matter how shameful. In fact, the more twisted my partner is, the more attracted I will be to him, because my ability to meet my lover's demands is the one way I can feel alive.

That is my virtue. It is also my biggest flaw. I can't deny a man. I'm like a vagina incarnate—female essence embodied. If I ever were to deny a man, I would stop being me.

I have tried to imagine any number of times what might, in the end, ruin me. Will I collapse of heart failure? Will I suffer an agonizing illness? Will a man kill me? It had to be one of the three. I'm not saying I'm not afraid. But because I can't quit, I suppose I'm the one responsible for destroying myself.

When I finally came to this realization, I decided from then on to keep a journal. It's neither a diary nor a list of appointments but a record just for me. Not one page that I've written here is fiction. I don't even know how to write fiction—it's beyond my creative abilities. I don't know who'll read my record, but I think I'll leave it open on my desk with a note attached that reads *For Johnson.* He's the only one who has a key to my apartment.

Johnson comes to my apartment four or five times a month. He's the only man I will see for free. And he's the only man with whom I've had a long-standing relationship. If someone were to ask me if I loved Johnson, I could easily answer *yes.* Or just as easily *no.* In fact, I myself don't know. What is certain is that Johnson somehow sustains me. It is perhaps a longing for a father figure? Maybe. Johnson is unable to stop loving me, so in a way he is like a father. My own father, of course, did not love me. Or at least his love for me was thwarted.

I remember when I asked my father to let me return to Japan. It was late one night about a week after Mother had died. I could hear the water dripping from the kitchen faucet, drop after drop. I don't know if the faucet started leaking right around the time Mother died or whether it had always leaked and she just made certain to twist the knob tightly whenever she turned it off. But it seemed all of a sudden that the faucet was always dripping. It terrified me—as if Mother were trying to tell us, *I'm still here.* No matter how many times I called, I couldn't get a plumber to come out to fix it. They were all too busy. Each time a drop of water hit the sink, both my father and I would turn and look toward the kitchen.

"Do you want to return to Japan because of me?" My father asked me this without looking me in the eye. It was clear he felt a bit guilty for having brought home his Turkish girlfriend, Ursula—don't ask me why she had a German-sounding name! But on the other hand, he was angry with me for reporting him to the police.

I called the police solely out of anger. My mother was lying there dead in her casket, and my father had to drag his pregnant girlfriend into Mother's home. I questioned his callousness, but I never once doubted his innocence. My father wasn't strong enough to dirty his hands with such a crime. He didn't possess a desire great enough to commit murder. So it came as no surprise that he stood on the sidelines and watched while my mother slowly collapsed. And when he could bear it no longer, he ran away. When the woman to whom he escaped got pregnant, he had no choice but to accept this burden. My father was a coward.

"It's got less to do with you than with me," I told him.

"What's that supposed to mean?" My father looked at me in confusion. His pale-blue eyes were drained of life.

"I don't want to be here."

"Because Ursula is here?" My father lowered his voice. Ursula was sleeping in the guest bedroom. Any kind of tension could bring on a miscarriage, and we were ordered to keep her quiet. Ursula had come by herself from Bremen on a work visa, and my father didn't have the kind of money it would take to hospitalize her for a long period.

"It's not because of Ursula."

Ursula was even more frightened by Mother's death than Father was, and she was suffering for it. She believed it was her fault that Mother committed suicide. She was just seventeen. Whenever I spoke to her, I sensed her childlike honesty and simplicity. I was not angry at Ursula. All I had to do was tell her that she had nothing to do with my mother's death and she was beside herself with joy. My father sighed with relief when he heard my answer. But he still couldn't look me in the eye.

"That's good. I was afraid you'd think my guilt was too great to forgive."

Well, he wasn't the only one with great guilt. Between Karl's infidelity and my mother's death, I grew up quickly.

"It's not a question of forgiveness. It's just that I want to return to Japan."

"Why?"

It wasn't only because I wanted to see Johnson again. I had loved Mother. And now that she was gone, why stay in Switzerland.

"With Mother dead there's really no reason for me to be here."

"I see. So, you've decided to live as a Japanese, then?" my father mumbled, with no attempt to hide his hurt. "You may have a hard time of it with your Western looks."

"Maybe. But I *am* Japanese."

At that point my fate was as good as sealed. I would live as a Japanese in that country thick with humidity. I would be pointed at by children shouting "Gaijin! Gaijin!" And behind my back the girls would whisper "Halves may be pretty now, but they show their age faster than we do." And the high school boys would torment me. I knew all that. And that is why I needed to build a protective wall around myself as thick as the one my sister had made. Since I couldn't construct one myself, I decided I'd use Johnson for that purpose.

"Where will you go? Will you live with your grandpa?"

My sister had already laid claim to our grandfather. And once she'd gotten her hands on something she would never let it go to anyone else. She'd bar the door with both arms before letting me set foot in the world they shared.

"I've asked Johnson to let me stay at his place."

"The American?" My father made an ugly face. "It's not a bad plan, but it'll cost."

"He said I didn't need to pay for room and board. So may I? Please?"

My father did not nod in consent.

"You let my sister stay in Japan!"

My father shrugged in resignation. "She never warmed to me."

That's because the two of them were too much alike. My father and I sat there silently. The leaky faucet broke through the quiet, drip after drip. My father shouted, as if unable to bear the dripping any longer, "All right, then! You can go back."

"And now you can live happily here with Ursula."

I hadn't really intended to end our conversation with those words, but a sad expression swept over my father's face.

The next day I skipped school and called Johnson at his office. I hadn't told him yet that I'd gotten my father's permission. Johnson was delighted to have gotten a call from me.

"Yuriko! How nice to hear from you. When I was transferred back to Tokyo, I thought I'd be able to see you. But we must have just missed each other. I was disappointed to learn that you'd moved to Switzerland. How is everybody?"

"My mother committed suicide and my father is living with his mistress. I really want to go back to Japan, but I have nowhere to stay. I would rather die than live with my sister. I just don't know what to do."

I wasn't trying to play on his sympathy. I was trying to seduce him. A mere girl of fifteen seducing a man of thirty! Johnson caught his breath and then came up with a plan.

"If that's the case, why don't you stay here—with us? It'll be like it was at the cabin. You'll be the little girl seeking refuge from your older sister's bullying. You can stay as long as you like."

Heaving a deep sigh of relief, I asked about Masami. If they had a child now, it would be hard for them to keep me as well.

"But what will Masami say?"

"She'll be thrilled. I promise. Masami is crazy about our cute little Yuriko. But what will you do about school?"

"I haven't decided."

"Well, then, I'll ask Masami to look into it. Yuriko, come live with us!"

Johnson's whispered entreaties were that of a man responding to a seduction. I leaned back on the sofa in relief. Overcome with the strange sensation that someone was watching me, I looked up to see Ursula staring at me. She winked. From the tone of my voice on the telephone, Ursula guessed what I was up to. I nodded and smiled. I'm just like you. From now on, I too will live relying on a man's favor. With a faint smile on her face, Ursula disappeared nimbly into the bedroom. From that day forward the faucet in the kitchen ceased to drip. I suspect Ursula had begun twisting it tightly. When my father wasn't around, Ursula walked with a spring in her step. I could hardly believe she needed to rest.

•

In the afternoon of the day before I was scheduled to leave Switzerland, Karl came sneaking around, knowing that my father would be at the factory. He pressed his lips against mine in a long kiss, right there in my room with my teddy bears and dolls.

"I'm sad I won't be able to see you anymore, Yuriko. Won't you stay? For me?" Karl's eyes were burning—and also calm. There could be little doubt that my departure and my mother's death freed him from any regret or guilt he may have felt.

"I'm sad too. But there's nothing else I can do."

"Can we do it now? One more time?" Karl began to unfasten his belt buckle.

"Ursula's here!" I told him.

"It's okay. We'll do it so she can't hear." Karl swept all the stuffed animals onto the floor and then pressed me down upon the narrow bed. I was unable to move under his weight. And then I heard a knock.

"Yuriko? It's Ursula."

Without waiting for Karl to jump up and straighten out his clothes, I reached out and flung the door open wide. Ursula smiled knowingly. Karl smoothed his tousled hair back with his hands and stood up, busying himself looking out the window as if he'd been standing there all along. Across the street was Karl's hosiery factory.

"What is it, Ursula?"

"Yuriko, if you're not going to take your teddy bears with you, I was wondering if I could have them."

"I don't care. Take whatever you want."

"Thanks!"

Ursula snatched up the koala and the teddy that had been tossed on the floor and looked over suspiciously at Karl.

"What's up, boss?" she asked.

"Oh, just came to say good-bye to Yuriko."

Ursula winked at me, as if to say, Yeah, right. Ursula was my accomplice. As soon as she left, Karl pulled an envelope out of the back pocket of his jeans with an air of resignation. When I opened the envelope, I found the nude pictures of me along with some money.

"Pretty, aren't they? I thought they might serve as a souvenir. And the money's a farewell gift."

"Thanks. Karl, where have you hidden your copies of these pictures?"

"I've got them glued to the back of the desk in the factory." Karl looked so earnest when he said this. And then he added, "I'm going to save my money and come to Japan."

But Karl never came to Japan once. And I hardly ever think of him these days. My first man—he was also my first customer. I still have the photos. I'm staring at the camera, posed like Goya's *Naked Maja* with a face that looks nearly frozen, spread across the sheets with skin so white it's translucent. My forehead is wide, my lips pouty. And in the pupils of my wide-open eyes is something I no longer possess: a fear of men and a longing. I seem to project an uneasiness over the fate that has befallen me. I am no longer afraid, desirous, or uneasy.

•

I sit in front of the mirror putting on my makeup. The face reflected there is that of a woman who has aged at terrific speed ever since passing thirty-five: me. The lines around my eyes and mouth can no longer be concealed, no matter how many layers of foundation I apply. And the round dumpiness of my body looks exactly like that of my father's mother. The older I get, the more I am aware of the Western blood coursing through my body.

In the beginning I was a model; then for a long time I worked at a club that hired only beautiful foreigners. Some would say I was a high-priced call girl. From there I moved to an expensive club, the kind no mere salary man would think to enter. But as I began wearing dresses with deeply plunging necklines, I myself plunged into cheaper and cheaper establishments. Now I have no choice but to work clubs that cater to men who have a fetish for "married women" and the more mature hostess. Moreover, now I have to struggle just to sell myself for cheap. I used to find my worth just knowing a man desired me, but not now; not only has my income shrunk but I realize that I have to search farther and wider for a reason to explain my existence in this world. While peering into my mirror, I stare at my eyes, which have lost their contours, and draw a thick line with my eyeliner pencil. I do this to create my vibrant professional face.

• 4 •

My sister had said she'd call again in the evening. I wanted to get out before she called. I wanted to avoid hearing her depressing voice. What the hell is she doing? I wondered. Drifting from one lousy job to another, searching for the perfect one—as if such a job exists in the first place. Or maybe, just maybe it does—in the form of prostitution! I laugh to myself as I stare into the mirror. If you can do it, be my guest. It's a job in which the finer points are as good as grasping emptiness. I've been a prostitute since I was fifteen years old. I can't live without men, yet men are my greatest enemies. I've been ruined by men. I'm a woman who has destroyed her female self. When my big sister was fifteen years old, she was just an ordinary junior high school student, studying herself silly.

Suddenly I'm struck by an idea. What if she's still a virgin? The younger sister's a whore, the older one a virgin. That's just too much. But now I'm curious. I dial her number.

"Hello? Who is it? Hello? Is that you, Yuriko? Come on, who is it?"

She picked up the minute the phone rang.

"Hello! Hello!" My sister is desperate to find out who is calling; her phone must never ring. Her solitude reverberates through the receiver. I let the telephone drop and convulse with laughter, my sister's voice still echoing at the other end. I can't decide if she's a virgin or a lesbian!

Once I hang up I begin to think about what I'll wear to the club tonight. My apartment consists of a bedroom, combination living-dining room, and a small kitchen. Not much space. The closet and dresser are combined—I hardly have that many dresses anyway. When I worked in Roppongi at the clubs for foreigners, I had a ton of gorgeous dresses. Valentino and Chanel dresses costing close to a million yen apiece. I must have had clothes worth a fortune. I'd slip into one or another of my beautiful dresses and fasten on a diamond as big as a glass bead without even giving it a second thought. Then I'd step into gold sandals that were too extravagant to wear for walking. I would never wear stockings—for the sake of customers who enjoyed kissing my toes. I'd take a taxi from my apartment. After work I'd set off in a customer's car to a hotel and from the hotel I'd return home by taxi. My muscles were only used while in bed with a man.

But as I began to fall from that world, my clothes also became the kind of cheap garments you can buy anywhere around here. I went from silk to polyester; from cashmere to wool blends. And now I have no choice but to cover my well-worn legs in bargain-basement stockings—legs that are dimpled with fat that refuses to melt away, no matter how I try to exercise.

What's changed the most is the quality of my customers. At the first club I worked in, the clients were actors, writers, young self-styled entrepreneurs. Many were at the level of company president or were distinguished foreign VIPs. Then at the next club they were mostly businessmen with no limits on the way they spent their company's accounts. From there I went to salary men with meager monthly paychecks. At present the customers I have are either weirdos who want wacky women or men without money. By wacky I mean grotesque. In this world there are people who prefer beauty after it's gone away or the dregs of a prosperity depleted.

With my monstrous beauty and my monstrous desire, I suppose I'll now become a full-fledged beast. My ghastliness has increased along with my age. I've written it any number of times already, but I do not feel lonely. This is the true figure of the woman who was once a beautiful girl. I daresay my sister must take great delight in my decline. That's why she calls me all the time.

•

I have more to say about Johnson.

When he came to meet me at Narita International Airport he wore a strained expression—and Masami was right beside him, beaming brightly. What a study in contrasts! Johnson was wearing a dark suit, white shirt, and regimental tie, and he was tapping his lower lip nervously with his index finger. I'd never seen him so attired. Masami was wearing a white linen dress—perhaps to show off her tanned skin and a veritable treasure trove of gold accessories that adorned her ears, neck, wrists, and fingers. The jet-black eyeliner at the corner of her eyes was way too dark. It was hard to tell what kind of expression she wore. Was she being serious or playful? That's why I started watching Masami when she put on her makeup because depending on how she applied it, I could tell—better than by anything she said—how she was feeling. That afternoon Masami revealed an exaggerated joy.

"Yuriko! What a long time since we saw you last. My, how big you've grown!"

Johnson and I exchanged glances. Now fifteen, I'd grown almost eight inches since I was in elementary school. I was five feet seven inches tall and weighed 110 pounds. And I was no longer a virgin. Johnson gave me a light hug. His body trembled slightly.

"It's so nice to see you again."

"Thank you so much, Mr. Johnson."

Johnson had told me to call him *Mark*, but I preferred *Johnson*. "Idiot Johnson!": that's what my sister had called him angrily just before she hung up on me. Whenever I thought of that I silently whispered in my heart, "God-sent Johnson." He was my one defense.

"I wonder if your sister's going to come?"

Masami looked around the airport dubiously. She needn't have bothered. I hadn't even told my sister of my arrival time.

"I didn't have time to call her before I left," I explained. "Besides, I heard my grandpa wasn't feeling well."

"Oh, I almost forgot!" Masami hadn't even heard what I'd said. "The admissions examination is this afternoon," she said, squeezing my arm happily. "We have to hurry home. Q Junior High School will accept you under the *kikokushijo* category, the one for students returning from overseas. It's going to be really convenient for you to commute to the school from our place—and I'll get to brag on you for going to a first-rate school like Q. I'm just delighted you got back in time for the exam."

Q School. That was my sister's school. I didn't want to go to a school like that. But Masami—ever the show-off—was determined to get me in. I looked to Johnson for help, but he just shook his head.

"You can put up with that much, at least," he said.

"Put up with it." That was the same thing Uncle Karl had said in the cabin that day when he took those pictures. I bit my lip in resignation. Masami led me by the hand and shoved me into the backseat of her flashy Mercedes-Benz. Next to me on the beige leather, I could feel Johnson's warm thigh pressing against mine. The incident in the cabin. Our secret. My eyes must have danced to have rediscovered the happiness. I waited for the next joy to unfold. Life doesn't happen according to plan. But we are free to dream.

On the way from the airport, Masami stopped the car to let Johnson out so he could go back to work. I was left in Masami's hands. She dragged me off to Q Junior High School in Minato Ward. The main building was made of stone and was very old-looking. The buildings flanking it were more modern; the high school was to the right. Without even thinking, I started looking to see if my sister was there. We hadn't seen each other since we parted in March. It had been more than four months. If I entered Q School, it would surely depress her. I can only imagine how angry she'd be. She'd studied herself silly so she could get into this school, all in order to get away from me. I saw right through her little ruse. When I laughed bitterly, Masami completely misinterpreted my feelings.

"Yuriko-chan, smile! You're so pretty when you smile. If you smile you're sure to pass the interview. Well, it's a paper test, but in name only. I know they'll want to have you around for a long, long time since you're so pretty. It was the same when I took my airlines exam. The competition was awful, but the girls with the best smiles were picked."

I doubted that a flight attendants' exam and the entry exam for this school were quite comparable. But since arguing wasn't worth it, I decided it would be easier to go with a sweet little smile. If I was accepted, what then? It would cost more than my father could pay to send me to this school. But then Johnson had agreed to put up half the tuition. Wasn't I little more than a prostitute then?

There were about ten students taking the exam to enter the school as "returnee students." All were kids who had been overseas because of their father's businesses. I was the only half, and I was the worst of the bunch when it came to the exam. I have no passion for school. What's more, I hardly have the vocabulary for conducting everyday conversations in either English or German.

That night I was so exhausted I ran a fever. Johnson's house was behind the Nishi-Azabu Tax Office. The room that Masami had prepared for me was on the second floor. The curtains, the bedspread, even the pillows were all done in the same Liberty print fabric, clearly Masami's taste. I had no interest in interior design and found the whole business overly fussy, but what did I care? The minute I crawled under the covers, I fell into a deep sleep. I woke in the middle of the night, sensing someone's presence. Johnson was standing by my pillow in a T-shirt and pajama pants.

"Yuriko? How are you feeling?" he asked in a low whisper.

"I'm just really tired."

Johnson bent his tall frame down and whispered in my ear, "Hurry up and get better. I've finally captured you."

Captured. A woman to be consumed by men. Unless I accepted my fate, I could never be happy. Again, the word *freedom* floated up in the back of my mind. I was fifteen years old. And in an instant I had become an old woman.

The next morning, we got the news from Q Junior High that I had been admitted. Masami was beside herself with joy. After she called Johnson at his office to tell him the good news, she turned back to me in great excitement and said, "We need to tell your sister!"

I had to give Masami my grandfather's phone number. I knew I'd have to meet my sister sooner or later. After all, we were now both in Japan. Even so, I knew my sister hated me. And for my part, I hated her. We looked nothing alike. We were like two sides of a coin. My sister reacted just as I knew she would.

"If by some chance you should run into me at school, don't you dare say hello. I'm sure you're very pleased to be getting all this attention. But I'm forced to do everything I can just to survive."

I too was doing everything I could just to survive. But I had no way to explain this to my sister.

"Well, aren't you the lucky one," she said.

"I want to see Grandpa."

"Well, he doesn't want to see you. He hates you. He said you have no inspiration. That you don't have what it takes to go after something with mad intensity."

"What's inspiration?"

"You idiot. Your IQ must not even top fifty!"

And so ended my conversation with my sister. When school started after the summer, she pretended not to know me. After I dropped out in my senior year of high school, all ties with the Q School system were cut. And for years I had no opportunities even to see my sister. Yet recently I've been getting all these phone calls from her. I'm suspicious of what she has up her sleeve.

· 5 ·

When they took me in, Masami was thirty-five and Johnson was five years her junior. Masami's sole purpose in life was to keep an eye on Johnson and ensure that he didn't lose interest in her. Because Johnson cared about me, Masami made it her business to make sure he knew that she was looking after me. It seems she worried his love for her would cool if by any chance she might overlook something in caring for me.

If I did not agree with what Masami did, I couldn't very well complain to Johnson. And even if I had, it was unlikely he would have gotten angry with Masami. Everyone was out for personal gratification. For Masami, without a child of her own, I was a pet. For Johnson I was a toy. That was all there was to my existence. I was born to be used.

I had to wear the clothes Masami bought me as if I loved them with all my heart—even though they were often pink and frilly or emblazoned so boldly with brand-name logos it was embarrassing, even if they were so ridiculous they made people turn around and stare. Masami enjoyed dressing me up in outlandish costumes that turned heads.

But for some reason she never once bought me underwear or socks. She felt she only needed to buy me things that Johnson would see. I had to buy those other things from my own measly allowance. Occasionally, when I got tired of trying to scrimp and save, I responded to the men who approached me in order to get money from them. *Enjo kōsai*, dating for profit. At the time there wasn't a term for it—as there is now.

Masami was very easy to manipulate. If others complimented her by saying, "Oh, what a pretty daughter you have," she would slip on her maternal mask and act deliriously happy. When my teachers informed her that "Yuriko-san is not self-assertive," she would explain—in her best martyr's voice—"She has had a difficult time since her mother committed suicide." When I brought friends home from Q School, she would revert to her years as a flight attendant and treat each and every one of us to first-class service. All I had to do was act submissive and all went well.

Whatever food Masami fixed I would eat, exclaiming all the while that it was delicious. This was true of the donuts, which she dusted so heavily with powdered sugar they looked as if they were covered in snow, and the cooking lessons she took once a week, which resulted in fussy French cuisine. And then there were the lunches she would make every night, in preparation for school the next day; they were ridiculously ostentatious. I've said it any number of times now, but it is really only in my heart that I was able to enjoy a sense of freedom, a freedom no one else could see. I suppose that is why I derived such pleasure—such a secret sense of affirmation—from deceiving Masami while I was with Johnson.

Johnson was superb at playing the part of the love-struck husband. When he was with Masami, he would pull her to him and wrap his arms around her hips. After dinner he would always help clear away the dishes. On weekend nights, he'd leave me at home and take her out for dinner. On those nights he locked their bedroom door when they returned, and they would spend the night together alone. Masami hadn't the slightest idea of what Johnson and I were up to—until it happened.

Johnson always made love to me early in the morning. Because of Masami's low blood pressure, she didn't wake easily. It was Johnson's job to make breakfast. He would slip quietly into my bed beside me as I slept. I enjoyed having my body—still half asleep—fondled by Johnson. First my fingers would awaken, and then the tips of my hair; slowly, slowly, the warmth would rise to my body itself until I would burn so brightly I could hardly stand it, and my body became suffused with heat. No sooner had he finished up than he'd nuzzle my hair and say, "Yuriko, don't ever grow up."

"Is it wrong for me to grow up?"

"That's not it. It's just that I love you best the way you are right now."

But I did grow. By the time I advanced to Q High School, I had grown tall. My bust had filled out and my waist became willowy. I had transformed almost overnight from a little girl into a young woman. I was afraid that Johnson would tire of me, now that I was no longer childlike. But in fact, the reverse was true. He began visiting my bed as soon as night fell. He desired me so badly he could not help himself. Masami—whose diet-induced thin figure looked terrific in the latest fashions—could not satisfy his craving.

My body—now womanly to perfection—seduced young men, to say nothing of the middle-aged. While on my way to school I was approached any number of times by interested men. I refused no one. My sense of autonomy existed deep within my heart. It never ever manifested itself on the exterior.

•

Well, I've gotten ahead of myself again. Summer vacation ended and the new school year began. I entered the junior high division of the Q School system and was placed in the East group of the third-year students. The instructor in charge of my group was Kijima, the biology teacher who had conducted the admissions interviews. I assumed he was also after me; in his perfectly starched white shirt, he stared at me so intently he might have bored a hole right through me.

"I hope you'll adapt quickly to the way we do things here so you will enjoy your time at Q School. If there's anything you don't understand, anything at all, please do not hesitate to ask me."

I gazed up into his eyes as they glittered behind his metal frame glasses. Kijima looked away as if in a panic and asked, with his gaze downcast, "So you have an older sister with us as well?"

I nodded and stated my sister's name. I suspected Kijima would immediately run off to the high school section and look her up. He would be disappointed to discover that my older sister and I looked nothing alike. Or perhaps he'd be suspicious. Perhaps he'd begin to look for faults in me as well. My sister's face was nothing like mine, so people who learned we were sisters were always curious.

As soon as homeroom was over, the boys and girls (the Q system was coed up to high school) clustered around me with unabashed curiosity. I was taken aback by their childlike straightforwardness. They were supposed to be such elite children, yet their inquisitiveness got the better of them.

"Why are you so pretty?" one boy asked with a straight face.

"Your skin's just like that of a porcelain doll!" a girl said, as she brushed my cheek with the palm of her hand. "You're the same color as one of those Meissen porcelains from Germany."

The girl overlapped her hand with mine to compare. Another girl touched my hair. Yet another shrieked out, "Oh, you're so cute!" and tried to hug me. The boys stared and stared, pressing into a tight circle around me until I felt my skin flush with the heat. But no matter how the boys may have fancied me, they were still, after all, just boys.

At that point I decided I would pretend to be an innocent child while attending this school. I realized it would be best not to engage the other students in conversation. Glancing to the side, I let out a big sigh, realizing that no one here would ever really understand me. As I turned my gaze down, I caught the eye of a boy with short hair sitting off to the side. His forehead was wrinkled; it gave him a weathered look of experience. He seemed to be criticizing me with his eyes. He was head instructor Kijima's son.

Young Kijima was the first male who did not feel desire for me. I sensed this immediately. He was also the second person to hate me, the first of course being my sister. Both my sister and Kijima were able to make me feel that in their presence there was no purpose to my existence. Because my sole reason for living was the fact that others desired me, I began slowly to peel Kijima's gaze off my skin. Your father wants me, I thought. I had always lacked the strength and free will to confront another this way, but now I channeled my emotions until they had a target for the first time: young Kijima.

Lunch hour arrived. A group of students went off together somewhere for lunch and took their time coming back. I sat alone and ate the lunch Masami had packed for me. But no matter how much of it I ate, the lunch just didn't seem to ever end. I looked around the classroom for a trash can.

I heard a voice above me. "My, my, what an elegant lunch! Were you expecting company?" A girl with tiny curls dyed a reddish brown was peering into my lunch box. She tried to pick up a portion of shrimp and olive mousse lodged in one corner, but the mousse slid through her fingers, landed on the desk, and lay glittering in the light of the mid-September sun, looking rather pathetic. She scooped up the olive.

"Kind of salty!"

"Have it all if you like."

"No. It's not very good."

The girl said her name was Mokumi, an unusual name, but that everyone called her Mokku. Her father was the president of a famous soy sauce corporation, and she was more brazen and entitled than any of the other students.

"So, is your father white or something?"

"Yes, he is."

"Well, if a half is going to turn out as gorgeous as you, I'll just have to go and have one of my own," Mokku said, in all seriousness. "But your older sister isn't pretty at all, is she? Everyone in class just went over to the high school to get a look at her. Is she really your sister?"

"Yes, she is."

Mokku snapped the lid of my lunch box shut without bothering to ask me if I minded.

"Well, it's unbelievable. When we went to get a look at her, she made an ugly face. She's a real dog, and creepy to boot. We were disappointed. She doesn't look like you at all. I'll bet she disappoints you too."

It wasn't unusual for me to encounter scenarios like this. When people first met me, they'd come up with all kinds of fantasies on my behalf. They'd imagine that I lived some kind of Barbie-doll life in a dream house with a handsome daddy, a pretty mama, and a good-looking older brother and gorgeous older sister protecting me. But then, when they actually saw my older sister—who looked nothing like the image they'd conjured up—their little fantasy about me disintegrated. They'd start to despise me—so I became everyone's little plaything.

I looked around the classroom. The students who had been so excited about my appearance that morning had returned and were sitting at their desks. Everyone struggled to avoid looking in my direction. My very existence was a riddle now. I had become a suspicious creature.

Just then something landed on my desk and rolled across it. It was a small wad of paper. I picked it up and stuffed it in my uniform pocket. I wonder who'd thrown it. The girl sitting across from me had her English textbook open and was poring over it studiously. But young Kijima, who was sitting in front of her, turned to look back at me. So it was Kijima. I took the wad of paper out of my pocket and threw it back at him. I didn't need to read it to know what it said. He'd seen my sister. He figured out that we were one and the same.

After class, Mokku came over to me and grabbed my arm.

"Come with me. I promised the seniors I'd show you to them."

She led me out into the corridor where a senior girl with a golden-brown tan and a ponytail was standing. Her eyes were narrow, her mouth large, and her garish face exuded self-confidence.

"You're Yuriko, right? I'm Nakanishi, the president of the cheerleader squad. I want you to join our club."

"I have no experience."

I'd never once even thought about joining a club and had little interest in the prospect. In the first place, I didn't have any money. More than that, I really didn't enjoy doing things in groups.

"It won't take long to learn. Besides, you'll be the main attraction. The students in the high school and university will be thrilled."

"I don't have any confidence."

Nakanishi ignored me and lifted my uniform skirt to get a look at my legs.

"Your legs are long and pretty. You really are a perfect beauty. We have to show you off!"

Johnson's words reverberated through my head. Yuriko is perfect. Perfect even down there.

Mokku spoke insistently from behind Nakanishi. "The president of the cheerleaders has personally scouted you out and invited you to join. You can't say no." My slowness to react irritated her and she pursed her lips. The pink lip gloss on her thick lips glistened. When I still refused to answer, Mokku snickered and said, "Maybe Yuriko's retarded or something."

Nakanishi gave Mokku a shove. "Mokku, you're going too far!"

"But she's so pretty—it wouldn't be fair if she was smart too!"

"Give her time." Nakanishi stepped in quickly in an effort to quiet Mokku. "It's all so sudden she's probably confused. We've got a lot of games coming up in October and we're going to be really busy anyway."

The president of the cheerleaders walked off with Mokku. When the other students noticed Nakanishi in the corridor, they called out to her in high squeaky voices, respectful and clearly doing their best to suck up and score points with her. I hated games like this. I thought about asking

Johnson to get a doctor to write me an excuse that would keep me off the squad. But then I thought about how much Johnson would enjoy seeing me in my little uniform.

Just then I felt a dark black cloud gliding over me. It was Kijima.

"Why'd you throw my letter back without reading it?"

• 6 •

Kijima's face was delicately chiseled for a boy and beautiful. His eyes were as sharp as a finely honed blade; the bridge of his nose thin. His attractiveness left one feeling both lack and excess. And, to be sure, with Kijima some things were missing, while others were overly abundant. Perhaps it was a combination of pride and self-consciousness. At any rate, this unbalance made Kijima look at once both pathetic and insolent.

"What! Can't answer?"

Kijima bit his lip in anger. Earlier, when I'd been surrounded by the other students in the class, I'd nodded to each question with a vague smile or answered with a word or two, passive and meek. It was only to Kijima that I stubbornly refused a response. I suppose this irritated him.

"I don't reply to strangers who address me so impertinently."

When Kijima realized I was rebuffing him, a contemptuous smile crossed his lips.

"So how would you like to be addressed, Your Royal Highness? Why should I respect someone as obtuse as you? My father brought home some files the other day and I saw your test scores. You've got to be the dumbest person ever admitted to the Q School system. The only reason they admitted someone as stupid as you is because of your looks. Did you know that?"

"Who let me in?"

"The school did."

"No. The school did not let me in. Your father did. Professor Kijima."

My words hit home. Kijima's slender frame trembled and he stepped back.

"Your father has his eye on me, you know. Ask him when you go home, why don't you? How tough it must be for you to have your own father as your head instructor."

Kijima stuffed his hands in his pockets and glowered at the floor. He shifted from foot to foot nervously. Having an elder sister who looks nothing like me may damage my image, but for Kijima it was worse. His own father would be discredited as the head instructor and would become the source of gossip. Kijima would lose his standing in the classroom. Both he and I faced the same dilemma. Kijima thought it over momentarily and then looked up. Having at last come up with an appropriate riposte, his face was flushed with victory.

"We've got specimens of butterflies and other insects all over the house, on account of my father being a biologist. It's not surprising he'd want to add you to his collection. You're a strange species."

"I suppose your father refuses to add you to his collection. You're hardly worthy of attention."

I'd hit Kijima's sore spot. His beautiful face turned crimson and then blanched white with anger.

"That's what everyone thinks. They think I'm a lousy student."

"I'm sure they do. That's the way rumors work."

"So are you a gossip?"

"And you aren't? You're the one who ran off to look at my sister and came back with the others to make fun of me."

Kijima looked like his words had gotten stuck in his throat. I wasn't by nature the kind of person who struck first—not like my sister. But for some reason I had felt compelled to go after Kijima. Why? It was simple. He hated me, just as much as my sister did. And so I hated him too. This was a first for me. With Kijima there was no desire. And on that score alone, Kijima was the only man I'd ever met who was different. Perhaps he was a homosexual. The suspicion would occur to me much later.

"So why'd you throw the letter back to me without reading it? Did you think I'd written you a love letter? Do you think all men are in love with you?"

"Hardly." I shrugged my shoulders the way I'd seen Johnson do. "Besides, I knew you'd written about my test scores."

"How'd you figure that out?"

I tilted my head to the side. "Because I hate you," I hissed.

It was going to be fun to attend this school and watch what would transpire. I left Kijima where he was—standing glued to the spot—and headed down the hall at a brisk clip. As I proceeded swiftly along the corridor, curious faces rose up and then receded into the background. Each classroom door I passed was clustered with the faces of gawking students.

"I hate you too."

Kijima was racing after me. I could hear him panting like some demon. I refused to respond, annoyed.

"I just have one more question for you. What is it you want? Here, I mean. Are you here because you want to study? Is it so you can play around in the clubs? Both?"

I stopped dead in my tracks and turned to look at Kijima straight on.

"Well, let's see. . . . I guess it's sex."

Kijima stared at me in disbelief.

"So, you like it?"

"I love it."

Kijima ran his eyes appraisingly over my face and body. He looked like he'd just come upon a rare species of animal.

"If that's the case, you'll need a partner. I can help you."

What? The gaze I turned back to Kijima said as much. I caught a glimpse of a T-shirt just beneath the collar of his white shirt. His gray uniform trousers were neatly pressed. Nothing was amiss, and yet he gave the impression of being somehow disheveled.

"I'll be your manager. No, your agent."

That's not a bad idea, I thought. Kijima's beautiful eyes flashed with light.

"You've already been approached by the cheerleading squad. You'll get invitations from other clubs as well. You're so noticeable, you'll want to be a star. I bet you don't know which club would be best for you. But I can ask around. I can find out what kind of acquaintances you can make in each club." Kijima looked back at the group of students who had gathered in a corner of the corridor to watch us converse. "Just look at them. There's one each from the ice-skating club, the dance club, the yachting club, the golf club. They all want to have an exotic creature like you to join so they can show you off—and not just to the boys in the high school and college clubs but also to those in other schools. They want everyone to know that Q School is famous for its beauty. They've already got the brains and the money. All they lack is the beauty."

I interrupted Kijima's little speech. "So which club should I join?"

"Well, if it's sex you want, you need a club that's good for sex. And since cheerleading is the flashiest, I would think it'd be the best. And look—Nakanishi already came personally to recruit you, so you can't afford to snub her."

I put up no resistance; becoming a toy was my destiny anyway. Nevertheless, I was curious as to why Kijima would be so interested in helping me. "Earlier you said you'd help me. What's in it for you?"

"If I were your manager, I'd earn respect." He grinned wickedly. "In less than half a year I'll be moving to the men's section of the school. The competition gets even worse there. We'll have to contend with students coming in from the outside. And it won't be just grades that matter. Every little thing will be a contest. But I'll be sure to come out on top. Know why? Because I'll have you. You'll be my weapon. All the boys in the high school will want to be with you. The students here—male and female—all think the world is theirs for the taking, just because they have money. I'll coordinate the transactions. How does that sound?"

Actually, it didn't sound bad at all. I nodded.

"Okay. And what's your take?"

"I get forty percent. Too high?"

"I don't care. There's just one condition. You mustn't ever call me at home."

Kijima looked down at my brand-new uniform shoes.

"You live with an American, don't you? I take it he's not a relative."

I shook my head no. Kijima dug a date book out of his pocket.

"A lover?"

"Sort of."

"You don't look a bit like your sister and you don't live with her. You are a complicated one."

Kijima wrote something in his date book and then tore the page out and handed it to me. "Let's always use this as our contact base. It's a café in Shibuya. Be sure to stop by after school."

And so, just like that, Kijima became my first pimp. Even after he moved on to the boys' high school and I to the girls' he continued to introduce me to other high school and university students. He had dis-

criminating tastes. Once he arranged for me to join the rugby team at
their overnight training camp—acting on special request for the club
president and vice president. Another time he set me up with the
teacher who supervised the yachting club. And I didn't just sleep with
students in the Q School system: I was also available to students, alumni,
and even teachers at other schools. Whoever it was, wherever, every man
I came across wanted to sleep with the beautiful young star cheerleader.
For his part, Kijima set it all up beautifully, so there were no complica-
tions afterward. I continued working with Kijima until I went out on
my own.

·

The day Kijima and I clinched our deal we bought Cokes at the school
store and sat on a bench by the pool, where we toasted our alliance. The
newly established synchronized swimming team was practicing in the
pool, under the direction of a coach who'd been brought in from outside
the Q School system. Kijima took one look at the transparent nose clips
the team members wore and burst out laughing.

"The coach is an Olympian. She charges fifty thousand yen for one
lesson, and she teaches three times a week. Unbelievable. But that's not
all. The coach of the golf club is a first-class pro who played in the British
Open. I guess they figure if they can hook up with the Q School system
now, they can get their kids in later."

"What about your father? Has he similarly benefited?"

"Yes." Kijima avoided my gaze. "He made an agreement off the books
to tutor a girl in the high school. Her family sent their driver to pick him
up for each lesson. He was paid fifty thousand yen for just two hours. We
used the money to take a vacation to Hawaii. All the students know
about it."

I remembered Kijima had said the students here believed they could
have anything for a price. Surely I'd be able to make a killing here as a
young prostitute. I looked up at the September skies of Tokyo, where the
summer heat still lingered. They were a smoggy gray and seemed to be
wrapped in the warmth emitted by the metropolis.

Kijima finished his Coke and looked over the high school playing
fields. Girls in navy-blue shorts streamed across the grounds. Kijima
tapped my shoulder. "I'll show you something funny. Come with me."

"What is it?"

"Your older sister's gym class."

"I'm not going to go. I don't want to talk to my sister."

"Come on. Just take a look. It'll be fun. There are a lot of famous people in your sister's class."

A bizarre form of rhythmic exercise class had just gotten under way. A judge of some kind was standing in the middle of the field and students were moving around her in a circle, as if it were a kind of summer festival dance. The teacher raised a tambourine and started to shake it fiercely. As soon as she started, the girls dancing in the circle around her began undulating in weird movements.

"Legs on the third beat, hands on the fourth!"

They stepped to the beat of the tambourine and moved their arms in unison. I wouldn't call what they were doing exercises, but it wasn't dance either. They looked ridiculous. I suppose you could say it looked like a folk dance with extra steps added.

"That's rhythmic exercise. It's been the pride and joy of Q High School for Young Women for generations, so you'd better get used to it. You'll be doing it before long too. Anyone who's ambitious learns to do it."

"Ambitious? For what?"

"Ambitious for good grades. You need good grades to get into the university—and students enter this high school so they can go on to Q University. But you have to be able to do more than just study. Unless you're the best in this rhythmic exercise routine, your overall grade point average will suffer."

Kijima's reply was laced with sighs, as if even having to explain as much to me was an excessive burden. He jiggled his legs nervously.

"So they're ambitious for something as stupid as that?"

"Well, most people in this world don't have the luxury of being as beautiful as you. They have to rely on something else."

It was all a battle of endurance. If you could last, you could get what you wanted. But I couldn't tolerate such long ordeals. If it were me I'd quit in no time. I didn't believe in endurance.

I wondered if my sister had an ambitious streak. I stared hard at the circle of dancers. My sister went around any number of times, but she couldn't keep up with the steps, and before long she quit. The students who couldn't keep up had to leave the circle and watch from the sidelines.

My sister folded her arms across her chest with apparent disinterest. She watched the students who were concentrating all they had on getting the steps right. She'd messed up on purpose. I saw through my sister's strategy.

"Now feet on the seventh beat and hands on the twelfth."

The movements grew even more complicated. One after another the students misstepped and had to leave the ring. They sat alongside my sister, watching the ones who remained. Before long there were more watching than dancing.

"Check it out, those two are in a dead heat!" Kijima mumbled to himself, barely able to hide his disgust.

Two girls were left. They danced around the teacher, reacting to her increasingly complicated instructions like acrobats. All the students' eyes were on them. In the distance, even the students in the junior high section had turned to watch. Kijima and I crept closer to the dancers' circle, careful not to attract my sister's notice.

"Feet on the eighth beat; hands on the seventeenth."

One of the students was of slight build with a nicely symmetrical figure. She looked very agile. She danced with amazing precision, as if not even thinking of what she was doing. It seemed she had even greater agility in reserve.

"That's Mitsuru. She's best in the school. She always wins. Everyone knows she's aiming for medical school."

"And the other girl?"

I pointed to a skinny girl who was moving jerkily like a puppet on a string. Her hair was thick and heavy, and the expression on her face and the way she moved her body made it look like she had reached the limits of her ability. She seemed to be in pain.

"That's Kazue Satō. She's an outsider student. She wanted to join the cheerleading squad but was shot down. She made a real stink about it too."

The skinny girl looked over at us as if she had heard what Kijima said. When she saw me she froze. Applause welled up from the onlookers. Mitsuru had won.

I suspect there are lots of women who want to become prostitutes. Some see themselves as valued commodities and figure they ought to sell while the price is high. Others feel that sex has no intrinsic meaning in and of itself except for allowing individuals to feel the reality of their own bodies. A few women despise their existence and the insignificance of their meager lives and want to affirm themselves by controlling sex much as a man would. Then there are those who engage in violent, self-destructive behavior. And finally we have those who want to offer comfort. I suppose there are any number of women who find the meaning of their existence in similar ways. But I was different. I craved being desired by a man. I loved sex. I loved sex so much I wanted to screw as many men as I could. All I wanted were one-night stands. I had no interest in lasting relationships.

I wonder why Kazue Satō became a prostitute. How strange that I met her last night for the first time in twenty years. And on a hotel-lined street in Maruyama-chō at that.

I admit that when money got tight, I took to the streets on my own. I'd stand on the corner and call out to anyone passing by. But the streets along Shin–Okubo with their bars and clubs had been claimed for whores shipped in from Central America and Southeast Asia. The competition there was fierce. The area was cordoned off by an invisible line and if you happened accidentally to cross into their territory you were in for a beating. Police enforced the law in the Shinjuku area, and it wasn't easy to get away with walking the streets there. Times were tough. I was on my own with no one to watch my back. And that's how I ended up at Shibuya that night—in an area I had rarely trolled.

I selected a street in front of a row of hotels near Shinsen Station and stood in the gloomy shadows on the corner in front of a statue of Jizō waiting for a man to come by. It was a cold night and a sharp wind was blowing from the north. I clutched at the collar of the red leather coat that I had pulled on over my silver ultra-minidress. I wore a thin slip under my dress and that was it. An outfit like this would allow me to get down to business without a lot of fuss, but it offered no protection from the cold. I took a drag of my cigarette and shivered, waiting.

I had my sights set on a group of drunks on their way home from an end-of-year party when a skinny woman stumbled down the narrow road sandwiched between cheap hotels. She looked like she was being blown along by the wind. Her black hair hung down her back nearly to her waist and swung from side to side with each step she took. She'd cinched the belt tightly around her flimsy white trench coat. Her legs, swathed in cheap flesh-colored nylons, were so skinny they looked as if they might snap in two. What was most remarkable about the woman was her appallingly impoverished body. She was so thin as to be nearly one-dimensional, a skeleton covered in skin. Her makeup was applied so thickly I at first thought she was on her way home from a costume party, and then I wondered if perhaps she was crazy. Under the glare of the neon light I could see the heavy black of her eyeliner and her bright blue eye shadow. Her lips glittered a deep crimson. The woman raised her hand and waved to me.

"Who gave you permission to stand there?"

I was startled by her words.

"Is it off limits?" I threw my cigarette down and crushed it with the toe of my white boot.

"I didn't say it was off limits."

The woman wore a strange expression. She spoke with such force that I worried she was with a yakuza gang. I looked around me to be sure. I saw no one else. The woman was staring at me.

"Yuriko." Her voice was so low and muffled it sounded like a curse. But there was no mistaking what she'd said.

"Who are you?" I asked.

She looked familiar, but I couldn't place her. Her features were distinct but nevertheless somewhat graceless. She looked like someone I knew but I couldn't remember who, and it was driving me crazy. I stared at her carefully. Of all her features, her long thin horselike face was most prominent. Her skin was dry. Her teeth protruded. Her hands were like little bird claws. She was an ugly woman, a middle-aged woman not unlike myself.

"Don't you remember?"

She laughed gaily. When she laughed the smell of stewed foods wafted up around her, a nostalgic smell. It lingered briefly in the cold winter air and then was snatched away by the northern wind.

"Might we have met at a club somewhere?"

"Guess again. My, you've grown old. Look at the lines on your face! And all that flab! I hardly recognized you at first."

I tried to remember the face I found behind the layers of makeup.

"When we were young we were like night and day, you and me. But just look at us now: we're not that different. I suppose you could say we're the same—or we might even put you a peg or two lower. What I'd give to show you to your friends now!"

The gloating words that spewed from her red mouth were tinged with bitterness. The black eyes beneath the layers of smeared eyeliner darted brightly. They resembled eyes that had glanced over at me one time long ago. Eyes that revealed—even as they tried to conceal—that their owner was at the end of her rope. I could tell that meeting me made the woman nervous by the way she sucked in her breath and chattered away. I realized that the disgusting-looking woman standing in front of me now was the student who had tried her hardest to keep up with the rhythm contest. Despite the years that had passed since then, I could still recall her name: Kazue Satō. She was in my older sister's class. A strange girl who had had some interaction with my sister. Kazue had had a bizarre interest in me, following me around like some kind of stalker.

"You're Kazue Satō, aren't you?"

Kazue gave my back a sharp push. "You got it! I'm Kazue. It took you long enough. Now get out of here! This is my turf, you know. You can't be picking up men here."

Her words were so unexpected they made me laugh bitterly. I repeated her own words. "Your turf?"

"I'm a hooker."

Her words pulsed with pride. I was so taken aback to learn that Kazue was a streetwalker that I didn't know what to say. Naturally, I thought I was special. Ever since I had reached the age of self-awareness I was convinced that I was different from other people. And I have to say the realization left me feeling somewhat superior.

"Why you of all people?"

"Well, why you?" Kazue shot back without hesitation.

I stared at her long hair, unable to answer. I could tell at a glance it was a cheap wig. Men don't go for women who try to turn tricks in wild getups. There was no way Kazue was going to get a good customer that way. But then, there weren't many good customers heading my way either. Even though they said nothing, I could tell by their expressions that they weren't interested in me. Quite a contrast from when I was young. Now we lived in a world where young amateurs played at being prostitutes. A professional like me or Kazue was practically worthless. Kazue was right: I was nothing like I was twenty years ago, and she and I weren't much different.

"But you know, Yuriko, I'm not like you. I work during the day. I bet all you do is sleep." Kazue pulled something out of her pocket and showed it to me. It was an ID card for some company. "During the day I earn an honest living," she said, somewhat sheepishly. "I'm a businesswoman in a first-rate firm. I do a difficult job that you could never even dream of doing."

Then why are you involved in prostitution? I caught myself just before the words left my mouth. I didn't want to know. She'd just add one more reason to the list of reasons women go into prostitution. And I didn't care.

"Do you come here every night?"

"I work the hotels over the weekends. I'd like to come every day but I can't."

Kazue spoke like a pro. At the edges of her words lurked a kind of happiness.

"Do you think you could let me use this spot on the nights you're not here?"

I wanted my own turf. I'd been a prostitute since I was fifteen, but I didn't have my own territory or a pimp to help me out.

"You want me to let you use my corner?"

"Do you mind?"

"Well, under one condition."

Kazue grabbed my arm roughly. Her fingers were so bony it was like being gripped by chopsticks. My arms prickled with goose bumps.

"I don't mind if you use the corner when I'm not here, but you have to dress like me, see?"

I saw her point. If the same woman worked the same corner, she'd build up a base of regulars. But would I really be able to look so hideous?

I found the prospect so unnerving that I began to tremble. But Kazue couldn't have cared less. She had set her sights on a pair of salary men on their way home.

"Hey, fellas, want to go somewhere for a cup of tea?"

The men looked at Kazue and then at me and hurried away as quickly as they could. Kazue dashed after them. The faster they went, the faster she ran.

"What's the rush?" she called after them, in a coarse voice. "There're two of us, one for each of you. We'll give it to you cheap and then you can trade partners. Look, she's half. And I'm a graduate of Q University."

"What a crock of shit," one of the men jeered.

"It's true. I'm not kidding," Kazue said, pulling out her ID card to show the man. He refused to look at it and knocked Kazue roughly out of the way as he pushed past her. Even as Kazue fought to keep her footing she chased after the man.

"Wait! Wait, why don't you?" Giving up, Kazue finally turned back to look at me and laughed. I didn't have experience chasing down johns. It looked like I would have a lot to learn from Kazue.

On my way home I stopped at a twenty-four-hour supermarket in Kabuki-chō and bought a jet-black wig with hair that fell as far as my waist, just like Kazue's.

•

I'm now standing in front of my mirror wearing the black wig. I've painted bright blue eye shadow over my eyelids and red lipstick on my lips. I wonder if I look like Kazue. I'd just as soon not look like her. Kazue had decked herself out to look like a prostitute so she could go stand on the corner in front of that statue of Jizō, benevolent protector of the damned, guardian of lost children. I've dressed myself in the same costume and will stand in the same place.

The phone rings. A customer, perhaps? I answer hopefully. It's Johnson. He's supposed to come see me the day after tomorrow but he has called to beg off. His mother in Boston has died, he says.

"Are you going to go to the funeral?"

"You know I can't. I don't have the money. Besides, I've been disowned, remember? I'll just go into mourning here."

Johnson says he'll go into mourning, but he doesn't do anything spe-cial. He said the same thing when his father died.

"Do you want me to go into mourning with you?"

"You don't need to. It has nothing to do with you."

"True, it's none of my business."

"That was cold, Yuriko."

Johnson's laugh was tinged with sorrow. Related. After he hung up I thought about my relations with others. Earlier I wrote that I imagine I became a prostitute because I didn't want to have long-lasting relation-ships with other people. Other than my father and my sister—to whom I'm related by blood—Johnson is the only person with whom I've had a lasting relationship. But this doesn't mean I love him. I've never loved anyone, not once. That's why I'm able to get along just fine without an intimate relationship with another person. Johnson's the only exception, and that's because I had a child with him fourteen years ago. No one else knows: not my father, not my sister, not even the child.

Johnson is raising the child himself: a boy. He's now a second-year student in junior high. Johnson told me his name but I forgot it. The rea-son Johnson stays in touch with me and comes to see me four or five times a month is because of the child. Johnson has faith that I secretly cherish a love for this child. I find his faith annoying, but I won't affirm or deny it.

"Yuriko, the boy seems to have a lot of musical talent. That's what they say at his school. Doesn't that make you happy?"

"The boy has really grown. He's already over six feet tall. He's such a handsome fellow, why won't you at least meet him?"

I have no use for a child who shares my blood. And Johnson's appeals to a mother's love only make me wince. Still, because I've been a prosti-tute for all these years and have only gotten pregnant once, it makes me think that my child with Johnson must have a very strong tie to this world.

•

I withdrew from Q High School for Young Women before I turned eigh-teen. I had just entered my senior year. It was because Masami found out about Johnson and me.

Around that time Johnson would sneak into my bed every night, knowing full well how dangerous it was. He didn't come just to have sex with me. He wanted to hear about the men Kijima had introduced me to.

"After the kid on the baseball team screwed you, what did he say?"

"He said that if I slept with him again he'd hit a home run."

"What a jerk!" Johnson laughed as he gazed appreciatively at my naked body. He enjoyed any sort of affirmation that I, his possession, was perfect. If Johnson had only just listened to my stories and then gone back to his own bed—but no, he'd get excited by the details I shared with him and would have to have me all over again. Just as Masami couldn't go to sleep without her nightcap—into which Johnson had secretly taken to putting sleeping pills—Johnson's day wouldn't end until he'd heard my stories.

That particular night he must have had a difficult day at the office. His face was drawn with weariness and he had me tell him stories again and again. He lay on the bed beside me, drinking bourbon straight out of the bottle. That was the first time I'd ever seen him so disheveled.

"Tell me more!"

I'd run out of my usual fare, so I started to talk about Kijima's father.

"If someone has an interest in me, he'll always let me know. But there's one person who won't approach me specifically *because* he's interested, and that's Kijima's father, Professor Kijima. The biology teacher."

"What kind of teacher is he?"

Usually when I stared at Johnson, his eyes looked like those of some kind of bird of prey—a vulture or a hawk. But tonight they were murky and dull.

· 8 ·

Johnson had absolutely no interest in my academic life. Not in my grades, my experience on the cheerleaders' squad, or even my first encounters with Mokku. But from time to time when he'd come to my room he'd make me put on my cheerleader outfit. He'd run his fingers over the gold and blue pleats of my miniskirt and smile bitterly. *Your school's just imitating American cheerleaders. What a bunch of copycats.* Johnson couldn't stand Japanese girls. Maybe he hated me too, and Japan as well.

Mine was a strange existence. Not Johnson's daughter and hardly his wife. To put it bluntly, I was nothing more than the daughter of an acquaintance who was there for his sexual pleasure, so of course he didn't feel the need to play a parental role. Sure, Johnson was immoral. It was clear that he expected me to provide him sexual services in return for the portion of the exorbitant tuition fees that he paid.

"Tell me about Professor Kijima," he said.

I was exhausted and wanted to sleep. But Johnson was drunk, his eyes awash with lust. I suppose he suspected my story about Professor Kijima would reveal a new source of sexual excitement, and it was to my benefit if I could entertain Johnson night after night with fascinating stories— just like the beautiful maiden Scheherazade in the thousand and one tales of the *Arabian Nights' Entertainments*. But I had no idea what about my stories would excite Johnson, so all I could do was just tell them as they happened. I rolled over on my back and began my story, slowly, haltingly.

"He is the professor who approved my admission to the Q School system. On the day of the interview, when I entered the classroom, there was a huge brown turtle that they were raising in an aquarium. I'd just flown in from Switzerland and was about to die of exhaustion. On top of that, my marks on the entrance exam had been really bad. I knew I wasn't going to get in so I was totally depressed. And then I saw the turtle. There was this snail crawling slowly along the glass of the aquarium, and the turtle just stuck out its neck and snapped the snail up, right in front of my eyes. Professor Kijima asked me what kind of turtle it was. I told him it was a tortoise, which apparently was the right answer. Since Professor Kijima is the biology teacher, that was enough to satisfy him and he decided to pass me."

Johnson erupted in laughter, letting the bourbon dribble out the side of his mouth.

"Ha! It wouldn't have made a bit of difference if you'd called it a tortoise or a terrapin. 'What's this square thing?' Kijima could have asked. 'Oh, it's a desk,' you'd have said, and he'd have passed you!"

Johnson was convinced that I was crazy about sex and too stupid to do schoolwork. Just like Kijima's son. Just like my sister. I normally never got angry when people made fun of me, but for some reason I suddenly felt like challenging Johnson. He'd spilled bourbon on the sheets and now they were stained with the brown liquid. Masami was going to have a fit, and it wouldn't be Johnson who'd get in trouble but me.

"I named the tortoise Mark, after you," I told him.

Johnson shrugged his shoulders exaggeratedly. "I'd rather be the snail. Let's name the tortoise Yuriko, after a woman who lives off of eating men. I bet Kijima what's-his-name would like to crawl into the aquarium and get snapped up by Yuriko. So why do you think Kijima has never tried to make it with you? Do you suppose he thinks you would sell yourself to a teacher?"

"No, it's because my manager is Professor Kijima's son."

Johnson rolled over on the bed in great gales of laughter, clapping his hand over his mouth to stifle the sound. "So that's why? Wow, this is just like some crazy soap opera!"

It wasn't that funny. After I'd advanced a grade, to Q High School for Women, I'd occasionally run into Professor Kijima. Whenever he saw me he'd greet me stiffly with a perplexed expression on his face. Just beneath his overly serious expression, I sensed a warm fear.

It happened at the end of my second year of high school. When Professor Kijima caught sight of me, he waved me over toward him with insistent gestures. He was wearing his usual starched white shirt. The long fingers that clutched his textbooks were coated white with chalk dust.

"I've heard something I'd like you to clear up. It's my hope that you'll be able to tell me it's not true."

"Why?"

"Because it concerns your honor." Professor Kijima spoke bitterly. "I've heard rumors that you've been involved in very inappropriate behavior, that you've completely shamed yourself. I can't believe what I've heard."

"What rumors?"

Professor Kijima looked down to his side and bit his lip. The disgusted expression did not suit such a good-natured man. In the blink of an eye he'd turned into an entirely different man, a sexual man. I found him very appealing.

"They say you're taking money to sleep with other students. If it's true you'll be expelled. Before the school launches its own investigation, I wanted to ask you myself. It's not true, is it?"

I was puzzled. If I said it was a lie I'd probably escape expulsion. But I'd already had enough of the cheerleaders' squad and the all-girl classes. Expulsion didn't sound so bad.

"It's true. I've just been following my own path, doing what I enjoy doing. It's my little moneymaker. Can't you just leave it be?"

Kijima started to tremble and his face reddened.

"Leave it be? But you're defiling the very core of your existence—your soul! You can't do that sort of thing!"

"My soul can't be damaged by something like prostitution!"

When he heard the word *prostitution* Kijima grew so angry that his voice shook.

"Maybe you don't notice it, but you're defiled. Your soul is defiled."

"Well, Professor, what about your decision to moonlight as a tutor making fifty thousand yen for a two-hour session and using the money to take your family on vacation to Hawaii? Is that not disgraceful? Have you not defiled your family?"

Kijima stared at me in blank amazement. How could I have possibly known about that, he seemed to be thinking. Clearly, he had no idea.

"Well, it is a disgrace. But my spirit is still pure."

"Why's that?"

"Well, I suppose because it's like a reward for hard work. I work hard at my job. But I don't sell my body, and neither should you. It's wrong. You're a beautiful woman. That's not something you chose to be or something you had to work hard to become. You were fortunate enough to be born beautiful. But to live off of exploiting yourself defiles who you are."

"I'm not exploiting myself. No more than you are with your moonlighting."

"It's not the same. In your work you hurt the people who care for you. They'll stop loving you. They won't be able to love you."

That was a new thought for me. My body is my own, why should anyone else think they owned it? Why should a person who loved me think he should be entitled to control my body? If love was that restricting, I was happy to live without it.

"I don't need anybody's love."

"What an incredibly arrogant thing to say. Just what the hell kind of person are you anyway?"

Kijima looked at his chalk-covered fingers in exasperation. His forehead was deeply wrinkled, and strands from his smooth hair slipped down over it. What startled me was the discovery that Kijima didn't want my body, he wanted to have *me*. He wanted to know what was going on in my heart. My heart. This was the first time I'd ever met someone who wanted to get to know that part of me I never showed to anyone else.

"Professor, is it that you want to buy me?"

Kijima was silent for a minute, unable to answer. then he raised his head and said plainly, "No. I'm a teacher and you are my student."

But you know I'm stupid, so why did you let me into this school? I started to ask this and then stopped, startled. Here was a man who wanted what no one had wanted before: he wanted to get to know the inner workings of the doll-like woman who was me. Karl wasn't interested in *me;* neither was Johnson. But Kijima's father liked me for who I was. The realization left me feeling numb. I was touched. But being touched is not the same as feeling desire. And I didn't exist without desire. If I didn't exist, then what?

"Professor, if you aren't going to buy me, I don't want you."

Kijima stared at me until his red face drained entirely of color.

"Besides, your son is my pimp. Did you know that?"

Kijima slipped deeper and deeper into silence until finally he drew in a deep breath.

"No, I didn't know. I'm very sorry."

Kijima bowed in apology and then turned and walked away. I watched his back as he retreated. I realized that he was going to have to expel both me and his son. I didn't tell Johnson that part.

In May, a month after beginning my senior year, I met up with Kijima, the son, outside the school gate. The navy-blue blazer of his school uniform was open, revealing a bright red silk shirt. He had a gold chain around his neck and was driving a black Peugeot. All were items bought on the sly from the money I'd earned. Kijima was born in April, so he'd just gotten his driver's license.

"Yuriko, get in."

I slipped into the snug seat alongside him. The girls on their way home from school glanced at us, their eyes flashing with envy. They weren't jealous of the car or of Kijima and his flashy clothes. They were jealous because Kijima and I were able to enjoy ourselves so freely, both inside school and outside it. And at the top of the list of jealous girls was Kazue Satō.

Kijima lit a cigarette angrily and took a deep drag before he turned to me and said, "What the hell did you say to my father? You bitch! We'll probably get expelled, you know. They're going to meet over the holidays and decide what to do with us. My father told me about it last night."

"Is your father going to resign too?"

"He might." Kijima turned away with a disgusted look. His expression was the spitting image of his father's. "What'll you do now?"

"Well, I could get a job as a model. The other day a scout showed up and gave me his business card. And there's always prostitution."

"Can I stay on with you then?"

"Sure," I nodded, staring at the girls who were walking in front of the car. One turned around and looked back at me. It was my sister. *Bitch.* She formed the words with her mouth without making a sound: *bitch, bitch, bitch.*

•

Johnson all of a sudden climbed on top of me and started to strangle me. Stop! I shouted and flailed away at him in an effort to get out from under his heavy body. But he pinned my arms and legs down and brought his mouth up close to my ear and shouted, "Professor Kijima likes Yuriko!"

"Probably."

"He'd be crazy to get mixed up with a girl like Yuriko. A first-class idiot."

"You're right. But it's too late. Professor Kijima has already gotten us both kicked out of school."

"What the hell?" Johnson let go of me as he spoke.

"We got caught. Me and Professor Kijima's son. We have to withdraw. And it looks like Professor Kijima's going to resign."

"Have you embarrassed Masami and me, Yuriko?"

Johnson's face flushed red, and not just from the bourbon. He was angry. I lay there waiting for him to do whatever he would. If he wanted to kill me, then that was that. Why is it that men who crave the flesh are so incapable of seeing the heart? Johnson was out of control. He knocked the bottle of bourbon over on the bed and I watched as the liquor seeped over the sheets, leaving an ever-widening brown stain. And not just the sheets—I was sure it was going through to the mattress as well. I was afraid of being scolded by Masami and grabbed for the bottle, but it fell to the floor with a thud

"You're just a heartless whore. A cheap slut. You make me sick!"

Johnson threw me down and started climbing over me violently, spewing out insults in a low voice. Was this a new game for him? I couldn't tell. I just lay back and looked up at the ceiling. I wouldn't feel anything. Ever since I became an old woman at the age of fifteen I haven't felt a thing, and ever since that night when I was seventeen I've been frigid.

All of a sudden there was a loud knock on the door.

"Yuriko-chan? Are you okay? Who's in there?"

Before I could answer the door burst open and Masami flew in with a golf club in her hand. She screamed when she saw me naked on the bed, a man savagely straddling me. But when she realized the man was her own husband, she collapsed on the floor.

"What are you doing?"

"Just what it looks like, dahling!"

Johnson and Masami stood at the side of the bed shouting insults at each other while I lay faceup, looking at the ceiling, naked.

•

I had just entered my senior year—and I had been living in Johnson's house for two and a half years—when I was advised to withdraw from school. It was the same for Kijima. Professor Kijima, assuming responsibility for his son's dereliction, resigned his own teaching post. I hear he became the superintendent at some company dormitory in Karuizawa. I imagine he's spending his time collecting all kinds of insect specimens. But I wouldn't know. I've not seen him since.

After Kijima and I withdrew from school we'd still meet up at the same café in Shibuya. Kijima would wave me over to where he sat in a dark corner of the restaurant. He'd always have a cigarette in one hand and a sports paper in the other; he never looked like a high school student. He looked more like a young tough who'd lost his gang. Kijima would fold his paper up with a rustling snap and stare at me.

"I'm going to transfer to another school. A man can't get by these days without finishing school. How about you? What'd Johnson say?"

"He told me to do whatever I wanted."

And so I had to live off the sale of my body, with no one to look out for me. Just as I do now. Nothing has changed.

FOUR · WORLD WITHOUT LOVE

Please listen to my side too. I can't let all the lies Yuriko wrote go uncontested. That wouldn't be fair, would it? You don't agree? But Yuriko's journal is so filthy I can't bear it. After all, I have a respectable job at the ward office. You have to let me try to explain.

I'm sure someone impersonating Yuriko wrote that journal of hers. I've already noted on a number of occasions that Yuriko didn't have the cleverness to organize her thoughts or write any kind of extended composition. Her schoolwork was always sloppy. I have an essay she wrote when she was a fourth-grader. Let me show it to you.

> Yesterday I went with my older sister to buy a red goldfish,
> but the goldfish store was closed on Sunday, so I couldn't buy
> a red goldfish and that made me sad so I cried.

This is all she could manage as a fourth-grader. But just look at the handwriting. It looks like a grown-up's, doesn't it? I suppose you're thinking that I wrote this and am now trying to pass it off as Yuriko's. But that's not the case. I found it the other day tucked in the back of my grandfather's closet when I was cleaning out his apartment. I used to correct every single one of Yuriko's wretched compositions, rewriting each word for her. I did everything I could to cover up the fact that my younger sister was dim-witted and morally corrupt. Now do you understand?

Well, then, shall I tell you more about Kazue in high school? I mean, since Yuriko wrote about her in her journal, I think I should. When Yuriko was admitted to the junior high division of the Q School system, even the girls in the high school went ballistic. Their excitement was only natural, I suppose, but it still posed considerable difficulty for me, as her older sister. I remember it very clearly.

Mitsuru was the first to ask about her. She came over to my desk during our lunch break carrying a large reference book. I had just finished eating the lunch I'd brought: stewed radishes with fried bean curd. It's what I'd fixed for my grandfather the night before. How can I remember such minute details? Well, I remember because I accidentally knocked the container over and the stew spilled on my English notes. Mitsuru looked at me sympathetically as I madly blotted away at my notebook with a damp handkerchief.

"I hear your little sister has entered the junior high division."

"So it would seem," I said, without looking up. Mitsuru tilted her head to the side, startled by the iciness of my answer. Her eyes grew wide and lit on me with bright alacrity. Mitsuru really was just like a squirrel! I was very fond of her, but at the same time I thought her rodent ways were often just too ridiculous.

"So it would seem? What kind of answer is that? Aren't you the least bit concerned about her? She is your sister." Mitsuru smiled warmly at me, flashing her big front teeth.

I stopped dabbing at my notebook and said, "No, actually I'm not the least bit concerned."

Mitsuru's eyes grew wide again. "Why? I hear she's very pretty."

"Who told you that?" I shot back. "And who cares anyway?"

"I heard it from Professor Kijima. Apparently your sister's in his group."

Mitsuru waved the book she was holding in front of my nose. It was a biology reference book written by a Takakuni Kijima. In addition to being in charge of the junior high division, Professor Takakuni Kijima was our biology teacher. He was a nervous type who wrote on the chalkboard with letters that were so perfectly square you'd have thought he'd measured them with a ruler. I couldn't stand the way he always looked: so proper, everything so perfect. I hated him.

"And I really respect him," Mitsuru said, without even waiting to hear what I had to say. "He's brilliant and he really looks out for his students. I think he's a great teacher. He was the one who took us on our overnight field trip when I was in junior high."

"What did he say about my sister?"

"He asked me if the older sister of a junior high transfer student was in my class. When I said I didn't know anything about it, he said that wasn't likely. So when I asked him for more details I finally figured out he had to be talking about you. It was such a surprise."

"Why? Is it hard to believe?"

"Because I didn't even know you had a younger sister."

Mitsuru was too smart to say that she found it hard to believe that I had a sister who looked so little like me, a sister who was so incredibly beautiful she looked like a monster. Just then we heard a commotion down the hall. A great crowd of students came pressing into the corridor, clamoring to look into the classroom where we sat. They were clearly from the junior high division. There were even a few boys among them, hanging back in the rear and looking a little sheepish.

"I wonder what's going on?"

But when I turned toward the door, a hush fell over the crowd of students. A large girl with curly hair dyed a reddish brown pushed her way through the crowd and stepped into the room. She was clearly the ringleader. From the haughty self-assured way she carried herself it was also clear that she was an insider, and the insiders in my class called out to her familiarly. "Mokku, what're you doing here?" This girl, Mokku, strode confidently into the classroom without answering and planted herself in front of my desk.

"Are you Yuriko's older sister?"

"Yes, I am."

I didn't want any dust to get into my lunch box, so I snapped the lid down. Mitsuru clutched the biology reference book to her breast, looking uneasy. Mokku gazed down at the stain that had seeped over my English notebook.

"What did you have for lunch today?"

"Stewed radish with bean curds," the student next to me answered. She was affiliated with the modern dance club and was a complete witch.

Every day she looked over my shoulder at what I was eating and snickered, screwing her face into a smirk. Mokku paid her no attention, completely disinterested. Instead she fixed her sights on my hair.

"Are you and Yuriko really sisters?"

"Yes, we really are."

"I'm sorry but I just don't believe you."

"I don't care whether you believe me or not."

I had no interest in talking to someone so presumptuous. I stood up and stared Mokku straight in the eye. She flinched and took a few steps back. I could hear the sound her big behind made as it bumped into the desk of the student in front of me. Everyone in the room was staring at us. Mitsuru, who was so short she barely managed to come up to Mokku's shoulder, grabbed Mokku by the arm and admonished her in a fairly sharp tone. "Stop poking your nose in other people's business and go back to your own classroom!"

Mokku turned back toward the corridor, still in Mitsuru's grip. Then, with an exaggerated flourish, she shrugged her shoulders and stomped out of the room. I could hear the students behind her sigh loudly with collective disappointment.

It was a good feeling. Ever since I was young I have loved bringing Yuriko down more than anything else. When people see a beautiful woman, they expect her to be perfect; they want her to remain beyond their reach. They feel she's safer that way, more adorable. So when they find out she's crude and unrefined, their admiration turns to scorn and their envy turns to hatred. Maybe the only reason I was born was to quash Yuriko's value.

"Wow, I can't believe he showed up too." At the sound of Mitsuru's voice I returned to my senses.

"Who?"

"Takashi Kijima. He's Professor Kijima's son and he's in his group."

One boy still lingered behind in the corridor after all the rest had left. He stood at the door to the classroom peering in at me. He looked exactly like his father: same compact little face, same slender build. His features were so nicely balanced you couldn't help but call him pretty. And there wasn't a hint of strength to him. Kijima's son's sharp eyes locked onto mine. I stared at him until he looked away.

"I've heard he's a problem kid," Mitsuri said.

She still clutched the biology book to her breast, brushing her fingers softly over the binding where Takakuni Kijima's name was written. I could tell from her gestures that she was in love. I wanted to say something mean to her, something to shock her back to reality.

"Well, what do you expect for a deviant?"

"How do you know he's deviant?" Mitsuru asked, startled.

"I've got eyes, don't I?"

Kijima's son and I had something in common. Kijima's son was the blight on his father's honor, and I was the blight to Yuriko's beauty. We were both giant zeros. I suppose Kijima's son had come to get a look at me because he harbored a distrust of Yuriko's monstrous beauty. Once he saw me, he was able to despise her. But Kijima's son was male after all, so I suppose he couldn't help feeling sympathy for a woman like Yuriko, who was just as stupid as she was beautiful. I was sick of being put in these difficult situations. I had to continue at this school, and Yuriko's presence was going to make my life unpleasant. I didn't want to end my time here as a giant zero, like Kijima's son. So from that day on I was determined to find a way to get rid of Yuriko.

"Hey, what's going on here?" I heard someone say in an overly friendly way. I turned to see Kazue Satō placing her hands on Mitsuru's shoulders in a chummy show of friendship. Kazue was always trying to make friends with Mitsuru and was constantly starting up conversations with her. Today she was wearing a ridiculously short miniskirt that only accentuated how skinny her legs were. Kazue was knobby and angular and so thin you could feel her bones if you touched her. Her hair was thick and lackluster. And of course there was that silly red logo. I could just picture her sitting in that pathetically gloomy room of hers with needle and thread, madly embroidering Ralph Lauren logos on her socks.

"We were talking about her younger sister," Mitsuru said, coolly brushing Kazue's hands off her shoulders. Kazue blanched for a second, feelings hurt, and then recovered with a look of feigned indifference.

"What about her sister?"

"She's enrolled in the junior high division. She's in Professor Kijima's group."

A look of uneasiness gradually crept over Kazue's face. I recalled her own younger sister—who was the spitting image of Kazue—and said nothing.

"That's great. She must be really smart!"

"Not particularly. She got in under the *kikokushijo* category. You know, for the children of Japanese who've been brought up abroad."

"So it pays to spend time abroad? It's true that you can get into a school like this without having to really study—just on the basis of living overseas?" Kazue let out a sigh. "I wish my father'd been transferred overseas."

"But that's not all, Kazue. Her sister's absolutely gorgeous on top of everything else."

I was sure Mitsuru hated Kazue. She kept tapping her front teeth with her fingernail while she talked to her. And the way she did it was different from when she talked to me. It was more random.

"Gorgeous? How do you mean?" Kazue scowled at me. What she meant to say was, How can you possibly have a gorgeous younger sister? You're not even remotely attractive.

"What I mean is, everyone's saying she's a knockout. Just a few minutes ago, all the junior high kids came running over here to get a look at the big sister."

Kazue looked down at her hands with hollow eyes as if she'd just realized that she held nothing—nothing to put up in comparison.

"My sister's set her sights on this school too."

"Tell her not to bother," I said crossly. Kazue flushed red and looked as if she were going to say something in response but bit her lip instead. "What I mean is, the insider students are so nasty they won't let you enter the clubs you want, will they?"

Kazue made a show of clearing her throat in an effort to avoid my obvious sarcasm. She'd joined the ice-skating team. But I'd heard others gossip that she was having a hard time coming up with the rink fees. The team had to dole out a lot of money to pay the Olympic-class coach they'd hired and cover the cost of renting the rink for lessons. Because of that, they'd accept any girl who wanted to join. It didn't matter if she couldn't skate a lick; as long as she could help with the costs, they didn't care. The students at this school were absolutely indifferent to the hardships their own pleasures imposed on those around them.

"Well, just so you know, I've joined the ice skating team. They were second on my list after the cheerleading squad, so I'm very happy with the way things turned out."

"Have they let you skate yet?"

Kazue ran her tongue over her lips a couple of times, apparently searching for the right words.

"It's the rich insiders who monopolize the rink, isn't it?" I said. "Or else the really pretty girls who look cute in their little outfits. That Olympic coach probably gives them private lessons anyway, so they get all the attention. Nothing like favoritism. The only other way to get noticed around here is to actually have talent. What a crock. The very idea of those high school students out there pretending to be ice skaters is a farce. It's just an amusement for the little princesses anyway."

At that, Kazue's eyes lit up and she smiled so broadly I thought she might rip her face open. Oh, yes. Kazue was nothing if not ambitious. And all she wanted—with a desire greater than anyone else's—was to be recognized as "a little princess" who was as talented in the classroom as she was on the ice. This had been Kazue's father's most fervent wish.

"I bet all they let you do is clean the rink and take care of their shoes. They may call it *physical training*, but it's more like hazing. And how many times did you have to run around the playing field the other day when it was over ninety-five degrees Fahrenheit? You looked like you were going to die! Is that the kind of amusement that's fit for a princess?"

"It's not hazing or anything of the sort!" Kazue finally regained the power to speak. "You have to train like that to build up basic strength."

"And once you build up your basic strength, then what? Are you going to try out for the Olympics?"

I had to say it. And I wasn't just being cruel. This dim-witted girl believed all you had to do was try your best and you could do anything. I wanted to set her straight. She knew nothing about the real world, and I wanted to explain the way things really worked. But more than that, I wanted to get my revenge on her father for having poisoned her with those stupid ideas in the first place.

When I looked up I noticed that Mitsuru was working her way over to the window where a group of girls were having a conversation. They admitted her into their little circle and soon they were all laughing. Mitsuru and I exchanged glances. She shrugged lightly without saying anything. What's the point? Her gesture seemed to say.

"I wasn't planning on trying out for the Olympics. But I'm still only sixteen, you know. If I wanted to, and trained like there was no tomorrow, there's no reason why I couldn't go to the Olympics."

I could hardly believe my ears.

"Boy, you really are an idiot. So do you think if you took up tennis and trained like crazy you could go to Wimbledon? Or if you decided to be beautiful and worked at it like nothing else you'd win the Miss Universe Pageant? Or maybe you think if you study like there's no tomorrow you'll be top in the class by the end of the year? You think you can beat Mitsuru? She's been at the top of the class since she was a first-year student in junior high and has never once had to give up her spot. You know why? Because she's a genius. You think all you have to do is try your best? You can try until you've worn yourself away to nothing, but there's a limit, you know. You can spend your whole life trying—hell, you can try until there's nothing left of you but a little stump—and you'll still never be a genius."

Lunch break was almost over but I was just getting started. I guess I was still irritated about being turned into a freak show by those junior high kids. Kazue's the one who ought to have been on display, not me. She'd insinuated herself into a place where she didn't belong and then was doing all kinds of asinine things without a care in the world. But Kazue had nerve, I'll give her that.

She turned to me and said condescendingly, "I have sat here and listened patiently to you, and I think you've got the attitude of a loser. You talk like someone who has never even tried to succeed at anything. I for one am going to keep on trying my best. Sure, it's probably foolish to think about entering the Olympics or Wimbledon, but I don't think it's a stretch to try to be first in the class by the end of the year. You may think Mitsuru's a genius, but I don't. She just tries really hard."

I recalled the way Kazue's family determined the pecking order in their household based on scholastic scores and laughed sarcastically. "Have you ever seen a monster?"

Kazue raised one eyebrow and looked at me with suspicion. "A monster?"

"Yeah, a person who's not human."

"Are you talking about geniuses?"

I paused for a minute. Genius doesn't quite cover it. A monster is a person with something twisted inside, something that grows and grows until it looms all out of proportion. I pointed silently toward Mitsuru. A few minutes ago she'd been laughing with her friends but now she had returned to her desk in order to get ready for the next class. She was wrapped in a strange aura of solitude. There was something about Mitsuru once she knew class was ready to get under way.

"I'm going to make it to the top of the class because I'm going to do my best," Kazue announced.

"Suit yourself."

"You say such hateful things!" Kazue was having a hard time selecting the appropriate words to challenge me. "My father said you were weird and didn't act like a girl. You're probably some kind of deviant. Maybe you do have a beautiful younger sister. Maybe you are smart. But I have a normal family with a father who has a good job—who works hard."

Kazue went back to her own desk. She could talk about her father's opinion of me all day long; what did I care? As I watched her walk away, I decided that from now on I would make it my business to keep an eye on her efforts to "do her best."

Quiet settled over the classroom. When I checked my watch I discovered it was already time for the next lesson. I scrambled to pick up the lunch box that I'd left on my desk and stuffed it away in my satchel. The door opened and in came Kijima in his white lab coat, a serious look on his face.

I'd completely forgotten that today was the day for our weekly biology class. First Yuriko, then the detestable Kijima Junior, and now Professor Kijima himself. What were the odds of running across all three in one day? I hurriedly searched for my biology book and put it on top of my desk. I was in such a rush that I knocked my pad off the desk and it fell to the floor with a thud. I saw Kijima briefly contract his brows in a frown.

Kijima put his hands on both sides of the lectern and looked slowly around the room. I knew he was searching for me; he had to be. I lowered my head. But before long I could feel his eyes hovering above my desk. Yes, that's right. Here I am, beautiful Yuriko's ugly older sister, the blight on Yuriko's life. But you've got a blight on your own life too, don't you? Your son. I raised my eyes and stared at him directly.

Like his son, Kijima's brow was wide, the bridge of his nose thin, and his eyes piercing. The gold-rimmed glasses he wore complemented his face and gave him a studious look. And yet there was something about his person that always looked disheveled. The trace of stubble the razor missed, perhaps? The strands of hair that strayed across his brow? The stains on his white lab coat? Those small marks of dishevelment symbolized something: he had a son who didn't live up to his expectations. Although father and son resembled each other in every other way, their eyes were different. Kijima looked at things head-on, his son in sideways glances. The father's direct gaze would never freeze on its subject but would trace its contours, taking in the details one by one, so it was always easy to tell what he was observing. Now he observed me, my face, my figure, without saying a word. Did you discover any biological evidence to link Yuriko to me? Don't look at me as if I'm some bizarre species of insect! I grew furious as I sat there soaking up Kijima's study. Finally he took his eyes off of me and began to speak in slow, measured tones.

"We've already covered the end of the dinosaur age, haven't we? We discussed the way the dinosaurs devoured all the conifers and other gymnosperms. Do you remember? Over time the dinosaurs' necks grew longer and longer so they could reach the highest plants. We talked about the way plants develop in accord with their environment, right? Interesting, don't you think? Gymnosperms got their name—naked-seed plants—because their seeds are not formed in an enclosed ovary. The angiosperms, in comparison, produce seeds in specialized reproductive organs called flowers, where the ovary or carpel is enclosed, so they are known as flowering plants. Now, because the gymnosperms depended entirely on wind dispersal for their reproduction, they were eventually eaten to the point of extinction. But in comparison, the angiosperms survived because they were in partnership with all the various insects. Are there any questions so far?"

Mitsuru kept her eyes riveted on Kijima without even shifting in her seat. I was very much aware of the electricity that ignited the air between those two. I had already suspected that Mitsuru was in love with Kijima. But even so I could hardly believe my eyes at the way the passion hovered in the air between them like a massive lump.

Earlier I told you that I cherished a kind of love for Mitsuru, didn't I? Perhaps that's not really accurate. Mitsuru and I were like a mountain lake formed by streams of subterranean water. The mountains are deep and lonely and the lake desolate. No travelers pass by. But in the earth beneath the surface, the waters are always flowing and always moving in unison. If I went beneath the surface, Mitsuru did as well. If I surged, so did she. For Mitsuru, Kijima must have represented an entirely different world, but for me he represented only an obstacle.

Yet there could be no doubt that Kijima was attracted to Yuriko. And the only reason he was taking notice of me now was because he was interested in her. Do you think I'm wrong? To be sure, I have never been in love. But if someone does love someone else, don't you think it's typical for that person to want to know all about the encumbrances his lover must contend with? And let's not forget that Kijima was a biology teacher. Don't you suppose he was also interested in Yuriko and me from a strictly scientific perspective as well? Kijima turned to the blackboard and wrote, *Flowers and mammalia—a new partnership is born.*

"Open your textbooks to page seventy-eight. The mouse eats the angiosperms, or flowering plants, and scatters the seeds in its droppings."

As if in chorus, the sound of pencils scribbling madly over notebooks arose from the classroom. I didn't write anything in my notebook and continued with my daydreaming. Yuriko must be a flowering plant. I am a naked-seed plant. The flowering plant attracts insects and animals with its beautiful blossoms and sweet nectar. I suppose Kijima must be an animal, then. If he's an animal, what kind of animal would he be? Kijima turned around and stared at me.

"Well, then, let's review. You there, do you remember why the dinosaurs became extinct?"

Kijima was pointing at me. Lost in my thoughts and completely caught off guard, I slumped down in my seat with a sour look.

"Stand up!" Kijima ordered reprovingly.

My desk creaked and my chair scraped across the floor as I pushed it back and stood up awkwardly. Mitsuru turned around and stared at me.

"Wasn't it because of giant meteorites?"

"That's part of it. What about the relation to plants?"

"I don't remember."

"Oh? Then what about you?"

Mitsuru stood up without a sound and launched effortlessly into a response.

"When they exhausted the food supply in their present location they would migrate to a new site until the plants there were gone as well. Gradually the forests that the dinosaurs depended on for sustenance were all depleted. From this example we can denote that the relationship between plant and animal is one to one. It is important to establish a cooperative partnership for survival."

"Exactly." Kijima nodded and then turned to the blackboard and wrote out word for word what Mitsuru had just said. Kazue looked over at me with a gloating sneer and thrust her shoulders back. What a bitch. From that moment on I harbored an intense hatred for Kazue, Mitsuru, and Kijima.

•

After biology we had gym class. Rhythmic exercises. We had to change into our gym clothes and gather outside, but I took my time. I still hadn't recovered from my earlier humiliation. I was certain that Kijima had intentionally tried to embarrass me in front of the entire class, just because I was Yuriko's older sister. No, because I was the beautiful Yuriko's older sister. It was as if people could not forgive me for being related to her. The only exception was Kazue.

Rhythmic exercises, as you now know, is a required course for girls in the Q School system. They say that when you move your arms and legs in different directions at the same time you exercise your brain; it's supposed to be the kind of exercise that prolongs your life. But I never practiced the steps at home, so I was never any good at it. Of course, if you were the first one to make a mistake, you attracted attention. So I tried to hang in there until others started to mess up and get disqualified. I was doing just that when Yuriko came by with Kijima Junior. I noticed them staring at the class.

I hadn't seen Yuriko for some time, and in the interim she had grown even more beautiful. Her breasts were now so full it looked as if they would come bursting through the white blouse of her school uniform at any minute, and her hips, high and round, pressed tightly against her tiny tartan skirt. Her legs were long and straight and perfectly shaped. And then there was her face: her white skin, her brown eyes, and her expression, so soft and beautiful; she looked as though she were constantly getting ready to ask a question. Even an immaculately crafted doll could not have been as lovely.

I was so surprised by the way Yuriko had matured that I lost my concentration and missed one of the steps. Those who made a mistake had to leave the ring of dancers. My exit from the ring was earlier today than I had hoped, and it was all because of Yuriko. I hated her for sneaking up on me. I hated her more than I could stand. Get the hell out of here! I screamed at her in my heart. Then I heard my classmates' derisive laughter.

"Look at Kazue Satō—dancing like a friggin' octopus!"

Kazue was doing her best to keep up with the music. She didn't want to lose to Mitsuru. Besides, she had to prove me wrong; hard work does pay off. Her face was creased with concentration while Mitsuru's was calm and cool, her arms and legs moving lithely left and right. She was so graceful she made it look more like a ballet than a gym exercise. And then Kazue caught sight of Yuriko and stopped dead in her tracks with a look of astonishment. At last she'd seen a monster. When I saw the shock on Kazue's face I couldn't help but burst out laughing.

"Sorry about earlier," Kazue said. She had come chasing after me as soon as class was over. "Shall we let bygones be bygones and just try to get along?"

I didn't answer. Kazue's sudden change in attitude made me wary.

"Your younger sister . . ." The sweat was pouring off Kazue's forehead in rivulets, and she didn't even try to wipe it off. "What's her name?"

"Yuriko."

I couldn't tell if Kazue was jealous or impressed or bitter. Her voice was thick with some kind of strange excitement.

"Wow, even her name is pretty, isn't it. I can hardly believe she's even the same species as us!"

Kazue's words were so inflamed with feeling that she continued to repeat the same lines over and over as the pungent smell of sweat wafted from her body. It really was a pungent smell—signalling the intensity of Kazue's feeling for Yuriko, I suppose. Without thinking I lowered my face. It was clear that Kazue's world was changing, now that she'd caught a glimpse of the monster.

Yuriko had just left the school grounds with Kijima Junior. To see the deviant little Kijima tagging along after Yuriko led me to suspect he was up to no good. I wanted to pay the little twerp back for the humiliation I had suffered in the earlier class. I decided then and there that I wanted to drive the Kijima father-and-son team out of school along with Yuriko as soon as I could.

•

A few days after this, as I was leaving school, I heard Kazue come bounding after me. She pressed a small envelope into my hand. I opened it up while I was on the train. The letter was written on two sheets of girlish notepaper printed with violets. Kazue's handwriting was pretty but lacked distinguishing characteristics.

> *Please forgive the informality of this letter.*
>
> *Both you and I are outsiders at Q High School for Young Women. You have come to my house, you have met my parents, and so you are perhaps the person with whom I am most likely to become friends. My father told me I shouldn't interact with you because your background is so unlike my own. But if we communicate in letters, I'm sure he won't know. Shall we send each other letters from time to time like this? We can confide in each other and talk about our studies.*
>
> *I think I have probably misunderstood you. Even though you are an outsider like me, you always seem so composed that I feel you've been a student at this school for a long time. And then you're always talking to Mitsuru, so it's hard for me to get close to you, and when I do you keep your distance.*
>
> *I don't know what the other students at Q High School for Young Women are thinking (particularly the insiders!), and I feel very out of place. But I am not ashamed of myself. I had my sights set on entering Q High School ever since first grade, and I got in on account of my hard work—and my hard work alone. So I have confidence in myself. Why shouldn't I? I believe I am going to achieve my goals. Things are going to turn out well for me, and I will lead a happy and successful life.*
>
> *But there are times when I'm not certain what to do, and I don't know whom I can talk to. And so without really thinking, I've written to you. There's something troubling me. May I please discuss it with you?*
>
> Yours,
Kazue Satō

Phrases like *Please forgive the informality of this letter* must have been something she copied from a letter-writing primer for adults. The very image of her sitting there copying from a manual made me laugh. I certainly had no interest in discussing her problems with her. But I was curious to know just what this troubling matter was, and I did want to know what was going on in her head. I suppose there's nothing more interesting than other people's problems.

●

That night, while I was absentmindedly turning thoughts like that over in my mind, I worked on my English homework. My grandfather, who was preparing the evening meal, stuck his head out of the kitchen and asked, "Did you say the Blue River bar is owned by the family of a kid in your class?"

"Yeah. Her name's Mitsuru and her mother works there."

"Well, that's surprising. I thought we were the only ones from a place like this with a kid at the Q High School for Young Women. But then the other day I met a fella who works security at the Blue River in front of the station. He's a graduate of the same school as the super here. They're good friends, it seems, and the super's always going over to his place. He called me to go by and look at some plants that were giving them trouble, and that's how I learned the daughter of the mama-san there goes to Q High too, and it sounded like she was in your class. So I've been thinking I might go by for a drink, given our connections. Coincidences like that make life worth living."

"Yes, why don't you? Mitsuru's mother told me to tell you to stop by sometime."

"Did she? I was afraid I'd just be a nuisance, being such an old fogy and all."

"I don't think that matters. As long as you're a customer, that's all that counts, right? I already told her about you—that you like bonsai—so I'm sure she'll be happy for you to come by."

I was mostly just humoring my grandfather. But it seemed he took my words to heart. The next thing I knew I heard him in the kitchen, happily rinsing the rice and chopping vegetables.

"I bet Blue River's pretty expensive. All the hostesses are young. I wonder if they'll give me a bit of a discount."

"Don't worry," I replied. I was more interested in Kazue's letter. I pulled it out, placed it on top of my English textbook, and read it again. I decided to ask her about it tomorrow.

•

"I read your letter. So what's this problem you wrote about?"

"Let's talk where no one else can hear us, okay?"

Acting like she was getting ready to reveal classified information, Kazue led me to an empty classroom. "It's kind of hard to talk about it with someone else," she said.

"But you want to talk about it, don't you?"

"Okay, here goes. I'm ready."

Kazue placed her hands on her cheeks shyly. She opened her mouth to speak any number of times but stopped each time to search for the words she wanted.

"Okay. It's like this. See, I like Professor Kijima's son, Takashi Kijima, so I want to know what's going on between him and Yuriko. I mean, when I saw Kijima with Yuriko it made me so upset I haven't been able to sleep."

"He really does have an attractive face, doesn't he?" As I said this I thought of Kijima's reptilian body and his darting eyes.

"I really like that kind of face," Kazue said. "He's so delicate and pretty for a boy, and tall, and cool, and—I'm just crazy about him! The first time I saw him was just before summer vacation. I ran into him at the bookstore in front of school and thought right then that he was really cute. I was completely shocked when I learned he was Professor Kijima's son. I've done a little background checking on the family, so I know that they live in Den'enchōfū, an upscale neighborhood. Professor Kijima's a graduate of the Q School system, and Kijima's younger brother is in the elementary division. I also learned that Professor Kijima always takes the family on a summer vacation and lets the children help him collect his insect specimens."

I gasped. So that's why Kazue lost the rhythmic exercise competition to Mitsuru! But that wasn't all. I knew Kazue was a gymnosperm but here she was trying to find insects and animals to partner with. Could there be another woman alive who was less self-aware? And Kijima of all people, with his shifty eyes! Such delicious irony. It was all I could do not to laugh in Kazue's face.

"Is that right? Well, I sure hope everything works out for you!"

"Do you think you could ask Yuriko about Kijima for me? I mean, she's so pretty and all, I'm sure Kijima likes her. And the thought of it makes me so crazy I can't even sleep. But I think there may be hope for me yet. The other day he smiled at me!"

Oh, I doubt that was a smile. We're talking about Kijima, after all. It was more likely a smirk brought on by Kazue's stupidity. But this information was a godsend. I'd been dreaming of a way to get rid of the Kijima father-and-son duo, and Yuriko too. I started scheming.

"I'll see what I can learn from Yuriko. I'll find out what her relation is with Kijima, and then I'll find out what kind of girl Kijima likes, okay?"

Kazue held her breath and nodded.

I looked at her anxious expression and added, "Is it okay if I let her know that you like Kijima?"

Kazue looked terrified and shook both her hands back and forth. "No, no, no! Please don't let her know. I don't want anyone to know yet. Maybe I'll tell her later."

"Got it."

"But there *is* one more thing I'd like you to find out, if you can do it without being too obvious." Kazue said, she pulled up her navy-blue knee socks, which had started to bunch around her ankles. "Find out if he'd be interested in a girl who's a year older than him."

"What difference does it make if the girl's a year older or not? We're talking about Professor Kijima's son. I'm sure he's more interested in a girl's intelligence than her age."

She squealed slightly and opened her tiny eyes as wide as I'd ever seen them.

"You're right. And Professor Kijima's handsome too. I love his biology classes!"

"All right. I'll call Yuriko tonight and see what she says."

I lied. I didn't even know the Johnsons' telephone number. But Kazue lowered her head with a worried look.

"Please be careful. Your sister's not the type to gossip, is she?"

"Oh we're both very tight-lipped. Don't even think about it."

"Really? That's a relief." Kazue glanced at her watch. "Well, I'd better go show my face at the team meeting."

"Have they let you skate yet?"

Kazue nodded uncertainly and picked up the navy-blue gym bag that all the team members carried.

"They told me when I made myself an outfit they'd let me skate. So I made one."

"Can I see?"

Reluctantly she pulled her skating suit out of her bag. It was navy and gold, the Q School colors. The cut and design was exactly like one of the cheerleaders' costumes.

"I put the spangles on myself," she said, holding the costume up to her chest.

"It looks like a cheerleader's uniform," I said.

"It does?" Kazue looked perturbed for a second. "You think I made it look like a cheerleader's uniform because I wasn't allowed to join the squad, don't you?"

"No, I don't think so, but others might."

Kazue's face clouded over when she heard my frank response, but then she mumbled—almost as if talking to herself—"Too late now, I've already made it. I made it like this because I like the Q School colors, that's all."

Kazue was very adept at deluding herself, I'll give her that much. In no time at all she could warp reality into meeting her own needs. I really, really hated that tendency of hers.

"What kind of girls do you think Kijima likes? I mean, girls from which clubs? What am I going to do if he hates girls on the ice-skating team? Or what if he's one of those frivolous types who only likes the girls on the cheerleading squad? Then what'll I do?"

"Don't worry. The ice skaters are just as vivacious as the cheerleaders. He's bound to like girls on that team. At least it's better than the basketball team! And I'll bet he likes girls who are good in school."

"Really? Do you think so too? Ever since I fell in love with Kijima, I've enjoyed my studies even more."

Kazue spoke happily, spreading her uniform across the desk. Then she balled it and stuffed it back in her gym bag. Kazue was too impossibly clumsy to do anything neatly.

"Oops, I've got to run. If I'm late I'll have to polish the senior girls' blades. See you later!"

Kazue snatched up the bag that contained her uniform and skates and bounded noisly out of the room. After she left I sat in the classroom for some time alone. It was autumn and nightfall was early. In no time at all it had grown dark. My rear end began to hurt. I noticed a line of graffiti on the edge of the desk where I was sitting. Someone had written *Love . . . love . . . I love Junji!* with a felt-tip pen. *Love . . . love . . . I love*

Takashi! Love . . . love . . . I love Kijima. . . . Without really thinking about it, I was led by association to imagine other lines to write, recalling the passion that had hovered in the air between Mitsuru and Kijima. I let out a long sigh.

I've never once in my entire life been in love with a man. Yes, I'm a human being who has gone through life just fine without ever experiencing that hovering lump of passion. And I have no regrets. Kazue was not so different from myself. Why was she not able to appreciate this?

•

It was past nine o'clock. I'd just gotten out of the bath and was heading to the sitting room to watch TV when the front door opened and my grandfather stepped into the apartment. He'd been out drinking. His face was bright red, and he was out of breath.

"Well, you sure are late. I went ahead and ate."

I pointed to the dishes with my grandfather's portion of the meal that I'd left on the little tea table: mackerel stewed in miso, boiled greens, and pickles. My grandfather had fixed it before he went out. My grandfather let out a long breath without saying anything. He was wearing a suit I'd never seen before, garish, with thick black stripes over a bright green background. His short-sleeved shirt was a pale yellow, and he wore a black string Texas tie with a strange-looking cloisonné fastener. Grandfather had small hands for a man, and as he loosened his tie strings he started to chuckle to himself, as if he'd just remembered something. No doubt he'd paid a visit to the Blue River.

"Grandpa, did you go to Mitsuru's mom's bar?"

"Uh-huh."

"Was Mitsuru's mom there?"

"Uh-huh."

My grandfather's reticence was odd, given his usual loquacity.

"So how was it?"

"What a wonderful person!" Grandfather mumbled in response, more to himself than to me. He turned to look at the bonsai he'd left outside and then stepped onto the veranda, obviously not interested in further conversation with me. He never left the bonsai out in the evening dew, so I found his behavior particularly disconcerting.

That night I had a bizarre dream. My grandfather and I were floating endlessly on an ancient sea. Everyone was there: my dead mother; my father, who is now living with a Turkish woman. Some of us sat on the black rocks scattered across the ocean floor while others lounged about on the gritty sand. I was wearing a green pleated skirt that I had loved as a child. I remember rubbing my hand along the pleats and thinking how wistful it made me feel. My grandfather was dressed in the same stylish outfit he'd worn to the Blue River. The ends of his string tie floated in the water. My parents were wearing what they always wore at home. They looked like they did long ago. They looked like they did when I was a child.

The sea began to fill with plankton, which looked very much like swirling flakes of snow. When I turned to gaze up at the surface of the water, I could tell that the sky above it was clear and bright, and yet for some reason my family and I were happily living our lives on the dark floor of the ocean. Such a weird and yet tranquil dream. And how telling that Yuriko was nowhere to be found. Without her I felt relaxed and peaceful, and yet I could also sense a tension as I waited, wondering when she might make her appearance.

Kazue came swimming along in her cheerleader's uniform, her hair jet black and her eyes set with determination. She was wearing flesh-colored tights, so I realized it was her ice-skating costume, not a cheerleader's uniform. Kazue moved with intense concentration to the tempo of the rhythmic exercise music, but because she was underwater her movements were slow and languid. I began to laugh. I wondered if Mitsuru was around too and looked around for her. Mitsuru was holed up in a wreck on the ocean's floor, studying. Johnson and Masami were sitting on the deck of the wreck. I thought I'd head in that direction when all of a sudden everything around me grew dark. A giant figure had cast a shadow over the surface of the water, blocking out the rays of the sun. I looked up in surprise.

Yuriko had finally put in an appearance. I was the size of a child, but Yuriko, with the face and body of an adult, was dressed in the flowing white robes of a sea goddess. Her ample breasts were visible through her clothing. Yuriko swam toward us with her long arms and long legs, a radiant smile on her beautiful face. I was terrified by her eyes as she looked around underwater. They emitted no light. I hid in the shadow of a rock, but Yuriko stretched out her exquisitely formed arms and started to pull me to her.

When I woke up it was just five minutes before my alarm was set to go off. I lay in bed, thinking about my dream. Ever since Yuriko showed up, Mitsuru, Kazue, and my grandfather all changed abruptly. Love . . . love . . . everyone was tangled up with love: Mitsuru for Professor Kijima, Kazue for Kijima's son, and my grandfather for Mitsuru's mother. Of course, when it comes to love I have no idea what kind of chemical reaction takes over the heart, never having experienced it myself. All I knew was that I had to do something to ensure that at least Mitsuru's and my grandfather's attentions returned to me. Would I be able to battle Yuriko? It didn't matter. I had no choice.

•

During lunch break, Kazue sauntered over to my desk, beaming with confidence. She placed her lunch box on an empty chair and dragged the chair over to my desk with a rattling screech.

"Is it okay if I eat with you?"

She'd already sat down before she asked. Typical. I turned a frosty gaze on her. Dog! Fashion nightmare! Jerk! She looked even more repulsive today than usual, so repulsive I just wanted to shout abuse after abuse at her. She'd tried to curl her hair. Usually it hung limply down over her head like a helmet, but today it stuck out on both sides like a wide-brimmed hat. You could still see the lines where the curler pins had pressed down on her hair. And to make matters worse, today she'd somehow rigged her tiny drowsy-looking eyes so that she seemed to be double-lidded.

"What'd you do to your eyes?"

Kazue brought her hands up slowly to her eyelids.

"Oh. These are called Elizabeth Eyelids."

She'd gotten hold of some beauty product that Japanese women glued to their eyelids to give them the extra fold they craved, because they thought it made their eyes look Western. She'd spied on one of the insider students attaching them to her eyes in the restroom. Just the very thought of Kazue holding that two-pronged toothpick-thin plastic wand up to her eye while she applied the device made my skin crawl. And then her skirt had shrunk so drastically that you could see halfway up her skinny thighs. She'd worked so hard at being attractive that she ended up looking more ridiculous than ever.

The other girls in the class poked one another in the ribs when they saw Kazue and made no effort to hide their laughter. It made me sick just to think that others thought we were friends. I hadn't minded so much when she'd just been the ugly know-it-all, but this new transformation was thanks to Yuriko, which made it all the worse.

"Satō, I've a favor to ask you." Two of our classmates who were also on the ice-skating team came up alongside Kazue. Both were insiders, but one was clearly subordinate to the other. They were very close. Both had fathers who served in ambassadorial positions in foreign countries. It seems that different ambassadorial assignments carried different levels of prestige, depending on the country. The two girls treated each other with the deference associated with their fathers' positions.

"What is it?" Kazue asked, turning to look up at them cheerfully. When they saw her Elizabeth Eyelids they both broke into smiles that they struggled to conceal. Kazue, however, did not notice. Instead she twirled her fingers through her curls as if to say, Look at my new hairstyle. When the two shifted their gaze to her hair, they could no longer stifle their laughter. Kazue watched them blankly.

"The team has designated a midterm review committee, and we've been put in charge. I hate to ask, but would you let us copy your English and Classics notes? You're the best student on the team."

"Of course," Kazue responded, beaming with pride.

"In that case, would you mind if we also had your social studies and geography notes? Everyone will be really grateful."

"No problem."

They hurried out of the room. I was certain they were in the hall laughing hysterically.

"You're such an idiot!" I said. "There's no such thing as a midterm review committee."

I knew it was none of my business, but I just couldn't help myself. Not that it mattered. Kazue was still luxuriating in hearing them call her "the best student in the club."

"We all need to help one another out."

"Oh, that's just terrific. And how are they going to help you?"

"Well, I don't know how to skate, so they can teach me what I need to know."

"Wait a minute. You joined the skating team and you can't skate?"

Kazue started to unwrap the handkerchief around her lunch box with a troubled look. She pulled out a squished rice ball and a piece of tomato. That was it. I had brought along the mackerel my grandfather had left uneaten and was enjoying my meal. But when I saw Kazue's meager fare I was too startled to continue. Kazue started to eat the rice ball with apparent distaste. It was just a plain rice ball, lightly salted, with nothing stuffed inside.

"It's not that I can't skate at all. I've been skating with my father any number of times at Kōrakuen Park."

"So what happened with your costume? Did they let you skate?"

"It's none of your business."

Kazue turned away.

"The cost of the costume and the rink charges are probably really high," I persisted. "Didn't your father complain?"

"Why should he?" Kazue pursed her lips angrily. "We've got the money."

They most certainly did not have the money. I bitterly recalled the gloom of Kazue's house and the way her father had dunned me for the international phone call I'd made.

"Let's not talk about my team anymore. I'm interested in hearing about Yuriko. Did you ask her?"

"I called her right away. Listen, you have nothing to worry about. Yuriko said Kijima was just giving her a tour of the school. She also said it doesn't seem that Kijima is going out with anyone else right now."

"That's great!" Kazue clapped her hands with joy. I found the thrill of lying even more entertaining than I had imagined.

"Oh, and one more thing. This is just Yuriko's opinion, of course, and it may have no significance, but it seems that Kijima likes older actresses and such."

"Who? Who?"

"Actresses like Reiko Ōhara."

I was on a roll and couldn't stop. At the time, Reiko Ōhara was one of the most adored actresses, or so I'd heard. "Reiko Ōhara!" Kazue wailed, and stared blankly ahead in frustration. How will I ever replace Reiko Ōhara? she seemed to be thinking. For a minute I remembered all the pleasure I'd had at tricking Yuriko with my lies when we were little, and my heart fluttered excitedly. But Yuriko had never believed me completely. There was always a part of her that resisted. If a kid knows she's not bright, she's always somewhat suspicious. But not Kazue. She swallowed my lies hook, line, and sinker.

"Oh, no! What do you think? What can I do to compete with her?"

Kazue peered over at me expectantly. In the end her narcissism had won out. Kazue was quickly regaining her self-confidence.

"Well," I declared convincingly, "you're good in school, for starters, and you know Kijima likes smart girls. But then he did mention Mitsuru. Maybe he's interested in her."

"Mitsuru?" Kazue wheeled around to stare at her. Mitsuru was sitting at her desk reading a book. It was covered with a book wrapper so I couldn't be sure, but it looked like an English-language novel. As Kazue scrutinized Mitsuru, I could sense the heat of the jealousy rising off her cheeks.

Mitsuru must have sensed Kazue's stare because she turned around and looked at us. She didn't reveal any interest in us. I thought it odd that Mitsuru hadn't even mentioned my grandfather's visit last night to her mother's bar. Maybe her mother hadn't told her he'd stopped by.

"Hey? Hey!" Kazue began to pester me. "Did she say anything about the kind of girl Kijima likes?"

"Well, I think we can assume he likes a pretty girl—he's male, after all."

"A pretty girl, right . . ."

Kazue took a few more nibbles of her rice ball and sighed. "I wish I looked like Yuriko! If I'd been born with a face like that . . . I can't even imagine how much better my life would be. A whole new world would open for me. Really, to have a face like that—*and* brains—what more could you want?"

"That's because she's a monster."

"I suppose. But if I could get where she is without having to study, I'd be glad to become a monster too."

Kazue was absolutely serious. And, in the end she did become a full-fledged monster. Of course, at that moment I couldn't have imagined how things would turn out. What? You think Kazue turned out the way she did in response to what I did back then? You're saying I'm responsible for her eccentricity? I don't believe that for a minute. No. What I believe is that there is something implicit in everyone, which forms that person's character and is responsible for everything else. There was something inside Kazue herself that was accountable for the change in her appearance. I'm sure of that.

"You really eat like a bird. You must overeat at breakfast," I said maliciously.

Kazue shook her head vigorously. "No way. I only drink a bottle of milk."

"Really? The other day when I was visiting you ate everything on your plate. You even gulped down the dipping sauce."

Offended, Kazue glared at me. "Well, I don't do that anymore. I'm watching what I eat. After all, I want to be as beautiful as a model."

Just then I thought of something very cruel. If she were to be any thinner than she already was, she would look so horrible there's no way anyone could be attracted to her.

"Yes, you're absolutely right. If you lost just a little bit more weight you'd be perfect," I said.

"I know. That's what I think too." Kazue lifted her skirt bashfully. "My legs are so fat. They've told me at practice that the thinner you are the lighter, which makes it easier to skate."

"All you need to do is try just a little bit more. Kijima is thin too, you know."

Kazue nodded with conviction when she heard what I said. Then she noted happily, "If I were a little thinner, I'd be pretty, and Kijima and I would look really good together."

She wrapped her empty lunch box in a tomato-stained handkerchief. Mitsuru appeared, her book tucked under her arm. She tapped me on the shoulder, "Yuriko's here. She said she has something to tell you."

Yuriko? How many times had I told her never, ever to come looking for me? Surprised, I turned toward the hallway. She was standing in the doorway with Kijima Junior, looking in at me. Kazue still hadn't noticed them, so I gave her a quick shove.

"It's Kijima."

Kazue's cheeks turned beet red and she became completely flustered. *What'll I do? What'll I do? I'm not ready for him to see me yet! What'll I do?* This was written all over her face.

I stood up. "Don't worry. They've come to talk to me."

"But you told Yuriko that I like Kijima, didn't you?"

"I didn't tell her."

I left her to her panic and headed toward my two visitors. Yuriko stared at me as I approached her. She stood straight as a ramrod and was now more than four inches taller than I was. The arms that hung from her short-sleeved blouse were long and slender and beautifully shaped. Even her fingers were gorgeous.

"What do you want?"

I noticed Kijima Junior flinch in surprise at the rudeness of my tone.

"Professor Kijima's my supervising instructor; I think you already know that. Anyway, he's asked me to fill out an information sheet about my family, and I don't know what I should write. I think it'll be weird if you and I don't have the same answers."

"Why don't you fill it in with information about Johnson and Masami?"

"But Johnson's not really family. Unless he's more than family?"

Kijima Junior smiled slyly and stared at Yuriko's face. At that moment I saw Yuriko blush. A light glimmered in her eyes. Anger gives birth to determination—and in Yuriko's eyes I saw the glimmer of determination. Yuriko had no business possessing determination. I would have to trample out whatever it was that had given birth to it.

"I filled the blanks in with information about you and Father. But if Professor Kijima asks me about it, I'll just tell him to come talk to you."

"Fine."

I looked at Kijima Junior. "Aren't you Professor Kijima's son?"

"Yeah. What's it to you?" He glared back at me. Clearly he hated nothing more than being asked about his father.

"It's just that Professor Kijima's such a great teacher, that's all."

"Well, at home he's a great dad too." Kijima parried.

"You and Yuriko are always together. You must be really good friends."

"Well, that's because I'm her manager," Takashi responded playfully. He stuffed both hands in his pockets and shrugged his shoulders. Those two were up to something. And I was so eager to find out what it was, I could hardly contain myself.

"What kind of manager would that be?"

"I do a little of this and a little of that. Oh, and by the way, Yuriko has decided she'll join the cheerleading squad."

Now isn't that ironic, I thought, as I turned to look back at Kazue. She was looking down, pretending she wasn't the least bit interested. But I knew every fiber in her body was trained on us.

"Kijima, what do you think of that girl there?"

Takashi glanced over at Kazue and shrugged without the slightest interest. Yuriko looked annoyed and tugged on his arm.

"Kijima, let's go."

When Yuriko turned to walk away, it suddenly dawned on me. She was no longer the little girl who had chased after me along the snowy road that night. Just six months ago, when she set off for Switzerland, she hardly ever spoke out, but now that she'd been separated from me she seemed much more assertive.

"Yuriko?" I asked, as I grabbed her arm. "What happened to you in Switzerland?"

Was her body temperature low? Yuriko's arm was icy cold. What was the point of my question? It was obvious, I suppose, and also extremely ill-tempered. But I wanted to induce her to tell me what I had already discerned—she'd had sex with a man. She was no longer a virgin.

But Yuriko surprised me.

"I lost the person I loved the most."

"Who?"

"Don't tell me you've forgotten already." The glimmer in Yuriko's eye intensified momentarily, as if it were a flame. "Our mother, of course."

She looked down at me with contempt. Her face twisted, the light in her eyes flickered, and her expression turned to one of sorrow. I longed to make that face of hers even more hideous than it was right then.

"And you don't look even one bit like her!"

"Resemblance is meaningless." With that as her parting shot, Yuriko latched onto Takashi's shoulder. "Kijima, I've had enough. Let's get out of here."

Kijima barely had time to turn around before Yuriko dragged him off. But he did manage to gaze back at me with a curious stare. Yes, that's right. I was completely taken with the question of resemblance, and I would continue to be. I am even now. I don't know why.

Before I could return to my seat, Kazue dashed over to me and began her grilling.

"Hey, what were you talking about with them? You were out there a long time."

"Oh, a lot of things. You didn't come up in the conversation, though."

Kazue lowered her unnaturally double-lidded lids and thought about it for a moment before asking, "What should I do to get Kijima to notice me?"

"Why don't you write him a letter?"

Kazue's face lit up at my suggestion. "What a great idea! I'll write a letter. But before I send it could I show it to you? It would help to get an impartial opinion."

Impartial? My lips twisted into a smile. I noticed that the smile was an imitation of the one Yuriko had used earlier.

· 2 ·

Can you guess what I did that night? I was imprisoned by the notion of resemblance. When I came to this realization, I made up my mind to press my grandfather for some answers. I wanted to know who my father was. Of course, I already knew I was half. There could be no denying that. I knew my mother was Japanese, and I was convinced that my father had to have been from a different country. Well, look at my skin. It's not yellow, is it? Well, is it?

But I was absolutely certain that my father could not be the same Swiss who had fathered Yuriko. Why? Well for starters we don't look a bit alike. And in the second place, how could such a mediocre man have fathered such a clearheaded child as myself? It certainly wasn't likely. Besides, my father's treatment of me was abusive. He always kept me at arm's length, and though he had no trouble scolding me, I never once felt any love from him.

Ever since we were children, Yuriko would pick on me because we looked so little alike. Oh? You can't imagine Yuriko ever picking on me? Why not? Is it because she's beautiful? Well, looks can be deceiving. Yuriko was ten times more spiteful and vicious than I ever was. She had absolutely no qualms about boring straight through my heart. "I wonder where your daddy is, huh?" she would chide me. "Because you don't look a bit like *my* daddy." This was always her ultimate weapon.

I realized that my Swiss father was not my real father when I first became aware of Yuriko's existence. True, Yuriko did not resemble anyone, but she clearly had both Asian and Western features. And the fact that she was dumb made her even more the spitting image of our parents. I also did not resemble anyone and yet, unlike Yuriko, my face was more clearly Asian-looking. And I was smart. So where did I come from? Ever since I was old enough to be aware of things I was racked with doubt about my parentage. Who was my father?

Once during science class I thought I'd found the answer to my question: I was a mutation. But the euphoria of my discovery soon evaporated. It was far more likely that the beautiful Yuriko was the mutant. Once that theory was shot to hell I was back where I started: perplexed, chagrined, and completely without an answer to the question that tormented me and would continue to torment me. Even now I have no answer. And Yuriko's return to Japan brought all my doubts back to the surface again.

.

My grandfather seemed to have gone out for the evening; at least he wasn't home. And he hadn't made any dinner preparations. So, lacking an alternative, I started rinsing the rice. I took the tofu out of the refrigerator and made miso soup. We had nothing else in the house—no side dish of any kind—so I suspected my grandfather had gone out to buy something and waited for his return. Night fell. I waited, and still he did not return. It was close to ten o'clock when I heard the front door open.

"You're late!"

"Oops," Grandfather mumbled. I went to the entry hall and found him bowing his head in a playful show of contrition, just like a child being scolded. Huh? I thought to myself, Grandfather's gotten taller! He was slipping out of a pair of snug-fitting brown shoes I'd never seen before. When I looked closer at them, sitting on the entryway floor, I saw they had heels as high as a woman's shoe.

"What's with the shoes?"

"These are known as *secret boots*!"

"Where on earth do they sell shoes like that?"

"What's wrong with them?" Grandfather scratched his head bashfully. The smell of pomade that wafted around his shoulders was particularly pungent. Grandfather was very self-conscious and never went without his pomade, even when he was just puttering around the apartment, but that night he had used more than twice the usual amount. I held my nose and scrutinized him. His brown suit, which I'd never seen him wear before, did not fit properly, and he had borrowed a blue shirt from his friend the security guard. I knew this was the case because I remembered seeing the security guard wearing the shirt with great pride sometime earlier. Besides, it was obvious he was wearing a borrowed shirt because the sleeves hung out below the sleeves of his jacket. To top it off, he was wearing a very bright silver-colored necktie.

"Sorry. You must be starved," he said, and handed me a small wrapped parcel. He was in good spirits. I caught the whiff of grilled eel. The odor was so strong I thought for a minute I might faint. The package was stained with sauce and still lukewarm. I took it in both hands and stood there for a moment without saying anything. My grandfather looked so strange. Maybe he had gotten over his obsession with bonsai. But how was he able to buy new clothes and shoes? Where was he getting the money?

"Grandpa, is that a new suit?"

"I bought it at the Nakaya in front of the station," he replied, as he smoothed the fabric with his hands. "It's a little large, but I think I look like a playboy when I wear it. You know me, I'm a sucker for luxury. And they recommended this tie. They said a silver tie would show up well on a suit like this. If you look closely you'll notice the material is patterned. It looks like snake scales, doesn't it? And when it catches the light it glimmers. I went over to the Kitamura Store on the other side of the station for the shoes. I'm a short fella, you know, and others tend to look down on me, which I can't tolerate. So I've been on a bit of a shopping spree. This shirt's the only thing I didn't buy—I was feeling a little guilty about all the spending—so I borrowed it from my buddy upstairs. But don't you think the color works well with the suit? It would be better if I had French cuffs, though. As soon as I can find a good shirt with French cuffs, I'm going to buy it. That'll be my next purchase."

Grandfather looked down regretfully at his shirtsleeves. They really did flap loosely, extending as they did all the way to his slender fingers. I pointed to the package, "So what's with the eel? Did someone give it to you?"

"Oh, right. Hurry and eat it. I thought you could use it for your lunch tomorrow so I bought extra."

"I asked if someone gave it to you?"

"And I said I'd bought it, didn't I?" Grandfather answered gruffly. "I had a little change left." He finally noticed that I was angry.

"Did you go to Mitsuru's mother's bar?"

"Yes, I did. Do you have a problem with that?"

"You went last night too. You sure have money to burn."

Grandfather opened the door to the veranda with a loud racket and gazed out. I suddenly had a sickening premonition and rushed to the veranda. Two or three of his plants were missing.

"Grandpa, did you sell your bonsai?"

Grandfather made no reply. He picked up the large pot containing the black pine and rubbed his cheeks affectionately against the pine needles.

"And do you plan to sell that one tomorrow?"

"No, I'll die before I sell this one. Even if the Garden of Longevity offers me thirty million yen for it."

If I let my grandfather do as he pleased, before long he'd sell off all his bonsai, and whatever profit they provided would be sucked up between the Garden of Longevity and the Blue River. Our life would hit rock bottom.

"Was Mitsuru's mother there?"

"She was."

"What did the two of you talk about?"

"She was busy, you know. She couldn't sit there and entertain me the whole time."

She. There was something about the way he said it that sounded so affectionate. A strong power seemed to emanate from my grandfather's body, an essence I had not encountered before, strong but soft. I could feel Yuriko's influence; her presence was changing everyone. I wanted to cover my eyes and ears. Grandfather turned around and looked back at me. There was a trace of fear in his face. I think he realized that I found his newfound love offensive.

"What did you and Mitsuru's mother talk about?"

"I told you we didn't have time for a real conversation. She's the owner of the bar, for crying out loud."

"But you went out and ate eel somewhere."

"True. She said she could slip away from the other girls for a spell and asked me to join her. She took me to some expensive place on the other side of the river. I was a bit nervous, never having been to such a fancy eel restaurant before. I drank liver broth for the first time, too. It's pretty good. I told her I wished I could give you a taste, that it was too bad you had to be at home alone, so she ordered this serving for me to bring home to you. She said it was really sad about you losing your mother and you were really brave to be coping so well on your own. She really is a nice lady."

Why, I wondered, would she speak to my grandfather as if she were some kind of heavenly maiden? Even Mitsuru criticized her—her own mother!

When I remembered that morning in the car I felt my breast fill with an anger for Mitsuru's mother that was so sharp it threatened to explode.

"So the eel was a gift?"

"Well, you got me there."

When Grandfather tried to brush it off I was ready. "And if I tell Mitsuru's mother that you've been in prison, what then? I bet it'd give her a shock."

Grandfather removed his suit jacket without saying a thing. The space between his eyebrows wrinkled into a crease. I wanted to say whatever I could to upset him, but that was because I wanted everything to stay just like it was, with the two of us living happily among his bonsai. Here he was, threatening to ruin everything by heading off into that repulsive realm of love—just like Yuriko. Traitor!

"If anyone's going to tell her it'll be me," my grandfather said, with a deep sigh. Just then he lost his footing and tripped over his trouser leg, stumbling a few paces before regaining his balance. Without his secret boots, the trousers were too long and trailed behind him like the hem of a samurai's court costume. I couldn't help but burst out laughing. First Kazue and her fake eyelids and now this. The lengths stupid people will go to for love! I was filled with hatred and an irritation so great I thought I would go insane.

"Grandpa, is she inspired?"

Grandfather looked back at me with surprise. Frustrated, I asked again, the anger in my voice rising. "Mitsuru's mother. I asked if she's inspired."

"Oh, that. Yes, she's nothing but."

I was racked with disappointment. How could my grandfather, who had spent his days puttering with his bonsai spewing out words like *crazy* and *inspiration*, now be calling a frumpy middle-aged woman inspired?

What was going on? Earlier, Grandfather had said Yuriko was too beautiful to be inspired; the change was too bizarre to imagine. I began to feel my love for my grandfather withering and spoke to him sharply. "Fine. Then I have something to talk to you about."

Grandfather hung his jacket neatly on a hanger and looked up at me. "What now?"

"Who's my father? Where is he?"

"Who's your father? Are you serious? You know he's that Swiss bastard." Grandfather slipped the belt off his trouser, now in a sour mood. "Who else would it be but him?"

"That's a lie. That man's not my father."

"Do we have to get into this now?"

Grandfather stepped out of his trousers and sat on the tatami mat, looking suddenly very tired. "Are you dreaming? Your mother is my daughter. Your father is that Swiss. I was opposed to the wedding but your mother wouldn't listen and went ahead with it anyway. So, you see, you're wrong."

"But I don't look like either of them—or anyone else, for that matter."

"Looks. Is that what this is all about? I already told you, the people in my family rarely look like anyone else."

Grandfather gazed at me perplexed, as if he couldn't quite understand why I would be so upset. I was disappointed, so distraught I just wanted to hurl that disgusting package of food to the floor. Before I could act on the impulse, I had a frightening thought. What if my mother went to her death with the secret hidden from us all?

"Check the family registry. It'll all be listed there," Grandfather said, as he pulled his necktie off, busily smoothing the wrinkles out with his hands. But I knew that wouldn't do any good. My father was a handsome and intelligent white man, perhaps French or British. He would have abandoned my mother and gone off to wander on his own. Maybe he's already dead. If so, I can never contact him. Or maybe he is waiting for me to grow up so he can contact me.

I had always lived with this strange sense of distance from my father, a distance I could not bridge. All you could say about our relationship was that we never got along. When my father spoke to Yuriko, his voice was always natural. But whenever he had to deal with me he was full of tension. I would immediately notice the way the lines would form at the sides of his lips. Whenever we came face-to-face, we had nothing to talk about, and it was clear he had to search long and hard for something to say.

Occasionally, when my father returned from work, he'd press me with questions. Whenever that happened I knew he was in a bad mood and I ought to exercise caution. But on the contrary, I would feel a rebellious urge course through me, compelling me to engage my father in an argument.

When my parents argued it was unbearable. But Yuriko would just sit there nonchalantly watching TV. When my father and I fought she would sneak out of the room, but when our parents fought she didn't seem to care. Was she really that dense? Or couldn't she bear to watch my father and me fight?

When my parents fought it was almost always about household expenses. In our family, our father was in charge of the money. Mother would get just enough from him every day to go to the market and buy provisions for dinner. As I said before, my father was a miser, and he tended to go over every little detail, far more thoroughly than anyone could possibly imagine.

"You bought spinach yesterday. There's no reason you need to buy more today."

My mother tried to launch a futile defense. "Do you know how much spinach you have after you boil it?" She took an imaginary bundle of spinach and piled it on her palm.

Father took the imaginary bundle up in his palm to show how the spinach would expand.

"Well, it's obvious you don't do any cooking," Mother would say, "because you don't know what you're talking about; it shrinks. If you split this much among four people, it'll be gone in a day's time. That's why you need two days' worth. If you boil it and make a chilled spinach salad it'll be gone in no time. If you slice it up with carrots and sauté it with meat that'd be fine, but it doesn't really go well with what we eat. I've tried to accommodate myself to the food you want me to serve in this house; you just don't know."

And on and on she went, to no avail.

My father just assumed that whatever he did was right, and he grew furious with anyone who tried to challenge that assumption. Next to Yuriko, I hated him the most. To cut to the chase, I had a very lonely childhood and grew up disliking everyone in my family. Really pathetic, don't you agree? That's why I thought it was so bizarre that Kazue Satō was able to accept her father's values so unconditionally. I just couldn't understand how someone could be such a daddy's girl. It made me despise her all the more.

My relationship with my father was as I just described it. And I never once loved a man or had sexual relations with one. I'm not a nymphomaniac like Yuriko.

I can't think of any creature more disgusting than a man, with his hard muscles and bones, his sweaty skin, all that hair on his body, and his knobby knees. I hate men with deep voices and bodies that smell like animal fat, men who act like bullies and never comb their hair. Oh, yes, there is no end to the nasty things I can say about men. I'm just lucky to have a job at the ward office so I don't have to commute to work every day on the crowded trains. I don't think I could stand riding jammed in a car with a bunch of smelly salary men.

But then, I'm not a lesbian either. I would never do something so filthy. True, I did have a bit of a crush on Mitsuru when we were in high school. But that was more like ardent respect, and it was short-lived besides. When I noticed Mitsuru honing her intellect like a weapon, I understood and felt a kind of admiration for her. But something happened that forced a falling-out between Mitsuru and me.

•

A number of weeks had passed since my grandfather started going off to the Blue River. He raised money for his little adventures by selling off his bonsai. I felt sad every time I looked at the emptying veranda—bitter and almost beyond despair. That's when it happened, one day when I was wrapped in a sense of desolation.

I'd just finished my art class. I had elected to take calligraphy. The art instructor had told us to write any word we liked, so I had splashed out the word *inspiration* in a wild scrawl. When I got back to homeroom, Mitsuru, who had just returned from music class, waved a sheet of music at me, signaling for me to come over. I was already in a foul mood, since I'd managed to get ink stains on my blouse. And Mitsuru's buoyant voice made me all the more irritable. She'd been studying hard for the upcoming midterms, and her eyes were red from lack of sleep.

"I've got something to tell you. Is now okay?"

I stared at the red veins that formed a crazy pattern in the whites of Mitsuru's eyes and nodded.

"My mother wants to have dinner with you, your grandfather, and me. The four of us. What do you say?"

"Why?"

I feigned ignorance. Mitsuru tapped her front teeth with her fingernail and cocked her head to the side.

"Well, it looks like my mother has taken an interest in you. You live nearby, so she said she'd like to have a chance for a nice leisurely talk sometime. If it's all right we can meet at our house, or we can go out somewhere for a meal, our treat."

"Why do you and I have to go? Wouldn't it make more sense for your mother and my grandfather to go out by themselves?"

Mitsuru hated unreasonableness. I saw the light flicker through her eyes as if she were struggling to solve a riddle.

"What do you mean by that?"

"You should ask your mother. It's not my place to explain."

That was the first time I'd ever seen Mitsuru angry. Her face flushed red and she looked as if her eyes would shoot daggers.

"You have no right to be rude. If you have something to say, say it. I don't like playing games."

When I heard the tears creep into her voice, I knew I had hurt her feelings. Mitsuru was touchy when it came to her mother. But I had to tell her what I thought.

"All right, then. My grandfather is head over heels in love with your mother. There's nothing wrong with that, in and of itself, and it really has nothing to do with me. But I don't want to get dragged into the middle of it. I refuse to be some kind of pawn in their little love game."

"What are you getting at?"

Mitsuru's face had turned from red to white and was growing whiter by the minute.

"My grandfather's become a regular at your mother's bar, you know. Since he doesn't have any money, he's sold off all his bonsai. It's got nothing to do with me. But why does your mother want to get involved with my grandfather? I think it's strange. I mean, my grandfather is nearly sixty-seven, and your mother's not yet fifty, is she? Of course, age doesn't matter when people are in love, but I'm just really, really uncomfortable when everything gets ruined with lust. Maybe it's on account of my sister—but you've changed recently too. And now my grandfather's acting weird. Ever since Yuriko's come back, everything seems to be falling apart and I can't stand it. Do you understand?"

"No, I don't understand." Mitsuru's response was calm. She shook her head slowly. "You're not making a bit of sense. But one thing I do understand: you won't permit your grandfather to spend time with my mother."

It wasn't a question of my permission; that was even worse. It was just that I hated people in love because people in love betray me. I fell silent. When I didn't respond, Mitsuru continued.

"You are a very childish person. I don't care what my mother does. But you make it sound like my mother's behaving despicably, and I can't stand to hear another word from you. I will never speak to you or spend time with you again. Satisfied?"

"I guess I have no choice in the matter."

I shrugged my shoulders. And so for half a year I did not have any contact with Mitsuru.

· 3 ·

Well, I think we need to work our way back to Kazue Satō, don't you? What's that? Yes, I can well believe you don't want to hear any more about my grandfather and Mitsuru's mother and their disgusting love story. But actually there's an interesting sequel. You see, Mitsuru passed the qualifying exam to enter Tokyo University Medical School, just as she'd intended. I know this because she contacted me after I'd matriculated into the German Language Division of Q University. At the same time, a number of problems occurred. It doesn't have a direct connection to the Yuriko and Kazue stories, but I'd like to talk about it eventually.

•

When was it that Kazue Satō's bizarre behavior began to grow really obvious? It was probably around the time we were in our second year of high school. Yuriko was in her first year, and I heard rumors that Kazue had started following her around. To use the current lingo, I suppose you could call her a stalker. It was horrifying. Kazue would peek into Yuriko's classroom. When she was in gym, Kazue would spy on her. If Yuriko attended a game with the cheerleaders, Kazue would be there. She was just like a dog following its master. She probably even sniffed around the Johnsons' house as well. And whenever she ran into Yuriko, she would follow her with her eyes, watching Yuriko as if she were under some kind of spell. What would motivate Kazue to want to stalk Yuriko? Even I couldn't figure that one out.

Wherever Yuriko was, there was always a commotion. Once Kijima Junior advanced to the Q High School for Young Men in a different part of the city, Mokku, the daughter of the soy sauce company president, took his place and trailed after Yuriko like poop from a goldfish.

Mokku was the manager of the cheerleaders' squad. As such she was, in effect, Yuriko's bodyguard, and she went wherever Yuriko went, protecting her from fans as well as from those who coveted her position and were envious of her. Yuriko was the squad mascot. Well, that's the point, isn't it? You couldn't expect an uncoordinated airhead like Yuriko to master the complicated moves in the cheerleaders' routines. All Yuriko was supposed to do was stand there like some kind of billboard, proving to the world that the Q School cheerleaders had raised their standards of beauty.

When the statuesque Yuriko strode through the school grounds with Mokku, her presence was so overwhelming that no one could take their eyes off her. I was amazed at how conceited she looked. She walked slightly ahead of Mokku, her face impassive, as if she were some kind of queen. Mokku, for her part, followed after her like a handmaiden. And then here'd come Kazue, right behind them, panting hard to keep up. It certainly was a peculiar sight.

Occasionally I'd notice that the minute Kazue ate her lunch, she'd run to the bathroom to throw it up. I say lunch, but there really wasn't much to it: just a tiny rice ball and a tomato or a piece of fruit. Kazue often brought a cheap kind of cookie made from soy flour. But as soon as she'd eat it she'd be so overcome with remorse that she'd rush off to the toilet to puke. Everyone in the class knew what she was doing, so whenever Kazue would start rustling through that sack of cookies, the other students would poke one another with their elbows and titter knowingly. Yes, Kazue had an eating disorder. Of course, at the time we didn't know there were such diseases. We just resented Kazue for her unbalanced diet and her habit of throwing up after a meal.

I heard that her reputation in the ice skating club was really bad. No matter how many requisitions she got, she never paid the rink fees. She wore her competition uniform even during practice sessions and swished around the rink oblivious to everything. It seemed like only a matter of time before she would be asked to leave the team, and yet surprisingly that never happened. That was because Kazue was useful when it came time to borrow her notes for exams. Kazue lent her notes to club members free of charge but from other classmates she demanded payment, one hundred yen for one class day's worth of notes. At that time Kazue was incredibly fixated on money. Most people grumbled behind her back that she was stingy.

Kazue had completely changed by the latter half of freshman year. At first she had tried her best to meld with the affluent atmosphere of Q High School for Young Women. But in the winter she suddenly changed. After I was in the university I heard someone say that the shift in her life came about later, when her father died, but as far as I could tell, Kazue had already undergone a change in appearance by the start of our second high school year.

I also noticed that Kazue had begun subjecting her teachers to an intense litany of questions during class. The teachers would soon grow impatient. "Okay, let's move on to the next question," they'd say, glancing at their watches, only to have Kazue complain, in a tear-choked voice, "But professor, I still don't understand." Even though the rest of the students in the class would roll their eyes in frustration, she didn't care. I don't think Kazue ever paid attention to the reactions of those around her. She gradually began to lose all awareness of her current reality. Whenever the teacher asked a question to which Kazue knew the answer, she would be the first to stick up her hand, a triumphant look on her face. And when she wrote down the answers to questions, she always covered her paper with her hand—just as if she'd returned to the days when she was a competitive elementary school student. Oh, yes. She was, without a doubt, such a weirdo no one wanted anything to do with her.

But I hung out with her. You understand, don't you? Kazue was hung up on a hopeless relationship and frustrated as a result. I'm talking about Takashi Kijima, of course. I wanted to see what I could do to ensure that the love Kazue harbored for Kijima swelled like a balloon. Kazue had taken my advice and written Kijima any number of letters. She always showed them to me first. I would make my corrections and send them back to her. And then Kazue would write them over again and again, never really certain that they were good enough to send. Would you like to see the letters? I'll show them to you. You wonder why I have them? Well, that's because I copied each one in my notebook before I sent it back to her.

Please forgive the informality of this letter. I realize it must seem rude to write you out of the blue like this. Please forgive me.

If I may, I'd like to begin with a self-introduction. My name is Kazue Satō and I'm in the B group of the first-year high school students. My goal is to advance to the economics division of the university and study economics. For that reason I apply myself to my studies every day, and if I say so myself I am a very serious student. I belong to the ice-skating club. I'm still too wet behind the ears to compete. (Or wet behind the toes, as the case may be.) But I'm practicing as hard as I can with dreams of someday competing. I fall a lot, so after practice I'm always covered in bruises. The seniors on the team tell me that's what it takes. So I'm really enthusiastic about training.

My hobbies are handicrafts and keeping a diary. I've kept a diary since I was in first grade and haven't missed a day yet. Now if I don't make an entry for the day, I'm so upset I can't sleep. I heard that you weren't in any club, Takashi. Do you have any hobbies?

I'm now in biology class with your father, Professor Kijima. He's a great teacher. He's able to explain even the most difficult things in very simple language. I have such respect for his skill in the classroom and his noble character. Q High School for Young Women has so many exceptional teachers like Professor Kijima, it just makes me grateful that I was able to enter the school. Takashi, I heard that you've been receiving your training in the Q system ever since you were little, on account of Professor Kijima being your father. You are so fortunate.

I'm a little embarrassed to do so, but I have a confession to make. Even though I'm a year ahead of you in school, I have a crush on you. I don't have any brothers, only a younger sister, so I don't know much about men. If you don't mind, would you write back? I'll dream of the day I hear from you. Until then, please accept this letter. And good luck with your midterm exams.

Kazue Satō

This was the first letter she sent. When I saw the second letter I burst out laughing in spite of myself. That's because of the poem "The Path Where Violets Bloom." When she showed it to me she said she wanted to have the folksinger Banban Hirofumi sing it.

The Path Where Violets Bloom

Wild violet, at my feet
The path where you have trod.
While plucking a broken bloom
I know you've passed this way.
Wild violet, blooming along the path
Into the sky overflowing with your heart,
I gaze afar and while I cry
I meet you on your way home.
Wild violet, I cannot see,
Cannot search for your love.
Bewildered, afraid,
The mountain road, the precipice below.

Once Kazue showed me a haiku or something by Toshizo Hijikata, the famous swordsman who tried to thwart the Meiji Restoration in the nineteenth century. I think it was his verse: "To know is to stray; to not know is to not stray—the path of love." Kazue copied the verse neatly onto a sheet of stationery with the note: *This is exactly how I feel.* She folded the stationery into four folds and slipped it into a regular envelope. Kazue may have been able to see her studies through successfully, but when it came to love she was not only immature but extremely old-fashioned.

"Hey, what do you think of this? Do you think I should go ahead and send it?" Kazue asked, as she showed me what she'd written. I was half terrified when I saw it and half elated. A week had gone by since her first letter. I advised her to send the second to his house as well. Why was I terrified, you ask? Because I knew that people in love are capable of behaving stupidly. Don't you find it scary too? Kazue had exposed her lack of sense and talent without the slightest qualm and had clearly revealed her shame to the recipient of her missives without even considering the consequences.

Of course Takashi didn't answer. Under normal circumstances the girl would have taken this as evidence that the boy had no interest in her. But Kazue was only confused.

"Why hasn't he responded? Do you think maybe he didn't get my letters?" Her eyes with their ridiculous double lids, compliments of Elizabeth Eyelids, opened wide. Her pupils glittered with light. And her body, which was even thinner than before, gave off a peculiar aura: her whole body glowed. She looked like some kind of swamp creature. So even a creature as ugly as this can fall in love? I was so creeped out by Kazue I couldn't bear to look at her straight on. But there she was, pulling on my arm and wheedling. "Hey, hey, what do you think? What? What do you think I should do?"

"Why don't you go call Takashi over and ask him yourself."

"I couldn't do something like that!"

Kazue blanched and shrunk back.

"Then get him a Christmas present and ask him when you hand it to him."

When Kazue heard my suggestion, her face lit up.

"I'll knit him a scarf!"

"That's a great idea! All boys are suckers for handmade goods."

I looked around the classroom. It was November and there were any number of girls clicking away at their knitting, making their boyfriends sweaters and scarves and such.

"Thanks! That's what I'll do."

Now that Kazue had a new goal, she calmed down. Once again a glimmer of confidence returned to her face. She was encouraging herself; I'm sure that's what she was doing. Her profile at such a time looked exactly like a certain man. You got it: like her father. On the day my mother died, when Kazue's father told me never to associate with Kazue again, he had that same haughty air about him.

•

It was close to Christmas, and the scarf that Kazue was knitting for Takashi was now over a yard long. It was incredibly ugly: black and yellow stripes that reminded me of a honeybee's butt. I imagined Takashi with the scarf wrapped around his neck and had a more difficult time than usual trying to stifle my laughter.

It was a winter afternoon, almost night, when I phoned Takashi's house. His father had a faculty meeting that day so I knew he wouldn't be home yet. Takashi himself answered the phone, his voice unexpectedly brisk and bright. No doubt about it, Takashi was a different person at home from who he was in school. It gave me the creeps.

"Hello? Kijima residence."

"This is Yuriko's older sister. Is this Takashi?"

"Yes. So you're the sister who looks nothing like Yuriko. What do you want with me?"

Kijima had quickly lost his pleasant telephone voice and brought his tone down an octave.

"Thank you for all you've done for Yuriko," I began formulaically. "To tell the truth, I have a favor to ask of you."

I could tell that Takashi was growing cautious. I thought of his shifty little eyes and began to feel queasy. Eager to hang up, I got right down to business.

"It's difficult to discuss by phone, but I know you won't meet me so I'll just cut to the chase. You've gotten letters from my classmate Kazue Satō, haven't you?"

I could hear Takashi catch his breath.

"Kazue wants to know if you'll return her letters. She's so embarrassed she can hardly stand it."

"Why doesn't she ask me herself?"

"She cried when I asked her and said she just couldn't bring herself to call you. So I'm doing it for her."

"She was crying?"

Takashi became quiet all of a sudden. I hadn't expected this. Suddenly I could feel unease rise within me. What would I do if things didn't go as I planned?

"Kazue bitterly regrets sending you those letters."

Takashi was silent for a while. Finally he answered, "Really? Well, I was impressed a bit. I thought the poem was especially nice."

"What part did you like?"

"Well, it was innocent and sweet."

"You're lying!" I found myself shouting. He was just too snide to bear. There was no way Takashi could have liked that pathetic poem.

But Takashi answered lightheartedly, "No, really. But Yuriko and I are involved in activities that have very little to do with purity."

"What are you talking about?"

My radar suddenly zoomed in on the secret passion emerging from Yuriko and Takashi. I could smell something evil brewing. I forgot all about Kazue and started thinking about what Takashi meant. But Takashi broke in hurriedly with exaggeratedly fast speech.

"It doesn't matter, does it? My little side job with Yuriko has nothing to do with you."

"A side job? What kind of work are you two doing? You should tell me, I *am* Yuriko's older sister, after all."

I braced myself for Takashi's response. They were doing something to earn money. And whatever it was had "very little to do with purity." I suddenly recalled that the last time I'd seen Yuriko, a thin gold chain glittered around her neck. Just visible beneath her uniform blouse was a lacy brassiere, and on her feet were slip-on shoes with red and green braided ribbon. No doubt they were Gucci. I was sure she didn't have much of an allowance. How was she able to afford clothes that were so well suited to the Q School atmosphere? No, more than just well suited, Yuriko was leading the pack when it came to fashion. I was now beside myself with curiosity. I held the receiver away from my ear and tried to think of a way to find out their secret. I guess I was silent too long because before long I heard Takashi shouting snidely, "Hello! You still there? Hello? What's going on?"

"Oh, sorry. Now, what was that job you two are doing?"

"Forget it. What is it you want me to do with Satō's letters?"

Takashi had changed the subject. I had no choice but to track down the answer to my question some other way. Resigned, I returned to Kazue.

"Kazue is embarrassed. She asked me to call you, so that's what I'm doing."

"This is weird. I'm the one who received the letters, but now I'm supposed to return them? Why does she want them back?"

"Look, Kazue is really upset about this. If you don't send them back she says she'll slit her wrists or something like that. Maybe she'll swallow sleeping pills, I don't know. Just send them back as soon as you can."

"Okay!" Takashi responded as if he were fed up. "I'll give them to her tomorrow."

"No, that's no good," I raised my voice. "You have to send them to her house."

"Should I mail them?"

I could tell Takashi was getting to be a bit suspicious.

"Mail is fine. Just write her address and last name on the envelope, that's all you need to do. Don't put anything else with the letters, okay? And if possible, send them registered express."

No sooner had I finished my sentence then I slammed the phone down. That should do the trick. I was sure Kazue would be horrified once the letters she'd sent had been returned to her. And if I had any luck at all, her father would discover them and go ballistic. Now, if I was really lucky, I'd manage to figure out what Yuriko and Takashi were up to. Suddenly going to school had become fun again.

•

Kazue missed school for several days. On the morning of the fourth day she turned up unexpectedly and stood in the doorway of the classroom like a giant roadblock. She surveyed the room with dark eyes. Her hair was no longer in curls and no longer was she hopelessly gluing those fake Elizabeth Eyelids over her eyes. The familiar dreary, uncool Kazue had returned, except for the fact that an unbelievably gaudy scarf, striped in yellow and black, was wrapped around her neck. The scarf she had knitted for Takashi curled around her like an enormous famished snake.

When the other students entered the class and saw Kazue, most looked flustered and quickly turned their eyes away as if they'd just seen something they were not supposed to see. But clearly oblivious, Kazue sauntered over to one of the girls on the ice-skating team who had earlier borrowed her notes.

"Kazue, what happened to you?"

Kazue stared up at the student as if in a daze, embarrassed.

"You can't go and take time off before the test!"

"I'm sorry."

"You can at least lend me your English and Classics notes."

Kazue nodded timidly, over and over. She plopped her school satchel down on the desk in front of her. Not surprisingly, the student who was sitting there looked up at Kazue angrily. She was an insider with very savvy fashion sense, well known for being good at baking cookies and cakes. She was reading a cookbook when Kazue interrupted her.

"Hey, you can't just go slamming stuff down on other people's desks, you know. I'm trying to figure out what cookies to bake. Show a little consideration."

"I'm sorry."

Kazue bowed again and again in apology. The unusual aura that had earlier suffused Kazue's entire body was now nowhere to be found. Instead she looked peaked and ugly, like a fruit squeezed of all its juice.

"Look here, you got some mud on my book! How can you be so rude?"

Miss Cookbook made a big show of wiping off her book. Kazue had probably set her satchel down on the train platform while she was on her way to school, or she'd rested it on the sidewalk and the bottom had gotten soiled. A number of students who heard what the girl had to say flushed slightly with excitement at her words, but the rest just pretended not to hear. Kazue handed over her notes and then, drenched in the student's belittling gaze, retraced her steps to her own desk. She turned back to look at me for support. I instinctively looked away, but not before I could sense what she was thinking. *Help me. Get me out of here!* I suddenly remembered that snowy night in the mountains when Yuriko had chased after me. That overwhelming impulse to use all my strength to ward off something horrible. The exhilarating feeling following the moment I thrust her away. I wanted to do the same to Kazue now, so badly I could hardly stand it. Finally, the first-period math class ended—without Kazue's badgering the teacher with her usual endless questions.

"Hey. Hey? Can I ask you something?" As soon as classes had been dismissed, before I could get away, I heard Kazue's pathetic voice coming up behind me. I had already begun heading down the second-floor corridor.

"What? What is it?"

I whirled around and looked at Kazue straight on, causing her to avert her eyes, a pained expression on her face.

"It's about Takashi."

"Oh? Did you get an answer from him?"

"Yes. Yes, I did," Kazue answered reluctantly. "Four days ago."

"That's terrific! What did he say?"

I pretended to be excited—all the while waiting gleefully to see how Kazue would answer. It was going to be so great. But Kazue pursed her lips and said nothing. I guess she was searching for a good excuse.

"Come on, what did he say?" I asked impatiently.

"He wrote that he wants to get together with me."

What a liar! I stared at Kazue's face in blank amazement. But she just looked bashful, a blush rising to her shrunken cheeks.

"This is what he wrote: *I've been interested in you for some time. Thank you for praising my father's class, that made me very happy. If you don't mind a younger man, let's continue sharing letters. Please feel free to ask me about my interests or anything.*"

"You're kidding!"

I almost believed her. I mean, Takashi said he was going to send back her letters, but there was no way I could be sure he had. And besides, he had shown an interest in that pathetic poem, so maybe he did write to her. Or maybe he was evil enough to be teasing Kazue. I realized my plan had backfired and I started to feel desperate.

"Can I see his letter?"

Kazue stared at my outstretched hand and a troubled look flashed across her face. She shook her head vigorously.

"No can do. Takashi wrote that I wasn't to show the letter to anyone. I'm sorry, I just can't."

"Then why are you wearing that scarf? I thought you were going to give it to Takashi as a present."

Kazue brought her hand quickly to her throat. Medium-width yarn, tightly woven, interspersed with elastic thread. Each band of color was four inches wide in alternating stripes of black and yellow. I watched carefully for her reaction. Go on, what kind of excuse will you have this time?

"I thought I'd use it as my own keepsake."

Ha! Caught you! I did a little dance.

"I deserve it! I had to wait for him, didn't I? I waited for a letter from him so I get to keep the present."

When I tried to grab Kazue's scarf she batted my hand away.

"Don't! Your hands are dirty!"

Her voice was threatening. I froze and stared at her. Within seconds she began to blush.

"I'm sorry. I'm really sorry. I didn't mean to say that."

"That's all right. It was my fault."

I turned on my heel and walked off as if I were angry. Let her chase me.

"Wait! I was wrong to say that. I apologize."

Kazue came after me but I kept walking, refusing to turn around. In fact, I didn't know what to do next. I was perplexed. What was the truth? Had Kazue really gotten a reply from Takashi or was she just making it up? The school grounds were lively with the sounds of students laughing and carrying on now that classes were over for the day. But even still I could clearly discern the sound of Kazue following me: the patter of her feet, her rough breathing, the sound her satchel made as it slapped against her short skirt.

"I apologize. Wait. You're the only person I have to discuss things with," she said.

I thought I heard her crying. I stopped and Kazue caught up. Her tearstained face crumpled and she sobbed like a child left behind by its mother. "I'm sorry. Please forgive me," she begged

"Why did you say such a thing? I've only been kind to you!"

"I know. It's just that the way you say things sounds so nasty that some-times it gets on my nerves. Besides, I didn't really mean what I said."

"But the two of you are really hitting it off, aren't you. It's just like I predicted, isn't it?"

Kazue stared at me blankly. Finally her face took on such a strange light it would be hard not to describe it as insane.

"That's right! We're really hitting it off. Ha-ha-ha!"

"So are you going to go on a date?"

Kazue nodded yes in response and then let out a scream. From the window of the corridor she could see Yuriko and Takashi walking through the school gate. I quickly flung the window open.

"Hey, wait! What are you doing?"

Kazue turned white and looked as if she would run off at any minute. I grabbed the scarf around her neck and tore it off.

"Stop! Stop it!" Kazue begged, as I held her against the corridor wall with all my might.

"Takashiiiii!"

Takashi and Yuriko both turned around at the same time and looked up at me. I hung the scarf out the window with both hands and waved it wildly. Takashi, wearing a black duffle coat, stared at me suspiciously. He grabbed Yuriko around the shoulders and escorted her out the school gate. A stylish navy-blue coat was thrown over her shoulders. She glared at me reproachfully. Crazy bitch of an older sister!

"What you just did was cruel." Kazue crouched in the corridor sobbing. Students passing along the corridor looked over at us curiously and then walked off whispering. I gave Kazue back her scarf. She hid it behind her back as if ashamed to have it seen.

"He's still with Yuriko, it seems. Did you lie to me?"

"No! He really sent me a response."

"Did he say anything about your poem?"

"He said it was a good poem. Honest."

"And about the self-introduction letter?"

"That he liked its straightforward honesty."

"That sounds like what a teacher would write about one of your compositions!"

I was angry so I started to shout. But don't you agree? Because Kazue lacked any imagination, she was only able to come up with a pathetic story. I wished she'd been able to lie more creatively. "What did your father say?" I asked coldly.

Kazue suddenly grew very quiet. Yes, that's right. From that day on, Kazue began to fall apart.

· 4 ·

That evening I received telephone calls from three different people—
quite an event for our household. The first call came while my grandfather and I were watching the detective series *Howl at the Sun*. The
phone startled my grandfather. He scrambled to his feet and ended up
tripping over the leg of the *kotatsu* table. When I thought about it later I
realized that Grandfather was probably waiting for a call from Mitsuru's
mother. I couldn't help but laugh at the way he looked as he rushed to
answer the phone. "Eh-hem. Hello," he said, his voice thick with phlegm.
But soon he was standing rigidly at attention. For a con artist my grandfather was timidly honest.

"Thank you for all you've done for my granddaughter. . . . Studying?
No chance of that. She ought to be, but she's just sitting here watching
TV. . . . What's that? She stopped by your house, did she? Well, thank
you for looking after her. . . . And she even made an international phone
call? I had no idea. . . . No, she didn't tell me. I'm very sorry for the
inconvenience."

Grandfather went way overboard. Chattering about stuff that was not
his business and bowing in apology with the telephone in his hand. My
mother was just like that—humbling herself unnecessarily. It gave me a
chill just looking at him. Ever since he started his affair with Mitsuru's
mother, I'd begun to close my heart to my grandfather. Finally he
handed the phone to me, his brow dotted with a nervous sweat.

"You shouldn't have said I was watching TV! We've got finals next
week, you know!" I said.

The call was from Kazue's mother, Kazue's fish-faced mother. I
recalled Kazue's dreary house and answered the phone with a curt greeting. Kazue's father's muffled voice hit my ears. He must have been standing next to his wife, fidgeting with irritation. Excellent! So my scheme to

ensnare that pathetic family was succeeding after all. I had a splendid chance to get my revenge for their being so horrible to me on the day my mother died. For using me as little more than a stand-in for Mitsuru. For coercing me to go home with Kazue. For the cost of the international phone call. I had my chance to trap them all.

"Has my daughter been acting strangely lately?" Kazue's mother asked nervously.

"Well, that's not easy for me to say—especially since I was told to have nothing to do with her. I really don't know."

"What's this? I had no idea you'd been told such a thing."

As Kazue's mother's voice grew more and more flustered, Kazue's father grabbed the phone. In no mood to mess around, he spoke forcefully and with his usual arrogance. "Listen here. What I want to know is whether or not Kazue is still seeing that Takashi Kijima fellow. I thought I could get it out of her, but I ended up losing my temper. You're just a second-year student in high school, I said. You're too young; you'd better not be doing anything shameful. But she just started crying and I haven't been able to get another word out of her. So I'm asking you. Is she involved in unseemly behavior?"

By the time he'd stopped talking I could sense the anger hovering around the edges of his words. I suspected that Kazue's father was jealous of Takashi. No doubt he wanted to be the only man ever to influence her; he wanted to control her for as long as he lived. Images of Kazue as a dark demon began to loom up in my imagination at that moment, one after another.

"No. She's not doing anything of the sort. All the other girls are writing love letters and knitting scarves and meeting boys at the school gate and such, but Kazue hasn't done anything unseemly. I think you must be wrong."

Her father's suspicions were particularly sharp because he wasn't willing to let it go.

"Well, then, who'd she make that ugly scarf for? No matter how many times I ask, she won't tell me."

"I heard she made it for herself."

"Are you saying she would spend all that precious time knitting something like that just for herself?"

"Yes. Kazue is good at handicrafts."

"And the letters that were sent back? Weren't they love letters?"

"In social studies class we had a creative writing assignment. I think she wrote those for class."

"I heard that this student Kijima is the son of one of the teachers there."

"Yes, that's right, so I guess she decided to use him as a fictional character."

"Creative writing, huh?"

My convoluted explanation had done little so far to allay his doubts.

"A parent worries, you know. If she goes on like this, she's not going to be in any shape for her final exams. She's got her sights set on the university economics department; she can't allow her grades to drop."

"You don't need to worry about Kazue. She always talks about how much she respects you, sir. She says she wants to be just like her father, and he graduated from Tokyo University. Kazue's really popular with the other students too."

Kazue's father seemed to appreciate my words.

"Good, good. That's what I always tell her. I tell her that once she gets into college she can date all the boys she wants. If she's a Q University student, she'll have her pick of anyone."

Hmm. I wonder. I could just picture Kazue at university. Unattractive, uncoordinated Kazue? I almost burst out laughing. Why, I wondered, did this clan who trusted "hard work" always defer their own pleasure, their own happiness, to some vague point in the future? It would be too late, wouldn't it? And why did they always believe so easily everything others told them?

"Well, you've certainly reassured me. Good luck with your exams. Please feel free to stop by and see Kazue at any time."

My, my, what an about-face that was! Is this really the same man who told me to have nothing more to do with his daughter? Kazue's father hung up the phone. My grandfather, who'd been eavesdropping on the conversation all the while, spoke with bright conceit.

"How about that! I'm not as timid as I used to be. I wasn't one bit nervous about talking to that Q School parent!"

I ignored him and went back to watching my TV show. I'd already missed the best part. I was spreading the evening paper out in front of me in irritation when the phone rang again. Once again Grandfather ran to get it. This time he called out cheerfully, "Yuriko-chan? What a nice surprise. How've you been?"

Grandfather looked like he wanted to chat for a bit, but I grabbed the phone from his hand. "What the hell do you want? Spit it out!"

Yuriko laughed brightly in response to my brusque command.

"I see you're still as grumpy as ever. And here I was calling you politely to tell you something. And I wanted to ask why you called out to Takashi today. You startled me."

"First say what you called to tell me."

"It's about Takashi. I know you probably like him, so I'm just calling to tell you not to get your hopes up."

"Why? Is he in love with *you*?"

"With me? No. I think he's probably gay."

"Gay?" Now I was startled. "Why do you think that?"

"Because he doesn't have the slightest bit of interest in me, that's why. Nice talking to you!"

How conceited can you get! She really got under my skin. I was furious on the one hand; on the other, things began to make more sense. "So that's it?" I mumbled to myself. Grandfather turned to look at me and then said somewhat reluctantly, "You know, you don't need to be so rude to your sister. She's the only sister you've got."

"Yuriko's not my sister!"

Grandfather was getting ready to reply, but when he saw how livid I was he thought better of it.

"You're so angry these days, even with me. Has something happened?"

"Why should something have happened? It's because of you, you know. Running around with Mitsuru's mother like that, it's disgusting. Immoral. The other day Mitsuru's mother made some stupid suggestion about how all four of us should go out for dinner: you, me, Mitsuru, and her mother. And now I'm not getting on with Mitsuru anymore either because of it. Ever since Yuriko came back, everybody's turned into a sex maniac. It's just disgusting."

Grandfather cringed and seemed ready to shrink into the floor. He turned to look at the bonsai that were lined up in a corner of the room. Now there were only three: the black pine, an oak, and a maple. It was just a matter of time before he sold those as well, and that also pissed me off.

The phone rang a third time. Grandfather moved listlessly toward the telephone but this time I answered first and heard a woman's hoarse voice calling my grandfather's first name.

"Yasuji?"

It was Mitsuru's mother. When she had spoken to me, that time in the car, her voice had been as raspy as her mannerisms were coarse. But when she called out my grandfather's name, she sounded so sweet you'd think she was the Virgin Mary. I thrust the receiver at my grandfather without saying anything. He snatched the phone from my hand, blushing redder and redder under my gaze, and spoke with a touch of formality. "It's really pretty there when the plums are in bloom, isn't it." It sounded like they were planning a trip, maybe to a hot spring. I sat down by the *kotatsu* table, stretched my legs out under heated quilts, and lay faceup on the floor pillows, watching Grandfather out of the corner of my eye. He knew I was watching him, so he pretended to be nonchalant but his voice betrayed his excitement.

"No, no, I wasn't sleeping yet. I'm a night owl, you know. What were you doing?"

Listening to their conversation, I could imagine the sludgy juices rising higher and higher in their bodies until they threatened to overflow. My grandfather's profile exuded joy, a joy that is unattainable if one tries to attain it. Does such a joy really exist? I've never experienced a feeling like that and I never want to. Whenever someone is on the verge of such joy, they always run away from me. Am I lonely? Don't be ridiculous. I had considered my grandfather an ally until he started mooning around. It was a betrayal. That's the way I felt. If someone finds it lonely to be abandoned, they should behave so others don't abandon them. But if they want to be left alone, they ought to induce disagreeable people to abandon them. I didn't want Grandfather or Mitsuru to leave me, but I wanted to get Mitsuru's mother and Yuriko as far away from me as possible.

To which group should I assign Kazue? She was an idiot who doted on her father like a little girl and who believed in the miracle motto, Try your best. I didn't have much use for a stupid girl like that, other than to keep her nearby to control.

•

Next morning, that idiot Kazue came over to thank me.

"I'm really grateful to you for not telling my father about me last night. My father was furious and I was terrified, but you denied it all and really bailed me out."

"So did your father forgive you?"

"Yes. Everything's okay now."

It would take time before Kazue could escape the spell her father had cast over her. Perhaps a lifetime. An interesting idea. I would create an opening for Kazue's escape, which I would then take delight in personally destroying. Yes. When I saw Kazue I felt like a god, manipulating that dunce like a puppet on a string.

•

You think Kazue started behaving strangely because I bullied her? No, that's not the case. I've said it any number of times before: Kazue was just too naïve, too pure. It's not just that she didn't see the world around her. She couldn't even see herself. I'd like the following to stay just between us: Kazue had a secret confidence in her own looks. I came across her countless times staring at herself in the mirror. She would smile at herself, and her face would take on a look of ecstasy. She was vain.

Both Kazue and her father could not accept the fact that there could possibly be anyone else with more intellectual ability than they had. And Kazue would never accept the fact that a woman with equal ability would always be more successful if she was beautiful. Put another way, could there have been anyone happier than Kazue?

In contrast to Mitsuru and me—who knew to polish our natural gifts in order to survive—Kazue was overly ignorant of her own self. A woman who does not know herself has no choice other than to live with other people's evaluations. But no one can adapt perfectly to public opinion. And herein lies the source of their destruction.

FIVE · MY CRIMES: ZHANG'S WRITTEN REPORT

· 1 ·

JUDGE: Please verify that your name is Zhang Zhe-zhong, a native of Dayi City, Baoxing County, in Sichuan Province of the People's Republic of China, born February 10, 1966.

DEFENDANT: Yes, that is true.

JUDGE: You presently reside at apartment 404 of the Matoya Building, 4–5 Maruyama-chō, Shibuya Ward, in the city of Tokyo; and you are employed by Dreamer. Is that correct?

DEFENDANT: That is correct.

JUDGE: You've stated that you do not need an interpreter. Are you certain?

DEFENDANT: Yes. My Japanese is good. I'm certain.

JUDGE: Very well. Will the attorney for the prosecution read aloud the indictment?

INDICTMENT

On this day of November 1, the twelfth year of Heisei (2000), the District Attorney for the city of Tokyo, as herein represented by D.A. Noro Yoshiaki, indicts Zhang Zhe-zhong, a citizen of the People's Republic of China, born February 10, 1966, currently a hotel employee and residing at Matoya Building #404, 4–5 Maruyama-chō, Shibuya-ku, Tokyo, before the Tokyo District Court on the following charges:

COUNT NO. 1

While the defendant was an employee at the Shangri-la, a Chinese restaurant in Kabuki-chō, Shinjuku-ku, he went to unit number 205 of Hope Heights apartments, 5–12 Ōkubo, Shinjuku-ku, on June 5, 1999, and at approximately 3 a.m. used both hands to strangle Yuriko Hirata (then 37), thus causing her death by asphyxiation. Thereafter the defendant removed from the purse of the afore-named victim ¥20,000 and took an 18-carat gold necklace (valued at the time at ¥70,000) from her person.

COUNT NO. 2

The same defendant went to unit number 103 of Green Villa Apartments, 4–5 Maruyama-chō, Shibuya-ku, on April 9, 2000, and at approximately midnight strangled with both hands Kazue Satō (then 39), thus causing her death by asphyxiation. Subsequently he removed ¥40,000 from the victim's purse.

CHARGES AND PENALTIES

Count No. 1: The defendant is charged with burglary and murder in accordance with Article 240, Part Two, of the Penal Code.

Count No. 2: The defendant is charged with burglary and murder in accordance with Article 240, Part Two, of the Penal Code.

JUDGE: We will begin the trial on the charges the district attorney has just read. But before proceeding I will inform the defendant of his rights. You have the right to remain silent, and so during these proceedings you may choose to remain silent. Should you answer a question, you are not under obligation to answer subsequent questions. However, should you choose to answer a question, anything you say may be used in evidence against you, so I urge you to exercise caution. You have heard the aforementioned conditions. I would like to take this opportunity to ask you if you have any response to the charges against you as read into the record by the prosecuting attorney.

DEFENDANT: I admit to killing Yuriko Hirata, but I did not murder Kazue Satō.

JUDGE: You plead guilty to the charges in the first count but not to the charges in the second count?

DEFENDANT: Correct.

JUDGE: And what about the charges of robbery?

DEFENDANT: I stole Miss Hirata's money and necklace, but I did not steal from Miss Satō.

JUDGE: Attorney for the defense, what is your statement?

DEFENSE ATTORNEY: I concur with the defendant.

JUDGE: Very well. Will the attorney for the prosecution please read your opening arguments.

OVERVIEW OF THE PROSECUTION'S OPENING ARGUMENTS: COUNT NO. 1 OF THE INDICTMENT

Item 1: The Defendant's Personal History

The defendant was born on February 10, 1966, in Sichuan Province of the People's Republic of China as the third son of Zhang Xiao-niu (currently 68) a farmer, and Zhang Xiu-lan (currently 61). The defendant has four siblings: his oldest brother, An-ji (currently 42); a second older brother, Gen-de; an older sister, Mei-hua (currently 40); and a younger sister, Mei-kun. Note that the second brother, Gen-de, died in childhood and the younger sister Mei-kun died in an accident in 1992. The defendant graduated from the local elementary school at the age of 12 and henceforth began to help the family with farming.

In 1989 the defendant decided to leave home to secure better employment. He and his younger sister, Mei-kun, boarded a train to Guangdong Province and sought employment in Guangzhou City. In 1991 they moved to Shenzhen City, also in Guangdong Province.

In 1992 the defendant and his younger sister, Mei-kun, stowed away on a ship sailing from Fujian Province, planning to enter Japan illegally. Although Mei-kun drowned in the process, the defendant was successful and entered our country illegally at Ishigaki Island. While concealing his illegal status, he found successive employment in the cleaning and cooking sectors. He also had jobs in construction. In 1998 he worked at a bar in Shinjuku known as Nomisuke, and in 1999 he began working at a tavern, also in Shinjuku, known as Shangri-la. In July of that same year he began employment at Dreamer, a love hotel in the Honmachi neighborhood of Kichijōji, Musashino City. The defendant is not known to be married. According to housing records, he lives with individuals known by the names Chen-yi, Huang, and Dragon, all Chinese nationals.

On June 30, 2000, the defendant was brought before the Tokyo District Court on the charge of entering the country illegally. He was sentenced to two years of incarceration with a suspended sentence of four years. (Decision dated July 20 of the same year.)

Item 2: Victim Yuriko Hirata

The victim Yuriko Hirata (hereafter Hirata) was born May 17, 1962, as the second daughter of Jan Maher (a Swiss national) who is currently employed by Schmidt, a textile manufacturer in Switzerland, and Sachiko Hirata. As her parents never legally married, the victim went by both Maher and her mother's name Hirata. Hirata and her parents moved from Kita-Shirakawa in Shirakawa Ward to Bern, Switzerland, in March of 1976. In July of that year, Sachiko died in Bern and Hirata left her father and returned alone to Japan. Because her elder sister was currently living with Sachiko's father, Hirata boarded at the house of an American acquaintance and entered the junior high division of the Q School system. Subsequently, Hirata advanced to the high school division but was expelled during her third year of high school due to inappropriate behavior.

After her expulsion she moved out of the American acquaintance's house and began to live alone. She signed on with a modeling agency and worked in advertising and magazine modeling until 1985, when she took employment as a hostess in Mallord, a club in Roppongi. In 1989 she moved to the club Jeanne, also in Roppongi, and after that she changed employment any number of times. While working as a hostess, Hirata engaged in prostitution in Shinjuku and Shibuya.

Item 3: Circumstances Leading to the Crime

The defendant, as previously stated, was employed as a waiter in the tavern Shangri-la in Shinjuku. But the salary was low and he felt ostracized by the owners of the business, who were natives of Fujian. The other employees criticized Zhang for being "a bumpkin who put on the airs of a sophisticated urbanite," so he did not have many personal associations with others at the establishment.

He was known to pinch off bites of food for himself when he carried food to customers; he poured the beer or whiskey left in the bottles he had served into a plastic container that he then carried home for his own consumption. He was warned about the inappropriateness of this behavior on numerous occasions.

Despite these lapses, he worked hard, was punctual, and never missed a day on the job. Claiming that he had to send money home to his family, he worked part-time at the neighborhood flophouse, Futo-momokko, heading there after his tavern job ended at 10 p.m. His duties at Futomomokko included taking out the trash and washing the towels. Once finished here he would rush through the streets of Kabuki-chō to catch the last train back to his apartment in Maruyama-chō, Shibuya Ward.

Every day of the week except Wednesdays, the defendant worked at the Shangri-la from noon to 10 p.m. He earned ¥800 an hour plus a monthly transportation fee of ¥6,500, so that every month he received approximately ¥315,000. In addition to this, his part-time job at the motel paid ¥2,000 for two hours.

The rent on unit 404, Matoya Building, came to ¥65,000 a month. But because he charged his three roommates, Chen-yi, Huang, and Dragon, ¥35,000 a month each, he made a profit of ¥40,000.

He often told his coworkers that his parents were rebuilding their house back home and he needed to raise ¥3,000,000 to send them. But he had expensive tastes and wore flashy clothes and accessories such as a

24-carat gold bracelet and a ¥50,000 leather jacket that he bought at the Isetan Department Store.

Item 4: Events Related to the Crime

At approximately 10 p.m. on June 4, 1999, the defendant came across Hirata in front of Ōkubo Park in the second block of Kabuki-chō as he was rushing to his job at Motel Futomomokko. She was holding an umbrella. He knew that streetwalkers frequented Ōkubo Park, but this was the first time the defendant had seen Hirata there. His interest in her was immediately piqued because he mistook her for an American, and he had always thought that eventually he would travel on to America.

"You have a nice face" were Hirata's first words to him. Since she spoke to him in Japanese, he realized she was not American, and initially he was disappointed. Her flattery, however, appealed to him and he was interested in following up but worried about missing work at the motel. So he just waved to her, smiled, and rushed ahead to the Futomomokko. There he went about his usual tasks.

Unable to get Hirata out of his mind, the defendant took the same route past Ōkubo Park on his way home. He reached the park at approximately 12:05 on the morning of the fifth and saw that Hirata was still standing there in the rain.

When Hirata saw the defendant, she called out to him cheerfully, "I'm about to freeze, standing here waiting for you!" At this point the defendant decided to have sex with her.

At that time the defendant had ¥22,000 on his person. When he asked Hirata what she charged, she replied that it would be ¥30,000. Since he did not have that much money, the defendant was ready to give up the idea; Hirata offered to lower the price to ¥15,000. The defendant then proposed that they move to a hotel. At this point Hirata informed the defendant that she had an apartment nearby. The defendant was relieved that he would not have to pay extra for a hotel and accompanied the defendant to her room.

On the way, Hirata stopped at a 7-Eleven and bought four cans of beer, a packet of chili peanut chips, and two bean-jam buns. The food cost ¥1,575, and Hirata paid for it out of her own pocket.

The room that Hirata led the defendant to was in a two-story building of wood and concrete construction just behind the Kitashin Credit Union on the fifth block of Ōkubo. The building, Hope Heights, had five units on the ground floor and five on the second. Hirata's apartment, number 205, was on the second floor, farthest to the north and just next to the exterior stairway. Hirata had been renting the room, under the name Yuriko Hirata, from December 5, 1996, at the rate of ¥33,000 a month. The sum was withdrawn monthly from her bank account. Hirata, it seems, rented the space for the purpose of prostitution. The unit consisted of a six-mat Japanese-style room with tatami flooring, and in the small space between the entry vestibule and this room were a kitchenette, toilet, and sink. Hardly any furnishings were on the premises, though a futon mattress was folded and ready for use.

The defendant and Hirata each drank two beers in the Japanese-style room, pulled the futon out, and had sex. The defendant wanted to fall asleep afterward but Hirata requested that he leave. When he asked her again to let him stay because it was raining and he had already missed the last train, she refused.

Hirata insisted that the defendant pay her ¥20,000 to cover the use of the room and the cost of the provisions she had bought at the 7-Eleven. When the defendant learned of these charges, he realized that not only would he have to spend all the money he had with him, he would also have to walk back to Shibuya in the rain. He refused to pay Hirata. When Hirata reproached the defendant, he decided to kill her. At approximately three o'clock in the morning on June 5, he strangled Hirata with both hands, bringing about her death by asphyxiation. The defendant then remained in the room, sleeping, until 10 a.m. that same morning.

At approximately 10:30 a.m., the defendant took ¥20,000 from Hirata's wallet. He removed the 18-carat gold necklace that she was wearing (valued at ¥70,000) and put it around his own neck. He then fled the apartment without locking the door, leaving Hirata's body just as it was.

Item 5: Events Subsequent to the Crime

The defendant arrived at the Shangri-la one hour earlier than his scheduled noontime start. He spoke to the owner about resigning effective immediately. When the owner refused to allow such a sudden resignation, the defendant cleaned out his locker and left the premises without any discussion of collecting the salary currently owed him. As he was leaving the Shangri-la, the defendant encountered Mr. A, another employee. They stood and spoke briefly in front of the restaurant. The defendant told A he had quit and then turned and headed toward Yasukuni Avenue. Mr. A noticed the defendant was wearing what seemed to be an expensive gold necklace that he had not seen before.

After the defendant left the Shangri-la, he took the Japan Railways Yamanote Line to Shibuya Station. From there he returned on foot to his apartment, number 404 in the Matoya Building on the fourth block of Maruyama-chō. This unit was rented by a certain Chen, a man the defendant met while a stowaway. Chen began renting the apartment in April 1998, and even after he moved out he kept the apartment under his name while the defendant remitted the monthly rent of ¥65,000 into Chen's bank account.

Matoya Building is a four-story ferroconcrete building. It has no elevator. The building and land are owned by Mrs. Fumi Yamamoto. Unit 404 consists of a six-mat and a three-mat Japanese-style room, a kitchen, and a bath. The defendant occupied the three-mat room. At noon on June 5, the man known as Dragon and the one named Huang were sleeping. Chen-yi (no relation to the aforementioned Chen) had already gone to his job at a pachinko parlor in Shinkoiwa and was not home. Dragon, Huang, and Chen-yi are all male Chinese nationals whom the defendant had met in Tokyo. They did not discuss their personal history or their work with one another.

The noise the defendant made when he entered the apartment woke Dragon and Huang, and they left shortly thereafter. After the defendant fixed himself a meal in the kitchen, he ate and went back to sleep. He awoke later that day, when Chen-yi returned, and the two of them went out to eat ramen at the Tamaryū Noodle Shop on the east side of Shibuya Station. They played a game at the Shibuya Meeting Hall bowling alley and returned to their apartment at around eleven o'clock that night.

When no news of the murder came to light, even after several days had passed, the defendant asked Chen-yi to help him find another job. Chen-yi suggested that the defendant join him at the pachinko parlor, an offer the defendant declined, saying the establishment was too noisy. Chen-yi promised to continue looking on the defendant's behalf.

Item 6: The Discovery of Hirata's Body and Subsequent Circumstances

Hirata's body was discovered ten days after the crime on June 15 when the occupant in the neighboring apartment, a Korean national, reported an offensive odor to the building owner. The owner went to the apartment to investigate and found the door unlocked. When he entered the apartment he found Hirata's corpse. She was clad only in a T-shirt, a light blanket covering her head.

Decomposition had already set in, but it was still possible to discern unusual marks on Hirata's throat and blood had pooled in the soft tissue of her neck region and the membrane along her thyroid gland. When the news of Hirata's death broke, the defendant realized he would not be able to return to the Shangri-la to collect his back wages. And fearing the necklace he had stolen would link him to the crime, he hid it in the pocket of one of his suitcases. Finally, worried about running out of money, he went back to Chen-yi and told him he would take any job he could find.

Chen-yi introduced the defendant to a part-time job as a janitor at the love hotel Dreamer, located at 1 Honmachi in Kichijōji, Musashino City. The defendant accepted the job and began work from July of that year.

OVERVIEW OF THE PROSECUTION'S OPENING ARGUMENTS: COUNT NO. 2 OF THE INDICTMENT

Item 1: The Victim Kazue Satō

The victim, Kazue Satō (hereafter Satō), was born April 4, 1961, the eldest daughter of Yoshio and Satoko Satō. Yoshio was employed by G Architecture and Engineering Firm. When Satō was in her first year of elementary school, her family moved from Ōmiya in Saitama Prefecture to the Kita-Karasuyama area of Setagaya Ward, Tokyo. Satō attended local elementary and middle schools, advanced to Q High School for Young Women, and from there entered the economics department of Q University.

Satō's father died when she was in her sophomore year of university, and as a result Satō had to take part-time jobs as a tutor and cram school instructor in order to pay her tuition fees.

Satō graduated from Q University in March 1984 and was employed in April by G Architecture and Engineering Firm, where her father had worked. As the largest firm in the industry, G was known for close relations among employees, earning the nickname G Family Company. Moreover, the company actively recruited the children of employees. When Satō, who had a distinguished university record, entered the company as a member of the General Research Department, she was the first woman to be assigned such a high position, and her future with the company held great promise.

In 1985, Satō was promoted to the position of assistant manager of the research office. This office is responsible for analyzing economic factors affecting construction, developing new analytical software programs, and so forth. Satō mostly conducted research on the economic effects of high-rise buildings. Her work was valued highly by others in the firm, and she was dedicated to her job.

However, she did not socialize with her superiors or colleagues after hours and, because she had no close acquaintances within the firm, no one really knew what she did after work. Satō never married. She lived with her mother and a younger sister. After her father died, Satō provided the main financial support for the family.

In 1990, when Satō was twenty-nine, she was sent provisionally to an engineering research laboratory affiliated with G firm. At this time she was hospitalized for anorexia. Satō had been diagnosed with and treated for anorexia when she was a sophomore in high school. In May 1991, Satō began to work part time as a hostess at a club in the evenings after work. In 1994, she started meeting men in hotels for compensated sex; finally, in 1998, she became a full-fledged prostitute working out of the Shibuya area.

Yuriko Hirata, the victim named in Count No. 1, and Kazue Satō both attended Q High School for Young Women, but they were in different classes and did not interact with each other either during or after their years in the school.

*Item 2: The Defendant's Personal Circumstances
as They Relate to the Present Case*

After the commission of the crime described in Count No. 1 of this indictment, the defendant resigned his jobs at both the tavern,

Shangri-la, and the flophouse, Futomomokko, and took up employment at the love hotel in Musashino City known as Dreamer. However, he did not change his domicile and continued to live at 404 Matoya Building, 4–5 Murayama-chō in Shibuya. Other than the aforementioned Dragon, Huang, and Chen-yi, two other Chinese nationals, by the name of Niu-hu and A-wu, stayed at the apartment from time to time.

The defendant worked at Dreamer every day of the week but Tuesday, from noon to ten at night, cleaning the guest rooms, washing the linens, and doing other menial tasks.

When he began working in 1998 he was industrious and dependable, but in the following year his attitude toward work gradually changed. He would arrive late and leave early and frequently missed work altogether. Cleaning the guest rooms was a two-person assignment. The defendant's behavior affected the work rotation and inconvenienced his partner, an employee from Iran, who lodged a complaint against him. Moreover, the defendant was written up for taking naps in the guest rooms; pilfering soap, shampoo, and towels; watching adult videos in the rooms; and other such inappropriate behavior.

In February of the same year, a local resident reported seeing the defendant take the condoms the hotel supplied its guests, fill them with water, and hurl the water-filled condoms from a hotel window at the cat owned by the sushi shop next door. At that point the hotel owner first considered terminating the defendant.

At that time the defendant earned an hourly wage of ¥750 yen for an average monthly salary of approximately ¥170,000. He received no additional allowance for transportation costs. The defendant, whose income had been reduced in comparison to what he had earned while working at the Shangri-la, began to borrow from his apartment mates. He borrowed ¥100,000 from Dragon, ¥40,000 from Huang, and ¥60,000 from Chen-yi. He told them his mother had been hospitalized back in China, and he had to send her more funds.

He also borrowed from Niu-hu and A-wu, who occasionally stayed over in the cramped apartment. And he continued to receive rent from Dragon and the others as before. Consequently, the relations between the defendant and his boarders grew progressively worse. Even Chen-yi, with whom the defendant had been on relatively good terms, grew embittered when the defendant lost his standing with his employers at Dreamer. Chen-yi had been the one to introduce the defendant to his employers.

On March 25, 2000, Dragon, Huang, and Chen-yi, knowing it was the defendant's payday, decided to press him to return the money he had borrowed from them. The defendant had planned to pay each man half the sum he had borrowed but, because the three knew he had over ¥240,000 in cash in a locked suitcase, they refused to accept his terms of repayment. They also argued with him for extorting so much rent from the three of them.

Under pressure, the defendant had no choice but to accede to the new terms his boarders presented. He agreed to pay a total of ¥200,000 back to the three men to cover the money he had borrowed and an additional ¥50,000 each to cover the past disparity in rent. The defendant had to resort to his Dreamer salary and the money he had until then been hoarding.

As a result, the defendant had only ¥60,000 left, which he had to stretch over the rest of the month, until his next paycheck. The hardship this imposed further weakened his relationships with Dragon, Huang, and Chen-yi.

About the same time, Chen, under whose name the apartment at 404 Matoya was being rented, had been pressuring the defendant to find another place to live. Beginning in January, Chen informed the defendant several times that he wanted him to vacate the apartment by mid-March. When the defendant complained that he had nowhere else to go, Chen offered to let him stay until the end of April. He also informed him that there was a vacancy in a neighboring building: unit 103 in the Green Villa Apartments at 4–5 Murayama-chō, Shibuya-ku. For a fee of ¥150,000 he would assist the defendant in renting the apartment. As these circumstances make clear, the defendant faced endless and escalating money problems.

The Iranian who worked with the defendant at the Dreamer later revealed that the defendant's reason for borrowing money—even though he had a sizable sum stashed away—was because he was saving up to buy a passport. It was his goal to travel to America.

Item 3: Conditions at 103 Green Villa Apartments

The Matoya Building at 4–5 Maruyama-chō in Shibuya-ku was a four-story ferroconcrete building about one hundred yards north on a narrow one-way road just across from the north side of Shinsen Station on the Inokashira-Keio Train Line. The Green Villa Apartments, scene of the crime under discussion, was a wooden building to the north of the Matoya Building. With one floor belowground and two above, space in the Green Villa was occupied by a number of small shops in addition to residences. Both buildings were owned by Fumi Yamamoto.

There were three residential units in the Green Villa Apartments. The crime under discussion took place in unit 103, which faced out on the one-way street. Unit 102 was unoccupied; Kimio Hara lived in unit 101. On the west side of the building was a metal exterior staircase leading to the second floor. In the basement, directly below unit 103, was a small eatery known as Seven Fortunes.

On the south side of the building was a narrow concrete sidewalk providing residents of the building access to their apartments from the road. On the south side of unit 103 was the exterior door that led to this sidewalk, as well as a window at about eye level. Upon entering the apartment, the kitchen was on the south wall and next to it a six-mat Japanese-style room with tatami flooring. Between the entry hall and the six-mat room was the toilet.

Chen had been introduced to Fumi Yamamoto by relatives and had rented unit 404 in the Matoya Building for ¥45,000. He in turn had rented the apartment to the defendant for ¥65,000. His relatives had opened a Chinese restaurant in Niiza City, Saitama Prefecture, and needed the apartment as a place to board employees. That is why the defendant had to vacate the premises. When the defendant complained that he had no other apartment to rent, Chen spoke with the landlady, Ms. Fumi Yamamoto, and made plans to rent the unit in Green Villa Apartments from her. When the defendant said he wanted to see the unit, Ms. Yamamoto gave him the key to unit 103 on January 28, 2000.

Shizu Kakiya had rented the apartment in question up until August 18, 1999, when she passed away. The apartment had been vacant ever since. The gas was cut off in September of 1999 and the electricity the following month.

There was only one key to the apartment, which Ms. Yamamoto possessed. She lent it to the defendant on January 28, 2000. Until that time, no one else had used the key.

Item 4: The Relations Between the Defendant and the Victim

On or around November 1998, the defendant learned from his apartment mate Huang that he had "met a Japanese woman on a dark street and had had sex with her." The woman's distinguishing features were that she was thin and had long hair. When he heard this, the defendant was convinced it was the same woman he'd seen in the neighborhood from time to time. Toward the middle of the next month, the defendant ran into Satō on his way home. Recalling Huang's story, he turned to look at her. When she saw this, she called after him, "Do you want to fool around?" When the defendant did not respond, she continued, "Can we go to your room?" The defendant declined, stating that he "had friends staying there." To this Satō replied, "How many? I'll do them all." When he heard that, the defendant brought Satō back to his apartment at 404 Matoya.

At that time two of the defendant's roommates were in the apartment, Dragon and Chen-yi. The three of them took turns having sex with Satō. Later, around January of the following year, the defendant was walking with Huang when they came across Satō in the Murayama-chō area. "Is that the woman you slept with?" the defendant asked Huang. When Huang nodded, the defendant said he'd slept with her too. Huang had already heard from Dragon around December 1998 that the defendant, Dragon, and Chen-yi had had sex with the woman in the apartment. When he told the defendant as much, the latter replied, "Well, actually, I first met that woman about a year ago."

Item 5: Events Leading to the Crime

On (Saturday,) April 8, 2000, at approximately 4 p.m., Satō left her home without saying where she was going. At approximately 6 p.m., she met up with a company employee whom she had seen on several occasions earlier. They met at the statue of Hachiko in front of Shibuya Station. From there they went to a hotel in Maruyama-chō, Satō received ¥40,000 from the man and, just before 9 p.m., she and the company employee parted ways at the top of Dogenzaka. Satō was seen heading toward Shinsen Station.

That same day the defendant had gone to work at Dreamer. At 10 p.m. the late-shift worker arrived and replaced the defendant. The defendant boarded the 10:13 Keio-Inokashira Line train bound for Shibuya and headed home. When he reached Shinsen Station, he got out and began walking toward the Matoya apartment building, which was only two minutes away.

The defendant encountered Satō within a few feet of his apartment building and decided that he would have sex with her again. But Dragon, Huang, and Chen-yi were at home by now, and he was no longer on good terms with them. He hesitated, therefore, not wishing to take her back to the apartment that he shared with them. As luck would have it, however, he happened to have the key to unit 103 in the neighboring Green Villa Apartments, for reasons already described. He took her to that apartment and had sex with her there.

Satō had condoms with her, taken from hotels she had visited with customers. She selected one from among her stash—a condom from the Glass Palace Hotel, as the wrapper read—and had the defendant put it on before they had sex. After the sex act, the defendant tossed the used condom along the sidewalk to the south of the Green Villa Apartments.

As previously noted, the defendant was short of money. When he saw Satō preparing to leave, he decided he would steal from her. Just after midnight, Satō put on her coat and began to pull herself together in preparation to leave. The defendant snatched her brown leather handbag. However, the victim struggled with him. He punched her in the face, and then, seized with the desire to kill her, he placed both hands around her neck and strangled her until she was dead. Then he unclasped the metal fitting on her purse and pulled out the wallet inside, taking from it ¥40,000 that she had received earlier. Leaving her body as it was, and leaving the door to the apartment unlocked, he fled back to his room at 404 Matoya.

Satoko Satō, the victim's mother, began to worry about her daughter when she did not return home on the evening of April 8. Up to this point, Satō had never been out all night. On Monday, April 10, when Satoko learned that her daughter had not gone in to work that morning, she filed a missing persons report.

Item 6: Events Following the Crime

The defendant calmly reported to work at Dreamer on April 9 as though nothing had changed. After work he went with two colleagues to

Inokashira Park to drink beer. At approximately 11:30 p.m., he boarded the Inokashira Line at Inokashira Station and headed home.

The next day, after he had finished work at Dreamer, the defendant met Chen-yi at Shibuya Station. They went to the ramen noodle shop Tamaryū on the east side of the station. Following this they went bowling at the Shibuya Meeting Hall alley. When they had finished, they discussed Green Villa and decided not to move there, as it was even smaller than their current apartment in Matoya Building. Further, the defendant indicated that he was planning to move to Ōsaka to find work there.

The eleventh of the month was the defendant's day off. He went to Niiza City in Saitama Prefecture to meet Chen. The defendant gave Chen ¥100,000, informed him he would not move into the Green Villa Apartments, and gave Chen the key to unit 103. That night Chen returned the key to the landlady, Ms. Yamamoto, at her residence in Suginami Ward. Yamamoto in turn handed the key to her son, Akira, who ran the company that supervised both the Matoya and the Green Villa apartments.

Item 7: Discovery of the Body

On April 18, when Akira Yamamoto was on his way to visit an acquaintance who lived on the first floor of the Matoya Building, he decided to check to be sure the door to unit 103 in the Green Villa Apartments had been locked. Once he approached the apartment, he looked through the eye-level window which was beside the apartment door. A small opening in the window allowed him to peer into the apartment where he saw, in the inner room, the upper body of someone who appeared to be sleeping. He speculated that the person was either an acquaintance of Chen's or a Chinese national who was employed in his restaurant. Akira Yamamoto called out and tried the door. It had been left unlocked. A woman's shoes were lined up just inside the entryway. Yamamoto was unpleasantly surprised when he realized the interloper was a woman. It was at this point he noticed a strange smell permeating the apartment and, without making a sound, he turned and left the apartment, locking the door behind him. The door was the kind that could be locked from the inside without a key. One only needed to push the button on the knob.

The following day, April 19, Akira Yamamoto grew concerned about the person he had seen sleeping in the apartment. What if the person continued to stay there? And what about that smell? Worried, Yamamoto headed back to the apartment with the key. When he looked in through the window he noticed that the individual was lying just as she had been the day before. Yamamoto unlocked the door, entered the apartment, and discovered Satō's corpse.

Other than the strangulation marks on Satō's throat, there were contusions on her head, face, and limbs—indicating that she'd been struck with a blunt object—and scratches on her as well, as though she'd been dragged. The soft tissue of her neck region and the membrane along her thyroid gland had hemorrhaged.

Item 8: Conduct of the Defendant Following Discovery of the Body

On the evening of April 19, 2000, shortly after the defendant returned home from his job at Dreamer, he was visited by a police detective who was conducting a routine investigation of the neighborhood. Dragon, Huang, and Chen-yi were still at work and had not yet returned to the apartment. The detective asked the defendant to answer numerous questions related to his current domicile and his work, and then he left. As soon as he had departed, the defendant tried to contact the others who shared the apartment.

The defendant called Chen-yi's cell phone and reached him while he was on the job in Dogenzaka. "The police were here," he said. "Lots of them. They showed me the picture of a woman I didn't know. They said they'd be back. If they find you here they'll figure out we're illegal."

When Chen-yi heard the defendant's account, he immediately called Huang at his place of work, the Mirage Café in Koenji, Suginami Ward. He planned to tell Huang not to return to the apartment. But Huang had already gotten off work and was on his way home. Chen-yi next raced to Dragon's place of employment—Orchard Tower—in the second block of Kabuki-chō, Shinjuku Ward. When he told Dragon what had happened, they both went to stay with an acquaintance of Dragon's.

While Huang was on his way home, unaware of the events that had transpired, he was met by a police detective and shown a photograph of the victim. Huang told the detective that he had seen the woman before. He also told him that the defendant had a key to one of the Green Villa apartments.

Around the same time, the defendant left unit 404 in the Matoya Building and stayed the night in a capsule hotel. Policemen went to question him at the Dreamer the next day, but he did not show up for work. The next day, April 21, the defendant left the hotel and went to Chen's house in Niiza City in Saitama Prefecture. He asked Chen to cover for him by telling the police that he returned the key to Green Villa apartments, unit 103, on April 8, the day before the crime. At that time he had also delivered ¥100,000 in cash. Chen informed him that he had already spoken to the police, and he refused to adhere to the defendant's request. Moreover, he told the defendant that the police were looking for him—since they knew he had had the key in his possession—and he ought to turn himself in. The defendant refused.

On the way back from Chen's the defendant began to worry about money. He decided to stop by his place of employment, resign, and ask to be given his back wages. So he headed toward the Dreamer in Musashino City.

When the police detective questioned the owner of the Dreamer, he discovered that the defendant had either entered the country illegally or was working without a proper visa. The defendant was therefore apprehended later that day and held on charges of entering the country illegally and working without appropriate documentation. He was brought to trial on June 30 of the same year and found guilty of the immigration and employment crimes for which he had been charged.

Subsequently it was discovered that the fingerprints found in unit 205 Hope Heights, the scene of Yuriko Hirata's murder, belonged to the defendant. Moreover, he was discovered to be in possession of the victim's necklace. After a thorough police investigation, the defendant was charged with the murders of both Hirata and Satō.

• 2 •

"MY CRIMES": THE DEFENDANT'S STATEMENT
BY ZHANG ZHE-ZHONG

JUNE 10, THE TWELFTH YEAR OF HEISEI (2000)

The original was written in Chinese. One of the examining officers instructed the defendant to write the statement after he had the defendant reenact the crime using a life-sized mannequin at the police station.

Detective Takahashi said, "Tell us everything about your life up to now; every rotten thing you've done, down to the last detail. Don't hide anything." Well, I've been living a rough life, hand to mouth, just trying to do the best I can. I haven't even had time to look back over the last few years of my life or pause for reflection. I can't remember the things that happened in the distant past, and I don't want to. They were too sad, too painful, and I've sealed them tightly in a forgotten chamber of my memory. I have many memories that I've tried to leave behind.

But Detective Takahashi has kindly given me this opportunity to tell my side of the story, and I would like to do my best to meet his request. It means, however, that I will have to think back on my pathetic life and recall all the many stupid mistakes I have made—mistakes that cannot be unmade. I have heard that I am suspected in the death of Miss Kazue Satō, but I am innocent of this crime. I hope this statement will clear my name where that is concerned.

•

In China, a person's fate is determined by where he is born. This is a saying we are accustomed to hear. But for me it is more than just a saying, it is the truth. If I'd been born in a city like Shanghai or Beijing or Hong Kong, not deep in the mountains of Sichuan Province, my life would have been filled with promise. It would have been bright and happy, of that I am certain. And certainly I would not have ended up making such a mess of things in a foreign country!

It's true that I am from Sichuan Province. Ninety percent of the total population of China lives in inland areas like Sichuan. Even so, those areas possess only 10 percent of the nation's wealth. The rest is controlled by Shanghai and Guangzhou and other port cities. Only 10 percent of the nation's population lives in port cities, yet those cities control 90 percent of the nation's wealth. The economic disparity between those who live on the coast and those in the inland regions only continues to deepen.

For those of us who live inland, we can only grit our teeth in despair as we smell the scent of the paper money and watch the glitter of the gold that we will never possess. We have no choice but to satisfy ourselves with millet and coarse grains, our faces and hair streaked with the dust of the fields we tend.

Ever since I was a boy my parents and my siblings always said, "Zhe-zhong is the smartest child in the village." I am not writing this to boast but to be sure that you understand the conditions under which I was raised. I was, to be sure, brighter than the other children my age. I picked up reading and writing in no time at all. And I was able to calculate finances without any effort. To stretch myself and expand my knowledge, I wanted to continue my schooling and go on to higher-level classes. But my family was poor. They could only afford to send me to the village elementary school. When I realized that my dreams would never be realized, I suppose—like a tree whose roots are stymied and twisted and not allowed to grow—I began to nurture a dark jealousy in my heart, an ugly envy. I believed fate had determined that I would be born into this miserable existence.

Going elsewhere to seek work was the only way people like me could escape this fate. When I went to Guangzhou and Shenzhen, I worked long and hard, thinking all the while that eventually I also would be able to enjoy a wealthy life and save money just like the people from those regions. But after I came to Japan, I was overwhelmed with the feeling that my plans were utterly hopeless. Why might that be? Because the wealth of Japan was beyond compare even to that of China's port cities.

If I had not been Chinese, if I had been born Japanese, I surely would not be experiencing these hardships now. From the minute I entered this world I would have had access to so many delicious dishes that half the food would go to waste. To get water, I would just turn a tap. I could bathe as often as I liked, and when I wanted to go to the next village or a neighboring town, I wouldn't have to walk or wait for a bus that might or might not ever come, I could take a train that rushes through the station every three minutes. I could study what I wanted when I wanted, I could pursue the career of my choice, I could wear attractive clothing, I'd have a cell phone and a car, and I'd end my life under the care of an excellent medical staff. The difference between the life I had in China and the one I might have had in Japan was so great, just imagining it caused me nothing but grief.

For so long I dreamed of this free and miraculous country, this Japan. I envied all who lived here. And yet it is in the country for which I longed so desperately that I now find myself imprisoned. How ironic! It's pathetic, in fact. Back home in my impoverished village, my mother—suffering from illness—awaits a letter from me, each day passing as slowly as a thousand autumn nights. If she ever finds out what has become of me, I will not be able to continue living.

Investigating officers, detectives, and Your Honor, I beseech you, after I serve my term for killing Yuriko Hirata, please let me return to my home in China. Let me spend the rest of my allotted time on earth plowing the barren land of my home village and contemplating my life and the crimes I have committed. I beg of you, please show me leniency. I throw myself on the mercy of the court.

•

I've been made a fool of all my life. My family was the poorest in our impoverished village. We lived in a cave, so the others looked down on us. There were those who spread rumors that my father was cursed by the gods of poverty. Even when we were invited to a wedding celebration or a festival, my father was almost always seated in the lowest seat.

My father was a Hakka Chinese. When he was a boy, my grandfather led him all the way from Hui'an in Fujian Province to a small village in Sichuan, and they began to live in a little corner there. The local toughs were all Han Chinese. Not a single Hakka had ever lived in the village, and they told my grandfather they would not allow him to build a house. That's how we came to live in a cave.

My grandfather was a diviner, a fortune-teller. I was told he started off with a successful business in the village but before long he lost favor because all his fortunes forecast bad luck. Eventually, he ran out of business altogether and our family slipped down to the depths of poverty. My grandfather refused to read anyone's fortune after that, even if they asked him to, and even at home he usually refused to speak to anyone. If he ever were to open his mouth, those around him would stand on guard, worried about his ill-omened prophecies. Even though he practiced his craft with great earnestness, people hated him for it. So he decided he'd be better off saying nothing at all.

After a while my grandfather ceased moving as well. His hair and beard grew long, and he sat inside all day long like Bodhidharma himself. I can still remember seeing him sitting perfectly still in the dark shadows of the innermost room of the cave. Everyone in the family got so used to him we stopped noticing if he was even there or not. When it was dinnertime, my mother would set a bowl of food in front of him. Before long the food would be gone, so we took that as a sign that our grandfather was still alive. When Grandfather did actually die, no one noticed for some time.

Once, when no one else was in the house, my grandfather called out to me. I was in elementary school at the time. Since I'd hardly ever heard him speak, his voice caught me by surprise and I swung around to stare at him. My grandfather was sitting in the dark of the inner cave, his eyes fixed on me.

"We've a murderer in the family," he said.

"Grandfather! What did you say? Who are you talking about?"

I asked my grandfather to explain, but he didn't say anything more. I'd been spoiled by then into believing I was a clever boy, a sensible lad, so I chalked my grandfather's comment up to the ramblings of a half-dead old fool and paid no attention. Before long I'd forgotten all about it.

Every day the members of our family cultivated fields halfway up the mountainside with the help of an emaciated old ox. Other than the ox, we had two goats. It was my older brother Gen-de's job to take care of them. He was the second son. The family grew an assortment of crops, mostly grains. My father, mother, and older brothers would awaken early, before the sun had risen, and head out to work. They wouldn't come home until past dark. Even so, the amount of food produced by those fields was inadequate to feed the entire family. Often we had to contend with droughts. When that happened we would go for months without ever getting enough to eat. All I could think, at those times, was how as soon as I reached adulthood I wanted to eat my fill of white rice, even if it killed me.

Because that's the kind of life we led, I was determined—from the moment I was aware of what was going on around me—to leave home as soon as I was old enough. I would head to one of the big cities—the likes of which I had yet to see—and find a job there. I assumed the family land would be passed down to the oldest son, An-ji. My older sister, Mei-hua, was sent in marriage to a neighboring village when she was fifteen. I knew that the crops from our fields and the food from our few goats was not enough to sustain my brother Gen-de, my younger sister Mei-kun, and me.

Eight years separated me from my eldest brother, An-ji. There was a three-year difference between me and my second brother, Gen-de. When I was thirteen, a catastrophe befell the family. An-ji caused Gen-de's death. It terrified me to think that my grandfather's prophecy had come true, and I clutched my younger sister, Mei-kun, and trembled with fear.

An-ji and Gen-de got in an argument, and An-ji hit Gen-de and knocked him down. Gen-de stuck his head on one of the crags in the cave and stopped moving. A police officer came to investigate his death, but my father concealed the circumstances, saying that Gen-de stumbled, accidentally hitting his head as he fell. If An-ji had been charged with killing his younger brother, he would have been sent to prison and there would have been no one left to tend the fields. After he got out of prison, he would have had nothing to come home to and would have needed to survive on his own.

In our village there was a surplus of men. It was so bad it was said that in a neighboring village four men had been forced to share one bride. That's how poor we were. My brothers had been arguing about a bride; that was the reason for their fight. Gen-de had made fun of An-ji.

But after An-ji killed Gen-de, he changed. He started to act just like my grandfather, refusing to speak to anyone. An-ji still lives in the village with my parents. He never married.

•

Perhaps my family is cursed. As the result of being pursued by a violent passion, both my older brother and I ended up murderers. As punishment, my brother will spend the rest of his life in solitude and poverty; and I, for the crime of killing Yuriko Hirata, must be incarcerated in a foreign country. My beloved younger sister met an untimely death on her way to Japan, and now I have nothing left.

My grandfather may have been forced to leave his home in Fujian and drift along to Sichuan, but if only his predictions hadn't been so dire, if only he hadn't chased everyone away, then . . . well, that is all I can think about these days. I am sure my grandfather saw the dark collapse of the family. Surely that is why he ended his days no better than a stone, sitting wordlessly in a dark cave.

At any rate, if my grandfather had said, "The murderer in the family is *you*; be careful," if he'd warned me, I could have been more cautious. I would not have come to Japan. And if I hadn't come to Japan, I would not have killed Yuriko Hirata, my younger sister would not have died, and I would not be suspected of Kazue Satō's murder. I could have gotten a job in a factory near the village and would have learned to content myself with one yuan a day. That's the way my life would have ended. When I think about what might have been, I'm consumed with grief.

What I did to Miss Hirata was unforgivable. I have no way to apologize. If it were possible, I would gladly replace her life with my own miserable existence.

However, when I was thirteen, I never would have imagined that this is the way I would end up. At the time, I could not forgive An-ji for what he had done. I could not bear to watch my parents grieve or listen to the malicious gossip the villagers circulated about us. I hated An-ji. But then, a person's emotions are a curious thing. At the very bottom of my heart, I couldn't help but sympathize with him.

After all, what he did was not unreasonable. Even I found Gen-de's behavior extremely offensive. He liked to fool around and was always out chasing women. He stole money from my father and spent it on booze. He was a complete good-for-nothing. Why, some of the villagers had even caught him having sex with the goats, and the gossip that ensued was a source of great shame for my father.

To be perfectly honest, Gen-de had brought so much shame to our family that I was relieved when he died and An-ji, who was to inherit my father's fields, escaped going to prison. If An-ji had been sent to prison, I would have inherited the fields, but it would have been more a curse than a blessing. Tied to a tiny parcel of land, I would have been forced to endure a life of hardship without ever knowing the civilized world.

The impoverished masses of China's inland people have one good thing going for them: freedom. But that's it. With no one to take particular notice of us, we were left pretty much to our own devices. And we clung to our freedom. So long as we stayed in the country, we were free to go where we wanted, do what we wanted, and die like dogs if we wanted. But all I could think about at the time was getting out of there and going to the city.

After my brother died, I had to take his place and look after the goats. Those were my father's wishes. But when I turned eighteen I took a job in a little factory nearby that made straw hats and wicker pillows. I was able to do that because we sold the goats when my mother started to suffer from a stomach ailment. I preferred working at the factory, making things from wheat straw, over tending the goats or working the fields. But the pay was low. I got only one yuan for every day of work. Still, even that paltry sum was a luxury in a family as financially strapped as my own.

Around that time, the second and third sons on the farm next to ours started preparing to go out to work in one of the port cities. The farm they had was not enough to feed all the mouths in the family, and the village already had too many workers. There were no jobs for young men and no marriage partners for them either. So most of them just loitered around the village like Gen-de had done—up to no good, getting into scrapes, and causing trouble.

A fellow I had known since we were children, Jian Ping, went off to Zhuhai in Guangtung, which later became designated as a Special Economic Zone. Here he took a job with a construction company, mixing cement and hauling building materials. With the money he sent back to the village, his family bought a color television, a motorcycle, and all kinds of other things that we considered great luxuries. I was so jealous I could die.

I wanted to set out for the city as soon as I could. But how was I to raise the money? The earnings I made at the straw factory—one yuan a day—were so measly, I couldn't even think of saving it. If I was going to get funds together, I'd have to take out a loan. But from whom? No one in the village was in a position to loan money. I had to raise the funds somehow so I could go off to the city like Jian Ping. That became my one and only dream.

In 1988, the year before the Tiananmen Square massacre, news shot through the village that Jian Ping had died. From Zhuhai City, he could see Macau just across the harbor, and apparently he had drowned while trying to swim across and smuggle himself into the country. At least, that is the information provided by the person who wrote the letter announcing Jian Ping's death.

Jian Ping had wrapped his documents and money into a bundle and tied it to his head. He waited for the sun to go down and headed to the outskirts of Zhuhai. Then, with his eyes fastened on Macau, he began swimming. It was pitch-black and he swam a number of miles, intending to slip secretly into Macau waters. To a Japanese, his action would probably appear unbelievably reckless. But I can understand his feelings so strongly it makes my heart ache.

Zhuhai and Macau are connected by land. You can stand on the streets of Zhuhai and look over at Macau. Just a breath away, a different country stretches out before your eyes, inhabited by the same race of people. And casinos. Macau has casinos. And money. Where there is money, one can do anything and go anywhere. In Macau people enjoy all kinds of freedoms, every freedom there is. But that freedom, we hear, is guarded by border patrols and surrounded by an electrified fence. Could there be a more cruel place on earth?

If caught trying to sneak across the border, we were told that you'd be sent to a prison where the conditions were worse than horrible. You'd be stuffed into a tiny room where bedbugs the size of animals crawl over everything, and where you're forced to fight others in the cell for the luxury of using the shit-encrusted slop jar.

But there is no high wall in the water. The waves cross the seas freely. I decided that I would try to swim for freedom too. I would swim to Macau, perhaps even Hong Kong.

In China, a person's fate is determined by where he is born; that is an inescapable fact. Jian Ping was willing to risk his life in an effort to alter his predetermined destiny. When I heard what had happened, my ideas underwent a change. I was determined to take Jian Ping's place in the effort to cross the ocean, to head for a free country where I could make as much money as I wanted.

•

At the end of that year my family began to discuss a marriage proposal for my younger sister, Mei-kun. The proposal was a good one for a family like ours, seeing as how we lacked financial resources. Although the suitor was a man from our village, he came from a fairly wealthy family. But there was a marked difference in ages. Mei-kun was just nineteen and her suitor was already thirty-eight. The suitor was short and homely. Small wonder that he was still without a wife!

"You're going to accept his offer, aren't you?" I asked my sister. "You'll be able to live a better life than you have until now."

Mei-kun looked down at her lap and shook her head.

"I absolutely refuse. I despise that puny little monkey of a man, even if he does have more money than we do. He's so short I'd still have to look down on him, wouldn't I! I won't go. If they do make me go, I'll agree to tending the fields, but that's it. I'm not going to become an old woman like my sister."

I gazed at my little sister. What she said was not unreasonable. Our older sister—six years my senior—had married into a family that was not much better off than our own, and she had had children one right after the other until now she was as dried up as an old woman. But Mei-kun . . . Mei-kun was an adorably attractive girl, the very apple of my eye. Her cheeks were round and her nose thin. Her limbs were long and slender and graceful when she moved. Sichuan is known for its beautiful women. I'd heard that a girl from Sichuan could go to any city in the world and be assured of a warm reception. My little sister had inherited a wanderer's blood from her grandfather. She was prettier than any of the girls in the nearby villages and she was headstrong.

"If I had a suitor like you, I'd marry," Mei-kun went on with great earnestness. "I've seen all the actors on the color television that Jian Ping's family has, and I don't think any of them come close to you."

I'm embarrassed if I seem conceited, but I have to admit that around my village people thought I was a handsome man. Of course, our village was small. If I went to the big cities I am sure I'd find any number of men better looking than I. Even so, my sister's compliment gave me confidence. And after I came to Japan, people often told me I looked like the actor Takashi Kashiwabara. Mei-kun looked me right in the eye and said, "We ought to appear on TV together, you and me. We're both good-looking, and we have a nice sense of style. I'll bet we could make lots of money in the movies. But of course we'll never get a chance, as long as we stay in a village like this. I'd rather die than stay here. Let's go to Guangzhou together. Really. What do you say?"

My sister looked around the cave where we lived—our dark, cold, damp home. Outside we could hear our mother and An-ji talking in gloomy tones about when it would be best to sow the millet. I couldn't take much more of this place. I'd had enough. As I listened to An-ji's voice, I supposed my sister had the same feelings. She reached out and took my hand.

"Let's get out of here. Let's go and live in a house made of concrete, just the two of us. A house with plumbing and no need to haul water, a house with electric wiring throughout the walls, a bright warm house with a toilet and a bath. We could buy a television and a refrigerator, a washing machine too. It would be so much fun to live in a house like that with you!"

We'd run electricity through the cave about two years ago. I'd stolen some electric wires and rigged them up to the closest utility pole.

"I want to go, believe me I do. But we'll have to save up the money. Right now I'm broke."

My sister looked at me like I was an idiot.

"What are you talking about? I'll be an old lady by the time you've saved up the money! And if we wait, I've heard, the train fares will go up as well."

I'd also heard the same rumor. They said train fares would be higher after the lunar New Year. That news made me want to leave all the sooner—certainly before the fares increased. But where was I going to find the funds to cover our travel? That's when Mei-kun murmured, "If I agree to marry that man, he'll have to bring me a gift of betrothal money, right? Why don't we use that?"

What my sister proposed was preposterous, yet we could think of no other way to get out of town. Reluctantly, I agreed to abscond with the money.

•

When Mei-kun's suitor heard she had agreed to marry him, he was overjoyed. He brought money over that he had been saving for several decades. All told it came to 500 yuan, more money than my entire family would make in a year. My father was delighted and stowed the money away in his chest. That's where it was when my sister and I stole it. We fled from the village the day following New Year's on the lunar calendar. Careful not to be seen, we raced toward the bus stop on the outskirts of town just before dawn, eager to catch the first bus of the morning.

As early as it was, the bus was already packed. Others had heard the same story we had been told about the hike in train fares, and everyone was eager to get to the cities before the rates went up. My sister and I crammed ourselves and our heavy bags onto the bus, not to be deterred. We would have to stand the whole way, a ride that would take more than two days. We've come this far, I encouraged my sister. Just hold out a bit more and we'll be in Guangzhou, just as we'd dreamed. I smiled.

When the bus finally reached its last stop, a lonely country station, a snow-laced rain had begun to fall. Dog-tired, I peered out in the hope of finding a shelter from the rain, but saw something so shocking I grabbed my sister's hand tightly.

A large crowd of people was sitting on the rain-soaked ground in front of the train station. There had to be as many as a thousand people, mostly young men and women, and they were being pelted by the rain, their clothes saturated and heavy with the weight. Clinging to plastic bags filled with pots and clothes and other possessions, they waited patiently for the train. Since there were only two inns, I was certain they were already filled to capacity. I saw no stores. All I could see were waves of people waiting in front of the silent station. From among the rain-drenched crowd, an occasional white puff of breath or steam drifted loosely skyward.

Our bus wasn't the only one to arrive. After we got out, bus after bus pulled up, each just as full as the last. The people on the buses looked to be coming from villages even more remote than ours and equally as impoverished. The number of people in front of the station continued to grow. It was impossible for those newly arrived to get close to the station. They pressed close to one another, and here and there little pushing matches and squabbles arose. The railway guards rushed around but there was little they could do.

We'd be lucky if we could get close enough to buy a ticket, I realized, let alone board the train. I was overwhelmed. We couldn't very well go home, not after we'd stolen the engagement money. Even my strong-willed little sister must have been feeling discouraged, because she looked like she was going to cry.

"What are we going to do? At this rate it'll be a week before we can even get on the train! And while we wait more people will come and the price will go up!"

"We'll think of something."

While I tried to comfort my sister I was recklessly pushing ahead, try-ing to ease the two of us into a group of people that was closer to the sta-tion. People began to shout angrily. "We're lined up here! Go back to the end of the line!" I glared in the direction of the voices. Among the group was one brute of a man who looked eager to start a fight. But my sister appealed to the man in a pathetic little voice. "Oh God, I feel so sick I think I'm going to die."

With little choice, the man reluctantly moved aside about six inches. I planted a foot in the space and set our cooking pot there. When I finally had enough room to sit, I pulled my little sister down on my lap. She buried her face in my shoulder and collapsed against me like a rag. I sup-pose we looked to the rest of the world like a loving couple, doing their best to comfort each other. But in fact, both my sister and I were so agi-tated we were ready to fall apart at any minute. We were so nervous we could hardly think straight. Yet we had no choice but to wait for the train.

Glancing at the people around us, my sister murmured, "All the peo-ple here seem to have tickets already. We've got to get tickets too."

The ticket window was already closed. I squeezed my sister's shoul-ders to silence her. If we stayed pressed as tight as this, there'd be no need for either of us to have a ticket. Besides, I was determined not to lose my place, even if it cost my life. I was going to get on that train. If that meant I had to clamber over the heads of all these people, that is what I would do—of that I was certain.

We waited for six hours, and during that time the number of people only increased, each and every one of us heading to the city in search of work.

Finally we heard people begin to shout, "The train's coming!" The farmers huddled in the station all began to scramble eagerly to their feet. Terrified by the surging mass of people, the station attendants abandoned the checking of tickets. There were a handful of station guards on duty, but we didn't let the fear of bullets stop us. We all pushed slowly toward the platform. Overwhelmed by the massive wall of people, fear flashed across the faces of the station guards. They knew they would not be able to stay the onslaught. The chocolate-colored train neared the platform and the crowds heaved forward before halting with a great sigh of disappointment. The windows of the train were fogged up so it was impossible to see inside, but people's feet and arms and belongings jutted out of the doors. The train was obviously already grossly overcrowded.

"If we don't do something," I told Mei-kun, "we'll never get out of this station. No matter what happens, do not let go of my hand. Do you understand? We're getting on that train."

I gripped my sister's hand, and we put our bundles up in front of our bodies. Then we pushed with all our might. I don't know if it was because my cooking pot was jamming into his backbone, but the man in front of me glanced over his shoulder with a pained expression, lost his footing, and stumbled to the side. Gradually the wall of people gave way. A number of people fell but I pushed ahead to the train without any apology, trampling bodies on my way.

Terrified of the stampede, the station guards and attendants had long since fled. Scarcely aware of their departure, we pushed recklessly ahead, climbing over people, being climbed on. It didn't matter. Everyone there had but one thought in mind: Get on the train! We were all wild with determination, not caring what happened to anyone else.

"Zhe-zhong! Zhe-zhong!"

I heard my sister's shrill scream. Someone had hold of her hair and was pulling her backward. If she fell, she'd be trampled and likely killed. I dropped the bags I was carrying and rushed to her rescue, punching the face of the woman who had grabbed her hair until she let go. Blood began to spurt from the woman's nose, but there was no one to care. It was insane.

I have no defense against anyone who might criticize my behavior at the time. I was in a situation that no one in Japan could possibly understand. The spectacle of all these people fighting to board one hopelessly overcrowded train may seem ridiculous, but for us it was a matter of life and death.

My sister and I managed to inch closer and closer to the train. But now I saw that there was a person in the nearest car waving a thick wooden rod and threatening to beat anyone who tried to push aboard. He clipped the man in front of me on the side of the head with the rod and sent him toppling to the side. Just at that moment the wheels of the train began to turn. Frantic now, I lurched at the person wielding the stick and, with the help of a strong man at my side, managed to yank him off the train. Then, using the people who had fallen as a stepping stool, I succeeded in hoisting my sister and myself aboard. Any number of people tried to follow suit, desperate to scramble after us. But now I took up the position of the man with the stick and did what I could to push them away. When I think back on it now it gives me goose bumps. It really was like a scene from hell.

Even after the train pulled out of the station, my sister and I remained in a state of extreme agitation. Sweat pored down our faces as we turned to look at each other. My sister's hair was tangled and her face was bruised and streaked with mud. I'm sure I didn't look much better. We said nothing—having no words to express our feelings—but I knew we were feeling the same way. We made it! We were lucky!

After a bit we regained our composure. We were once again crammed in with other people who were as heavily bundled as we, with no option but to stand in the aisles between the seats. We couldn't sit down, much less stretch out. After half a day we would reach Chongqing. It would be two more days before we made it to Guangzhou. Neither of us had ever set foot outside our village, and here we were traveling by bus and train for the first time, heading for a place we'd never seen. Would we be able to endure the stress? I wondered. And what awaited us at our destination?

"I'm thirsty," my sister whined as she leaned against my chest. We'd used up all our water and food on the bus. Afraid of losing our space at the station, we had not tried to get our hands on more. We'd had no choice but to board the train with no provisions. I ran my fingers over my sister's tangled hair, smoothing it down as best I could.

"Put up with it."

"I know. I just wonder if we're going to have to stand like this the whole way."

My sister glanced around. Among the other passengers standing in the aisle, some were drinking water or eating steamed bean-jam dumplings with one hand and holding on with the other without losing their balance. What really surprised us was a woman standing and cradling a baby in her arms. Chinese peasants are certainly sturdy.

A group of four girls who looked to be no more than sixteen or seventeen years old were standing together in one corner at the end of the aisle. They had clearly worked hard to look fashionable, tying their hair with red or pink ribbons. But one glance at the way their round cheeks were sunburned, and their hands swollen red with chilblains, and I could tell they were country girls used to the harsh conditions of fieldwork. My sister was so much prettier there was no comparison, I thought, and a wave of pride washed over me.

Every time the train swayed, the ugly girls shrieked coquettishly and grabbed hold of the men standing around them. My sister glared at them contemptuously. One of the girls pulled out a jar of Nescafé instant coffee that had long since been emptied of its original contents. She had filled it with steeped tea, which she now drank with a grandiose gesture, as if to taunt my sister. For us, foreign import goods like instant coffee were magnificent luxuries. We'd only seen empty jars of the product and then only at the houses of the village wealthy.

My sister gazed enviously at the tea. When she saw this, the girl turned her torture up a notch, pulling a tangerine out of her bag and peeling off the skin. It was only a small tangerine, but the sweet citrus smell suffused the train compartment. Oh, that scent! Just thinking of it brings tears to my eyes. That scent defined the difference between the haves and the have-nots, an unimaginably wide difference! A difference that is enough to drive a person crazy, disrupt his life. I don't think you Japanese can ever really understand this feeling. And you are fortunate as a result.

The scent of the tangerine suddenly disappeared and was replaced by a horrible odor. The door to the toilet had opened. Everyone immediately turned their heads away and trained their eyes downward. This was because a yakuza type had emerged from the toilet. Most of the people on the train were dressed in soiled Mao suits. But this fellow was wearing a smart-looking gray suit jacket, a red turtleneck sweater, and baggy black trousers. He had a white scarf tied around his neck. His clothes were good quality. But his eyes glinted shiftlessly just like Gen-de's had. He was clearly a tough customer. When the toilet door opened I could see two other men inside, both dressed just like him, smoking cigarettes.

"Those bastards have laid claim to the toilet and now no one else can use it," the man standing alongside me muttered bitterly. He was a head shorter than I.

"Well, then what are we supposed to use?"

"The floor."

I was shocked. But when I looked down at my feet I saw that the floor was already damp. I thought I'd smelled something foul when we got on the train. Now I knew what it was: human piss.

"What if you need to take a shit?"

"Well. . . ." The man laughed, revealing that he only had one tooth in the front of his mouth. "I have a plastic bag with me, so I'm going to use that."

But once the bag was full I had no doubt that he'd drop it on the floor of the train. He might just as well take a crap on the floor to start with. "Why don't you just do it in your hands?" the pimple-faced teenager behind me cut in.

The people around us laughed, but half of them looked pretty desperate. It was pathetic. No matter how poor my family was, even though we lived in a cave, we never would have considered soiling our home with our own excrement. Human beings just don't live that way.

"Are all the cars like this?"

"They're all the same. The first thing a person does when he gets on is try to secure the toilet. A seat comes second; he heads right for the toilet. See, if the train gets packed like this, even if the toilet is empty you can't get to it. Far better to try to occupy the toilet. Sure, it may stink. But if you bring a board with you and place it over the hole, at least you can sit down in there; you can even stretch your legs out and sleep. And you can lock the door, see, and ensure that no one gets in but you and your friends."

I craned my neck to look around me in the car. People were packed together, standing in the aisles and even in between the seats, and small children and young women were stretched out in the luggage racks above the seats. The seats accommodated four people, face-to-face, but all I could see of those seated was the black hair on the top of their heads. They were crammed so tightly into their seats that they couldn't move and had no choice but to do their business right there in front of everyone.

"It's not so bad for men, I suppose, but it must be hard on the women."

"Well, they can pay those fellows to let them use the toilet."

"They have to pay?"

"Yep, that's the business they're in: charging money for the toilet."

I looked stealthily at the yakuza. He must have gotten bored inside the toilet and come out to look around. He stared at the group of girls, seeming to size them up. Then he watched the mother nurse her baby. When the group of girls turned away bashfully, the man next set eyes on my sister. I was alarmed and tried to hide her from his line of vision. I began to feel worried by her beauty. The man glared at me. I looked down.

The man shouted in a loud voice, "The toilet costs twenty yuan to use. Any takers?"

Twenty yuan would amount to about three hundred yen in Japan. A paltry sum, perhaps. But I made only one yuan a day when I worked at the factory.

"That's expensive," said the girl who had been eating the tangerine, throwing out a challenge.

"Well, then, I guess you won't be using the toilet."

"If we don't we'll die."

"Suit yourself. Go ahead and die."

The man spit this out and slammed the door shut. Three men were in that tiny toilet. What were they doing? I had no idea. All I knew was that there was far more room in the toilet than standing in the aisle.

"I wish I were a baby," my sister said, as she gazed enviously at the infant in its mother's arms. "I could wear diapers, drink breast milk, and not worry about a thing!" My sister's face was pale and streaked with dirt. Dark circles had formed under her eyes. That was to be expected. Before we waited hours to board the train we had stood on a cramped and jostling bus for two days. We were totally exhausted. I told my sister to lean on me and try to get some sleep.

I'm not sure how much time had passed, but over the tops of people's heads I caught a glimpse of the sun setting outside the window. Everyone in the train was quiet, squished together. We swayed to the rhythm of the train, everyone moving as one. My sister awoke and looked up at me. "How much farther to Chongqing, do you think?"

I didn't have a watch, so I had no idea what time it was. The man with no front teeth overheard her question. "We get to Chongqing in about two more hours. And there'll be people there who'll want to get on. It'll be interesting."

"At Chongqing will we be able to buy food and water?" I asked.

When he heard my question the toothless man snickered. "What kind of wishful thinking is that? Do you suppose you can get back on the train if you get off? That's why everyone brought water and food with them."

"Is there anyone who'll share with us?"

"I will." I swung around when I heard someone answer. A man in a tattered and patched Mao suit was waving a grimy-looking bottle filled with water. "One drink for ten yuan."

"That's too much."

"Then go without. This is all I've got; I'm not giving it away."

"Let us each have a drink for ten yuan." I looked at my sister's face in surprise. She wore a determined look.

"You drive a hard bargain. All right then."

When he struck the deal a young woman at the other end of the aisle held up a tangerine and shouted, "You want this for ten yuan?"

My sister's response was curt. "I'll let you know after I've had a drink of water." When she had drunk her fill she handed the bottle to me and mumbled, "If you're smart, you'll drink as much as you can. We're paying ten yuan for it, after all."

"True."

My sister's expression startled me. I brought the bottle to my lips and drank. The water was warm and tasted rusty. But it was all the water I'd had in over half a day. Once I started drinking, I couldn't stop. "That's enough!" the man shouted angrily, but I played the fool. "I'm just taking my drink," I said. The people around us laughed scornfully.

"Pay up now!" the man said.

I pulled the money out of my pocket. I had all the bills rolled up together and bound with a rubber band. The murmur that shot through the crowd around me when they saw the wad of bills was nearly deafening. Of course, I had not wanted to show all my money to strangers, but I had no other way of getting ten yuan out of my pocket.

My hand trembled so badly I could hardly count the bills. Not just because everyone's eyes were riveted on me, but because I'd never paid ten yuan for anything back home. I heard my sister swallow. I suppose she too was anxious.

How absurd to have to lay out so much money just for a drink of water. I was appalled by such meanness. And yet I had to pay. The callousness of those around me was shocking. And yet it was a valuable experience. We were heading for the city, where we were sure to see and hear things we had never before imagined. This was a good introduction. I can still remember how shocked I was when I came to Japan and saw the way people spent money like water, without a care. It made me so angry I wanted to curse them all.

At any rate, I finally counted out ten one-yuan bills and handed them to someone who gave them to the man who'd sold us the water. When I did, the man grew even more irritated. "You act like such a country bumpkin, and there you are with all that cash, you bastard! I ought to have charged more!"

The young woman who had earlier tried to sell us the tangerine started to ridicule the man. "Don't be so greedy. You only have yourself to blame, not knowing the first rule of sales! Before you start criticizing our country cousins here you ought give your own hollow head a whack! It might knock some sense into you!"

The people standing around her laughed.

"Those two are loaded! They have to be carrying close to five hundred yuan!" The man with only one front tooth spoke so loudly everyone in the train car heard. Everyone started to mumble and murmur. The group of four girls turned to stare at us, their mouths agape.

"Mind your own business," I told the man. But he just laughed at me like I was an idiot.

"You don't know shit about the world, do you?" he taunted. "You ought to divide your cash into smaller wads and tuck it in different places. That way one person can't make off with it all at once."

Right. Right. The people surrounding the man—people who had nothing to do with any of this—nodded in agreement. Mr. Tooth continued ribbing me.

"No doubt about it, you're a bona fide hick. Haven't you ever heard of a wallet? I bet you come from a village that's so poor you've run out of wives."

"Well, it takes one to know one! You sure do stink. Haven't you ever heard of a bath? Or maybe peeing on the floor is the custom at your house. Hey, I've a favor to ask you. Take your filthy hand off my ass!" my sister shouted.

When they heard the way my sister responded, the rest of the car burst into laughter. Mr. Tooth turned beet red and looked down with embarrassment. I clasped my sister's hand. "Way to tell him, Mei-kun."

"You can't let people get away with stuff like that, Zhe-zhong. Before long they're going to be throwing themselves at our feet, each and every one of them. We're going to become movie stars, beloved throughout the land and rich to boot."

My sister poked me in the ribs with her elbow to emphasize each of her points. Yes, it is true. I had come to depend on my little sister with her quick wit and strong will to pull me along in life. And yet I ended up in this foreign country without her. I hope you can understand just how difficult it has been for me, how lost I have been.

Sometime later, the train jerked suddenly and the passengers toppled forward. Outside I could see telephone poles and the lights of tall buildings. It was a city. I started to grow excited. We'd reached Chongqing! It's Chongqing! Chongqing! The people around me began to clamor nervously, expectantly, uneasily.

Mr. Tooth, who had grown quiet after being shamed by my sister, said just behind me, "You two don't have tickets, do you? I know you sneaked on." He waved a pink-colored ticket in my face. "If you don't have a ticket, they take you off the train and throw you in jail."

My sister looked up at me in shock. Just at that point the train glided into the station. Chongqing was a big city, but it was the first station the southbound train had entered. The platform was swarming with people, all farmers, waiting there to transfer to our train. They began scrambling to board. The yakuza type picked up a heavy stick and walked toward me. I assumed he was going to use the stick to menace anyone who tried to board the train, but he handed the stick to me. "Give me a hand, why don't you?"

I had no choice but to comply. I got ready to spring into action, but when the door opened no one was there to get on. I was caught off guard. And then a young pistol-wielding station guard appeared in front of me, so I quickly brought the stick down to my side.

The guard shouted roughly, "Ticket inspection. Present your tickets for inspection. If you don't have a ticket, get off the train." The passengers around me lifted their pink-colored tickets high above their heads.

My sister and I looked down. Packed in like sardines among all those people, we were the only ones without tickets.

"You have no ticket?" I started to explain to the station policeman that I'd had no time to purchase one, but before I could the yakuza type held me back with his hand.

"He'll pay no matter the cost."

The guard turned immediately to the station official at his side and whispered in his ear. After a moment's consultation he said to me harshly, "It's two hundred yuan to Guangzhou." As a rule the ticket was usually no more than thirty yuan a person.

"Haggle!" I heard someone say from within the car.

"Two hundred yuan for two," I said.

"Get off the train," the station official said. "You're under arrest for boarding the train without a ticket."

The guard pointed his gun at me.

Desperate, I tried again. "Two for three hundred yuan."

"It's two for four hundred yuan."

"That's no better than when we started. How about two for three hundred and fifty yuan?"

Again the guard conferred with the station official. I waited nervously. In a minute he turned back to me with a solemn countenance and nodded. When I pulled the money from my pocket, the station official pressed two tickets on thin pink paper into my hand and shut the door.

•

My younger sister and I had endured hunger and thirst as we headed to Guangzhou, refusing offers from surrounding passengers to sell us food and water. My hands had barely stopped trembling from the ordeal of counting my money in front of others. But of everything we had started out with, we had only a tiny sum left. I was overcome with remorse. If only I'd thought to stock up on food and water before we got on the train, I would not have had to squander my sister's precious betrothal gift. I certainly was naïve. Why hadn't I realized that there would be others, lots of others, trying to migrate to the city just like us? By the time we got to Guangzhou we had barely one hundred yuan left.

In the farming villages of China there are over two hundred and seventy million people, more than the arable land can feed. The farms produce only enough to support a hundred million, fewer than half. Of the remaining hundred seventy million people, about ninety million work in local factories. The other eighty million have no choice but to head to the cities to look for work. At the time this influx of surplus labor was referred to in China as the Blind Flow. Now of course it's known as the Pool of the People's Workforce. But *blind flow* better captures the reality of a desperate people groping about in darkness, struggling to follow the beacon of light glittering off the money available in the city.

All this I learned while aboard the train from the pimple-faced college student who stood behind me. Pimple's name was Dong Zhen. He was tall and lanky, with shoulders that jutted out like a clothes hanger. His face was covered with festering pimples that oozed a yellow pus. "Zhe-zhong," Dong Zhen asked me, "can you guess how many people will migrate from Sichuan to Guangzhou after New Year's on the lunar calendar has passed?"

I tilted my head to the side. I came from a village of four hundred. It was impossible for me to imagine a large gathering of people. Even if I'd been told it would be the whole of Sichuan, it wouldn't have made much impact on me because I'd never seen a map.

"I don't know."

"About nine hundred thousand people."

"Well, where are they all going to go?"

"Just like you—to Guangzhou and Zhu Jiang, the Pearl River Delta."

I couldn't believe there'd be enough work to go around if more than nine hundred thousand people crowded into the same city. I was being carried along by bus and train, but I still had no idea what a city was.

"Will there be a place we can go to get help finding a job?"

Dong Zhen laughed. "You really are an idiot. No one will help you. You have to do it on your own."

When I heard this I was beset by doubts. All I'd done up to now was tend goats and make straw hats. What kind of work was I going to be able to find? I recalled that my friend Jian Ping had worked in construction, so I asked Dong Zhen. "What about construction work?"

"That's the kind of job anyone can do, so the competition's stiff."

Dong Zhen took a swig of water out of his canteen as he answered. I gazed at the water longingly.

"Would you like a sip?" he asked. And he let me take a drink. The water smelled stale and fishy, but I was grateful all the same to have been given a swallow without having to pay. In the entire train car only one person was heading to university, and that was Dong Zhen. I imagined that as a member of the intelligentsia he would look down on simple farmers, but Dong Zhen was unexpectedly kind.

"I'm sure there's a section of town where they pick up day laborers. You ought to go there and wait. I've heard that if you carry your own shovel and tools you'll get hired right away."

"What about my little sister? What kind of work could she get?"

"Women can get all kinds of jobs from babysitters, maids, nurses, laundresses, and the like to mortician assistants in the morgue. Then there're jobs as guides at the crematorium, tea servers, and so on—every one of them low paying."

"How come you're such an expert?"

"It's just common sense. But I guess I would look smart next to you; you really don't know much about anything! You'll see. Fellows who come to the city looking for work tend to talk a lot, and news travels by word of mouth. Before you know it, you'll have heard it all."

Dong Zhen leaned over to me.

"Your little sister doesn't look the type to take to the kind of dreary jobs I mentioned," he whispered in my ear.

Mei-kun had gone to the toilet, and I suddenly noticed that she had not yet returned. I looked around and saw that she was standing by the toilet, the door open wide, talking intimately with the group of young thugs. What was so funny? I wondered. They had suddenly started to laugh. All the other passengers on the train turned—as if on signal—and stared at the four of them. I kept my eye on my sister as she gazed up at the yakuza. She was flirting with him. It made me feel queasy. Dong Zhen poked me in the ribs.

"Looks like your little sister is making friends with the gangster."

"No, that's not it. She just doesn't want to spend money on the toilet, so she's trying to manipulate him."

"She seems very adept at the game. Look, she's giving him a beating!"

My sister was patting the yakuza on the arm and laughing. For his part, he was pretending that it hurt and flinching from her touch with exaggerated gestures.

"Let it go."

Dong Zhen realized I was angry and started to tease me. "My God, you two act more like lovers than siblings!"

He'd struck a nerve. I flushed red with embarrassment. Yes, I was ashamed to admit it, but I was very fond of my sister. When I worked at the straw hat factory, there were ten female employees in addition to the men. They were all teenagers. They'd call out to me and follow me around, but they didn't interest me in the slightest. Not one of them could hold a candle to Mei-kun.

"At the rate she's going, your little sister's going to be heading off with that gangster."

"Mei-kun wouldn't do something so stupid."

It never occurred to me that Dong Zhen's words would turn out to be true, but when the train finally pulled into the station at Guangzhou, my sister leaped to the platform with an animated expression and said to me excitedly, "Zhe-zhong, do you mind if we say good-bye here?"

I couldn't believe my ears. "Are you sure?" I asked her again and again.

"Yes, I've already found a job," she said, with great pride.

"What kind of job?"

"Working in a first-class hotel."

Exhausted after traveling for two days and nights with nothing to eat, I stumbled to the platform.

"Those fellows said they'd help me find a job, so I'm going to go with them." My sister pointed to the yakuza and his two friends. I walked over toward them. Pointing to the man who'd handed me the stick at Chongqing, I demanded angrily, "What the hell do you want with my sister?"

"You must be Zhe-zhong. My name's Jin-long. Your sister here says she's looking for a job, so I'm going to introduce her to someone I know. She can work at the White Swan Hotel. Everyone wants a job there. Must be your lucky day." Jin-long adjusted his white scarf at his throat as he responded.

"Where is this White Swan Hotel?"

"It's a first-class hotel built in the former concession on Shamian Island."

"Shamian?"

Jin-long looked back at my sister and me and burst into raucous laughter. "Man, you really are a hick!" Mei-kun joined him in laughing at me. That's when I realized my sister was angry at me: for getting on the train without knowing what I was doing, for spending four hundred yuan.

I grabbed her shoulder angrily. "You have no idea what kind of trouble you can get into, do you? He's a gangster. Don't you get it? That first-class hotel is all a big lie. It's just a ruse to get you into prostitution."

My sister looked troubled by what I'd said. But Jin-long just scratched the side of his nose and answered, as if annoyed, "I'm not lying. I'm friends with the hotel cook so I've got influence. If you're worried about it, come by the hotel yourself."

When my sister heard what he said, she held her hand out to me.

"Give me half of what's left of the money."

I had no choice but to do as she asked. I counted out half of the one hundred yuan and handed it to her. As soon as she tucked it away in her pocket, she looked up at me happily. "Come by and see me, Zhe-zhong!"

I watched my sister walk across the station platform with Jin-long and his gang, the bag with all her worldly possessions dangling from her hand. And then she disappeared through the gate. I was supposed to protect my little sister, yet wasn't I the one who had depended on her? Suddenly I felt as if one of my arms had been ripped from my body. I was petrified. Hordes of weary travelers pushed past me, racing to get to the gates of the station.

"Well, that was a shock! Your sister's not one to wait around, is she?"

It was Dong Zhen.

"I messed up."

When he heard my weak reply, Dong Zhen looked at me sympathetically. "Well, that's the way it goes. I was all alone from the very beginning. Better go buy a shovel," Dong Zhen advised, and disappeared into the crowds, pushing his way through with his bony shoulders. When I came to my senses, I realized that I was soaked with sweat. It was only the beginning of February, but Guangzhou was farther south than Sichuan and much warmer.

I walked off with my back to Guangzhou Station. The men and women who passed me by were stylish and walked with confidence and pride. Tall buildings, so big they might have been palaces, loomed overhead; the sun, reflected off the window glass, shone in my eyes. I had no idea how to cross the broad road buzzing with traffic. An old woman looked at me in disgust, as I stood confused on the side of the road, and pointed to a pedestrian overpass. Great swarms of people were on the bridge crossing over the street. I too climbed the stairs and crossed but I was so tired and so hungry that I could not stop my knees from trembling. I have to say that I began to feel an intense hatred for my sister. She had betrayed me.

Just at that moment a policeman appeared in front of me, blocking my way. Remembering the incident at Chongqing Station, I immediately handed the man five yuan and asked him to direct me to the day laborers' pickup site. He pocketed the money without batting an eye and told me something. But I couldn't understand a word he said. He spoke Cantonese. I was flustered. This was China, but somehow I'd forgotten that the dialect spoken here would be different. Day laborer! Day laborer! I shouted my question countless times and finally in desperation began to imitate digging with a shovel. The policeman just pointed to the square in front of the station.

Finally it dawned on me. The station was the pickup site. With so many people to compete with, it would be next to a miracle if I managed to get a job. And while I waited to be picked, I'd run through all the money I had left and then would have no choice but to beg. I'm the kind of person who has to always be moving ahead. I can't just sit quietly and wait.

The farm folk who'd come to town searching for jobs had little choice but to live on the streets, and I was not unlike them. The figure we cut here wasn't much different from life back in the village, praying for rain. We entrusted ourselves to the whims of nature and depended entirely on the heavens for our survival. I was determined to be different. I was going to search for work on my own. That's what I said to encourage myself, at any rate. I was not going to end up just another member of the crowd in front of the station. I had to get away from them. I walked with determination down the road alongside the cars and motorcycles.

Finally I reached a section where the traffic wasn't so heavy. I was on an avenue lined with plantain trees that stretched as far as the eye could see. On both sides of the avenue were old houses with peeling paint. The frontage of each house was narrow, and wooden shutters bordered the second-floor windows. The houses were built in the bright and airy South China style that I had not had an opportunity to see in my village. While I walked along the avenue, I thought I could imagine how Guangzhou natives must feel. The winters are warm, the greenery luxuriant—what a refreshing place to live.

I had always been insanely jealous of the people who lived such wealthy lives in port cities. As I rambled down the avenue, I could feel my heart growing lighter and brighter the farther I walked. Gradually I could feel my courage return. I was young. I was strong. I was neither bad-looking nor unintelligent. I could easily see myself finding success in this city and living in a house like one of these. If someone would just give me a chance, I could do anything.

I came to a fashionable street. There were girls with long hair eating ice cream as they strolled by. Young men wore snug-fitting jeans. I stopped in front of a shop window lined with glittering gold necklaces. In a restaurant I saw a fish tank lined with fat fish and large shrimp. The people inside the restaurant were happily dining on stir-fried meat and fish. How delicious it all looked!

The sun was setting. I was exhausted by the energy of the city and sat down alongside the road. I was thirsty and famished, but I didn't want to spend my money unwisely. All I had was a meager fifty yuan, and out of that I'd already squandered five. A child rode past on a bicycle and tossed a soda bottle on the side of the road. I hurried to pick it up and drained the liquid that remained in the bottom. It was Coca-Cola. Only a small bit was left, but I will never forget how delicious it was on my tongue—just like sweet medicine. I put tap water in the bottle and drank until I had exhausted the lingering sweet taste.

I'd have to earn money. I wanted to drink this beverage every day of the week until I'd had my fill. I'd go to the restaurant that I'd passed to buy more. And I'd eat their delicious food and live in one of those fine old houses. I started to walk again, my mind made up.

Eventually, I came to a construction site. I wondered if perhaps it was past quitting time. A group of men in the filthy clothes that immediately identified them as day laborers were sitting in a circle sharing stories and laughing. I asked the men if they knew where I could go to pick up a construction job. One of the men pointed a dirty finger and said, "Go back to Zhongshan Avenue and head east. You'll come to Zhu Jiang—it's a big river. There's a pickup site just along the riverbank."

I thanked the man. When he returned to his circle of friends, I grabbed a shovel and ran off.

It didn't take me long to find the laborer pickup site. There was a concrete retaining wall alongside the road, and just beyond it I could see the brown water of the Pearl River. Twenty to thirty men were already there. Off to the sides were shacks made of scrap lumber and old cement sacks:

makeshift barracks for the laborers. There was even a roadside food stall. With little to do, the men either sat in a circle talking in loud voices or squatted exhausted on their haunches. I asked a young man, "Is this where you pick up work?"

"Yeah," he answered abruptly. He eyed my shovel enviously. I gripped it tightly, prepared to fight if he tried to take it from me. I wanted to be sure I was in the right place, so I continued to question him.

"Can I line up here too?"

"You gotta get here early to get picked, but if you want to line up no one'll mind. Besides, there won't be any jobs left by the time they get to us."

So that was how it worked. This fellow had been too far back in line to get picked today, but he would be at the head of the line tomorrow. If you missed the pick one day, you got it the next. But conversely, when you did get picked, you'd miss it the next day. The only way to get a job, it seemed, was to push to the front of the line.

"What time do they start hiring tomorrow?"

"There's no particular time. They send a truck around, fill it up with workers, and then off they go. If you're not on the truck, you don't get work. You can't afford to goof around."

I took up my position right behind the man. Maybe it was the exhaustion of the journey finally catching up to me, but I fell asleep right where I was with my arms wrapped around the shovel.

I was awakened by the cold and the sound of people talking. Day was dawning, the blue sky spread directly in front of my eyes. I was surprised to find that I had slept straight through the night on the cold hard surface of the retaining wall. I staggered to my feet and found that several hundred men were milling anxiously around as if the work crew selection would begin any minute. I rubbed my eyes and took a drink of water from the bottle. Just then a truck came barreling toward us at top speed.

"Carpenters and coolies for bridge construction!" the man standing on the bed of the truck called out in a loud voice. "Fifty men."

As soon as they heard him, men began to run in his direction waving their hands. Using a long pole to keep them at bay, the man continued, "Only men with shovels or pickaxes."

I ran to the front of the crowd. The man took one look at my size and the shovel in my hand and nodded. Then he motioned me aboard the truck with his chin. Once he did all the men surrounding the truck started to clamber onto the bed, pushing and shoving, each determined to secure a place for himself. There was little the man could do to control them. The truck bed shuddered and shook. A number of men fell, or were pushed, and tumbled to the ground. It was just like the train. The truck bed was packed with people, and when no one else could squeeze on, the truck took off. A number of the men fell off when the truck pitched and swerved, but no one seemed to care. I clutched the shovel to my chest, careful so no one else would make off with it. The cool morning breeze off the river stung my cheeks.

•

I did construction work for three months. It was simple work but physically demanding. I'd work from seven in the morning until five at night. I'd mix concrete on-site or else help carry iron girders. I worked with every ounce of strength I possessed and made seventeen yuan a day. I didn't think that was enough, so as soon as I finished for the night, I'd head to town and get part-time jobs cleaning or picking up trash. I was satisfied with the way things were going because I was earning seventeen times what I'd made at the straw hat factory. There was just no way to compare the opportunities I had in the city with what I'd had back home, and I was delirious with joy.

In order to save money I'd picked up scrap lumber and plastic on the job sites and used the materials to make my own little shack back at the laborers' pickup place. I would stay there all night so when the truck came in the morning I was able to run out and line up. The other men who lived on the grounds were kind. If they made a stew of pig entrails, they'd give some to me. Or they'd call me over when they were sharing a bottle of cheap wine. But only the men from Sichuan Province did this. That's because we only trusted those from our own region, those who spoke the same language.

When I'd saved up one thousand yuan, I decided to quit working construction. I'd had enough of life in the barracks. Moreover, whenever I went to town for some entertainment, I'd see other men my age out with girls, and they seemed much happier than I was. I wanted to find a job in the city—something that would be easier and more attractive. But the kind of work a day laborer could do was just about limited to what they

now call the Three Ds: anything that was dangerous, dirty, and difficult.
This was true of work in the cities as well. In this respect, China is no different from Japan. In order to get advice about finding a job, I decided to
try to find my sister. I hadn't done so until then because I was still angry
about the way she had abandoned me.

I went to Zhongshan Avenue and bought a new T-shirt and a new pair
of jeans. I didn't want to embarrass her by showing up in my tattered
work clothes. Because I'd been working in construction, my skin was
tanned and my body had grown muscular. I imagined that when my sister saw me looking masculine and urbane, she would be impressed. I
was itching to confront Jin-long, as I was still angry with him for taking
my sister away from me. I hadn't forgotten for one second how strong he
had looked, how in control.

It was a hot day in early June. I carried a bag with a pink T-shirt in it,
a gift for my sister, and headed down Huangsha Avenue alongside the
Pearl River toward the White Swan Hotel. The hotel towered over
the Pearl River side of Shamian Island. It was massive, at least thirty stories high. As I gazed up to the top of the chalk-colored building, I felt
myself flush with pride to think that my younger sister, Mei-kun, was
working in such elegant surroundings. But I felt so uncomfortable when
confronted with all the foreign tourists walking in and out of the hotel
and strolling around the grounds that I found it hard to step through the
magnificent front doors. Four stocky doormen were standing alongside
the driveway in front of the hotel, each dressed in matching maroon uniforms. They glared at me suspiciously. The doormen skillfully greeted
guests arriving by taxi and guided them inside. And when foreign guests
returned to the hotel on foot, the doormen spoke to them in fluent
English. These doormen didn't look as if they would welcome an inquiry
from me, so I approached a man who was tending a patch of garden to
the side of the entry doors. From his appearance and attitude, I could
tell he was a migrant.

"Zhang Mei-kun is working here, and I was hoping you could tell me
how I might find her."

"Shall I ask for you?" the man replied in the northeastern accents of
Beijing. He put his rake down and went off. I waited and waited but he
did not return. I gazed at the rays of the sun glittering off the Pearl River
and grew more and more apprehensive. At last I felt a tap on my shoul-

der. It was the gardener. He spoke to me sympathetically. "There doesn't seem to be a Zhang Mei-kun working here. I asked one of the personnel staff to look the name up, and she's not listed anywhere. I'm sorry."

I was shocked, but in fact I had suspected as much. No one is that lucky. I had come to feel more and more certain that my sister had been tricked by Jin-long, but what could I do? Realizing I would never see Mei-kun again, tears began to roll down my cheeks.

"Well, what about a guy named Jin-long? He's a big guy who looks like a gangster. He said he had a friend who worked in the kitchen here."

"What's his family name? Do you know which restaurant he works in?"

I had no idea. I just shook my head from side to side.

"The cooks here all make good wages. It's not likely they'd run around with gangsters."

The man shrugged his shoulders as if to laugh at my ignorance and returned to his work. I was crestfallen. I followed the sidewalk around the hotel and walked off in the direction of Shamian, a natural island at a fork in the Pearl River. I'd heard that before the Revolution it had been a foreign settlement, and no Chinese were even allowed to set foot on the island. Now it was public land and anyone could enter.

This was my first trip to Shamian. A wide avenue spread out alongside rows upon rows of European buildings. Down the center of the avenue was a green median bursting with the bright red blooms of salvia and hibiscus. The houses lining the streets were even more beautiful than the tidy little houses I was so fond of in Guangzhou, one of which I intended someday to make my own. I sat on a bench and gazed along the avenue. Each day, it seemed, I discovered something that was even better than what I'd seen the day before. My thoughts returned to Mei-kun. Why hadn't I stopped her from leaving me?

"Hey, you!" A man's voice interrupted my thoughts. I turned to see a man who looked like a police official. He called to me in an arrogant tone. My heart froze. I'd come out with neither a residency permit nor any identification papers. The man was dressed in the kind of blue suit a government official would wear. His build was slight, but he walked with self-assured determination. Surely he was involved in some high-level position. The last thing I wanted to do was get nabbed for something, so I decided to act like a witless country bumpkin.

"I'm not doing anything wrong."

"I know. Just come with me for a minute."

The man took my arm and pointed to a black car parked beside one of the European buildings.

"Get in."

I couldn't get away. The man had me by the arm and was leading me to the car. It was a large Mercedes. The driver looked at me through his sunglasses and smirked. I was pushed into the backseat. The man in the suit got in the front passenger seat and turned around to look at me.

"I have a job for you. But you have to agree not to talk about it. That's the condition. If you can't agree to my condition, I'll let you out right now."

"What kind of job?"

"You'll see when we get there. If you aren't up for it, get out now."

I was terrified, but I was also intrigued. What if this was just the break I'd been waiting for? I couldn't get out. I'd had enough of life as a coolie, and I'd lost my beloved little sister. What else did I have to lose? I nodded in agreement.

The Mercedes headed back to the White Swan. When I'd left the hotel earlier, I never imagined I'd ever go back. The car pulled around to the front and the doormen who had earlier menaced me dashed out to greet us, opening the car doors adroitly. When the doormen saw me get out of the car they were not able to conceal their surprise. My spirits suddenly soared. No matter what kind of fate may be in store for me, it would have been worth it just to have experienced that feeling.

I entered the hotel for the first time, following the man in the suit. The lobby was crawling with wealthy people dressed in elegant clothes. I stopped in my tracks and stared, unable to help myself. The man grabbed my arm and tugged me roughly. He shoved me into the elevator and took me up to the top, the twenty-sixth floor. When the doors opened, I was assailed with anxiety and unable to move. If I step off the elevator now, I told myself, I can never go back to my old life.

· 3 ·

"Hurry up and get out," the man ordered impatiently. I stared at him in a daze.

"I don't think I can go through with this. I don't have my papers with me. Please, let me go home."

Heedless of my wishes, the man grabbed me roughly by the arms, yanked me out of the elevator, and forced me to walk alongside him. He was strong; I had little choice but to follow. My legs trembled in fear. The man dragged me off to a dimly lit corridor and pulled me along deeper and deeper into the hotel. No one else was around.

The hallway was covered with a thick beige carpet woven in an ornate design of water lilies and phoenixes. It was so luxurious I felt it wrong even to step on it. A dim lamp illuminated a far corner of the corridor, and from somewhere came the strains of elegant music. A marvelous scent wafted along the hallway. My fear gave way to a sense of gentle ease. I found the abruptness of the shift incredible. Had I never left the countryside, I would have died without ever even realizing such a wondrous place existed.

The man knocked on the last door. A woman's shrill voice called in answer and the door opened immediately. A young woman stood in front of us, dressed in a navy-blue suit and wearing bright red lipstick. "Come in," she said, as if it were a command. I looked around nervously and then drew a sigh of relief. There were three other men in the room. They looked to be my age. I suppose they had also been picked up, as had I, and brought to this place. They were sitting nervously on a sofa watching television.

I sat down gingerly on the edge of the sofa. The other men were migrants, just like me. I could tell at a glance from the clothes they wore. They were also nervous, having been dragged by a strange man and woman into a room more elegant than they could have ever imagined. They too were uncertain what would happen to them.

"Wait here," the man said, as he stepped into the adjoining room. He was gone for a long time. The woman with the bright red lipstick did not open her mouth once. She just sat there watching TV along with the rest of us. Her eyes were so cunning and sharp, I assumed she was either a police officer or a government agent. I'd been in the city now for three months, toiling as a migrant laborer; it didn't take me long to sniff out one of their kind. They gave themselves away with their haughty manner and high-handedness.

The television was tuned to a news story, covering some kind of riot. Young men were shouting with blood streaming down their faces; tanks were rolling in the streets, and people were running for cover. It looked like a civil war. Later I learned that this was the day following the killing in Tiananmen Square. I had not heard anything about the demonstrations, and had a hard time believing what I was seeing. The woman with the crafty face took up the remote control and turned off the television. The men, looking nervous, quickly averted their eyes, trying to avoid the woman's gaze, and exchanged uneasy glances.

The room we were in was massive. It looked like it could sleep up to twenty or thirty people. I suppose it was done in what you would call the rococco style. There was a lavish Western-style sofa set in the room and an enormous television set. In the corner of the room was a bar. The curtains across the large window were pulled back and I could see the rays of the afternoon sun glittering over the Pearl River. It may have been hot outside, but the air-conditioning was on in the room and it was cool and dry. In a word, refreshing.

The woman pierced me with her keen gaze but, undeterred, I stood up and stared at the scene outside the window. Off to the right I could see makeshift shacks that a group of migrant workers had slapped together. What a filthy sight. They shouldn't be allowed to build their shacks in such a beautiful place as this, I thought. Tiananmen Square seemed far away, like something completely unrelated to me.

The door to the adjoining room opened softly, and the man who had brought me there poked his head in and pointed to me.

"You, come here. The rest of you can leave."

The men who had been waiting looked relieved on the one hand and disappointed on the other, as if they'd missed an opportunity. They got to their feet and shuffled out. I headed for the next room, completely baffled as to what was to transpire. There I found an enormous bed in the center of the room. A woman was sitting in a chair by the bed, smoking a cigarette. She was short, and her body was firm and compact. Her hair was dyed a reddish brown and she was wearing large pink-rimmed glasses. A bright red gown was draped across her shoulders. She was garish and looked to be in her forties.

"Come over here."

Her voice was surprisingly soft. She beckoned me to a small settee. When I sat down, I noticed that the man who had brought me had left the room. It was just me and the woman now, sitting face-to-face. The woman raised her eyes—which looked twice as large as they were due to the magnification of her glasses—and examined me carefully. What on earth is going on? I wondered, as I returned the woman's gaze.

"What do you think of me?" she asked.

"That you're scary," I answered in all honesty, and the woman pulled her lips into a tight grimace.

"That's what everyone says."

She stood up and opened a small lockbox on a shelf next to the bed. She pulled out what looked to be a cupful of loose tea and poured some into a pot. Her hands were large. Then she poured hot water efficiently into the pot. She was making me a cup of tea.

"This is delicious tea," she said.

I would have preferred Coca-Cola, I thought to myself. But not wanting to anger the woman, who clearly saw things differently, I kept nodding.

She continued, saying triumphantly, "This oolong tea is of the highest quality. It's from fields that I own in Hunan. And every year we only produce a little tiny bit."

The woman made a circle with her hands the size of a soccer ball. I'd never been given a taste of such rare tea.

"What's your name?"

The woman sipped the tea and stared at me as if she were appraising merchandise. Her gaze was soft but penetrating. I felt my heart tighten instinctively. I didn't know what was going on, and I'd never been in a situation quite like this before: left alone with a woman whose purpose I did not understand.

"Zhang Zhe-zhong."

"Such a common name. My name is Lou-zhen. I make my living as a songwriter."

I couldn't imagine how one could make a living writing songs, but even a naïve country bumpkin like myself had had enough experience in the world to know that a woman who stayed in a luxurious hotel like this was not run-of-the-mill. Lou-zhen, a songwriter, had hired a man to go out and find men like me. Why? Was she involved in some kind of organized crime? I began to tremble at the thought, assailed by a fear I couldn't even name. But Lou-zhen said, as if it irked her, "I want you as my lover."

"Your lover? What do you mean?"

"It means you'll sleep with me."

She stared right at me as she said this. I felt my cheeks burn red hot.

"I couldn't do that."

"Yes, you could," she replied smoothly. "And in return I will give you a nice sum of cash. You want to make money, don't you? That's why you came to this city as a migrant laborer, isn't it?"

"Well, yes, but . . . I've been paid to *work*."

"I suppose you could say this will be work too!"

The woman seemed to realize that what she'd just said was peculiar, because she gave an embarrassed laugh. I couldn't tell if she was from a good family or not by the way she behaved.

"How much money are we talking about?"

"If you can satisfy me, I'll give you all you want. What do you think? A pretty good deal, huh?"

For a minute I couldn't respond. My heart was torn. On the one hand I didn't think I could ever possibly be a male prostitute, no matter what the compensation. On the other hand, I was sick and tired of working in construction, and the idea of making such easy money was extremely tempting. More than tempting, in fact. In the end the money won out. I slowly nodded my consent. Lou-zhen smiled and filled my cup with tea.

In truth, it takes considerable courage to write about this. I hesitated to divulge all these details in the written report I submitted earlier to this court, Your Honor. But now I've been given an opportunity to reflect on my past life. I just pray that you will read what I have written here without prejudice or contempt.

So that is how I allowed the wealthy middle-aged Lou-zhen to buy me. I knew she was only interested in my body, but still I wondered if perhaps she might love me. Because even though she always spoke to me in rough suggestive tones, she doted on me as if I were her favorite pet dog. The reason she had picked me from among the other men, she said, was because my face came closest to resembling that of her ideal. And she liked the fact that I stood off on my own looking out the window, instead of sitting with the others watching television. I didn't realize it at the time, but there was a two-way mirror in the room where we had been asked to wait, and Lou-zhen had watched us from here.

I was ordered to live in Lou-zhen's suite. While there—in that magnificent hotel—I saw and heard things I had never before experienced: things like Western-style food and table manners, the decadence of breakfast in bed, a rooftop swimming pool. I'd been raised in the mountains and did not know how to swim. Reclining beside the pool, tanning myself, I would watch Lou-zhen swim laps, her strokes powerful and smooth. The pool was limited to club members, all of whom were either wealthy Chinese or foreigners. I was particularly taken with the stylish Western women and was ashamed to be seen there with the unattractive Lou-zhen.

I began drinking: beer and whiskey or brandy and wine. Lou-zhen enjoyed watching videos of American movies. She very rarely watched news shows. I wanted to find out what had happened at Tiananmen Square and afterward, but since Lou-zhen didn't get a newspaper I had no way to find out. Lou-zhen let it slip that once, when she was young, she had visited America. At that time the only people who ever went abroad were either government officials or exchange students, so it was a mystery to me how Lou-zhen got out. But I never asked her any questions. I played my role of the young lover to perfection. I did what I could to master the life I led in the penthouse of the White Swan Hotel, this room next to heaven itself.

The room may have brushed heaven, but Lou-zhen was a disgusting person. If I gave voice to just the slightest opinion about anything, she flew into a rage. With haughty self-assurance she forbade me to express any of my own ideas. At those times I wanted to cut all ties with her and run away someplace where I could live my own life. But my whole sphere of existence was now confined to the penthouse and the pool on the twenty-sixth floor. I was not allowed to walk freely about the hotel or to leave it on my own. Within a week of agreeing to live with Lou-zhen, I began to regret my decision.

About ten days after the incident at Tiananmen Square, something happened. The phone by the side of the bed rang, and when Lou-zhen answered it she turned strangely pale. Her voice was tense.

"Well, then, what should I do? I suppose I should come back immediately."

She was still agitated after she hung up. She leaned over to me, and I made as if to embrace her from behind.

"Something troublesome has happened in Beijing."

"Does it have anything to do with you?"

Lou-zhen got up and put a cigarette in her mouth. She didn't answer. "Deng Xiaoping's gone and done it!" she mumbled. That was all, but it was enough to make me realize that the reason her background was mysterious was that she was probably the daughter of a high-level Communist Party member. After Tiananmen, her father undoubtedly was facing difficulties.

Lou-zhen remained in a nasty mood for the rest of the day. She got more phone calls, which left her depressed, anxious, and angry. I sat watching a Hollywood movie until Lou-zhen told me, "I have to go back to Beijing for a bit, Zhe-zhong. You wait for me here."

"Can't I go with you? I've never been to Beijing."

"No, that won't do." Lou-zhen shook her head abruptly, like a man.

"Well, then, will it be okay if I wander around the hotel?"

"I guess I don't have much choice. But be sure you always have him with you."

Him was her bodyguard, the man who had brought me to Lou-zhen in the first place.

"You can't run off without telling me where you're going, and you can't fool around with other women. If you do pull that kind of trick on me, I'll be sure to have you locked up."

With that threat, Lou-zhen set off for Beijing. She took Bai Jie, the crafty-faced woman, with her. Bai Jie was her secretary and lived on the same floor of the hotel. That woman must really have despised me, because whenever she came near me she would look away in disgust. The bodyguard and the limo driver were no better. They must have figured Lou-zhen would tire of me sooner or later, so whenever she wasn't around they were rude to me.

I wanted to get out somehow. On the day after Lou-zhen and her secretary left for Beijing, I set off to explore the hotel under the watchful eye of the bodyguard.

"So, who's Lou-zhen's father?" I asked, as we rode the elevator. The first time I'd met the man, when he brought me here, I was afraid of him. But now my attitude had changed completely, which did not please the bodyguard. He said nothing and looked away.

I put the screws to him: blackmail. "You know, when Lou-zhen gets back I'll no problem telling her about the way you and her secretary pilfer her cigarettes and booze and sell them on the side."

The bodyguard went pale. "If you want to know so bad I'll tell you"—he scowled—"but an ignoramus like you isn't going to recognize the name anyway."

"Try me."

"Li Tou-min."

I couldn't believe my ears and nearly collapsed on the floor with shock. Li Tou-min was the number-two man in the Chinese Communist Party. Lou-zhen had threatened me with prison if I tried to escape, but I hadn't realized how serious she was. I'd gotten tangled up with a really dangerous woman.

"Are you kidding?"

I grabbed the bodyguard's shoulders but he shook free of my grip roughly.

"She's Li's eldest daughter. Whether things go well for you or not depends on how you behave. All the ones before you were idiots. They got caught up in this life of luxury and forgot that we were the ones who yanked them out of the stinking mud of the countryside. That's when Lou-zhen can really be vile. She makes sure they know just what they are."

"So you're saying I'll be okay as long as I watch my step?"

The bodyguard didn't answer. He just smiled. I braced myself, thinking I'd try to knock him out here in the elevator. But just when I was ready to attack, the car jolted as we reached the first floor, the doors opened, and I was confronted with an entirely new world.

I forgot Lou-zhen completely. Families were milling about the lobby in T-shirts, businessmen rushed through at a brisk pace, and there were the doormen in their maroon livery. I'd been holed up in Lou-zhen's suite so long, it had been at least two weeks since I was last out. A Western woman wearing a dress that was cut low in back sauntered past and smiled when she caught my eye. How big the world is! I was absolutely captivated by the different people I saw walking this way and that throughout the spacious lobby. These were people awash with luxury and the richness of peace. I wanted to become just like them. No, I was determined to *be* one of them. My heart, dominated by a desire for wealth and a longing for freedom, was filled with bitterness. I was seized with the desire to escape. As if reading my mind, the bodyguard whispered gruffly in my ear, "Remember, watch your step. Your clothes belong to Lou-zhen, your shoes, everything. If you even think of skipping off, she'll have you brought up on charges of theft."

"Bastard."

"Hick."

"It takes one to know one."

"Not me. I'm from Beijing."

While we exchanged murmured insults, we sauntered through the lobby, this way and that, without a flicker of nastiness on our faces.

Indeed, the white polo shirt, jeans, and shoes I was wearing had all been provided by Lou-zhen. The polo shirt was designed by Fred Perry of London. The jeans were Levi's. And the shoes were Nike—black leather with white stripes. At that time you could probably count the number of Chinese people in the world who were able to afford to wear Nikes. When I first got the pair I had on, I was so happy I could hardly stand it. Every morning I'd take them up in my hands as if they were the most precious gift ever imagined. And precisely because I was dressed so impeccably, the people who saw me regarded me with respect.

Ah, he may be young, but you can be sure he's rich. That's what I assumed the doormen were thinking as I saw them look enviously at the Nikes on my feet. Up till then I had been overwhelmed by Lou-zhen. I sucked in the air of her wealth until I felt my lungs would explode. But wealth glitters all the brighter when it is accompanied by admiration. If no one is there to appreciate your wealth, it loses half its value. When I made this discovery, I realized that I had to get away from Lou-zhen. I had to break free of her grasp.

I took a seat on the sofa in the corner of the lobby, to enjoy more fully the way I looked in my expensive clothes. There was a window directly across from the couch, and in it I could see my reflection. When the bodyguard saw me admiring my clothes, he smirked with pleasure.

"The tailor makes the man! Those fine threads of yours looked just as good on the guy before you, you know."

I was dismayed. The clothes were hand-me-downs? I had assumed they were new.

"What happened to him?"

"Well, let's see. The little shit was from Heilongjiang Province. We caught him helping himself to Lou-zhen's prize tea, and that was that. The asshole before him was from the Inner Mongolia Autonomous Region. He wore Lou-zhen's ruby ring in the swimming pool and lost the stone. He said he wanted to see what a gem looked like underwater. Just the sort of thing to expect from a little hick like that! They're both enjoying prison hospitality now."

When I heard that I was assaulted by a new wave of fear. Was this the fate that awaited me? Only two weeks had passed since I moved in with Lou-zhen. I could tell she was taken with me, but I couldn't stand her. From then on, all I could think about was getting away from her—and also helping myself to a few of her things.

You'll have to forgive me, but I didn't think that would be stealing. Why? Because I had not been adequately compensated for my hard work. At the outset Lou-zhen had promised me a salary, but she paid me no more than twenty yuan a day. I didn't think this was fair; she'd promised more, after all. But when I asked her she said, "No, no. I am paying you one hundred yuan a day. But once I subtract the room and board, this is all that remains. Of course, I don't charge for your cigarettes and drinks."

The bodyguard jabbed my arm. "Time to go back." With little choice I rose to my feet, feeling as miserable as a prisoner. A pathetic peasant boy kidnapped by the daughter of the ruling party.

"Look." The bodyguard nudged me. "Look at the kid in the stroller."

A white man and woman, presumably an American husband and wife, were making their way through the lobby with a baby stroller. They stopped to stand by the fountain. I stared at the couple in disbelief as they stood there smiling blissfully. How could anyone be so fortunate that they could go overseas on vacation with their family? The husband was wearing shorts and a T-shirt. The wife had on a matching T-shirt and blue jeans. They were a robust healthy-looking white couple. But the baby in the stroller—so small it looked like it could barely sit—was Asian. Had these charitable foreigners adopted this pathetic little Chinese orphan? I wondered.

"What's going on?"

The bodyguard pointed discreetly around the lobby. There were white couples all over, just like this one, pushing baby strollers; in every case the babies in the strollers were Chinese, both boys and girls. And each was dressed in brand-new pure-white baby clothes.

"Adoption mediation."

"Who?"

The bodyguard turned his eyes up to the ceiling.

"Lou-zhen's involved in this? She said she was a songwriter."

"That's what she says. Tell me, have you heard any of her songs?"

When I shook my head, the bodyguard snorted.

"Adoption mediation is her real work. She runs a charitable organization."

I doubted there was much charity involved. Lou-zhen liked luxury. She wouldn't work if it didn't pay handsomely. But I don't know all the facts, so I won't describe something that isn't my business. What I want to write about is not the adoptions per se. Rather, it is this: when I looked at those babies in the strollers, I couldn't help but feel jealous. They were so lucky to be able to go to America while they were still too little to know anything. How easy it would be for them to be raised as Americans.

I was born and raised in China. But never once, even though I lived there for a long time, did anyone ever do anything for me. If you're born in the country, you're expected to stay in the country. If you want to move to the city, you have to have a permit to do so. And forget about going overseas. Those of us who came to the city as migrant laborers had to live hand to mouth, constantly trying to avoid the snares of the law.

I was lost in these thoughts when suddenly the bodyguard pinched my elbow. "Hey! Wake up! And just so you know, my name's Yu Wei. *Sir* to you, asshole. Don't forget it."

Later Yu Wei told me that Lou-zhen had had to rush back to Beijing because her younger brother had been badly injured in the riots that followed the Tiananmen Square protests. Apparently he'd broken his arm and been arrested. Lou-zhen had two stepbrothers, quite a bit younger than she. One was an artist, specializing in prints, who lived in Shanghai. The other lived in Beijing and had a rock band with some of his buddies; his band had given a number of performances in front of the tent in Tiananmen Square where the students were staging their sit-in.

•

Lou-zhen stayed in Beijing longer than she had expected. She wasn't able to help her brother and had to keep extending her stay. If her father had flexed his political muscle they could have had the boy out in no time. But the boy's performance had been televised, and shown on the news; it had captured the attention of the country—even the world—so it wasn't a simple matter to get him released. There would have been an uproar if they'd let him go. If anything, Yu Wei insisted, the authorities ought to be even harsher on him.

Li Tou-min's three children had each been sent to study in America, given lavish allowances, and encouraged to work in fancy Western-style businesses in the cities of their choosing. They'd been blessed beyond belief. As a high-ranking member of the Communist Party, Li was able to use his authority to line his own pockets.

When Yu told me this I was less angry than I was envious. There it was again: In China, a person's fate is determined by where he is born. If I'd been born to a member of the Party's inner cabinet, I would not have ended up committing this crime. I am torn with regret over my misfortune.

Two weeks passed and Lou-zhen still had not come back. She was too busy running around Beijing trying to secure her brother's release. If it had been me, I am sure I wouldn't have cared what became of one of my stepbrothers. But for someone like Lou-zhen, born into the lap of luxury, it was impossible, I suppose, to think only of herself while her family's profits were threatened.

Lou-zhen called Yu Wei every day. While Yu Wei talked to her, he would wink knowingly at me and go out of his way to grimace and make faces. It was all I could do not to burst out laughing.

I got to be good friends with Yu Wei while Lou-zhen was gone. We'd watch TV together, help ourselves to Lou-zhen's liquor, and basically enjoy ourselves. Our favorite topic of conversation was the Tiananmen Square protests. Yu Wei called my attention to one of the young women activists on the news program we were watching. She was organizing the others around her. "That one's trouble, Zhe-zhong," Yu Wei said. "I can tell by her eyes. You get hooked up with a girl like her, and no good can come of it."

Yu Wei was thirty-two. He said he was from Beijing, but he was really from a farming village on the outskirts of the city. His mother had been a maid for the Li family for years and had gotten Yu Wei his body-guard job.

Yu Wei was also a bad influence. He brought in a bottle of cheap whiskey and mixed it with Lou-zhen's good scotch. He rifled through the wastebaskets, picking out drafts of letters that Lou-zhen had thrown there. He said he was going to hold on to them as insurance, in case he ever needed to blackmail her. He also went through the drawers of her desk, looking for the key to her lockbox. I was worried that if by some chance he should be found out, I would be the one who took the blame, but he just laughed and said I was a chicken-shit.

On the day we got the news that Lou-zhen would return the following afternoon, Yu Wei and I went to the rooftop pool. For Yu Wei it was a forbidden pleasure.

"Some kind of fucking paradise this is!" Yu Wei scoffed. The water in the twenty-five-meter pool was clear, and the blue-painted bottom of the pool wavered in the rays of the sun. The breeze blowing over the roof was hot. The streets below may have been noisy, but no sound disturbed the stillness on the roof. There were fewer than ten people in the pool area, and no one was swimming. They sat with absolutely no interest in one another, just enjoying the rays of the sun baking their bodies.

There was a small bar in one corner of the patio. I don't know when she'd arrived, but a young woman was sitting there, drinking a cocktail with an expectant look, as if she were waiting for someone. She had long hair that hung down her back, and she was wearing only a pair of stylish sunglasses and a little bikini. Respectable women never came to a pool alone, so I knew she must be a prostitute waiting to pick up a customer.

"Wonder if she'd take us on?"

When Yu Wei heard what I said, he showed me a roll of cash he had hidden under his towel. "With this she will!"

"Where'd you steal that from?"

It had to be Lou-zhen's money. We could get away with diluting her scotch, but sneaking off with her money was going to be a problem. I turned pale.

"Shit! What if she thinks I did it?"

"Relax!" Yu Wei replied, annoyed. He lit a cigarette. "We'll get it back from that woman when we're done with her and return it before the night is over."

"Well, let's go, then."

Yu Wei pulled a few of the bills off the roll and pressed them in my hand. The woman was chewing on her straw, looking in the other direction. She didn't notice us approach. She really was attractive. Her limbs were long and slender, her face small and oval.

"Hello, there," I called out.

The woman wheeled around and gasped as she removed her sunglasses. I gazed, stunned, into Mei-kun's big eyes, watching as they filled with tears.

"Zhe-zhong!"

"What's going on?" Yu Wei asked suspiciously.

"She's my little sister!"

"You don't say. Brother and sister? I can see the resemblance."

It made me extremely angry to see the way the expression on Yu Wei's face turned from surprise to scorn. No doubt he was telling himself that he'd come across a pair of brother-sister prostitutes.

The closer I was to Mei-kun, the more like a prostitute she looked. The makeup she wore was much too garish for a woman at a pool, and her hair was dyed a reddish brown just like a cheap streetwalker. I was happy to see her again, but I couldn't let go of my feelings of bitterness. You dumped me at Guangzhou Station and slid into this despicable state? Just as I predicted! I couldn't get past wanting to shout at her. My emotions were so jumbled, I hardly knew what to think. So I just stood there in shock until Mei-kun tapped Yu Wei on the shoulder and said, "Do you mind? We have a lot to talk about. A little privacy, please."

Yu Wei shrugged his shoulders in disgust, bought a beer, went off to sit in a chair some way away, and spread out a newspaper.

"Oh, Zhe-zhong, I'm so glad to see you! Get me out of Guangzhou, okay? That Jin-long has a heart as black as a snake. He sends me off to snag customers and then takes all my money. If I complain he hits me. Right now he's waiting for me down in the lobby. He sent me up here to find a customer. Let's run away together."

Mei-kun nervously surveyed the people around the pool. I was shocked to see her this way—Mei-kun, who had always been so self-confident, so quick to turn a situation to her advantage. But who was I to talk? As soon as Lou-zhen returned, I would go right back to being her little pet dog. What could have been more pathetic than a brother and sister ending up this way? I felt bitter, as if I were being overwhelmed by an existence much greater than my own, a being I was powerless to resist. Unless you've experienced this kind of helplessness, you cannot understand. I could not escape. But why was I so afraid of Lou-zhen?

"Easy to say we should run away. But where would we go?"

My question was feeble and unfocused. But Mei-kun's response was quick and certain. "Let's go to Shenzhen."

And so Mei-kun determined, as she had earlier, the next location in my pilgrimage: Shenzhen. It was another of the designated Special Economic Zones, I'd heard others say. There are all sorts of jobs in Shenzhen, and the salaries are good. I've lived in Tokyo for many years now. Every time I take the train past Shinsen Station I think back to China. The pronunciation of the two place names are so very similar. *Shinsen Station is next*, the conductor will call over the loudspeaker, and for a minute I'm transported back to this very moment in time. It's a strange sensation.

"Well, that's a great idea, but how are we going to pull it off?"

I gazed hopelessly up at the sky. Once she learned I'd run off, Lou-zhen would hunt me down, taking full advantage of her influence and connections. I did not want to end up in prison; that was the bottom line. Mei-kun grabbed my arm tightly and planted her heels firmly on the ground.

"Look, you've got to come to some decision. We're not going to get another chance like this."

I turned to look back at Yu Wei. He was glaring at me. Did he suspect something?

"Zhe-zhong, do you want me to be a whore for the rest of my life?"

No. I shook my head, feeling as though I'd been slapped. I suppose it would be next to impossible for anyone else to really understand how I felt. I had grown up with Mei-kun and she was very dear to me, a very important presence. But ever since she abandoned me, a black hatred toward her had been born in my heart. Hatred is a terrifying thing. It filled me with a cruel desire, a hope that Mei-kun too would suffer a bitter fate. But even though I knew she was suffering, I still wasn't happy. And that's because the sight of Mei-kun in distress caused me to suffer as well. In the end, I decided to escape with Mei-kun for one reason. I couldn't bear the idea of Mei-kun sleeping with other men. It made me jealous. I felt as though something I possessed—something of my own— had been damaged.

"But what am I supposed to do? Yu Wei keeps a close eye on me."

As soon as I began to go over the details of my own situation, Mei-kun spoke up briskly. "No problem. Just tell him I want to sleep with him. We'll put on a little performance, shall we?"

I took Mei-kun by the arm and led her to Yu Wei.

"Yu Wei, my sister tells me she's interested in you."

Yu Wei pushed his chair back and stood up. His face registered pride.

"Is that so? You put in a word on my behalf, did you?"

Yu Wei headed off, his steps full of swagger. We followed behind. The three of us returned to Lou-zhen's penthouse. Mei-kun was amazed by the luxurious accommodations. She looked up at me enviously.

"Zhe-zhong, do you live here? This is amazing. Just like a dream. You have AC, TV, and room service!"

Yu Wei fought to bite back a sardonic laugh. This made me angry and I turned on him.

"Yu Wei, my sister doesn't come cheap. You'll need to pay one thousand yuan. In advance."

Without protest Yu Wei handed my sister the roll of money he had shown me at the pool. It was the money he had stolen from Lou-zhen's lockbox. I was troubled and put the money on top of the desk. If Lou-zhen blamed me for the missing money I'd be in serious trouble. While Yu Wei stepped into Lou-zhen's room to turn on the air conditioner, Mei-kun whispered, "We'll slip out while he's in the bath. Zhe-zhong. Get everything ready and wait."

Mei-kun took Yu Wei by the hand and disappeared with him into Lou-zhen's room. I could hear the sound of the shower. I was so nervous, I didn't know what to do. I'd sit down and then the next minute I'd be up again, pacing. I couldn't relax. Suddenly Mei-kun rushed out of the room.

"Zhe-zhong, come on."

I took her hand and left Lou-zhen's penthouse. While Mei-kun was racing down the corridor she started to laugh, "Ah, this feels great!" But I was too worried about what would happen to share her happiness.

Once we were in the elevator I suddenly remembered the pink T-shirt I had bought earlier to give to her. I had left it in the penthouse. Without thinking I let out a cry. But Mei-kun was only interested in the money.

"Wow, I've never earned this much before!"

She fanned the bills out in front of me. It was the money I had left on the desk.

"Why did you bring that? That's not Yu Wei's money!"

"Don't be silly. We can't make our getaway without money!"

Mei-kun stuffed the bills away in her brand-name shoulder bag.

"I'll be charged with a crime."

Mei-kun paid no attention. In the brief four months since we had parted at Guangzhou Station, my sister had changed. I gazed at her profile—the profile of the little sister I had loved. Her nose was slightly upturned. Her lips were slightly crooked, her face plump and adorable. Without thinking I wanted to hug her slender body. She was so beautiful and her heart was so wicked.

I was certain we were running off with Lou-zhen's money, a crime that was going to stick to me like a wet shirt. My heart grew heavy. In some ways, the pink T-shirt I had left behind symbolized everything that had happened to me. It was the innocence that had once belonged to Mei-kun and myself. I had forgotten it in Lou-zhen's room. And I would live without ever getting it back.

When we dashed through the lobby, I saw a man sitting on a sofa in a Hawaiian shirt smoking a cigarette. He looked up in alarm when he heard us approach. It was Jin-long. He was wearing sunglasses but there could be no doubt. He leaped to his feet and chased after us. "Taxi!" I called impatiently to the doorman. And so the two of us made our painful exit from Guangzhou.

•

All right, Detective Takahashi has just reprimanded me for writing too much about unrelated matters. I've been given a precious opportunity to write about the crime that I committed. I killed a woman I did not even know, and I should be reflecting on my own stupidity in this testament. But here I am going on about my own trivial upbringing and all the shameful activities that I became involved in. I apologize to you, Detective Takahashi, and to you, Your Honor, for forcing you to read this long and insignificant ramble.

However, I have written about the life I led back in my home country because I want you to understand that all I ever wanted was the chance to earn the kind of money I would need to live independently and comfortably without having to resort to unseemly behavior. And yet, here I am in prison all the same—forced to endure day in and day out the constant questioning by detectives and even made to suffer the humiliation of being suspected of murdering Kazue Satō. I had no part whatsoever in her death. I have made this very clear on numerous occasions. But let me state it once again for the record: I had nothing to do with Kazue Satō's murder. I don't know anything about her, and so I cannot write about her here. Detective Takahashi has told me to write only what I know about the crimes under consideration, so I will hurry to complete my account.

•

You needed a pass to enter the Special Economic Zone of Shenzhen, which of course we did not have. So we decided to settle first in Dongguan City, which was a small municipality not far away, and set about looking for work. Known as a second border zone, Dongguan is prosperous, and the Chinese who work over in Shenzhen can afford to throw their money around. Interestingly, the Chinese nationals who live in Hong Kong think that prices in Shenzhen are cheaper, so they come over to the city to shop and enjoy themselves. The Chinese who live in Shenzhen have the same opinion of Dongguan City, because Dongguan is close to one of the Special Economic Zones. Mei-kun found a job babysitting the children of women who worked in hostess bars, and I got work at a cannery.

I think that period was the happiest in my life. The two of us lived in harmony, helping each other out just like husband and wife, and after nearly two years of hard work we had saved up enough money to buy permits for Shenzhen. We moved there in 1991.

We succeeded in landing jobs at the best karaoke club in Shenzhen. Mei-kun worked as a hostess and I was an assistant manager. Mei-kun is the one who helped me get the job. She'd been scouted earlier, and she said she'd work on condition that they hire me. I wasn't particularly fond of the idea of her working as a hostess. It made me uncomfortable because I felt it would be too easy for her to slip back into prostitution. Mei-kun, for her part, worried that I would fall for one of the other girls who worked in the club. So we kept an eye on each other as we worked, a very peculiar state of affairs for a brother and sister.

•

Why did I come to Japan? It's a question I am frequently asked. My younger sister was, as always, the one to determine my fate. To be perfectly honest, I had always been keen on moving to America. But Mei-kun was strongly opposed. In America, Chinese laborers are taken advantage of and paid only one dollar an hour. But in Japan we could earn more, save it, and then move to America with our savings. Mei-kun's logic always won out over my weak-willed indecisiveness. I did not agree with her, but as usual I was not able to stand up to her.

One day, something happened that persuaded me to head to Japan sooner rather than later. The club owner called me to his office.

"A man came by from Guangzhou looking for a fellow named Zhang from Sichuan. It looks like he's been asking around all over the place. Are you the one he's after?"

"There are a lot of people from Sichuan named Zhang," I answered nonchalantly without batting an eye. "What does the man want?"

"He said it had something to do with Tiananmen. It seems he's offering a reward."

"What did he look like?

"He was with a woman. The man was a mean-looking bastard, and the woman had beady little eyes."

The owner of the club, who did not like trouble, eyed me suspiciously. Lou-zhen had sent Yu Wei and Bai Jie to look for us. I could feel the blood drain from my face, and I struggled to maintain my composure. If they were offering a reward, it wouldn't be long before someone gave us up. Everyone working in Shenzhen was after money.

That night when I got back to our apartment, I discussed the situation with Mei-kun. She raised her eyebrows.

"To tell the truth, I didn't tell you, Zhe-zhong, but the other day I saw a guy in front of the station who looked just like Jin-long. I've been terrified that he'd show up at the club sooner or later. Our luck may have run out here."

The karaoke club where we were employed was expensive and well known. It wasn't the kind of club that inlanders frequented. Most of the clientele were from Hong Kong or Japan. I didn't think it was likely that Jin-long would come by, but Shenzhen wasn't that large. We were bound to run into him sooner or later. Things were getting dangerous for us here.

The next day I began searching for a snakehead—a smuggler—to help us get to Japan. If we went to Shanghai, I assumed we could find any number of snakeheads willing to get us away from Jin-long. But Lou-zhen was another story. Her younger brother lived in Shanghai and it's not likely there'd be many willing to tangle with the authority she could bring to bear. This wasn't going to be easy. And then a hostess from Changle in Fujian Province told me about a snakehead she knew there. I called him immediately and asked him to smuggle us into Japan.

The snakehead wanted a down payment of only ¥1,000,000 to cover the cost of two forged passports. The rest of the money we would pay once we got to Japan and started working—an additional ¥2,000,000 per person. The total charge, therefore, would be ¥5,000,000. I let out a sigh of relief. Ever since I learned we were being hunted, I was so busy looking over my shoulder, it was like I had a permanent crick in my neck.

•

February 9, 1992: I will never forget that day for as long as I live. That was the day we set sail for Japan. Completely by coincidence, it was on the same date three years earlier that Mei-kun and I had fled from our village. Only someone who has traveled on that journey into this country can possibly understand the dangers my countrymen and I faced. And when I think of my sister's death, I am overcome with bitterness. I've not wanted to talk about this to anyone, so I will keep my account brief and without great detail.

Forty-nine of us boarded the boat. Most were young men from Fujian Province. A few women Mei-kun's age were also aboard. They were married, I surmised, by the way they sat close to their male companions, their eyes downcast. Terrified of the dangerous sea voyage that now confronted them, they were nevertheless determined not to be a burden to their husbands. But Mei-kun was unfazed. She took out her brown-covered passport again and again and stroked it happily, the passport she had thought she would never get.

The first boat we boarded was small, a regular fishing boat. We sailed out of Changle harbor squeezed rail to rail in the hold. The seas were calm and the weather warm. I let out a sigh of relief. But once we pulled away from shore and entered the high seas, the winds grew strong. The boat was buffeted mercilessly by rough waves. Finally we reached a large freighter. The captain of our boat handed each of us a screwdriver and told us to board the ship. I had no idea what we were supposed to do with the screwdriver, but I clambered onto the deck.

When we were all aboard, we were led into a narrow wooden container. They closed it up so no one could tell from outside that it contained people. It was pitch black inside. And with forty-nine people crammed into such a narrow space, the air soon grew stale and thick.

"Poke holes in the sides with your screwdrivers," I heard someone shout. The sound of pounding that arose all around me was freakish as everyone worked feverishly to pierce airholes in the side of the container. I banged on my part with all my might, but no matter how I tried I managed to bore a hole that was only a quarter of an inch wide. I stuck my mouth to the hole and sucked in the fresh air. I wouldn't die. Gradually the panic I had felt over the prospect of suffocating abated. It wasn't long, however, before we were all covered in stench. At first we had designated a corner of the container for our personal business, but by the second day, practically the entire bottom was covered in waste. Mei-kun, who had started the trip in such a buoyant mood, grew taciturn. She clung to my hand and refused to leave my side. Mei-kun was claustrophobic.

•

On the fourth day of our voyage, the ship's engine stopped. We could hear the crew running busily around the deck. We had reached Taiwan. But because no one told us anything, I thought we'd probably gotten to Japan.

Mei-kun, who had been leaning listlessly against me, nauseated with seasickness on top of claustrophobia, suddenly sat up and grabbed my coat with great intensity.

"Are we in Japan?"

"Maybe."

I wasn't sure, so I shrugged uncertainly. But Mei-kun leaped to her feet and began busily combing her hair, barely able to suppress her joy. If we'd had more light in the container, I'm sure she would have put on makeup. But after a solid day, the ship still remained at anchor. No one came for us. Mei-kun could not sit still. She kept getting up and running her hands over the wall of the container, slapping it fiercely with her palms.

"Let me out!"

One of the men from Fujian Province who had been squatting in the dark spoke to me in a husky whisper. "You need to settle her down. This is just Taiwan."

When Mei-kun heard the word Taiwan she was horrified. "I don't care if it is Taiwan. I have to get out. I can't take this anymore! Somebody help me!" She began banging on the walls of the container, screaming hysterically.

"Hey, do something with your woman. If they hear her we'll all be fucked."

I should have been gentler, but I could feel forty-seven pairs of eyes boring into my back, and I struck Mei-kun across the face to silence her. As soon as I hit her, she collapsed just like a puppet with its strings snapped. She fell where the floor was filthy with vomit and feces and lay there, faceup, her eyes staring into the darkness. I worried when she didn't move, but I couldn't allow Mei-kun to endanger the lives of all the others in the container. As long as she was quiet, I thought it best to leave her where she was. Later, when I looked back on this horrible tragedy, I could not believe that I might have ended Mei-kun's life with just a smack across the face. Not Mei-kun. She was so strong, so determined.

The next day the ship finally sailed out of Taiwan. It slowly plied the rough winter seas on its way to Japan. Mei-kun lay just where she was, a semi-invalid, neither eating nor speaking. On the sixth day they finally opened the container. The air off the seas was cold, nearly freezing. But after being closed up in the dank stench of the container, it felt clean and exhilarating. I gulped in giant breaths of the air. Mei-kun managed to stand up on her own, feeble though she was. She looked at me and smiled weakly.

"That was awful."

I would not have believed in a million years that those would be Mei-kun's last words, but less than twenty minutes later, as we boarded a small boat that would carry us through the darkness to the Japanese shores, the accident occurred. For some reason, the second Mei-kun set foot on the boat, the sea, which had up to that moment been placid, surged mysteriously into a huge wave. Mei-kun tumbled into the water before anyone could catch hold of her. I had boarded the boat ahead of her and tried to grasp her hand but it all happened too quickly. When I reached out to her, my hand clutched nothing but air. As she slipped into the sea, Mei-kun looked up at me with an expression of utter shock. And then she disappeared beneath the waves. Her hand moved back and forth for a second—as if she were waving good-bye—and all I could do was stare after it in a daze. Even if I had tried to help her, I couldn't swim. I screamed her name. But there was nothing anyone could do. We just stared at the dark water. My darling little sister died in the cold midwinter seas, the Japan she had so longed for drifting just before her eyes.

·

I am now nearly finished with my long and rambling tale. Detective Takahashi, Your Honor, please indulge me and read on to the end. Detective Takahashi titled this account "My Crimes" and instructed me to reflect on my wrongful behavior by writing about my upbringing and all my past mistakes. Now, as so many different memories come to mind, I am choked by tears of regret. Truly I am a despicable man. I was unable to rescue Mei-kun, I murdered Yuriko Hirata, and I have continued to live comfortably. How I wish I could go back in time and start all over. Once again I could become the boy I was when I left home with my little sister. How bright the future looked to me then, how full of promise! And yet all I have to show for it now is this crime. A horrible crime only a reprehensible creature could have committed. I killed the first woman I met in this foreign country. I believe I ended up becoming this evil person because I lost Mei-kun, my very soul.

·

An illegal alien in Japan, I lived like a stray cat, dodging here and there, constantly afraid of inviting the attention of others. Chinese people are accustomed to close-knit communities, never living far from home and depending on the support and guidance of family members. But here I was many miles from home and family. I had no one to help me find a job or a place to live; I had to do that all by myself. And when I lost my sister, I had no one to console me. After three years of hard work, I was finally able to pay off the snakehead for the money he'd fronted in getting my sister and me to Japan. But after that I had very little else to aim for, and I lost even the will to save money. Most of the other men I knew in Japan had wives and children back in China and were working to send money to them. I envied them.

Around that time I met a Taiwanese woman who was working in Kabuki-chō. I just wrote that Hirata was the first woman I met in Japan, but actually I went with this Taiwanese woman to see the movie *Yellow Earth*. She was ten years older than I and had two children she'd left in Kaohiung. While she was working as the mama of a club, she attended a Japanese-language school and saved her money to send back to her children. She was a very gentle person and took great care of me when I was feeling desperate.

But no matter how gentle a person is, if the upbringing is different, that person cannot know how you truly feel. She could not really understand what it was like to be brought up in such an impoverished village and then to have suffered the hardships of migrant labor and the agony of losing a sister. This annoyed me, and eventually I separated from her. It was at that point that I decided to set my sights on traveling by myself to America.

A stray has no choice but to live like a stray. Even though I shared lodgings with several others in the apartment at Shinsen, we were all, each in our own way, loners. I didn't even know that Chen-yi and Huang were fugitives until I heard it from Detective Takahashi. If I'd known they were criminals, I certainly would have had nothing to do with them. The reason I started to fall out with the other men I lived with was because I was secretly planning my trip to New York. It wasn't simply a disagreement over money.

Detective Takahashi has criticized me for extorting the apartment rent from my companions. I was responsible for renting the apartment from Chen. I had to make sure the apartment was clean and in order and I had to cover the cost of the utilities. So it only made sense that they paid more. Who do you think cleaned the toilet? Who took out the trash? I did all that, and I made sure the bedding was hung out to dry.

To have been betrayed by the men I lived with wounded me deeply, especially Huang. Everything he said was a lie. That I'd known Kazue

Satō for a long time; that the three of us had relations. Those were nothing but bald-faced lies. He must have had his own reasons for trying to pin the blame on me. Please think about it, Detective Takahashi, Your Honor. I beg of you. I know I've said this already many, many times, but I never met Kazue Satō. That charge against me is false.

•

When I met Yuriko Hirata, it spelled misfortune for us both. I heard from Detective Takahashi that Ms. Hirata had once been beautiful and had worked as a model. Detective Takahashi went on to say that "as she grew old and ugly she became a cheap streetwalker." But I thought she was still beautiful.

When I first saw her in Kabuki-chō I was attracted to her beauty and youthfulness. I didn't care how late it was, I made a point of taking the route through Kabuki-chō on my way home from Futamomokko that night. When I saw that Miss Hirata was standing there in the rain waiting for me, I was filled with joy. She looked at me and smiled faintly. Then she said, "I'm about to freeze standing here waiting for you!"

I can still remember that rainy night very clearly. Miss Hirata was holding an umbrella, and the black hair that hung down her back, nearly to her waist, looked exactly like Mei-kun's. My heart began to pound. Her profile, too, was the spitting image of Mei-kun's. That was the main reason I was attracted to her. I had been searching for Mei-kun. The men around me would always say, "Your sister's dead. Get over it!" But I couldn't help fantasize that she was still in this world and that I would run into her again someday.

There can be no doubt that she disappeared that night in the sea. But what if a fishing boat passing by had rescued her? She could still be alive. Or maybe she swam to a nearby island. I thrived on such hope. Mei-kun had been brought up in the mountains, just like me. She wasn't able to swim. But she was a strong-willed, talented woman. I can still remember running into her again at the pool in Guangzhou. "Zhe-zhong!" she'd called out to me then, her eyes filling with tears. And so I walked the streets around me, hoping—expecting—to see her again.

Miss Hirata complimented me the first time she saw me. "You have a nice face." And I had said to her in return, "You look exactly like my younger sister. You're both beautiful."

"How old is your younger sister?" Miss Hirata asked, as she walked along beside me. She threw the cigarette she'd been smoking into a puddle and turned to look at me. I gazed into her face head on. No, she wasn't Mei-kun after all. I was disappointed.

"She's dead."

"She died?"

She shrugged her shoulders. She looked so sad I found myself being drawn to her. She seemed like the kind of person to whom I could unburden myself. And then Miss Hirata said, "I'd like to hear about it. My place is nearby. Why don't we go there and share some beers?"

Detective Takahashi said that's just the kind of thing prostitutes say. He does not believe my testimony. But when I met Miss Hirata, I was not encountering a prostitute; rather, I was meeting someone whose hair and profile looked just like my little sister's. I think the fact that Miss Hirata bought the beer and the bean-jam buns with her own money when we stopped at the convenience store is all the proof I need to support my testimony, don't you? I think Miss Hirata was interested in me. Of course, we did negotiate a price, that much is true. But that she went from ¥30,000 down to ¥15,000 should prove that she was fond of me.

As soon as Miss Hirata got to her apartment in Ōkubo, she turned to me and asked, "So what would you like to do? We'll do whatever you want; just tell me."

I told her exactly what I'd been repeating to myself in my heart over and over. "I want you to look at me with tears in your eyes and call out 'Brother!'"

Miss Hirata did as I asked. Without thinking, I reached over and embraced her.

"Mei-kun! How I've wanted to see you!"

While Miss Hirata and I were having sex I was beside myself with excitement. I suppose it was wrong. But it confirmed everything. I did not love my sister as a sister. I loved her as a woman. And I realized that when she was alive this is exactly what we had wanted to do. Miss Hirata was very sensitive. She looked up at me and asked, "What would you like me to do next?" It drove me wild.

"Say 'That was awful' and look at me."

I taught her the words in Chinese. Her pronunciation was perfect. But what really surprised me was that real tears began to form in her eyes. I realized that the word *awful* resonated with something in Miss

Hirata's own heart. We cried together in her bed, holding each other. Naturally, I had no desire to kill her, far from it. Even though we were racially different and from different cultures, I felt we understood each other. Things I could not communicate to the woman from Taiwan I was able to communicate to Miss Hirata, even though I had only just met her. It was amazing. Miss Hirata seemed to share my feelings, for the tears rolled down her cheeks as I held her in my arms. Then she took the gold necklace off her neck and hooked it around my own. I don't know why she did such a thing.

So why did I kill her? you ask. I don't even understand it myself. Perhaps it was because she pulled the wig off her head as easily as if she were doffing a hat. The hair that emerged from beneath the wig was light brown flecked with white. Miss Hirata was some kind of foreigner who looked nothing like my Mei-kun!

"Okay, the game's over."

She suddenly grew cold. I was shocked.

"Was it all just a game?"

"Well, what did you think? That's the way I earn my living. It's time for you to settle up."

I felt a chill creep down my spine as I pulled the money out of my pocket. That's when the trouble started. Miss Hirata told me to hand it all over, all the ¥22,000. When I asked why the price had changed, she said with disgust, "Playing incest games costs more. Fifteen thousand yen is not enough."

Incest? The word made me furious. I shoved Miss Hirata down on the futon.

"What the hell are you doing?"

She scrambled to her feet and rushed at me, as mad as a demon. We began to push and shove each other violently.

"You cheap bastard! God, I wish I hadn't fucked a Chinaman."

I wasn't angry about the money. I was angry because I felt Mei-kun had been tarnished. My precious Mei-kun. I suppose this is what we had been heading toward all along, from the minute we ran away from home; tragedy was all that awaited us. Our unattainable dream. Our impossible dream so easily transformed into a nightmare. The Japan that Mei-kun had longed to see. How cruel. I had to survive. I had to continue living in the country that Mei-kun never lived to set foot in. And I had to endure all of its ugliness. What kept me going was the hope of finding a woman like Mei-kun. And when I finally did, all she wanted was to play games for money. How stupid I was not to see it coming. I felt as though I were being swept along by a rapid current, unable to understand what was happening. When I came to my senses, I saw that I had strangled Miss Hirata. I did not kill her because I wanted to steal her money. But I made a mistake I can never undo. I would like to dedicate the rest of my life to praying for the repose of Miss Hirata's soul.

Zhang Zhe-zhong

· 1 ·

was so determined to attend the first public hearing in the Apartment Serial Murders trial that I asked to take a leave from my job at the ward office. Do you find that surprising? The courtroom looked like any other courtroom, but it was the largest one in the courthouse, and I was astounded to learn that they had had to dispense spectator tickets by lottery to those who wanted to view the proceedings. Nearly two hundred people lined up for a chance at a ticket. That just goes to show you how fascinated people were with Yuriko and Kazue. A lot of reporters and people from the media came to cover the case, but I heard they wouldn't let the cameras in. When I asked my boss to let me have the time off, his lips twitched. I knew he was dying to ask me about it.

Earlier, I noted that I had absolutely no interest in whether or not that Chinese man named Zhang had actually murdered Yuriko and Kazue. I still feel the same way. I mean, those two were streetwalkers. They met freaks and perverts all the time. They had to know they might be killed if they weren't lucky; it was precisely because they knew this, I assume, that they found what they did so thrilling. Moving from customer to customer, never knowing if this day might be their last; when they left home, they couldn't be sure that they'd ever return. And then when the night was done and they did make it home in one piece, they must have felt such relief as they counted the money they'd earned. Whatever danger they might have faced, that night and others, they stored away in their memory to draw on again and again as they learned to survive by their wits.

The reason I went to court in the first place was because I had read the copy of Zhang's deposition that Detective Takahashi gave me. "My Crimes," he titled it. What a ridiculously long and tedious piece of work. Zhang goes on and on about completely irrelevant matters: the hardships he faced in China, all the things his darling little sister did, and so on. I skipped over most of it.

But throughout the report Zhang repeatedly refers to himself as "smart and attractive," noting at one point that he looks like Takashi Kashiwabara. When I read this I began to feel curious about what kind of man he was. According to Zhang, on the day he killed her, Yuriko told him, "You have a nice face." All her life, Yuriko was praised for her own beauty. If she thought Zhang had a nice face, I had to get a look at him.

You see, I've never been able to forget little Yuriko, back in the mountain cabin, snuggling up to Johnson's knees. One of the most handsome men in the world with one of the most beautiful girls. No wonder they were attracted to each other and unable to separate for as long as they lived. What? No, I most certainly was not jealous. It's just that beauty seems to function as its own compass; beauty attracts beauty, and once the connection has been made it remains so for life, the arrow holding steady, pointing in the opposite direction. I was half, myself, but unfortunately I had not been blessed with a similarly fantastic beauty. Rather, I knew my role in life was to be the observer of those who had been so blessed.

For the event at the courthouse I borrowed a book on physiognomy and took it with me. I planned to study Zhang's features. A round face indicates a carnal personality: someone who is easily contented, does not fuss over details, but is indecisive and promptly loses interest in things. An angular face indicates someone who has a calculating personality, is physically robust, hates to lose, and possesses a stubbornness that makes it difficult to get along with others. On the other hand, those with triangular faces are delicate and sensitive; they are physically fragile and tend to be artistic. These categories are then further divided into three positions—upper, middle, and lower—starting from the top of the face and working toward the sides. By reading these various positions, you can determine someone's fortune. For example, I suppose I would conform to the "sensitive personality." I am physically delicate, drawn to beauty, and fit the artistic type. But the part about not being sociable is me in a nutshell.

Next we have the five endowments, the major areas or landmarks of the face: eyebrows, eyes, nose, mouth, and ears. One item of particular note is the brightness of the eyes; the more penetrating the gaze, the more substantial the individual's vital force. A nose with a high bridge indicates an equally high sense of self-pride. A large mouth suggests aggressiveness and self-certainty.

If it is possible to predict someone's character and fate by observing their face and physical attributes, how is it that the beautiful Yuriko met such a tragic end? Beautiful, brainless Yuriko! There must have been an imperfection in her face that brought her to this fate. Perhaps it was her perfect beauty?

A young detective, clearly on the side of the prosecution, leaned close and peered into my face. The eyes he turned to me behind brown-framed glasses were full of pity, as if he'd marked me as the grieving sister of the victim. "They'll be starting soon. Take a seat on the front row to the right," he said.

I had been given special treatment from the very beginning, not needing to line up for a ticket or for admission. I went directly to the front of the courtroom. I was the only one present who was related to Yuriko, which was to be expected. I had not told my grandfather that Yuriko had died. Grandfather is currently being cared for at Misosazai Nursing Home, where he is off chasing the dreams of his past—or perhaps being chased by his past nightmares. The present has been cleared completely from every corner of his memory. The simple happy time I spent with Grandfather was very brief. He moved in with with Mitsuru's mother once I entered the university. It was fine with me if she wanted to take care of a senile old man, but as soon as Grandfather started showing signs of dementia, she abandoned him. Well, none of it really matters now.

It was time for the trial to begin. The spectators made a great fuss scrambling for seats. I sat in the far corner of the very front row with my head bowed, looking like a relative of the victim. With my long hair hanging down over my cheeks, I doubt if it was possible to see much of my face from the spectators' gallery.

At last the door opened and a man appeared, sandwiched between two fat courtroom guards. He was manacled, a chain leading from his handcuffs to a belt around his waist: Zhang. Wait a minute! Where was the resemblance to Takashi Kashiwabara? I was appalled as I stared at the shabby man in front of me. He was squat, pudgy, and bald. His face was round and his eyebrows short and bushy. To top it off, he had a pug nose. Most notable about him was the expression in his eyes; they were squinty and gleamed with light as he looked out over the spectators, darting here and there. He looked desperate, as if he were searching for someone he knew, someone who would help him. His mouth was small and constantly dropped half open. If I were to make a physiognomic analysis of Zhang's character, I would say he is easily bored and he must have a difficult time getting along with others, because he is stubborn and yet is weak-willed. I sighed audibly from my seat in the gallery, disappointed.

Perhaps my sigh created a ripple in the air that was transmitted to Zhang. He turned and looked directly at me from where he was seated, ramrod straight, in the defendant's chair. Maybe he'd already been told that I would be there as a connection to Yuriko. When I returned his stare, he averted his eyes timidly. *You killed Yuriko.* I glared at him with accusing eyes. He seemed to sense my scowl. He squirmed in his chair and swallowed so loudly I could hear it.

Well, I glared at him, but in fact I did not blame him for his crime. How can I explain this? If Yuriko and I were compared to the planets, she'd be the one closest to the sun, always basking in its rays; I'd be the one off in the dark on the far side. Planet Yuriko would always be there between me and the sun, soaking up its rays. Am I wrong? I managed to enter Q High School for Young Women in a desperate attempt to escape Yuriko, but it wasn't long before she followed after me and I sank back into the misery of being her older sister, confronted regularly with unflattering comparisons. Yuriko, whom I hated down to the very marrow of my bones, was killed so easily by this pathetic man. Yes, I despised Yuriko from the bottom of my heart.

The court proceeding was over in no time. Zhang was once again handcuffed, manacled, and led from the room. I felt as if I'd been tricked by a fox. For a time I was unable to move from my seat in the gallery.

Where did that jerk Zhang get off, telling such a pack of lies—things like "My sister and I were attractive," and "I look like Takeshi Kashiwabara!" These had to be the most flagrant lies I'd ever encountered. And since he was so fervent in declaring his innocence in Kazue Satō's murder, I was all the more convinced he did it. I mean, think about it. If a person is so incapable of viewing himself objectively, if he's convinced that he is good-looking when he's not, obviously he's going to come up with all sorts of outrageous lies.

"Excuse me, may I speak with you for a minute?"

I was cornered in the corridor in front of the courtroom by a pale woman. My book on physiognomy notes that people with combination pale and blotchy complexions have bad kidneys, so I felt a twinge of concern for this woman. But then she said she was from some television station, a fact about which she clearly felt considerable pride.

"I believe you are Miss Hirata's older sister, is that correct? What did you think of the court proceedings today?"

"I was unable to take my eyes off the defendant."

The woman began scribbling furiously in her notebook, nodding encouragingly as she did so.

"I hate the man for killing my only sis—"

"The defendant has clearly admitted to Miss Hirata's murder," the woman cut in, without waiting to let me finish. "The problem lies with the Kazue Satō case. What do you make of the fact that an educated career woman turned to prostitution? After all, weren't you and she classmates?"

"I think Kazue—I mean Miss Satō—was after the thrill. She thrived on it; she lived for it. I imagine the defendant was one of her customers. I think he has a carnal personality, or—oh, I don't know."

While I was blundering through my explanation of physiognomy, the reporter stared at me, perplexed. She continued to nod, but she was only pretending to take notes. And before long she'd lost interest in anything I said. No one cared about Yuriko's death. It had no impact on society. But Kazue? Kazue had worked for a respectable firm. Isn't the attention she was now garnering just so typical of her?

The woman left me alone, standing on the highly polished floors of the courthouse corridor. Then a skinny woman with uncommonly large eyes stepped in front of me. It seemed she'd been waiting for me to be alone. She looked carefully around, ensuring that no one was nearby. Her hair was long and hung straight down her back. She was wearing an outfit that resembled an Indian sari, but it was cotton, not silk, and stiffly starched. She stared at me intently and then smiled lightly.

"What's the matter, you don't remember me?" When the woman got closer, I caught a whiff of chewing gum on her breath. "It's Mitsuru."

I was so shocked I couldn't move. Of course, the papers had recently been full of articles about her. Mitsuru had been one of the central figures in a religious organization, whose members several years ago had been involved in carrying out terrorist activities and been imprisoned.

"Mitsuru! Are you out of jail already?"

My words caused her to flinch. "Oh, that's right. Everyone knows all about me."

"Yeah, everyone knows."

Mitsuru looked back down the corridor with an irritated expression.

"I'll never forget this courthouse. My case was tried in room four-oh-six. I had to appear at least twenty times. And no one came to support me. My one and only ally was my defense attorney, But even he, deep in his heart, thought I was guilty. He didn't understand," Mitsuru grumbled. "All I could do was sit there wishing it would be over." Then she tugged gently at my arm. "Look, if you've got time, let's go get a cup of tea. I want to talk to you."

She was wearing a black jacket over her sari. I was reluctant to be seen with her, her outfit was so bizarre, But when I saw how happy she looked I didn't have the heart to say no.

"There's a coffee shop in the basement that should be okay. Ah, what a luxury this is—to be able to move about freely!" Mitsuru's voice was buoyant, but she kept looking nervously over her shoulder. "I'm followed by detectives, you know."

"That's awful."

"But what am I complaining about? You're the one who's really had it rough, aren't you?" Mitsuru said sympathetically. She gave my arm a squeeze as we stepped into the elevator. Her hand was warm and damp and I found it annoying. I pulled away.

"Why do you say that?"

"Well, Yuriko. It's so awful—to have had something like that happen. I just can't believe it. And Kazue! What a shock!"

When the elevator reached the basement, I moved to get out and collided with Mitsuru, who had stepped ahead of me. She had stopped square in the doorway, too nervous to go farther.

"I'm really sorry! I'm just not used to being out in public."

"When did they release you?"

"Two months ago. I was in for six years," she whispered.

I looked at Mitsuru from behind. There wasn't the slightest trace of the bright studious girl she had been in high school. Squirrel-like, sagacious Mitsuru! Now she was thin and flimsy and rough like a nail file. She looked like her mother—her mother who was so frank and so pathetic. Her mother who had betrayed my grandfather. I'd heard it was her mother who encouraged Mitsuru—and also her husband, who was a doctor—to join that religious group. But I wonder if that was true.

"How is your husband?"

"He's still in. I have two sons, you know. They're being brought up by my husband's family, and I worry about their education."

Mitsuru sipped her coffee. A few drops dribbled off her lip and onto the front of her sari, staining it, but she didn't seem to notice.

"Still in?"

"In confinement. I imagine he'll serve the maximum sentence. It's to be expected." Mitsuru looked up at me, somewhat embarrassed. "But what about you? I just can't believe what happened to Yuriko. And Kazue too. I can't imagine that Kazue would do such a thing. She was such a hard worker. Maybe she just got tired of trying so hard."

Mitsuru pulled a pack of cigarettes out of the cloth bag she was carrying and lit one. She started to smoke, but she didn't look used to it.

"We've put on the years, you and I! I think the gap between your teeth has grown larger."

Mitsuru nodded in agreement. "You've aged too. Maliciousness just gushes from your face now."

The words triggered thoughts of the events in the courtroom that day. If anyone had a face from which maliciousness gushed forth, it was Zhang! *That's* the face of a lying scoundrel if ever there was one. His ridiculous deposition was just varnished with lies. It's clear that he killed a whole host of people in China to get their money. He raped his younger sister and killed her. And there's no doubt he murdered both Yuriko and Kazue.

"Tell me," I asked Mitsuru. "A face that gushes with maliciousness: is that someone dogged by bad karma? I'm wondering what kind of karma I have, and I figured that if anyone could tell me, it's you."

Mitsuru stubbed her cigarette out and frowned. She looked nervously around the room and finally spoke in a hushed voice.

"Please don't say such crazy things. I've quit the organization; I smoke now as proof. But you've misunderstood the doctrines of my former religion. Buying into all the garbage the mass media spews out just makes you despise people who are really sincere about what they believe."

"Are you showing me a face that gushes maliciousness, then?"

"I'm sorry! I was wrong. I keep doing these things ever since I got out. I have no self-confidence, and I don't know how I'm supposed to act. I mean, I've forgotten. I really need to get into some kind of rehab. I came here specifically because I thought I'd see you. I just used the Yuriko-and-Kazue trial as an excuse to see you again. Since I hate class reunions and gatherings of that kind, I figured it was the only chance I'd have."

Mitsuru raised her face as if she suddenly remembered something. "The letters I sent you from prison—did you get them?"

"I got four: New Year's cards and midsummer wishes."

"Sending New Year's cards from a place like that was hard. They played the 'Red and White Singing Contest' on the radio. I'd listen to it, sitting *zazen* style, and cry. What the hell am I doing here, contemplating my navel? I'd wonder. But you never answered. Weren't you pleased to learn that the straight-A student had ended up in prison? I'm sure you thought it appropriate. You must have thought it justified." Her voice grew rough. "I made a royal mess of things, and I'm sure all the world rejoiced."

"Mitsuru, you've come to resemble your mother, haven't you?"

Whenever Mitsuru's mother wanted to say something, she just blurted it out, letting the chips fall where they might. It always had an avalanche effect. Things would take on a momentum of their own; before she knew it, she'd said more than she should have and ended up where she hadn't anticipated. The liar Zhang was the exact opposite, I thought, and once again I recalled his crafty face in the courtroom.

"Hmm, have I?"

"I remember your mother gave me a ride to school in her car once. It was on the same morning I learned that my mother had committed suicide. Your mother said she probably killed herself because she was menopausal."

"Right. I remember. How I wish I could go back in time! If only I could return to the days when I was able to live without knowing any of what I know now. If I could, I wouldn't spend all my time studying like a maniac. I would fool around like the other girls and have fun dressing in the latest fashions. I would join the cheerleading squad or the golf team or the ice-skating club. And I would hang out with boys and go to parties. I just wish I'd lived the life of a normal happy teenager. You probably feel the same way, don't you?"

Hardly. I had never once thought of returning to the past. But if there were a time in the past that I would have wanted to return to, it would have been those peaceful days I spent with my grandfather when he was obsessed with his bonsai. However, then he got all tangled up in the lustful ripples that reverberated from Yuriko, went crazy over Mitsuru's mother, and changed completely. So, no, there really was no time in the past I would want to visit. I suppose Mitsuru had completely forgotten the way we had convinced each other of our talents for survival. She began to irritate me, rather like the irritation I had felt earlier for Yuriko and her stupidity.

Mitsuru peered at me anxiously. "What are you thinking about?"

"About the past, of course. The distant past that you say you want to return to. I'd go back to the point in time when Yuriko was a flowering plant, and I was a naked-seed plant. Except, of course, Yuriko would be all dried up."

Mitsuru stared at me quizzically. I didn't try to explain. When she saw I wasn't going to continue, she blushed and turned away. There it was! There was the expression that was unique to her in high school.

"Sorry, I know I'm acting strangely," Mitsuru said, as she gripped her cloth bag. "It's just that I can't help feeling that everything I worked so hard for, everything I believed in, is now meaningless—and I can't bear it. When I was in prison I did my utmost not to even think about it. But now that I'm out, it's all coming back to haunt me, and I just panic. Of course, what we did was horrible, a huge mistake. I don't know how I could have killed all those innocent people. But I'd been brainwashed. The leader of the sect could read what I was thinking and he controlled me that way. There was no way I could have escaped. I think it's all over for me. I'm sure my husband will die in prison. I just cling to my children and wonder what to do. I've got to try my hardest to ensure they're brought up safely, since I'm all they have left. But I don't think I can do it. I've got no confidence. Here I am: I studied my brains out, I got into Tokyo University Medical School, I became a doctor—yet I can never make up for those six years I spent in prison. And because of that, no one will ever hire me."

"What about Doctors Without Borders?" I asked, though I knew nothing about them myself.

"Oh, so you don't care because it's not your problem," Mitsuru mumbled darkly. "Talking about not one's problem, everyone acts like they were shocked when they found out about Yuriko and Kazue. But I wasn't. Those two were always defiant, swimming against the tide. Especially Kazue."

Mitsuru echoed what the female reporter had said earlier. No one seemed particularly interested in Yuriko. Kazue was the only one they treated as a celebrity. Mitsuru's eyes were empty, completely devoid of the sparkling brilliance and bold independence they had once had.

"Where are your children now?" I asked.

Mitsuru had lit another cigarette. She squinted in the smoke. "They're with my husband's parents. The older boy is a sophomore in high school. The younger is preparing for his junior high entrance exams. I hear he wants to get into the Q School system, but there's no way he'll succeed. It's not a question of his grades, he'll never escape the curse of having us for parents. It's as if he's been branded."

Branded—that's a good way to put it, don't you think? It so perfectly suited my own situation and the way I had to go through life *branded* as the older sister of the monstrously beautiful Yuriko. I was seized with an intense desire to see Mitsuru's children. I wondered what kind of faces they had. I was fascinated by the way genes are passed along, the way they are damaged and mutated.

"I know you resent my mother," Mitsuru said, breaking into my thoughts by saying something completely unexpected.

"Why do you think so?"

"Because she abandoned your grandfather. You probably don't know, but your grandfather caused Mother to join the organization. She's still in it too. She says she'll hold her ground until the end. She's looking after those members who are still practicing."

My grandfather would be shocked if he heard this. I knew Mitsuru's mother supported her decision to join the organization; she'd joined too. But I could not for a moment entertain the idea that my grandfather was somehow responsible. Was it the enactment of some kind of karmic retribution?

"My mother has said that disrupting your grandfather's life like that was what she regretted most in life. And it wasn't just your grandfather's life, was it. She upset your life as well."

When I entered Q University, my grandfather decided to move in with Mitsuru's mother, who bought a luxury apartment nearby. I went there once. I remember that the front door to the building locked automatically and you had to call up on the intercom to be let in. It was a new system at the time and my grandfather was terribly proud of it. But, ironically, it was because of that locking system that we knew he was growing senile. Each time he went out, he'd forget to take his key. Then he'd push the intercom button for the wrong apartment and stand there shouting, "It's me! Let me in!"

"It was on account of the love affair between my mother and your grandfather that both you and I were forced to live on our own. And then Mother came running back to live with me. She left everything in a shambles: my place, your place, the place she shared with your grandfather. She couldn't forgive herself for what she'd done, so she decided to take up religious training. That's what got her started."

"Was she able to forgive herself through religious training?"

"No." Mitsuru shook her head proudly. "That's not it. She selected the path she took because she wanted to know more about the laws governing the human realm. She wanted to understand how human beings could possess such dark, selfish passions. At that time, my husband and I were tormented by questions of death. All humans die. But what happens to them after death? Is transmigration possible? As doctors, we could not avoid direct confrontation with death as an inevitable outcome—but now and then we encountered some inexplicable cases. That's when my mother recommended that we meet the leader of the organization she had joined and talk with him. And that's how we ended up joining too."

I was growing annoyed with this conversation and began avoiding Mitsuru's gaze. It seems in the final analysis that people who get involved in religion are only after their own personal happiness. Am I wrong?

"Well, my grandfather doesn't care now," I said. "He's completely senile now and spends all his time in bed."

"He's still alive?"

"Very much so, though he's now past ninety."

"Really, I'd just assumed he was dead."

"Well, I suppose that's what your mother thinks too."

"We seem to be missing each other's points." Mitsuru hung her head so low I thought her neck would snap. "It's probably because I haven't properly returned to society yet." A vacant gaze swept over her face. "In high school, I tried so hard to remain number one. Med school too. And I got everything I wanted. I was at the top of my department and was one of the best at the hospital. But gradually, things began to feel less clear than they had before. It makes sense when you think about it. A doctor is not evaluated by test scores. Of course, I know it's important for doctors to save lives. But in the ear, nose, and throat specialty we rarely encounter cases that are life-threatening. Day after day I was faced with allergy-induced nasal inflammation. Only once did I see a patient who was in critical condition, owing to a tumor on the lower jaw. But that was it. That was the only time I felt my work was really worthwhile. So I lapsed into a kind of fog. That's when I thought that if I underwent religious training I could bring my life to the next level."

I let out a long sigh. This was excruciating! You understand why, don't you? I had loved Mitsuru. I had believed that we polished our respective talents—me my maliciousness and Mitsuru her brilliance—not because we wanted to be cool but because we needed them as weapons in order to survive the Q School for Young Women.

Mitsuru glanced up at me uncertainly, "Did I say something to upset you?"

I decided to give her some indication of the dark mood building inside me. If I didn't, she'd lapse back into her "while I was in prison" routine.

"When you were in college, were you able to keep your position at the top of the class?"

Mitsuru silently lit her third cigarette. I waved the smoke away with my hand and waited for her to answer.

"Why do you want to know?"

"I'm just curious."

"Well, then, I'll tell you the truth. I wasn't first in the class, not by a long shot. I probably came in around the middle. No matter how hard I tried, how carefully I listened in class, or how many all-nighters I pulled studying, there were always others I could not beat. But what do you expect? I mean, the school admitted the brightest students from throughout the nation. To make it to the top you had to be naturally gifted, an absolute genius—otherwise you could study forever and it was still hopeless. After a few years I finally realized that far from being first, I'd be lucky if I ended up twentieth. It really gave me a shock. That's not like me, I thought, and I began to suffer from an identity crisis. So do you know what I decided to do?"

"I can't imagine."

"I decided I would marry someone who really was a genius. That's my husband. Takashi."

When she said his name was Takashi I immediately drew the association to Takashi Kashiwabara. But I remember seeing her husband's photograph in the newspapers, and he didn't look a thing like Takashi Kashiwabara. He was skinny, wore glasses, and looked like an overly studious scholar. No matter his genius, he was much too ugly for me to ever want to marry! From the point of view of physiognomy, his ears were pointy like a demon's and his mouth was small. The middle and lower phases of his face indicated weakness. His was a face that foretold great tragedy in the middle to late years of life. When I consider Takashi's fate, I can only conclude that physiognomy is amazingly on target.

"I've seen your husband's face."

"Right. He's famous."

"And so are you."

Mitsuru flushed red—whether because of my sarcasm or a hot flash, I couldn't tell. As a cult member, Mitsuru had been involved in a number of cases involving the kidnapping of believers. If these so-called believers tried to escape, Mitsuru and the others would lock them in a room, force them to take drugs, and then begin the initiation. If they weren't careful, the victims would overdose and die.

Still, those deaths were nothing compared to the time Mitsuru's husband dropped poison gas from a Cessna airplane on a number of farmers and their families. The leader of their religious organization suffered from some kind of persecution complex, which was triggered when local farmers staged protests against the establishment of his religious headquarters near their farmlands, so he ordered Mitsuru's husband to drop mustard gas on their fields. At the time, as luck would have it, a group of elementary students were visiting the farms for a little hands-on agriculture study, and they were caught up in the gas. Fifteen people died.

Mitsuru tried to change the subject.

"Do you know about osmotic pressure? I thought, if I married a brilliant man, that some of his genius would brush off on me."

I noticed that as she began to talk, her body started to cave in on itself, like a sail that loses the wind. Her thin body grew all the flatter. I could see the veins crawling over the fingers clutching the cigarette. I was amazed by how empty-headed Mitsuru had become.

"By that time, my mother had separated from your grandfather. She joined the organization, saying she wanted to eliminate her illusions. By illusions she meant her selfish passions."

"Well, wouldn't that be good, to eliminate them, I mean. It's not as if she had actually cared for my grandfather," I said harshly.

Mitsuru responded mockingly. "You can't forgive me, can you? You think you're better than I am because I ended up in a religious cult."

I tilted my head to the side. "Are you sure you haven't lost a few marbles?"

"Oh? So we're going to resort to insults, are we?" Mitsuru raised her head suddenly. "I remember not so long ago you were more than a little obsessed with looks. How should I put this? You just cared about faces. I knew you had an inferiority complex because Yuriko was so pretty. But you went way beyond a complex; you were a fanatic. Ever since high school you've been really proud of yourself for being half, haven't you? Everyone laughed at you behind your back, you know. You weren't even remotely pretty. But you can transcend your body with how you discipline your soul."

I never would have believed I would hear such abusive lies from Mitsuru. It was too much. I could not, however, bring myself to speak in my own defense.

"Your hatred of Yuriko was really bizarre," she continued. "It was more like jealousy. I know you were the one who leaked the news about Yuriko and Kijima's son. Whatever Yuriko was doing with the boys in the boys' side of the school had nothing to do with you. But Yuriko was popular. Everyone idolized her. Still, to get your own sister expelled from school by spreading rumors about her being involved in prostitution— that was really vicious. And until you lessen your store of bad karma, you have very little chance of transmigration any time in the future. If you are reborn, it'll be as some bug that crawls through the dirt."

I was furious. I had tried to let Mitsuru have her say, knowing she'd been brainwashed, but she'd gone too far.

"Mitsuru, you are a complete idiot. I've listened to you go on and on about being at the top of the class, getting into Tokyo University Medical

School, and all that crap about osmosis, and I'm just fed up. All this time I had thought you were a clever little squirrel, but you were nothing but a slug. You were just a puffed-up little show-off, no better than Kazue!"

"You're the one who's crazy. Look at you—you look absolutely evil. Why do you think you're any more sincere than I am? You go through life telling nothing but lies. And even now you're sitting here thinking how wonderful you are because you're half. I sure wish I could trade you for Yuriko."

I stood up angrily, kicking the chair back as I did. The waitresses, suddenly noticing us, looked up from what they were doing and stared. Mitsuru and I glared at each other until she hid her face. I shoved the bill for our coffee over to her.

"I'm leaving. Thank you for treating."

Mitsuru pushed the bill back across the table. "We'll split it."

"I had to sit here and listen to what you wanted to say; we're not splitting the bill. You say I have a complex about Yuriko. I have to hear this today, on the day of the trial? I'm here as a bereaved member of the victim's family. What gives you the right to insult me like that? I demand compensation for damages."

"You think I'm going to pay compensatory charges?"

"Well, you have that rich family of yours. Your mother owned how many cabarets? And you rented that luxury apartment in Minato Ward just to flaunt your wealth, didn't you? Then your mother went out and bought a condominium with a fancy intercom in that swanky Riverside area. All I've got is my measly job."

Mitsuru launched into her response with apparent relish.

"My, you pick a convenient time to start complaining about your measly job. Just amazing. And here I remember you ever eager to boast about the way you were going to become some famous translator of German. But your marks in English class were just deplorable, weren't they? Hardly what you'd expect from a half! And for your information, my family is not wealthy. We sold our house and our business, and the money we made on that and on the sale of our two cars and our resort property in Kiyosato all went into the coffers of the religious organization."

I placed my coins begrudgingly on the table. Mitsuru counted out the change and continued.

"I'm going to go to the next hearing too. I think it'll be really good for my rehabilitation."

Suit yourself, I wanted to say, but thought better of it. I turned and exited the coffeehouse, walking away briskly. As I did I heard the pitter-pat of Mitsuru's canvas sneakers following me.

"Wait! I almost forgot the most important part. I got letters from Professor Kijima."

Mitsuru dug through her bag, pulled out an envelope, and waved it in my face.

"When did you get letters from Professor Kijima?"

"While I was in prison. I got quite a few. He was really worried about me, so we corresponded."

Well, wasn't Mitsuru just beside herself with pride. I hadn't heard anything about Professor Kijima for such a long time, I'd just assumed he'd died. And all this time he'd been sending Mitsuru letters.

"Well, how kind of him."

"He said it wounded him terribly for one of his students to be involved in a scandal—just like I would worry over my patients."

"Your patients weren't out murdering people, were they?"

"I'm still recuperating, you know. Still only halfway in my struggle to return to society, and your cruelty is not appreciated." Mitsuru gave a big sigh. But I'd had just about all I could take, I wanted to get out of there. Still, if she wanted to talk about cruelty, she ought to examine the way she was using Yuriko and Kazue's trials as her own personal class reunion.

"He wrote about you too, so I thought you'd like to see. I'll let you borrow them. But you have to be sure to give them back to me at the next hearing."

Mitsuru passed the thick envelope over to me. The last thing I wanted was a packet of letters I had no interest in reading. I tried to hand them back to Mitsuru but she was already walking away, staggering slightly. I watched her depart, trying to find in her something that resembled the girl she had been in the past. The Mitsuru who had been good in tennis. The Mitsuru who had been so light on her feet during our rhythmic dance routines. I'd been vaguely fearful of her—with her physical agility and her brilliant mind. She had seemed like something of a monster to me.

But the Mitsuru I saw now seemed awkward, uncoordinated, even in the most casual of movements. Concerned about being followed by detectives, she was so busy looking over her shoulder that she practically ran into someone who was right in front of her. Anyone who had known Mitsuru in the past would have had a hard time recognizing her in the idiot she'd become. This hollow Mitsuru had transmigrated into an entirely different monster.

I remembered that when we were in high school, I used to think of both Mitsuru and myself as mountain pools formed by underground springs. If Mitsuru's spring was deep beneath the surface of the ground, so was mine. Our sensibilities were complementary and our train of thought was exactly the same. But now those springs had disappeared. We were now two separate pools, lonely and remote. Moreover, Mitsuru's pool had already gone dry, exposing the cracked earth at the bottom. I wish I hadn't seen her again.

I heard someone calling to me. "Aren't you Miss Hirata's older sister?"

I hurriedly stuffed Kijima's letters in my pocket and looked up. A familiar-looking man was standing in front of me. He was around forty and wore a fairly expensive brown suit. His beard was flecked with white whiskers and he was as rotund as an opera singer, a "carnal personality" who clearly ate delicious food.

"I'm sorry to bother you," he said, "but might I have a brief word?"

I was trying to figure out where I'd seen him before, but I couldn't place him. As I stood there with my head cocked to the side, the man launched into a self-introduction.

"I see you don't remember. I'm Zhang's lawyer, Tamura. I hadn't expected to see you just now. I had thought I would try to call you later this evening." Tamura led me to a corner of the corridor, clearly annoyed. We were next to the cafeteria. Lunch was over, the cafeteria had closed, and the employees inside were moving the tables around, carrying bottles of beer, and setting up for some kind of private function. Upstairs in the courtrooms they're deciding someone's fate, while downstairs in the basement they're whooping it up. Easy for them. I'm just glad I'm not the defendant.

"Sensei, I don't know what you think, but I'm certain Zhang killed Kazue."

Tamura straightened the knot to his mustard yellow tie while he prepared his lines. "I can certainly understand how you must feel, as a member of the family, but I have to say I think he's innocent."

"Surely not. The study of physiognomy makes clear Zhang's a killer. There can be no doubt."

Tamura looked troubled. He didn't dare try to refute my argument. I suppose he realized that he had to let the victim's family members say whatever they pleased. But I wasn't some sentimental idiot who sympathized blindly with the victim, I was trying to explain things from the scientific perspective of physiognomy.

I needed to make that clear, but Tamura said in a whispery voice, "Actually, what I wanted to ask you is whether you had had contact recently with either Yuriko or Kazue. I can find no proof for this in the investigation, but it seems such an unlikely coincidence, don't you think? I mean for your younger sister and your former classmate to be killed the same way, less than a year apart. It's just too bizarre to be happenstance. So I was wondering if you'd heard anything from either of them?"

Yuriko's diary immediately came to mind, but I didn't want to tell him about it. Let him find out about it on his own. "I don't know. But then, I hadn't seen either Yuriko or Kazue in some time. Don't you imagine they both just hit a patch of bad luck? If you'd consider the physiognomy, Zhang is somewhere between a 'calculating personality' and a 'carnal personality'—the type to go for prostitutes. He killed them both. Kazue too. There's no doubt—"

Flustered, Tamura interrupted me. "Yes, yes, I see. That's fine. Zhang's case is now under deliberation, and it's best if I don't discuss it with you."

"Why? I'm related to the victim. I'm the one whose only sister was murdered! Her precious sister."

"I understand. Really I do."

"What do you understand? Tell me."

Perspiration had begun to dot Tamura's forehead, and as he patted through the pockets in his suit searching for his handkerchief, he changed the subject.

"I believe I saw one of those cult members here not too long ago. Wasn't she also a former classmate of yours? You certainly had a—well, what should I say?—unique high school class."

"Yes, it's been a virtual class reunion here today."

"Well, yes, you could look at it that way. Excuse me," Tamura said. He turned to leave, heading hastily into the coffeehouse. And here I had more to say, I thought, as I glared at his muscular back. First of all there was his remark about my *unique* class. The more I thought about it, the angrier I got. And then there were the words Mitsuru had said to me earlier; they started spinning around and around in my head as well.

When I finally managed to slink back to my apartment in the government housing complex, I found it cold. The tatami was old, stained here and there where miso soup had been spilled on it. And it smelled. I lit the kerosene heater and looked around the room. It was shabby and small. Back when bonsai pots crowded Grandfather's veranda, we were poor, but oh, I was happy! Yuriko was still in Bern, I'd just entered Q High School for Young Women, and I had dedicated myself enthusiastically to looking after my grandfather, my true flesh and blood. I suppose I liked my grandfather so much because he was an affirmed scam artist. And yet he was so timid, even more so than I. Yes, it was odd. He was not a bit like me. The "class reunion" had brought me down.

The letters? Once night fell I pulled them out and looked through them with disgust. Here they are. The handwriting is shaky—written by an old man's trembling hand—so they're hard to read. And, as I expected, they are preachy. But if you want to read them, go ahead. I don't mind.

> *Greetings and Salutations.*
> *My dear Mitsuru:*
>
> *Are you well? The winters in Shinano Oiwake are particularly severe. The ground in my garden has frozen over into tiny pillars of frost. Before long it'll all be frozen and then the long winter will set in. I'm sixty-seven now and heading into the winter of my life.*
>
> *I'm still running the dormitory for the N Fire Insurance Company. Not much has changed. Now that I'm past retirement age, I fear I'm not much use anymore, but the director of the company has very kindly asked me to stay on. He's a graduate of the Q School system.*
>
> *Well, then, let me begin by congratulating you on your release from prison. Now I can finally send letters to you— and hopefully receive them—without worrying about the prying eyes of the censors. You have certainly put up with so much and weathered it all with such fortitude. I feel deeply for you and the way you must worry over your husband and the children you've left with others to raise.*
>
> *But Mitsuru, my dear, you are not yet forty. Your future lies ahead of you. You have awakened from the nightmare of mind*

control, and if you struggle to live an upright life from here on, never forgetting to pray for the souls of those whom you harmed and beg their forgiveness—I am confident that you will be all right. If there is anything I can do for you, please do not hesitate to ask.

Dear Mitsuru,

You were the brightest student I ever had, and I never once worried about your future. To have seen the way you have stumbled, however, has urged me to reconsider the past. I feel responsible for your slide into criminality; my careless manner of teaching must be held accountable. I have determined that I shall repent alongside you.

To tell you the truth, ever since the religious organization you were affiliated with committed those crimes, I have hardly had a day free of turmoil. And then with the tragedies last year and the year before, I have had cause to grieve all over again. I am sure you are aware that both Yuriko Hirata and Kazue Satō were killed. They say the same murderer is responsible. To think of the way they were both so cruelly murdered, and their bodies abandoned, is more bitter than I can bear. I remember them both so well.

Kazue Satō's case has garnered particular attention, with headlines screaming OFFICE EMPLOYEE BY DAY, PROSTITUTE BY NIGHT! *She was such a serious student when she first entered my classes—and then to have her turned into fodder for the rapacious media! To think of how this must mortify her family makes me want to rush to her house and throw myself before her mother and apologize. My dear, I imagine you must be mystified as to why I might feel this way. But I cannot overcome the feeling that somehow I failed as a father—consider my eldest son—and as an educator.*

We at Q High School for Young Women espoused an educational tenet that advocated self-sufficiency and a strong sense of self-awareness in our students. And yet, among the girls who have graduated from Q High School for Young Women, there are data to prove that the rate for divorce, failure to marry, and suicide is much higher than that in other schools.

Why is it that girls who come from such privileged back-grounds, who are so proud of their academic accomplishments, and who are such excellent students must meet so much more unhappiness than students elsewhere? Rather than suggesting it is because the real world is crueler for them, I think it more accurate to suggest that we allowed the creation of an environment that was too much of a utopia. Or, to put it another way, we failed to teach our girls the strategies that would enable them to cope with the frustrations of the real world. It is this realization that continues to haunt me, and the other teachers feel the same. We realize now that it was our arrogance that prevented us from coming to grips with the real world.

I've mellowed now that I have been living here in a severe environment, going about the mundane job of looking after a dormitory. The naked human is powerless against nature. As a scientist, I clothed myself with knowledge and believed that one could not live without the study of science. But now I realize that science alone is not enough. I suppose that when I taught school, all I taught was the heart of science; I am ashamed to think of it now. I wonder if there are similar teachings in your religion?

My dear Mitsuru,

I believe I need to rethink my approach to education. But when I finally came to this conclusion, I was well along in years and no longer actively teaching. I was retired—forced to resign because of my own son's delinquent behavior. My regret over my failure to realize this sooner has only deepened over the years, made more painful still by what befell you, my dear, and the horrible business with your classmates Miss Hirata and Miss Satō.

While tending to the dormitory I've also been busy with my life work of studying the behavior of the Kijima Tribolium castaneum. T. Castaneum is a species of beetle, aka the Red Flour Beetle. I discovered a strain quite by accident in the woods behind my house, so I was allowed to give it my name. Being that I was the one who discovered the strain that now bears my name, it's necessary for me to follow up with an appropriate study.

The behavior of a living organism is really a fascinating subject. If furnished with sufficient food and favorable living conditions, the reproduction rate of an organism will increase exponentially. As the rate of individual reproduction increases, the group population expands, as you well know, my dear. But if the increase in food supply is not commensurate with the increase in population, fierce competition will ensue among the population, at which point the birthrate falls while the death rate increases. Eventually this has an impact on the development, formation, and physiology of the organism—which is the foundation of physiology.

In my research on the Kijima T. castaneum, I discovered a mutation—a beetle with longer wings and shorter legs than the others. This mutation was clearly the result of the intensification of a sense of individuation. I believed that modifications resulted in the insect's shape and structure so as to enhance its speed and mobility. I want to study this mutation, to verify it with my own eyes. But I doubt I will live as long as will be necessary to complete the study.

My dear Mitsuru,

I wonder if perhaps your religion—or Miss Hirata's work in prostitution, or Miss Satō's double life—is not an outcome of shifts in the structure and makeup of our populations. Is not this intensification of individuation—this heightened sense of awareness of self—a result of the suffocating burden of being trapped within the same social community? It is from the pain this produces that we find changes occurring in our makeup and structure. Without a doubt the experiences that unfold are cruel and bitter. Perhaps it is not possible for us to teach about these bitter experiences. More likely it is impossible for us to articulate the findings we extract from our painful experiments in life.

As bright as you are, I am sure that even you are not able to figure out just what it is I am trying to say. Let me be more direct.

When I first read about the Yuriko Hirata incident in the newspapers, I was just as shocked as I had been when I learned about your crimes. No, I was even more shocked. More than twenty years had passed since Yuriko and my son were expelled from school. I remember that Miss Hirata's older sister (I forget her name, but you must remember her; she was in your class, a fairly drab person) came to me and asked me what she should do about her sister, who was going off with my son to engage in prostitution. At the time I said, without even thinking, "I will not tolerate this. Most likely we will expel them."

If I am to be perfectly frank about what I was thinking at the time, it was Yuriko, rather than my own son, whom I was disinclined to forgive. I was feeling selfish, and my behavior was utterly unbecoming to a teacher. But as ashamed as I am to admit it, I am committed to describing things just as they happened. I am not trying to write a confession. But I realize that the decision I made lacked a basis in either pedagogical wisdom or prudence, and I deeply regret it now.

Ironically, I was the one who saw that Yuriko Hirata was admitted to the Q School system in the first place. Miss Hirata had just returned from Switzerland, and her scores on the entrance exam for transfer students were not good. Her marks in Japanese classics and mathematics were particularly low. The other instructors all felt that she did not meet our minimum requirements, but I saw that she was admitted over their objections. I had a number of reasons for doing so. First among them was the fact that Miss Hirata was so beautiful she stole my heart away. I was a junior high school teacher, but even so I was not immune to wanting to have a pretty girl around to observe. But what was foremost in my mind was the potential of conducting a biological study of what happens when a mutant member of a species is introduced into a population.

I had dual motives in admitting her, but my plan backfired and cost me my job. I should have known better than to introduce such an abnormally beautiful creature into a population of her normal peers. To deepen the irony, it was my own son who served as Miss Hirata's procurer, humiliating me with the *filthy money he earned as a result. Now I am haunted all the more by the unsettling belief that it was my unreasonableness in admitting Miss Hirata and then seeing to her expulsion that led to her further depravity and ultimately to her death.*

When I decided to expel Miss Hirata, I called her guardians, Mr. and Mrs. Johnson, and spoke to them about it. Mrs. Johnson was furious, much more so than her husband; I remember her saying that she wanted to throw her out of their house immediately. I encouraged her to do so. I was angry with Miss Hirata. But no matter what she had done, she was still under-age and should not have been held responsible for her actions. Rather, the blame lay with the environment in which she was being raised. Even though I realized this, I was still unable to overcome my anger at the girl.

And her elder sister as well. I heard that after Miss Hirata was expelled, far from growing more lively, the elder sister turned more and more morose. I don't think it would be an exaggeration to say that I was responsible for creating the dis-cord between them. The older sister entered this school by her own hard work. Only my curiosity permitted the admission of her younger sister, Yuriko. Human beings are not subjects in biological experiments.

The fate of Kazue Satō also weighs heavily on my mind. It is true that Miss Satō was the target of bullying while she was in Q High School for Young Women. I cannot help but conclude that the cause of this bullying was directly related somehow to the fact that Yuriko Hirata had been admitted into the school system. Because Miss Satō admired Miss Hirata and had a crush on my son, Miss Hirata's older sister treated her terri-bly. News of her behavior reached me, I'm quite sure, and yet I did nothing—pretending not to be aware of any of it. For Miss Satō, life at Q High School for Young Woman—a life she had struggled long and hard to enjoy—must have been a tor-turous nightmare. Believing competition to be an inevitable aspect of any population of species, I stood on the sidelines and watched.

Effort has nothing to do with the changes to structure and physiology that develop as a consequence of the intensifi-

cation of individuation. Indeed, it is futile. That's because changes are carried out at whim. And yet I, as a teacher—no, the educational system itself—pushed Miss Satō toward this futility. She drove herself to work hard while at the university and again at her workplace, until she finally just wore herself down. Tragically, that's when the change to her structure finally took place, and unfortunately it was a change that depended entirely on attracting male desire. That this change was diametrically opposed to our school motto of self-sufficiency and self-confidence is a consequence of my own selfish whimsy. I am convinced of this. If I had not admitted Miss Hirata into the school, Miss Satō might have completed her high school years without suffering from bulimia.

When population figures are low, individual life-forms learn to survive independently in isolation. When individuation intensifies, life-forms develop group survival strategies, changing in size and structure as they do. But girl students can't help but feel that they can't survive in isolation. The competition among them is severe. The basis for this competition is grounded in scholastic performance, personality, and financial security, but the greatest of these is physical beauty, which is determined entirely by birth. And here's where things get very complicated. Some girls may be more beautiful than others when it comes to one aspect of their looks but will not pass muster when a different aspect is compared. The competition between them thus intensifies. I placed Yuriko Hirata into this mix: the super-beauty. I learned, after Miss Hirata and my son had been expelled, that even in the boys' section of the school the competition she inspired was tremendous. But I continued to close my eyes. That is to say, I left things to resolve on their own. I was the one who triggered the events that have unfolded over the last twenty years. Do you understand now why I say I feel responsible?

My dear Mitsuru,

I do not think even a brilliant student such as yourself escaped this battle. Perhaps you managed to stay on top because of a fierce effort. You were very pretty, and your grades excelled all others. But on the dark side of that bright offense, I know you were working tirelessly, weren't you? And the power that urged you on was born of your fear of losing, was it not? The minute you forgot this fear, that was the minute you would fail to attain your goal.

I ignored this as well. And I call myself an educator! How I regret that I failed to offer anyone the kind of education that might have saved them from this "failure." But it is all in the distant past. So many lives have been lost. And the years when you should have been laying a foundation for your maturity have been spent locked away in prison. How sad this makes me. I feel I should at least try to convey my sentiments to Miss Hirata's older sister, but I regret to say that I cannot remember her name. Yes, that's right, I can remember that even back then I was so entranced by Miss Hirata's beauty that I was overcome with jealousy for my own son. How it shames me to admit it!

I cut ties with my son Takashi. I do not know where he is or what he is doing or even if he is dead or alive. Strictly through rumor, I learned that after he was expelled he continued in the same line of work. He is drowning in a sweet poison (making a living off exploiting women is the darkest of poisons), and I find it highly unlikely that he will ever be able to drag himself from the mire that claims him. My wife may have been in touch with him secretly for all I know. But he has not once tried to contact me. My anger was that great.

My wife died three years ago of cancer. My younger son's family took care of the funeral. I have no idea if Takashi knows of his mother's death. My younger son has also cut ties with him. Although he did not understand the reason why, he had to change schools when Takashi was expelled and I was dismissed from the Q School system.

My wife loved Takashi dearly, and she was consumed with regret over the turn our life took. She could never forgive me. But whether she liked it or not, hadn't our son introduced his own classmate to customers and accepted the money he got from the transaction? What Takashi did was shameful and deviated from my own sense of values. I don't think it would be an exaggeration to say that what Takashi did led to my destruction.

Based on an investigation the school conducted, Takashi had earned several hundred thousand yen! He took the money he earned and his license and went out and got a foreign-import car. He sneaked around behind my back, living a wild and extravagant life. He paid Miss Hirata nearly half of the money he pulled in. His behavior was despicable, no better than that of a beast. He was lining his pockets by wounding her body and spirit. My wife and I had no inkling of any of this. We all lived in the same house; how could we have not noticed? I'm sure you find it hard to accept. But when he was at home, my son kept everything secret and acted just as he always had. He lived a double life.

Now I've come to the conclusion that Takashi must have harbored some kind of resentment of me, some need for revenge. I was his father, but I was also an instructor at the school he attended. And my feelings for Miss Hirata defy easy explanation. If Takashi had really shared my feelings for the girl, could he have prostituted her like that? To think of calling what he was doing a business is so cold-blooded it makes me tremble with horror. Depriving me of my love for another person and for my enjoyment of my imagination was another way he wounded me. Gradually I began to realize the grievous mistake I'd made in enrolling my sons in my own school. That is what started it all off. I am responsible, therefore, for everything that happened afterward.

I suppose you could say that mine was a strange fate. I knew that Miss Satō had sent my son any number of letters. At the time, I told Takashi, "Reply in all sincerity." I said this because I knew he had no interest in the girl. I have no way of knowing if he followed my advice or not. But the fact that Miss Satō developed an eating disorder leads me to wonder if perhaps Takashi was involved. There is nothing I could have done about it, but I do feel pangs of regret for having placed Takashi in the school.

Mitsuru, dear,

I'm nearly seventy years old, and here I am reflecting on the past, seeing how cruel youth was. It's not unusual for young people to be overly fixated on themselves and to exclude others. But the students in the Q system were far worse than most. And it's not just the Q system that is at fault. Surely, Japanese education as a whole should accept the blame. Earlier I wrote that all I taught students was to think and feel scientifically. But now I have something far worse to write about.

Not only did I not teach the truth at school, I was beside myself with worry that I would end up burying a different kind of "weight" in my students' hearts. That was brought on by the fact that I participated in encouraging their belief in an absolute value system, a system in which one sought to outdo everyone else. In a word, I am afraid I advocated a form of mind control. And that is because those students who worked as hard as they could but received no reward for their efforts have been forced to live a life burdened by this weight. Wasn't this the way it was for Kazue Satō or even for Miss Hirata's older sister? Both were different from the other girls, but they were no match for you, my dear, when it came to scholastic abilities.

The weight we buried in their hearts was powerless against those who would destroy them. They lacked beauty. And no matter how hard they tried, there was nothing they could do to change that.

Mitsuru, dear,

In a letter that you sent to me earlier from prison you confessed to having been attracted to me. Your letter surprised and gladdened me. To be perfectly honest, while I was teaching you in high school, my heart was captivated by the beautiful Miss Hirata. She was so much more beautiful than any woman I'd ever seen before, that just to gaze upon her filled me with joy. I suppose this is what rendered me powerless in the face of the tremendous weight we all felt—the need to be better than others. Or rather, I should say, the weight became *utterly meaningless. You see, natural beauty creates such excitement that the existence of the weight is negated. And once it is negated, the heavier it is to bear. Therefore, Yuriko Hirata was hated just for existing. We could not help but want to run her out of school.*

Perhaps what I've written is a bit exaggerated. But am I wrong? I do not know. When I spend these quiet days here in Oiwake, I remember bits and pieces about the past. If only I'd done this, that person would not be dead now, I think to myself. Or if only I'd said such-and-such, that person would not have done those things. I am overwhelmed with shame.

Mitsuru, dearest,

I can see the good and the bad in the actions you and your husband took. What you did was absolutely unforgivable. I say this because I believe your religious faith is another problem altogether. Religious faith in and of itself is neither good nor bad. But how could it lead you to believe it was all right to kill other people? You were such a superior student, easily a match in your own way for Miss Hirata. But you lost the power to reason. And Miss Hirata? Did she think she had no other way to survive in this world than as a prostitute, accepting any man who came along and selling herself to him? How is that possible? Was the education she received so easily overturned?

I wrote that I want to throw myself at the feet of Kazue Satō's family and beg their forgiveness. In the same way I would like to meet Miss Hirata's older sister and apologize for the horrible mess my selfish whimsy created. A precious life has been lost. It's such a tragedy.

While I go about my study of insects, I shall remain tucked away here in my frozen mountain fastness. It is for the best, I think. But what shall I do to relieve myself of the mourning I feel for you, my dear, for Miss Hirata's older sister, and for Miss Satō's family? Ah, I shall never rid myself of this turmoil.

Well, here I've gone and written another long and meandering letter to you, just as you have been released from prison. Please forgive me. And when you are feeling stronger, please come to Oiwake for a visit. I should like to show you my fieldwork.

Most sincerely,
Takakuni Kijima

What do you think? Aren't these letters from Professor Kijima a riot? It's a little late to be feeling regret now, but he goes on with his tedious convictions. I really can't make any sense of them. I'd completely forgotten that Kijima's son's name was Takashi. When I saw the name in his letter, I burst out laughing. Mitsuru's husband is also named Takashi. Neither one has the kind of looks I fancy. And then Professor Kijima goes and writes that he's completely forgotten me! "I forget her name, but you must remember her; she was in your class, a fairly drab person." Shit! A little rude, don't you think? And he a former teacher! What a farce! The old fart must be going senile. And now all I am is "Yuriko's older sister."

Professor Kijima wrote about the intensification of the individual's sense of self and the changes in the shape of life-forms and such, but I don't think that's what's going on. Mitsuru and Yuriko and Kazue didn't mutate; they simply decayed. A biology professor certainly ought to be able to recognize the signs of fermentation and decay. Isn't he the one who taught us all about these processes in organisms? In order to induce the process of decay, water is necessary. I think that, in the case of women, men are the water.

• 2 •

The next hearing was a month later. It was to begin at two o'clock, so I asked my boss if I could leave the office early that day. I was a part-timer, and the boss was none too happy about my arriving late and leaving early. But when I told him I was asking because I wanted to go to the trial, he completely changed his tune. "Fine, fine. Go on then," he said, and waved me off. Zhang's trial was becoming a convenient excuse for getting out of work. But I really did not look forward to attending the hearings. I did not enjoy seeing the prisoner's gloomy face, for a start, and trying to dodge the media was getting to be annoying. Still, Mitsuru had made me promise to give Kijima's letters back to her at the next trial, so I couldn't very well avoid going. I'm a stickler for following through on responsibilities. And I was eager to see what kind of weird outfit Mitsuru would show up in. Curiosity on a number of fronts drew me to the courthouse.

When I reached the courtroom early, a woman with a short haircut waved me over. She had on a yellow turtleneck sweater, a brown skirt, and a stylish scarf wrapped smartly across her shoulders. I cocked my neck to the side, pretty certain that I didn't know anyone that well dressed.

"It's me! Mitsuru."

That's when I saw the big front teeth and the bright eyes. What had happened to that strangely outfitted middle-aged woman?

"You've changed," I said.

I threw my belongings roughly down on the seat behind me. When I did, I knocked Mitsuru's purse to the floor and she bent over to pick it up, a frown on her face. Gone was the frumpy canvas bag. This was a black Gucci shoulder bag.

"What's with the bag?"

"I bought it."

Didn't she tell me the last time we met that she had no money? And there I'd stupidly split the bill with her like I had to dole out charity. With the money she spent on her Gucci bag, I could have bought at least ten of the bags I was carrying. I wanted to chew her out but I just nodded.

"That's nice. You look well."

"Thank you. I've been feeling a bit more settled." Mitsuru smiled slightly. "The last time I saw you I was a nervous wreck. I think I've grown more accustomed to being back in society, but for a while there I felt like Rip Van Winkle. Everything was so different. The neighborhood had changed, prices had gone up. Every part of me was aware of how different things had become in the six years I'd been away. Actually, I went to visit Professor Kijima at his dormitory last week. We talked about all kinds of things, and I felt better after that. I'm going to start over."

"You saw Professor Kijima?"

Why, I wondered, did Mitsuru's cheeks suddenly redden?

"That's right. I thought about the letters I lent you and began to feel so nostalgic that I decided to go see him. He was delighted. We walked together through the woods of Karuizawa. It was freezing, but I was overwhelmed to realize there really are such warm people in the world."

I was shocked. I stared at Mitsuru, as she sat there blushing, and pressed the packet with Professor Kijima's letters into her hand.

"Professor Kijima's letters," she said. "Did you read them?"

"I read them. But I can't make much sense of them. Are you sure he's not senile?"

"Why? Because he couldn't remember your name?"

Mitsuru was perfectly serious—which made me even more annoyed.

"That's not why."

"I told Professor that I showed you his letters, and he seemed to grow concerned for you. He was afraid you'd think badly of him for writing the things he did. He's worried that you're depressed over what happened to Yuriko."

"Well, I'm not! Even if I am just Yuriko's older sister."

Mitsuru released a long sigh. "I probably shouldn't say this, but you've been warped for as long as I can remember. I feel sorry for you, I really do. I wish you could pull yourself out from under whatever spell Yuriko cast over you. Professor Kijima said what you were suffering was nothing short of mind control."

"Professor, Professor . . . you sound just like a broken record. Did something happen with the two of you?"

"Nothing happened. But his words touched a chord in my heart."

It sounded like Mitsuru was in love with Professor Kijima, just like she had been in high school. There are people who make the same mistakes over and over without ever learning. I couldn't take any more of Mitsuru, so I turned around and faced the front of the courtroom. Zhang was being led into the room, sandwiched between two guards, his hands in manacles connected to a cord around his waist. He looked over at me timidly and quickly glanced away. I could feel all the others in the courtroom staring over at me. They didn't want to miss the showdown between the victim's family and the assailant, and I didn't want to disappoint them. I glowered at Zhang for all I was worth. But Mitsuru interrupted me. "Look over there," she said as she grabbed my arm. "Look at that man."

Annoyed, I turned to look. Two men had just claimed empty seats in the spectators' gallery. One was fat, the other a handsome youth.

"I wonder if that's Takashi Kijima."

Takashi Kijima had the same perversely precocious look that I had despised. But what was mortifying was that he was still so attractive and youthful. His body was long and slender: snakelike. And his head was small, compact and nicely shaped. His face had delicate lines, and his nose was high and thin, reminding me of the blade of a finely honed knife. His lips were fleshy, the kind girls would surely find sexy and swoon over. Right, girls like Kazue Satō. But surely he was too young. Besides, Kijima was never quite as attractive as this boy. I could hardly take my eyes off him. When the judge entered the courtroom, I looked back at the men again and stared at them.

The man I took for Kijima held a duffle coat that he had folded neatly. When we had to rise for the judge, he got to his feet clumsily. After everyone else had taken their seats again, he still stood there, staring into space. The fat man had to grab him by the arm and pull him down. The bones in his shoulders and the muscles of his chest that I could detect through the simple black sweater he wore were perfectly balanced. He was at that age caught between childhood and youth where he was growing like a young tree. His face was lovely—the features as becoming for a woman as they were for a man. The shape of his dark eyebrows was beautiful, a perfect arch as if formed by hand. No, this wasn't Kijima. I was certain.

"No, now that I look at him carefully, it's not Takashi Kijima."

"It is. It's Kijima. It has to be," Mitsuru whispered in my ear after the courtroom had quieted down.

"There's no way Kijima would be that young. Besides Kijima always looked much more disagreeable."

"No, not him, the fat one!"

Startled, I almost fell out of my chair. The man had to be close to 220 pounds. If I carved some of the fat off his face, I might be able to find a likeness to Kijima in there somewhere. The trial had begun but I was too busy trying to look at the men behind me to pay attention. Besides, the focus of the hearing today was Zhang's upbringing and background, and the deliberations were so boring I thought I would die.

"I was an excellent student in elementary school. I was born intelligent."

How could he sit there in front of everybody and brag about himself like that without the slightest embarrassment? I couldn't take much more of this. While trying to stifle a yawn, I thought about Takashi Kijima sitting behind me. How had he gotten so ugly? He looked like a completely different person. He'd changed so much, I wanted to call up Professor Kijima and let him know what had become of his son since he saw him last. That's what I'd do! I'd take a picture of him and send it to his father with a letter.

•

When the hearing ended for the day and Zhang left the courtroom, Mitsuru let out a shallow sigh, her shoulders dipping slightly.

"Sitting through these procedures is more difficult than I thought. It makes me remember my own trial. I never felt more naked, more exposed, in all my life. Listening to the questions that the defendant was asked today brings it all back. My entire life history was spread out for all to see. I felt I was hearing about someone else, someone entirely different from me. It was strange. Once I realized that people were dying during those initiations, I was too afraid to do anything to help them in their final moments. Let karma have its way, I thought. Yet when my own time came, I was so terrified and trembled so badly I couldn't even stand up. I was a doctor, trained to save human life. How was I able to do something so cruel? My trial continued amid great confusion. The only thing that got me through was my mother, who came with a group of other believers. When she entered the courtroom, we exchanged glances. Very subtle. But in her glance I understood that she was telling me to be strong, that I did nothing wrong. I was judged there in that courtroom, before the whole world, but I scarcely saw anyone but my mother."

"So are you saying you feel no remorse?"

"Not that. What I'm saying is, everything was confused. It was like a TV drama."

I held up my hand in an effort to put an end to Mitsuru's convoluted tale of tangled emotions. If I wasn't careful, Takashi Kijima was going to get away. I wasn't interested in him so much as I was in the youth with him. I had to speak to him. Why are you with Takashi Kijima? You rarely find such handsome boys. Was he Takashi Kijima's son? If not, who on earth was he? I was consumed with curiosity. If he was Kijima's son, no matter how hateful Kijima might be or how ugly he'd become, his worth in my eyes had just skyrocketed. And Mitsuru looked like she still had more to say.

"Let's have a class reunion," I suggested.

"What are you talking about?"

The courtroom was now nearly empty and Mitsuru's voice reverberated against the walls. I could hardly believe it when Takashi Kijima turned and headed toward us. He was wearing a gaudy sweater with jeans, trying to look youthful. Under his arm he clutched a small brand-name men's purse, making him look like an out-of-date gangster. I imagined he had an overstuffed wallet, a cell phone, and a case of name cards stuffed inside, along with an assortment of other little things. Unfortunately, his young companion did not seem to be interested in coming along with him. He stayed seated, his eyes straight ahead, as he had been all through the trial.

"You're Mitsuru, aren't you?"

His voice was thick, in keeping with his body. It had a nasal sound, unpleasant to listen to. Proof of too many cigarettes, too much booze, and too many late nights. The skin on his face was grayish, the pores conspicuously large. I imagined if I put my finger on his cheek, it would feel slick with grease.

"And you're Kijima-kun, right? It's been a long time," Mitsuru said.

"Mitsuru, you had a rough time of it. I read what happened in the paper and couldn't believe it. But you look fine now. You've worked that out, right?"

Kijima pointed toward the judge's bench with an air of comfortable familiarity. Not just his physique but the way he spoke was round and soft. Like a woman. Mitsuru's face clouded over.

"Thank you very much for your kind concern. I am very sorry to have caused my associates from Q School system such hardship, but it is all behind me now."

"Congratulations."

Kijima gave a deep bow. Mitsuru bit back her tears. It looked just like a scene from some gangster movie. I was not at all interested, however, and turned to look at the boy. Mitsuru's tear-choked voice had caught his attention, and he was now looking this way. His face was exquisite. Why did he look so familiar?

"You recognized me right away, didn't you, Mitsuru? Most people have no idea who I am, now that I've put on some weight. The other day I ran into a former Q classmate down in the Ginza, but he walked right past me. He was the same guy who was so smitten with Yuriko he'd throw himself on the ground in front of me, begging me to fix them up. And now for Yuriko to wind up getting murdered by a stranger! But when you come right down to it, that was probably her long-cherished dream."

"Long-cherished dream?" Mitsuru burst out.

"Yuriko always told me she knew she'd be killed by one of her customers someday. It frightened her, but she seemed to be waiting for it to happen. She was a smart, complicated woman."

Mitsuru started tapping her front teeth with a troubled look: *tap, tap, tap.* I suppose she felt she couldn't go along with what he'd said. Thanks to Takashi Kijima's father, Mitsuru had finally returned to society. I pursed my lips and said, "Well, I can't say I don't agree that it was a long-cherished dream, but there's no reason why you should stand here talking about it."

Takashi Kijima smiled bitterly. I despise people who smile when they mean to be sneaky. That's just like my supervisor at the ward office.

"You're Yuriko's older sister, aren't you? You have my deepest condolences." Kijima greeted me politely, just as he had done with Mitsuru. "I understand what you must be going through. Still, am I wrong to assume that you also believed Yuriko would wind up like this someday, once she went down the road she selected for herself? I think you and I are the only ones who truly understood her."

What impertinence. As if he might have actually understood my sister.

"It was your fault. You're the one who chased her down that wretched road in the first place. You're the one who taught Yuriko all about the business. If she hadn't met you, she'd probably still be alive. And that's not all. There was Kazue too. You bullied her."

I went after him. I didn't mean a word of it. I just wanted to harass him.

Kijima hesitated. "I did not bully Kazue or anything of the sort. I just didn't know what to do about all those letters she sent me. She was so pathetic. I didn't like her, but I didn't want to hurt her. I wasn't that insensitive."

When she saw Kijima wipe away the globules of sweat that had beaded along his forehead with his thick hand, Mitsuru tried to change the topic.

"Never mind that. What are you doing these days? Your father disinherited you, didn't he?"

"Well, like they say, As the boy, so the man. I'm still in the business, though we refer to it now as an *escort service*. I introduce women to men."

Kijima rifled through his wallet and pulled out two cards, handing one to both Mitsuru and me. Mitsuru read hers out loud.

"*Mona Lisa Women's Club. High-class ladies are waiting for you.* But Kijima-kun, you've used the wrong character to write *high-class*. And the card's design—it seems so outdated."

"There are customers who prefer it that way—old-fashioned, I mean. It's not a mistake, it's intentional. By the way, Mitsuru, how *is* the old man?"

"He's great. He's working on his insect study and supervising the dormitory in Karuizawa. You knew your mother passed away, didn't you?"

Mitsuru gave the news as delicately as possible.

"When was that?"

"I think it was three years ago. She had cancer."

"Cancer? That's awful."

Kijima shrugged his shoulders dispiritedly, but because his neck was swathed so thickly in flesh it was hard to notice the movement.

"I gave my mother no end of grief. I'm going to be forty next year, and I'm still doing the kind of work a mother can't be proud of. There was no way I could face her."

"Professor Kijima worries about you, you know."

"Well, he didn't write that in his letters, did he?" I snapped. "He says he wants time to reconsider his son's conduct. What an asshole!"

At my outburst, a nervous look washed over Mitsuru's face.

"Are there letters?" Kijima asked. "If he wrote about me I'd like to see them."

Mitsuru began to open her handbag, but I stopped her.

"Make copies. Those are important letters. You don't want to lose them. And you don't know when you two will see each other again. Everyone in the office where I work makes copies of everything. Mitsuru, you trust people too much."

"I suppose you're right."

Takashi Kijima pressed his hands together in mock prayer. "I just want to look at them. I'll give them right back."

Mitsuru grudgingly handed the packet of letters to Kijima, and he sat down in the courtroom and started to read through them. I asked about the youth.

"Kijima, who's the kid? Is he yours?"

Kijima raised his eyes from the letters. A jeering light shot through them. I felt uneasy.

"You mean you can't recognize him?"

"No. Who is it?"

"That's Yuriko's son."

Horrified, I turned back to look. Yuriko had mentioned in her journal that she had had a son with Johnson. So this was the child of those two beautiful people. He would be a high school student by now.

Mitsuru smiled faintly. "Hey, he's your nephew!"

"That's right."

Confused, I combed my fingers busily through my hair. I wanted to lure Yuriko's son away from the ugly Kijima. But the boy—the focus of our discussion—did not look our way. He sat quietly, waiting for Kijima to complete his business.

"Kijima, what's the boy's name?"

"It's Yurio. I think Johnson gave him the name."

"What is Yurio doing here?"

"Yuriko's death was such a shock that Johnson went back to the United States. He wanted to take Yurio with him, but he was still in the middle of high school, so I agreed to take care of him."

I started toward Yurio. I was delirious with the happiness that was coursing through me, the happiness once again to have before my eyes a beautiful person.

"Yurio-chan? Hello."

Yurio raised his head and stared at me. "Oh. Hello."

His voice had already changed. It was thick and deep but also strong and youthful. His eyes were beautiful. They seemed to look right through me. I felt my heart racing in my chest as I said, "I'm Yuriko's older sister. That means I'm your aunt. I don't know anything about you, but we're related. Why don't we put this horrible event behind us and get on with our life, shall we?"

"Um—okay."

Yurio searched the room around him, looking perplexed. "Excuse me, but where did Uncle Kijima go?"

"He's standing right over there, isn't he?"

"Oh? Uncle Kijima? Where are you?"

I noticed something very strange just then. Yurio did not seem to see Kijima, even though he was sitting only a few feet away. Kijima raised his eyes. They were full of tears, no doubt from reading his father's letters.

"I'm over here, Yurio. Relax." And then he said to me, "Yurio's been blind since birth."

•

How does the world exist for a person who is so exceptionally beautiful but who cannot see to acknowledge his own beauty? Even if he hears the way people sing his praises, he cannot affirm the concept of beauty, can he? Or, does he pursue a beauty that has nothing to do with the beauty one perceives with one's eyes? I was dying to know what shape the world took for Yurio.

I wanted to have my nephew live with me so badly I could hardly stand it. If Yurio was with me I could live freely; I could live happily, I thought. You could say I was selfish. I don't care. I felt I had to have him. He was completely free of the bias that is implicit in the eyes of others. That's right. Even if I was reflected in Yurio's beautiful eyes, the image would never be transmitted to his brain. So the meaning of who I was would also change. Because for Yurio, I would exist only as voice or as flesh. He would never see my thick squat body or my ugly face.

I don't accept my own self? Is that what you think? I recognize that I am homely enough to have harbored an inferiority complex toward my younger sister, Yuriko. What about my theory that she was born of a different father? You say that's a deception? You're wrong. It's a game I play in my head. I tell myself that I want to become a woman who was born beautiful, who is brilliant and a much better student than Yuriko, and yet who hates men. Gradually my imaginary self closes the distance—if only slightly—between reality and my make-believe. The malice with which I arm myself is simply the spice of my game. Am I wrong? Are you saying the body that contains the imaginary me is a fool? If that's the case, you ought to try to live with a younger sister who is monstrously beautiful. Can you possibly imagine what it is like, I wonder, to have your own individual nature denied before you are even born? From the moment of your infancy the way people react to you is so clearly different from the way they react to others. How would you feel if you had to experience that, day in, day out?

We moved to the coffee shop in the basement and sat around a table. But the only one I paid attention to was Yurio. He sat in a chair some distance from us, his posture straight and erect. Yuriko's beautiful son. No matter how adoringly I gazed at his face, he had no idea that my eyes were on him. I could stare to my heart's content. The waitresses, the waiters, even the middle-aged man who looked like the manager shot self-conscious glances at Yurio from time to time. Did he make them restless too? The coffeehouse—such a shabby little place—suddenly seemed to sparkle. To see all these people admiring Yurio only increased my pleasure. I took delight in feeling so much more superior than they.

Seating Yurio at some remove from our table was Mitsuru's idea. She had some things related to Takashi Kijima and Yuriko she wanted to talk about and she didn't want Yurio to hear.

"What did you and Yuriko-san do after you left high school?" she asked Takashi.

Takashi Kijima looked at me as I gazed over at Yurio.

"Do you know?" Mitsuru asked me.

"No. Once Yuriko left the Johnsons and started living on her own, we never communicated. I didn't know what to do. My father would call from Switzerland all the time, worrying about her. And then my grandfather went crazy over your mother; keeping up with Yuriko was the last thing on my mind."

"There was talk among the other students," Mitsuru said. "They said Yuriko became a model for the magazine *an-an*. I was amazed. I went to the bookstore and thumbed through the copy they had on the shelf. I can remember it even now. She was modeling the latest surfer fashion, so the lines of her body were exposed but they were absolutely perfect. And the makeup she had on was so stunning it just took my breath away. But I didn't see any more pictures of her after that."

Mitsuru tried to draw me in but the smile soon vanished from her face. Yes, it was unlikely that I would have followed her career.

"Yuriko-san appeared in all kinds of magazines," she said. "So why did she disappear so suddenly? She didn't specialize in a particular look, and she never appeared in the same magazine twice."

She was known as the phantom model. I can imagine what happened. More than likely Yuriko, with her lust for men, had affairs with either the photographer or the art director or one of the men around her. She got a reputation for being an easy lay, the people at the magazine lost respect for her, and then she didn't get any more work there.

Kijima's fat ugly face broke into a smile; it was clear he was recalling those days from the past. "That's right. Yuriko was just too gorgeous, her face too perfect to appeal to the needs of the magazines of the time. And she exuded too much sexuality. If she'd still been a junior high student they might have been able to use her. But once she turned eighteen, she became such a stunning beauty she even outdid Farrah Fawcett. At the time there just wasn't much one could do with a woman like that. It's different, now that we have models like Norika Fujiwara."

Kijima spoke like a true professional. He took a cigarette out of his purse and lit it.

"She was only about five feet seven inches tall, which doesn't quite cut it as a runway model, and she was too Western-looking to make a good actress. There weren't any other opportunities. Nothing else but to go after men who were rolling in dough. It was during the height of the Bubble Economy. I had men who were making a killing in real estate come up to me—since I was her agent—and fan a whole handful of ten-thousand-yen notes under my nose. All that for one or two hours with Yuriko. They'd pay three hundred thousand yen."

Mitsuru glanced in my direction. "Kijima, do you have to talk like that? It's not appropriate."

"Oh, sorry." Kijima apologized.

"You made a killing too, didn't you?" I asked.

Kijima, lost in dreams of his days of wine and roses, avoided looking at me. He scratched his saggy jowls with a fat finger.

"Well, yes. I did make some mistakes in my youth. But after all, I was thrown out of school very suddenly—thanks to your betrayal."

"It wasn't a betrayal. Professor Kijima wrote in his letters that she came seeking advice," I said.

Kijima shrugged it off.

"It was a betrayal. Your friend here had long nurtured a violent jealousy of Yuriko. It was her nature."

"You're wrong. She was worried about Yuriko," Mitsuru said.

"Is that what you think? Well, I suppose we should just let bygones be bygones, but I have a whole host of things I'd like to get off my chest." Takashi Kijima spoke sarcastically. "I was going into my senior year of high school, you know. I was eighteen. When I got home my old lady was crying and my little brother just stared at me angrily and refused to speak. As soon as my old man got home, he started smacking me on the side of the face. Ever since then, I've had trouble hearing out of my right ear. My old man was a southpaw, and when he struck you he packed a bigger wallop than expected. I didn't cry, but it stung like hell. My dad yelled, 'I don't want to have to look at you. Don't ever show your face to me again!' My mother tried her best to smooth things over, but it was hopeless. My old man was stubborn. So I told him, 'You wanted to do her too. Yuriko told me. You threw us out of school because you couldn't have her!' As soon as I said that he popped me again in the ear, right in the same place, with even more force. Then I yelled, 'You idiot! I'll see you at my hearing!' He said, 'I've tolerated quite enough. Just put yourself in Yuriko's place.' But the truth was, Yuriko enjoyed doing what she did. When I think of it now, I realize I should have just agreed with whatever he said. I guess that's why I cried when I read the old man's letters. He's getting along in years. And I suppose I'm still haunted by the past."

"Come on, get to the point," I said. "What became of you and Yuriko?"

"Oh, once we both got thrown out of our homes we decided to live together, so we went out to find a condominium. We needed about three million yen, but between the two of us we had a lot of money stashed away. We rented a high-class apartment in Aoyama. We wanted a place in Azabu, but it was too close to the school, so we let it go. The place we got was a two-bedroom apartment; we each had our own room. The next day, I took Yuriko out with me and got to work. I took her first to modeling agencies and got her set up with jobs there. But the modeling work never lasted long; I already told you why that was. Sooner or later Yuriko started picking up her own customers, dragging them back to her room in our apartment. No, it's not a lie. Yuriko was a natural slut."

I nodded with an exaggerated gesture. That's it. Yuriko was the kind of woman who couldn't live without "water." She needed water to promote her decay.

"Around that time a man turned up asking to be her patron. He'd made an instant killing in real estate. I thought I would have to find another apartment, but I ended up not having to move out because he took Yuriko off with him to Daikanyama. He put out the capital and kept Yuriko for a mistress. Soon, Yuriko had no use for a manager. I was left with the apartment in Aoyama; after a while the rent got too much for me, so I had to move out. Thus began my fall. Quite a story, huh?"

Mitsuru, who had been listening silently, pursed her lips and said, "What I don't understand is, if you and Yuriko were living together, why'd you let her go into prostitution? What was it between you two?"

"What was it, I wonder?" Kijima gazed up at the ceiling. "To be perfectly blunt, the two of us had a business arrangement, and our only concern was making a profit."

"You weren't romantically involved, even with Yuriko as beautiful as she was?"

"Not a chance. I'm homosexual."

I gasped. How reprehensible! How could Yurio have been left in the hands of such a monster? I looked instinctively toward the boy. At some point Yurio had put on a set of headphones and was nodding lightly in time to the music, his eyes closed. Mitsuru started tapping her front teeth with her fingernail: *tap, tap, tap.*

"Have you been that way since high school?"

"I don't know. I have to admit it's strange myself—for a homosexual to have tailed after Yuriko that way. I guess there was something about her that excited men, but I never felt it myself. After we started living together, I found myself attracted to a man who occasionally came to visit her. He was a middle-aged yakuza. And I noticed I was feeling jealous of Yuriko. That's when I knew." Kijima closed his eyes slightly, clearly taking delight in his self-revelations. "After Yuriko and I split, I began managing others, men as well as women. I had the know-how, so business was good. Yuriko and I would meet up again once in a while and I'd pass her some business. But for a number of years we went out of our way to avoid each other."

"Why?" Mitsuru asked.

"We'd both changed. I got fat and Yuriko got old. We both knew all about the other's glory days. There had been a time when all Yuriko had to do was walk down the street and she'd have men tripping over themselves to get to her. They were like putty in her hands. But in later years she couldn't get a decent customer if she tried. I knew she'd lost her selling power. And I couldn't lie about it. So Yuriko grew distant. I was relieved when she stopped contacting me. That's when it happened, you know. When I learned about her murder. And not much later, news of Kazue's murder made the rounds. I started to realize how dangerous my line of work had become. That's why, when Johnson asked me to look after Yurio, I was eager to accept. It was like some kind of penance for me."

"You shouldn't keep Yurio at your place," I said.

"Why not?"

Mitsuru looked up in surprise. And so I said with perfect clarity, "Well, I'm his family. And besides, you can't say that Kijima's line of work or that Kijima himself offers a good environment for a young man. I'll take care of Yurio. He can go to school from my place. I'll contact my father in Switzerland. I'm sure he'd send a little money to support Yurio."

To tell the truth, ever since Yuriko's death I hadn't had any contact with my father in Switzerland. What a cold man. But if he knew about Yurio, I was sure he'd send money.

"Well, you're entitled to your opinion, but . . ." Kijima gave my face and body the once over and smirked. I suppose he didn't think it appropriate for a spooky-looking woman like me to be taking care of such a handsome boy. I stood up angrily.

"Fine. Let's just ask Yurio himself."

I went over to where Yurio was sitting. He had his eyes closed and was swaying to the music. I don't know if he sensed my presence or not. But he opened his blind eyes. His eyelashes were long, the irises brown, and the whites of his eyes translucent. He was so beautiful. Dark eyebrows hemmed his eyes dramatically.

"Yurio-chan," I began, "won't you come to your aunt's house? I'll be happy to look after you. You've been living with your father for such a long time, I think you should live with a Japanese woman for a bit. Wouldn't you like that?"

Yurio smiled, flashing brilliant white teeth.

"I'm the only family you have to look out for you now. Come to my house. Let's live together, shall we?"

I could feel my heart pound as I tried to persuade Yurio. To have had this sprung on him so suddenly . . . he could easily say no, and that would be the end of it.

"Will you buy me a computer?" Yurio asked, as he gazed off into space.

"Are you able to use a computer?"

"Sure. I learned in school. All I need is the right software. If I have a sound-based system I can use all kinds of technology. I create music on the computer, so I really need to have one."

"Well, then, I'll buy one for you."

"Great. Then I guess I'll go live with you."

I was lost in my fantasy. All I could do was repeat over and over to myself, "I'll buy one for you. I'll buy one for you."

• 3 •

I brought Yurio to live with me in P Ward in my grandfather's government-sponsored apartment. While Yurio was under Johnson's care, he had been placed in a facility in Osaka that specialized in caring for the blind. Since he had been there from his first year of elementary school, practically raised there, in fact—he would occasionally lapse into the Ōsaka dialect when he spoke. It made me laugh. He had a face that was so beautiful it was out of this world, but he was straightforward and taciturn. His only interest was listening to music. He was a very bright young man who hardly needed any special attention. He was so beautiful. And here I was so closely related to him. I could hardly believe it was true.

A person's fate is a curious thing. I truly believed I was reliving those quiet, peaceful days I had enjoyed earlier with my grandfather. Back when he had depended on me—helpless, vulnerable. And now here was Yurio, blind, who had to rely on me as well. I imagined he enjoyed living with me.

"Have you heard from your father?" I asked Yurio.

I was worried about Johnson trying to take Yurio away, so I would ask him this tentatively from time to time.

"He called Uncle Kijima's place any number of times. But I never actually lived with my father for long. I like Uncle Kijima much better."

You like him? I thought, racked with jealousy.

"What do you like about that irresponsible creep?"

"He's not irresponsible. He was very kind to me. He told me if I needed one he would buy me a computer. He promised."

I didn't have much money at the moment and his talk of computers was making me anxious. "But he never got one for you," I countered. "Kijima is a schemer. He'd just use the computer as bait to reel you in— and then you'd realize your mistake. No, I rescued you from a devil."

"What are you talking about? It doesn't make any sense."

"It's okay. It's nothing for you to worry about. It's just that I had some unpleasant experiences with him in the past and there's bad blood between us. It's a long story. I think it's better if you don't know. Kijima brought about your mother's misfortune. I'll tell you about it when you get older."

"I never met my mother, so I don't care what you tell me about her. I heard about her from my father. I think she probably hated me. When I was small it made me sad, but I'm used to it now. I don't really think much about it anymore."

"Yuriko was a woman who thought only of herself. She wasn't like me. She used to torment me, so I know just how you feel. I'm going to look after you for the rest of my life, so don't you worry. You can stay with me forever."

Because Yurio had no interests except music, he'd answer a question perfunctorily and then pop his headphones back on. The music that leaked out was some kind of rap in English that I did not understand. At school Yurio had been studying to be a piano tuner. Although his studies were cut short midstream, he didn't seem to care. He just spent the day listening to music through his headphones, from the time he got up until the time he went to bed.

"Yurio, what do you want to be when you get older?"

When Yurio heard me ask another question, he pulled his headset off again. But he didn't look irritated. "Well, something related to music, I guess."

"A piano tuner?"

"No. I'd like to make music. That's why I need a computer. I know it sounds strange for me to say this, but I think I have talent."

Talent. The word thrilled me. Yuriko had been as beautiful as a monster; now her child, who was her equal in looks, was also blessed with a talent that surpassed others. I wondered how I could help him develop this talent further.

"I understand. I'll see what I can do." I let out a deep sigh and looked around the shabby room. "What if you went to Johnson's?"

"Well, I'd like to go to America to get a taste of real rap music. I know my father has family in Boston. He went back after he divorced his Japanese wife. I heard that he just got married again over there, to a woman with a ten-year-old son, and that boy's his heir, so there's no reason for me to go see him. I'd only be in the way." Yurio sounded relieved to get that off his mind. "All I have is music," he continued. "It's my fate to be surrounded by music."

I stroked Yurio's cheek. It was tense. I would replace Yuriko and be the mother he never had. Yurio smiled sweetly.

"I was starving for a mother's affection. So I'm really happy to be living here with you, Aunt."

Yurio was not able to see, but he more than made up for it by speaking from the heart. I took his hand and pressed it to my cheek.

"I'm the exact image of your mother. Your mother had a face like this. Just touch it and see."

Yurio timidly stretched out his other hand. I grabbed his big, cool hand and brought it to my nose and eyes.

"People always said your mother and I were really pretty. Here, feel this? Double-fold eyelids. My eyes are large and my nose is thin. My eyebrows look like yours—with a nice elegant arch. My lips are full and pink. They're like yours too, but I don't suppose you can tell."

"No, I can't."

For the first time Yurio's response was tinged with sorrow.

"But I don't think of my sightlessness as a handicap. I've been blessed with a talent to allow me to live immersed in beautiful music. My desire is to hear music and also to make music that no one has yet heard before."

Such a simple, wonderful desire. I felt I'd struck oil by coming across a boy as pure as Yurio. Like thick black liquid bubbling up from the earth's core, my maternal instincts bubbled up within me. I would earn money for him. I had to buy him a computer. I decided to beg money from my father in Switzerland. I searched for my old address book and found my father's phone number.

"Hello. It's me. Your daughter."

A woman responded in German. It had to be the Turkish woman my father had married. She put my father on the phone right away. He sounded old, and he could hardly understand Japanese anymore.

"No press please."

"Father. Did you know Yuriko had a son?"

"No press."

He hung up. I looked back at Yurio, disappointed. He had an expression on his face that seemed to say, I could have told you this would happen. He turned his face away—his profile the spitting image of Yuriko's—and closed his eyes. I wondered if in his world he created beautiful shapes out of sound. I couldn't accept anything I couldn't see. I could see beauty. Yurio's sightless beauty held no meaning for me. Even though I had a beautiful child in my life, I wasn't able to share his world. It was terrifying, wasn't it? And sad. I felt my heart fill with a giant sorrow, as if I were suffering unrequited love. I wanted to curl up in pain. I had never in all my life had these feelings before.

"Someone's here."

Yurio pulled the headphones off and listened but I couldn't hear a thing. Just as I was looking around the apartment suspiciously, I heard a knock at the door. Yurio's sense of hearing was uncanny.

"It's me! Mitsuru."

Mitsuru was standing in the filmy darkness of the housing complex hallway. She was wearing a vivid blue suit and had a beige coat folded over her arm. It was an outfit for spring and she made the dingy hallway pulse with brightness.

"I can't believe you're still living exactly where you lived when you were in high school! Do you mind if I come in?"

Mitsuru peered past me into the apartment somewhat timidly, as if she were afraid of barging in. I had no choice but to invite her in. She offered the perfunctory greetings, removed her high heels, and placed them neatly by the door. Her gaze landed on Yurio's big sneakers lined up next to her shoes, and she gave a slight smile. I wondered why she'd come. She was even livelier than she had been when I saw her at the courthouse. Yet she seemed completely poised. She was gradually returning to her old self.

"Sorry to pop in like this. I had some news I wanted to share with you."

Mitsuru settled down by the tea table and placed her coat and handbag neatly at her side. They were both brand-new and without a doubt expensive. I boiled a kettle of water, keeping an eye on Mitsuru out of the corner of my eye, and made us each a cup of tea. I used the same kind of Lipton tea bags I'd used when Grandfather was living here. I was stubborn that way. Once I found something I liked, I hated to have to change it.

"You said you had some news?"

"I've gotten a divorce and I'm going to marry Kijima."

Kijima? Which Kijima? Surely not Takashi Kijima. Had she come to take Yurio away? Seeing my look of panic, Mitsuru laughed and shook her head.

"The father, you dummy. Professor Kijima. We've been corresponding, and we finally decided to marry. This is the way Professor Kijima put it: Marrying you will be the last task I have as an educator."

"My, my. Well, congratulations."

I offered my best wishes stiffly. Of course, I had Yurio so I wasn't particularly jealous. I was just feeling sad that Yurio had a world of music I couldn't enter, that was all. I couldn't muster up genuine joy. My armor of malice was gradually growing thin. Mitsuru was glowing with happiness.

"So Professor Kijima feels duty bound to rescue his brilliant student, does he?" I asked, somewhat snidely. "And is he going to make you the stepmother of his corpulent son?"

"I suppose. That's why I'm here today, with a message for you from Takashi." Mitsuru pulled an envelope out of her purse. "Here. My stepson, as you say, told me to hand this over to you. Won't you please accept it?"

I peered into the envelope, hoping it contained cash. Instead I found two notebooks that looked like old ledgers of some sort.

"Those are Kazue Satō's journals. She sent them to Kijima just before she was murdered. Kijima felt he should give them to the police when he learned about the crime. But she writes about his occupation, so he was afraid he'd get arrested for aiding and abetting prostitution. He came to the courthouse that day to see how to get rid of them. He tried to give them to me, but of course I'm worried myself about being under police surveillance and don't need to get involved in any more trouble. But you're the older sister of one victim and friend to the other. No one had a closer relationship to the two of them than you. If anyone should have the diaries, it's you. So, please don't make a fuss; just take them."

Mitsuru spilled all that out in one breath and then shoved the package across the table toward me. Kazue was murdered and now here were her journals. Somehow they seemed ominous. Without thinking, I pushed the package away. Mitsuru slid it back across the table in front of me. We played our little game of back and forth a few more times, shoving the package across the narrow table, and then Mitsuru grew frustrated. She stared at me hard. I glared back. The last thing I wanted was Kazue's journals. I mean, really! I didn't care whether Zhang killed Kazue or if she was killed by someone completely different; it had nothing to do with me, but Mitsuru would not let up.

"Please," she begged. "Just take them. And read them!"

"I don't want them. They're bad luck."

"Bad luck?" Mitsuru looked offended. "Are you saying they're bad luck because they're affiliated with a woman like me? A woman with a criminal history?"

I could feel an incredible power coursing through Mitsuru, one I had never felt before now. I shrank back. I suppose it was the power of love. Water a plant and it comes to life, sinking its roots deep into the black earth and raising its head up high, afraid of neither rain nor wind. That's the impression Mitsuru made on me. Women who need water all become domineering. Yuriko had been the same way. Finally, I replied, "I don't think you're bad luck or anything of the sort. With you it was a question of religion."

"Blaming it on religion is a bit facile, don't you think? I was undone by my own weakness. That's what led me to join that organization in the first place. I get confused even now when I think about it. Staring at your own weakness is horrible. Unimaginably painful. But you've never once even thought about your weaknesses or tried to overcome them, have you? I know about the complex you harbor toward Yuriko. It's practically debilitating. Especially because you don't fight it."

"Don't patronize me. What have these journals got to do with me?"

It was all so baffling. Why did Mitsuru want me to read the diaries so badly?

"I think it would be best for you to read them yourself and find out. Takashi said so too. Because you and Kazue were close. You ought to read them. Kazue sent them to Takashi because she wanted someone to read them; of that there can be no doubt. She didn't want them read by the police or a detective or the judge. She wanted them read by someone from the real world . . . her world."

What kind of proof, I wonder, did she have for making such assertions? As you well know, Kazue and I were not very close at all. We entered high school at the same time. She started talking to me, and I had no choice but to answer. That's all there was to it. We had misunderstandings and would patch them up from time to time. But after the incident of the love letters she sent to Takashi Kijima, her pride was wounded and she avoided me.

"You're the only one who ever visited her house, aren't you? She was a loner, just like you."

"I think Takashi should keep them. She sent them to him because she liked him. Wasn't there a letter?"

"There wasn't a letter. This is all there was. If you ask how she knew his address, I'll answer but it's not easy. It seems Takashi knew the owner of the hotel where there was an escort agency that Kazue used. He ran into Kazue once in front of the hotel. I think he gave her his card."

"Then why don't I send them to her family? If I mail them from the ward office, it won't cost me a thing."

Mitsuru shot me a look. "Don't you dare. I don't think Kazue's mother will want to read these. I don't care how close a daughter might be to her mother, there are some things she doesn't need to know."

"Well, then, why is it so important for me to know them? Explain yourself."

Explain yourself. That was exactly the same phrase Kazue always used in high school. I smiled sardonically when I remembered it. Mitsuru looked to the side and started tapping her front teeth with her finger. She still had that same space between those teeth. Yurio was in the other room, his back to me, sitting cross-legged on the floor with his headphones on. But he wasn't swaying to the rhythm. I wondered if perhaps he was eavesdropping with his amazing sense of hearing. I didn't want him to know about my weaknesses. I began to regret letting Mitsuru into the house. Then she suddenly stopped tapping her teeth and fixed her eyes on mine.

"Don't you want to know why Kazue got into prostitution? I do. But I don't want to get any further involved in this. I have my hands full just trying to sort out the mess I got myself into. I can't afford to think about Kazue. I have to think about myself and the people I'm involved with now: my family, Professor Kijima, all the people I killed. Until I've straightened my own life out, I don't think I'll be going back to the trial. I was able to see you after all these years—and talk to Takashi—but I have to start thinking about my problems and only my problems now. It's different for you. You're going to keep going to the trial because of Yuriko's murder, right? And you'll take care of her son, Yurio. You have to because she's your sister. Why do you have to be involved with Kazue? Well, read her journals."

I remembered reading in Yuriko's diaries that she ran into Kazue in one of the love-hotel alleys in Murayama-chō. Maybe what happened after that was recorded in Kazue's journals. I wanted to read them, but at the same time I didn't want to. I hesitatingly picked up the package and peered inside.

"What'd she write about?"

"Ha! See! You're curious already," Mitsuru chirped triumphantly. "Don't you want to know what she was thinking about? She studied her head off, just like I did. Then she went out in the world and got herself a good job. And yet that wasn't the half of it. I don't know what led Kazue to do what she did, but she became a common streetwalker, standing on the corner picking up men. That's the most dangerous way to go about it. It wasn't at all like what Yuriko had done in high school, turning a few tricks on the side. You want to know what happened to Kazue, don't you?"

Why did I have to be told this by Mitsuru? Why was I being blamed? I was furious. Mitsuru drained her tea and placed the cup back on the saucer with a light clink. As if that sound was the signal she'd been waiting for, she let loose.

"This is what I think. I probably shouldn't say this, but I will. You and

Kazue were exactly alike in many ways. You both were insanely studious. You studied all the time and always did your best, and you made it into Q High School for Young Women. But once you were in, you discovered that you were way out of your league and could not possibly compete with the other students. So you gave up. Both you and Kazue were amazed, when you entered high school, by the disparity between yourselves and the other girls there. How you wished you could narrow the gap a bit. Fit in more. So first you started adjusting the hem of your school uniform to make it shorter. Then you started wearing knee socks like the other girls. Did you forget? I know it's not polite for me to say this, but you finally just gave up because you didn't have the money to compete. You pretended not to have any interest in fashion or boys or studying. And you decided you'd manage to endure your time at Q High School for Young Women by arming yourself with malice. You got nastier and nastier with each year. Meaner in the second than the first, meaner in the third than the second. That's why I kept my distance from you.

"On the other hand, Kazue put all her energy into trying to fit in with the others. She came from a family that had some money. She was smart. So she thought she could wiggle her way in with the rest of us. But it was her very determination that marked her as a target for bullying. The harder she tried the worse it was. There's really no one more cruel than adolescent girls, and Kazue was uncool about everything. And then, when you of all people laughed at her, it set you up as a target as well. I can still remember how you cried when someone called you a 'penniless loser.' It was during gym class. You had decided to act like a lone wolf; that was your strategy for survival. But there were plenty of times when you let your defenses down. You liked the school ring everyone ordered at graduation, didn't you?"

Mitsuru looked at the fingers of my left hand. I hurriedly hid the ring.

"What do you mean?"

My voice trembled with bitterness. Mitsuru had attacked me as though she were a completely different person. I didn't know how to react. I wanted to argue with her, to set her straight. But my beloved nephew was sitting in the next room listening.

"Don't you remember? It's hard to say, but since I probably won't ever see you again, I will."

"Why, where are you going?"

My voice must have sounded anxious. Mitsuru's face softened and she broke into a laugh.

"I've told you that Kijima and I are going to live in Karuizawa. But you're not going to want to see me after I finish telling you all that I think. I've stopped worrying about hurting other people's feelings and curtailing my opinions. I may offend you with what I have to say, but now's my chance.

"When we graduated from Q High School for Young Women, many students went on to Q University, right? That's when they all got together and decided to make a school ring to commemorate our class. Everyone there ordered the ring. It was gold with the imprint of the school emblem. I lost mine long ago so I can't remember exactly what design it was. Wait a minute. Don't tell me you're wearing the ring!"

Mitsuru pointed at the hand I had hidden. I shook my head emphatically.

"No, this is different. I bought this ring at the Parco Department Store."

"You did? Well, I really don't care one way or the other. The students who'd been in the Q School system from the very start didn't really pay much attention to the rings and never wore them. They just wanted one as a keepsake. But the girls who brandished the rings around proudly after they went on to university were inevitably those who'd entered the first year of high school. That's what I heard later. And they wore them with such bravado because they could finally be proud of having advanced up from a lower division. I know this is really trivial, so don't laugh, but when I first heard this I was very surprised to learn that the one who was most determined to wear her ring night and day was you. Now this may be just a silly rumor. I mean, I don't know if it's true or not. But it caught me by surprise because I thought for the first time I had seen inside your heart."

"Who told you?"

"I forget. It was really all so silly. But is it? Is it really just a silly story? If anything, it's terrifying. That's because it represents precisely the value system that holds sway in Japan today. Why do you think I got involved in a religious organization with such a similar structure as Q School? I believed that if I renounced my family and entered the religious organization, I could advance my social position, make my way up the ranks of the hierarchy. But even though my husband and I practiced all kinds of austerities, we would never have been permitted to become executives in the innermost circle of power, and we would never have been in line to assume leadership of the organization. Only the founder and his entourage were 'born into the privilege.' They were the true elite. See? It's exactly the same as what we faced at Q, don't you think? I figured this all out while I was in prison. I realized that my life took a turn down the wrong path when I entered the Q system in junior high and tried so hard to blend in with those who were born to power. You and I are the same. And Kazue too. We all had our hearts wrested away by an illusion. I wonder how it looked to others. I wonder if we looked like victims of mind control.

"If you look at it that way, the one who was freest of all was Yuriko. She was so liberated, I wondered if she didn't come from an entirely different planet. Such a free spirit. She couldn't help but stick out in Japanese society. The reason she was such a prize among men goes beyond her beauty. I suspect they instinctively saw her true spirit. That's why she was able to captivate even a man like Professor Kijima.

"The reason you haven't been able to overcome your sense of being Yuriko's inferior is not just because she was beautiful but because you could never share her sense of freedom. But it's not too late for you. I've committed a horrible crime and will spend the rest of my life repenting. But for you it's not too late. That's why I'm telling you: Read these notebooks."

Mitsuru stepped into the next room and spoke affectionately to Yurio, with no sign whatsoever that she had just spoken to me harshly.

"Yurio, I'll be going now. Please take good care of your aunt."

Yurio turned toward Mitsuru, his beautiful eyes fixed on the space above her head, and slowly tilted his head down. I was so smitten by the color of his eyes, I didn't care one way or the other what Mitsuru had said to me. By the time I came to my senses, she was gone.

For a brief second the love I had once harbored for Mitsuru bubbled back into my heart. Wise, clever, squirrel-like Mitsuru. She had finally returned to the nest in the safe, luxuriant woods with Professor Kijima. I knew she would never leave again.

Yurio ran his fingers across the tea table, came to the package with the notebooks, and pulled them out of the envelope. He clutched them briefly and announced in a clear, calm voice, "I feel hatred and confusion here."

SEVEN · JIZŌ OF DESIRE: KAZUE'S JOURNALS

• 1 •

APRIL 21
GOTANDA: KT (?), ¥15,000

Rain since morning. I left work at the usual time and headed toward
the Shimbashi Station entrance to the Ginza Subway Line. The
man ahead of me kept glancing back vigorously over his shoulder
as he walked. I assumed he was trying to spot a cab. The rain bouncing
off his umbrella splashed onto the front of my Burberry trench coat,
causing it to stain. I fumbled angrily through my purse, looking for my
handkerchief. I pulled out the one I'd stuffed in my bag yesterday and
patted busily at the raindrops. The rain in Shinibashi is gray and stains
whatever it hits. I didn't want to have to pay for dry cleaning. I quietly
cursed the man as he climbed into his cab. "Hey, asshole, watch what
you're doing!" But as I did so I recalled the vibrant way the rain had
bounced off his umbrella, and that led me to think about how strong
men are in general. I was seized with a feeling of desire, soon to be followed by disgust. Desire and disgust. These two conflicting emotions
always accompanied my thoughts of men.

The Ginza Line. I hate the orange color of the train. I hate the gritty wind that whips through the tunnels. I hate the screech of the wheels. I hate the smell. Usually I wear earplugs so I can avoid the sounds, but there's not much I can do to avoid the smell. And it's always worse on rainy days. It's not just the smell of dirt. There's the smell of people: of perfume and hair tonic, of breath and age, sports pages and makeup and menstruating women. People are the worst. There are the disagreeable salary men and the exhausted office ladies. I can't stand any of them. There aren't very many high-class men out there who catch my attention. And even if they did, it wouldn't be long before they'd do something to make me change my opinion of them as well. There's one more reason I hate the subway. It's what links me to my firm. The instant I step down into the subway and head toward the Ginza Line, I feel as if I'm being pulled into a dark subterranean world, a world lurking beneath the asphalt.

As luck would have it, I was able to get a seat at Akasaka-mitsuke. I peered over at the documents the man sitting next to me was reading. Was he in my line of work? Which company does he work for? How did his company rank? He must have felt my gaze, because he folded the page he was reading so I could no longer see it.

At my office I am surrounded by papers. The stacks piled on my desk form a veritable wall all the way around me and I don't let people peek at my desk while I'm working. I sit there hidden behind the wall of paper, earplugs in place, lost in my work. A pile of white pages stretches in front of my eyes, and to my left and right are other piles. I sort them carefully so they won't tumble over. But they're stacked higher than my head. I want them to grow so high they'll brush the ceiling and cover up the fluorescent bulbs. Fluorescent lights make me look so pale—I have no choice but to wear bright red lipstick when I'm at work. It's the only way to counteract the washed-out look. Then, to balance out the lipstick I have to wear blue eye shadow. Since that makes my eyes and lips stand out too starkly, I draw my eyebrows in with a dark pencil; if I don't I won't look balanced, and if things aren't balanced it is very difficult—if not impossible—to live in this country of ours. That's why I feel both desire and disgust for men and both loyalty and betrayal for the firm I work for. Pride and phobia, it's a quagmire. If there were no dirt, there would be no reason for pride. If we had no pride, we'd just walk around with our feet in the mud. One requires the other. That's what a human being such as myself needs to survive.

Dear Ms. Satō,

All the noise you make is annoying. Please do everyone a favor and try to be a little quieter when you're working. You are inconveniencing others in the office.

This letter was on top of my desk waiting for me when I got in this morning. It had been typed on a computer, but I couldn't care less who wrote it. I snatched it up and walked to the office manager's desk, waving the paper noisily as I went.

The office manager had graduated from the economics department of Tokyo University. He was forty-six. He'd married another woman in the firm, who had graduated from junior college, and they had two children. The manager had the tendency to squash whatever achievements other men made and to steal the successes women attained. Earlier, he had ordered me to revise a report I had written. Then he stole my original thesis and represented it as his own work: "Avoiding Risks Related to the Cost of Construction." This kind of misappropriation was an everyday occurrence with the research office manager, and the only way I could succeed was to learn to outmaneuver him. For that reason, I had to try to protect my spirit, to keep things in balance, and accent my most impressive abilities. That was the only way I was going to get to a clear understanding of the true meaning of things. I had to remain firm and concentrate.

"Excuse me, but I just found this note on my desk. I'd like to know what you intend to do about it," I said to him.

The office manager took out his metal-framed reading glasses and put them on. As he slowly read over the note, a sardonic smirk rose to his lips. Did he think I wouldn't notice?

"What do you expect me to do? It looks like a private matter to me," he said, scrutinizing the clothes I was wearing. Today I had on a polyester print blouse and a tight navy-blue skirt accessorized with a long metal chain. I had worn the same outfit yesterday, the day before yesterday, and the day before that.

"So you might think. But private matters influence the workplace environment," I told him.

"I wonder."

"Well, I'd like some kind of evidence that the noise I make really is annoying and, moreover, just what it takes to be annoying."

"Evidence?"

The office manager glanced at my desk with a perplexed look. My desk was piled high with papers. Next to it sat Kikuko Kamei. Kamei was staring at her computer monitor, her fingers flying feverishly over the keyboard. After a minor restructuring last year, all the office personnel who were in managerial positions got their own computers. Of course, I was the assistant office manager, so I was given one. But the rank-and-file Kamei did not. Undeterred, she proudly came to work each day with her own laptop. She wore a different outfit every day as well. At some point one of my colleagues said to me, "So, Ms. Satō, why don't you wear a different dress to work every day like Ms. Kamei does? It would give us all more to enjoy on the job." To that I had replied tartly, "Yeah? Well, are you going to increase my salary so I can go out and buy a new outfit for every day of the year?"

"Ms. Kamei, sorry to bother you but would you mind coming here for a minute?" the office manager said. Kamei looked at the two of us. The color of her face changed as she hurried to our side. Her high heels clicked noisily, which caused all the other people working at their desks to look up in surprise. I could tell that she had intentionally made the noise.

"What can I do for you?" Kamei asked, as she looked from the office manager to me, clearly comparing us as she did. Kamei was thirty-two, five years younger than I. Five years but a world apart. She'd joined the company after the enactment of new equal-employment laws. A graduate of Tokyo University Law School, she was extremely conceited. And to top it off, she wore flashy clothes. I'd heard that she spent over half her salary on them. She still lived at home, and since her father had been a bureaucrat of some sort and was still in good health, she was affluent. I, on the other hand, had a mother who was a full-time housewife, and I had had to work to provide for her and my sister once my father died. How was I supposed to have money to spend on clothes?

"I have a question to ask you," the office manager began. "Does the noise that Ms. Satō makes disturb the others around her? I realize this is an awkward question and I apologize, but your desk is right next to hers, so I figured you'd know."

The office manager hid the letter I'd received, and spoke to Kamei with feigned nonchalance. Kamei glanced over at me and took a deep breath.

"Well, I'm busy with my typing so I imagine I create a lot of noise myself. I get wrapped up in what I'm doing and don't really pay much attention to the racket I make."

"I'm not asking about the noise *you* make, Ms. Kamei. I'm asking about Ms. Satō."

"Oh." Kamei acted embarrassed, but I spotted a glimmer of nastiness beneath her mask.

"Well . . . Ms. Satō always uses earplugs, so I don't think she really notices the noise she makes. I mean, it's small things, like when she puts her coffee mug down or rifles through her papers. And I guess you could say she bangs the drawers a lot when she opens and closes them. But it's not really a problem for me. I mean, I just mention this because you asked."

After she said that, Kamei turned to me and said softly, "I'm sorry."

"Well, is it loud enough that we should ask Ms. Satō to be more careful in the future?"

"Oh, no . . . I didn't mean . . ." Kamei vigorously denied anything. "It's just that you asked me—I suppose because my desk is next to hers—so I answered. That's all. I don't think you should make a big deal out of it."

The office manager turned to me.

"Okay? Are you satisfied? I don't think you have anything to worry about."

The office manager always behaved this way. He never took responsibility for the problems that came his way but always tried to pass them along to someone else. Kamei looked at him disconcertedly.

"Excuse me, sir, but why did you call me over? What does this have to do with me? I really don't understand."

"Well, you wrote it, didn't you?" I was practically shouting at her.

Kamei pursed her lips together in shock, as if she had no idea what I was talking about. She really did a good job acting the fool. The office manager turned to me and raised his hand as if to try to calm me down.

"Look, this is a matter of personal sensitivities. A person with tightly honed sensitivities wrote this, don't you imagine? Let's just leave it at that. Don't make it worse than it is."

The office manager picked up the phone on his desk and started dialing as if he had just remembered something he needed to do. Acting as if she had no idea what was going on, Kamei returned to her desk, her head hanging low. I couldn't bear the thought of going back to my desk and sitting next to her, so I headed off to get some coffee.

The part-timer in the filing department and our office assistant were already in the kitchen preparing tea for a horde of people. The part-timer was a freelancer and the assistant had been sent over from a temp agency. Both had dyed their hair a brassy brown, cut short, with bangs pinned back off their foreheads. Both of them looked uncomfortable when they saw me enter, so I knew they'd been bad-mouthing me. I pulled a clean coffee cup off the counter and asked, "Is there any hot water?"

"Yes." The part-timer pointed to the thermos. "We just poured it in the pot."

I poured hot water over the instant coffee I had just purchased. The part-timer and the assistant stopped what they had been doing and watched me. They looked annoyed. I spilled some of the hot water on the counter, but I just left it there and returned to my desk. Kamei looked up and turned to me when I walked by.

"Ms. Satō, please don't take offense at what I said earlier. I think I must be pretty noisy too."

I said nothing in reply, retreating behind my mountain of papers. I was on my fourth cup of coffee that day. I left each cup on my desk when I was finished with them, making space for the empty mugs. Each and every one of them had red lipstick stains on the rims. I figured I could carry them all back to the beverage counter when I was ready to leave for the day. That made the most sense to me. Kamei began to tap away softly at her keyboard. The sound drilled its way into my head. She may have been pretty, and she may have graduated from Tokyo University, but she couldn't do what I did—and that filled me with a sense of superiority. What would she say, I wondered, if she saw the large pack of condoms I had in my purse? That thought alone gave me pleasure.

•

The subway emerged from underground and headed into Shibuya Station. It was the moment of the day I loved best: rising from deep underground to the surface. It gives me such an immense feeling of relief, liberation. Ahh. From here I head into the night streets, right smack into a world where Kamei would never tread, a world before which the part-timer and the assistant would flinch in fear. A world the office manager could not even imagine.

I reached the call girl agency just before seven o'clock. The office was in a studio apartment among the shops lining Dogenzaka Avenue. It consisted of a tiny kitchen, a toilet, and a minuscule shower. There was a sofa in the ten-mat carpeted room, as well as a television. The office desk, where a man sat answering the phones, was off in the corner. The man shook his bleached-blond head in boredom and thumbed through a weekly magazine. He dressed like a teenager, but he was in his thirties. There were already about ten girls in the room, watching TV and waiting for phone calls. Some of the girls played with their Game Boys or looked through magazines. It was rainy tonight, and when it rains business is always slow. Everyone was settling in for a long wait.

This is where I transform from Kazue Satō into Yuri, my street name. I took the name from the Yuriko I knew in high school, a beautiful but dim-witted girl. I sat on the floor and spread the economic newspaper that I hadn't yet read over the glass-topped coffee table.

"Hey! Who left a wet umbrella here? You're getting everyone's shoes wet!"

A woman in a sloppy gray sweatshirt, her hair in a braid, shouted angrily. She wasn't wearing any makeup and her face—lacking any evidence of eyebrows—looked freakish. Even so, once she put on her makeup, she was a reasonably attractive woman so she got lots of requests—which made her bossy and smug. I apologized and got up. I'd forgotten that I needed to leave my umbrella in the hallway out front. Once she knew I was the culprit, the Braid began to make a fuss, hoping to earn a little sympathy from the man operating the telephones.

"You left your umbrella right on top of my shoes, and now they're so wet—even on the inside—that I can't possibly wear them. You need to pay me for this, don't you think?"

I glared at her, folded my umbrella up, and stepped out to leave it in the hallway. There was a blue plastic bucket by the door where everyone else had put their umbrellas; I stuck mine in as well. To get revenge for her outburst, I decided to take a bigger, nicer umbrella out of the bucket on my way out, pretending to do so by mistake. When I went back inside the office, the Braid was still giving me sour looks.

"You know, I don't know who you think you are, rustling your stupid newspaper when you can see the rest of us are trying to watch television. And why do you think you can spread your stuff out all over the table here? Other people use the same space, you know. Try being a little considerate. You can't go around acting like you're the only one here. And the same goes for the jobs. You've got to take your turn."

The girls here were nothing like Kamei; they said just what they thought. I nodded begrudgingly. But it was clear the Braid was jealous of me. She had some inkling of the fact that I had a good education and a job in a top-notch firm. That's right, you little bitch, by day I have an honest job. I graduated from Q University, and I am able to write intelligent and probing essays. In short, I'm nothing like you. Well, I could tell myself that all day long, but at night, on the street, a woman has only one thing going for her. And once she's past thirty-five, she can't help but despair over the fact that she is losing it. Men have excessive demands. They want a woman to be educated and to have a proper upbringing and a pretty face, and they want her to have both a submissive character and a taste for sex. They want it all. It is difficult to meet those demands and to live in a world where demands like this take precedence. No, more than that, it's ridiculous even to expect that one could. And yet women have no choice but to try to manage, searching as they go for some redeeming value to their lives. Well, my greatest value was my ability to achieve a balance—and to earn money.

The phone rang. I turned to look hopefully at the dispatch operator. I wanted him to pass me the job. But he pointed to the Braid. She went to the vanity in the corner, pulled out her makeup kit, and began putting on her face. The other women continued watching television or reading their magazines, hoping they'd be the next to go. I started to eat the food I'd bought earlier at the convenience store, pretending I didn't care. I returned to reading the newspaper. The Braid let her hair down and wiggled into a tight red minidress. Her legs were straight but heavy and her hips were wide. What a pig. I looked away. I hate fat people.

It was nearly ten o'clock, and the phone still had not rung again. The Braid had long since returned. She sprawled out on the floor, seemingly exhausted, and watched television. The mood suffusing the apartment was one of resignation. I was depressed, figuring it was now too late for much of anything. And then the phone rang. Everyone perked up their ears and looked over at the dispatcher. He had a troubled look on his face as he pushed the HOLD button on the phone.

"It's a request to visit a private residence. An apartment in Gotanda that doesn't have a bath. Do I have anyone who'll go?"

A woman with a face like a horse whose only redeeming feature was her youth lit a cigarette and said, "I'm sorry, but I draw the line at men who don't have their own bathing facilities."

The Braid ripped into a bag of chips and spoke in agreement. "What a jerk. If a man doesn't have a bath in his apartment, he's got no business calling for a girl to visit him there."

A number of angry voices concurred here and there.

"Okay then, I guess I'll have to tell him no." The dispatcher glanced over at me as he spoke.

I stood up. "I'll go."

"Will you, Yuri? That's great. I'll make the arrangements."

The dispatcher looked relieved, but after he told the man on the other end of the phone okay, I noticed that he was smirking to himself. I realized that he might have been grateful to me for my willingness from a business point of view, but from a personal point of view it was clear that he despised me.

I pulled out my compact and touched up my makeup. The other women looked at me in disgust. I knew they were thinking, My, my, you certainly pay a lot of visits on men without bathrooms!

Don't be so squeamish, girls, I wanted to say. You're too soft. If you do business with a man who has a handicap like that, you can turn it to benefit yourself. Serve him shorter and charge him more for the inconvenience. Laugh at me now, but you wait and see what it's like when you're thirty-seven. Then you'll understand. I wasn't going to let those silly girls get me down.

In three years' time, I'll be forty. That's when I'll retire from this group. I'll have to. My time will be up for this line of work. If I can't get work as a call girl, I'll market myself as a "mature lover." Or I'll start trolling the streets and procure my own customers. And if I can't stand it, I'll have to quit all together. But once I'm no longer able to find liberation in my night work, I imagine my day job will fall apart as well. That's what I fear, but I have to keep on living even so. So my biggest obstacle is my own insecurity. If I can't keep my balance, I need to harden myself further.

I stepped into the tiny bathroom and changed into a blue miniskirted suit. I'd bought it off the bargain racks at the Tokyu Department Store for ¥8,700. Next I put on a long-haired wig. The hair fell all the way to my waist. Kazue Satō had turned into Yuri. I felt I could do anything. I picked up the slip from the dispatcher with the address and phone number of the client and walked out the door. I searched through the bucket, selecting what was probably the Braid's long stylish umbrella, got in a cab, and headed toward the man's apartment in Gotanda.

The apartment was beside the train tracks. I paid the cab fare and made sure to get a receipt. Some agencies have their own cars and drive girls to their customers, but my office has us pay for cabs. Then they reimburse us later.

Mr. Hiroshi Tanaka, Apartment 202, Mizuki Heights. I took the flight of stairs on the outside of the building and knocked on the door to apartment 202.

A man opened the door. "Thanks for coming," he said.

He was nearly sixty and had the rugged physique of a construction worker. His face was brown from the sun, his body hard. The apartment smelled of mold and cheap liquor. I peered in, quickly scanning the interior. I wanted to be sure there were no other men inside. We didn't have to take this kind of precaution when we were sent to a specific love hotel. But at a private residence it was important to be careful. A girl I know went to service one man and then had several others show up, one right after the other. She ended up being gang-raped by four men. That meant they only paid once for the price of four. What a ripoff.

"I don't mean to be rude, but I really expected them to send someone younger." Tanaka looked me up and down without the slightest hesitation and sighed with audible disappointment. The furniture in his apartment was cheap. How the hell did he expect to get some hot young thing with the pathetic kind of life he lived? I turned to look back at him, my trench coat still wrapped over my shoulders.

"Yeah? I was hoping for a younger client, myself."

"Well, then, I guess that makes two of us, huh?"

Resigned to his disappointment, Tanaka tried to laugh it off. I looked around the apartment without so much as a smile. "Hardly. I understand you don't have a bathroom on the premises. Nobody wanted to come over, but I took the call as an act of kindness. You should be grateful."

My complaint had hit home. Tanaka scratched the side of his face, clearly embarrassed. I had to take precautions to ensure he didn't try to abscond without paying. The first thing I did in the apartment was call the office to let the dispatcher know I'd arrived and all was well.

"Hello. It's Yuri. I'm here."

I put Tanaka on the phone.

"She'll do. I mean, I don't have any complaints. I guess I can't expect too much, without a bath. But next time won't you send a younger one?"

His gall really pissed me off, but I was used to it, so I didn't take any real offense. Instead, I took my anger and applied it to my eagerness to get the job done. I wanted to get my money and get out of there. I'd get my revenge by gouging Tanaka a bit on the price.

"What do you do for a living?" I asked.

"Oh, a little of this and a little of that. Mostly construction."

Well, I work for an architectural firm, you asshole. I'm the assistant manager of the research office, and I make ¥10,000,000 a year. In my heart I screamed this at him. I could feel my anger rising; it was what sustained me. I despised the man. Customers who are passive and weak-willed tend to be a lot of fun even for the prostitute.

"Save the small talk. I'm paying by the hour." Tanaka looked at his watch as he spoke. He wasted no time spreading out a wafer-thin futon. The quilt he dragged out had been wadded up and looked filthy. I felt my resolve slipping. To bolster my courage I asked curtly, "So did you clean yourself there?"

"I washed, yeah."

Tanaka pointed to the sink.

"Just a little bit ago, I washed it real good, so how about sucking it some?"

"I only do straight-up sex," I said brusquely, as I fished a condom out of my purse. "Here, put this on."

"I can't get it up just like that," Tanaka mumbled uneasily.

"Well, I get paid whether you do or not."

"You're a cold bitch."

I took off my trench coat and folded in neatly. The rain marks were still there on the front. I put some spit on my finger and tried to rub them out.

"Hey, why don't you stand there and take your clothes off? Give me a striptease."

Tanaka hoisted his T-shirt over his head and pulled off the workman-type trousers. Men are such pigs, I thought, as I looked at his shriveled sex organ under the mound of white pubic hair. Thank God he was small. I don't like large men because it always hurts later.

"No, I don't do that sort of thing," I reminded him gently. "I'm just here for the main event."

I hurriedly got out of my underwear and lay down on the thin mattress. Tanaka looked at my naked body and started to rub his penis. Twenty minutes had already passed. I looked at the watch that I'd set beside the bedding. I had one hour and ten minutes to go. But I planned to trick him into shortening that to fifty minutes.

"I'm sorry, but would you mind spreading your legs apart and giving me a look?"

I gave in to Tanaka's request, slightly. He was so meek and mild, I figured it wouldn't hurt to indulge him just this much. If I were too cold it could backfire and make him angry. That would be dangerous. But he was a complete stranger, someone I'd never seen before, and for some reason that always allowed me to act more audaciously. It was strange. I'd heard about one prostitute who killed her john in an Ikebukuro hotel. It wasn't really self-defense, so it was somewhat unusual. But those things happen, now and then. The john had tied her up and was videotaping her. He stuck a knife in front of her face and threatened to kill her. I can well imagine how scared she must have been. I haven't yet had an experience like that, but you never know when you're going to end up with some weirdo. It's scary, but I almost want to have something like that happen, as long as I don't die. Being scared out of your wits helps affirm that you are alive.

Once Tanaka finally got an erection, he picked up the condom with trembling hands and tried to put it on. It took him forever. I normally help the guy out in those situations, but since Tanaka didn't have a bath in his apartment, I refused to touch him. Sheathed, Tanaka fell on me and started to squeeze my breasts clumsily.

"That hurts!" I complained.

"I'm sorry, I'm so sorry," Tanaka apologized over and over as he tried to stick his penis in me. I was afraid if he didn't get it in soon he'd lose his erection. I certainly didn't want to start all over and was beginning to be irritated. So, with little other choice, I grabbed his penis and guided it into place. Finally we got it all the way in. Because he was old, it took him awhile to come, which thoroughly disgusted me. But before long he finished up and then rolled off to lie beside me. He started stroking my hair.

"It's been a long time for me."

"Well, then that was good, wasn't it?"

"God, it's good to fuck."

Yeah, well, I do it every night, you old fart. I certainly didn't want to lie there exchanging pleasantries with Tanaka, so I got up to get dressed. Tanaka, left behind on the futon, looked up at me, disappointed.

"Stay beside me for a while and let's talk dirty. Isn't that part of the deal? The whores in the old days always did."

"What era was that?" I asked, and laughed as I wiped myself off with tissues before stepping back into my underpants. "Just how old are you, mister?"

"I've just turned sixty-two."

To be living such a pathetic life at that age! I looked around his shabby apartment. One room, six mats big. That was it. No bathroom. He had to go down the hall to use the toilet. I sure as hell didn't want to end my life like this. But then, if my father were still alive, he'd be about the same age, I thought, and I took a closer look at Tanaka's face. His hair was sprinkled with strands of white. The flesh on his body sagged. When I was in school I suspected that I had a father complex, but that was a long time ago. Here I was with a man the same age that my father would have been.

Suddenly Tanaka was angry. "Don't laugh at me!" he shouted.

"I'm not laughing at you! What're you talking about?"

"You are. You're standing there staring at me like you think I'm stupid or something. I'm the customer, remember? And you're nothing but a fucking whore. You're no spring chicken yourself, you know, and standing there naked like that—why, you're nothing but a bag of bones. I can't get hard with a body like that. It just pisses me off!"

"I'm sorry. I said I wasn't making fun of you." I hurried to finish dressing. No telling what Tanaka might do now that he was mad. At any rate, this was his house. He could easily pull out a knife or who knows what. I had to calm him down. But more than that, I had to get my money.

"Are you leaving already? You're really pissing me off."

"Call me again, okay? Business is slow for us, too. I'll give you an extra treat."

"Extra? What'd you mean?"

"I'll go down on you."

Tanaka started grumbling as he climbed into his briefs. He looked at the clock. There was still more than twenty minutes left. I didn't care, I wanted to leave.

"You owe me twenty-seven thousand yen."

"The flyer said twenty-five thousand."

Tanaka pulled out the flyer and checked it to be sure. He must have needed glasses, because he had to squint his eyes up into a ridiculous grimace to read.

"Didn't he tell you? If you don't have a bath in your house, the price goes up."

"But I washed! I didn't hear you complaining."

It was going to be a pain to explain so I just rolled my head to the side in revulsion. Only a minute ago I'd had a strange man's cock inside me. I wanted to wash myself off. Wasn't it obvious? Men can't ever think about anything but themselves.

"It's expensive," Tanaka complained.

"All right, then. For you I'll come down to twenty-six. How's that?"

"Fine. Hey, wait a minute, there's still time left."

"Oh? Do you think you can go again before the twenty minutes is up?"

Tanaka clucked his tongue as he pulled out his wallet. He handed me ¥30,000 and I gave him ¥4,000 in change. I put my shoes on fast—hoping to get out of there before he changed his mind—dashed out the door, and flagged down a cab. I crawled in, and as the cab splashed through the pouring rain I pondered my own bitterness. The pain of being treated like a mere object. And a sense that this pain would turn into pleasure. It would be best if I could just think of myself as a thing. But then my existence at the firm would become a nuisance. There I was Kazue Satō, and not some thing. I had the taxi drop me off some distance from the office and walked the rest of the way through the rain. That cut about ¥200 off the taxi charge. I could have the office reimburse me for double the amount of the taxi receipt that I got on the way over to Tanaka's place.

I saw the Marlboro Hag at Murayama-chō— in front of the statue of Jizō, the gentle Buddhist bodhisattva, protector of those condemned to hell and all who wander between realms. The Marlboro Hag got her name because she was always wearing a flimsy jacket with a white Marlboro logo on the back. She was well known around the office. She had to be around sixty years old. Maybe she was a loony, but she always stood next to the Jizō statue and called out to the men who walked past. Because of the rain tonight, her cheap Marlboro jacket was soaked and her black bra showed through underneath. Not a single man presented himself, but she stood there beside the Jizō as always, like some kind of ghost. She would most likely stay on the streets until the day she died. Once you get fired as a call girl, you have no choice but to go out trolling for your own men. As I stared at the Marlboro Hag's back, I was terrified that a similar fate awaited me in the not-so-distant future.

It was close to twelve o'clock when I got back to the office. Most of the girls, resigned to a lousy take for the evening, had gone home. The only people left in the office were the dispatcher and the Braid. I handed ¥10,000 to the dispatcher and put ¥1,000 in the kitty for snacks and drinks and such. All the girls who'd had customers for the night were required to do this. Thanks to having gotten an extra ¥1,000 out of Tanaka, my contribution to the kitty did not affect my overall take for the evening. I chuckled to myself at the thought. The dispatcher glared at me as I walked by.

"Yuri! I just got a call from your last customer. He says you over-charged him, and he was plenty upset. Did you trick him into believing he had to pay more because he didn't have a bath?"

"Sorry."

What a prick! Tanaka's ugly face floated before my eyes and I found myself growing furious. What a coward! But now the Braid started in on me.

"Did you run off with my umbrella? I've had to sit here and wait for you to get back. You can't just go off and use other people's things, you know!"

"Oh, I'm sorry. I just borrowed it for a bit."

"Oh, I'm sorry? That's not good enough. You did it to get back at me."

I'm sorry, I'm sorry. I kept repeating my empty apologies until the Braid shrugged her shoulders.

"I'm leaving!" she shouted, as she flounced out of the office. I hurried to straighten up my things, afraid I'd miss the last train.

At Shibuya Station I dashed onto the 12:28 Inokashira Line train bound for Fujimigaoka. At Meidaimae Station I transferred to the Keio Line and got off at Chitose-Karasuyama. I would have to walk another ten minutes before I got home. It had rained all day long and I felt depressed. What the hell was I doing anyway? I came to a stop in the falling rain. I'd been cooped up in the office all evening and only had ¥15,000 to show for it. I persisted because I wanted to save ¥200,000 a week, but at this rate I wasn't going to meet my goal. I needed eight to nine hundred thousand a month, ten million a year. If I could maintain that rate, I could save up one hundred million yen by the time I turned forty. I enjoyed thinking about my savings, seeing the money multiply before my eyes. I just wanted to reach my goal; then I could enjoy looking at all I'd saved. In a way, saving money meant the same to me now as studying had earlier.

· 2 ·

MAY 30
SHIBUYA: YY, ¥14,000
SHIBUYA: WA, ¥15,000

I gazed at the photograph of my father atop my beat-up old piano. It's the same photograph we used at his funeral service. He has a stern expression on his face as he stands, looking very dignified and dapper in a sharp suit with his office building in the background. I loved my father. Why? I wonder. Probably because he treated me as if I were the most important thing in his life. He doted on me. He, more than anyone else, was able to discern my true strengths—and as a consequence was distraught that I had been born female.

"Kazue's the smartest girl in our family," he would say to me.

"Well, what about Mother?"

"Once your mother married she stopped studying, didn't she? Why, she never even reads the newspaper."

My father whispered that in my ear as if I were his co-conspirator. It was Sunday, and my mother was in the garden tending to her plants. I was in junior high at the time, studying for the high school qualifying examinations.

"Mother reads the newspaper!"

"Only the society page and the television schedule. She doesn't even glance at the articles on economics or political affairs. That's because she can't understand them. Kazue, I think you should get a job with a first-class company. You'll be able to meet an intelligent man, someone who will stimulate you intellectually. There's no need for you to marry, though. You could just stay on in this house. You're bright enough to out-do any man out there."

I was convinced that women who married and became housewives ended up as laughingstocks. I wanted at least to avoid that. Or if I did marry, I'd have to marry a man who was more intelligent, so he could appreciate my abilities. At that time, I didn't understand that smart men don't always select smart women. Because my parents did not get on that well, I believed it was because my mother wasn't very smart and never really tried to apply herself. She treated my father with respect and put him on a pedestal in front of others, but behind the scenes I knew she despised him because he'd come from a rural upbringing.

"When your father married me," she'd say, "he didn't even know what cheese was. When I made breakfast he thought I'd let the cheese spoil because it smelled sharp, and he asked me what it was. I was shocked at his ignorance."

Mother laughed when she told this story, but her laugh disclosed a sense of disgust. My mother had grown up in Tokyo, where her father, grandfather, and great-grandfather had all been either upper-level bureaucrats or lawyers. My father, on the other hand, was from some hick town in Wakayama Prefecture, where he had to struggle just to make it into Tokyo University. He had no choice after that but to enter a company and work as an accountant. My father was proud of using his wits to succeed. My mother was proud of her pedigree.

And what about me? After I graduated from Q University, I entered a top-notch firm. I was fashionably thin and men paid attention to me. I had it all, which in and of itself was extremely cool, I thought. By day I was respected for my brains; by night I was desired for my body. I felt like Superwoman! It made me grin as I thought about it.

"Kazue! Watch what you're doing! You're spilling your coffee!" I heard Mother scream angrily. I realized I'd dribbled here and there. A brown stain was spreading on my polyester skirt. Mother picked up the dishcloth and threw it at me. I tried to wipe the coffee off but only succeeded in making the stain worse. Once it had set, it was not going to come out. Resigned, I picked the newspaper off the table and began to spread it out.

"Aren't you going to change?" my mother asked, without looking in my direction. She began clearing away my younger sister's breakfast things. She always made my sister's breakfast: toast, fried egg, coffee. My sister worked for a manufacturer and had to leave at the crack of dawn. I only had to be at work by nine-thirty, so I usually didn't have to leave home until eight-thirty.

"No. The skirt is navy so it's not that noticeable."

I heard my mother release an especially loud sigh, so I looked up.

"What?"

"I just think you could pay more attention to your appearance. You've worn the same outfit how many days in a row now?"

This made me angry. "Look, I'm old enough to dress myself, so just mind your own business, will you?"

Mother was quiet for a minute after that. But then she started in again.

"I don't want to bring this up now, but there is something I simply must speak to you about. Lately you've been coming home very late. What have you been doing? Plus your makeup has gotten so heavy, you're thinner than ever, and I just wonder if you're eating properly."

"I'm eating."

I chewed up a gymnema pill and washed it down with a swig of coffee. Gymnema was a popular weight-loss product. It was distilled from natural sources and helped break down fat cells in the body. I bought a bottle in the convenience store and ate the pills instead of breakfast.

"That's not food, it's medicine. You'll get sick if you don't eat well."

"If I get sick, there will be no one around to keep earning money, will there?"

Mother had gradually begun to look like a nasty old woman. Her hair had thinned and her face—with her eyes spaced so far apart—had begun to look more and more like that of a flounder. When she heard my taunt, Mother let out a big sigh and then she said, "You've really become a monster. It's frightening."

She pointed to the bruises I had on my wrists. "Are you into something weird?"

"Oh-oh! I've gotta run!"

I looked at my watch and jumped up. I slapped the newspaper down on the table. Mother covered her ears with her hands and glared at me angrily.

"Was that loud enough?" I shouted. "You ought to be able to grant me that much. I mean, you're living off my wages, aren't you? Why do you think you can tell me what to do?"

"Why shouldn't I?"

"Because I'll do whatever I damn well please and there's nothing you can do about it."

I felt better once I got that off my chest. Back when I first entered the same company where my father had worked, I was so proud of the fact that I was able to provide for my mother and sister. But now it had become a big weight around my neck. My father had collapsed in his bath. If we'd discovered him right away, we might have been able to save him. I couldn't help secretly blaming my mother. She was at home, but she'd already gone to bed. I just couldn't get it out of my mind that she was somehow to blame.

After my father's death, my income was the sole support for the family, and I began to feel the pressure. I took on as many tutoring jobs as I could and spent all day running from one to the next. And what did she do, my mother? She just sat at home fussing over the plants in her garden. What a big fat zero. A worthless woman. I looked at my mother in total disgust.

"If you don't hurry, you're going to be late," my mother said, without glancing over at me. What she meant was, Hurry up and disappear. I threw on my trench coat and grabbed my shoulder bag. Mother did not go with me to the front door to see me off. Here I was, setting off to earn the money that enabled her to live in this house, and she couldn't even say good-bye. She'd always managed to send my father off.

I slipped into my dust-covered black high heels and left the house. I was tired, and my legs felt heavy. I hadn't had enough sleep. As I walked to the station, I looked down at the bruises on my wrists. The customer I had last night was into S&M play. He'd tied my wrists tightly. I encounter that kind of customer from time to time, and each time I add an extra charge to the usual fee. "If you want to get kinky, give me another ten thousand yen and I'll play along," I tell them.

At work I was so sleepy I couldn't take it, so I went into the conference room and stretched out on the table to nap. It was as close as I could get to crawling into bed. I lay there on my back and slept. Someone came into the room, but seeing that I was on the table, he closed the door in a hurry and left. I was sure someone would call me on it before long, but at that point I didn't care.

I slept for about an hour before I returned to my desk. As I walked past Kamei's desk I saw her hurriedly cover up one of her papers. I knew what it was: an invitation to one of the social gatherings that the others in the company organized. I never attend, so nobody bothers to invite me anymore. At that moment I was seized with the desire to have a little fun with Kamei. "What's that you have?" I asked. Kamei took a deep breath, preparing her answer.

"Ms. Satō, can you come? They'll be having a party next week."

"When?"

"On Friday."

I could feel the air in the office go still. Everyone held their breath, awaiting my response. I glanced over at the office manager. He was sitting at his computer pretending to type something.

"I'm afraid I can't."

The air began to stir again. Kamei nodded nervously.

"Oh, well, that's too bad."

Kamei's outfit was garish. Today she was wearing a pantsuit made of some kind of glossy material. Her blouse was bright white and open at the throat, revealing a gold necklace underneath. She really stood out in a conservative work environment like ours. And when she left at night, I suspect she exuded the aura of a "career woman." I felt a flash of superiority as I compared her double life to my own.

"Ms. Satō, you haven't ever joined us on one of our nights out, have you?"

Kamei seemed to be launching some kind of offensive strike. I ducked down behind the piles of papers on my desk and did not answer. Just as I stuck the earplugs in my ears, I heard Kamei apologize for overstepping her bounds.

"Sorry."

Actually, I *had* gone to one of the events, shortly after I'd entered the firm. There were about forty people there, as I recall. They held the event at a bistro next to our office building. I figured it would be like an extension of work and I probably should go. Other than the old-timers, there were about ten other new employees. Only two of us, another woman and I, had graduated from a four-year university.

There were hardly any other women in the company with university degrees. Out of the 170 new employees, there were only seven of us. There was no particular title or special section for us, so I assumed we would all demand to be given the same kind of positions that men graduating from university received. But I was assigned to the research post along with another woman with a degree from Tokyo University, just like Kamei, so I was certain that we were considered the talented employees. I think her name was Yamamoto. But I'm not sure, because she quit after working a little over four years.

When I attended the after-work gathering, all I saw were my peers and superiors running around drunk. What was particularly distressing was to see the way the male employees were checking out the new females. They were most interested in the women who had attended junior college and were assigned to lower assistantship positions. Amid all the chatter and hoopla, I sat with one other Tokyo University graduate. We both looked rather stunned. There were other women around us, but they seemed used to this sort of event and were shrieking with laugher and trading jokes with one another. Before long the men started running a poll to find out who the most popular female employee was.

"Okay, out of all the women here, which one would you pick for a trip to the beach?"

A male employee five years ahead of me started it off. The section head and the office manager both started to applaud when it came time to vote for their favorite. In the end an assistant in the design section was selected for the beach. Then the situation was changed. Who would you want to take to a concert? Who for a walk in the park? And so on. Finally they asked, "Who would you most want to marry?" And the bistro erupted in unanimous applause for a sweet modest girl who worked as one of the operations assistants.

"Just look at them all." The Tokyo University graduate turned to me. I didn't answer. I just sat there stiffly on my cracker-thin floor cushion. My dream was falling apart. Men who were competent at work were carousing around and getting drunk.

A man who entered the company when I did called over to us. "How about Ms. Yamamoto?" he said.

The men who had been voting on women turned and pretended to look awed with respect. "No, not Ms. Yamamoto. She's too smart for us!" All the men laughed. Yamamoto was a beautiful woman, the kind most men found it difficult to approach. Yamamoto stared at them coolly and shrugged her shoulders.

"Well, then, what about Ms. Satō?"

The speaker pointed to me, and the men from the research department—all my seniors—looked at me, their faces red from the alcohol.

"Be careful what you say about Satō. She got her job through connections!"

I always believed that I'd gotten the job on account of my own abilities and hard work, but I guess that's not how it looked to the others. I came to realize for the first time in my life that mine was an existence that would never meet the approval of society.

• 3 •

I want to win. I want to win. I want to win.

I want to be number one. I want to be respected.

I want to be someone whom everyone notices.

I want people to say, What an awesome employee Kazue Satō is. So glad we hired her!

But even if I was at the top of the list, who would know? My job was not one where it was easy to distinguish yourself. The work I did was not easily quantified. I wrote reports, and it was difficult for others to recognize my excellence. This drove me crazy. What could I possibly do to ensure that the others in the office noticed me and my abilities? My superiors claimed I'd been admitted to the firm on account of my family connections. I had to think of a way to prove them wrong—to prove myself.

Later, when I heard that Yamamoto had passed the top level of the Government English Language exam, I started studying for the exam myself. After I'd studied like a maniac for a full year, I took the exam and passed the top level also. But it wasn't particularly unusual to have people in our firm who had top-level credentials; that still wasn't good enough. I started taking all my notes and writing memos in English. I wrote Japanese with English grammar structure. As a result, those around me stared at me in amazement, and I was delighted by my own success.

Another time, I decided I would contribute an article to the newspaper. With my breadth of knowledge and superior verbal skills, I knew I could write not just on domestic economic issues but on international politics as well. I submitted a short article called "What Gorbachev Should Do" to the readers' column of one of the national newspapers. When the paper printed the article in the morning edition, I bounded off to work in fine spirits. I was sure everyone would come up to me and compliment me on the piece. "Hey, I saw the paper this morning!" they would say. "Your piece is great!" But contrary to expectations, no one at the office seemed to have even noticed. They all went busily about their work. What, no one here even reads the paper? I found that really hard to believe.

During lunch the office manager frequently read the paper, so I assumed he'd have something to say to me about it. I loitered around his desk during my lunch break, not able to eat anything myself. The office manager looked up and glanced over at me.

"Did you write this, Satō?"

He thumped the paper with his finger. My chest swelled.

"Why, yes, I did."

"You're really clever, aren't you?"

And that was that. I can still remember the disappointment I felt. There must be something wrong here. I could think of only one reason for this oversight, one reason that could redeem me in my own eyes. They were jealous of me.

Two years or so had passed since I entered the firm. Once, while I was writing a report in English, I felt someone hovering over me.

"You write like a native speaker, don't you? Did you study overseas?"

Occasionally the head of the research division would stop by to check on things. He was now peering over my shoulder, interested in what I was writing. The division head was named Kabano. He was forty-three, a good-natured fellow who'd graduated from a mediocre university and was the kind of person who was often treated with contempt. I ignored him. I didn't think there was any particular reason to reply. Kabano looked at me—set adrift in that office with no one really to rely on—and smiled compassionately.

"I knew your father well, Satō. He was in accounting when I first joined the firm. He helped me a good deal."

I looked up at Kabano. A number of people had mentioned my father, but most of them had only been on the fringes of power. Kabano was no different, but I couldn't help feeling that he was trying to belittle my father for some reason.

"Such a shame about your father—and him still so young. But having an exceptional daughter such as yourself must have made him happy. I'm sure he was very proud of you."

I said nothing and turned back to my work. Kabano must have been shocked by my lack of response; he left the office immediately. That evening as I was preparing to leave, a male coworker who was five years my senior came over to me. He had been the one who had accused me at the office party of using connections to enter the firm.

"Satō, it really isn't any of my business, but I'd like to talk with you about something. Do you have a minute?"

He barely spoke above a whisper, glancing around nervously the whole time.

"What is it?"

I could feel my defenses rising. I still hadn't forgiven him.

"It's kind of difficult to talk about, but I feel it's my obligation. I don't think your attitude earlier was appropriate. In fact, I think you were rude to Mr. Kabano."

"Really. And what about your own attitude? Weren't you the one who announced to everyone that I used connections to get into the firm? Don't you think that was rude?"

I imagine he had not expected me to launch this kind of defense, because his face wilted.

"If I insulted you, please understand it was just the liquor talking. I apologize if I hurt your feelings. That hadn't been my intention. I meant it as a warning to others that you are part of the G Corporation family and that they shouldn't be rude to you. That's what Mr. Kabano was trying to express earlier. That's why I think your attitude was rude. In a family such as ours, everyone supports and encourages everyone else. That's just the way we are, and you'd do well to recognize it. Getting sulky about an imaginary offense is counterproductive."

"You're welcome to think whatever you like, but I entered this firm through my own ability. Of course I wanted to follow in my father's footsteps, but I earned my position here on my own. Naturally I'm very proud of my father. But I'm tired of hearing about him."

My older colleague folded his arms across his chest. "Do you suppose it was really through your own ability?"

When I heard him say this, I practically burst out in tears of rage. "If you don't believe me, check it out yourself! And stop going on about *connections.* I've had enough."

"No, that's not what I meant," he continued. "I got in because of connections, too. My uncle worked here. He's already reached retirement age and isn't around now. I don't care if people say I'm here on account of connections or not. There are times I felt protected because of my uncle. Of course, there are always people who will hassle you because of connections. But life is full of enemies anyway. It doesn't hurt to form strong alliances and turn negatives to your advantage. That's the way the corporate world operates in Japan."

"I think it's wrong."

"That's because you don't understand the first thing about a man's world."

With that as his parting shot, my colleague turned and walked away. I was so angry I thought I'd explode. *A man's world!* Men trotted that out when it suited them, forming alliances with one another and excluding women at their convenience. If G Architecture and Engineering Firm was supposed to be one big happy family, women ought to be included in these alliances also. I was pretty sure there was a Q University alumni ring in the firm, but no one had told me about it. I was surrounded by the enemy. I really was cast out into the wilderness. Suddenly I heard Yamamoto speaking to someone in a hushed voice.

"Okay. I'll meet you in front of the movie theater."

She hung up hurriedly, before anyone could know she was making a private phone call, and looked around her. She looked radiantly happy. Undoubtedly she was going to meet a man. "It's important to make strong alliances as best you can and turn the negatives to your advantage." That's what my senior colleague had advised. If that was the case, the best alliances a woman could have were with men. Yamamoto couldn't take being here much longer, and that's probably because she had a man. I returned to my desk feeling dejected, flopped down in my chair, and laid my head on my desk.

"I'm going now," Yamamoto called, as she headed for the door. She was wearing freshly applied bright red lipstick and her whole body was suffused with joy. I straightened up abruptly and followed her.

The man waiting for Yamamoto in front of the movie theater wore the drab uniform of a graduate student: jeans, jacket, and sneakers. There was nothing particularly remarkable about his face, and everything about him looked ordinary. But there was Yamamoto waving to him as if she were the happiest woman in the world. The two then disappeared into the theater. What the hell? I had assumed Yamamoto's boyfriend would be incredibly handsome and was bitterly disappointed to find things so contrary to my imagination.

Once the bell for the movie sounded and I was left standing alone in the street in front of the theater, my heart would not stop racing. Small black insects began to crawl their way through my heart. First one, then two, then three, and finally four. The more I tried to chase them away, the more they came. Before long I felt like my entire heart was little more than a wriggling black mass. The feeling was so oppressive, I wanted to break into a run.

Yamamoto had what I would never be able to obtain. And it wasn't just Yamamoto. The female assistants who taunted me for not being able to do my work, my male peers whose rudeness knew no bounds, the marginal old men like Kabano—all of them had the ability to interact with others: friends, lovers, someone to whom they could open their hearts, someone with whom they could share conversation, someone they longed to see once work was done. They had people outside the workplace who made them feel happy.

The May breeze was cool and delightful. The setting sun dyed the thicket of trees in Hibiya Park orange. Even so, the dark mood that had encircled my heart would not leave me. The black insects swarmed around one another, wiggling, multiplying, dangling along the edge of my heart, and finally spilling over. Why only me? Why only me? I continued to ask myself this as I fought against the breeze, making my way to the Ginza, my back bowed with the effort. Once I returned to my dark lonely house, the only person who would be there to greet me would be my mother. That was all I had to look forward to. The thought of returning to work the next day was more depressing than I could bear. My disappointment, my irritation, fed the insects in my heart.

The life I was living was no different from that of a middle-aged man. I went to work and then I went home. I existed solely to carry home a paycheck. Whatever I earned was turned immediately into household expenses. First Mother put my check in the bank. Then she bought cheap food for our meals, paid my sister's tuition costs, and made our house payments. She was even responsible for doling out my own meager allowance. If I took off somewhere and never returned, my mother—who had already used most of the savings—would be completely at a loss. I couldn't run away. I would have to continue looking after my mother until she finally died. Weren't my responsibilities exactly like those faced by men? I was only twenty-five years old at that point, yet I was already shouldering the weight of a family. I am forever a child with a paycheck.

But men have secret pleasures that they are able to enjoy. They slip off with their buddies for drinks, they play around with women, and they enjoy all kinds of intrigues on the side. I had nothing outside of work. And I wasn't even able to enjoy work because I wasn't considered the best; Yamamoto took that title. I had no friends in the firm. And when I looked back to high school, I could think of no one there whom I could have called a friend. No one! The insects in my heart squirmed as they whispered their taunts. I was so overcome with loneliness and despair that I came to a halt right there on the streets of the Ginza and started to cry. The insects writhed.

Someone speak to me. Call out to me and take me out. Please, please, I'm begging you, say something kind to me.

Tell me I'm pretty, tell me I'm sweet.

Invite me out for coffee, or more. . . .

Tell me that you want to spend the day with me and me alone.

As I continued on my way along the Ginza streets I gazed pointedly into the eyes of the men I encountered, beseeching them wordlessly. But every man who happened to glance in my direction quickly averted his eyes with an irritated look. They would have nothing to do with me.

I turned off the main avenue and darted down a side street. Women who looked like they worked in hostess bars brushed passed me, their faces thick with makeup, the air around them heavy with perfume.

These women refused to look at me too, assuming I'd accidentally stumbled onto their turf. They only had eyes for men—potential customers. But the men who stumbled by all looked to be the type who worked in a firm just like mine—just like me. The insects squirmed, addressing the women. One of the women standing in front of a club stared long and hard at me. She looked to be in her mid-thirties. She was wearing a silver kimono with a burgundy obi. Her jet-black hair was swept up atop her head. She glared at me suspiciously through upturned eyes.

The insects in my heart accosted the woman: What are you looking at? And when they did, the woman began to preach to them.

An amateur like you—you're an eyesore here. Leave. You don't understand much of anything, do you, you pathetic little princess. These are bars for company men. What goes on here is directly related to what goes on in the company. And both are a man's world. All for men and men alone.

I shrugged my shoulders.

Women who polish their skills and capture a man are the shrewdest. The kimono woman looked me up and down, clearly unimpressed by my drab appearance. She snorted scornfully. Impossible for you, I suppose. Did you abandon your femininity?

I didn't abandon anything. If you compare me to a woman like yourself, I look pretty drab; but as a result, I'm able to work a real job. I'll have you know I graduated from Q University and I work at the G Firm.

All totally worthless, I imagined that the woman replied. As a woman you're less than average. You'd never be able to get a job in the Ginza.

Less than average. Less than the fiftieth percentile on a standard scale. No one would want me. The thought made me go nearly crazy. How horrible to be less than average.

I want to win. I want to win. I want to win. I want to be number one.
I want people to say, What a great woman, I'm glad I got to know her.
The insects in my heart continued to squirm.

A long thin limousine pulled up. The smoked glass on the windows prevented me from seeing inside. While the people walking down the street paused to watch the car pass, the limousine, almost too big for the narrow lane, turned the corner and came to a halt in front of an elegant-looking establishment. The driver leaped out and opened the passenger door. A fortyish man, looking very enterprising in his double-breasted suit, stepped out with a young woman. The hostess-club women, the waiters, and all the others passing on the street took notice of the woman, expressing awe at her exceptional beauty. She wore a glimmering black cocktail dress. Her skin was pallid, her lipstick bright red, and her hair was long, light brown, and wavy.

"Yuriko!"

I called her name without even thinking. There she was in the flesh: my love rival from high school, licentiousness incarnate. She had no need for diligence or study; she was a woman born exclusively for sex. Yuriko heard me and turned around. She glanced at me briefly, turned back to the man, and took his arm without saying a word. I'm Kazue Satō! You know that perfectly well. Why are you pretending you don't recognize me? I bit my lip in anger.

"Do you know her?" The kimono-clad woman asked me suddenly. All this time I'd been having an imaginary conversation with this woman. To have her suddenly address me took me by surprise. Her real voice was surprisingly youthful and kind.

"We were in high school together. I was good friends with her older sister."

"You're kidding. Her older sister must be a beauty, too."

The woman could hardly conceal her admiration. I was quick to reply, "No, she was a real dog. They didn't look a bit alike."

I left the kimono-clad woman standing there looking shocked and hurried home. I felt a great sense of satisfaction; I think the sight of Yuriko set it off, knowing how humiliated her older sister would be to know what Yuriko was up to. The knowledge released me from my own misery. Here was someone even more pathetic than I was! Yuriko's older sister was not as intellectually gifted as I. She reeked of poverty, and she would never be able to get a job with a first-rate firm. I was still better than her, I told myself, appeasing my earlier despair. All it took was a petty incident like that and the insects in my heart vanished into thin air. That night I was freed from the anxiety I thought would hound me forever. But I still feared the insects would return to torture me—a foreboding that still seemed very real.

•

I don't have any good memories of my childhood. I have tried to forget it. Gazing at my reflection in the bathroom mirror, I cannot help recalling unpleasant times from the past. I'm now thirty-seven. I've still retained my youthful looks. I diet, so I'm thin. I can still wear a size two. But I'll be forty in three years and it terrifies me. By the time a woman is forty, she's basically an old hag. When I turned thirty I was afraid I was slipping over the hill, but it's nothing like turning forty. At thirty there was hope for a future. By hope, I mean I thought I might finally get selected for something good at work that would seal my success, or I might meet Mr. Right, or something equally ridiculous. Now I don't entertain any such notions.

I always get a little crazy when I reach a turning point in age—like when I was teetering between nineteen and twenty or twenty-nine and thirty. I was thirty when I first started the prostitution business. I was annoyed that I had no sexual experience. When I said I was a virgin, I got a customer right away just because he was curious. I don't want to remember that encounter. But at the time I figured I wouldn't ever be fifty. I doubted I'd even live to be forty. At any rate, I thought it would be better to die than become an old hag. That's right. I'd rather die. Life has no meaning for an old hag.

"Would you like a beer?"

I heard the customer calling to me from the other room. I was in the shower washing myself, washing every nook and cranny, washing away the sweat and spit and semen that glistened all over my body—fluids from a man I didn't know. Even so, the customer that night was not particularly bad. He was in his late fifties. From his clothes and his manners, I would say he was employed by a respectable company. He was gentle. And he was offering me a beer. That was a first for me.

From the perspective of a fiftyish man, I must have appeared young, even at thirty. If I always had customers like him, I'd be happy; I could continue in the business even after I passed forty. I wrapped the bath towel around my body and returned to the room. My customer was sitting in his underwear smoking a cigarette while he waited for me.

"Here, have a beer. We've still got time."

His relaxed manner calmed me. If he'd been younger he'd want to try to do it again and again.

"Thank you." I used both hands to lift the glass to my lips, and the customer's eyes narrowed in a smile.

"You've got good manners. You must have been brought up to be a proper young lady. Tell me then, why are you doing this?"

"I wonder . . ." It made me feel good to hear him say I had good manners, so I smiled at him politely. "I guess at some point I just got bored with going back and forth to work, day in and day out. Women sometimes want adventure in life. A job like this—I mean, for a woman, I see all kinds of people I might not otherwise have ever had the chance to meet. I guess I get to know a little bit more about the world."

I do it for the adventure? Oh, please, that had to be the oldest line in the book! But the customer was the type who wanted the fantasy. He wanted a woman who would give him a story.

"Adventure?" He fell for it.

"Selling your body is the ultimate adventure. I'm sure a man couldn't do it."

I smiled sweetly and adjusted my wig. Even when I shower I don't get my face wet, and I never remove the wig.

"You work for a firm?"

"That's right. But it's a secret!"

"I won't tell; let me in on your secret. Which firm is it?"

"If you tell me, I'll tell you."

I did my best to build the suspense. If I played my cards right, he might ask for me again. At least that was what I was banking on.

"It's a deal. I'm kind of embarrassed to say, but I teach at a university. I'm a professor."

I could tell he was proud of what he did and who he was. If I could get a bit more information I would have scored a great success.

"You're kidding. Which university?"

"I'll give you my business card. And if you have one, I'd like to have it."

And so, naked, we exchanged cards. My customer's name was Yasuyuki Yoshizaki. He was a professor of law at a third-rate private university in Chiba Prefecture. Putting on reading glasses, Yoshizaki peered at my card respectfully.

"Well, this is a shock! So you're the assistant manager of the research office at G Architecture and Engineering. My, my, what a distinguished person. Your job must come with considerable responsibility."

"It's not so bad. I do research and write reports about the economic factors affecting our markets."

"Well, then, we're practically in the same line of work. Did you go to graduate school?"

Yoshizaki's eyes revealed both fear and curiosity. I was driven to take advantage of his excitement.

"Oh, no. After I graduated from the economics department at Q University, I didn't go on. Graduate school was too much for me!"

"You graduated from Q University and you're working as a hotel call girl? Well, that's a first! I'm impressed."

Clearly excited, Yoshizaki filled my glass with beer.

"I hope you'll see me again. Let's drink a toast to our next meeting."

We clinked glasses. I'll look forward to it, I offered. I queried Yoshizaki as I studied his name card.

"Professor, may I call you at your office? I'd like to meet you without having to go through the escort service. If I go through the office, they take a cut and I lose. If it's all right, could I have your cell phone number?"

"Oh, I don't carry a cell phone. But you can call me at my office. If you tell them you're Satō from Q University I'll know who it is. Or you could say you're Satō from G Firm. That'd be fine too. My assistant would never suspect a graduate of Q University of being a call girl!"

Yoshizaki chuckled. Doctors and professors were the most lascivious of all. From what I knew of their world, most men who were obedient to authority figures, as well as those who had earned authority positions, were always idiots. When I recall the anxiety I once felt about being at the top of that world, I laugh so bitterly it makes my teeth ache.

•

When we left the hotel, Yoshizaki stepped into the street away from me as if he had never met me. But I didn't care. Instead, it made my heart throb with excitement. Yoshizaki was interested in me as a woman, and surely this was proof that he was destined to become one of my loyal customers. I'd be able to meet him privately, without the escort management taking a cut from my pay, which was the ideal way of earning money in this business. Women use their bodies to earn money—so it seems unreasonable that we can't stand on street corners alone. Yet there isn't anything more dangerous than trying to procure your own customers off the street. But Yoshizaki was different. He was an affable university professor who seemed to have a real interest in me. I was counting on him to become a good customer.

I hummed happily as I strolled through the night with Yoshizaki. I forgot the chilly reception that awaited me at the escort service office, the Braid's belligerence, the way my colleagues at the firm snubbed me, my mother's nagging, even my fear of growing old and ugly. I was flushed with a sense of victory. The future was bright. Good things were in store for me. I hadn't felt this sense of optimism for a long time. For the first time since I entered the escort agency at the age of thirty, my position as an elite businesswoman was appreciated, and I was being celebrated and sought out.

I grabbed Yoshizaki's arm and linked my own around it. Yoshizaki broke into a grin and looked over at me.

"Well, well, don't we look like a fine pair of lovers."

"Shall we become lovers, professor?"

The young couples we passed along the hill turned to stare at us and then broke into whispers. A bit old for it, aren't you? they seemed to say. I couldn't care less what they thought and didn't pay any attention, but Yoshizaki brushed my arm away, looking confused.

"This doesn't look good. You're young enough to be mistaken for one of my students—and a mistake like that could cost me my job. Let's be a bit more discreet, shall we?"

"I'm very sorry."

I apologized politely for causing any inconvenience, to which Yoshizaki waved his hand in front of his face timidly. "No, no, don't get the wrong idea. I'm not blaming you."

"I know."

He still looked upset, though, and looked nervously around him. When a cab approached he flagged it down.

"I'm going to take a taxi the rest of the way," he said, as he began to climb in.

"Professor, when will I be able to see you again?"

"Next week. Call me. Say it's Satō from Q University. I'll have my assistant put you through."

The way he said it was a bit haughty, but I didn't mind. I was happy. Yoshizaki had recognized my talent, my superiority. What a fortunate chance meeting ours had been.

Once I made the crest of the hill on Dogenzaka Avenue, I turned to look back toward Shibuya Station. The road rose in a gentle curve. It was past midnight and a breeze had come up, fairly strong for October. It ruffled the hem of my Burberry coat. My armor during the day was a flowing cape; at night it became Superman's cape. By day a businesswoman; by night a whore. Inside my cape was an attractive woman's body. I was capable of using both my brains and my body to make money. Ha!

The taillights of a taxi winked at me between the trees along the avenue as it slowly made its progress up the hill. A little faster and I would catch it, I thought. Tonight I looked beautiful, full of life. I turned down a narrow street lined with small shops. Perhaps I'd run across someone I know. Tonight of all nights I wanted to give the people at the firm a glimpse of my other self.

"You look like you're having a good time."

A businessman who appeared to be in his fifties called out to me, squinting as if into a dazzling light. His suit was gray and his dust-covered shoes were worn and shapeless. His suit jacket was open and the sleeve was being tugged down his arm by the strap of the heavy black shoulder bag he was lugging. I could see a men's magazine stuffed inside the bag. His hair was mostly white and his face was gray and discolored as if he suffered from some kind of liver disease. He looked like the kind of man who'd spread out the pages of a sports paper on a crowded train, oblivious to the discomfort of others; the kind of man always short of cash. Definitely not the type who'd have a job at a prestigious firm like mine. I smiled at him sweetly. Few men ever called out to me in the streets, even when I addressed them first.

"Are you on your way home?" he asked, somewhat timidly. His voice bore a trace of some kind of accent. Clearly he wasn't from the city.

I nodded. "Yes, I am."

"Well, would you like to stop off for a cup of tea with me or something?"

He clearly wasn't interested in food or even booze. What were his intentions? I wondered. Was he trying to pick me up? Had he figured out I was a prostitute?

"That would be nice."

I've got another customer! I felt my heart tighten with excitement. And to have found him so soon on the heels of Yoshizaki. I had to be careful not to lose him; this was my lucky night.

The man looked down nervously. He wasn't used to women. I could tell that he was afraid of what was going to transpire and I reverted back to my former self. When I first entered the water trade—you know, prostitution—it was the same for me. I didn't really understand what men would want and I was full of anxiety. But now I knew. No, that's not true. I still don't know. Perplexed myself, I put my hand on the man's arm. He wasn't as pleased with my gesture as Yoshizaki had been and he shrank back instinctively. The hawker in front of the cabaret looked at me and laughed. Looks like you've snagged yourself an easy mark there, haven't you, girlie? You bet I have, I thought, as I gazed back at the hawker, my confidence soaring. I'm having fun tonight.

"Where do you want to go?" the man said.

"What about a hotel?"

The man was startled by my directness. "I don't know. I don't have that much money. I just thought I'd like to sit and talk with a woman, that's all. And then you walked past. I didn't know you were that kind of woman."

"Well, how much can you pay?"

Embarrassed, the man answered in a small, timid voice.

"Well, if I have to pay the hotel costs, probably around fifteen thousand yen."

"We can find a cheap hotel. Some only charge three thousand yen. And I'll charge you fifteen thousand yen."

"In that case, I think I can manage. . . ."

When I saw him nod, I began to head in the direction of a hotel. The man followed. His right shoulder dropped slightly under the weight of the bag he was carting. He really was a slob. A shabby excuse for a man. But he had called out to me, so I had to treat him like gold.

I turned back and asked, "How old are you, mister?"

"I'm fifty-seven."

"You look younger. I thought you were probably around fifty."

Yoshizaki would have appreciated the compliment. But this man just frowned. Before long we made it to the hotel. It was a love hotel near Shinsen Station, just on the border of Murayama-chō. When I pointed it out to the man, he couldn't hide his discomfort. I suppose he was regretting his decision to come with me. I glanced at him warily. What if he tried to back out now? I'd need to think of something to keep him, I told myself, surprised at my own temerity. I was used to the agency making all the arrangements.

When we got to the entrance of the hotel, the man fished out his wallet. I glanced inside and saw that he really did only have two ¥10,000 bills.

"Don't worry about it now. You pay later."

"Oh? I didn't know."

The man slowly slipped his puny wallet back in his pocket. Looks like he'd never come to a love hotel before either. I was going to have to come up with a way to make him one of my regulars. He wasn't an ideal customer, but if I could get men like him and Yoshizaki to patronize me regularly, I wouldn't need to depend on the escort agency. That seemed like the only way out of the rut I was in, my only defense against the onslaught of old age. I picked the smallest room on the third floor and we squeezed into the tiny elevator. It looked as if it could hardly hold more than one person at a time.

"Let's talk for a while in the room, shall we? You might not realize it, but I work in the corporate world myself."

The man looked at me in surprise. I could tell he was feeling mortified at having been snagged by a prostitute. He was blushing.

"No, I really do. Once we get to the room I'll give you my business card and tell you all about it, okay?"

"Thanks. That'd be nice."

The room was small and dirty. The double bed filled it from wall to wall. The paper shoji screen covering the window was torn in places, and the carpet was mottled with stains. The man dropped his shoulder bag to the floor and sighed. He'd removed his shoes and his socks smelled.

"This for three thousand yen?"

"It's the best I could do. This is the cheapest place in Maruyama-chō."

"Thanks for trying."

"Would you like a beer?"

The man smiled, and I pulled a bottle of beer out of the minibar. I poured the beer into two glasses and we toasted. The man drank in little sips, almost as if he were lapping it up.

"What kind of work do you do, mister? Would you mind giving me your business card?"

The man hesitated for a moment and then pulled a wrinkled card holder out of his suit pocket. "Wakao Arai, Deputy Chief of Operations, Chisen Gold Chemicals, Incorporated." The company was based in

Meguro, it said. I'd never heard of it. Arai stuck out a bony finger and pointed to the name of the company. "We sell chemicals wholesale. The firm is based in Toyama Prefecture, so I doubt you've heard of it."

I handed him my business card with a self-important flourish. A look of shock washed over Arai's face.

"I'm sorry if it's rude for me to ask, but why do you do this sort of thing if you have such a good job?"

"Why, you wonder?" I gulped down my beer. "At work nobody pays any attention to me."

I'd let slip a bit of my true feelings. It was only until I was thirty that I worked with such zeal. When I turned twenty-nine I was sent to a separate research facility. My rival Yamamoto worked only for four years and then quit to get married. That left only four of the women who'd originally entered the firm with me. One was in advertising. Another in general affairs, and the other two in engineering. They were responsible for architectural planning. When I turned thirty-three, they finally brought me back to the research office. But there wasn't a single interesting person there anymore. All the men I had entered the firm with had long since been promoted to higher positions in the inner administration, where women would never be accepted. The younger female office assistants clearly didn't like me. University women who had entered the firm after me were working less and getting ahead. In short, I had slipped off the fast track. I had clearly been shifted from the winners to the losers. Why would that be? Because I was no longer young. And I was a woman. I was doing a lousy job aging and I could no longer build a solid career.

"It's really gotten to me. I feel like I want to get revenge."

"Revenge? On who?" Arai looked up at the ceiling. "I suppose everyone feels like that from time to time. We all want revenge. We've all been hurt one way or another. But the best thing to do is keep on going as if none of it matters."

Well, I didn't agree. I was going to get revenge. I was going to humiliate my firm, scorn my mother's pretentiousness, and soil my sister's honor. I was even going to hurt myself. I who had been born a woman, who was unable to live successfully as a woman, whose greatest achievement in life was getting into Q High School for Young Women. It had been all downhill since. That was it—that was why I was doing what I did, why I turned to prostitution. When it finally struck me, I started to laugh.

"Mr. Arai, I'd like to keep talking about this, so it'd be great if we could get together again. Fifteen thousand yen will be fine. We can meet here and drink beer and talk. How about that? I'm quite good at economics, you know, and I'll spring for beer and the snacks and bring them along."

When he heard me make my request in all earnestness, desire flashed across Arai's eyes. It was the first sign I'd had all evening. Men are weird. They have to think they're the ones in control.

· 4 ·

OCTOBER 4
SHIBUYA: E (?), ¥15,000

Today I napped on the table in the empty conference room all morning long. My back was killing me, lying on the table, but I ignored it. I'd spent last night until about eleven-thirty cooped up in the office of the hotel escort agency, and I was the only one not to be called. Not once.

"What's this? You picked a fine place for a nap!" A man's voice startled me and I snapped to, swinging my legs over the table. It was Kabano, the man who had told me that my father had been kind to him when he first joined the firm. Kabano had risen higher in the firm than I had predicted. He'd been promoted from division manager of general affairs and was now an executive officer. At our firm we almost never saw the executives. They were much too exalted, with offices on the top floors. They even had an elevator that only they could use, and they were driven to and from the building in private company cars.

Kabano wasn't particularly talented, but he was affable and had no enemies to speak of, and that was enough to propel him up the ladder to success. That was one aspect of the company structure I just could not understand.

"I heard snoring so I peeked in, and lo and behold there was a woman fast asleep. Not at all what I expected!"

"I'm sorry. I have a headache."

I climbed slowly down from the table and slipped into the shoes I had left on the carpet. I couldn't suppress a tiny yawn. Kabano looked me over with an expression of displeasure. That pissed me off. What's your problem? I wanted to ask. You think just because you're some high-and-mighty executive you can come in here and lord it over me? You old fart. You have some nerve waking me up!

"If you have a headache, you should go to the infirmary. That's what it's there for, you know. Miss Satō, are you sure you're all right?"

"What do you mean?"

I combed my fingers through my long hair. It was tangled and too messy to be easily smoothed without a proper brushing. But what on earth was he staring at? Kabano finally averted his eyes.

"Don't you know? You're awfully thin. Why, you're practically skin and bones. You're much thinner than you were when you were young; I almost didn't recognize you just now."

So I'm thin, so what's wrong with that? Men like women to be thin and have long hair; isn't that practically a given? I'm five feet five inches tall and I weigh a hundred pounds. I'd say that's just about perfect. For breakfast I eat a gymnema tablet. For lunch I go to the company cafeteria in the basement and buy a prepared lunch, mostly seaweed salad. Sometimes I just skip lunch, and I hardly ever eat the white rice that comes with it. I will eat the vegetable tempura, though. At any rate, anytime I see a fat woman it revolts me. I think she must be stupid to look like that.

"If I put on weight my clothes won't look right anymore."

"Concerned with clothes, is it? I'm sure that's an issue for a young woman, but . . . Miss Satō, I really think you ought to see a doctor. I'm worried that there may be something seriously wrong with your health. Are you working too much?"

Am I working too much? Well, yeah, maybe at night! A smile quickly overtook my lips.

"I'm not working all that hard. It's just that last night was a bit of a drought."

"What are you talking about?" Kabano asked, alarm spreading over his face. Whoops, things are getting tangled up in my mind. This old fart's an executive here. I need to revert back to my daytime self—fast. I'm not handling my double life too well today.

"Oh, nothing. I just meant that I haven't had much leftover work to do, that's all."

"Well, I'm sure the work here in the research office can be very intense. I recall someone remarking earlier that you wrote a report that received considerable praise."

"That was a long time ago. Conditions were a lot more positive then."

I was twenty-eight when I wrote that report: "Financial Investment in Construction and Real Estate: Creating New Myths" was the title. It won a prize from the Economic News Publishing House. That was the happiest period in my life. Japan was still floating on the Bubble Economy, the market for new construction was promising, and times were heady. There was a jerk who criticized my article, though, for lacking any clear strategic suggestions. I've never forgotten how bitter his remarks made me feel.

"That's not true. You still have a lot of potential." Kabano suddenly looked over at me with a pained expression. "Miss Satō, your mother must be really very worried about you."

"My mother? What do you mean?"

I pushed my index finger against my chin and tilted my head to the side. Ever since Professor Yoshizaki admired this pose as looking particularly cute and young ladylike, I had been trying it out every chance I got. Professor Yoshizaki seemed to like women who acted like well-bred young ladies.

"What I mean is your mother might be worried that you're not well, and you're all she's got."

Well, you've got that right. I'm her cash cow. No way she wants to lose me. If I stop pulling in money, she won't know what to do. But what would I do? Suddenly I felt a stab of fear. What was going to happen as I grew older? If I got fired from the firm and wasn't able to keep up my night work, I'd lose all my sources of income. If that happened, you can be sure my mother would turn me out of the house.

"I understand. I'll try to be more dependable."

When he saw the change that swept over me, the seriousness with which I listened to his suggestion, Kabano nodded with approval.

"We'll just keep what happened today between the two of us, so don't worry about it. I'm glad I was the one who found you; I'm not often over this way, you know. But I have to say, and I know this may seem harsh, that you've really changed. You look like you've got a few screws loose."

"What's wrong with the way I look?"

I tried out my pose again, tilting my head.

"You wear too much makeup, for one thing. Hasn't anyone told you that? I mean, some makeup is fine, but you've crossed the line. It's not appropriate for the workplace. My advice may seem overly solicitous, but I really think you should consult a mental health counselor."

"A counselor?" I was so taken aback I nearly shouted. "Why do you say that?"

I had been required to see a psychiatrist at the end of my second year in high school, on account of my eating disorder. They said my life was in danger and made all kinds of ridiculous predictions that made my mother cry and my father blow up with anger. It was ludicrous. But had they cured me? How about when I was twenty-nine? Hadn't I been told the same thing then?

The door to the conference room burst open and the secretary poked her head in. I guess she'd heard me shouting. She stared at me in shock.

"Mr. Kabano, is that you? It's past time now."

"Well, then, I'd best be on my way."

Kabano rushed out of the conference room. The secretary glared at me suspiciously. What are you looking at, bitch? You don't know what it's like to run freely through the night, do you? Bet you've never had a man want you. Whoa, I've already reverted to my whore self.

When I got back to the research office, the manager looked at me fixedly. "Satō, I'd like to see you for a moment." What now, another sermon? Utterly disgusted, I headed to the manager's desk. He looked up from his computer screen and swiveled in his chair to look at me when I came over.

"You know, it's okay for you to step away from your desk. But you have to be careful not to be gone so long."

"I'm sorry. I have a bad headache." I glanced at Kamei out of the corner of my eye. She was her usual gaudy self. Today she was wearing a red T-shirt with black pants. She had her hair pulled back and she'd buried her face in the documents she was reading, the spitting image of a proper career woman. God, I hated her. She had perfected the charade exquisitely.

"Satō, are you listening?"

The office manager raised his voice in irritation. Everyone in the office turned to stare at me. Kamei glanced over at me and met my gaze before casually looking away.

"All I'm saying is if it happens again, tell me before you take off."

"I'm sorry. I understand."

"You're no kid, you know. You need to act more responsibly. You're pushing the envelope here. Let me be frank, I have no idea how much longer we can keep you on in this office. The good days are over and none of us are indispensable anymore. Ours is a surplus department. I've heard that both research and planning are in for a major overhaul. So I advise you to pay attention to what you do."

It was a bluff. I gazed at the floor in a fit of sulkiness. I was the assistant manager, for crying out loud, how could they fire me? It wasn't right. Was it because I was a woman? Because I was a prostitute by night? A sense of superiority bubbled forth at the thought. I was awesome. A superstar able to outperform anyone else at this crummy firm. I'd earned prizes for my essays, all while serving this firm as the assistant manager of research, an assistant manager who sells her body. My chest swelled with pride.

"Thank you for your advice. I'll be more careful."

After being chewed out like that, I had to do something to calm myself down, so I left the office to go fix myself a cup of coffee. When I stepped into the corridor, the employees who were heading my way quickly scattered left and right to avoid me. Cut it out! I'm not some kind of freak, you know. I felt the blood rise to my head, but then I thought about my secret night life and calmed down. I ought to do something to get back at the Braid, I thought to myself. So I went down to the first-floor lobby to use the pay phone.

"Hello, you've reached Juicy Strawberry."

I recognized the dispatcher's voice. I could just imagine the excitement and anticipation now racing through the hearts of the girls stuck in the office during the day. I pressed a handkerchief to the telephone receiver in an effort to disguise my voice.

"I wanted to talk about the girl named Kana that you sent over the other night. The customer had a complaint and asked me to relay it to you."

Kana was the Braid's street name.

"What is it?"

"Looks like that Kana girl took money out of the customer's wallet. She's a thief."

I hung up. God, that felt good. I couldn't wait to get to the agency office tonight.

I made myself look busy for the rest of the day and then left the firm. I stopped at a convenience store and bought *oden* stew and a pack of rice balls. I even bought a carton of cigarettes for the dispatcher. Then I rushed along the streets to the hotel office in high spirits. I've got to get sent out tonight, I thought, somewhat testily. My goal of saving up a hundred million yen before I turned forty was growing more and more unlikely, but there was little I could do if they didn't share the customers with me. I was sure it would piss the Braid off, but I wanted to get sent out ahead of her tonight. I burst through the office door.

"Good evening, ladies!"

The dispatcher looked over at me and then turned away. There were already five or six girls in the office lounging around reading trashy magazines, watching television, or wearing headphones and listening to music. The Braid ignored me.

"Here you go!" I said, as I handed the dispatcher the carton of Castor Mild cigarettes. I'd paid for them out of my own pocket, but since it was a bribe to get him to send me some work, there was little help for it.

"Are these for me?"

I couldn't tell if the dispatcher was surprised or annoyed.

"Yes, they are. I'm hoping for a little work tonight."

That should do it. I headed over to the table feeling confident and put down my bag of food. I slurped away at the *oden* broth and nibbled on my rice balls. The phone rang and everyone turned in anticipation. *Send me,* I implored the dispatcher with my eyes. He pointed at the Braid.

"Kana-chan, he's asking for you."

"All right."

The Braid pulled reluctantly away from the television. I had scarfed down my dinner and now felt very dissatisfied. Why hadn't the Braid gotten the ax? As soon as she left, the dispatcher called me over to his desk. There wasn't a call waiting for me, so I couldn't figure out what he wanted. I smiled endearingly as I approached.

"Yes?"

"Yuri-san, uh—"

I could feel a sermon coming on. I steeled myself for what was next.

"Yuri-san, we'd prefer you not to use our agency anymore. That prank phone call earlier; that was you, wasn't it? Don't try another trick like that again. Kana-chan's our best girl."

I'd been fired. I couldn't believe it. I just stood there with my head hanging. The other girls sat there pretending not to know what was going on, but I was sure they'd heard.

"Then give me back the cigarettes," I said to the dispatcher.

•

I hurried down Dogenzaka in the grips of a new plan. I needed to find a department store so I could go in one of the restrooms there and touch up my makeup. I was going to horn in on the Marlboro Hag's business. I had no problem standing around for hours at a time. I'd wanted to have my own clientele. And since I'd been fired from the hotel escort service, now seemed like the time to get started. Moreover, there was no better time than the present to get past all the bitterness I had tasted today.

I could see the 109 Building. It stood like a veritable beacon of fashion at the crotch of a Y-shaped intersection: Dogenzaka on one side and the road leading to the Tokyu Department Store shopping arcade on the other. Throngs of people poured through the streets on both sides of the building. I pushed myself past young men scoping out the girls in their midst and clawed my way through clumps of office ladies engrossed in shopping. Finally I reached the restroom on the basement floor. The room was teeming with young women, but I staked out a place for myself in front of one of the mirrors and began coating my face with makeup. I painted my eyelids with blue eyeshadow and slathered lipstick that was even redder than usual on my lips. The pièce de resistance, of course, was the black wig that I had tucked away in my shoulder bag. My transformation was complete. Yuri-san stood before the mirror, hotel call girl par excellence, ready to take on the night. While I stared at the change in myself, I felt my heart throb with confidence. I don't need that stinking agency. I'll handle my own business.

I felt the same sense of accomplishment and triumph I'd felt earlier, when Yoshizaki had affirmed my value. Now I was ready to acknowledge my own worth, to set my own price. The time had come for me to take charge. No firm, no agency, no escort dispatcher. I was going to stand on my own two feet, and I was going to start by standing in front of that Jizō statue. There I would be able to be myself, to be free. I wondered why I had earlier felt sorry for the Marlboro Hag. She was a woman to be respected, a woman among women after all.

I headed back up Dogenzaka, the long hair of my wig swinging from side to side with each step I took. I passed by the row of love hotels and headed to the statue of Jizō. Benevolent bodhisattva, Jizō pledged to ease the suffering and shorten the sentences of those serving time in hell. In the pale light filtering down over the dark streets I could see the Marlboro Hag standing in front of the statue waiting for a man. She was smoking a cigarette. The Jizō statue wore a benignly sweet, gentle expression and stood on a triangular patch of land facing an old Japanese restaurant. The area in front of the statue glistened slightly from all the water that had been poured over it in supplication. That is where I would stand.

"How's it going?" I called out to the Hag.

She glared at me suspiciously, the cigarette dangling from the corner of her mouth. But in contrast to her demeanor, she spoke with a stilted politeness. Gone was the earlier abusiveness she had once used to drive me away.

"What do you want? I don't do women, you know."

"How's business?"

The Marlboro Hag looked back at the Jizō statue. It looked as if she and the statue were in cahoots, as if she had to consult it before she answered.

"Business, you say? It's the same as always."

When she turned to look behind her, the skin on her neck wrinkled like crepe fabric. As dark as it was, her wrinkles were still visible. She was wearing a flossy chestnut-colored wig. Her body was short and stocky and so decrepit it was pathetic. There was no doubt in my mind that I surpassed her with my youth and my slim physique. I felt flushed with a sense of superiority. The Marlboro Hag returned my gaze and looked me over from head to foot.

"I thought I would give it a try."

"Humph!" The Marlboro Hag gave a short snort and laughed. Then she turned to the Jizō statue and said, "Well, only Jizō knows whether you'll succeed or fail. Isn't that right?"

I made up my mind to state my business straightaway. I'd tell her I'd decided that from tonight on I'd be standing here, so she could just move herself somewhere else.

"I'd like you to give this spot to me now."

The old woman tossed her cigarette down angrily. When she spoke she sounded like a different person.

"What? You think I'm going to give you my spot?"

"Well, everyone gets replaced at some point; that's just the way life is. Besides, you're not really active anymore, are you?" I shrugged my shoulders. "It's time for you to retire, don't you think?"

"Oh, I see, and you think you're here to give me notice? But I still have a whole host of customers who expect to find me right where I am."

The Marlboro Hag was bluffing. The black bra wasn't the only thing you could see through her flimsy jacket. You could also see the sagging skin on her chest. It was crystal clear that the person to whom that chest belonged had to be nearing seventy.

"Well, I don't see any customers now," I said, as I pointed to the empty streets. It was already close to eight o'clock and no one was around. A young man wearing a white kitchen uniform stepped out of the sushi shop across the way. He glanced over at us with disgust and looked as if he were going to say something, but when the Marlboro Hag waved at him he made a face and pursed his lips. He pulled a hose out from the side of the shop and began watering the plants out front and washing the pavement.

"You don't know shit, you know. Customers will be by before long, you'll see."

I pulled the carton of Castor Milds out of my bag and handed them to her. "Look, I'll give these cigarettes to you if you'll leave and let me have the spot."

The Marlboro Hag lifted her heavily mascaraed eyes and stared at the cigarettes. Then she grew angry. "Don't fuck with me, girlie. You can't buy me off with a lousy carton of cigarettes. I'm a hot item around here, okay? I've got a body men will pay to see. I've got something you don't have. Do you want to look? I don't care if you want to or not, I'm going to show you anyway."

The Marlboro Hag yanked the zipper down on her jacket exposing her black bra and fetid flesh. In the next instant she grabbed me by the wrist, forcing my hand up to her breasts. I fought her off, but the Marlboro Hag was much stronger than I had expected. Too strong for me, anyway.

"Stop!"

"No, I won't stop. I told you I was going to show you and that's what I'm going to do. Here, touch me."

The Marlboro Hag pressed my hand up under the right side of her bra. I stared into her eyes in horror. Instead of a saggy breast she had just a ball of tattered cloth. She pushed my hand over to the left side of her chest, and there I found the softness I had expected to find—warm springy flesh that squished through my fingers as if trying to escape when I squeezed down.

"Now do you understand? I've got no right breast. I lost it ten years ago to cancer. And I've been standing here ever since. In the beginning I was nervous, ashamed. I figured I wasn't complete anymore as a woman. But among my customers I had more than a few who took a fancy to me because of what was missing. What do you think? Do you think it's strange? Do you get it? No, I doubt you do. How could you? But that's the way it works, this business. And so, no, I will not give you my spot. This is where men who want a one-breasted woman come. And come they do! You're too skinny anyway. You may be younger than me, still young enough to be a woman. It's too soon for you to be standing under the Jizō statue. Besides, you've still got too much stuff. If you think you can go me one better, I'd like you to show me what *you* don't have."

The Marlboro Hag spoke like she'd won that round. I pulled out my corporate ID.

"Yeah, well, take a look at this."

"What's that?"

"My corporate ID card."

"I can't read it without my glasses." Even so, the Marlboro Hag took the card in her hand and squinted. "What's it say?"

"It says: Kazue Satō, Assistant Manager, Research Office, G Architecture and Engineering Corporation. That's me."

"Well, isn't that something? It's a first-rate firm, isn't it? But if you're really one of the managers, why the hell do you want to horn in on my business? Besides, I asked you to show me something you *don't* have. I'll bet you're proud of this."

"I'm not proud. I just don't know what else to show you."

I really didn't know. Somehow I couldn't articulate how my school-age goals, my current pride, and the firm that should have been the source of my identity had something in common with her missing breast. But it did seem that the thing we are most proud of and the thing we are most ashamed of are but the front and back of the same coin. They torture and thrill all at once.

The Marlboro Hag lit a cigarette. A man was heading in our direction. He had on a gray suit, white shirt, and black shoes. Looked like an office worker from the sticks. Even his eyebrows were droopy.

"Let's make a wager," I said. "The one who can get that man to buy her gets to stand here."

"Fine, but he's one of my regulars."

The Marlboro Hag smiled like she had gotten the best of me.

"Hey!" the man called out to her. No one ever came by this way, so any woman waiting there was an easy buy. It was stupid. But even so it looked like the Marlboro Hag had a surprising number of regulars. That's why I was determined to win her spot.

"Mr. Eguchi," the Marlboro Hag called to the man.

"How're you doing tonight?" The man called Eguchi looked at me without smiling. Determined not to lose, I propositioned him.

"Want to fool around?"

"Who's this?"

"A new kid. I didn't have the heart to chase her away," the Marlboro Hag answered, as she straightened her wig.

"Mr. Eguchi, how about it?" I went on.

Eguchi knitted his droopy eyebrows and thought it over. He looked like he was in his late fifties. The Marlboro Hag thought she had the contest sewn up. She laughed and said, "She really is pushy."

"I'll give you a discount," I blurted out, without even thinking.

Eguchi responded immediately. "In that case, I'll buy you."

The Marlboro Hag picked up her shoulder bag and frowned.

"You're really a cold bastard, Eguchi. She doesn't have what I have, you know."

"Well, a change does everybody good now and then."

I felt triumphant. I handed the Hag the carton of cigarettes. She took it with a look of resignation, but then a smile washed over her face. This annoyed me.

"What's so funny?"

"Oh, nothing. But you'll see, sooner or later," she mumbled to herself.

Well, you should know; it's time for you to retire, you old bitch, I grumbled in my heart. Ha! I won!

"Feel free to stay here until I get back," I said cavalierly, as I linked my arm in Eguchi's. His arm was thick for his age and muscular.

"That place'll be good. It's cheap."

Eguchi pointed to the hotel where I'd gone earlier with Arai. It was the cheapest love hotel in the area. It seemed Eguchi knew his way around.

"How long have you been standing on corners?"

"Since tonight. I've taken over the Marlboro Hag's turf, so I hope to keep your patronage."

"Well, you work fast. What's your name?"

"Yuri."

We continued to chat as we stepped into the tiny elevator. Eguchi's eyes were full of curiosity as he looked at me. Eguchi, Yoshizaki, Arai— they were all the same. And now they were my regulars. I felt my mood grow buoyant, realizing I was doing pretty well in the business.

We went in the same room Arai and I had used. It had just been a few days ago, but I ran the water in the bath as if I'd never been there before and took out two glasses. Then I pulled a bottle of beer out of the mini-bar and opened it. Eguchi sat on the bed and watched what I was doing. He looked displeased.

"Don't bother with that now. Help me with my clothes."

"Yes, sir, right away."

I looked at Eguchi in surprise. He was angry and his face had turned red. I wondered if he was going to be a difficult customer. What if he were dangerous? I tried to remember the names of the men who had been listed in the hotel agency as troublemakers.

"Hurry up!" Eguchi shouted. I helped him out of his suit jacket, still reeling in shock. I wasn't used to doing it, and I didn't do a very good job. The smell of his cheap pomade was sickening. I folded his threadbare shirt and trousers on a hanger and hung them up. Once he was down to his baggy undershirt and his yellowed briefs, he pointed down at his feet.

"Hey, you forgot my socks!"

"Oh, sorry."

When I'd pulled off his socks, Eguchi stood there in his underwear with his arms crossed and his legs spread apart like he was the frigging King of Siam.

"Well, get a move on!"

When I looked up at him to see what it was he wanted, he slapped me hard on my cheek. Instinctively I tried to defend myself.

"Don't be so violent!"

"Shut up, bitch, and get your clothes off. I want you naked and standing on the bed."

He was a sadist. Was he into some kind of sick game? Just my luck to pick a sicko for a customer, I thought. I trembled as I took my clothes off. When I was completely naked I climbed up on the bed and stood there, terrified. When Eguchi barked his command, I thought my ears were deceiving me.

"Let me see you shit."

· 5 ·

DECEMBER 2
SHIBUYA: YY, ¥40,000
SHIBUYA: HOMELESS GUY(?) ¥8,000

Once I started standing in front of the Jizō statue, I was happy. Of course there were times when the cook at the restaurant across the way would throw water at me or passersby would hurl insults, but the sensation of actually making my way through the world on my own, with my own body, was something I never got to experience at my day job. And I was thrilled to be able to bank all the money I earned and not have someone else skimming off my profits. This, I believed, was precisely what it meant to be in business. No doubt about it, the Marlboro Hag had enjoyed it so much, she hadn't wanted to quit.

I really hadn't expected the old bag to relinquish her turf so readily.

After I left Eguchi that night I headed straight back to the Jizō statue. Eguchi had been such a disgusting sadist, I was certain the Marlboro Hag had tricked me into going off with him.

"What a pervert!" I exclaimed when I saw her. She was squatting down on the roadside like a child and drawing something with a rock. The sound the rock made dragging over the asphalt was like fingernails on a blackboard. She looked up when she heard me and laughed.

"So did ya do it?"

"I did, and I imagine I won't be permitted back in that hotel anytime soon!"

"Well, you're braver than I am," she said, as she got to her feet. "If you want my turf, you can have it." It all seemed a little too easy.

"Really?"

"Yeah, I've had enough. I can't keep up with Eguchi's demands. I think this means it's time for me to retire."

The next night the Marlboro Hag was not to be found in front of the Jizō statue. Such a smooth exit and such a stunning debut. It was all so laughable.

But even so, working the corner all night long was hard, and I was always exhausted the next day at the firm. The upshot was that I hardly did any real work. About all I did was clip interesting articles from the economics newspapers. I figured I could give them to Yoshizaki. Since I didn't have to pay for the photocopies, I copied all the articles and compiled them into scrapbooks. Soon I had enough to fill three notebooks. Other than that I wrote seductive letters, birthday cards, and other such notes, all the while pretending to be hard at work on my reports. Moreover, I made a habit of slipping out of the research office and taking naps in the empty conference room just as before. And since my own desk was covered in mountains of papers, I ate my lunch in the ladies' restroom. People in the office began to avoid me more and more. Once while I was in the elevator I overheard a woman whisper behind me, "I hear she's known as the office ghost." But I really didn't care what anyone else thought of me. I was only real at night. The hope of achieving a balance was now just a farce.

One day in December after I had met Yoshizaki and had holed up with him in a hotel, I was walking back to my spot in front of the Jizō statue when I pulled my wallet out of my shoulder bag and gave it an appraising squeeze. I was content. Yoshizaki gave me ¥30,000 each time we met, but tonight, after I gave him the scrapbook full of clippings that I had made him as a present, he gave me an extra ¥10,000. With a reaction like that, I was determined to continue clipping articles for him. That's when I noticed that a man was already standing in front of the Jizō.

"Hey, girlie."

He was wearing black pleated pants with a white bomber jacket. A lion was embroidered in gold thread on the front of the jacket. His hair was close-cropped. I picked up the pace, thinking I had a customer.

"Were you waiting for me?" I asked cheerily. "Want to fool around?"

"Fool around? With you?"

The man laughed derisively and ran his hands through his short hair.

"I don't charge that much."

"Just hold up a minute. You don't know who I am, do you?"

"What do you mean?"

The man thrust both hands into his pants pockets causing the front of his pants to swell up like a paper lantern.

"I'm with the Shōtō Organization that runs these parts. You're new, aren't you? We got word down at the office that there was a new girl in front of the Jizō, so I came by to check it out. How long have you been here?"

Once I realized he was a member of a yakuza gang who had come to extort money from me, I put up my guard and took a few steps back. But his whole demeanor and his manner of speech were surprisingly gentle.

"I've been here for two months. I took over from the Marlboro Hag."

"That old lady? She's dead, you know."

"No kidding? How'd she die?"

"I guess she was sick, wasn't she. It got so bad that she couldn't even stand here."

The man answered brusquely as if it were clearly no concern of his.

"But that's yesterday's news. What's more important is for you to think about counting on my organization for protection. It's dangerous out here for a woman alone. Why just the other day a hotel call girl was roughed up bad by her customer. He smashed her skull in. You look the wrong way at some of these fellows and they go ballistic. It's too dangerous for a woman without protection."

"Thanks, but I'm fine."

I clutched my bag, worried about my money, and shook my head.

"You think that now because you haven't seen what I've seen. But it just takes one bad customer and then it's too late. My organization will look out for you. And it'll only cost you fifty thousand yen a month. Cheap, don't you think?"

Fifty thousand yen? He had to be kidding! There was no way I'd agree to that.

"I'm very sorry, but I don't make enough to cover your fee. I can't afford to pay fifty thousand yen."

The yakuza looked me square in the face. I could tell he was trying to size me up, so I held his gaze. That made him laugh.

"All right then. Let's just see how it goes. I'll let you think it over. But you'll be hearing from me again."

"Got it."

The yakuza headed down the street toward Shinsen Station. I knew he'd be back. There had to be some way I could get out of this, I thought to myself, running my tongue over my lips. It shouldn't have surprised me that the yakuza would try to horn in on someone working alone. I assumed they were testing me. I pulled my notebook out and in the darkness tried to add up the money I'd made over the last two months. It came to about ¥50,000 a month. I certainly didn't want to see all that going to the yakuza. I was reluctant because I was still only halfway to meeting my goal of a hundred million yen.

"Hey, you! Are you in business or what?"

I was so engrossed in adding up my income that I failed to notice the man standing right in front of me. For a minute I thought the yakuza had come back with his buddies, and I looked around suspiciously. But the man standing in front of me was clearly a homeless person. He was around fifty with a blackish coat over a pair of gray uniform-type pants. He held two grimy-looking cloth bags and was pulling a rickety shopping cart.

"I'm in business." I hastily stashed my notebook in my bag.

"What happened to the old lady who used to be here?"

"She died. She was sick."

The homeless man gasped. "You're kidding! I miss coming by one time and then she's dead, just like that? She was a nice lady too. Real kind."

"Mister, were you one of the Marlboro Hag's customers? If so, I can take care of you."

"Really?"

"You're homeless, aren't you?"

The clothes the man was wearing were not as filthy as the stuff he was carting around. The man flinched when he heard my question and hung his head.

"Yeah. So what?"

"I don't mind."

Homeless or not, a customer was a customer. I nodded to him again in agreement and started to make arrangements. The man let out a sigh of relief and surveyed the area around him.

"The thing is, I don't have any money for a hotel, so the old lady would do me in an empty lot by the station."

An empty lot? This was a bit much, but if we could just get it over without a fuss I figured it wouldn't be too bad. So long as money changes hands, who cares where it happens?

"How much will you pay?"

"About eight thousand."

"How much did you pay the old woman?"

"Sometimes three thousand, sometimes five. But you're young. I'd feel bad if I didn't pay a bit more."

It was nice to hear someone call me young. I held up eight fingers, my spirits boosted.

"Okay, then. Eight it is."

We headed off toward Shinsen Station side by side. When we got to a level spot overlooking the station, about halfway up the hillside, there was an open lot. It looked like it had been cleared for a new building. Scaffolding had been set up and building materials lay in piles. It was as good a spot as any. I took off my trench coat in the shadow of the scaffolding. The homeless man set his bags off to the side and whispered in my ear.

"Let me do it from the back."

"Fine."

I handed the man a condom, turned around, placed my hands on the scaffolding, and tilted my hips up. "It's cold, so be quick about it."

The man slipped inside me. What kind of man was he? Where was he from? So long as I got paid, I didn't care one way or the other. My feelings were now that simple, that strong. It made me happy when I realized it. The man thrust himself into me insistently before finally finishing. I took the packet of tissues I'd gotten at Shibuya Station—compliments of the Takefuji Loan Company—and used them to clean myself. The man pulled up his pants and said, "Thanks. You're really nice. I appreciate that. I'll find you again when I have some money."

Then he pressed a wad of dirty bills in my hand. I smoothed the wrinkles out of the bills as I counted them; sure enough, there were eight of them. I watched the homeless man walk away from the empty lot and put the bills in my wallet. The used condom that he had thrown down in the trampled, withered grass was one I'd picked up in the hotel room I'd visited earlier with Yoshizaki. That's right, I'll trash the place, I'll run havoc through the streets; I'll do as I please! I looked up at the night sky—the cold, cold sky. The tree branches trembled but I felt exhilarated. I had never been so free or so happy. I could satisfy any demand a man might make of me. I was a good woman.

•

When I returned to the Jizō statue later that night I saw a woman standing on the turf I had rightfully inherited from the Marlboro Hag. To make matters worse, she was a foreigner. I was furious. But as soon as I got closer, I saw it was Yuriko. For her part, however, Yuriko had no idea who I was. She stared at me blankly, just as dim-witted as she had been in high school. I scrutinized her. How proud she had once been of her voluptuous breasts. Now her ample chest just looked shapeless, even matronly. The wrinkles at the edges of her eyes were deep and caked with foundation. To add insult to injury, the former beauty had a double chin. But there she was in a red leather coat, wearing a flashy silver ultra-miniskirt. I wanted to burst out laughing but somehow managed to control myself.

"Yuriko!"

Yuriko stared at me in amazement. She still hadn't figured out who I was. "Who are you?"

"Don't you remember?"

I've become such a spectacular woman, Yuriko doesn't recognize me. On the other hand, Yuriko looks hideous. It made me feel good. I had to laugh. A cold north wind was blowing. Yuriko looked chilled and clutched her skimpy leather coat to her chest. I wasn't fazed by cold winds or anything of the sort. After all, I'd just come back from taking care of business in an open field. I doubt you could do anything like that, you former beauty. Slut! Hell, you may have been born a whore, and you may still be turning tricks for all I know, but my God you're ugly now.

"Might we have met at a club somewhere?" Yuriko asked, in a prissy voice.

"Guess again. My, you've grown old. Look at the lines on your face! And all that flab! I hardly recognized you at first!"

Yuriko frowned and craned her neck to get a better look at me. The way she moved was still exactly the same. She was so used to being the center of attention that she had a regal way about her most mundane movements. She'd been so beautiful, so celebrated, that people naturally wanted to pick on her.

"When we were young we were like night and day, you and me. But just look at us now. We're not that different. I suppose you could say we're the same—or maybe it would be more accurate to put you a peg or two lower. What I'd give to show you to your friends now!"

Yuriko stared at me. Yes, in her eyes I could see the hatred she bore me. Eyes that understood every little thing around her, no matter how she tried to feign ignorance. I remembered Yuriko's older sister. Did she know how ugly Yuriko had grown? I wanted to call her up right away. She had a complex about Yuriko that she could never kick, so I imagined she was off now living a miserable life.

"You're Kazue Satō, aren't you?"

Yuriko finally saw through my disguise. She sounded like she was speaking down to me. Unable to check my anger, I gave her a sharp push. My hand sank immediately into her soft flesh.

"You got it! I'm Kazue. It took you long enough. This is my turf, you know. You can't be picking up johns here."

"Turf?"

What an idiot. She still hadn't figured out what I was doing there. I couldn't believe anyone could actually be that dense. Was it so hard to believe that I would be into prostitution?

"I'm a hooker."

"Why you, of all people?"

"Well, why you?"

My response seemed to startle Yuriko. She looked as if she were going to stumble, but I asked again.

"So, why do you do it?"

It was a moot question. Ever since she was in junior high school, Yuriko had made her way in the world by toying with men. A bimbo like Yuriko would not have been able to survive without men. I, on the other hand, was a clever girl who could have survived just fine without a man. And yet, here we both were—prostitutes—running into each other in front of the same Jizō statue. Two streams flowing in the same direction. I figured it had to be fate, and that made me happy.

Yuriko started to beg. "Do you think you could let me use this spot on the nights you're not here?"

Naturally it would be difficult for me to mind the shop here three hundred and sixty-five days a year. No matter how tenuous my existence at the firm was to become, it was not likely that I would ever actually quit. I needed the salary I earned there to support my mother. Besides, far better for Yuriko to borrow my turf occasionally than to have some woman I didn't know at all poaching it in my absence. And then there was always the question of the yakuzas. I was afraid they would keep hounding me to put up protection money. As I stared at Yuriko's corpulent body, I began to hatch a plan.

"You want me to let you use my corner?"

"Do you mind?"

"Well, under one condition." I grabbed Yuriko's arm. "I don't mind if you use the corner when I'm not here, but you have to dress like me, see?"

On the nights I couldn't come, Yuriko would stand in for me—as me. I thought it was brilliant.

· 6 ·

DECEMBER 3
SHIBUYA: SOME FOREIGNERS (?), ¥10,000

The day after I met Yuriko, we had a spell of balmy springlike weather. It's hard to pick up a customer while battling the freezing December winds;

frigid weather tends to chill romantic notions. It's much easier when the nights are warm and the customer is in high spirits. Seeing the good weather, I figured I'd have a good night. One of the interesting aspects of standing on the corner is seeing how the weather and the mood affect business. Every day it's different. When I worked for the hotel escort agency, I never had an opportunity to make observations like these.

I headed toward the Jizō statue in a good mood, humming a song. Once I got there I waited for Yuriko. I only half believed she'd show up. What on earth could she be thinking? I couldn't even imagine. When we were in high school she stood out from all the rest. She was so beautiful it was difficult even to approach her. And because she was always gazing off into space, clearly focused on nothing, she seemed even more inaccessible. I was always too intimidated to speak to her. It wasn't that she was absent-minded; she was a master of measuring the subtle differences between herself and others. If someone asked her a question, she'd answer. Otherwise, she kept her mouth clamped shut. That was Yuriko. And I despised the sober self-aware look in her eye. But our cool Yuriko grew ugly as she grew older. Fate chased her down and devoured her. Time has a way of leveling the playing field. As I grew older, I gained a sense of self-worth and superiority. Compared to the lonely impoverished Yuriko, I now had a great job at a great firm. I suppose the fact that I had once been a properly raised lady in a decent family had a lot to do with it. As I stood there thinking that, I wanted to burst out laughing. Decent family! What a joke. It was falling apart.

"Saint Jizō, I'm an entirely different person now. And I'm insanely happy!"

My face wreathed in smiles, I looked up at the Jizō, who was smiling quietly, as if to match my excitement. I fished through my purse for the shiniest ten-yen coin I could find, placed it in front of the statue, and brought my hands together in prayer.

"Saint Jizō, please give me four customers tonight. That's the goal I'm setting for myself. My mission is to meet my goal. Please do what you can to help me out."

Before I could even finish my prayer, two student types started walking toward me from Shinsen Station, speaking to each other in subdued tones. I turned back to Jizō. "Hey, quick work! Thanks a million."

The students noticed me standing there in the dark and looked over at me as if they'd seen a ghost. I called out to them, "Hey, fellas, would one of you like to party?" They looked bewildered and poked each other with their elbows.

"Come on. It'll be fun. Let's party."

The students were young. They looked at me in disgust, turned away, and ran. I recalled how people at work tried to avoid eye contact with me, as if they'd seen something disgusting. Even my mother, my younger sister, all they had to do was look at me and they'd cringe. It seemed that whoever looked at me could not help but recoil.

Was I completely out of bounds? I had no idea how I looked to others. I headed off in the direction the two boys had taken.

"Let's party our brains out. Come on. I'll do you both. We can go to a hotel and I'll do you both for fifteen thousand yen. What do you say?"

The two were speechless. They practically started running when they saw me behind them. But I can't let my prey get away! And then, at that instant, I heard someone call out, "Try me. I'll do you each, one by one."

I couldn't believe it. The woman on the street ahead of me, with her arms stretched out wide, was done up exactly like me. She tried to block the boys from going past her. The boys, completely taken aback, came to a halt.

"I'll give you a better deal—five thousand yen each."

Her black wig fell to her waist. She had a Burberry trench coat like mine, black high heels, and a brown shoulder bag. She'd painted her lids with thick blue eye shadow, and her lips were bright red. It was Yuriko. The boys, now completely panicked, ran past her. She looked back after them and then turned around and shrugged.

"They got away."

"Well, of course, you terrified them."

I was angry, but Yuriko didn't seem to care. "Don't sweat it. The night is young. What do you think, Kazue? Do I look like you?"

Yuriko opened her trench coat. Underneath she was wearing a cheap blue suit. It resembled the one I wore. I stared at the thick layer of white foundation Yuriko wore. She looked like a clown. It was hideous. Is that what I look like? I was furious.

"Do you think I look like that?"

"You do, Kazue. You look like a monster."

"Well, whatever happened to the beautiful half you used to be? You're fat and ugly now."

Yuriko smiled scornfully, her lips curling up the way foreigners' mouths do.

"Laugh all you want but you're no better."

"What do you mean, I'm no better?" I asked. "Don't I look like a businesswoman?"

Yuriko turned an unfocused gaze on me and snorted. "No. I don't see it. You don't look like a businesswoman or even a young woman. In fact, you don't even look like a middle-aged woman. All you look like is a monster. M-o-n-s-t-e-r."

I stared at Yuriko, my mirror image. Both of us were monsters.

"Well, if I'm a monster, you're one too, Yuriko."

"Yeah, I suppose so. A pair of whores standing around in the same outfits must be terrifying. But you know, there are men in this world who like monsters. It's weird when you think about it. On the other hand, I suppose you could say it's men who made us into monsters. Kazue, when is it okay for me to stand here? If it's going to be a problem I'll go over and stand in front of Shinsen Station."

"Absolutely not," I said, in no uncertain terms. "Shinsen Station's included in my turf. I inherited the area from the Marlboro Hag, and if you don't follow my instructions I won't share any of it with you."

"The Marlboro Hag?" Yuriko asked, looking up at the Jizō statue, clearly with little interest in the question.

"That's the old woman who used to work this area. She died right after she retired."

Yuriko smirked. Her teeth were stained yellow from cigarettes.

"What a shitty way to go. I suspect I'll be killed by a john. Probably you too, Kazue. That's the way it goes when you're on the prowl. The minute a man turns up who likes monsters, you can be sure he'll be the one who'll do us in, you and me."

"Why the hell do you think that? You've got to have a more positive attitude!"

"I don't think my attitude is negative." Yuriko shook her head in denial. "After whoring for twenty years, I've come to know men for what they really are. Or wait. Perhaps I should say I know who *we* really are. At heart, a man truly hates a woman who sells her body. And any woman who sells her body hates the men who pay her for it. You get two people together with all that hate, somebody's going to kill someone before too long. I'm just waiting for my day to come. When it does, I don't plan to fight. I'm just going to let myself be killed."

I wondered if Yoshizaki and Arai hated me. What about the sadist Eguchi? I couldn't understand Yuriko's perspective. Had she seen into the future? Had she looked at the hell that lay ahead of her? It was different for me, wasn't it? I frequently enjoyed selling my body, though it was true that there were times when it was little more than a miserable moneymaking scheme.

The neon lights over the love hotel were flickering. At that instant Yuriko's profile floated in the dark like some kind of heavenly visage. I was reminded again of the ethereal beauty she possessed in high school. It was as if I'd slipped back in time.

"Yuriko, do you really hate men? I always thought you liked men so much you could never get enough of them."

Yuriko turned back to look at me. When I saw her face straight on, she looked like a dumpy middle-aged woman again.

"I hate men, but I love sex. It's the opposite for you, isn't it, Kazue?"

I wonder. Do I love men and hate sex? Do I walk the streets just so I can get close to men? That's the wrong way of going about it. Yuriko's question shocked me.

"If you and I became one, we'd be perfect. We'd be able to live the ultimate life. But on the other hand, if it's the perfect life you want, best not to be born a woman."

"So, Kazue? When are you going to let me work your corner?"

"Come after I've gone home. I always take the last train to Fujimi-gaoka at twelve-twenty-eight. If you want to come by after I've left, that's fine with me. You can stand the rest of the night if you want."

"You are too kind. Thank you so very much," Yuriko said sarcastically.

She walked off toward Shinsen Station, the hem of her coat flapping in the breeze. I looked up at the Jizō statue in irritation. I felt Yuriko had soiled me and the ground I stood on with her presence.

"Saint Jizō, am I a monster? How was it that I became this monster? Please teach me, I pray."

Of course, the Jizō does not speak. I looked up into the night sky. The neon signs along Dogenzaka had dyed the sky pink. I could hear the sound of the wind rushing high above my head. It was growing colder by the minute. Seeing the tips of the treetops shivering brought an end

I detected a glint of derision in the man's eyes. I fished my corporate ID out of my purse.

"Well, then, let me set the record straight. I'm employed as a staff member at one of the biggest firms in the nation. I graduated from Q University, so you know I have to be intelligent."

The man walked over to a streetlamp and studied my ID card. After he pored over it, nodding as he did so, he brought it back.

"I'm impressed. The next time you try to pick up a customer you should show him your ID. I'll bet a lot of men would be drawn to a woman who's employed at such a distinguished firm."

"I do show them."

When the man heard my response he laughed, flashing his white teeth. The way he laughed took my heart away. I hardly ever saw men laugh like that, and I found myself drawn to him. I enjoy it when men make a fuss over me—especially men who are my superiors. It was like this with my father. It was the same when I first joined the firm. All my superiors there treated me to praise and I loved it. And now here I was, wrapped in nostalgia. I peered up into the man's face and said in a little-girl voice, "Did I say something funny? Why are you laughing?"

"God, you're so cute. I thought you were doing this to raise your value. But things aren't what they seem, are they?"

I could not understand what he was trying to say. There were men out there, like Yoshizaki, who got off on the fact that I was a graduate of Q University and an employee at a top-rate firm. And that's why I made a habit of showing my ID card to all potential customers. So what was this guy going on about?

"Why do you say things aren't what they seem?"

"Forget it."

He brushed my question aside and turned to leave.

"Hey, wait. Where'd you like to do it? I'll do it wherever you want. I'll even do it outside, if you want."

The man waved for me to follow and I rushed after him awkwardly. I was willing to do it for ¥8,000 and do it anywhere. I didn't want this man to get away. I'm not sure I understood why. The man turned left at a dark intersection and followed the road that dipped down before ending at Shinsen Station. I wondered if he was taking me to his room. I could feel the damp night air on my cheeks as I followed him, full of nervous excitement. The man turned down a narrow road in front of Shinsen Station, walked about three hundred feet, and stopped in front of a four-story apartment building. The building was old and the entry hall looked as if it hadn't been cleaned in ages. Torn newspapers and empty cans lay scattered about. But it was close to the station and the individual units themselves didn't seem particularly small.

"You live in a nice place. Which room do you rent?" I asked.

The man pressed his finger to his lips, signaling for me not to speak. Then he headed up the stairs. There was no elevator, and the stairs were strewn with garbage.

"What floor are we going to?"

"I've got friends staying in my apartment, so we can't go there," the man muttered, in a low voice. "So I thought we'd go to the roof. Okay?"

"I don't mind. It's warm tonight."

I was going to do it outside again after all. Being in the open air had its advantages. But it also seemed so dirty, like going to the bathroom in the woods. My feeling of freedom did not really overcome the filthiness. I climbed the stairs in a state of confusion. The flight of stairs from the fourth floor to the roof was littered with all kinds of stuff, as if someone had dumped the contents of their dresser drawers there. There were sake bottles, cassette tapes, stationery, photographs, sheets, torn T-shirts, and English-language paperbacks. The man picked his way through the junk, kicking it to the side as we went. I glanced at one of the photographs that he kicked aside. It was a picture of a white man surrounded by young Japanese men and women. They were all smiling. There were other photographs of this man too.

"That's a Canadian language teacher. He defaulted on his rent and ended up living on the roof for a couple of months. He said he didn't need this stuff so he just left it behind. It's all garbage."

"Photographs and letters are garbage? A Japanese person would never throw away a letter someone had sent him or pictures of himself."

I could hear the man laugh in the darkness.

"If you don't need it anymore, it's garbage." He turned back to look at me. "I suppose Japanese people don't like to see this kind of thing. But as a foreign laborer myself, let me tell you that I'd like to forget all about Japan. I'd leave it as a big empty gap in my life if I could. It wouldn't bother me. The most important things are in our home country."

"I suppose it's nice to have a home country."

"It is."

"Are you Chinese? What's your name?"

"I'm Zhang. My father was a government official from Beijing, but he lost everything in the Cultural Revolution. I got sent down to a small commune in Heilongjiang Province. Once I got there, I'd get picked on if I even mentioned my father's name."

"So I guess you were a member of the intelligentsia."

"No. I was a smart kid, but I was always prevented from advancing my education. Someone like you wouldn't be able to understand."

Zhang offered me his hand. I grabbed it and he helped me onto the trash-strewn roof. It was surrounded by a concrete wall about three feet high, and in one corner a refrigerator stood alongside a mattress—just as if it were a room without walls or ceiling. The mattress was soiled and torn in places so that the springs showed through. There was a rusty toaster oven and a suitcase with a smashed lid. I looked over the wall at the street below. There wasn't a person in sight, but the cars whizzed past at an immoderate speed. I could hear a man and a woman talking in one of the second-floor apartments of the building next door. I saw a train on the Inokashira Line bound for Shibuya pull into Shinsen Station.

"No one can see, so let's do it here," Zhang said. "Please take off your clothes."

"All of them?"

"Of course. I want to see what you look like naked."

Zhang crossed his arms and sat on a corner of the filthy mattress. With little choice I stripped until I was completely naked. While I stood there shivering with cold, Zhang shook his head, "I'm sorry to have to tell you this, but you're too skinny. A skinny body like yours just doesn't turn me on. I'm not going to pay you eight thousand yen."

I yanked my Burberry coat over my shoulders, furious.

"How much will you pay?"

"Five thousand yen."

"Okay then, five thousand."

When he heard me agree, Zhang asked incredulously, "Why? I don't believe it!"

"Well, you're the one setting the price here."

"I'm negotiating. You give in too easily. I guess that's what you've always done. But in China you wouldn't last a day. Lucky for you you were born in Japan. My little sister wouldn't have let me get away with a bargain like this."

I couldn't figure out what Zhang was trying to say and was just about at my wits' end. It was freezing. A cold north wind had come up, and there was no trace of the earlier warm night air. I stared down at the torn blanket covering the mattress and said nothing. Zhang began to grow impatient as well.

"So? What's it going to be?"

"You decide. I only try to please the customer."

"Aren't you in this for the business? I can't believe you're so lacking in ambition. You are really an unattractive woman, you know. I'll bet you aren't any better at your other workplace either. Japanese people are all the same. If you had a little more individuality, you might be a better prostitute. You would, wouldn't you?"

What a pain in the ass he was turning out to be. I had an easier time figuring out Eguchi and his disgusting demands. I began to collect my clothes.

"What are you doing? Did I tell you you could put your clothes back on?" Zhang asked, bemused. He drew closer to me.

"Well, you're being difficult, and I really don't feel like standing here listening to your lectures."

"You look the type who would like lectures."

Zhang grabbed me tightly and I leaned into him. His leather coat was cool against my bare skin.

"Hurry up and take off your clothes."

"I'm not undressing. I want you to suck me off just like this."

I got down on my knees and pulled the zipper on Zhang's jeans. He pulled his dick out from his shorts and pushed it into my mouth. He rambled away while he had me suck him.

"You're really a submissive girl. You do everything I tell you to do, since I'm your customer. I wonder why that is. I don't know much about Q University, but I imagine it's one of the more prestigious institutions in Japan. In China, girls who graduate from university wouldn't dare do what you're doing. All they can think about is their own career—making it to the top. It looks like you've given up on your career. I guess you got tired of being submissive at work, so instead you submit to men you've never met. Am I wrong? You know, men don't really like women who are submissive. My little sister was extremely attractive. Her name was Mei-kun. She's dead now, but I really respected her. I loved her. No matter how difficult things became or how she had to struggle, she always fought her way to the top. She was always looking for the next challenge. I hate a woman who looks back. I could never love a woman like you. That's what lets me treat you like this."

Zhang gradually grew more excited as he talked. I took my mouth off his penis and quickly fumbled through my purse for a condom. Zhang was still sitting on the mattress. He drew me closer and started kissing me roughly. I was startled. I'd never been embraced that way by a customer. Zhang started to move his hips on top of me and I felt a change taking place inside me that I had never experienced before. What was happening? I was burning. All this time I had been faking orgasms and now I was finally having the real thing? It wasn't possible! Oh, God! I clung to Zhang's leather jacket.

"Oh, God, save me!"

Startled by my cry, Zhang looked up and stared into my face. And then he came. I held my breath and clung to him, trying to draw him closer, but he quickly pulled away.

"Why did you say *save me* just now?" Zhang asked, with an earnest expression. "I held you just now as if you were my little sister; that's why it made you feel good, isn't it? I think you should thank me."

Was he still haggling over the price? I was panting so hard I could hardly focus. When I came to my senses, I realized that my wig had slipped off and Zhang was playing with it.

"My little sister had long hair too. About like this. Poor thing, she fell into the ocean, and I watched her die."

Zhang's face had grown dark.

"Mr. Zhang, I'll be glad to listen to your story, but that'll bring the price back up to eight thousand yen."

Zhang raised his head. He looked irritated, as if I had interrupted his thoughts.

"Well, that doesn't surprise me. You have to devote all your energy to selling your body. No wonder you aren't much interested in what your customers have to say. All you can think about is yourself." He spat these words out angrily and stood up to leave.

A northern wind had suddenly come up, swirling the trash on the rooftop. Zhang hooked the zipper on his jacket, which fell to about his waist, and pulled it up to his chin with a harsh yank. I wanted to give him a piece of my mind but hesitated because I didn't want to get into a big argument before I'd gotten my money. But it was so typical of a foreigner. So typical of a man to be insensitive to my distress. I hurled all kind of expletives at Zhang—silently. But what irked me most was the fact that this was the first time I had ever really enjoyed sex, and yet he pushed me away so coldly. Was it the completely indifferent way he treated me that had turned me on? As for my own distress, what exactly did I have to be distressed about?

With utter seriousness, I told Zhang, "I'll have you know that not all my clients patronize me just for sex. One is a university professor who enjoys conversing with me on a variety of subjects. We discuss his current research projects and he keeps me informed of their progress. Our relationship extends into the academic. And there are others as well. Another is deputy chief of operations for a chemical manufacturer. He tells me about the difficulties that go on in his company, and I give him advice on how to deal with it. He's always very grateful. So, you see, I do listen to my clients. But those are men who take me to hotels and pay me a proper fee. And furthermore, they are all intelligent men who are able to carry on substantive conversations."

I couldn't tell if Zhang had heard anything I'd said. He looked bored and scratched listlessly at the edge of his mouth. The wind blew his hair back off his face and I could see he had a receding hairline. Go figure: a handsome enough face but balding! I began to grow bitter over the fact that I'd been coerced into doing my business atop this windblown garbage dump of a roof. I threw the used condom against the rough concrete surface of the rooftop and watched as Zhang's semen splashed out.

"Just going to toss it away like trash, huh?" Zhang asked, when he saw what I'd done with the condom. A twinge of emotion leaked through his words.

I laughed.

"Didn't you just say you wanted to forget all about Japan and everything that's happened here?" I asked. "You're going to have no trouble tossing me aside just like the trash on the stairs back there."

Zhang turned back to look at me but said nothing. He opened the door to the staircase, and I could see a dull orange glow. The entrance to the trash-strewn stairway looked like the mouth to a dark cave. I continued my assault.

"While we were in the midst of things back there, you kept talking about your sister. Are you into *hentai,* some kind of perversion? Isn't that off limits?"

"Why?" Zhang glanced up in surprise. "What's wrong with it?"

"What's wrong with it? It sounds like you were having sex with your sister. That's incest! And if you weren't actually doing it, it seems like you wanted to, didn't you? I mean, isn't that bestial?"

"Bestial?" Zhang shook his head. "No, it's beautiful. We might have been brother and sister, but we were also like husband and wife. What relationship could be more intimate than that? We'd been together our entire lives. When my sister came to Japan, she betrayed me. She decided she'd come first, and she tricked me so she could get away. But I used every resource I had and tracked her down. I think her drowning at sea was an act of fate. I stuck out my hand to try to save her but I couldn't reach her. Maybe I didn't want to reach her; I've thought about that. I feel sorry for her now, but at the time I thought she got what was coming to her. Do you think I'm a devil? What would that make a whore like you?"

I had no idea how to respond. This man had let his sister die—but then, that wasn't any business of mine. I belted my trench coat around my waist and used the tissue I'd gotten at the station to blot my lipstick. I looked over toward the hills of Maruyama-chō. Surrounded by these hills, Shinsen Station looked like it was down in the bottom of a valley— and my own feeling was bottoming out as well. I wanted to get back to the lights of Dogenzaka. I had the sneaking suspicion that Yuriko was staking out my turf in front of the Jizō statue, and the idea was making me nervous. I wanted to get paid and be on my way. I stole a glance at Zhang, but he looked as if he were going to keep talking forever. He took out a cheap lighter and lit up a cigarette.

"Do you have any brothers or sisters?" he asked.

I nodded, an image of my younger sister's dour face floating up before me.

"Yes, I have a younger sister."

"What's she like?"

She's a nose-to-the-grindstone sort who works for a manufacturing firm. She leaves the house every morning at seven-thirty and she's back at six every night, like clockwork, after stopping first at the grocery store on her way home. She's very simple. She carries her lunch to work and is able to save over a hundred thousand yen of her salary every month. Talk about frugal! I've hated her ever since we were children. She was always back in the shadows, silently watching my successes and failures, determined not to follow in my footsteps. She was a sensible girl. She went to college with money I provided, and she and my mother are now much too fine for me! I thought all this but of course I didn't say it aloud.

Zhang looked over at me.

"Have you ever wished that your younger sister was dead?" he asked.

"The thought never leaves my mind. But there are other people I'd like to see dead as well!"

"Like who?" Zhang was absolutely earnest.

Who would I like to see dead? My mother, Kamei, the office manager—lots and lots of people, I thought. So many I can't even remember their faces now, let alone their names. I don't really like anyone. And I've never been loved by anyone, I suddenly realized. I simply ply the waters of the night on my own. I could well imagine the way Zhang's younger sister looked as she lifted her hand above the surface of the dark sea. Stretching, stretching for help. I wasn't like Zhang's sister. I wasn't asking for help. I would tread the frozen waters of this sealike city until my hands and feet were too numb to move. Drifting down, down, until my lungs collapsed under the pressure of the water, I would let the waves carry me away. There was no better sensation than this! Feeling liberated, I gave a big stretch. Zhang flicked his cigarette butt away.

"So who's the most revolting customer you've had?"

I thought immediately of Eguchi. "I had a customer who wanted to watch me shit."

Zhang's eyes flashed. "So what did you do?"

"I did it. I knew he was deadly serious, which literally scared the shit out of me!"

"Well, then, I guess you'll do anything, huh?"

"Probably."

"You're badder than me, that's for sure. I've done a lot of things in my time; I was the gigolo for a famous woman once. But you take the cake."

Zhang took a neatly folded ¥10,000 bill out of his pocket and handed it to me. I took ¥2,000 out of my wallet and offered it to him as change, but he pressed it back in my hand.

"Do you want your change? Or are you giving me ten thousand yen?"

"No, I'm not going to give it to you. We made a deal. I want you to earn the ¥2,000."

Zhang murmured this, his mouth next to my ear. I hurriedly put the thousand yen notes back in my purse.

"What do you mean by earn it?"

"My room is right below where we are. I have a friend there. He doesn't have a girlfriend and is really lonely. He's always complaining about it. Kind of pathetic, huh? I'd like you to help him out, okay? Do him as an add-on. He's a friend, so I'd like to treat him."

"It'll take more than two thousand yen."

I flashed Zhang a disgusted look. But I was freezing up on the roof and the idea of thawing out in his room was appealing. Besides, I had to use the bathroom.

Zhang looked at me slyly. "Please. It won't take long. And he'll wear one of those so there'll be no danger." He pointed at the condom I'd thrown down earlier.

"Can I use your bathroom?"

"Help yourself."

I followed Zhang down the stairs. He stopped in front of the apartment on the corner of the fourth floor. The paint on the front door was chipping, and all kinds of empty liquor bottles and beer bottles were lined up beside it. You could tell at a glance that the apartment was occupied by messy men. Zhang turned the key in the lock and stepped in ahead of me. The smell of greasy hamburgers and male body odor wafted out. The narrow entryway was cluttered with dirty shoes and sneakers with the backs flattened to look like slip-ons.

"They're young, not neat like me." Zhang laughed as he tried to explain the untidiness. "I make my own meals. But young people today, they just eat McDonald's!"

"Your friend is young?"

If he were young he'd make lots of demands. Since I usually only deal with older men, I felt a small spark of excitement—along with a touch of fear—at the prospect of doing a young man. Zhang gave me a shove and I stepped into the entryway.

"There's a young one and then another who's about my age."

Two men? I was taken aback. And then at that instant I heard a conversation in Chinese. The sliding door opened and a man wearing a black shirt and an equally black expression stuck his head out. He looked to be Zhang's age. His long hair was unkempt, jet-black, and lusterless. His shirt was open at the front.

"This guy is called Dragon."

Is he the one I'm supposed to do? I wondered. I smiled at him sweetly.

"Good evening," I said.

"Who're you, a friend of Zhang's?"

"That's right. It's nice to meet you."

I caught Dragon and Zhang exchanging glances and felt my guard go up. I tried to look as far back in the apartment as I could. There wasn't much to it. It consisted of a six-mat room and a three-mat area, attached to which was a tiny kitchen and bath. How many men are bunking down here? I wondered. It's hardly big enough for one! Zhang said he wanted me to do his friend, so I assumed he meant Dragon.

"Take your shoes off and go on in."

Zhang bent over as if to help me out of my shoes, but I took them off just fine on my own. I lined my high heels up neatly in the filthy tangle of men's shoes. How long had it been since they'd bothered to clean? I wondered. The seams of the tatami were thick with grime and dust, the filth of another world.

That's when I saw another man sitting in the corner by the sliding door that partitioned off the rooms. When he realized that I was looking at him, the man raised his sparse eyebrows, but his expression hardly changed at all. He was wearing a gray warm-up suit and glasses.

"That's Chen-yi. He's got a part-time job at a pachinko parlor in Shinkoiwa."

"What do you do, Dragon?" I asked.

"Oh, a little of this and a little of that. Not something you can easily sum up in one word."

Dragon was not very forthcoming. From the way he answered, I could surmise that he was involved in some kind of suspicious activity. Dragon stared at me fixedly, shifting his eyes only to exchange glances with Chen-yi.

"Who is it you want me to do? You with your measly two thousand yen."

Standing defiantly with my hands on my hips, feet planted firmly on the tatami matting, I got down to business. It was nice being in the warm apartment, but I wanted to find out who I was doing and where we were supposed to do it. Though apparently it wasn't going to be that easy.

"Well, who do you want to do first, Dragon or Chen-yi?"

"Wait a minute. I'm not doing two for two thousand yen. That's outrageous."

"You said yes." Zhang grabbed me by the arms. "You never asked how many, did you. So I figured you understood. You can't go now, you'll go back on your word."

With little choice, I pointed at Chen-yi. Young and seemingly reticent, Chen-yi was far preferable to the spooky-looking Dragon.

"No way!" Dragon interrupted. "We go according to age. That's the Chinese custom. Zhang is first."

"I just did him. He doesn't need a turn," I shouted. Zhang laughed caustically and barked some kind of order to Dragon in Chinese. Zhang in turn said something to Chen-yi. I was getting angry.

"What are you talking about?"

"We're just wondering if we'd rather do it one at a time or all at once."

"You're out of your mind!" I screamed. "It's one by one or not at all."

"But you said it yourself, didn't you? You said you'd do anything. You were pretty cool about it, weren't you? I think you'll enjoy doing what we ask."

Chen-yi stood up and came toward me, and Dragon made a be-my-guest gesture. Then he said something to me in Chinese that I didn't understand.

"Dragon says you're too skinny—not much of a lay—but it's been over half a year since he's had a woman, so you'll do."

"That's going too far!"

"Too far, is it?" Zhang laughed. "Ever since we came to your country that's the kind of thing we hear. We're constantly having our value appraised. 'He's bright' or 'he's strong' or 'he's shrewd' or 'he's a hard worker.' People evaluate us like they'd rate animals. Surely it's the same for you. You're in the business of selling your body, so you ought to be used to people sizing you up before they settle on a price. I bet you do what you do because you like it. Am I wrong?"

I was going to protest but Dragon began to tear at my coat. He knocked me down on the tatami. His violence caused my blue suit jacket to rise up around my chest; then Dragon started trying to push up my skirt. I was being accosted right there while Zhang and Chen-yi watched. That was a first for me. I was trash, the cheapest prostitute a man could have. I squeezed my eyes tight.

"Look at me! It'll turn you on!" Zhang shouted gleefully.

I opened my eyes reluctantly and saw Zhang's white socks and Chen-yi's bare feet.

•

The one named Dragon had not taken a bath in weeks. He reeked. It was all I could do not to throw up, just guiding him into place. Instinctively, I covered my nose with my hand. Dragon didn't seem to notice or else he didn't care. He was too busy flailing about on top of me. I squeezed my eyes shut, held my nose, and lay there as cold as a stone Jizō. That's the way it always was. I never felt a thing. I would lie there while a man stuck his thing in me and all I had to do was be patient. It wouldn't take long. And that was it. Sometimes I would put on a little act of my own. But there was no need for that here.

I knew Zhang and Chen-yi were right there watching, but by then I didn't really care. If I hadn't gotten excited, like Zhang said, then I would not be embarrassed or even angry about doing it in front of them. But to do two men for two thousand yen? I did the math in my head. There was clearly no profit in it, only loss. Then why did I agree? That's when I remembered that I had come to Zhang's apartment because I wanted to use his toilet. How could I have forgotten something like that? Had I become completely numb even to my own feelings? Or perhaps even more aware? I couldn't decide and my thoughts became a jumble. I had enjoyed my time with Zhang up on the roof. That was the first time I had felt such pleasure, and I wondered if it would happen again. Each time sex seemed the same, even though it was with different men. Sex certainly was strange. Ever since I ran into Yuriko, I'd felt uncertain, as if I were drifting around in a dream, and it felt good.

Dragon grabbed my shoulders roughly and let out a sharp groan. Then he came. Without really thinking anything much at all, I gazed up at the ceiling, which was covered here and there with brown stains. On the roof, right above where we were now, was where I'd had sex earlier with Zhang. I recalled throwing the condom and watching the semen leaking out over the roof. Perhaps it had seeped down into the ceiling here. Perhaps it was what had made those stains.

From time to time I find myself amused by the paucity of semen a customer will spew out after all that panting and moaning. And it's for a puny product like that that a man will buy a prostitute like me? My nighttime self always excels my daytime self. If it weren't for my night-time self, what would become of my customers and their lame products? Tonight, for the first time I experienced joy that I was not born a man. Why? Because I thought men's desires trivial. And because I had become the entity that acknowledged those desires.

I felt I could finally understand Yuriko's freaky calm. Ever since Yuriko had been a little girl, she brought the world to her feet by using her sexuality. In her treatment of male desires of all kinds, she had built a world entirely out of men—even if only for the briefest of moments. It made me bitter. She didn't have to study; she didn't even have to work. She was able to bring the world to her feet by one method and one alone—because she was able to make men ejaculate. Now I would do the same. For a brief second I was drunk with the feeling of mastery.

I heard an exchange in Chinese and opened my eyes. Zhang and Chen-yi were sitting down by Dragon and me. They were staring right at me. Chen-yi, who didn't look like he was older than his mid-twenties, was blushing and pressing his hands between his legs. Did you feel it? I wanted to ask. How'd you like it? I gazed over at Chen-yi from where I was on the floor. Chen-yi averted his eyes from my face as if he were angry and turned away.

"Chen-yi's next." Zhang gave Chen-yi a nudge.

Chen-yi looked reluctant to have sex in front of an audience and glared sulkily at Zhang as if in protest. But Zhang would have none of it. For a mere two thousand yen he had taken me and Dragon and Chen-yi and had us bending to his will. I could see I had not yet come to terms with Zhang's world. I was going to have to conquer Zhang. I raised my arms and wrapped them around Zhang's knees.

"You next."

But he just brushed me aside and pushed Chen-yi over to me.

"Go on. Hurry up."

Chen-yi reluctantly began removing his track suit. When Dragon saw Chen-yi's erect penis, Dragon said something. I pulled a condom out of my bag and handed it to Chen-yi. Unaccustomed to them, Chen-yi was awkward, but he managed to put it on; then he took off his glasses and set them beside him on the tatami. What a jerk. Dragon snatched up the glasses and put them on, like a fool. The condescension and bitterness had faded from Dragon's expression and I noticed that he looked relaxed and gentler. I expect my expression was similar.

Chen-yi embraced me, and then he started planting sloppy kisses on my face, which completely took me by surprise. Zhang had done the same thing. I opened my eyes and looked up to see Zhang staring down at me. My customers never kissed me. We just fucked. That was true even of my regulars like Yoshizaki and Arai. None of them kissed me, and none of them wanted to. Zhang urged me on with his eyes. I remembered having my first orgasm with him on the roof. If I could have more, I could master my own world. I wrapped my arms around Chen-yi's back and began to kiss him back, writhing together with him as if our bodies were one. I felt Zhang's hand on my left thigh, rubbing. His hand was warm. Dragon followed suit, touching my right thigh. I was being teased and touched and fondled by three men. I couldn't have asked for more. I was a queen! God it was great. At that moment Chen-yi and I both came; for me, it was the second orgasm of my life.

Zhang put his hand on my head, brought his lips down to my ear, and whispered, his voice rough with excitement, "Did it feel good?"

I sat up and retrieved my wig, which had found its way to the other side of the room. Chen-yi looked back at me shyly, then quickly got dressed. Dragon sat there staring at my body while he smoked a cigarette. I put my wig back on and anchored it with a pin, then I started getting dressed.

"Let me use the bathroom."

Zhang pointed to a set of veneer doors by the entryway. I was dizzy when I stood up. I guess that's to be expected. I mean, that was the first time that I'd serviced three men one after the other like that. So many firsts in one day had worn me out, and I staggered to the bathroom door. It was filthy. The floor was wet with urine. Why do men have to be such pigs? It made me retch. The toilet, the trash on the stairs, the gunk in the seam of the tatami—they were all the same. I guess that's why I began to feel a new sensation welling up inside me, a feeling of wretchedness I couldn't shake. Fighting back the tears, I finished my business as quickly as I could.

"Want to do me again?" Zhang asked, as I came out of the bathroom.

I shook my head. "No. Your toilet is so filthy I feel like I'm going to throw up."

"Well, welcome to reality."

Was this reality, a place like this? Then what were the orgasms I'd had? And that momentary taste of control? The feelings I had earlier welled up again. But why? Welcome to reality. That's precisely why I wanted to live forever in the dream where I get to rule the world.

"I'm going."

I put myself back together and glanced back into the room as I slipped into my high heels. Not one of the men looked at me as I left.

·

It was eleven-thirty when I got back to the Jizō statue. Yuriko would be coming around soon. I looked at my watch and I scanned the street for signs of her, but she didn't turn up. Cold, tired, and irritated, I started to head for the station. And then I heard Yuriko calling to me from behind.

"Kazue, how'd it go tonight?"

She made her way slowly down the hill, dressed exactly like me: long jet-black hair, white face powder, blue eye shadow, and bright red lipstick. I felt I was beholding my own ghost, and a cold shiver went up my spine. Rock-bottom whore. A woman who exists only for the benefit of a few lousy cc's of sperm. Monster. I deflected the question.

"What about you?"

Yuriko held up one finger. "One. A sixty-eight-year-old man. He said he saw a sex flick at the Bunkamura and got a hard-on. It made him want to go out and buy a woman—the first for him in ten years, he said. Kind of cute, don't you think?"

"How much did you get?"

Yuriko resorted to hand gestures again, this time holding out four fingers. ¥40,000? I felt a rush of envy.

"Lucky you!"

"Hey, it was only four thousand yen!" Yuriko laughed as if she weren't even referring to herself. "I'd never done a customer that cheap. But he said that was all he had, so I agreed. Can you believe it! When I was in my twenties I'd pull in three million, just in one night! And look at me now. Why is it that the older you get the less you can make? Even when you're young and beautiful, the man is still after the same thing. I can't figure why people make such a fuss over youth. You end up having sex the same way whether you're young or old, don't you?"

"So long as you're not ugly, I don't see why it matters if you're old."

"That's not what I mean." Yuriko shook her head solemnly. "It has nothing to do with looks. All men care about is whether the woman is young."

"I guess. Hey, I'm curious. How'd you turn out to be so ugly?"

My nasty comment didn't so much as provoke a blush out of Yuriko.

"Hmmm. I guess it was just fate. I was never that aware of my looks anyway. It was always the people around me who made such a fuss. It's a lot easier this way, though."

Yuriko pulled a pack of cigarettes out of her shoulder bag and asked, "So what kind of customer did you have tonight, Kazue?"

"Three foreigners. They were Chinese. I got thirty thousand yen for each, so I came away making ninety thousand."

I lied through my teeth. Yuriko exhaled a sigh of cigarette smoke.

"Ah, I'm so jealous. If you find good customers like that, you should introduce me."

"No way."

"I'm not jealous because you made some money. It's because if those men are willing to pay that kind of money to you, Kazue, they must be the type who like monsters. I mean, you're ugly too. If some kid came across you in the dark, you can be sure he'd burst into tears. And you don't have much of a future. You're just going to keep falling lower and lower. You're going to have to quit your job at the firm before long because no one's going to be able to bear looking at you."

Yuriko's eyes glittered. I may have been a rock-bottom whore but the thought of slipping even lower frightened me. According to Yuriko's prophecy, at some point a monster-loving man would appear and kill me. I wondered if I'd be killed by Zhang. I remembered the humiliation I'd felt when he tossed me aside after sex. He hated me. He hated sex. But he liked monsters.

A strong wind blew up, and I clutched the front of my trench coat closed, wishing I could peer inside Zhang's heart. He might have spoken gently, but his world was a sordid one, full of lies. And yet I felt only joy at having been admitted to that sordid world. I was much more terrified of Zhang's impenetrable nature than I had been of Eguchi.

"Hey, Yuriko, what do you think of your older sister?"

Yuriko smiled faintly at the Jizō statue.

"Tell me."

I gave Yuriko's fatty shoulder a squeeze. At least a head taller than me, Yuriko turned slowly around. Her gaze was unfocused, a glimmer of suspicion in her eyes.

"Why do you want to know about my sister?"

"Zhang, my customer, prattled on and on about his younger sister, which reminded me that you had an older one, that's all. She died—Zhang's sister, I mean. He seemed to have been crazy about her."

"My sister was madly jealous of me from the minute I was born. It was almost as if she were in love with me. I was completely negated by her."

Oh, God, Yuriko was getting ready to go off on another one of her philosophical jags. Her ramblings confused me. I was in no mood for thinking on such an abstract level. All I wanted to do was cover my ears and hope she'd shut up. But Yuriko kept on going.

"Sisters? Ha! We didn't get along then and we don't get along now. My sister and I were two different people, but we were really one. She is a virgin, too timid to take on a man, and I'm the opposite: I can't live without men. I was born to be a whore. We're like opposite ends of the spectrum. Interesting, huh?"

"I don't think it's interesting at all," I spat out. "Why is it, in this world of ours, that women are the only ones who have a hard time surviving?"

"Simple. They don't have delusions." Yuriko let out an earsplitting laugh.

"So we'd be able to live if we had delusions?"

"It's too late for us, Kazue."

"Oh, really?"

I had worn away the reality of my job at the firm with my delusions. In the distance I heard the sound of the train on the Inokashira Line. It wouldn't be long before the last train had gone by. I decided to stop by the convenience store and buy a beer and drink it on the way home. I left Yuriko standing there, stamping her feet against the cold.

"Well, work hard!"

This was Yuriko's answer: "Death awaits."

•

I caught the last train. When I got home, the chain was on the front door and I couldn't get in. They'd turned all the lights off and latched the door, clearly to lock me out. That made me so furious I rang the doorbell over and over. Finally I heard someone pull the chain out of the latch. My sister stood in the doorway, looking pissed off.

"Don't you dare lock me out again."

My sister lowered her gaze. She must have been sleeping. She had pulled a sweater over her pajamas. Her gaze had brushed up against something deep inside me, and it irritated me.

"What the hell kind of look is that? You got something to say to me?"

My sister didn't answer. She shivered slightly as the cold air—and the depravity I had brought home with me—swept in from behind. While I slipped off my shoes, she returned to her bedroom. Our family was falling apart. I stood in the chilly corridor, petrified.

• 7 •

JANUARY 25
SHIBUYA: A DRUNK, ¥3,000

I hit a patch of bad luck after running into Zhang. Two weeks ago I went to a hotel with a guy into bondage and sadomasochism, and he beat my face pretty badly. I had to take a week off work as a result. Once I finally healed, I still had no luck getting customers. The sadist was someone I'd picked up after a five-day drought. I'd called Yoshizaki any number of times to get him to see me, but he told me he was too tied up with entrance exams to get away. Then I tried Arai, but apparently he'd been sent to the main office in Toyama and wasn't available. So I spent my nights in vain, standing silently in front of the Jizō statue waiting for customers who never came. I began to feel impatient with the hopelessness of my situation. In the cold months, there weren't many men loitering around. So I decided that tonight I'd walk through the brightly lit Dogenzaka entertainment area.

My night work was strictly cash-based. The money I made had a completely different feel from the salary that was deposited directly into my bank account. I loved the touch of the paper bills so much I could hardly stand it. Every time I put them into the deposit slot at the ATM, I felt such a flicker of sadness as I watched them disappear that I frequently called out *good-bye!* But no customers, no bills. And if I couldn't earn money, I wouldn't be able to continue my life on the streets. It was as if I were being completely negated as a human being. Was this what Yuriko meant when she said, "Death awaits"? I was terrified of finally meeting that day.

I rushed down to the Ginza Line subway platform. I needed to get to Shibuya before the other prostitutes grabbed up all the customers.

"No way! I can't believe she'd be doing something like that!" It was noisy down on the platform, but I could hear what two office-lady types were saying as they stood in front of me waiting for the next train. One was wearing a fashionable black coat, the other a red one. They were both carrying name-brand handbags and had their faces made up prettily.

"One of the guys in the business department said he saw her hanging out around Maruyama-chō. Said it sure looked like she was trying to pick up guys."

"You're kidding! That's disgusting. And her? I can't believe any guy would actually pay money to sleep with her."

"I know. It's incredible, but it seems to be true. She's gotten even more repulsive than usual lately. Everyone avoids using the toilets on the eleventh floor because she eats her lunch in there. She drinks the tap water straight out of the sink faucet; she doesn't use a glass. That's what I heard."

"Why haven't they fired her?"

They were talking about me. I stood there stunned, my head whirling. So I'd become the focus of attention. But with all the men and women standing in proper formation—three lines to a door—waiting for the subway as they gazed down the dark tracks, the two took absolutely no notice of me. It made me feel calm but somehow disappointed. But I hadn't done anything wrong! I tapped the black-coated office lady on the shoulder.

"Excuse me."

The woman turned around and stared at me, stunned.

"I'll have you know that I correctly perform all my work in the research office. I'm the assistant manager and, what's more, a report I wrote won a newspaper award. There's no reason why I should be fired."

"I'm sorry."

The women stepped out of line and rushed from the platform. That felt good! Stupid bitches. No way I'd be dismissed from work. Every day, all day long, I busily clip articles from the newspaper. The office manager said nothing about the purple bruises on my face from the beating I took the other week. All anyone in the office has to do is look at me and they admire my work. Ha! I stood there humming happily to myself as I waited for the train to glide into the station.

I put my makeup on in the bathroom of the basement of the 109 Building. The bruises were still faintly visible around my cheekbones. I covered them with a thick layer of foundation. Then I brushed blush over my cheeks. The false eyelashes I attached to my upper and lower eyelids made my eyes look bigger. With the wig as the finishing touch, I was done. I smiled at myself in the mirror. You are pretty! Perfect! I noticed that the young women nearby were all gaping at me. I shouted at their reflection in the mirror without turning around.

"What are you looking at? This isn't a circus, you know."

They quickly averted their eyes and acted innocent. One of the young women smirked, but I didn't care. I pushed roughly past the high school student who was standing in line to use the toilet and walked out.

The wind was blowing, rattling the tips of the trees as I trudged up Dogenzaka. A middle-aged man lugging a briefcase was a few feet ahead of me, by himself. I called out to him when I got closer.

"Hey, there, how'd you like to have some fun?"

The man glanced quickly into my face and kept walking as if he hadn't heard me.

"Come on. We don't have to take long. And it won't cost much."

The man pulled up abruptly and growled at me. "Get lost."

I stared at him as if I hadn't understood.

"Fuck off!" he spat, as he scurried away. What's his problem? I felt my anger rising but managed to control it. A fiftyish man was headed my way, just your basic gloomy-looking nine-to-fiver.

"Hey, mister, want to have some fun?"

The man brushed roughly past me without bothering to answer. As I continued up the hill I propositioned one middle-aged man after another. Most of them just ignored me and went on their way. I even called out boldly to a man in his late twenties, but he glared at me, repulsed, and waved me away. Just then I felt something strike the side of my face and fall to the ground. I looked at the pavement; it was a balled-up tissue. When I glanced up, I saw a young man wearing jeans leaning on the guardrail beside the sidewalk blowing his nose. The man laughed and threw another wad of filthy tissue at me. I hurried away. There are a number of men who enjoy tormenting prostitutes, and it's best just to try to avoid them. I dashed into a shop-lined alleyway and caught the sleeve of a salary man leaving a cheap tavern. His cuff was frayed. The man didn't look like he had much money.

"Hey, want to party?"

He shouted at me, with breath reeking of booze, "Get the hell out of my face. I got a good buzz on and don't want you ruining it."

The hawkers in front of the cabaret saw this and had a good laugh at my expense. They slapped each other on the shoulder and looked over at me, eyeing me derisively. "What a freaking monster!" one said to the other.

What's so monstrous about me? Confused, I continued to wander along the busy alley. Even though this is the exact same spot where Arai first propositioned me, and even though there are so many drunks around here now, and even though I'm so much prettier than I was then, why are the men so obnoxious when I call out to them?

I came to the office building where the hotel escort agency I had worked for, Juicy Strawberry, was located. I wondered if they'd take me back. But then I remembered the conditions the dispatcher had laid down when he fired me and realized it was highly unlikely that they'd give me another chance. I stood there for a while looking up at the narrow stairway to the office and weighing my options.

Just when I'd made up my mind and was starting up the stairs to the Juicy Strawberry office, the door opened and a man walked out, heading down the stairs. It wasn't the owner or the dispatcher. This man was hugely overweight; his double chins were so massive, I could hardly see his face as he made his way down the stairs. The stairway was narrow, so no matter how thin I was, there was no way the fat man could squeeze past me. I headed back down the stairs and waited there impatiently for him to get out of the way. As he walked past me he held up his hand in greeting. "Sorry," he said, staring at me, taking me in from head to toe. Clearly sizing me up.

Without wasting a beat I trotted out my usual phrase: "No problem. But hey, you want to party?"

"Are you hitting on me? *You*?"

The man snickered. His voice was painfully offensive—as if the sounds he produced were drenched in grease. But still, it was somehow familiar. I cocked my head to the side, perplexed. Naturally, I did not forget to bring my finger up to my chin in an effort to make my gesture as charming as possible. It looked like the man had tilted his head to the side as well, though it was hard to tell under all that fat.

"Have we met somewhere before?"

"I was just now thinking the same thing."

Once the man had made it down the stairs, I could tell he was barely taller than I am. He peered at my face, staring rudely. His eyes were snakelike.

"Maybe you've come by my business before? I know we've met."

As the man was speaking, I suddenly caught a glimmer of someone I'd known earlier. It was Takashi Kijima, no doubt about it. He was the boy I'd loved so much in high school that I'd sent him love letters. And here he was, the boy who had been as thin as a knife, buried under a mound of flesh.

"Wait a minute! Are you the one who was friends with Yuriko's older sister?" He thumped his head in annoyance, trying to remember my name. "You were a year ahead of me. . . ."

"I'm Kazue Satō."

I had to help him out or we'd have been there forever. Kijima let out a long sigh of relief. "Well, it's certainly been a long time!" he said, in a surprisingly friendly tone. "I guess more than twenty years have passed since I left school."

I nodded with annoyance, making special note of Kijima's clothing. He had on a camel-colored overcoat that looked like cashmere, a gold diamond-studded ring on his right hand, and a heavy-looking bracelet on his wrist. His permed hair was out of style, but even so it looked like he was doing really well. So why was he still pimping? And why the hell had I ever been attracted to him? The very thought made me laugh.

"What's so funny?"

"I was just wondering why I was so crazy about you."

"I remember you sent me letters. They were really something."

"I wish you'd just forget that ever happened." That had been the most humiliating event in my life. But I curbed my tongue and my anger and propositioned Kijima again.

"Kijima-kun, what do you say we go party?"

Kijima started fanning his hand in front of his face in a vigorous effort to end my question.

"Not going to happen. I'm gay, and I'm out. So don't even go there."

So that was it! What a fool I was. Far from lacking merit, what I had hoped for wasn't even in the realm of possibility.

"Yeah? Well, see you later then."

I shrugged my shoulders and walked away.

Kijima pursued me, breathing heavily, and grabbed hold of my shoulder. "Kazue, wait. What happened to you?"

"What do you mean, what happened to me?"

"I mean you look completely different. Are you really turning tricks now? I heard you'd been hired by G Architecture and Engineering. What happened with that?"

"Nothing happened with that." I shook my shoulder free. "I'm still working there. I'm the assistant manager of the research office."

"Impressive! So you're moonlighting at night? Women are lucky. They can earn money leading double lives."

I turned to look back at Kijima. "You look different too, you know. You're so fat I hardly recognized you."

"Well then, I guess we're both not what we used to be," Kijima replied, with a short snort.

That's not true, I contradicted him silently. I was always thin and beautiful. Aloud, I said, "I ran into Yuriko the other day. She's changed too."

"Yuriko? No kidding!"

Kijima repeated Yuriko's name over to himself several times, clearly full of emotion. "Yuriko. Was she well? I lost contact with her a while back and I've been wondering how she was doing."

"She's a mess. She's fat and ugly. I can't believe someone so beautiful could have turned out to be so ugly. We used to be like night and day. Well, we still are! Only now I can't understand how I could have felt so much jealousy and resentment for her."

Kijima nodded, silently mouthing his agreement.

"She's now standing on corners just like me. She says she wants to hurry up and die and doesn't care what happens anymore. You're the one who pushed Yuriko into the business in the first place, aren't you?"

Kijima looked wounded by my accusation. He frowned and fumbled with the buttons on his coat; they looked like they'd pop off at any minute. Then he gazed up at the sky and exhaled a long dramatic sigh.

"Kijima, are you working here?"

"No. The owner of Juicy Strawberry is an acquaintance of mine, and I just came by to see how he's doing. What about you?"

"I used to work here. And since it turned cold I thought I'd come back and see if I couldn't get a temporary position. Hey, might I ask you to put a word in for me?"

Kijima's face froze and he shook his head firmly.

"No can do. If I were the owner, I wouldn't hire you. You're not fit to be a call girl anymore. You're even too old to play the mature-woman role. You should forget about working at a place like this."

"Why?" I asked indignantly.

"Well, look at you! You've already crossed the line. If you're stooping to propositioning someone like me, you must be desperate. There's nothing left for you but to stand on corners. Besides, you're doing the kind of job those frail little escort girls can't do with their thin skin and their neuroses."

"I'm easily wounded too, you know. I'm always upset about something."

Kijima eyed me doubtfully, the corners of his mouth turning down in a smirk.

"Right. You don't look like you ever even catch cold. And when your adrenaline kicks in, I'll bet nothing gets in your way. You're out on the stroll because you enjoy it, don't you? And you probably enjoy thumbing your nose at your company."

"Well, what do you expect? It's the only way I can exert a little control over my life. I've been treated like dirt from the minute I entered the company. I do a good job, but no one finds me very attractive, so I never win. And I don't like losing."

Kijima listened to me without interrupting, but he had pulled his cell phone out of his coat pocket as if he was wondering just how much longer I would take. I quickly shifted gears.

"Do you have a business card with you? I'd appreciate one if you do. I don't know, I may need to call you sometime if I need help."

Kijima looked aggrieved. I suppose he didn't want anything to do with me.

"Well, I mean if Yuriko dies or something."

Kijima's expression turned serious, and he hurriedly retrieved a card from his coat and handed it to me.

"If you see Yuriko again, tell her to contact me."

"Why?"

"No real reason," Kijima replied pensively, clutching his cell phone in his flabby hand. "I guess I'm just curious."

Curious. Yes, that was a satisfying answer.

"Kijima-kun, men used to be attracted to me out of curiosity. So why is it that my business is so poor these days? It happened practically overnight."

Kijima rubbed his flabby jowls with a thick finger. "I figure any man who hooks up with you now is doing so because he wants to know how you've come to stoop so low. I wouldn't say it's curiosity. I'd say it's something deeper, darker. I mean, a normal man would be afraid of the truth. I hate to say it, but I doubt there's any man out there who'd want to pay to sleep with you. And if there is, you can be sure he's got the balls to look evil in the face."

"Fallen? Me?" I was so taken aback I couldn't help but shout. "Where do you get off insulting me? I do what I do for revenge. And looking evil in the face? Isn't that a bit of an overstatement!"

"Revenge? For what?"

Kijima seemed to take a sudden interest. He peered at me and then quickly averted his eyes.

"Oh, I don't knoooow!" I cried, with an exaggerated pout, and rocked from side to side. "For everything! For everything that goes wrong!"

"What's with the little-girl act?" Kijima snorted, staring at me with feigned disbelief. "Look, I've got to go. Watch yourself, Kazue. You've really gone into the deep end." He gave a perfunctory wave, turned on his heels, and headed down the narrow alley to the main avenue.

"You can't talk to me like that, Kijima-kun! You think I'm crazy? Is that it? No one's ever said anything like that to me before, you bully!" I shouted at him, watching his back as he walked away.

My confidence shattered, I gave up on the idea of trying to get a job with Juicy Strawberry or trying to work the passersby on the main avenue along Dogenzaka. I pulled my trench coat tight and wrapped my arms around my chest. I wanted to hurry back to my spot in front of the

Jizō statue. I was much better suited to standing patiently in the dark, waiting for customers to pass.

When I cut through a narrow alley of love hotels, I noticed an older woman watching me from the shadows. She stepped forward and gently tugged my arm.

"Do you mind if I ask you a few questions?" she said.

She was wearing a crocheted hat of white wool with matching wool gloves, and she'd draped a polyester floral scarf around her gray coat like a sailor collar. Her outfit was so unusual I couldn't help but burst out laughing. She tenderly wrapped my hand in her own gloved hand and whispered in a soft high-pitched voice, "You mustn't let yourself fall into this shameful profession. God's love is great and all encompassing. But you have to try to raise yourself up too, you know. If you do, you can start anew. Your pain is my pain; your submission shall be my submission. I will pray for you."

It felt good to have my frozen hands cradled in her warm grip, but even so I shook her hands off mine.

"What are you talking about? I'm already working so hard to raise myself up I'm about to die! I'll have you know I was an outstanding student."

"I know. I know. I know so well it nearly hurts."

I detected a whiff of old-lady breath mints when the woman exhaled.

"What do you know?" I asked, with a derisive laugh. "I'm managing to get by just fine without any help from you. I work at a corporation during the day, you know."

I hurriedly pulled out my ID card to show the woman, but she hardly even glanced at it. Instead, she pulled a black book out of the bag she was carrying and pressed it to her breast.

"You enjoy selling your body, don't you?"

"Yes, I do. I certainly do."

The woman shook her head. "Now, that's not true, is it? Your lies wound me deeply. Do you enjoy being treated cruelly by men? It pains me to see how foolish you are. My heart aches each time I encounter unfortunate women like you. You've been deceived by your employers, haven't you, dear? And at night you are betrayed by men. That's the horrible limbo you must endure. You're even deluded by your own desires. My poor, pathetic darling. Hurry and open your eyes to the truth."

As the woman stroked my head, she knocked off my wig. I slapped her hand away and shouted angrily, "Pathetic? Don't you look down your nose at me!"

Startled, the woman took a step backward. I ripped the Bible from her hands and flung it against the wall. It made a smacking sound and slipped to the asphalt with a soft thud. The woman gasped and started to run to retrieve it, but I pushed her out of the way and stomped on the book. I could feel the onion-thin pages ripping under my sharp heel. I felt elated to be doing something I knew I shouldn't do.

I began running along the dark road. The chill north wind stung my cheeks and the sound of my high heels clattered through the silence as I ran. It had felt good to humiliate that woman. I came to a convenience store, went in, and bought a can of beer and a packet of dried squid. I pushed open the can and drank the beer as I walked along. Refreshed by the cool liquid washing down my throat, I gazed up into the night sky. I was free. I was even thinner and more beautiful than before. And I enjoyed my independence to the hilt.

I could no longer bear the idea of standing patiently in front of the Jizō, so I raced down the stone stairs that led to Shinsen Station. On the way I passed the empty lot where I had done the homeless man. I entered the lot and stood there drinking my beer and gnawing on the squid. I couldn't have cared less about the cold. A sudden urge to pee came over me, so I squatted down over the withered grass and let go. I was reminded of the filthy toilet in Zhang's apartment. I much preferred this empty lot.

"Hey, sister! Whatcha doin down there?"

A man was watching me from the stone steps. He must have been plastered because the wind picked up the smell of liquor on his breath and carried it all the way down to where I was.

"Something fun."

"Yeah? Can I join you?"

The man stumbled down the stairs. I propositioned him.

"Mister, I'm freezing out here. Let's go somewhere where we can be inside."

As soon as I saw the man nod genially, I grabbed his arm and led him back toward Maruyama-chō. There I pulled him into the first love hotel we came to. He looked like he was a salary man, late forties, maybe early fifties. His skin was warm from the sake he'd drunk and his complexion was murky. I dragged him down the hall, barely managing to stay on my feet because he was stumbling so badly, and pushed him into a room.

"I charge thirty thousand yen."

"I don't have that kind of money on me."

The man lurched forward slightly as he fished through his pockets. He produced a receipt and his commuter pass. I figured we'd already come this far, might as well get it over with. So I pushed him down on the bed, threw myself on top of him, and planted a kiss on his alcohol-laden lips. He roughly pulled his head away and stared at me.

"Cut it out!" he protested. "Let's not do this."

"Wait a minute. You're the one who brought me here. I'll take my thirty thousand before you try to cheat me out of it."

I hadn't had a customer in so long, I didn't want him to get away. I was desperate. The man relented and pulled several thousand-yen bills out of his wallet. Then he hung his head.

"I'm sorry. This is all I've got on me. But I won't ask any more of you. I'll leave now."

"Hey, I'm a professional in a major firm. Don't you want to know why I turn to prostitution at night?"

I turned over on my side on the bed and tried to look alluring. The man snapped his wallet closed and pulled on his coat. I hurried to collect my things as well. I didn't want to get stuck with the room bill. The man left the room and marched up to the registration desk to haggle over the fee. He had clearly lost his earlier buzz.

"We didn't mess the room up or anything, so why don't you just charge me half price. We weren't even there for ten minutes."

The receptionist glanced quickly at me. He was a middle-aged man very obviously wearing a toupee.

"All right, I'll let you off for fifteen hundred yen."

The man handed over two thousand-yen bills with obvious relief. When the attendant handed him a five-hundred yen coin in return, the man told him to keep it for his troubles.

"It's not much. But I appreciate your understanding."

When I heard the man say this, I immediately stuck out my hand. "Hey, wait a minute. I think that belongs to me. After all, I was the one who had to endure your kisses for a lousy three thousand yen!"

Both the man and the receptionist stared at me in amazement. But I didn't bat an eye, and in the end the receptionist gave me the coin.

•

It was nearing time for the last train of the evening. I bought another can of beer and drained it. I walked down the stone stairs again and headed back to Shinsen Station. My earnings for the night amounted to ¥3,000–¥3,500 if you add the tip I wormed out of the hotel receptionist. But with the cost of the beer and squid, I was in the red. As I walked down the street to the station, I could see the apartment building where Zhang lived. I turned to look up at the fourth-floor windows. A light was on in his unit.

"Well, we meet again. You're looking well."

I heard a voice behind me. It was Zhang. I tossed the empty beer can to the side of the street, where it bounced with a clatter. Zhang was wearing his leather jacket and jeans, just as he had the other night. The expression on his face was serious. I glanced at my watch.

"I still have a little time. Do you think the fellows in your apartment would want to fool around again?"

"I'm really sorry," Zhang said, somewhat apologetically, "but you didn't make a big hit with them. Both Dragon and Chen-yi thought you were too skinny. They like a woman with a bit more meat."

"Well, what about you?"

Zhang rolled his big eyes. His brows were thick and his lips full and other than the fact that he was balding, he was really my type. For some reason I wanted to be with him.

"I don't care. Any woman will do for me." Zhang laughed. "Any woman other than my sister."

"If that's the case, will you hold me?"

I threw myself against Zhang's body. The Shibuya-bound train on the Inokashira Line had just pulled into the station and passengers were crowding the platform. They stared at us, but I didn't care. Zhang did. With an embarrassed look, he wrapped his arms around me, trying to keep me at bay, but I continued to squirm, trying to force my way deeper into his embrace. I felt suddenly beset with sorrow.

"Will you be good to me?" I asked Zhang, in a cloying tone.

"Do you want me to be good to you? Or do you want me to have sex with you?"

"Both."

Zhang pushed me aside roughly so he could look into my face. Then he said coolly, "Unn-uh, you have to choose. Which one?"

"Be good to me."

As soon as I murmured my response, I knew I meant it. I hadn't been after the money. So why the hell had I been standing there on the corner night after night? Did I just want someone to be nice to me? Surely not. I was confused. Maybe I was drunk. I pushed my hand against my forehead.

"If you want me to be good to you, will you pay me?" he asked.

I looked up at Zhang in surprise. Leering in the darkness, he looked sinister.

"Why do I have to pay? Shouldn't it be the other way around?"

"But what you're asking for is skewed. You don't like anyone, do you? Not another person, not even yourself. You've been duped."

"Duped?" I cocked my head to the side, clueless as to what he meant. I didn't try to pull my cute-girl pose; I didn't have the energy for it.

Zhang continued cheerfully. "That's right, duped. I just learned this expression. Technically speaking, it means someone who gets screwed or conned. You've let yourself be duped by everyone you meet—in your office, on the street. In the past you were duped by your father and your school."

The last train would be leaving Shibuya Station by now. As I listened to Zhang prattle on, I looked toward the tracks. I had no choice but to go home. Just like I had no choice but to go to work the next morning. I couldn't help it. So was I being duped by society? I remembered what the Bible lady had said to me: "It pains me to see how foolish you are."

· 8 ·

JUNE 5

During the rainy season, business all but dried up. And with the constant rainfall I didn't feel like standing outside all night getting drenched. To top it off, the low-pressure fronts made my eyes puffy, and I felt sleepy all day long. It was harder and harder to get out of bed in the morning. All I wanted was to take the day off, and the internal battle I had to wage to get myself out the door became exhausting. Why is it that even though the spirit may be willing, the body falters? Today I got up even later than usual and sat at the table listening to the rain. My mother had already fixed my sister's breakfast and seen her off to work. She'd retreated to her own bedroom and the house was perfectly still. I poured some water from the electric kettle and made myself a cup of instant coffee. Then, instead of eating breakfast, I crunched on a gymnema tablet. The waistband of my navy-blue skirt was now so loose, the skirt spun around on my hips. I was trimmer now than ever. The lighter I grew, the happier I felt. At this rate I was just going to melt away into thin air. I was ecstatic. The weather might be oppressive, but I was in a jubilant mood.

The rain had begun to come down in torrents. The flowers in the garden that Mother was so proud of had been flattened: hydrangea, azaleas, roses, little flowering grasses. They were all bent down. I turned to the garden and cursed the stupid plants. As soon as the rains let up they'd bounce right back, perkier than ever from all the moisture. The little bastards! I despised my mother's precious garden.

I looked out at the sky. No doubt business would be hopeless tonight as well. I'd only been able to work one week during the whole month of June and barely managed to pull in ¥48,000. I'd had four customers, including Yoshizaki and some drunk. I squeezed ¥30,000 out of Yoshizaki and the drunk gave me ¥10,000. Then I had two homeless guys. The first was the man I'd done before in the empty lot, but the other was a newcomer. I did them both outside under a rain-laced sky. It had gotten to the point where men would pay me to watch me pee out in the lot. Nothing fazed me anymore. But as a consequence I was finding it harder and harder to concentrate at work; I was always so tired. I just sat at my desk and clipped newspaper articles, and I didn't even care which articles I clipped. Sometimes I amused myself by clipping out sections of the television listings. My boss would glare at me out of the side of his eyes, but he never said a word. The other people in the office looked at me and huddled together in whispers, but I didn't care. Let them talk. I was strong.

I opened the morning edition of the newspaper, and after I scanned the weather report I thumbed through the society page. My eyes were caught by the crumbs of toast my sister had left behind in the paper— she'd gotten to it before me. She must have stopped to read this page. The headline read: WOMAN'S BODY DISCOVERED IN APARTMENT. The victim's name was Yuriko Hirata. Yuriko! It occurred to me that I hadn't seen her recently. So you've gone and gotten yourself killed. It was just as you predicted, wasn't it? Congratulations. As I spoke these words in my heart, I heard the sound of laughter. Who was it? I wondered, as I looked around.

Yuriko's spirit was hovering between the grimy ceiling and the cluttered dining table; she was looking at me. Only the upper half of her body was visible in the blue-white glow of the fluorescent light. Her face was no longer the fat, ugly face that I had seen recently. She'd returned to the luminous beauty of her youth. I spoke to her.

"It happened just the way you wanted it to, didn't it?"

Yuriko smiled, flashing her brilliantly white teeth. "Thanks. I've gone ahead and died before you. What will you do now, Kazue?"

"Business as usual. I still have money to make."

"Quit while you can." Yuriko laughed. "You'll never make enough to be satisfied. Besides, sooner or later the man who killed me will kill you too."

"Who?"

"Zhang."

Yuriko's answer was unmistakable. But how'd she come to know Zhang? I began to work it out in my mind. Yuriko must have drawn him to her; Yuriko's a monster; Zhang likes monsters; one thing led to another. But if that's the way it went, was Zhang really going to kill me too?

The other day when I threw myself at him, he held me, didn't he? I wanted Zhang to be good to me. I wanted him to hold me. Yuriko raised a slender index finger in front of her face and waved it back and forth vigorously.

"No, no, no, Kazue. Mustn't entertain any desires of your own. No one's going to be good to you. They don't even want to have to pay you. Old whores like us, you know, all we're good for is making men face the truth. That's why they hate us."

"Face the truth?" Before I was even aware of what I was doing I had brought my hand to my chin and tilted my head to the side.

"Oh for heaven's sake, Kazue, are you still trying to pull that cute-girl stunt? Give up already. It's hopeless. You just don't get it, do you?"

"I do too. I do get it. I get the fact that I'm thinner and prettier than ever."

"Who was it gave you that bad advice?"

What was she talking about? Then I remembered that it came from someone. Was it back in high school? Yuriko's older sister?

"It was your older sister."

"And you believe something someone told you so long ago?" Yuriko sighed. "Kazue, you really are gullible! You've got to be the most credulous person I know."

"Whatever. Yuriko, look. Tell me what you meant about facing the truth."

"That it's all empty. A big fat nothing."

"Am I a big fat nothing?"

As soon as I asked I caught myself wrapping my arms around myself. I'm nothing! Empty. When did I disappear? All that was left of me was just a suit of clothes—the clothes that belonged to a graduate of Q University, an employee of G Architecture and Engineering. There was nothing inside. Then again, what is it that's inside, anyway?

When I came to my senses I had spilled coffee all over the open page of the paper. I quickly dabbed at the table with a cloth. The paper had turned completely brown.

"Kazue, what's wrong?"

I looked back to see my mother standing in the door to the living room. Her tiny makeup-free face was twisted in fear.

"You were talking just now. I heard your voice and I thought you were talking to someone."

"I *was* talking to someone. I was talking to this person here."

I pointed to the newspaper. But the article had become so stained with coffee, it was difficult to read it anymore. Mother didn't say anything, just pressed her hand to her mouth in an effort to suppress a shriek. I didn't pay her any attention but yanked my shoulder bag off the chair.

"I've got to make a phone call!" I shouted.

As I pulled my date book out of my bag, a snot-encrusted wad of tissue flew out, along with a dirty handkerchief. They both landed beside me on the floor. Mother stared at them angrily, but I just shooed her away.

"What're you looking at? Get out of here."

"You're going to be late for work."

"It's no big deal if I'm just a little late. The office manager was a whole hour late the other day. And the day before that, one of the secretaries was late. Everyone does it, so why shouldn't I? Why do I always have to be the one who's so serious about my job? I've been slaving away all this time to keep you in this house. You're damn right I'm tired of it!"

"Kazue, dear, are you doing what you do because of me? Is that it?"

My mother was mumbling. Lines of worry creased her face as she peered at me.

"It's got nothing to do with you! I work because I'm a dutiful daughter."

"Yes, you are." My mother's stammer was nearly inaudible. She didn't seem to want to leave, but she finally went back to her room with a sour face. I flipped through my date book, looking for the address section. Yuriko's older sister. It had been over ten years since I'd had any contact with her, but suddenly I felt I couldn't settle down until I heard her voice. As I slowly dialed her number, I tried to figure out what it was I needed so desperately to confirm. I was absolutely baffled.

"Hello. Hello? Who is it?"

The voice on the other end of the line was sickeningly gloomy, cautious. I stated my business directly without bothering with any small talk.

"It's me. Kazue Satō. Hey, I read Yuriko-chan's been murdered."

"That's right."

Her voice gave a hint of depression, but at the same time reverberated with a kind of calm.

Yuriko's older sister started to make some weird sound on the other end of the phone. It was low and constant like the idling of a motorcycle. She was laughing. Hers was the laughter of one relishing a sense of relief, a laughter that revealed the joy she felt over finally being free of Yuriko. I felt the same way. To me she'd been my senior in the night trade, and she'd come out of nowhere to encroach on my turf: the former high school beauty. So I suppose we both felt that we'd somehow been set free. And then, at the same time, there was something that bound us to her.

"What's so funny?" Yuriko's sister demanded.

"Nothing."

I wasn't even laughing. Why'd she ask something like that? Yuriko's sister was crazy. So I returned the question.

"Well, I suppose you're sad, aren't you?"

"Not really."

"Oh, that's right, you and Yuriko-chan weren't particularly close, as I recall. It was as if you two weren't even related. Others might not have realized you were sisters, but I picked up on it right away."

Yuriko's sister interrupted me. "Enough about that. What are you doing these days?"

"Guess." I threw my shoulders back defiantly.

"I heard you'd gotten a job with an engineering firm."

"Would you be surprised if I told you Yuriko-chan and I were in the same line of work?"

It was silent at the other end. Yuriko's older sister must have been thinking it over. I knew she was jealous of me. She was a woman who longed to be like Yuriko but couldn't imitate her if her life depended on it. But I was different.

"Well, I intend to be careful!"

That shut her up! I hung up hastily. But really, what had Yuriko's older sister and I been freed from? From living? Maybe I wanted to be killed the same way Yuriko did. Because I was also a monster. And I was tired of living.

•

By evening the rains still had not relented. I opened my folding umbrella, dashed out into the downpour, and wandered around Shinsen

Station, hoping to run into Zhang. I stood in front of his apartment building and looked up at his unit, but it was pitch-black. No one had returned yet. Just when I thought I'd give up and go home, I caught sight of Chen-yi walking in my direction. He was wearing a thin white running shirt and shorts with beach sandals, even though the rain had cooled things off. I drew up alongside him.

"Good evening."

When Chen-yi noticed me he stopped walking. The eyes behind his glasses darted wildly, as if he were being forced to behold something distasteful.

"I need to see Zhang, and I was wondering if he was home."

"Zhang is probably not in. He changed jobs so he's gone both day and night. I don't know when he'll come back."

"May I wait for him in his room?"

"No. You can't do that." Chen-yi shook his head aggressively. "We have others staying here. It won't do."

He acted as if he was ashamed of having had sex with me in front of everyone else.

"Well, can I see for myself?"

I started to head up the stairs, but Chen-yi grabbed me roughly and made me stop.

"I'll go see if he's in or not. You wait here."

"If he's in, tell him that I'll be waiting for him on the roof."

Chen-yi regarded me with suspicion as I headed toward the stairs, but I didn't care. The trash that littered the staircase between the fourth floor and the roof had multiplied, as if it were some kind of living organism. The entire staircase was now carpeted with garbage: wastepaper, scraps of English-language newspapers, plastic soda bottles, CD covers, torn sheets, and condoms. I kicked the junk aside with the toes of my wet shoes and made my way up the stairs. I passed the door to Zhang's apartment and headed on up to the roof. The rain-soaked mattress was stretched across the stairs and stuck out onto the roof like a corpse—the mattress the language teacher had left behind. The mattress where Zhang now sat, his head hanging. Dingy T-shirt, blue jeans. His hair over his ears. He looked like he hadn't shaved in days. Zhang was no different from the multiplying garbage. I was suddenly reminded of the plants in Mother's garden, wrecked by the rain. Once the rains stopped, those plants would spring back up.

"What are you doing sitting up here?"

"Ah, it's you?" Zhang looked up at me in surprise. My eye lit on a gold chain glittering around Zhang's neck.

"That's Yuriko's necklace, isn't it?"

"What, this?" Zhang touched the necklace as if he'd just remembered it was there. "So, her name was Yuriko?"

"Yes, she was an acquaintance of mine. She always dressed exactly like me."

"She did, didn't she, now that you mention it."

Zhang twisted the chain around his fingers. Rainwater dripped off my umbrella and pooled onto a corner of the mattress like a spreading stain. Zhang didn't seem to notice.

"You killed Yuriko, didn't you?"

"That's right. I killed her because she asked me to. It was the same with my sister. I said my sister fell into the sea and drowned, but that was a lie. I killed her. In the container, on the voyage to Japan, we had sex every night. She was repulsed by the idea of living like a beast and asked me, with tears in her eyes, to kill her. I told her not to worry about our relationship and asked her any number of times to go ahead and live with me like husband and wife, but she wouldn't do it. So I threw her in the sea. I could see her hands waving from between the swells as she drifted farther and farther from me; it was as if she were bidding me good-bye. She was smiling. She seemed happy to be waving good-bye to her life with me. We borrowed so much money just to make it to Japan. I couldn't believe how stupid she was. So whenever I meet a woman who says, 'Kill me,' I'm only too happy to oblige. If she just can't deal with her life, I'll step up to settle things for her. How about you?"

Zhang smiled slightly in the darkness. The wind had grown strong and lashed our faces with rain. I turned aside, trying to avoid the rain, but Zhang just grimaced as he let the rain pelt his face. His forehead glistened with moisture.

"I don't want to die yet. But I may before too long."

Zhang grabbed my legs. "You're so thin! Like a skeleton. I can't understand why you can't gain any weight. Do you suppose you're sick? My sister and that Yuriko woman were both healthy. Why are you the one who's sick? It's sad, isn't it?"

"You think I'm sick? But I don't want to die."

"There are people out there who are already on the road to death, and they don't even know it. And then there are people who are a picture of health but choose to die anyway. Don't you agree?"

I was suddenly assailed by sorrow. Why was it that when I talked to Zhang I felt so lonely, so sad? I sat down on the filthy, sodden mattress. Zhang grabbed me by the shoulders and pulled me to him. He smelled of sweat and dirt, but I didn't mind.

"Be good to me. Please."

I burrowed my face in Zhang's chest, playing with the chain that glittered at his neck.

"All right. And in return, you be good to me."

We held each other, murmuring over and over, "Be good; please be good to me."

· 9 ·

JANUARY 30
SHIBUYA: WA (?), ¥10,000
SHIBUYA: FOREIGNER, ¥3,000

Zhang's a big liar. A piece of shit. And a murderer! I placed my can of beer, packet of dried squid, and bottle of gymnema pills on the counter at the convenience store and thought about him.

"Hey!" Someone poked me in the back. I realized I'd cut in line but I didn't care, I stood where I was and placed an order for *oden* stew.

"I want fish cake, radish, and *konnyaku*—one of each. And fill the bowl up with broth, will you."

The man behind the counter gave a snort of annoyance, but the female clerk—who was used to seeing me there—went to the cauldron of *oden* and picked out what I wanted without any expression at all. The two young women standing in line behind me mumbled something—either an insult or a complaint—so I turned and glared at them. They looked intimidated. It amused me. I'd taken to staring people directly in the eye—in the office, at home, wherever. I am a monster. Everyone treats me like I'm special. And if you have a problem with it, just try to be like me!

I went outside and quickly slurped the broth. The smooth warm liquid slipped down my throat. I knew the heat of the liquid would shrink my stomach. It would grow smaller and smaller. A train rumbled passed on the Inokashira Line tracks. I straightened up and watched it pull into Shinsen Station. I wondered if Zhang was in it.

More than half a year had past since Zhang and I clung to each other that rainy night. It was now January. We'd had a mild winter so far, which made things a lot easier for me. Whenever I got to Shinsen Station, I always looked for Zhang. Once, as I peered up through the fence from the road, I thought I saw a man who looked like him standing on the platform. But I hadn't run into him since that rainy night. That was just as well. He was nothing to me. I put all my energy into my night work. Zhang will continue to live in this country, forgetting that he's killed Yuriko.

That night we'd both been desperately sentimental. But still, I had had to burst out laughing when I heard Zhang's ridiculous little soliloquy.

"I loved that prostitute. The one you said was Yuriko."

"Oh, give me a break! That's not really likely, is it? I mean, you had just met her. And Yuriko wasn't anything more than a shabby whore. Besides, I doubt even she would have believed you. She hated men, you know."

Zhang grabbed me by the throat as I squirmed in laughter, as if he was going to strangle me.

"Oh, so you think it's funny? Well, how about I do you the same way? You stupid bitch."

The orange light illuminating the entry to the staircase reflected in Zhang's eyes, making them glitter. He looked possessed, creepy. Frightened, I slapped Zhang's hands away and stood up. The rain struck my cheeks. I raised my hand to wipe it off and realized it wasn't water, it was Zhang's spit. Sperm, spit: a woman receives what men excrete.

"Get lost." Zhang waved me away, and I rushed down from the roof. I scrambled down the slippery staircase, kicking the wet garbage aside as I went. What was it about Zhang that I wanted to try to escape? Even I wasn't sure. As I got to the front door of the building, I collided with a man who was dashing in from the outside. His body, damp with rain and sweat, emitted a peculiar odor. His black T-shirt was soaked, revealing a slender build. It was Dragon. I adjusted my wig and called out to him.

"Hello!"

Dragon did not reply. Instead he riveted me with his needle-sharp gaze.

"Zhang's on the roof," I informed him. "Do you know why he's hanging out up there? He's running from something."

I had planned to tell Dragon that Zhang had murdered Yuriko, and that was why he was on the lam. But before I could, Dragon surprised me with an explanation of his own.

"He's running from us, the asshole. He's cheated us out of all our money, and until he pays us back we've told him he's not welcome to come back."

The night I had slept with Chen-yi and Dragon one after the other, Dragon had been kissing Zhang's ass. But tonight, Dragon was arrogant.

"Yeah, well, he killed a prostitute, you know. He killed a prostitute in Shinjuku," I said, smirking at him.

"A prostitute? Let him kill all the prostitutes he wants. They're easily replaced. But money, that's different!"

Dragon shook the cheap vinyl umbrella he was carrying, sending raindrops scattering in all directions.

"Well, don't you agree?"

I nodded, yes. He had a point. Money was definitely more valuable than life. But then, when I died, my money would be meaningless. My mother and younger sister would end up with it. The thought irritated me, but what could I do? I was disgruntled by the fact that I couldn't figure out something so simple. Dragon looked at me and laughed derisively.

"Do you believe what that asshole tells you? Zhang's a liar, you know. No one here trusts a thing he says."

"Everyone lies."

"But nothing that loser says is true. Oh, he acts like he's such a hard worker, talking about how he left his village to seek his fortune in the big cities back home. But the fact of the matter is, he bumped off his grandpa, his older brother, and the man who was supposed to marry his little sister and he had no choice but to skip town. He says he forced his sister into prostitution when he got to Hangzhou and he started running drugs for a gang. He pretends that he was kept by some politician's daughter to cover his tracks. He's an asshole. Hell, the only reason he came to Japan was to escape the police."

"He told me he killed his sister."

Dragon looked up in surprise. A look of bemusement flashed across his eyes. "Well, well. I guess the son-of-a-bitch does tell the truth now and then. That seems to be true. I heard it from another guy who made the trip on the same boat with Zhang. He said he pretended to grab for his sister's hand, but it looked to the guy like he'd pushed her overboard. Well, whatever happened, the bastard's a criminal. And he really screwed us over."

Dragon headed for the stairs. I saw the muscles in his back ripple under his wet T-shirt.

"Hey, Dragon?"

He turned back to look at me.

"Do you want to party with me?"

Pure loathing washed over Dragon's face as he eyed me up and down.

" 'Fraid not. I'll keep my money for a woman who's better than you. Besides, I like a woman with a little more meat."

"Motherfucker! You know you enjoyed sleeping with me."

I picked up the umbrella that Dragon had left by the doorway and hurled it at him, but it landed halfway up the stairs. Dragon burst out laughing and turned to continue up to the roof. Motherfucker! Goddamn motherfucker! I had never used such filthy language before in all my life, but I couldn't help myself. I hope they all die. Motherfuckers! I remembered their dirty apartment. I'd told myself then that I'd never go back. So why had I propositioned Dragon? It must have just been a moment of weakness brought on by the embrace I had enjoyed earlier on the roof. Or maybe it was as Yuriko predicted. Maybe it was because whores like us expose men. I'd exposed Zhang's weakness and Dragon's maliciousness. I was so furious with myself that I intentionally broke the cover to the mailbox slot for unit 404.

•

I wondered what had become of Zhang. That's what was on my mind as I trudged off to the Jizō statue, the plastic grocery bag dangling from my hand. I had an appointment to meet Arai there. It had been a long time: four months. Both Yoshizaki and Arai had invited me out to dinner in the past. But now they just wanted to meet in hotels. First it was twice a month, then once, and now about once every two months or so. To make up for the infrequency, I was determined to try to get more money from them for each session.

When I reached the alley that ran in front of the Jizō statue, I saw Arai's rounded back. He was lurking in the shadows in front of the statue, wearing the same shabby gray coat he had worn last year and the year before that, his shoulder weighed down, as always, by the strap of a black vinyl bag. And, as always, a weekly paper poked out over the edge of the bag. The only thing different was that his hair had grown thinner and whiter than it had been two years ago.

"Mr. Arai, have you been waiting long? You're early, aren't you?"

Arai frowned when he heard my high-pitched voice, and he brought his finger to his lips, signaling me to be quiet. No one was around. Why did he have to be so nervous? I wondered if he was ashamed to be seen with me in public. Arai said nothing but turned and headed off to our regular love hotel. The ones in Murayama-chō were the cheapest around, ¥3,000 for a short stay. I hummed as I strolled along, making sure to stay a few feet behind Arai. I was in a good mood. I was pleased that Arai had decided to call me. It had been awhile, but I felt things might be returning to the way they had once been, when I felt I owned the Shibuya night. I may have been a lowly street-corner prostitute, but I still didn't want to die. I wasn't going to end up like Yuriko.

When we got to the hotel room I turned the hot water on in the tub and scanned the room for anything valuable to take. I decided to help myself to the extra roll of toilet paper that had been put there. I might be able to use the night-robe sash for something. And then of course there were the condoms by the pillow. I noticed that they'd only provided one tonight. Usually they leave two. I called the front desk to complain and had them send up one more. I would leave one there for Arai and pocket the other.

"You'll have a beer, won't you, Mr. Arai?"

I opened the grocery bag I was carrying, pulled out the can of beer and the snacks I'd bought earlier, and set them on the rickety table. The *oden* was my evening meal, so I ate it without offering him any.

"God, you like a lot of broth in your *oden*," he said with disgust.

This was the first time we'd seen each other in I don't know how long, and this was all he had to say to me? I didn't answer. *Oden* broth is diet food; anyone knows that! It fills you up and then you don't eat a lot of other stuff. How come men don't know simple things like this? I drank the rest of the broth. Arai looked at me in annoyance and headed to the bathroom. He used to be so hesitant about saying the wrong thing in front of me, so conscious of his own small-town manners: Mr. Arai from a chemical company in Toyama. When did he change? I sat there for a bit, staring blankly into space, while I thought it over.

"I want this to be our last session."

Arai's pronouncement caught me completely off guard. I stared at him in shock, but he avoided my gaze.

"Why?"

"Because I'm going to retire this year."

"So what? Does that mean you have to retire from me too?"

I couldn't help but laugh. Company and prostitute were one and the same? That would make me a company employee both day and night. Or, maybe it's the other way around: I'm a prostitute both night and day!

"No, that's not what I'm suggesting. It's just that I'll be home all the time and it'll be hard to get away. Besides, I doubt I'll have many complaints that I'll need you to listen to."

"Okay, okay. I get the picture," I said impatiently, as I held my hand out in front of Arai. "Then give me what I'm owed."

Arai went to the closet where he'd hung his wrinkled suit jacket and sullenly reached into the pocket to pull out his paper-thin wallet. I knew he only had two ten-thousand-yen notes inside. He always brought just enough to cover my charge of ¥15,000 and the ¥3,000 room fee. He never walked around with anything more than the amount he needed. Yoshizaki was the same way. Arai placed the two bills on my upturned palm.

"Here's your fifteen thousand yen. Now give me five thousand in change."

"You're short."

Arai stared at me. "What do you mean? This is what I always pay."

"That's just my salary. If I'm an employee in your nighttime company, you need to pay my retirement allowance."

Arai stared at my open palm but said nothing. Then he looked up at me, clearly growing angry.

"You're a prostitute. You have no right to that!"

"I'm not just a prostitute, I'm also a company employee."

"Right, right, I know: G Corporation, G Corporation. All you ever do is brag about it. But I bet you're an enormous burden to your firm. If you'd been employed at my company, you'd have been let go long ago. The era of your debut is long past, you know; you're no longer the flower-faced office lady you used to be. You're really weird, to tell you the truth, and you get weirder by the minute. Each time I sleep with you, I ask myself what the hell I'm doing. I can't figure it out. You disgust me. But then, each time you call, I feel so sorry for you I can't help but agree to meet you."

"Oh, is that so? Well, then, I'll just take what you've given me here for the time being. The additional hundred thousand yen you can deposit in my bank account."

"Give that back. You bitch!"

Arai grabbed the bills from my hand; I couldn't let him take them. If I lost that money, I'd lose myself. But Arai struck me hard across the face, sending my wig flying.

"What do you think you're doing?"

"That's what I'd like to know! What are you doing?"

Arai was breathing heavily. "Here, bitch," he hissed as he threw one ten-thousand-yen note at me. "I'm leaving."

Arai yanked his suit jacket on and folded his coat over his arm.

Once he hoisted his bag onto his shoulder, I shouted at him. "You have to pay the hotel costs too. And you owe me seven hundred yen for the drinks and the snack."

"Fine."

Arai reached into his pocket and pulled out a handful of change. He counted out the coins and threw them on the table.

"Don't ever call me again," he said. "The more I see you the more you terrify me. You make me sick."

Look who's talking, I wanted to say. Who was the one who always wanted to get me off with finger play? Aren't you the one who had me pose for Polaroid pictures; who tied me up and got off on S and M play? And who was the one I had to suck on until I was nearly blue in the face because he couldn't get it up? I did all this for you—I freed you—and this is the thanks I get?

Arai opened the door and addressed me curtly. "Satō-san, you ought to be careful."

"What do you mean?"

"You've got the shadow of death over you."

With that he closed the door. Once I was alone, I looked around the room. Well, thank God I hadn't pulled the tab on the beer can! Funny, that's all I could think of at the time. I was more offended by Arai's claim that I was tantamount to a corporation than I was by his sudden change of heart. A man's work and prostitution are the same? If a man has a retirement age in the corporate world, then should he also retire from buying prostitutes? It was the same as the lecture I'd been given long ago by that woman in the Ginza. Well, enough of that! I stuffed the beer and snacks back in the plastic bag and turned off the hot water.

•

I returned to the Jizō statue. There was a man standing there waiting for me. At first I thought Arai might have changed his mind, but then I noticed that the man was taller than Arai and was wearing jeans.

"You look well," Zhang said, breaking into a smile.

"Really?"

I opened my trench coat as wide as I could. I wanted to seduce Zhang. "I've been hoping to run into you."

"Why?"

Zhang brought his hand up to my cheek and stroked it softly. I quivered. Be good to me. I flashed back to that rainy night. But I wasn't going to say those words again. I hated men. But I loved sex.

"I'd like to do a little business," I told him. "What do you say? I'll give you a good price."

"Three thousand yen?"

Zhang and I started walking. I keep a record of the men I have liaisons with in my prostitute's journal. But the marks that I've used in my journal tonight are in reverse order, aren't they? They're backwards. This time I've marked Arai, WA, instead of the foreigner, with a question mark. This indicates those men with whom I will probably not have sex again. In other words, it marks the men I think are rotten.

•

Zhang and I linked arms and walked from one dark alley to the next. Past the kitchen assistant, who threw water at me and told me to get lost; past the man who told me no one does that anymore, when I tried to exchange beer bottles for money; past the sake shop owner who treated me callously; past the convenience-store clerk who refuses to say a word to me, even though I'm constantly buying stuff in her store; past the punks who shine their flashlights on me and burst out laughing when I'm in the empty lot having sex. I wanted to shout at them all, Look at me now! I'm not just some street-corner whore, some bottom-feeding slut. Here I am walking for all the world to see with a man who was waiting for me in front of the Jizō statue. A man who is good to me. I am the sought-after, the desired, the capable: the queen of sex.

"We look like a pair of lovers!"

I squealed in delight. I'm with Zhang. I'm an employee of G Corporation. My article won a newspaper prize. I'm the assistant office manager. How come I was never able to get by without saying all these things? Was it simply that I wanted to say them to customers? No, it was more than that. I had to say what I said because if I didn't I would feel they were making fun of me. I had to be the best at everything I did. It was important to me as a woman. And that made me want to show off. I wanted men to watch me, to appraise me. Moreover, I wanted them to approve of me. That was me in a nutshell. In the final analysis, I was really just a sweet girl who needed approval.

"What are you mumbling about over there?"

Zhang peered at me. His eyes were wide and awash with uncertainty.

"I was talking to myself. Could you hear?" I asked Zhang, surprised by his question. But he just shook his balding head.

"Are you feeling okay? I mean, mentally?"

Where'd he get off asking such a question? Of course I was okay! Nothing wrong with my mental abilities! I got up on time this morning, boarded the train, changed to the subway, and worked like an aggressive career woman in one of the biggest corporations around. At night I transformed into a prostitute sought out by men. Suddenly I remembered the argument I had had earlier with Arai and stopped short. I'm a company employee day *and* night. Or is it that I'm a prostitute night and day? Which is it? Which one is me? Is the area in front of the Jizō statue my headquarters? Then was the Marlboro Hag the chief of operations before I took over? That thought amused me so much I burst out laughing.

"What are you doing?"

Zhang turned around to stare at me as I stood there laughing. When I looked around me, I saw that we'd arrived in front of Zhang's apartment building. I put my hands on my hips and declared, "Tonight, I'm not doing a whole host of men!"

"Don't worry, none of them want to sleep with you anyway," Zhang said. "No one but me, that is."

"Do you like me?" I asked Zhang, reeling with excitement over his last words. Say it! Say it! Say, "I like you." Say, "You're a good woman. You're attractive." Say it!

Zhang didn't say anything. He fished around in his pockets.

"Where are we going? To the roof?"

I was afraid the roof would be too cold. I leaned against one of the walls and looked up at the night sky. But then, if Zhang was good to me, I wouldn't mind the cold. Suddenly I was seized with doubt. What did it mean for a man to be good to you? Did it mean he'd give you lots of money? But Zhang didn't have money. More likely he'd try to haggle over the ¥3,000. Was it something that you felt, then? But I was afraid of feeling. I mean, for a prostitute it's supposed to be about work.

"Did you hear what I just said?"

Zhang walked past his apartment building and stopped in front of the one next to it. It was a peculiar building. There was a bar in the basement, and I could see orange lights leaking out onto the asphalt from windows that were at street level. When I peeked in the windows, I saw customers seated with their drinks, their heads about level with our feet. The building was three stories tall, but it looked to be only about as high as a two-story building. The top of the basement windows were at street level, and the first floor started just above that. The boisterous noise coming from the basement bar seemed oddly incongruous with the quiet loneliness of the surrounding buildings. I found it a little unnerving. Even though I'd come to Zhang's apartment any number of times, I'd never once noticed this shabby apartment building that was right next door.

"Has this building been here all along?" I asked.

Zhang looked taken aback by the dim-wittedness of my question. He pointed up to the top of the building.

"It's been here all this time. Look over there; that's my room. I can see this building from my window."

I looked up to the fourth floor of the other building and could see two windows that opened out above us like eyeballs. One of the windows was dark, the other was bright with a fluorescent lamp.

"You've got a direct view."

"That I do. I can see if someone's in or not. The super of this building sometimes gives me a key to one of the apartments."

"Then, if I lived in this apartment, you would know exactly what I was doing at any given time."

"If I wanted to."

The idea made me happy. Zhang looked puzzled. He swung his head down. He stopped in front of the apartment at the end of the other shabby building—Number 103—and pulled a key out of his pocket. The apartment next to it was pitch-black. It didn't look as if anyone was living there. It looked as if there were vacant units on the second floor too. Three grimy-looking mailboxes were tacked to the thin Sheetrock wall at the entryway. Above these was a sign that read GREEN VILLA APART-MENTS. Condoms and leaflets were strewn across the concrete floor. I shivered. The filth in the apartment foyer reminded me of the garbage on the roof of Zhang's building and the stench of his bathroom. I sensed this was a place I shouldn't see and shouldn't be visiting. I shouldn't do this.

"Hmm, I wonder if I'm doing something I shouldn't?" I asked Zhang, without thinking.

"I doubt there's one thing in the world that fits that category," Zhang answered, as he opened the door.

I looked inside. It smelled like an old person's breath. It was pitch-black inside; the odor that greeted me seemed to have risen out of a vast emptiness. We could do it in here and no one would know, I thought to myself. Zhang left me standing there and disappeared into the darkness. It seemed he knew his way around. He'd probably brought any number of women here already. Well, I wasn't going to let them get the better of me, I thought, as I slipped quickly out of my high heels, causing them to shoot off in both directions.

"There's no electricity, so watch your step."

Brought up to be a polite young lady, I turned around and straightened my shoes neatly in front of the entry step. The step was cool on my feet. And even though I was wearing stockings, I could tell it was covered in dust. Zhang was already sitting on the tatami in the back room.

"I can't see. I'm scared," I called out in a syrupy voice, hoping Zhang would hold out his hand. But he didn't come to me. I groped my way to the back room. The apartment was entirely bare, so I had no reason to fear bumping into anything. It didn't take long for my eyes to adjust to the dark. Light from the outside filtered in through the kitchen window, so it wasn't pitch-black. It was a small apartment. I could vaguely make out Zhang sitting cross-legged at the back of the six-mat room. He held up his hand to motion me over.

"Come in here and take off your clothes."

I pulled off my coat as I shivered in the cold. I stripped off my blue suit. I took off my underwear. Zhang sat there fully clothed, wrapped in his leather jacket. I lay back on the tatami and looked up at the ceiling. Zhang looked down at me.

"Haven't you forgotten something?"

"What?" I asked, my teeth chattering against the cold.

"Why did you take your clothes off before you got your money? You're a prostitute, aren't you? I'm here to buy you, so you ought to make sure you get your money first."

"Well, give it to me then."

Zhang placed three thousand-yen notes over my body. One on my chest, one on my stomach, and one on my crotch. A measly three thousand. I wanted to scream, I want more! But on the other hand, I would have been happy to do Zhang for nothing. I wanted to experience normal sex. I wanted to be held tenderly. I wanted to make love.

Zhang said, as if reading my heart, "You're not worth more than three thousand yen. What do you think? Do you want the money? If you don't, you'll become a normal woman, not a prostitute. But you know I'm not interested in normal women, so I don't sleep with them. So what will you be, a whore who's worth no more than three thousand yen or a normal woman I don't want to touch?"

I collected the thousand-yen notes off my body and clung to them. I still wanted him to hold me. I could hear Zhang pulling the zipper down on his jeans. And in the dim light I could see his erect penis. Zhang put his penis in my mouth and began moving his hips. His breathing grew labored.

"I can't do it with a woman unless I pay for it. Even if it's just a paltry three thousand."

Zhang lay down and entered me. He was still dressed, and it was only where he entered me that he was warm. It felt strange. His leather jacket was cool on my skin, and every time he moved the friction of his jeans rubbing against my thighs hurt.

"You like prostitutes because your sister was one?"

"That's not it." Zhang shook his head. "It's just the opposite. I liked prostitutes, so I made my sister become one. I didn't do it because I wanted to sleep with my sister. I did it because I wanted to sleep with my prostitute sister. There's nothing in this world that's off limits. But people who get duped wouldn't understand."

Zhang gave a high-pitched laugh. He began to move on top of me. I wanted him to kiss me. I stretched my face up to his, but he turned his head away, intentionally avoiding my lips. Only our lower bodies touched, moved, machinelike, methodically. Was this really what sex was? I felt so empty, like I was on the verge of going crazy. The other time he'd been gentle. And I'd felt like I'd never felt before. What would happen today? I heard Zhang laugh. He was growing excited, breathing heavily. He was completely alone now, wasn't he? That was sex.

I heard Yuriko's voice. I saw her sitting on my left. She was wearing a wig with hair that fell to her waist. Her eyelids were painted blue, her lips bright red. A prostitute dressed just like me. Yuriko began to tickle my left thigh with her slender fingers.

"Go on! See, I'm going to help you. I'm going to help you come."

Slowly, softly she began to massage my thigh.

"Thanks, you're so nice to me. I'm sorry I bullied you in high school."

"Silly, the one who got the worst bullying was you. Why didn't you see it? You never could see your own weaknesses." Yuriko spoke ruefully. "If you'd known, you might have been happy."

"Maybe."

Zhang had begun to thrust into me violently. He was getting heavier, pressing down on my chest so hard I couldn't breathe. Zhang didn't even notice the woman who had to bear his weight. Most of the men I took as customers were like that. Did they think I was going to go on forever without noticing their contempt? The stunt with the money really brought it home. Was that really my worth? Not likely! Not for an employee of G Corporation who pulled down a salary of ¥10,000,000 a year.

"There are customers out there who are attracted to a woman like me without a breast. Pretty odd, wouldn't you say?"

I remembered that voice. I turned in surprise to my right and saw the Marlboro Hag sitting there. She was wearing a black bra with a wad of material where her breast should have been—the breast she'd lost to cancer. I could see the bra through her flimsy nylon jacket. The Marlboro Hag massaged my right thigh. Her hands were dry and calloused but strong. The massage felt good. It was like it had been in Zhang's apartment when I was doing Chen-yi. Dragon was on my right and Zhang on my left, both stroking my thighs.

"Don't think about anything. You think too much! Give in to your body, relax, enjoy life!" The Marlboro Hag laughed. "I gave you the turf in front of the Jizō statue because I thought you'd do a good job—a better job than you've done, anyway."

"That's not true!" Yuriko shouted at the Marlboro Hag. "You knew all along that Kazue would turn out like this."

The two of them continued talking, completely oblivious of me or Zhang. But they never stopped their hands. They continued stroking my thighs. Zhang was nearing orgasm. He let out a loud cry. I wanted to come too. I heard a voice above my head.

"Your foolishness wounds my heart."

It was the crazy woman with the Bible. I didn't know what to believe anymore. I was so confused, I started to scream in the darkness.

"Save me!"

Zhang came just as I screamed. Panting heavily, he finally rolled off my body. At the same time, Yuriko disappeared and then the Marlboro Hag, and I was alone in the room, lying by myself on the tatami, naked.

"You're talking to yourself again!"

Zhang opened my handbag without asking, pulled out a packet of tissues, and used them all on himself. Then he caught sight of the crumpled ten-thousand-yen note that I had squeezed out of Arai.

"Don't try to steal it. That's mine."

"I'm not going to steal it." Zhang laughed and snapped my purse shut. "I don't steal from prostitutes."

Liar. Didn't he just say there was nothing in the world he wouldn't do? I suddenly felt cold and got up to dress. Lights from a passing car raced across the walls of the room. In that burst of light I could see that the walls were spotted with stains and the paper room dividers were torn. How strange that someone with as good an upbringing as I would end up in a room like this. I tilted my head to the side. Zhang opened the window in the kitchen and threw his spent condom outside. He turned back to look at me.

"Let's meet here again."

•

I'm home now and have opened my notebook. I think it won't be long before I have to bring my journal writing to an end. It's supposed to be a record of my activities as a prostitute, but I'm having more and more days without customers. Therefore, Kijima-kun, these notebooks are for you. Please don't send them back to me like you did with those love letters in high school. Because, you see, what you've read in these journals is another true side of me.

EIGHT · SOUNDS OF THE WATERFALL
IN THE DISTANCE: THE LAST CHAPTER

Well, everyone, I've reached the conclusion of this long and convoluted tale. Please bear with me a little longer while I wrap things up.

I have tried to tell you as much as I possibly can about the tragic death of Yuriko, my younger sister, who impressed all who saw her with her beauty; daily life at Q High School for Young Women, the epitome of the classist society so firmly embedded in Japan; the sensational events involving Kazue Satō, a former student of that school; the successes and setbacks of Mitsuru and Takashi Kijima, also associated with the school, who happened to find each other years later; and the scoundrel Zhang, who came from across the seas to encounter, strangely enough, both Yuriko and Kazue. To that end I have made public the records, diaries, and letters I have in my possession. And I have persisted with my account, hoping you would understand at least a fraction of my story. And yet—and this is what I have struggled with—what exactly is it that I want you to understand? Even now I am not certain.

After Yuriko and Kazue died, you would think that I would have tried to counteract all the humiliation that the crime and the succeeding trial—so widely publicized throughout the mass media—had generated.

But you would be wrong. I had neither that kindness nor that sense of justice. And why was that? I don't have a definite reason.

I can only come up with one suggestion: Perhaps Yuriko and Kazue and Mitsuru and even Takashi and Zhang are all part of me—whoever "I" am. Perhaps I exist in order to remain behind as their spirits—floating, recounting their tales. If that's the case, I am sure there are some among you who will observe that mine is a black spirit. And you would be right. A spirit, you should know, assumes a black form. It is painted with hatred, dyed with bitterness, and has a face disfigured by curses and resentment. And that's why it lingers on. Perhaps you could say my existence was like that of grimy snow packed darkly in the pit of Yuriko's heart—and of Kazue's and Mitsuru's and Zhang's. Having said as much, I realize I have probably taken the comparison too far. But I have no other way to express it. I was flesh and blood—just an everyday, ordinary person rife with intolerance, resentment, and jealousy.

Once I graduated from college I took a completely different path from my model-turned-prostitute younger sister. I chose to be inconspicuous. In my situation, inconspicuousness meant living forever as a virgin, a woman who would have no contact with men.

A permanent virgin. Do you know what this signifies? It may sound wholesome and pure to you, but that was not actually the case. Kazue articulated it brilliantly in her journals, didn't she: to miss the only chance one has to have power over a man. Sex is the only way a woman has to control the world. That was Kazue's twisted view, at any rate. But now I can't help but wonder about whether or not she was right. When a man enters me (the very idea is even more ridiculous than I could have imagined) and ejaculates inside me, am I not overwhelmed by satisfaction. . . feeling as though I am finally in touch with the world? At least that's what I feel for the moment. But this is a complete delusion. The delusions arise from believing that prostitution is the only way—that the only way for a woman to have any control over her world is to do what Kazue did. A woman who awakens to this fact will know it was all just a big mistake.

I have said, haven't I, that I preferred a nondescript life. But in truth that's not quite correct. All I ever wanted was not to be compared to Yuriko. And since I was going to lose whatever competition we had, I decided to withdraw from the game altogether. I was very strongly aware of the fact that I lived to be Yuriko's other side, her negative image. A person like me—a negative image—is profoundly sensitive to the existence of shadows in those who live in sunlight. Those radiant creatures carry their black thoughts furtively, not wanting others to see. But they get no sympathy from me. I am immediately aware of their blackness, having lived so long as a negative myself. Far from sympathizing, it would be more accurate to say that I survive off the dregs I manage to collect from the shadows cast by those who live in the sun.

Kazue's record of her life as a prostitute was so sad it gave me new will to go on living. The sadder she was, the more I resented her. I enjoyed her failures. Do you understand? And for the very same reason, Yuriko's diary gave me nothing. Beneath it all, Yuriko was really a strong cunning woman. This much became obvious to me. She was absolutely hateful. And I had nothing I could use against her.

I was imprisoned by Yuriko. I had no choice but to trail after her all my life as though I were her shadow. Zhang's deposition, therefore, held no surprises for me. It was a tedious affair. That's because Zhang, a villain through and through, did not possess even a mote of shadow. There are villains, you see, who live in the sunlight.

•

Kazue's journals were different. Zhang's deposition may have been predictable, but not Kazue's. The dissolute loneliness she depicted was awful. When I finished reading her words, I felt a change come over me—something I'd never felt before. Before I was even aware of it, I started to weep in sympathy. Me! I couldn't hold back the tears as I thought about how completely alone Kazue had been: her outward appearance so grotesque she was like the Incredible Hulk. The reverberations that echoed through Kazue's empty heart made my own heart tremble, paralyzing me so I couldn't speak. I've never experienced an orgasm, but I wonder if this feeling was not similar?

Her journals fill two large notebooks, one bound in brown leather, the other black. Each is lined with neat precise handwriting, reminding me very much of the notebooks she used to keep in high school. Kazue recorded the amount of money she received from her customers with absurd vigilance. She had a personality that was so honest, so meticulous, she could not bear to go without writing about the encounters she had. Kazue, the excellent student who only wanted to be praised for her intelligence, the nice girl who longed to be admired for her proper upbringing, the professional who aimed for a career at the top levels. Even at her best, Kazue was always somehow lacking—and here she had unintentionally revealed herself and her spirit in the pages of her journals.

I suddenly recalled Mitsuru's words: "You and I are the same. And Kazue too. We all had our hearts wrested away by an illusion. I wonder how it looked to others." No, she was wrong. *That's wrong!* I cried out in my heart. Don't you see? "Hatred and confusion." That's what Yurio had said when he touched Kazue's journals, and that's what I held in my heart. It couldn't be otherwise. I was a woman sensitive to the shadows in others. So where was the hatred and confusion in me? The dregs that I lived off were only what I gleaned from other people, their hatred and confusion. I was not like Kazue. I was not a grotesque monster.

I swept Kazue's journals off the tabletop. And in an effort to calm myself, I touched the ring on my left hand, the one Mitsuru had made fun of. It is the source of all my feelings. What's that? Yes, I am contradicting myself. I did make fun of the classist nonsense at Q High School for Young Women. But at the same time I liked that society. Don't you suppose everybody lives a contradiction in one form or another?

"Is something wrong?"

Yurio, sitting beside me, could sense that I was trembling. He put his hands on my shoulders. Such a sensitive boy. He covered my shoulders with his strong young hands. I could feel the heat from his palms sinking into my skin. I wondered if sex was like this. I nervously pressed my cheek to those hands. Yurio sensed the dampness of my tears and asked in alarm, "Aunt, are you crying? Was there something in those notebooks that upset you?"

Alarmed, I pulled Yurio's hands from my face.

"They're sad. And they contain a few items about your mother too. But I don't want to tell you what they say."

"That's because it describes hatred and confusion, right? But what? Tell me. I want to know. I want to know every single thing that's written in those notebooks, from A to Z."

Why did Yurio want to know? I wondered. I gazed up at the boy's beautiful eyes. His irises were brown with flecks of green, the most exquisite color I'd ever seen. They were like perfectly clear pools, reflecting nothing. And yet, Yurio was like me. He too was sensitive to the dark shadows that others cast, wasn't he? If he were able to perceive instantly the darkness in others and turn it into something that he himself could enjoy, then I most definitely wanted to share the contents of the journals with him. I had so sated myself on the remains of all the others that my heart had begun to throb. I wanted to sully Yuriko and Kazue with the poison of words and fill Yurio's ears with those words so that he might grow up with the truth. I wanted to leave behind my genes. It was the same as wanting to give birth, was it not, because if I were able to fill Yurio with the poisoned truth, then wasn't it likely that he too—this beautiful boy—would become just like me?

"Kazue's journals depict an absolutely sublime struggle, the struggle between an individual and the rest of the world. Kazue lost the battle, ended up completely alone, and died hungry for some measure of kindness from another person. Don't you think it's a sad story?"

Shock flashed in Yurio's face. "Was it the same for my mother?"

"It was. Yes, you're right. You were born of a woman just like that."

I lied. Yuriko was far from being like Kazue. From the very start, Yuriko had never believed in the rest of the world—in other people. Yurio lowered his eyes, took his hands off my shoulders, and pressed them together as if he were praying.

"Your mother was weak. She was worthless."

"It's just so sad. If I'd been there, I could have helped her."

"How?"

No one could have done anything, I thought. Besides, you were just a child, you couldn't possibly have understood. I wanted to challenge Yurio's idealism, but he continued with determination.

"I don't know what I would have done, but I would have done something. If she was lonely, I would have lived with her. I would have selected music for her and let her listen to it. And I would have made music for her that was even more beautiful. That way I would have helped to make her at least a little happier."

Yurio's face glowed as if he'd thought of the most wonderful solution. I could not get over how beautiful he was, and how tender. His notions were childish and yet weren't they particularly sweet? Was this a man's true form? Before I was even aware of it, a new emotion began to bud within me: love. But that's impossible. Yurio is your nephew! So? What's wrong with that? I could hear the angel and the devil inside me doing battle.

"You're exactly right, Yurio-chan. Your aunt is too easily discouraged. I wonder why Yuriko didn't take you in. I just can't imagine."

"I was strong enough not to need my mother."

"Are you saying I'm weak?"

Yurio pressed his hands to my shoulders and back, as though to understand how I was built. I trembled under his touch. It was an entirely new feeling. I was being evaluated by someone else. No, not evaluated. I was being experienced by another.

"Aunt, I don't think you're weak. I think you're poor."

"Poor, you say? More like impoverished. There's no doubt that I'm impoverished."

"No. What I mean is that your heart has grown thin. It's a shame. It's just as that woman said earlier. But it's not too late. I agree with her on that."

I thought he'd been listening to his rap music through his head-phones. But given his keen sense of hearing, Yurio had picked up every-thing Mitsuru had said. I felt that Mitsuru and Yurio were in cahoots, and it made me so bitter that I ached with resentment.

"Are you strong, Yurio-chan?"

"That's right. I've always lived alone."

"Well, the same goes for me. I've always lived alone too."

"Really?" Yurio tilted his head to the side. "I get the sense that you depended on my mother."

Living in Yuriko's shadow: was that a kind of dependence? It was a form of weakness and poverty, surely. The realization stung. I stared at Yurio's fleshy lips. Tell me more! Teach me more about myself. Guide me.

"By the way, Aunt. About the computer. When am I going to get it? If I had a computer, I could make your life a lot easier."

"But I don't have the money."

Yurio's cheeks drained of color. To see him gazing off into space—a space he could not see—while lost in thought was adorable, I thought.

"You don't have any savings?"

"I've got about three hundred thousand yen. But that's it. And I'm holding on to it for an emergency."

Yurio turned suddenly. "Ah, there's the phone."

I hadn't heard anything, but the phone started ringing. I knew Yurio's intuition was acute, but this was overwhelming. I picked up the receiver with a feeling of dread.

The call was from the ward-sponsored old-people's hospital. It was Grandfather: he'd passed away a few minutes before, at the age of ninety-one. What need did I have to know about his last moments? In his senility he'd returned to a period fifty or sixty years in his past, when he was a young man. My bonsai-freak con-artist grandfather had forgotten all about his daughter's suicide, and he never knew his granddaughter had been murdered. He slipped into death while enjoying himself in the euphoria of his senility. But talk about timing! Here we'd just started to discuss finances. I assumed I'd have to apply the meager savings I had to my grandfather's funeral expenses. And that wasn't the worst of it. With my grandfather dead I'd have to vacate the apartment, because the lease was in his name. There'd be the moving expenses. And now I had to buy a computer.

"Yurio, Grandpa has died. I can't let you use my savings. Plus, we're going to have to leave this apartment. Why don't you ask Johnson to buy you the computer?"

"Why don't you go out and earn money?"

"Earn money?"

"On the streets. Like my mother."

What on earth was he thinking? I slapped his cheek with my palm. Not hard, of course. But when my palm struck his soft cheek, I could feel the row of his pretty teeth. His youthfulness made me tremble. Yurio said nothing but pressed his hand to his cheek and looked down. Such cool beauty. Just like Yuriko. I could feel my breast swell with love, and I knew from the depths of my heart that I wanted the money. No, it wasn't just the money that I wanted. Nor was it the computer. It was the boy who wanted the computer. I wanted Yurio. I wanted a life together with Yurio. Because that is where I could find happiness.

•

In her diaries, Yuriko made some interesting comments about prostitution. If you'll indulge me, I will quote them here:

> I suspect there are lots of women who want to become prostitutes. Some see themselves as valued commodities and figure they ought to sell while the price is high. Others feel that sex has no intrinsic meaning in and of itself but allows individuals

to feel the reality of their own bodies. A few women despise their existence and the insignificance of their meager lives and want to affirm themselves by controlling sex much as a man would. Then there are those who are actuated by violent, self-destructive behavior. And finally we have those who want to offer comfort. I suppose there are any number of women who find the meaning of their existence in similar ways. But I was different.

Yuriko was different. As she continues she explains that she became a prostitute because she was lascivious to the very core of her being.

Now, if I were to become a prostitute, my reason would be different still. Unlike Yuriko, I don't crave sex. I don't even like men. They're sneaky, and their faces, their bodies, and the way they think are boorish. They're selfish and will do anything to get what they want, even if it means injuring the people close to them; they don't care. Besides, all they worry about is the façade; they have absolutely no concern for what's beneath. Do you think I'm exaggerating? Well, I don't agree. Every man I've ever met over the forty years or so of my life has been pretty much the same. My grandfather was a pleasant fellow but not particularly attractive. Takashi Kijima, by contrast, was attractive but completely twisted.

But now I've found an exception: Yurio. I don't think there's another man around who's as attractive and gentle in spirit as Yurio. When I think of the possibility of his turning into one of those horrid men when he grows older, it makes me miserable! What if I did become a prostitute? I would then have the money to ensure that Yurio would never turn into a repulsive man and the two of us could live happily together forever. How's that for a reason? Pretty original, wouldn't you say? I wonder what my life as a prostitute might be like.

•

I see myself walking through Maruyama-chō wearing a black wig that comes down to my waist, blue eye shadow, and bright red lipstick. I flow through the streets and alleys. I see a middle-aged man standing in front of a hotel, looking like he wants something. He has a lot of hair on his body and little on his head. I call out to him.

"I'm a virgin, you know. I really am. A virgin at forty. Why don't you give me a try?"

The man looks at me with mild annoyance, but I can see he's curious. Has he seen the determination in my eyes? Suddenly he turns serious, and I find myself crossing the threshold of a love hotel for the first time in my life. Needless to say, just imagining what will happen next makes my heart race. But my determination takes control. I have been confronted with a desire to transform both myself and the hatred I feel for Yurio, who has begun to despise me. I struggle to breathe under the man's weight, and as I accept his caresses, which lack even a mote of gentleness, you can be sure this is what I am thinking. Kazue grew hideous and exposed her ugly body to others. She took her revenge on herself and on the rest of the world by making men buy her. And now I am selling my body for the same reason. Yuriko was wrong. Women have only one reason for turning to prostitution. It's hatred for others, for the rest of the world. No doubt this is incredibly sad, but then men have the capacity for countering such feelings in a woman. Still, if sex is the only way to dissolve these feelings, then men and women really are pathetic. I will launch my boat on a sea of hatred, my eye on the far shore, wondering when I might make land. Ahead I hear the roar of water. Might my boat be headed for a waterfall? Perhaps I must first plunge into the falls before I can set out upon the sea of hatred. Niagara? Yguazu? Victoria? My body trembles. But if I can make the first descent, the path that opens from there will be surprisingly pleasant, won't it? That's what Kazue expressed in her journals. So let me shoulder my baggage of hatred and confusion and set sail undaunted. In honor of my courage, there on the other shore, Yuriko and Kazue are waving to me, urging me on, applauding my gallant determination. Hurry up! they seem to say. I recall what Kazue recorded in her journal, and I too want to enfold myself in a man's embrace.

"Be good to me, please."

"I will. And in return, you be good to me."

Was I with Zhang? I strained my eyes to see.

A NOTE ABOUT THE AUTHOR

Natsuo Kirino, born in 1951, is the author of sixteen novels, four short-story collections, and an essay collection. She is the recipient of six of Japan's premier literary awards, including the Mystery Writers of Japan Award for Out, *the Izumi Kyōka Prize for Literature for* Grotesque, *and the Naoki Prize for* Soft Cheeks. *Her work has been published in nineteen languages worldwide; several of her books have also been turned into movies.* Out *was the first of her novels to appear in English and was nominated for an Edgar Award. She lives in Tokyo.*

A NOTE ABOUT THE TRANSLATOR

Rebecca L. Copeland, professor of Japanese literature at Washington University in St. Louis, Missouri, was born in Fukuoka, Japan, the daughter of American missionaries. She received her Ph.D. in Japanese Literature from Columbia University in 1986. She has published numerous scholarly studies on and translations of modern Japanese women's writing.

A NOTE ON THE TYPE

This book was set in New Caledonia, a type-face designed by W. A. Dwiggins (1880–1956). It belongs to the family of printing types called "modern face" by printers—a term used to mark the change in style of the type letters that occurred around 1800. Caledonia borders on the general design of Scotch Roman, but it is more freely drawn than that letter. This version of Caledonia was adapted by David Berlow in 1979.

COMPOSED BY
Creative Graphics,
Allentown, Pennsylvania

PRINTED AND BOUND BY
Berryville Graphics,
Berryville, Virginia

DESIGNED BY
Iris Weinstein

F
KIR

Kirino, Natsuo,
   1951-

Grotesque.

$24.95

MAR '07